THEODORA SARAH ORNE JEWETT was born in Maine on September 3, 1849, growing up in the small town of South Berwick, where she was to spend the principal part of her life. Ill health prevented her from fulfilling her ambition to become a doctor; she turned to writing instead. Her first story was published when she was eighteen, and her literary production continued unabated until a crippling accident in 1902 ended her creative career. She died on June 24, 1909, leaving behind a remarkable literary legacy that includes her classic *The Country of the Pointed Firs*.

MARY WILKINS FREEMAN was born Mary Ella Wilkins in Randolph, Massachusetts, on October 31, 1852. Not until she was twenty-nine was her first story published; before that, her life had been shadowed by ill health, straitened circumstances, unrequited love, and the death of her beloved mother. Twenty prolific years of writing followed, accompanied by growing recognition and financial reward, but her unfortunate marriage in 1902 led to a decline in her work. She died in New Jersey on March 15, 1930.

Short Fiction of Sarah Orne Jewett and Mary Wilkins Freeman

Including
The Country of the Pointed Firs

Edited and with an Introduction by
Barbara H. Solomon

A MERIDIAN CLASSIC

NEW AMERICAN LIBRARY

NEW YORK AND SCARBOROUGH, ONTARIO

Library of Congress Catalog Card Number: 79-84605

SIGNET, SIGNET CLASSIC, MENTOR, ONYX, PLUME, MERIDIAN AND
NAL BOOKS are published *in the United States* by NAL
PENGUIN INC., 1633 Broadway, New York, New York 10019;
in Canada by The New American Library of Canada Limited, 81
Mack Avenue, Scarborough, Ontario M1L 1M8

First Meridian Classic Printing, June, 1987

1 2 3 4 5 6 7 8 9

PRINTED IN CANADA

This book is for my mother and father,
Rose and Lothar Hochster

Acknowledgments

I wish to express my gratitude to Michael Palma of the English Department and Stanley J. Solomon of the Communication Arts Department of Iona College for their invaluable reading of my manuscript. Barbara Beauzethier and Doris Viacava of Ryan Library were extremely helpful as was Kathryn Moczydlowski, English Department student secretary. At the college's secretarial center, I would like to thank Mary A. Bruno and the following members of her staff: Hyacinth M. Fyffe, Mariann A. Gallello, Patricia M. Heiles, and Teresa F. Martin.

Contents

Introduction

The reputations of writers of real literary merit are frequently as susceptible to the change of fashion as are styles of clothing or popular entertainments. By 1925 (the year in which Fitzgerald's *The Great Gatsby* was published), the subject matter of two of America's best-known writers, Sarah Orne Jewett and Mary Wilkins Freeman, had become distinctly unfashionable. These late nineteenth-century writers had depicted small New England villages; the American public wanted to read about burgeoning cities. They wrote about patient heroines, waiting hopefully for an eligible suitor to come courting; readers craved descriptions of the new woman—the flapper, the popular daughter, the vamp who applied lipstick, pulled on her flesh-colored stockings, and bobbed her hair. In the Roaring Twenties, the Jewett and Freeman portraits began to seem quaintly irrelevant—especially those of opinionated old women who went to Sunday services or the village store and for whom the purchase of a spring bonnet was an occasion of momentous significance. Instead the public was fascinated by the romantic entanglements of college sophomores who drove fast cars and attended crowded cocktail parties.

Now, half a century later, a glimpse of the activities of the inhabitants of a tiny village provides to jaded city dwellers a scene as exotic as a South Pacific Island, and a hopeful heroine sitting at her kitchen table often reveals a great deal more integrity and strength than a nervous flapper striving to create an image of popularity and desirability. And the struggles of individualistic, stubborn old women to live according to their convictions seem as dramatic as any conflict between egotistic young lovers.

Although the reputations of both Jewett and Freeman declined in the 1920s, and their fiction went virtually unread in the 1930s and 1940s, a rediscovered enthusiasm for these New England writers has emerged. A significant number of

critics attracted to the contributions of regional writers have
re-evaluated their literature. Feminists have found a surprising modernity in the roles dramatized by Jewett and
Freeman. For, strange as it may at first seem, their reticent
heroines, dressed in sprigged muslin and carrying silk shawls,
were women who valued their identity and who contributed
meaningful work, women who had not yet been relieved of
household chores to become the leisured but despised "just a
housewife" of the decades to come.

What were to the readers of the 1920s serious defects in
the subject matter of Jewett and Freeman no longer appear
as such to us. For example, the contemporary reader has an
entirely different attitude toward the settings of their stories.
A generation raised on concrete streets and frustrated by
long lines, traffic jams, uncollected garbage, and irrational urban
violence is naturally attracted to the quiet New England villages of these writers' fiction and curious about the customs,
routines, and attitudes which were common knowledge to the
reader of a century ago.

Jewett and Freeman also depicted extensive and close
family relationships which often seemed oppressive to both
their fictional characters and readers at the end of the nine-
teenth century. But in our own era of dissolving family bonds,
wide geographical separation of relatives, and frequent di-
vorce, there is an attractive element in stories about relatives
who accept the necessity of getting along in spite of one
another's faults, who experience the continuity of generations
of living in close proximity, and who accept unquestioningly
the responsibilities, pleasures, and pains of family ties.

Finally, we have grown tired of an American youth cult
which tells us that the most interesting people in the world
are eighteen-year-old girls and that adults over thirty are to
be pitied, distrusted, or simply ignored. Thus, we turn with
reawakened interest to the attitudes and activities of the mature women created by Sarah Orne Jewett and Mary Wilkins
Freeman.

The 1920s revolution in manners, morals, and literary taste
was created in part by an exciting group of young writers
who shaped modern American literature in many significant
ways. But their rebellion against their literary predecessors is
no longer our rebellion. Now we can return to what they la-
beled "old-fashioned" and "outdated" and recover these poi-
gnant stories of American life, handled with the consummate
literary skills of Sarah Orne Jewett and Mary Wilkins Freeman.

SARAH ORNE JEWETT

THE COUNTRY OF THE POINTED FIRS

In 1896, at the age of forty-seven, Sarah Orne Jewett published her finest work, *The Country of the Pointed Firs*. She had been publishing sketches and stories for more than twenty-eight years, beginning with the melodramatic "Lovers of Jenny Garrow." Returning again and again in her writing to the women and men of small New England towns, she chronicled the everyday lives of industrious farm wives and traced the patterns of life of the impoverished, lonely inhabitants of once-prosperous coastal towns. Fittingly, her best novel shares these elements with her finest short fiction, giving us a detailed view of the people of the imaginary seacoast town of Dunnet Landing, Maine. Yet, in spite of its great charm and artistry, *The Country of the Pointed Firs* is undoubtedly America's least-read masterpiece, probably because of problems of both genre and subject matter.

To begin with, most critics are at a loss as to whether to consider it a novel at all. Many, in discussing it, refer to it as a series of sketches or stories; others vaguely call it a "work," or a "volume of episodes," or even, as Richard Cary does, a "paranovel."

Yet the book certainly *is* a novel, a stylistic precursor of such works as John Dos Passos' *Manhattan Transfer* (1925). Just as that novel chronicles the lives of many New Yorkers—sometimes drawn together by their interaction with one another, but more often by a collective sense of place, by the ways New York affects the multitudes that swarm in its streets—so *The Country of the Pointed Firs* is the chronicle of numerous lives in and around Dunnet Landing. Here lives are molded by the long Maine winters, by the surrounding rock-filled fields (so rocky, in fact, that one old seaman marks the buried rocks with stakes painted yellow and white in the fashion of buoys), and by the harvest of the sea, a necessary supplement to the poor yield of the soil. If Manhattan stimulates in Dos Psasos' characters a sense of the excitement of things to come, of wealth to be gained, of adventure just around the next corner, by contrast, Dunnet Landing is redolent of voyages long since made and now evidenced only by a conch shell, a tea caddy from Tobago, a piece of goods from a distant land. It evokes images of a freshly made fish chowder or newly picked blackberries eaten with intense savor and of a deeply emotional family reunion. In a world of weathered, paintless farmhouses, a "quiet outlook upon field and sea and sky" from a cherished old rocking chair becomes important, as does the sensibility of a narrator which is finely enough developed to determine where her friend is treading in the herb garden by the different odors of the crushed plants wafting through the windows.

The critics' problem with the structure and classification of *The Country of the Pointed Firs* is further complicated by the existence of four additional pieces dealing with Dunnet Landing, all written after the publication of the novel in 1896. Three years after that edition appeared, Jewett published "The Queen's Twin" and "A Dunnet Shepherdess" in *The Atlantic Monthly*, followed by the publication in 1900 of "The Foreigner" in the same magazine. At the time of her death in 1909 she was still at work on "William's Wedding," which was first published in *The Atlantic Monthly* in 1910. These pieces have not been integrated into the 1896 text in this volume because Jewett never authorized their inclusion during her lifetime.[1] As Willa Cather has noted, Jewett never referred to the four pieces as stories, but used the terms "papers" or "sketches."[2] In addition, she referred to "The Queen's Twin" as "a new chapter about Mrs. Todd and one of her friends."[3] Thus, there are several indications that had Jewett been able to complete "William's Wedding," she might well have revised and reordered the concluding chapters of her novel.[4] This process is certainly not unprecedented, and Dickens' alternative ending to *Great Expectations* comes readily to mind as an example of such a revision. It is also possible that had Jewett retained her health, she might have

[1] In several editions, however, publishers have placed three of the sketches within the novel.

[2] *Not Under Forty* (New York: Alfred A. Knopf, 1936), p. 89.

[3] Richard Cary, editor, *Sarah Orne Jewett: Letters* (Waterville: Colby College Press, 1956), p. 89.

[4] She suffered from a debilitating accident in 1902 which prevented her from writing fiction thereafter.

completed a sequel to *The Country of the Pointed Firs*, since "William's Wedding" begins what is obviously a return visit to Dunnet Landing, which clearly takes place after the first summer described in the novel. Therefore, although the four sketches have been placed at the end of the 1896 text of *The Country of the Pointed Firs* in this volume, the reader may well prefer to read these directly after finishing Chapter XX, "Along Shore," where they seem to fit most plausibly.

In structuring *The Country of the Pointed Firs*, Jewett relies, as she does in an overwhelming number of her stories, on the paying of visits as the center of her dramatic action. These visits range from the summer-long stay of the unnamed narrator at Mrs. Todd's house in Dunnet Landing, to Captain Littlepage's afternoon visit to the schoolhouse where the narrator is engaged on her writing project, to the narrator's and Mrs. Todd's visit to Mrs. Blackett and William on Green Island, to Mrs. Fosdick's visit to Mrs. Todd. Even the trip to the Bowden reunion is obviously an elaborate day-long visit.

There are also several tales of visits within visits, as Mrs. Fosdick and Mrs. Todd reminisce about the secluded life of the once-jilted Joanna Todd on Shell-heap Island and Mrs. Todd describes the visit she and the minister made to Joanna's island hermitage. By design, the plot is composed both of episodic incidents in the past of various characters (Joanna's and Captain Littlepage's, for instance) and the narrator's experience of her summer at Mrs. Todd's house.

But there is very likely a second reason why *The Country of the Pointed Firs* has been so undeservedly neglected: it is so thoroughly a woman's book about the world of women— old women at that. The keynote to the thoroughly feminine world of the novel is sounded as Almira Todd and the narrator make their plans to visit Green Island. The narrator thinks about arranging for a ride on one of the big boats, but Almira insists that she and Johnny Bowden, a young boy, will easily be able to handle a small dory. Once there, Johnny will be no trouble, occupying himself with the herring weirs. Almira adds: " 'we don't want to carry no men folks havin' to be considered every minute an' takin' up all of our time.' "

This is a world in which women prepare medicinal teas and syrups, doctor the sick, make their own shoes, reweave the carpets, go fishing and clamming, raise sheep, chickens, and vegetables, sew and repair clothing, and cook and preserve foods. Most male critics who comment on the novel emphasize the deterioration of shipping activity which has ended much of the prosperity once enjoyed by Dunnet Landing. They are not so much impressed by the vital domestic activities of the women as depressed by the town's lack of an outlet for traditional masculine activities which might provide more interesting or exciting roles for the men of Dunnet Landing.

But in this fictional universe, as in so much of Jewett's work, there is no masculine leadership or authority. This fact is not necessarily the result of economic conditions. When we examine the male characters who appear in *The Country of the Pointed Firs,* we find that their failures generally result from traits of character rather than from age or circumstance. For example, William Blackett, who is excessively timid and shy, has not made much of his life (according to Mrs. Todd) because he lacks his mother's "snap." And the Reverend Mr. Dimmick is both a poor sailor (endangering his and Mrs. Todd's lives during their trip) and a poor spiritual guide. He fails to give any comfort to the reclusive Joanna Todd and is sent off like a small boy to look for Indian artifacts while Joanna and Mrs. Todd discuss their deeply felt emotions and Joanna explains her decision to remain a recluse on Shell-heap Island. Santin Bowden, who marshals the participants at the Bowden reunion, is still another example of failure, spending his life as a shoemaker while always longing for a military career. Rejected when he tried to enlist in the Civil War because he was not considered "a sound man," he suffers from "gloomy spells . . . an' then he has to drink."

The women of Dunnet Landing, capable, busy, and sensible, are Jewett's subject, and as long as the topic of women's activities and their relationships with one another seemed unfashionable, the novel was invariably thought of as a "minor" masterpiece or a "quaint" classic.

Another difficulty with Jewett's subject matter has been the age of her characters. In many respects, *The Country of the Pointed Firs* celebrates the lives of the elderly. Foremost among the aged characters is Mrs. Blackett, Almira Todd's eighty-six-year-old mother. Almira herself is sixty-seven, and although we do not know the exact age of the narrator, her remarks on the topic of growing old indicate her own awareness of the passing of time.

On the way home from the Bowden reunion, she is briefly concerned about the possible strain of the day for Mrs. Blackett, but notes that neither Mrs. Blackett nor Mrs. Todd was troubled by the burden of years. "I hoped in my heart that I might be like them as I lived on into old age, and then smiled to think that I too was no longer very young. So we always keep the same hearts, though our outer framework fails and shows the touch of time."

Virtually every character in the book is nearly sixty years old, and a number are in their seventies or eighties. Jewett's vision was, no doubt, partially determined by the realities of small-town life along the Maine coast. With such limited opportunity for economic advancement in the small towns, and the difficulty of farming on the surrounding thin soil and rocky hills, young people frequently left for the cities in order to have a wider range of possibilities. But Jewett's treatment of her older characters is so obviously marked by a genuine respect and liking for them that in this case there was a fortuitous combination of necessity and preference. As Susan Allen Toth has noted:

> Miss Jewett is interested in her old people not only because they are vital and alert, but also because their age gives them a special sensitivity. Looking back upon their lives, they have a deepened awareness of what Miss Jewett believes are the most important moments of life. . . .[5]

In analyzing the characteristic attitudes of the older characters, Toth finds a Wordsworthian quality in some who experience a dual pleasure in their activities. They value the happiness of the present, but they also know that it will provide enjoyable memories for the future.[6] The desire to experience pleasure fully and to absorb it without distraction is exemplified by a comment of Almira Todd's on the way home from the Bowden reunion. Some of the guests have not yet returned home, visiting elsewhere to finish out the day, but Mrs. Todd believes " 'Those that enjoyed it best want to get right home so's to think it over.' "

Nevertheless, Jewett does not romanticize old age, nor does she suggest that longevity confers admirable traits on the elderly. She also depicts such characters as Captain Littlepage, who must be cared for by Mari' Harris, a hired house-

[5] "The Value of Age in the Fiction of Sarah Orne Jewett," *Studies in Short Fiction*, VIII (Summer 1971), 435–36.
[6] *Ibid.*, 436–37.

keeper, and who is generally scorned or unheeded by the townspeople; Elijah Tilley, who has never recovered from the death of his dear wife; and who is patiently awaiting death himself; and Mrs. Hight, an invalid made extremely demanding and querulous by her infirmities and by the loss of her independence early in life through illness.

An important unifying element of the novel is the tenor of the comments of Almira Todd, who is the narrator's and our guide through the woods and fields and over the sea to the houses of the country of the pointed firs. Her judgments and sympathies set the tone for each of our visits, and she is an admirable teacher both indoors and out. She tells us that the woods, which make many people uncomfortable or fearful, have always seemed like home to her. Nature has enriched her vision of human behavior, and the following are typical descriptions of her experience. She is pleased to find that an ash tree which was formerly "kind of drooping and discouraged" now appears healthy and strong: "Grown trees act that way sometimes, same's folks; then they'll put right to it and strike their roots off into new ground and start all over again with real good courage." Similarly, Mrs. Todd describes her preference for the tansy that grows near the schoolhouse lot, and which she characterizes as having a great deal of "snap" to it: "Being scuffed down all the spring made it grow so much the better like some folks that had it hard in their youth, and were bound to make the most of themselves before they died."

In assessing the virtues and failings of her neighbors, Mrs. Todd exhibits considerable tolerance, a sincere enjoyment of good company, and a capacity for imagination and sympathy that enables her to understand and empathize with the diverse characters in and around Dunnet Landing. Not in the least disturbed by harmless eccentricity, she wishes that Mari' Harris would have the tact to listen to Captain Littlepage's stories; and she comprehends the impulse behind Mrs. Martin's preparation of a supper to be shared with Queen Victoria, who will obviously never arrive to eat it. And when Mrs. Fosdick suggests that a trip to Massachusetts or out West might have cured Joanna Todd's depression, it is Mrs. Todd who objects to this oversimplification of the problem, explaining: " 'No. . . .'T is like bad eyesight, the mind of such a person: if your eyes don't see right there may be a remedy, but there's no kind of glasses to remedy the mind.' "

With her much broader perspective on the world, the narrator nonetheless is entertained, instructed, and refreshed by her visits in and around the country of the pointed firs. Although she never has cause to pity Mrs. Todd, she does make a discovery about her friend at the Bowden reunion:

> The excitement of an unexpectedly great occasion was a subtle stimulant to her disposition, and I could see that sometimes when Mrs. Todd had seemed limited and heavily domestic, she had simply grown sluggish for lack of proper surroundings. She was not so much reminiscent now as expectant, and as alert and gay as a girl. We who were her neighbors were full of gayety, which was but the reflected light from her beaming countenance. It was not the first time that I was full of wonder at the waste of human ability in this world, as a botanist wonders at the wastefulness of nature, the thousand seeds that die, the unused provision of every sort.

This is one of the rare passages in which the narrator, who will return to the larger sphere of the world, acknowledges the limitations of the narrower sphere of Dunnet Landing. She, however, is free to enjoy the best of both worlds, using the Landing as a retreat from the pressures of a harried city existence. But her respect for her independent friend forces this admission that Mrs. Todd has abundant vital forces which are insufficiently utilized in her calling in life.

Nonetheless, the narrator has a just appreciation of the beauties and restorative powers of this small Maine community. Her simple but rich experiences there may be reminiscent of what his Walden experiences represented to Henry David Thoreau. He retreated to a one-room cabin in which to write; Jewett's narrator bargains for a summer's use of a one-room schoolhouse overlooking the town and the sea for the same purpose. She explores a great deal of both human character and nature's scenes in the neighborhood of the seacoast village. As Thoreau was to claim that he had traveled much in Concord (scorning those tourists who merely traversed vast spaces without truly learning and living), so the narrator of *The Country of the Pointed Firs* might justly claim that much had she traveled in Dunnet Landing. She sums up her relationship with this special place as follows:

> When one really knows a village like this and its surroundings, it is like becoming acquainted with a single

person. The process of falling in love at first sight is as final as it is swift in such a case, but the growth of true friendship may be a lifelong affair.

SHORT STORIES

The stories of Jewett in this volume were selected with three basic considerations in mind. First, they are among her best pieces of fiction; second, they present typical techniques and subject matter; and finally, they rarely, if ever, appear in anthologies. Generally, Jewett has been represented in fiction collections by one of four stories: "A White Heron," "The Courting of Sister Wisby," "The Dulham Ladies," or "Miss Tempy's Watchers." Although these are among her finest stories, they are only four of a large group of stories deserving attention. This collection affords those four tales a well-deserved rest and provides an opportunity for readers to become acquainted with several equally valuable Jewett stories.

Jewett (as well as Freeman) wrote numerous stories on a topic that has become overwhelmingly important in America: the problem of living with dignity and security in old age. From a number of her stories, it becomes clear that in New England homes of a century ago middle-aged and even elderly parents commonly retained control of a household where married children had moved in, enlarging the number of working members of the family. A widow of some means generally prided herself on her fortunate independence and had sufficient relatives and friends so that she could still feel herself a vital and respected member of the community. She usually managed to remain in the house where she had spent her adult life and dreaded the time when she would be forced to make a series of long "visits" to her married children, thus becoming a dependent in their households. The most deplorable situation of all was that of the ill or totally impoverished old woman who could not afford help to run her farm or who could no longer "do for herself." If she had outlived all close relations, she could only anticipate with horror the arrangements that outsiders would make for her.

Two of the Jewett stories, "The Town Poor" (1890) and "Aunt Cynthy Dallett" (1899), deal with the failure or success of arrangements for old age. Within the framework of the short visit paid by Mrs. Trimble and Miss Wright to the Bray sisters in "The Town Poor," the author depicts the bleak, impoverished existence of two handicapped old women, without the means to support themselves and left to the mechanism of the New England town's "welfare" system—a system which has failed dismally in the case of these two sensitive gentlewomen. Their father, generous in matters of township repairs and renovations, did not, however, "put by" for his unmarried daughters. When the well-to-do Mrs. Trimble recalls Mr. Bray's lack of forethought, she quotes the adage for the letter "B" that she learned as a child from her copy book: "Be just before you are generous."

Forced by the selectmen to relinquish their village house and to put all their possessions up at auction, the honest Bray sisters have kept back only four of their mother's prized sprigged china cups. Thus, they have been stripped of all the familiar objects which give the New England housekeeper a sense of pleasure and remind her of the continuity of her family.

After the town of Hampden had collected whatever could be raised through the auction, the two old women were "bid off" for five dollars a month by Abel Janes. His wife, an unskilled housekeeper of an unpromising and isolated farm, feels that taking in the sisters at that price for their room and board was indeed a bad bargain on the part of her husband, and after four visits to the selectmen, Mrs. Janes has managed to extract the promise that they will provide the money for a few amenities and some firewood. In fact, the pitiable sisters still lack the "stout shoes an' rubbers" which would allow them to walk to Sunday meeting. Their room contains only a single usable chair and their bed.

Jewett concludes this tale of the dismal existence of the old and impoverished sisters on an optimistic note—but it is not of social reform. The help to be had for Ann and Mandana Bray will come from the efforts of Mrs. Trimble, a good-hearted acquaintance. One individual will relieve the suffering of two deserving friends and will force the officials of the town to rearrange the "welfare" plans based entirely on the desire to handle the Bray sisters with the least possible expenditure for the town.

In "Aunt Cynthy Dallett", Jewett once again used the action of paying a call to dramatize the attitudes and needs of her characters. Aunt Cynthy, now eighty-five years old and somewhat lame, has spent her life in her hillside house. She is visited on New Year's Day by her niece, Abby Pendexter, who is also elderly and who lives in the village below. Although Abby is the younger of the two, she feels the anxieties of old age more strongly since she is also troubled by poverty. She has had to sell her hens in order to pay the quarterly rent of twelve dollars on her house in the village.

Abby's kindly friend, Mrs. Hand, who accompanies her on her call to Aunty Cynthy, perceives the trauma involved when an independent and solitary woman must think of giving up her own house. She realizes that the best solution would be for Abby to join Cynthy, but adds: " 'I know just how you both feel. I like to have my own home an' do everything just my way too!' "

In this tale a seemingly trivial action takes on great significance for the women. When Abby has been in the sitting room while the others remained in the kitchen, she thoughtfully "opened the window to let the sun in awhile." Mrs. Dallett, who at one time would have been provoked by anyone's taking such a "liberty" in her house, now feels comforted by the presence of a caring and affectionate relative. In addition, noticing the carefully darned places in her niece's dress, she thinks compassionately: " 'She begins to look sort o' set and dried up, Abby does. She oughtn't to live all alone; she's one that needs company.' "

By the end of the visit, the aunt and niece have come to an understanding through which the needs of both will be satisfied. Neither woman need lose her dignity: Abby sees herself as moving up to the hillside house her aunt loves in order to keep an aging relative company; Mrs. Dallett comes to realize that Abby, though younger, is having a difficult time and needs someone too. Jewett demonstrates the desire each woman has to be treated with tact and consideration as well as with warmheartedness.

Two of Jewett's stories, "Miss Esther's Guest" (1893) and "Miss Peck's Promotion" (1888) deal with a potential marriage, but these could hardly be called tales of courtship. Typically, both depict characters who are not young. In "Miss Esther's Guest," the refined and timid Esther Porley, who is sixty-four years old, overcomes her reticence and decides to accept a city guest, who will be sent to her village from Boston through the arrangements of the Committee for the Country Week, a charitable, church-related organization.

Although Esther has carefully specified that she would "know how to do for a woman that's getting well along in years, an' has come to feel kind o' spent," the guest assigned to her, through an oversight, is Mr. Rill, an elderly retired engraver who lives in Boston in a fourth-floor garret room where the only view from his window is of a brick wall.

Jewett skillfully sketches the ways in which these two lonely people supply important comforts to one another and the pleasure which this accidental coming together has provided. The discovery of a truly suitable mate at any age is a touching theme, and in Jewett's fiction such experiences among the elderly are not rare.

In "Miss Peck's Promotion," Eliza Peck is called upon by the Reverend Wilbur Elbury to take over as housekeeper upon the death of his wife. Thus Eliza, who is forty, leaves her hillside farmhouse to reside at the busy parsonage in the village below. The parishioners expect that Eliza will become the minister's second wife, and Eliza herself slowly begins to entertain the prospect, as she and the Reverend spend a number of enjoyable evenings reading aloud together.

It was all a new world to the good woman whose schooling and reading had been sound, but restricted; and if ever a mind waked up with joy to its possession of the world of books, it was hers. She became ambitious for the increase of her own little library; and it was in reply to her outspoken plan for larger crops and more money from the farm another year, for the sake of bookbuying, that Mr. Elbury once said, earnestly, that his books were hers now. This careless expression was the spark which lit a new light for Miss Peck's imagination.

The hard-working and competent woman is attracted not so much by the minister, whose selfishness and indolence she well knows, but by the glimpse of the world of excitement and delight made accessible through the books in his house.

Throughout the period of her belief (which will prove erroneous) that she and the minister are drawing closer together through the friendly activities and interests which she expects would make a sound basis for marriage, Eliza checks her impulses to make any outward display of her feelings. And when the minister unexpectedly brings home the new bride he has chosen, a pretty but pretentious and unskilled young girl, Eliza recovers quickly from the illusions she had had about Elbury.

Jewett's tale involves two undesirable marriages—one consummated, the other contemplated. The reader, like Eliza, is

convinced that Wilbur Elbury has married a woman who will
be neither strong enough to balance the weaknesses of his
character nor competent enough to make the parsonage the
comfortable place it was under Eliza's rule. Yet Jewett
clearly considers the match that Eliza contemplated as also
distinctly unsuitable. A remarkable woman of strength and
common sense, Eliza frequently misses her hilltop view and
farm while living in the village. The lure of the parsonage is
that of a place where greater use could be made of her energy and intelligence. But on her return to her own home,
Eliza will take with her the best part of life at the minister's
household, an enthusiasm for and determination to continue
exploring the literary horizons which have opened before her.
The insensitivity of the minister's behavior during his secret
courtship of a woman in another town strongly indicates his
moral unworthiness, and the reader comes to see Eliza not as
a rejected woman, but as an enriched individual.

The last of the Jewett selections, "The Passing of Sister
Barsett" (1893), is another tale with a social call as a framework for the action. Miss Sarah Ellen Dow, who has been
nursing the ailing Sister Barsett, stops at the house of her
friend Mrs. Mercy Crane to recount the events of the last few
days and to bring the news that Sister Barsett has
passed away. During the course of Sarah Ellen's narrative we
learn a considerable amount about Sister Barsett's history of
hypochondria, her medical and religious opinions, and her
flaws as a housekeeper; we also learn of her kindly treatment
of Sarah Ellen, who works as a nurse for the elderly or dying
and does not have a permanent home of her own. Sarah Ellen is smarting from the tactless treatment she has received at
the hands of Sister Barsett's two sisters, who arrived at the
house when they were finally convinced that their sister's
death was imminent. She gleefully describes one of Sister
Barsett's final actions:

> "She was herself to the last. . . . I see her put out a
> thumb an' finger from under the spread and pinch up a
> fold of her sister Deckett's dress, to try an' see if it was
> all wool. I thought 't wa'n't all wool, myself, an' I know
> it now by the way she looked. She was a very knowin'
> person about materials; we shall miss poor Mis' Barsett
> in many ways, she was always the one to consult with
> about matters o' dress."

Mercy Crane, eager to discuss all the details of this momentous occasion, invites Sarah Ellen in for a rather elaborate tea, which gratifies and pleases both women. Their all-too-human rehearsing of Sister Barsett's shortcomings is nicely balanced by a sincere appreciation of her finer traits. The women are soon to find, however, that they have not yet quite finished with the indomitable Sister Barsett.

In this, as in most of Jewett's fiction, the incidents are not world-shaking. Typically the author records the way in which an old woman carefully wears a mended glove so that the tear will not be too noticeable, or the way in which a long afternoon may be pleasurably shortened by a visit from an acquaintance who can produce a bit of gossip or a shrewd observation about family relationships. The lives of the characters are never lived out on a grand scale. Yet there is much that we recognize and enjoy of enduring human nature, which the author so meticulously and tenderly renders for us.

BIOGRAPHY

Sarah Orne Jewett was the second of three daughters of Caroline Perry and Theodore H. Jewett. Born on September 3, 1849, she was christened Theodora Sarah Orne Jewett, her first name a feminized form of both her father's and paternal grandfather's. Although the family soon dropped the "Theodora" from use, it had been a significant—almost prophetic—choice, since her father was to be the single most influential figure in Sarah Orne Jewett's development. Dr. Jewett, a dedicated physician, provided the young Sarah with the two indispensable sources of growth and inspiration that would later inform her creative adulthood. First, he shared his love and knowledge of literature with her, encouraging her to read and discuss his favorite authors. Second, because she suffered from attacks of arthritis (diagnosed at the time as rheumatism) from childhood and did not seem to flourish indoors at school, he often allowed her to forego long days in the classroom. Instead, she accompanied him as he visited his patients. During these lengthy trips, Sarah learned to observe closely and appreciate the scenes of nature before her. And at each stop at a farmhouse where some ailing child or adult required the doctor's care, she began to glimpse the underlying drama of these country people whose lives often seemed so bland or routine on the surface.

The countryside around her home in South Berwick,

Maine, had rich associations for Sarah which went beyond farm life. An inland port on the banks of the Piscataqua River, about twenty miles from Portsmouth, Berwick had been a prosperous and energetic ship-building center. Some vestiges of the excitement of this seagoing community still remained during Sarah's childhood. Her grandfather, who in his youth had been an adventurous sea captain and shipowner, attracted men of similar seafaring experience to his general store, and there Sarah could hear tales of past glories, when South Berwick provided men and supplies for voyages to all the exotic ports of the world. Those voyages had by then become only cherished memories, since a series of circumstances had conspired to leave such New England towns as South Berwick mere relics of what they had been. But because these memories were an integral part of the lives of Sarah's relatives, the influence of the sea on the texture of life along the Maine coast became woven into the fabric of her art.

Her formal education consisted essentially of four years at Berwick Academy, from which she was graduated at the age of sixteen. Her literary career was initiated with the publication of a short story, "Jenny Garrow's Lovers," in *The Flag of Our Union* (Vol. XXIII, Jan. 18, 1868) a few months after she turned eighteen. Her next two stories were rejected by *The Atlantic Monthly,* but another, "Mr. Bruce," was accepted and appeared in 1869.

Sarah had a desire for a career as a doctor, but because of her poor health and her knowledge of the physical strains of that profession, she realized how difficult fulfilling her goal might prove. Instead, she began regularly to contribute children's poems and stories to magazines, and in 1873 her first Maine story, "The Shore House," appeared in the *Atlantic.* By then, she knew that she was meant to be a writer.

Sarah seemed always to believe that she would not marry, and there are no indications that she ever fell in love. Financially secure because of a comfortable legacy from her grandfather, she seems not to have experienced any family or social pressures to conform to nineteenth-century traditions of feminine behavior. Both she and her older sister Mary—also unmarried—cherished a sense of their independence and general competence in the world.

The death of her father from a heart attack in 1878 caused Sarah intense grief. She had dedicated her volume *Country By-Ways* to him with an inscription to "My dear father; my dear friend; the best and wisest man I ever knew." Fortunately, a few years after Dr. Jewett's death, her friendship with Annie Fields, the wife of publisher and editor James Fields, became an increasing source of pleasure and consolation. Sarah had been a fond friend of both James and Annie, and, after James's death in 1881, she discovered a similarity in tastes and interests with Annie that led to extended visits at her home in Boston. The friendship deepened, becoming a nurturing and enriching force for both women. Soon Sarah was dividing her time between Boston and South Berwick, spending summers at Annie's cottage at Manchester-by-the-Sea. In South Berwick, she had a great deal of freedom to write, since her sister Mary had charge of the household, and even the care of her invalid mother was not a difficult responsibility. Her time at South Berwick was often spent productively, and the slower pace of the small Maine town provided a balance for the busy social activities at Annie Fields' house in the city.

These comfortable arrangements were disrupted on September 3, 1902, when Sarah fell from a carriage. The accident had crippling effects, both physical and psychological, from which she never fully recovered. One of the most devastating of these effects was that the accident brought to an end her writing career of thirty-four years. Although she was still capable of writing letters, she was unable to resume writing short stories. In March of 1909, while visiting Annie Fields, she was taken ill and, after being returned to South Berwick, suffered a cerebral hemmorhage. Her death came on June 24 of that year.

SELECTED BIBLIOGRAPHY

❧❧

THE FICTION OF SARAH ORNE JEWETT

Deephaven. Boston: James R. Osgood, 1877.

Old Friends and New. Boston: Houghton, Osgood, 1879.

Country By-Ways. Boston: Houghton, Mifflin, 1881.

The Mate of the Daylight, and Friends Ashore. Boston and New York: Houghton, Mifflin, 1884.

A Country Doctor. Boston and New York: Houghton, Mifflin, 1884.

A Marsh Island. Boston and New York: Houghton, Mifflin, 1885.

A White Heron and Other Stories. Boston and New York: Houghton, Mifflin, 1886.

The King of Folly Island and Other People. Boston and New York: Houghton, Mifflin, 1888.

Strangers and Wayfarers. Boston and New York: Houghton, Mifflin, 1890.

A Native of Winby and Other Tales. Boston and New York: Houghton, Mifflin, 1893.

The Life of Nancy. Boston and New York: Houghton, Mifflin, 1895.

The Queen's Twin and Other Stories. Boston and New York: Houghton, Mifflin, 1899.

The Tory Lover. Boston and New York: Houghton, Mifflin, 1901.

The Uncollected Short Stories of Sarah Orne Jewett, edited by Richard Cary, Waterville, Maine: Colby College Press, 1971.

Selected Biographical and Critical Materials

Auchincloss, Louis. *Pioneers and Caretakers.* Minneapolis: University of Minnesota Press, 1965.

Bender, Bert. "To Calm and Uplift 'Against the Dark': Sarah Orne Jewett's Lyric Narratives," *Colby Library Quarterly,* 11 (December 1975), 219-29.

*Berthoff, Warner. "The Art of Jewett's Pointed Firs," *New England Quarterly,* 32 (March 1959), 31-53.

*Chapman, Edward M. "The New England of Sarah Orne Jewett," *Yale Review,* 3 (October 1913), 157-72.

Brooks, Van Wyck. *New England: Indian Summer*. New York: E. P. Dutton and Co., Inc., 1940.

*Buchan, Alexander M. *"Our Dear Sarah"; An Essay on Sarah Orne Jewett*. Washington University Studies New Series. Language and Literature—No. 24 (St. Louis, 1953).

Cary, Richard. *Sarah Orne Jewett*. New York: Twyane Publishers, Inc., 1962.

Cary, Richard, ed. *Sarah Orne Jewett: Letters*. Waterville, Maine: Colby College Press, 1956.

———. *Appreciation of Sarah Orne Jewett: 29 Interpretive Essays*. Waterville, Maine: Colby College Press, 1973.

Cather, Willa. *Not Under Forty*. New York: A. A. Knopf, 1936.

*Eakin, Paul John. "Sarah Orne Jewett and the Meaning of Country Life," *American Literature*, 38 (January 1967), 508-531.

Frost, John Eldridge. *Sarah Orne Jewett*. Kittery Point, Maine: The Gundalow Club, Inc., 1960.

Green, David Bonnell. "The World of Dunnet Landing," *New England Quarterly*, 34 (December 1961), 514-17.

*Magowan, Robin. "Pastoral and the Art of Landscape in 'The Country of the Pointed Firs,'" *New England Quarterly*, 36 (June 1963), 229-240.

Matthiessen, Francis Otto. *Sarah Orne Jewett*. Boston: Houghton, Mifflin, 1929.

Parrington, Vernon Louis. *The Beginnings of Critical Realism in America*. New York: Harcourt, Brace and Co., 1930.

Quinn, Arthur Hobson. *American Fiction. A Historical Survey*. D. Appleton Century Co., 1936.

Stevenson, Catherine Barnes. "The Double Consciousness of the Narrator in Sarah Orne Jewett's Fiction," *Colby Library Quarterly*, 11 (March 1975), 1-12.

Thorp, Margaret Farrand. *Sarah Orne Jewett*. Minneapolis: University of Minnesota Press, 1966.

*Toth, Susan A. "The Value of Age in the Fiction of Sarah Orne Jewett." *Studies in Short Fiction*, 8 (Summer 1971), 433-41.

———. "Sarah Orne Jewett and Friends: A Community of Interest," *Studies in Short Fiction*, 9 (Summer 1972), 233-41.

Vella, Michael W. "A Reading of 'The Country of the Pointed Firs,'" *ESQ: A Journal of the American Renaissance*, 19 (1973), 275-82.

*Voelker, Paul D. " 'The Country of the Pointed Firs': A Novel by Sarah Orne Jewett," *Colby Library Quarterly*, 9 (December 1970) 201-213.

Westbrook, Perry D. *Acres of Flint: Writers of Rural New England, 1870-1900*. Washington, D.C.: The Scarecrow Press, 1951.

* Articles marked with an asterisk have been republished in Richard Cary's *Appreciation of Sarah Orne Jewett: 29 Interpretive Essays.*

MARY WILKINS FREEMAN

❧❦

SHORT STORIES

The typical Mary Wilkins Freeman story deals with a heroine who is generally over forty years old, and frequently over fifty or sixty. Whereas in the stories of Sarah Orne Jewett, the people of the surrounding villages and towns are generally sympathetic onlookers, in the stories of Freeman, the independent and courageous heroines often find that they need to defend themselves and their opinions against the scorn or criticism of the larger community. Thus, there is a great deal more conflict in the Freeman stories. Typically, in the stories of both writers somewhat impoverished characters exist in rather restrictive circumstances. There are few luxuries in most of the households they depict, yet their characters have an enviable capacity for experiencing joy in the blooming of a potted plant or in a spoonful of good preserves at teatime. The need to conserve material goods gives an intensity to their enjoyment which is often absent from works in which the characters live in a world without material cares.

A number of Freeman's finest stories have as their central theme a woman's determination to maintain her own identity and to live by her own values in old age, in spite of oppressive circumstances, harsh criticism, or opposition. Among such stories in this volume are "A Mistaken Charity," "A Church Mouse," "An Independent Thinker," "A Village Singer," and "A Poetess." In addition, a related theme, the discovery of a woman's separate identity, no matter how late in life, is the subject of "The Lombardy Poplar."

In "A Mistaken Charity" (1887), the two elderly Shattuck sisters live together in the house in which they were raised. Harriet, the elder, is somewhat deaf as well as rheumatic, and Charlotte is blind. But they manage to survive through occasional gifts of food from kindly neighbors and such treats as berries from their own currant and gooseberry bushes, apples from their two trees, and the pumpkins which Harriet, with great pride, raises. As the story opens, they are anticipating with pleasure a dinner of a "mess of dandelions" which they will boil with a bit of pork.

When a well-meaning neighbor arranges for the sisters to enter an "Old Ladies Home" in a nearby city, she cannot understand their reluctance to leave. But the new circumstances, which most people would consider a change for the better, make Harriet and Charlotte miserable. Both the food and manner of dressing at the "Home" offend them:

> . . . nothing could transform these two unpolished old women into two nice old ladies. They did not take kindly to white lace caps and delicate neckerchiefs. They liked their new black cashmere dresses well enough, but they felt as if they broke a commandment when they put them on every afternoon. They had always worn calico with long aprons at home, and they wanted to now; and they wanted to twist up their scanty gray locks into little knots at the back of their heads, and go without caps, just as they always had done.

Feeble but undaunted, the two old women make their escape to return home, and Harriet enjoys the idea that the people who run the "Home" will learn that " 'folks ain't goin' to be made to wear caps agin their will in a free kentry.' "

Freeman brilliantly portrays the simple pleasures of these women's lives through Charlotte's insistence that she experiences "chinks" of light in her otherwise black world when something truly delightful happens. She tries to explain what this phenomenon is like to her incredulous sister:

> "If you had seen the light streamin' in all of a sudden through some little hole that you hadn't known of before when you set down on the door-step this mornin', and the wind with the smell of the apple blows in it came in your face, an' when Mis' Simonds brought them hot doughnuts, an' when I thought of the pork an' greens jest now—O Lord, how it did shine in! An' it does now. If you was me, Harriét, you would know there was chinks."

Only in their weathered old cottage with their coarse but hearty meals can these women please themselves and be themselves. Theirs is the triumph of an independent spirit that evades the "system."

Two other stories which end triumphantly for women in conflict with society are "A Church Mouse" (1891) and "An Independent Thinker" (1887). In "A Church Mouse," which also deals with the arrangements to be made for an impoverished old woman, Hetty Fifield's conflict with society is much more dramatic than that of the Shattuck sisters. Hetty struggles in order to secure a dignified niche in the small town where she has always lived.

Upon the death of the employer with whom she shared a run-down old house, she has been evicted, and her possessions, which consist of a cookstove, a bed, a sunflower quilt, and a few framed wool flower samplers, have been set out in the yard. Thus, she engages in a desperate argument with Caleb Gale, a deacon of the town's church and, in spite of his many objections, manages to get herself appointed church sexton—a position never before held by a woman in the history of the village. Her arguments could hardly have been more effective or modern if they had been written by a feminist of this decade:

> "Men git in a good many places where they don't be-
> long, an' where they set as awkward as a cow on a hen-
> roost, jest because they push in ahead of women. I ain't
> blamin' em; I s'pose if I could push in I should, jest the
> same way. But there ain't no reason that I can see, nor
> nobody else neither, why a woman shouldn't be sax-
> ton."

When the deacon questions Hetty's ability to perform such physical tasks as sweeping the meeting house, tending the fires, and tolling the bell, this tough and resilient old woman points out that she has been doing those and more difficult kinds of chores all her life.

In Hetty Fifield, Freeman depicts a character who not only stands up to individual male figures of authority, but who must withstand a virtual onslaught by a community intent on ousting her from her new shelter, the meeting house. The author characterizes her as a woman who has always functioned as an outsider:

> She was held in the light of a long-thorned brier among
> the beanpoles, or a fierce little animal with claws and

teeth bared. People were afraid to take her into their families; she had the reputation of always taking her own way, and never heeding the voice of authority. "I'd take her in an' have her give me a lift with the work," said one sickly farmer's wife; "but, near's I can find out, I couldn't never be sure that I'd get molasses in the beans, nor saleratus in my sour-milk cakes, if she took a notion not to put it in. I don't dare to risk it."

Certainly, the story provides an unusual portrait of a heroine, one who finds no precedent inviolable and who manages to gain understanding from those around her. To change the opinion of an entire New England congregation is no mean achievement.

In "An Independent Thinker," Esther Gay, a proud old woman refuses to perform the meaningless ritual of attending church on Sunday when she is so deaf that she will not be able to hear the preacher. Since she considers services a waste of two valuable hours of her life each week, she chooses instead to knit stockings that she then sells, donating her earnings to the needy.

The pressure on her to conform is intense. It is manifested when her granddaughter's suitor, Henry Little, ceases to come calling. His mother has no objection to the girl, Hatty Gay, but doesn't want her son to marry "any girl whose folks didn't keep Sunday, an' stayed away from meetin'. . . ." Esther hotly responds that she isn't going to give up her princi ples for Henry nor any of his family, and, if anything, she knits more furiously than ever on the succeeding Sundays.

Through her ingenuity and determination, Esther undertakes an important new charitable occupation to avoid attending Sunday meeting and to bring Henry and Hatty together without compromising herself. This tale affects us with a profound sense of the inexorable demands that a narrow-minded community can make and of the pressures that are brought to bear on the nonconformist.

Two women who do not fare as well as Esther Gay in maintaining their self-image are Candace Whitcomb of "A Village Singer" (1891) and Betsey Dole of "A Poetess" (1891), Both of these women have defined themselves in terms of the possession of a special talent or function and suffer extraordinarily when the larger world no longer shares their vision of this special identity.

In "A Village Singer," Candace Whitcomb has been dismissed after forty years from her paid position as the leading soprano of her church's choir. Freeman vividly describes what singing her solos had meant to Candace: "To this obscure woman, kept relentlessly by circumstances in a narrow track, singing in the village choir had been as much as Italy was to Napoleon—and now on her island of exile she was still showing fight."

On the Sunday when the new soprano, Alma Way, takes her place for the first time, Candace, who lives close to the church, waits for Alma to begin her solo. Then she plans and sings another hymn so that it can be clearly heard inside the church, disconcerting the new performer and irritating the entire congregation.

When Mr. Pollard, the minister, visits Candace during his noontime break to remonstrate about her unseemly behavior, he finds, to his great shock, a rebellious and bitter adversary, who decries the way she has been treated:

> "My voice is as good an' high today as it was twenty years ago; an' if it wa'n't, I'd like to know where the Christianity comes in. I'd like to know if it wouldn't be more to the credit of folks in a church to keep an old singer an' an old minister, if they didn't sing an' hold forth quite so smart as they used to, ruther than turn 'em off an' hurt their feelin's. I guess it would be full as much to the glory of God. . . . Salvation don't hang on anybody's hittin' a high note, that I ever heard of."

Interestingly, although Mr. Pollard and William Emmons, the choir leader, have served as long as Candace, the congregation has no intention of replacing them with younger, more energetic men. Only the old woman is considered incompetent. Although Candace lashes out at those who have hurt her, there is no possibility that she will prevail, and her anger becomes a self-destructive force. Her powerful sense of her own identity and of the beauty of her own singing voice never desert her. Even on her deathbed, at a scene of reconciliation with her nephew, Wilson Ford, and with Alma Way, she is true to her standards for her art; she says, after Alma has sung for her: " 'You flatted a little on—soul'. . . ."

Whereas Candace Whitcomb's reaction to criticism of her voice is a rebellion against authority and continued confidence in her own judgment, Betsey Dole of "A Poetess" reacts with characteristic meekness to criticism of her poetry. No one suspects the damage inflicted on her beautiful sense of self by a minister's evaluation of her work. Mrs. Caxton, upon the death of whose young son Betsey had composed a memorial poem, reports this cruel comment to her: " '*Sarah Rogers says that the minister told her Ida that that poetry you wrote was jest as poor as it could be, an' it was in dreadful bad taste to have it printed an' sent round that way.*' " He concludes that Betsey "had never wrote anything that could be called poetry, an' it was a dreadful waste of time."

Freeman wants us to be certain that the criticism is justified and that indeed Betsey writes dreadful, sentimental verses. She has Mrs. Caxton explain some of the qualities of her dead child that she would like to see included in the poem:

> "You could mention how—handsome he was, and good, and I never had to punish him but once in his life, and how pleased he was with his little new suit, and what a sufferer he was, and—how we hope he is at rest—in a better land."

After reading the resulting poem, Mrs. Caxton feels comforted and gratified that Betsey was able to include a reference to Willie's new suit.

Betsey's poetry may be execrable; nevertheless the loss of her identity as a poet is tragic. For the reader has witnessed the sacrifices Betsey gladly makes to write her poem (going without lunch, eating a meager dinner of bread and jelly), knows the exquisite pride and pleasure she takes in the printed copy of the verse, and thus can gauge the devastation caused by the minister's casual criticism. It is virtually a death blow for the impoverished and ailing woman.

In Freeman's portrait of Betsey Dole, we have a simple lover of beauty, who raises flowers in her garden when a larger supply of vegetables would be much more suitable and practical. A life of deprivations does not seem to bother her. With her own well run dry, she must carry water for her garden some distance each hot and dusty evening. Her good summer dress is very old, but she cannot afford another. Obviously, a serene sense of her particular talent as a poet sustains her, rendering her poverty and lack of comfort unimportant. "The Poetess" dramatizes not merely the disillusionment of a good woman, but also expresses that sense of betrayal experienced by a religious person. How can Betsey trust in a creator who permits such a disparity between desire and ability within his creation? Betsey can only ask—not answer—this question.

In "The Lombardy Poplar," (1903), Freeman depicts an undistinguished old woman who has lived near a look-alike all her life. First, Sarah Dunn had always dressed exactly like her twin sister, Marah. "They were alike not only in appearance, but in character. The resemblance was so absolute as to produce a feeling of something at fault in the beholder. It was difficult, when looking from one to the other, to believe that the second was a vital fact; it was like seeing double."

Upon Marah's death, her sister had given the entire "twin" wardrobe to a second cousin, also named Sarah Dunn. Since the two cousins already shared many physical characteristics of the Dunn family, "the clothes of the deceased twin completed all that had been necessary to make the resemblance perfect." Thus, as the two women walk regularly through town on their way to Thursday evening meeting, Sarah is once again mirrored by a double. Not only do the cousins reflect a great similarity in their appearance, but they seem in their preferences, opinions, and conversations to be in complete accord.

Sarah is moved to create a separate identity for herself only after her cousin's ridicule of her preference for a particular tree rouses her from her undifferentiated existence. After she has described the comfort she gets from seeing a poplar, the only one of a row of five poplars to survive, she answers her cousin's criticism that the Lombardy poplar is not pretty like an elm or a maple, and doesn't even look like a tree, but more like "a stick tryin' to look like one." A sudden metamorphosis seems to occur as Sarah defends the tree:

She appeared straighter, taller; all her lines of meek yielding, . . . of utter passiveness, vanished. She looked stiff and uncompromising. Her mouth was firm, her chin high, her eyes steady, and more than all, there was over her an expression of individuality which had not been there before. "That's just why I like the popple," said she, in an incisive voice. "That's just why. I'm sick of things and folks that are just like everything and everybody else. I'm sick of trees that are just trees. I like one that ain't."

Sarah reveals the inner change she feels in the very tangible change of appearance which she adopts. At last she stands in an individual relation to the universe.

"One Good Time" (1900) dramatizes the drive with which a heroine asserts herself and secures the single experience which she believes is essential to her happiness. Narcissa Stone, who is probably close to forty years old, has led a life of restriction and deprivation. Prevented from marrying her suitor, William Crane, while her sickly and tyrannical father required her help, she has spent fifteen years serving the old man, whose rheumatism had confined him to a chair. After her father's death, she explains to William how she feels about those years:

> "I 'ain't never had anything like other women. I've never had any clothes nor gone anywhere. I've just stayed at home here and drudged. I've done a man's work on the farm. I've milked and made butter and cheese; I've waited on father; I've got up early and gone to bed late. I've just drudged, drudged, ever since I can remember. I don't know anything about the world nor life."

Narcissa has determined that she and her mother will use most of the $1500 of the insurance money they have inherited to spend a year in New York. She is convinced that she would not make any kind of wife for William if she were merely to move from her father's farm and take up life at William's farm without the "one good time" she has planned to have. Both her mother and William are bewildered by Narcissa's fierce convictions, yet both submit to her will.

The trip might simply be described as one to buy the clothes and jewelry the women have never had, or to visit the theater, but it is more than that. It represents the world of pleasurable experiences and freedom that Narcissa has known only in her imagination. Narcissa's account of her trip to New York is delightful and entertaining in spite of her recollection of the painful circumstances of her departure. Much as the trip differed from Narcissa's imagined experience, and much as it causes her some pangs of guilt, it was truly a success. Now the heroine can move toward her marriage to William gladly and freely.

Of the stories in this volume which depict courtships, only one, "A Conflict Ended" (1887), shows the woman and man resolving their problems and marrying. In fact, by the end of this story, there are two couples who are reunited. The other two tales, "Louisa (1891) and "A New England Nun," (1891) portray women who—for differing reasons—do not wish to marry the suitors who are courting them.

In "A Conflict Ended," Freeman describes a most unusual quarrel which has prevented the marriage of Esther Barney and Marcus Woodman for over ten years. Marcus, in a moment of anger, had sworn that he would never enter the Congregational church if the Reverend Mr. Morton were appointed minister over the objections of a part of the congregation. He has kept his vow not to enter the church, and for ten years has instead taken his place on the church steps each Sunday as services begin. Esther, who was engaged to Marcus at the time has broken her engagement, since she cannot bear to marry any man who could make such a fool of himself. She recognizes the comic aspect of her situation explaining to her apprentice milliner, Margy Wilson: " 'That makes it the hardest of anything, according to my mind— when you know that everybody's laughing, and you can hardly help laughing yourself, though you feel 'most ready to die.' "

A subplot of the story concerns the argument between Margy and her young suitor George Elliot. Their dispute, which leads to a break between them, is over the question of whether George's mother will live with them after they are married. Margy has a strong dislike for Mrs. Elliot, and insists that she will not live in the same household as her future mother-in-law. As a result, George ceases to call. But upon separation, Margy suffers more intensely than George, and she relents, pleading with him to let his mother come live with them, promising to "get along with her," and, even further, asserting that she will "do anything." There is a good deal of cold calculation in George's behavior, because he has learned that his mother will probably live with his brother, Edward. When Margy wonders why George has never told her this good news, his reply is, " 'I thought it was your place to give in, dear.' " His attitude is echoed by Margy when she describes her reconciliation to Esther: " 'I've about made up my mind it's a woman's place to give in mostly. I s'pose you think I'm an awful fool.' "

Esther's own reconciliation is based partly on Margy's advice and partly on the pity she feels for a man trapped by his own stiff-necked will. In an unusual analysis from one of

Freeman's characters, Esther both describes Marcus' flawed
character and suggests that her love for him is not founded
on the rational basis of his possessing sound and pleasing
traits, but stems from a force beyond her judgment.

> ". . . he's got too much will for his common-sense,
> that's all, and the will teeters the sense a little too far
> into the air. I see all through it from the beginning."
> ". . . I s'pose love's the strongest when there ain't any
> good reason for it. They say it is. I can't say as I ever
> really admired Marcus Woodman much. I always see
> right through him; but that didn't hinder my thinking so
> much of him that I never felt as if I could marry any
> other man."

But the message which Freeman communicates through the
actions of both Esther and Margy is certainly an ambiguous
one. For each in submitting to the will of her lover finally has
her own way.

Esther's decision to accept Marcus as a husband is made
utterly without Margy's sense of desperation in capitulating to
George. Freeman informs us that during the past ten years
Esther has enjoyed numerous pleasures as an independent
woman in spite of her need to keep her emotions for Marcus
in check.

> She was more fixed in the peace and pride of her own
> maidenhood than she had realized, and was more shy of
> disturbing it. Her comfortable meals, her tidy housekeep-
> ing, and her prosperous work had become such sources
> of satisfaction to her that she was almost wedded to
> them, and jealous of any interference.

Despite the ludicrous aspects of the quarrel, and the town
of Acton's obvious amusement at Marcus' behavior, the two
old lovers achieve surprising stature as Esther's preferred
submission—even to the point of sharing her husband's igno-
minous place on the church steps—provides him with the
means of saving himself from a pattern which has virtually
become the obsession of his life. Esther's love is the means of
rescuing a man drowning in a sea of his own implacable will.

In "A New England Nun" probably the best known of
Freeman's stories, the author elaborates on the idea of a satisfied solitary woman. While for Esther Barney the satisfac-

tions of her ordered, tidy life are outweighed by feelings of love and pity for Marcus Woodman, Louisa Ellis no longer has such feelings for her fiancé, Joe Dagget. After a separation of fourteen years, Joe has returned home sufficiently wealthy to wed the girl he left behind when he went to seek his fortune.

In a sympathetic and unusual portrait of a single women, Freeman depicts a person who has created a narrow but pleasing life for herself and whose faint stirrings of love for Joe have disappeared with the passing of time. To Louisa, her fast-approaching marriage (to which she believes herself morally committed) means only a series to losses. She loves her own home but will have to give it up to move to Joe's larger house and take on the responsibility of caring for and satisfying a domineering mother-in-law. She knows she must relinquish some of her favorite occupations, such as distilling the aromatic essences of roses and peppermint, and must cease sewing dainty seams for the pure pleasure of putting in the stitches.

On the one hand, one might be tempted to categorize Louisa as a stereotypical spinster who rejects the dirt and disorder of the processes of life. But Freeman will not permit us to dismiss her with this easy judgment. Instead, she catalogues the joys of Louisa's quiet existence, from her evening tea, artistically set on a starched linen cloth with "a damask napkin on her tea-tray, where were arranged a cut-glass tumbler full of teaspoons, a silver cream-pitcher, a china sugar-bowl, and one pink china cup and saucer," to her "throbs of genuine triumph at the sight of the window-panes which she had polished until they shone like jewels." The tale suggests a considerable range of feminine behavior and goals. Typically, the "old maid" has been portrayed as a bitter, deprived creature whose unmarried state has brought her little but envy of the more fortunate members of the species—married women. Freeman, however, suggests that some women may not be suited for marriage, perhaps by temperament or through long years of solitary living. Like the canary who flutters wildly when Joe comes to visit, Louisa is made to feel uncomfortably fluttered by his disruption of her peaceful daily routine. Freeman would no more have us condemn Louisa Ellis' timid and meticulous nature than she would have us condemn Louisa's canary for not having been born an eagle.

The heroine of "Louisa" twenty-four-year-old Louisa Britton, seems to have only three options open to her: teaching, marrying, or starving. Since the first possibility has been taken from her, and since she has a strong aversion to the second, she must struggle valiantly to prevent the third from becoming a reality. Louisa had been supporting her mother and a senile old grandfather since the death of her father when she lost her job as a teacher. After eight years during which she had done her work superbly, her position was given to a relative of a member of the school board.

Louisa's distaste for a marriage without love causes her to discourage the visits of Jonathan Nye, a wealthy bachelor and the only eligible one in the small community. Mrs. Britton bitterly criticizes her daughter's behavior because she visualizes the Nye household as a haven of plenty where meat is enjoyed every day of the week. In her own bare household, she and Louisa must settle for a supper of bread and butter.

Freeman dramatizes the limited possibilities for her determined heroine, who has planted a field of potatoes only to have much of her crop destroyed by her grandfather. Louisa's mother is horrified to think of her daughter planting potatoes "out there jest like a man, for all the neighbors to see." She wants to sew additional lace around the collar and cuffs of Louisa's Sunday dress to help cover the shameful tan Louisa has acquired by working in the fields. Later, in an effort to earn some money, Louisa hires herself out to a neighbor to rake hay. Her mother becomes physically ill at the idea.

> Mrs. Britton had turned white. She sank into a chair. "I can't stan' it nohow," she moaned. "All the daughter I've got."
>
> "Don't, mother! I ain't done any harm. What harm is it? Why can't I rake hay as well as a man? Lots of women do such things, if nobody round here does. He's goin' to pay me right off, and we need the money."

Obviously, if Louisa were a male, no one would object to any of the jobs she attempts to do, but for a female to insist on supporting herself and on rejecting the rescue from poverty and toil embodied in Jonathan's offer of marriage seems incomprehensible to those around her. Significantly, Freeman's "happy ending" for Louisa comes not in the form of a new suitor, but in the return of her economic independence. Knowing that she has her teaching job once again, she can turn contentedly to her dreams of love yet to come.

Three of Freeman's stories dramatize a family conflict or

crisis: "Gentian" (1887), "The Revolt of 'Mother'" (1891), and "The Selfishness of Amelia Lamkin" (1909). In all three stories a basic unity in ongoing family life exists despite a serious conflict. Although characters may judge poorly, fail to communicate their profound needs, or even cause physical harm to one another, an underlying sense of good intentions prevails, convincing us that when a person has been enlightened about the feelings or needs of a member of the family or made to realize the consequences of his or her actions, he or she will modify the harmful behavior. Typically, the misguided person in all three stories is a male, though female members of the family share in the blame equally in "The Selfishness of Amelia Lamkin."

"Gentian" and "The Revolt of 'Mother'" both concern women who have been submissive wives for their entire married life. But while Lucy Tollet of "Gentian" welcomes that role and will continue in it, Sarah Penn in "The Revolt of 'Mother'" decide that she must overrule her husband's judgment that the Penns need a new barn instead of a new house and willingly engages in an unusual public and dramatic conflict. Her lifelong submission has been the result of a conscious decision to accept this role, whereas Lucy's behavior seems to be so thoroughly a part of her character that she has no conscious choice.

The source of the conflict between Lucy and Alfred Tollet, who have been married for almost fifty years, is the small amount of gentian which Lucy surreptitiously sprinkles in his tea and in her pies and bread—in fact, in all her cooking—because her husband has been feeling sick and she is certain that this is the only way to cure him. Alfred, who vehemently refuses to see a doctor or take any medication, had "complained of great depression and languor all spring and had not attempted to do any work," an unusual condition for the generally healthy old man.

Fearful that he will grow worse and perhaps even die, his timid and obedient wife takes, in her desperation, the extreme measure of deceiving her husband. She thinks nothing of the fact that since they share all their meals she is forced to share his dose of gentian. Her deception takes a physical toll on her: as Alfred begins to recover, she seems to wither and suffer. When he has fully recovered by September, Lucy can no longer stand the strain of her situation and confesses to having dosed the food with the bitter tonic. Alfred is outraged. Lucy will not be allowed to handle his food again, as he makes clear when he purchases a supply of food at the local store and announces his plans to do all of his own cooking. Crushed, Lucy suggests that if her husband no longer wishes her to serve him, perhaps he would prefer her to leave entirely. Significantly, she phrases the matter in the terms of a dismissed employee: "Alfred, if you don't want me to do nothin' for you, mebbe—you'll think I ain't airnin' my own vittles; mebbe—you'd rather I go over to Hannah's." Although Lucy's suggestion that she live with her sister takes Alfred by surprise, he concurs in order to demonstrate how relentless his anger is.

Freeman delineates Lucy's total lack of an identity apart from that as Alfred's wife by showing her suffering through a fall and winter of separation. She is entirely loyal to Alfred, refusing to allow her sister to utter a word of criticism about him. Since serving Alfred is both her vocation and avocation, she can begin to be truly alive again only when they are reunited the following spring.

In contrast, Sarah Penn in "The Revolt of 'Mother'" is an industrious, capable farm wife who exhibits considerable inner strength. Quite early in the story, when Freeman sketches Sarah's physical appearance, she suggests that this wife's submissiveness is self-imposed:

> She was a small woman, short and straight-waisted like a child in her brown cotton gown. Her forehead was mild and benevolent between the smooth curves of gray hair; there were meek downward lines about her nose and mouth, but her eyes, fixed upon the old man, looked as if the meekness had been the result of her own will, never of the will of another.

When Sarah discovers that her husband, Adoniram, is building still another barn while his family is expected to continue living in the small, shabby dwelling he had promised to replace forty years before, her anger and frustration are completely justified. Adoniram refuses to answer her arguments or to change his plans. In a startling and courageous act, Sarah moves herself and her two children into the commodious, well-constructed barn while her husband is away for a trip of a few days. By the following morning all the villagers have heard of Mrs. Penn's extraordinary move: "Some held her to be insane; some, of a lawless and rebellious spirit." Mr. Hersey, the town minister, visits Sarah at the barn with the obvious intention of getting her to return to her former house. Recognizing no authority but her own in this matter, she splendidly sends him on his way:

> "I don't doubt you mean well," said she, "but there are things people hadn't ought to interfere with. I've been a member of the church for over forty years. I've got my own mind an' my own feet, an' I'm goin' to think my own thoughts an' go my own ways, an' nobody but the Lord is goin' to dictate to me unless I've a mind to have him."

Upon his return, Adoniram is bewildered and dismayed to find his family comfortably preparing for dinner in the new barn. Sarah quietly but firmly explains that she has made up her mind that their old house wasn't fit to live in and that they are going to live in the barn. She then describes the windows and partitions which will be necessary to turn the barn into the house promised her so long ago.

Certainly the dispute between Sarah and Adoniram is deeply felt by both, but during the course of their arguments, the wife continues to bake her husband's favorite pies, to sew new shirts for him, and to process the milk of their six cows. Family solidarity is sacred, and Mrs. Penn's actions are not a threat to it. When their daughter Nancy criticizes her father's building of the barn, Sarah attempts to defend her husband, even though these thoughts reflect her own bitter ones, asserting that his perceptions differ from those of a woman. Sarah suggests that there is some consolation in the fact that Father has kept their own roof well shingled and that it has never leaked—but once. Sarah's ultimate victory restores harmony to the family and dramatizes that there is more than one variety of "submissive wife."

Amelia Lamkin in "The Selfishness of Amelia Lamkin" is not merely a submissive wife, but an utterly self-sacrificing wife and mother, a martyr to the demands of family life. Freeman opens the story with a catalogue of the dishes Amelia believes necessary for her to cook for her family's breakfast. Catering to the whims of every member of the family, she herself exists virtually on table scraps.

Ironically, as her sister Jane Strong points out, Amelia's complete unselfishness can also be seen as a subtle form of selfishness. Jane explains: "You've been doing your duty all your life so hard that you haven't given other people a

chance to do theirs. You've been a very selfish woman as far
as duty is concerned, Amelia Lamkin, and you have made
other people selfish." Jane perceptively concludes that Addie,
one of Amelia's three children, will make a poor wife because
she is totally unused to waiting on herself.

Amelia's behavior, as a wife and mother, however, only
partly caricatures that often considered desirable by society.
Trained from childhood to put aside personal preferences, to
regard the nurturing of others as the highest good, to defer to
male authority, and to imbue the roles of wife and mother
with exalted spiritual idealism, women such as Amelia no
doubt often achieved high praise and regarded themselves as
models of feminine behavior. But Freeman insightfully provides a counter-description of Amelia as a woman who has
paid a terrible price for playing the role of the angel in the
house:

> Amelia was faded almost out as to color, and intense so-
> licitude for others and perfect meekness had crossed her
> little face with deep lines, and bowed her slender figure
> like that of a patient old horse, accustomed to having his
> lameness ignored, and standing before doors in harness
> through all kinds of weather. Amelia's neck, which was
> long and slender, had the same curve of utter submission
> which one sees in the neck of a weary old beast of bur-
> den.

Important comparisons are made between Amelia's appearance and those of both her sister and her husband. Although
Jane Strong, who is unmarried, is ten years older than her sister, she has retained much more of her youthful good looks
than has the worn Amelia and is far healthier. Even Amelia's
husband, Josiah, "although older than she, was still fresh-
colored and full-faced, and he had not a gray hair." The example of the Lamkins might admirably support the
generalization that every marriage is two separate marriages—his and hers—and that the two may be very different.
When Amelia collapses in a serious state of exhaustion,
Josiah, along with his children, begins to recognize the culpa-
bility of using another person. His repeated question as to
whether Amelia's continual struggles to put in his sleeve-buttons and shirt studs had hurt her becomes almost a comic re-
frain.

Amelia, of course, has always been a willing victim of her

own ideals and conscience, convinced that no one else in the
household could perform her tasks. Freeman wishes us to
comprehend that the lure of this sort of self-image is not an
isolated eccentricity of Amelia's. Overwhelmed by feelings of
guilt at her mother's illness, Addie seems on the verge of
being seduced by a similar image. She replies to a proposal
from Edward Emerson:

> "I have resolved never to marry, never to allow any
> other love or interest to come between me and my own
> family. If mother—" She went on, with a word omitted:
> "I must make all the restitution to her in my power, by
> devoting my whole life to her dear ones, to Tommy and
> the baby and father."

Freeman employs the phrase "life of self-immolation"
when she describes Addie's plan for devoting herself exclu-
sively to the care of her mother and the rest of her family.
Just as Amelia had perverted the roles of mother and wife so
that they became painful and destructive, so Addie seems to
be embracing a similar existence. The prospect that her
daughter is contemplating such a choice gives Amelia the will
to live, to rise after many months from her bed so that she
may exorcise Addie's burden of guilt.

Finally, "Old Woman Magoun" (1909) is an unusual
Freeman story, virtually the only one of its kind in her short
fiction. Its subject matter might well have been handled by
such naturalists as Stephen Crane or Frank Norris, and it
does rather self-consciously make references to the overwhelming forces of heredity and environment. In addition,
the story conveys a distinct contempt for and fear of the separate world of the masculine characters; the women quite
clearly view them as alien beings to be managed or avoided,
who do not exist in the reasonable, ordered, and nurturing
feminine world.

At first it seems that Mrs. Magoun, referred to as "Old
Woman Magoun" throughout the story, can control her personal existence and even exert strong pressures on the other
inhabitants of the hamlet of Barry's Ford. She berates the
men of the community for failing to put a log bridge across
the Barry River:

> She spread her strong arms like wings, and sent the
> loafers, half laughing half angry, flying in every direc-

tion. "If I were a *man*," she said, "I'd go out this very minute and lay the fust log. If I were a passel of lazy men layin' round, I'd start up for once in my life, I would."

Freeman indicates that in this situation Mrs. Magoun's criticism and determination are effective: "The weakness of the masculine element in Barry's Ford was laid low before such strenuous feminine assertion." Even as the old woman and her friend Sally Jinks watch the work being done on the bridge, they note that the men rely heavily on drinking liquor and chewing tobacco to keep themselves going. The women agree that "men is different" as they reflect on all the work they have done throughout their lives without depending on such stimulants to keep their spirits up. When the men come to her house to eat the dinner Mrs. Magoun has promised them as a reward for getting the bridge built, she sends her fourteen-year-old granddaughter, Lily, upstairs, out of the way of the "passel of hogs."

Lily is the illegitimate child of Mrs. Magoun's dead daughter and Nelson Barry, a handsome but degenerate son of the once-great Barry family, who now spends his days hanging around the general store or gambling. He has never paid any attention to his illegitimate child, until he discovers that she is on the verge of becoming a beautiful young woman and that he can make use of her. When he comes to demand the girl, whom Mrs. Magoun has always acknowledged to be his child, Barry pitilessly asserts, " 'I am going to have the girl, that is the long and short of it.' " The old woman guesses his true motive after hearing that another gambler, Jim Willis, had seen Lily: " 'You have been playing cards and you lost, and this is the way you will pay him.' " Barry is the one man she cannot control or intimidate.

Although she tries every means, Mrs. Magoun soon realizes that she will be unable to save Lily from her father's plans to exploit her as a sexual possession. Lily has, in fact, met Jim Willis, and found the handsome, well-dressed stranger attractive. Several times throughout the story, she asks hopefully whether she will see him again. When Lily encounters her father at the store where she has come on an errand, Freeman suggests that there is a strain of the Barry family sensuality in her. At first repelled by Nelson's kiss, she responds differently when he softly strokes her cheek: "Now Lily did not shrink from him. Hereditary instincts and nature itself were asserting themselves in the child's innocent, receptive breast."

Mrs. Magoun has attempted to protect Lily by extending her childhood and emphasizing her childlike behavior. In Barry's Ford, adult femininity is a threatening responsibility. For the grandmother, sending Lily to the Barry household—where her father and his feeble-minded sister live in the decay and squalor of a once-magnificent house—is worse than sending her to her death. For as Old Woman Magoun is an extremely religious and moral person, she considers that she would be sending the child to a life of vice and evil, in effect to her spiritual death. Thus Freeman's tale is of a strong, protective woman faced with a choice between what she sees as two different kinds of death for the beloved child she has raised. The tale is indeed a grim one for a writer who generally chooses to portray conflicts which do not lead to violent conclusions.

Freeman, like Jewett, writes essentially about women's activities, taking as her perspective that of the most important female character. (In only a few of her stories does she employ a man as her central character.) Her stories depict the intensity and range of the experiences of a variety of women who have only one limitation in common: the geographical boundaries of the small New England town they inhabit. What these women may lack in terms of a vast landscape as the setting for their actions is more than compensated for by the richness of their inner landscape. Theirs is a world sometimes endowed with rich earth, but more often with only thin soil which must be carefully cultivated, a world occasionally luxuriant with nature's fecundity, yet often marked by rough gray crags, the stony ledges of their individuality which jut unexpectedly outward.

BIOGRAPHY

Mary Ella Wilkins was born in Randolph, Massachusetts, on October 31, 1852. Her parents, Eleanor Lothrop and Warren Wilkins, had previously lost their first child in infancy, and they were later to lose another child, a son, at the age of three. Their second daughter, born seven years after Mary, died at the age of seventeen, and thus Mary was their only child to live to adulthood. The Wilkins family was significantly influenced by strong religious convictions. As an Orthodox Congregationalist, Mary would spend a total of six hours each Sunday participating in prayer services and educational activities at the church.

Her secular education took place at Randolph's public school, where a single teacher instructed all children in grades one through seven. Like Jewett, she suffered from ill health during her childhood and was prevented from enjoying some of the usual playtime activities. Just as the demise of the shipbuilding trade had brought serious economic problems to Jewett's Berwick, the decline of the small shoe factories, as well as the decline in profits from farming, began to cause severe hardship in Randolph, and Warren Wilkins determined to move his family to Brattleboro, Vermont, where he planned to give up his trade of carpenter and house builder to become a partner in a dry-goods store.

Thus, at the age of fifteen Mary enrolled in Brattleboro High School and upon graduation in 1870 attended Mt. Holyoke Female Seminary. Finding the strenuous atmosphere at Mt. Holyoke too intense (as had Emily Dickinson before her), Mary remained at the school for only a year, concluding her formal education by attending classes for a year at Glenwood Seminary for girls in West Brattleboro.

In contrast to Jewett's early success with publication, Mary was unable to earn any money from her writing until, at the age of twenty-nine, she was paid ten dollars for "The Beggar King," a children's ballad which was accepted by the juvenile magazine *Wide Awake*. Again, unlike Jewett, who was financially secure, Mary had an intense need to supplement the family income, which had been steadily diminishing over more than a decade. The Wilkinses had suffered so many reversals in Brattleboro that in 1877 Mrs. Wilkins accepted the job of housekeeper for the Reverend Thomas Pickman Tyler, and the Wilkins family moved into the Tyler household. This move must have been particularly painful for Mary, then twenty-five years old. Not yet a successful writer, having earlier given up the profession of teacher after finding it uncongenial, she was unable to help with the burden which had fallen upon her parents. To complicate matters, Mary had long been in love with Tyler's son Hanson, and although the young navy ensign was attentive and kind to Mary, he did not love her.

In 1880 Eleanor Wilkins died, leaving a terrible void in her daughter's life. It was soon after this event that Mary, who had been christened Mary Ella, changed her middle name to Eleanor, thus memorializing her love for her mother.

Within a year or two of her first publication, Mary had begun to sell both children's poetry and stories, and in 1882 she had two adult stories accepted for magazine publication: "The Shadow Family" in Boston's *Sunday Budget* and "Two Old Lovers" in *Harper's Bazaar*. She had found her life's work and had finally been recognized as a writer of talent.

About a year after the death of her father in 1883, she left Brattleboro to return to Randolph, the town of her childhood. Just as Jewett's friendship with the lively and affectionate Annie Fields became a mainstay for a young woman grieved by the death of her father, so a friend from Mary's childhood, Mary John Wales, provided the security and companionship which Mary had lost through the deaths of all the members of her immediate family. The Wales household, consisting of Mary John, her parents, and a brother, was distinctly dominated by the women of the family. Obviously Mary had found a congenial setting in the Wales farmhouse, where over a period of almost two decades she wrote prolifically, drawing, as did Jewett, on the small New England towns as the background for her depiction of human drama. Although Mary and Sarah Orne Jewett never met, Mary received a letter from Jewett commending the stories of *A Humble Romance*, to which she somewhat modestly replied that she believed she had never written a story which was the equal of Jewett's "A White Heron," which she considered among the finest stories she had ever read.

Although she met her future husband, Dr. Charles Manning Freeman, in 1892, it was not until January 1, 1902, that Mary, at the age of forty-nine, married after a two-year engagement. Thereafter, she made her home in Metuchen, New Jersey. The marriage was generally considered a dismal one. Seven years younger than his wife, Dr. Freeman had a medical degree but preferred to earn his living as a prosperous lumber dealer. He suffered from alcoholism which later contributed to severe emotional disorders, and in 1922 the couple were legally separated. In the following year, Dr. Freeman died.

Although Mary Wilkins Freeman received numerous honors during the 1920s—among them the William Dean Howells Gold Medal for Fiction and a membership in the National Institute of Arts and Letters—the work which she did after her marriage is generally considered far inferior to that in her early volumes of short stories. She died in Metuchen on March 15, 1930.

SELECTED BIBLIOGRAPHY
THE FICTION OF MARY WILKINS FREEMAN

A Humble Romance and Other Stories. New York: Harper and Brothers, 1887.

A New England Nun and Other Stories. New York: Harper and Brothers, 1891.

Jane Field. New York: Harper and Brothers, 1893.

Giles Corey, Yeoman: A Play. New York: Harper and Brothers, 1893.

Pembroke. New York: Harper and Brothers, 1894.

Madelon. New York: Harper and Brothers, 1896.

Jerome, A Poor Man. New York: Harper and Brothers, 1897.

Silence and Other Stories. New York: Harper and Brothers, 1898.

The People of Our Neighborhood. Philadelphia: Curtis Publishing Company, 1898.

The Jamesons. New York: Doubleday and McClure Company, 1899.

The Heart's Highway, A Romance of Virginia. New York: Doubleday, Page and Company, 1900.

The Love of Parson Lord and Other Stories. New York: Harper and Brothers, 1900.

Understudies. New York: Harper and Brothers, 1901.

The Portion of Labor. New York: Harper and Brothers, 1901.

Six Trees. New York: Harper and Brothers, 1903.

The Wind in the Rose-Bush and Other Stories of the Supernatural. New York: Doubleday, Page and Company, 1903.

The Givers. New York: Harper and Brothers, 1904.

The Debtor. New York: Harper and Brothers, 1905.

By the Light of the Soul. New York: Harper and Brothers, 1906.

"Doc" Gordon. New York: The Authors and Newspapers Association, 1906.

The Fair Lavinia and Others. New York: Harper and Brothers, 1907.

The Shoulders of Atlas. New York: Harper and Brothers, 1908.

The Whole Family, A Novel by Twelve Authors (including Mary W. Freeman, William D. Howells, Henry James, et al.). New York: Harper and Brothers, 1908.

The Winning Lady and Others. New York: Harper and Brothers, 1909.

The Butterfly House. New York: Dodd, Mead and Company, 1912.

The Yates Pride: A Romance. New York: Harper and Brothers, 1912.

The Copy-Cat and Other Stories. New York: Harper and Brothers, 1914.

An Alabaster Box (with Florence Morse Kingsley). New York: D. Appleton and Company, 1917.
Edgewater People. New York: Harper and Brothers, 1918.

Selected Biographical and Critical Materials

Bentzon, Th. (Mme. Thérèsè Blanc-Bentzon). "Un Romancier de la Nouvelle-Angleterre," *Revue des Deux Mondes,* 136 (August 1, 1896), 544-69.

Brooks, Van Wyck. *New England: Indian Summer.* New York: E. P. Dutton and Company, Inc., 1940.

Crowley, John W. "Freeman's Yankee Tragedy: 'Amanda and Love,' *Markham Review,* 5 (Spring 1976), 58-60.

Foster, Edward. *Mary E. Wilkins Freeman.* New York: Hendricks House, 1956.

Hartt, Rollin Lynde. "A New England Hill Town," *The Atlantic Monthly,* 83. (April and May, 1899), 561-74; 712-20.

Herron, I. H. *The Small Town in American Literature.* Durham, N.C.: The Duke University Press, 1939.

Kendrick, Brent L. "Mary E. Wilkins Freeman," *American Literary Realism, 1870-1910,* 8 (Summer 1975), 255-57.

Machen, Arthur. *Hieroglyphics.* New York: A. A. Knopf, 1923.

Matthiessen, F. O. "New England Stories," in *American Writers on American Literature,* ed. John Macy. New York: Horace Liveright, 1931.

"New England in the Short Story," *The Atlantic Monthly,* 67 (June 1891), 845-50.

Parrington, Vernon L. *The Beginnings of Critical Realism in America.* New York: Harcourt, Brace and Company, 1930.

Pattee, Fred Lewis. *Sidelights on American Literature.* New York: The Century Company, 1922.

Quina, James H., Jr. "Character Types in the Fiction of Mary Wilkins Freeman," *Colby Library Quarterly,* 9 (December 1971), 432-39.

Thompson, Charles M. "Miss Wilkins: An Idealist in Masquerade," *The Atlantic Monthly,* 88 (May 1899), 665-75.

Toth, Susan A. "Mary Wilkins Freeman's Parable of Wasted Life," *American Literature,* 42 (January 1971), 564-67.

———. "Defiant Light: A Positive View of Mary Wilkins Freeman," *New England Quarterly,* 46 (March 1973), 82-93.

Westbrook, Perry D. *Acres of Flint: Writers of Rural New England, 1870-1900.*" Washington, D.C.: The Scarecrow Press, 1951.

———. *Mary Wilkins Freeman.* New York: Twayne Publishers, Inc., 1967.

Williams, Blanche C. *Our Short Story Writers.* New York: Dodd, Mead and Company, 1926.

Wright, Austin McGiffert. *The American Short Story in the Twenties.* Chicago: The University of Chicago Press, 1961.

Ziff, Larzer. *The American 1890's.* New York: Viking, 1966.

Sarah
Orne Jewett

The Country
of the Pointed Firs

Alice Greenwood Howe

CONTENTS

I.

THE RETURN

There was something about the coast town of Dunnet
which made it seem more attractive than other maritime villages of eastern Maine. Perhaps it was the simple fact of acquaintance with that neighborhood which made it so attach-
ing, and gave such interest to the rocky shore and dark
woods, and the few houses which seemed to be securely
wedged and tree-nailed in among the ledges by the Landing.
These houses made the most of their seaward view, and
there was a gayety and determined floweriness in their bits of
garden ground; the small-paned high windows in the peaks
of their steep gables were like knowing eyes that watched the
harbor and the far sea-line beyond, or looked northward all
along the shore and its background of spruces and balsam
firs. When one really knows a village like this and its surroundings, it is like becoming acquainted with a single person.
The process of falling in love at first sight is as final as it is
swift in such a case, but the growth of true friendship may
be a lifelong affair.

After a first brief visit made two or three summers before
in the course of a yachting cruise, a lover of Dunnet Landing
returned to find the unchanged shores of the pointed firs, the
same quaintness of the village with its elaborate conventionalities; all that mixture of remoteness, and childish certainty of
being the centre of civilization of which her affectionate
dreams had told. One evening in June, a single passenger
landed upon the steamboat wharf. The tide was high, there
was a fine crowd of spectators, and the younger portion of
the company followed her with subdued excitement up the
narrow street of the salt-aired, white-clapboarded little town.

II.

MRS. TODD

❧❧

Later, there was only one fault to find with this choice of a
summer lodging-place, and that was its complete lack of seclusion. At first the tiny house of Mrs. Almira Todd, which
stood with its end to the street, appeared to be retired and
sheltered enough from the busy world, behind its bushy bit of
a green garden, in which all the blooming things, two or
three gay hollyhocks and some London-pride, were pushed
back against the gray-shingled wall. It was a queer little
garden and puzzling to a stranger, the few flowers being put
at a disadvantage by so much greenery; but the discovery was
soon made that Mrs. Todd was an ardent lover of herbs, both
wild and tame, and the sea-breezes blew into the low end-
window of the house laden with not only sweet-brier and
sweet-mary, but balm and sage and borage and mint, wormwood and southernwood. If Mrs. Todd had occasion to step
into the far corner of her herb plot, she trod heavily upon
thyme, and made its fragrant presence known with all the
rest. Being a very large person, her full skirts brushed and
bent almost every slender stalk that her feet missed. You
could always tell when she was stepping about there, even
when you were half awake in the morning, and learned to
know, in the course of a few weeks' experience, in exactly
which corner of the garden she might be.

At one side of this herb plot were other growths of a rustic
pharmacopoeia, great treasures and rarities among the com-
moner herbs. There were some strange and pungent odors
that roused a dim sense and remembrance of something in
the forgotten past. Some of these might once have belonged
to sacred and mystic rites, and have had some occult
knowledge handed with them down the centuries; but now
they pertained only to humble compounds brewed at intervals
with molasses or vinegar or spirits in a small caldron on Mrs.
Todd's kitchen stove. They were dispensed to suffering neighbors, who usually came at night as if by stealth, bringing

their own ancient-looking vials to be filled. One nostrum was called the Indian remedy, and its price was but fifteen cents; the whispered directions could be heard as customers passed the windows. With most remedies the purchaser was allowed to depart unadmonished from the kitchen, Mrs. Todd being a wise saver of steps; but with certain vials she gave cautions, standing in the doorway, and there were other doses which had to be accompanied on their healing way as far as the gate, while she muttered long chapters of directions, and kept up an air of secrecy and importance to the last. It may not have been only the common ails of humanity with which she tried to cope; it seemed sometimes as if love and hate and jealousy and adverse winds at sea might also find their proper remedies among the curious wild-looking plants in Mrs. Todd's garden.

The village doctor and this learned herbalist were upon the best of terms. The good man may have counted upon the unfavorable effect of certain potions which he should find his opportunity in counteracting; at any rate, he now and then stopped and exchanged greetings with Mrs. Todd over the picket fence. The conversation became at once professional after the briefest preliminaries, and he would stand twirling a sweet-scented sprig in his fingers, and make suggestive jokes, perhaps about her faith in a too persistent course of thoroughwort elixir, in which my landlady professed such firm belief as sometimes to endanger the life and usefulness of worthy neighbors.

To arrive at this quietest of seaside villages late in June, when the busy herb-gathering season was just beginning, was also to arrive in the early prime of Mrs. Todd's activity in the brewing of old-fashioned spruce beer. This cooling and refreshing drink had been brought to wonderful perfection through a long series of experiments; it had won immense local fame, and the supplies for its manufacture were always giving out and having to be replenished. For various reasons, the seclusion and uninterrupted days which had been looked forward to proved to be very rare in this otherwise delightful corner of the world. My hostess and I had made our shrewd business agreement on the basis of a simple cold luncheon at noon, and liberal restitution in the matter of hot suppers, to provide for which the lodger might sometimes be seen hurrying down the road, late in the day, with cunner line in hand. It was soon found that this arrangement made large allowance for Mrs. Todd's slow herb-gathering progresses

through woods and pastures. The spruce-beer customers were
pretty steady in hot weather, and there were many demands
for different soothing syrups and elixirs with which the unwise curiosity of my early residence had made me acquainted. Knowing Mrs. Todd to be a widow, who had little beside
this slender business and the income from one hungry lodger
to maintain her, one's energies and even interest were quickly
bestowed, until it became a matter of course that she should
go afield every pleasant day, and that the lodger should answer all peremptory knocks at the side door.

In taking an occasional wisdom-giving stroll in Mrs. Todd's
company, and in acting as business partner during her frequent absences, I found the July days fly fast, and it was not
until I felt myself confronted with too great pride and
pleasure in the display, one night, of two dollars and twenty-
seven cents which I had taken in during the day, that I
remembered a long piece of writing, sadly belated now, which
I was bound to do. To have been patted kindly on the shoulder and called "darlin'," to have been offered a surprise of
early mushrooms for supper, to have had all the glory of
making two dollars and twenty-seven cents in a single day,
and then to renounce it all and withdraw from these pleasant
successes, needed much resolution. Literary employments are
so vexed with uncertainties at best, and it was not until the
voice of conscience sounded louder in my ears than the sea
on the nearest pebble beach that I said unkind words of with-
drawal to Mrs. Todd. She only became more wistfully affectionate than ever in her expressions, and looked as
disappointed as I expected when I frankly told her that I
could no longer enjoy the pleasure of what we called "seein'
folks." I felt that I was cruel to a whole neighborhood in cur-
tailing her liberty in this most important season for harvesting
the different wild herbs that were so much counted upon to
ease their winter ails.

"Well, dear," she said sorrowfully, "I've took great advantage o' your bein' here. I ain't had such a season for
years, but I have never had nobody I could so trust. All you
lack is a few qualities, but with time you'd gain judgment an'
experience, an' be very able in the business. I'd stand right
here an' say it to anybody."

Mrs. Todd and I were not separated or estranged by the
change in our business relations; on the contrary, a deeper in-
timacy seemed to begin. I do not know what herb of the

night it was that used sometimes to send out a penetrating odor late in the evening, after the dew had fallen, and the moon was high, and the cool air came up from the sea. Then Mrs. Todd would feel that she must talk to somebody, and I was only too glad to listen. We both fell under the spell, and she either stood outside the window, or made an errand to my sitting-room, and told, it might be very commonplace news of the day, or, as happened one misty summer night, all that lay deepest in her heart. It was in this way that I came to know that she had loved one who was far above her.

"No, dear, him I speak of could never think of me," she said. "When we was young together his mother didn't favor the match, an' done everything she could to part us; and folks thought we both married well, but 't wa'n't what either one of us wanted most; an' now we're left alone again, an' might have had each other all the time. He was above bein' a seafarin' man, an' prospered more than most; he come of a high family, an' my lot was plain an' hard-workin'. I ain't seen him for some years; he's forgot our youthful feelin's, I expect, but a woman's heart is different; them feelin's comes back when you think you've done with 'em, as sure as spring comes with the year. An' I've always had ways of hearin' about him."

She stood in the centre of a braided rug, and its rings of black and gray seemed to circle about her feet in the dim light. Her height and massiveness in the low room gave her the look of a huge sibyl, while the strange fragrance of the mysterious herb blew in from the little garden.

III.

THE SCHOOLHOUSE

For some days after this, Mrs. Todd's customers came and went past my windows, and, haying-time being nearly over, strangers began to arrive from the inland country, such was her widespread reputation. Sometimes I saw a pale young creature like a white windflower left over into midsummer, upon whose face consumption had set its bright and wistful mark; but oftener two stout, hard-worked women from the farms came together, and detailed their symptoms to Mrs. Todd in loud and cheerful voices, combining the satisfactions of a friendly gossip with the medical opportunity. They seemed to give much from their own store of therapeutic learning. I became aware of the school in which my landlady had strengthened her natural gift; but hers was always the governing mind, and the final command, "Take of hy'sop one handful" (or whatever herb it was), was received in respectful silence. One afternoon, when I had listened—it was impossible not to listen, with cottonless ears—and then laughed and listened again, with an idle pen in my hand, during a particularly spirited and personal conversation, I reached for my hat, and, taking blotting-book and all under my arm, I resolutely fled further temptation, and walked out past the fragrant green garden and up the dusty road. The way went straight uphill, and presently I stopped and turned to look back.

The tide was in, the wide harbor was surrounded by its dark woods, and the small wooden houses stood as near as they could get to the landing. Mrs. Todd's was the last house on the way inland. The gray ledges of the rocky shore were well covered with sod in most places, and the pasture bayberry and wild roses grew thick among them. I could see the higher inland country and the scattered farms. On the brink of the hill stood a little white schoolhouse, much wind-blown and weather-beaten, which was a landmark to seagoing folk; from its door there was a most beautiful view of sea and shore. The summer vacation now prevailed, and after finding the door unfastened, and taking a long look through one of the seaward windows, and reflecting afterward for some time in a shady place near by among the bayberry bushes, I returned to the chief place of business in the village, and, to the amusement of two of the selectmen, brothers and autocrats of Dunnet Landing, I hired the schoolhouse for the rest of the vacation for fifty cents a week.

Selfish as it may appear, the retired situation seemed to possess great advantages, and I spent many days there quite undisturbed, with the sea-breeze blowing through the small, high windows and swaying the heavy outside shutters to and fro. I hung my hat and luncheon-basket on an entry nail as if I were a small scholar, but I sat at the teacher's desk as if I were that great authority, with all the timid empty benches in rows before me. Now and then an idle sheep came and stood for a long time looking in at the door. At sundown I went back, feeling most businesslike, down toward the village again, and usually met the flavor, not of the herb garden, but of Mrs. Todd's hot supper, halfway up the hill. On the nights when there were evening meetings or other public exercises that demanded her presence we had tea very early, and I was welcomed back as if from a long absence.

Once or twice I feigned excuses for staying at home, while Mrs. Todd made distant excursions, and came home late, with both hands full and a heavily laden apron. This was in pennyroyal time, and when the rare lobelia was in its prime and the elecampane was coming on. One day she appeared at the schoolhouse itself, partly out of amused curiosity about my industries; but she explained that there was no tansy in the neighborhood with such snap to it as some that grew about the schoolhouse lot. Being scuffed down all the spring made it grow so much the better, like some folks that had it hard in their youth, and were bound to make the most of themselves before they died.

IV.

AT THE SCHOOLHOUSE WINDOW

❧

One day I reached the schoolhouse very late, owing to attendance upon the funeral of an acquaintance and neighbor, with whose sad decline in health I had been familiar, and whose last days both the doctor and Mrs. Todd had tried in vain to ease. The services had taken place at one o'clock, and now, at quarter past two, I stood at the schoolhouse window, looking down at the procession as it went along the lower road close to the shore. It was a walking funeral, and even at that distance I could recognize most of the mourners as they went their solemn way. Mrs. Begg had been very much respected, and there was a large company of friends following to her grave. She had been brought up on one of the neighboring farms, and each of the few times that I had seen her she professed great dissatisfaction with town life. The people lived too close together for her liking, at the Landing, and she could not get used to the constant sound of the sea. She had lived to lament three seafaring husbands, and her house was decorated with West Indian curiosities, specimens of conch shells and fine coral which they had brought home from their voyages in lumber-laden ships. Mrs. Todd had told me all our neighbor's history. They had been girls together, and, to use her own phrase, had "both seen trouble till they knew the best and worst on 't." I could see the sorrowful, large figure of Mrs. Todd as I stood at the window. She made a break in the procession by walking slowly and keeping the after-part of it back. She held a handkerchief to her eyes, and I knew, with a pang of sympathy, that hers was not affected grief.

Beside her, after much difficulty, I recognized the one strange and unrelated person in all the company, an old man who had always been mysterious to me. I could see his thin, bending figure. He wore a narrow, long-tailed coat and walked with a stick, and had the same "cant to leeward" as the wind-bent trees on the height above.

54

This was Captain Littlepage, whom I had seen only once or twice before, sitting pale and old behind a closed window; never out of doors until now. Mrs. Todd always shook her head gravely when I asked a question, and said that he wasn't what he had been once, and seemed to class him with her other secrets. He might have belonged with a simple which grew in a certain slug-haunted corner of the garden, whose use she could never be betrayed into telling me, though I saw her cutting the tops by moonlight once, as if it were a charm, and not a medicine, like the great fading bloodroot leaves.

I could see that she was trying to keep pace with the old captain's lighter steps. He looked like an aged grasshopper of some strange human variety. Behind this pair was a short, impatient, little person, who kept the captain's house, and gave it what Mrs. Todd and others believed to be no proper sort of care. She was usually called "that Mari' Harris" in subdued conversation between intimates, but they treated her with anxious civility when they met her face to face.

The bay-sheltered islands and the great sea beyond stretched away to the far horizon southward and eastward; the little procession in the foreground looked futile and helpless on the edge of the rocky shore. It was a glorious day early in July, with a clear, high sky; there were no clouds, there was no noise of the sea. The song sparrows sang and sang, as if with joyous knowledge of immortality, and contempt for those who could so pettily concern themselves with death. I stood watching until the funeral procession had crept round a shoulder of the slope below and disappeared from the great landscape as if it had gone into a cave.

An hour later I was busy at my work. Now and then a bee blundered in and took me for an enemy; but there was a useful stick upon the teacher's desk, and I rapped to call the bees to order as if they were unruly scholars, or waved them away from their riots over the ink, which I had bought at the Landing store, and discovered too late to be scented with bergamot, as if to refresh the labors of anxious scribes. One anxious scribe felt very dull that day; a sheep-bell tinkled near by, and called her wandering wits after it. The sentences failed to catch these lovely summer cadences. For the first time I began to wish for a companion and for news from the outer world, which had been, half unconsciously, forgotten. Watching the funeral gave one a sort of pain. I began to wonder if I ought not to have walked with the rest, instead of hurrying away at the end of the services. Perhaps the Sunday

gown I had put on for the occasion was making this disas-
trous change of feeling, but I had now made myself and my
friends remember that I did not really belong to Dunnet
Landing.

I sighed, and turned to the half-written page again.

V.

CAPTAIN LITTLEPAGE

⊰⊱

It was a long time after this; an hour was very long in that coast town where nothing stole away the shortest minute. I had lost myself completely in work, when I heard footsteps outside. There was a steep footpath between the upper and the lower road, which I climbed to shorten the way, as the children had taught me, but I believed that Mrs. Todd would find it inaccessible, unless she had occasion to seek me in great haste. I wrote on, feeling like a besieged miser of time, while the footsteps came nearer, and the sheep-bell tinkled away in haste as if some one had shaken a stick in its wearer's face. Then I looked, and saw Captain Littlepage passing the nearest window; the next moment he tapped politely at the door.

"Come in, sir," I said, rising to meet him; and he entered, bowing with much courtesy. I stepped down from the desk and offered him a chair by the window, where he seated himself at once, being sadly spent by his climb. I returned to my fixed seat behind the teacher's desk, which gave him the lower place of a scholar.

"You ought to have the place of honor, Captain Littlepage," I said.

"A happy, rural seat of various views,"

he quoted, as he gazed out into the sunshine and up the long wooded shore. Then he glanced at me, and looked all about him as pleased as a child.

"My quotation was from Paradise Lost: the greatest of poems, I suppose you know?" and I nodded. "There's nothing that ranks, to my mind, with Paradise Lost; it's all lofty, all lofty," he continued. "Shakespeare was a great poet; he copied life, but you have to put up with a great deal of low talk."

I now remembered that Mrs. Todd had told me one day that Captain Littlepage had overset his mind with too much reading; she had also made dark reference to his having "spells" of some unexplainable nature. I could not help wondering what errand had brought him out in search of me. There was something quite charming in his appearance: it was a face thin and delicate with refinement, but worn into appealing lines, as if he had suffered from loneliness and misapprehension. He looked, with his careful precision of dress, as if he were the object of cherishing care on the part of elderly unmarried sisters, but I knew Mari' Harris to be a very commonplace, inelegant person, who would have no such standards; it was plain that the captain was his own attentive valet. He sat looking at me expectantly. I could not help thinking that, with his queer head and length of thinness, he was made to hop along the road of life rather than to walk. The captain was very grave indeed, and I bade my inward spirit keep close to discretion.

"Poor Mrs. Begg has gone," I ventured to say. I still wore my Sunday gown by way of showing respect."

"She has gone," said the captain—"very easy at the last, I was informed; she slipped away as if she were glad of the opportunity."

I thought of the Countess of Carberry, and felt that history repeated itself.

"She was one of the old stock," continued Captain Littlepage, with touching sincerity. "She was very much looked to in this town, and will be missed."

I wondered, as I looked at him, if he had sprung from a line of ministers; he had the refinement of look and air of command which are the heritage of the old ecclesiastical families of New England. But as Darwin says in his autobiography, "there is no such king as a sea-captain; he is greater even than a king or a schoolmaster!"

Captain Littlepage moved his chair out of the wake of the sunshine, and still sat looking at me. I began to be very eager to know upon what errand he had come.

"It may be found out some o' these days," he said earnestly. "We may know it all, the next step; where Mrs. Begg is now, for instance. Certainty, not conjecture, is what we all desire."

"I suppose we shall know it all some day," said I.

"We shall know it while yet below," insisted the captain, with a flush of impatience on his thin cheeks. "We have not looked for truth in the right direction. I know what I speak of; those who have laughed at me little know how much reason my ideas are based upon." He waved his hand toward the village below. "In that handful of houses they fancy that they comprehend the universe."

I smiled, and waited for him to go on.

"I am an old man, as you can see," he continued, "and I have been a shipmaster the greater part of my life—forty-three years in all. You may not think it, but I am above eighty years of age."

He did not look so old, and I hastened to say so.

"You must have left the sea a good many years ago, then, Captain Littlepage?" I said.

"I should have been serviceable at least five or six years more," he answered. "My acquaintance with certain—my experience upon a certain occasion, I might say, gave rise to prejudice. I do not mind telling you that I chanced to learn of one of the greatest discoveries that man has ever made."

Now we were approaching dangerous ground, but a sudden sense of his sufferings at the hands of the ignorant came to my help, and I asked to hear more with all the deference I really felt. A swallow flew into the schoolhouse at this moment as if a kingbird were after it, and beat itself against the walls for a minute, and escaped again to the open air; but Captain Littlepage took no notice whatever of the flurry.

"I had a valuable cargo of general merchandise from the London docks to Fort Churchill, a station of the old company on Hudson's Bay," said the captain earnestly. "We were delayed in lading, and baffled by head winds and a heavy tumbling sea all the way north-about and across. Then the fog kept us off the coast; and when I made port at last, it was too late to delay in those northern waters with such a vessel and such a crew as I had. They cared for nothing, and idled me into a fit of sickness; but my first mate was a good, excellent man, with no more idea of being frozen in there until spring than I had, so we made what speed we could to get clear of Hudson's Bay and off the coast. I owned an eighth of the vessel, and he owned a sixteenth of her. She was a full-rigged ship, called the Minerva, but she was getting old and leaky. I meant it should be my last v'y'ge in her, and so it proved. She had been an excellent vessel in her day. Of the cowards aboard her I can't say so much."

"Then you were wrecked?" I asked, as he made a long pause.

"I wa'n't caught astern o' the lighter by any fault of mine," said the captain gloomily. "We left Fort Churchill and run out into the Bay with a light pair o' heels; but I had been vexed to death with their redtape rigging at the company's office, and chilled with stayin' on deck an' tryin' to hurry up things, and when we were well out o' sight o' land, headin' for Hudson's Straits, I had a bad turn o' some sort o' fever, and had to stay below. The days were getting short, and we made good runs, all well on board but me, and the crew done their work by dint of hard driving."

I began to find this unexpected narrative a little dull. Captain Littlepage spoke with a kind of slow correctness that lacked the longshore high flavor to which I had grown used; but I listened respectfully while he explained the winds having become contrary, and talked on in a dreary sort of way about his voyage, the bad weather, and the disadvantages he was under in the lightness of his ship, which bounced about like a chip in a bucket, and would not answer the rudder or properly respond to the most careful setting of sails.

"So there we were blowin' along anyways," he complained; but looking at me at this moment, and seeing that my thoughts were unkindly wandering, he ceased to speak.

"It was a hard life at sea in those days, I am sure," said I, with redoubled interest.

"It was a dog's life," said the poor old gentleman, quite reassured, "but it made men of those who followed it. I see a change for the worse even in our own town here; full of loafers now, small and poor as 't is, who once would have followed the sea, every lazy soul of 'em. There is no occupation so fit for just that class o' men who never get beyond the fo'cas'le. I view it, in addition, that a community narrows down and grows dreadful ignorant when it is shut up to its affairs, and gets no knowledge of the outside world except from a cheap, unprincipled newspaper. In the old days, a good part o' the best men here knew a hundred ports and something of the way folks lived in them. They saw the world for themselves, and like's not their wives and children saw it with them. They may not have had the best of knowledge to carry with 'em sight-seein', but they were some acquainted with foreign lands an' their laws, an' could see outside the battle for town clerk here in Dunnet; they got some sense o' proportion. Yes, they lived more dignified, and their houses were better within an' without. Shipping's a terrible loss to this part o' New England from a social point o' view, ma'am."

"I have thought of that myself," I returned, with my interest quite awakened. "It accounts for the change in a great many things—the sad disappearance of sea-captains—doesn't it?"

"A shipmaster was apt to get the habit of reading," said my companion, brightening still more, and taking on a most touching air of unreserve. "A captain is not expected to be familiar with his crew, and for company's sake in dull days and nights he turns to his book. Most of us old shipmasters came to know 'most everything about something; one would take to readin' on farming topics, and some were great on medicine—but Lord help their poor crews!—or some were all for history, and now and then there'd be one like me that gave his time to the poets. I was well acquainted with a shipmaster that was all for bees an' bee-keepin'; and if you met him in port and went aboard, he'd sit and talk a terrible while about their havin' so much information, and the money that could be made out of keepin' 'em. He was one of the smartest captains that ever sailed the seas, but they used to call the Newcastle, a great bark he commanded for many years, Tuttle's beehive. There was old Cap'n Jameson: he had notions of Solomon's Temple, and made a very handsome little model of the same, right from the Scripture measurements, same's other sailors make little ships and design new tricks of rigging and all that. No, there's nothing to take the place of shipping in a place like ours. These bicycles offend me dreadfully; they don't afford no real opportunities of experience such as a man gained on a voyage. No: when folks left home in the old days they left it to some purpose, and when they got home they stayed there and had some pride in it. There's no large-minded way of thinking now: the worst have got to be best and rule everything; we're all turned upside down and going back year by year."

"Oh no, Captain Littlepage, I hope not," said I, trying to soothe his feelings.

There was a silence in the schoolhouse, but we could hear the noise of the water on a beach below. It sounded like the strange warning wave that gives notice of the turn of the tide. A late golden robin, with the most joyful and eager of voices, was singing close by in a thicket of wild roses.

VI.

THE WAITING PLACE

"How did you manage with the rest of that rough voyage on the Minerva?" I asked.

"I shall be glad to explain to you," said Captain Littlepage, forgetting his grievances for the moment. "If I had a map at hand I could explain better. We were driven to and fro 'way up toward what we used to call Parry's Discoveries, and lost our bearings. It was thick and foggy, and at last I lost my ship; she drove on a rock, and we managed to get ashore on what I took to be a barren island, the few of us that were left alive. When she first struck, the sea was somewhat calmer than it had been, and most of the crew, against orders, manned the long-boat and put off in a hurry, and were never heard of more. Our own boat upset, but the carpenter kept himself and me above water, and we drifted in. I had no strength to call upon after my recent fever, and laid down to die; but he found the tracks of a man and dog the second day, and got along the shore to one of those far missionary stations that the Moravians support. They were very poor themselves, and in distress; 't was a useless place. There were but few Esquimaux left in that region. There we remained for some time, and I became acquainted with strange events."

The captain lifted his head and gave me a questioning glance. I could not help noticing that the dulled look in his eyes had gone, and there was instead a clear intentness that made them seem dark and piercing.

"There was a supply ship expected, and the pastor, an excellent Christian man, made no doubt that we should get passage in her. He was hoping that orders would come to break up the station; but everything was uncertain, and we got on the best we could for a while. We fished, and helped the people in other ways; there was no other way of paying our debts. I was taken to the pastor's house until I got better; but they were crowded, and I felt myself in the way, and made excuse to join with an old seaman, a Scotchman, who had built him a warm cabin, and had room in it for another. He was looked upon with regard, and had stood by the pastor in some troubles with the people. He had been on one of those English exploring parties that found one end of the road to the north pole, but never could find the other. We lived like dogs in a kennel, or so you'd thought if you had seen the hut from the outside; but the main thing was to keep warm; there were piles of birdskins to lie on, and he'd made him a good bunk, and there was another for me. 'T was dreadful dreary waitin' there; we begun to think the supply steamer was lost, and my poor ship broke up and strewed herself all along the shore. We got to watching on the headlands; my men and me knew the people were short of supplies and had to pinch themselves. It ought to read in the Bible, 'Man cannot live by fish alone,' if they'd told the truth of things; 't aint bread that wears the worst on you! First part of the time, old Gaffett, that I lived with, seemed speechless, and I didn't know what to make of him, nor he of me, I dare say; but as we got acquainted, I found he'd been through more disasters than I had, and had troubles that wa'n't going to let him live a great while. It used to ease his mind to talk to an understanding person, so we used to sit and talk together all day, if it rained or blew so that we couldn't get out. I'd got a bad blow on the back of my head at the time we came ashore, and it pained me at times, and my strength was broken, anyway; I've never been so able since."

Captain Littlepage fell into a reverie.

"Then I had the good of my reading," he explained presently. "I had no books; the pastor spoke but little English, and all his books were foreign; but I used to say over all I could remember. The old poets little knew what comfort they could be to a man. I was well acquainted with the works of Milton, but up there it did seem to me as if Shakespeare was the king; he has his sea terms very accurate, and some beautiful passages were calming to the mind. I could say them over until I shed tears; there was nothing beautiful to me in that place but the stars above and those passages of verse.

"Gaffett was always brooding and brooding, and talking to himself; he was afraid he should never get away, and it preyed upon his mind. He thought when I got home I could interest the scientific men in his discovery; but they're all taken up with their own notions; some didn't even take pains to answer the letters I wrote. You observe that I said this crippled man Gaffett had been shipped on a voyage of discovery. I now tell you that the ship was lost on its return, and only Gaffett and two officers were saved off the Greenland coast, and he had knowledge later that those men never got back to England; the brig they shipped on was run down in the night. So no other living soul had the facts, and he gave them to me. There is a strange sort of a country 'way up north beyond the ice, and strange folks living in it. Gaffett believed it was the next world to this."

"What do you mean, Captain Littlepage?" I exclaimed. The old man was bending forward and whispering; he looked over his shoulder before he spoke the last sentence.

"To hear old Gaffett tell about it was something awful," he said, going on with his story quite steadily after the moment of excitement had passed. " 'T was first a tale of dogs and sledges, and cold and wind and snow. Then they begun to find the ice grow rotten; they had been frozen in, and got into a current flowing north, far up beyond Fox Channel, and they took to their boats when the ship got crushed, and this warm current took them out of sight of the ice, and into a great open sea; and they still followed it due north, just the very way they had planned to go. Then they struck a coast that wasn't laid down or charted, but the cliffs were such that no boat could land until they found a bay and struck across under sail to the other side where the shore looked lower; they were scant of provisions and out of water, but they got sight of something that looked like a great town. 'For God's sake, Gaffett!' said I, the first time he told me. 'You don't mean a town two degrees farther north than ships had ever been?' for he'd got their course marked on an old chart that he'd pieced out at the top; but he insisted upon it, and told it over and over again, to be sure I had it straight to carry to those who would be interested. There was no snow and ice, he said, after they had sailed some days with that warm current, which seemed to come right from under the ice that they'd been pinched up in and had been crossing on foot for weeks."

"But what about the town?" I asked. "Did they get to the town?"

"They did," said the captain, "and found inhabitants; 't was an awful condition of things. It appeared, as near as Gaffett could express it, like a place where there was neither living nor dead. They could see the place when they were approaching it by sea pretty near like any town, and thick with habitations; but all at once they lost sight of it altogether, and when they got close inshore they could see the shapes of folks, but they never could get near them,—all blowing gray figures that would pass along alone, or sometimes gathered in companies as if they were watching. The men were frightened at first, but the shapes never came near them,—it was as if they blew back; and at last they all got bold and went ashore, and found birds' eggs and sea fowl, like any wild northern spot where creatures were tame and folks had never been, and there was good water. Gaffett said that he and another man came near one o' the fog-shaped men that was going along slow with the look of a pack on his back, among the rocks, an' they chased him; but, Lord! he flittered away out o' sight like a leaf the wind takes with it, or a piece of cobweb. They would make as if they talked together, but there was no sound of voices, and 'they acted as if they didn't see us, but only felt us coming towards them,' says Gaffett one day, trying to tell the particulars. They couldn't see the town when they were ashore. One day the captain and the doctor were gone till night up across the high land where the town had seemed to be, and they came back at night beat out and white as ashes, and wrote and wrote all next day in their notebooks, and whispered together full of excitement, and they were sharp-spoken with the men when they offered to ask any questions.

"Then there came a day," said Captain Littlepage, leaning toward me with a strange look in his eyes, and whispering quickly. "The men all swore they wouldn't stay any longer; the man on watch early in the morning gave the alarm, and they all put off in the boat and got a little way out to sea. Those folks, or whatever they were, come about 'em like bats; all at once they raised incessant armies, and come as if to drive 'em back to sea. They stood thick at the edge o' the water like the ridges o' grim war: no thought o' flight, none of retreat. Sometimes a standing fight, then soaring on main wing tormented all the air. And when they'd got the boat out o' reach o' danger, Gaffett said they looked back, and there was the town again, standing up just as they'd seen it first, comin' on the coast. Say what you might, they all believed 't was a kind of waiting-place between this world an' the next."

The captain had sprung to his feet in his excitement, and made excited gestures, but he still whispered huskily.

"Sit down, sir," I said as quietly as I could, and he sank into his chair quite spent.

"Gaffett thought the officers were hurrying home to report and to fit out a new expedition when they were all lost. At the time, the men got orders not to talk over what they had seen," the old man explained presently in a more natural tone.

"Weren't they all starving, and wasn't it a mirage or something of that sort?" I ventured to ask. But he looked at me blankly.

"Gaffett had got so that his mind ran on nothing else," he went on. "The ship's surgeon let fall an opinion to the captain, one day, that 't was some condition o' the light and the magnetic currents that let them see those folks. 'T wa'n't a right-feeling part of the world, anyway; they had to battle with the compass to make it serve, an' everything seemed to go wrong. Gaffett had worked it out in his own mind that they was all common ghosts, but the conditions were unusual favorable for seeing them. He was always talking about the Ge'graphical Society, but he never took proper steps, as I view it now, and stayed right there at the mission. He was a good deal crippled, and thought they'd confine him in some jail of a hospital. He said he was waiting to find the right men to tell, somebody bound north. Once in a while they stopped there to leave a mail or something. He was set in his notions, and let two or three proper explorin' expeditions go by him because he didn't like their looks; but when I was there he had got restless, fearin' he might be taken away or something. He had all his directions written out straight as a string to give the right ones. I wanted him to trust 'em to me, so I might have something to show, but he wouldn't. I suppose he's dead now. I wrote to him, an' I done all I could. 'T will be a great exploit some o' these days."

I assented absent-mindedly, thinking more just then of my companion's alert, determined look and the seafaring, ready aspect that had come to his face; but at this moment there fell a sudden change, and the old, pathetic, scholarly look returned. Behind me hung a map of North America, and I saw, as I turned a little, that his eyes were fixed upon the northernmost regions and their careful recent outlines with a look of bewilderment.

VII.

THE OUTER ISLAND

❦

Gaffett with his good bunk and the bird-skins, the story of the wreck of the Minerva, the human-shaped creatures of fog and cobweb, the great words of Milton with which he described their onslaught upon the crew, all this moving tale had such an air of truth that I could not argue with Captain Littlepage. The old man looked away from the map as if it had vaguely troubled him, and regarded me appealingly.

"We were just speaking of"—and he stopped. I saw that he had suddenly forgotten his subject.

"There were a great many persons at the funeral," I hastened to say.

"Oh yes," the captain answered, with satisfaction. "All showed respect who could. The sad circumstances had for a moment slipped my mind. Yes, Mrs. Begg will be very much missed. She was a capital manager for her husband when he was at sea. Oh yes, shipping is a very great loss." And he sighed heavily. "There was hardly a man of any standing who didn't interest himself in some way in navigation. It always gave credit to a town. I call it low-water mark now here in Dunnet."

He rose with dignity to take leave, and asked me to stop at his house some day, when he would show me some outlandish things that he had brought home from sea. I was familiar with the subject of the decadence of shipping interests in all its affecting branches, having been already some time in Dunnet, and I felt sure that Captain Littlepage's mind had now returned to a safe level.

As we came down the hill toward the village our ways divided, and when I had seen the old captain well started on a smooth piece of sidewalk which would lead him to his own door, we parted, the best of friends. "Step in some afternoon," he said, as affectionately as if I were a fellow-shipmaster wrecked on the lee shore of age like himself. I turned toward home, and presently met Mrs. Todd coming toward me with an anxious expression.

"I see you sleevin' the old gentleman down the hill," she suggested.

"Yes. I've had a very interesting afternoon with him," I answered; and her face brightened.

"Oh, then he's all right. I was afraid 't was one o' his flighty spells, an' Mari' Harris wouldn't"—

"Yes," I returned, smiling, "he has been telling me some old stories, but we talked about Mrs. Begg and the funeral beside, and Paradise Lost."

"I expect he got tellin' of you some o' his great narratives," she answered, looking at me shrewdly. "Funerals always sets him goin'. Some o' them tales hangs together toler'ble well," she added, with a sharper look than before. "An' he's been a great reader all his seafarin' days. Some thinks he overdid, and affected his head, but for a man o' his years he's amazin' now when he's at his best. Oh, he used to be a beautiful man!"

We were standing where there was a fine view of the harbor and its long stretches of shore all covered by the great army of the pointed firs, darkly cloaked and standing as if they waited to embark. As we looked far seaward among the outer islands, the trees seemed to march seaward still, going steadily over the heights and down to the water's edge.

It had been growing gray and cloudy, like the first evening of autumn, and a shadow had fallen on the darkening shore. Suddenly, as we looked, a gleam of golden sunshine struck the outer islands, and one of them shone out clear in the light, and revealed itself in a compelling way to our eyes. Mrs. Todd was looking off across the bay with a face full of affection and interest. The sunburst upon that outermost island made it seem like a sudden revelation of the world beyond this which some believe to be so near.

"That's where mother lives," said Mrs. Todd. "Can't we see it plain? I was brought up out there on Green Island. I know every rock an' bush on it."

"Your mother!" I exclaimed, with great interest.

"Yes, dear, cert'in; I've got her yet, old's I be. She's one of them spry, light-footed little women; always was, an' light-hearted, too," answered Mrs. Todd, with satisfaction. "She's seen all the trouble folks can see, without it's her last sickness; an' she's got a word of courage for everybody. Life ain't spoilt her a mite. She's eighty-six an' I'm sixty-seven, and I've seen the time I've felt a good sight the oldest. 'Land sakes alive!' says she, last time I was out to see her. 'How you do lurch about steppin' into a bo't!' I laughed so I liked to have gone right over into the water; an' we pushed off, an' left her laughin' there on the shore."

The light had faded as we watched. Mrs. Todd had mounted a gray rock, and stood there grand and architectural, like a *caryatide*. Presently she stepped down, and we continued our way homeward.

"You an' me, we'll take a bo't an' go out some day and see mother," she promised me. " 'T would please her very much, an' there's one or two sca'ce herbs grows better on the island than anywheres else. I ain't seen their like nowheres here on the main."

"Now I'm goin' right down to get us each a mug o' my beer," she announced as we entered the house, "an' I believe I'll sneak in a little mite o' camomile. Goin' to the funeral an' all, I feel to have had a very wearin' afternoon."

I heard her going down into the cool little cellar, and then there was considerable delay. When she returned, mug in hand, I noticed the taste of camomile, in spite of my protest; but its flavor was disguised by some other herb that I did not know, and she stood over me until I drank it all and said that I liked it.

"I don't give that to everybody," said Mrs. Todd kindly; and I felt for a moment as if it were part of a spell and incantation, and as if my enchantress would now begin to look like the cobweb shapes of the arctic town. Nothing happened but a quiet evening and some delightful plans that we made about going to Green Island, and on the morrow there was the clear sunshine and blue sky of another day.

❈

VIII.

GREEN ISLAND

One morning, very early, I heard Mrs. Todd in the garden outside my window. By the unusual loudness of her remarks to a passer-by, and the notes of a familiar hymn which she sang as she worked among the herbs, and which came as if directed purposely to the sleepy ears of my consciousness, I knew that she wished I would wake up and come and speak to her.

In a few minutes she responded to a morning voice from behind the blinds. "I expect you're goin' up to your school-house to pass all this pleasant day; yes, I expect you're goin' to be dreadful busy," she said despairingly.

"Perhaps not," said I. "Why, what's going to be the matter with you, Mrs. Todd?" For I supposed that she was tempted by the fine weather to take one of her favorite expeditions along the shore pastures to gather herbs and simples, and would like to have me keep the house.

"No, I don't want to go nowhere by land," she answered gayly—"no, not by land; but I don't know's we shall have a better day all the rest of the summer to go out to Green Island an' see mother. I waked up early thinkin' of her. The wind's light northeast—'t will take us right straight out; an' this time o' year it's liable to change round southwest an' fetch us home pretty, 'long late in the afternoon. Yes, it's goin' to be a good day."

"Speak to the captain and the Bowden boy, if you see anybody going by toward the landing," said I. "We'll take the big boat."

"Oh, my sakes! now you let me do things my way," said Mrs. Todd scornfully. "No, dear, we won't take no big bo't. I'll just git a handy dory, an' Johnny Bowden an' me, we'll man her ourselves. I don't want no abler bo't than a good dory, an' a nice light breeze ain't goin' to make no sea; an' Johnny's my cousin's son—mother'll like to have him come; an' he'll be down to the herrin' weirs all the time we're there,

70

anyway; we don't want to carry no men folks havin' to be considered every minute an' takin' up all our time. No, you let me do; we'll just slip out an' see mother by ourselves. I guess what breakfast you'll want's about ready now."

I had become well acquainted with Mrs. Todd as landlady, herb-gatherer, and rustic philosopher; we had been discreet fellow-passengers once or twice when I had sailed up the coast to a larger town than Dunnet Landing to do some shopping; but I was yet to become acquainted with her as a mariner. An hour later we pushed off from the landing in the desired dory. The tide was just on the turn, beginning to fall, and several friends and acquaintances stood along the side of the dilapidated wharf and cheered us by their words and evident interest. Johnny Bowden and I were both rowing in haste to get out where we could catch the breeze and put up the small sail which lay clumsily furled along the gunwale. Mrs. Todd sat aft, a stern and unbending law-giver.

"You better let her drift; we'll get there 'bout as quick; the tide'll take her right out from under these old buildin's; there's plenty wind outside."

"Your bo't ain't trimmed proper, Mis' Todd!" exclaimed a voice from shore. "You're lo'ded so the bo't'll drag; you can't git her before the wind, ma'am. You set 'midships, Mis' Todd, an' let the boy hold the sheet 'n' steer after he gits the sail up; you won't never git out to Green Island that way. She's lo'ded bad, your bo't is—she's heavy behind's she is now!"

Mrs. Todd turned with some difficulty and regarded the anxious adviser, my right oar flew out of water, and we seemed about to capsize. "That you, Asa? Good-mornin'," she said politely. "I al'ays liked the starn seat best. When'd you git back from up country?"

This allusion to Asa's origin was not lost upon the rest of the company. We were some little distance from shore, but we could hear a chuckle of laughter, and Asa, a person who was too ready with his criticism and advice on every possible subject, turned and walked indignantly away.

When we caught the wind we were soon on our seaward course, and only stopped to underrun a trawl, for the floats of which Mrs. Todd looked earnestly, explaining that her mother might not be prepared for three extra to dinner; it was her brother's trawl, and she meant to just run her eye along for the right sort of little haddock. I leaned over the boat's side with great interest and excitement, while she skillfully handled the long line of hooks, and made scornful remarks upon worthless, bait-consuming creatures of the sea as she reviewed them and left them on the trawl or shook them off into the waves. At last we came to what she pronounced a proper haddock, and having taken him on board and ended his life resolutely, we went our way.

As we sailed along I listened to an increasingly delightful commentary upon the islands, some of them barren rocks, or at best giving sparse pasturage for sheep in the early summer. On one of these an eager little flock ran to the water's edge and bleated at us so affectingly that I would willingly have stopped; but Mrs. Todd steered away from the rocks, and scolded at the sheep's mean owner, an acquaintance of hers, who grudged the little salt and still less care which the patient creatures needed. The hot midsummer sun makes prisons of these small islands that are a paradise in early June, with their cool springs and short thick-growing grass. On a larger island, farther out to sea, my entertaining companion showed me with glee the small houses of two farmers who shared the island between them, and declared that for three generations the people had not spoken to each other even in times of sickness or death or birth. "When the news come that the war was over, one of 'em knew it a week, and never stepped across his wall to tell the others," she said. "There, they enjoy it: they've got to have somethin' to interest 'em in such a place; 't is a good deal more tryin' to be tied to folks you don't like than 't is to be alone. Each of 'em tells the neighbors their wrongs; plenty likes to hear and tell again; them as fetch a bone'll carry one, an' so they keep the fight a-goin'. I must say I like variety myself; some folks washes Monday an' irons Tuesday the whole year round, even if the circus is goin' by!"

A long time before we landed at Green Island we could see the small white house, standing high like a beacon, where Mrs. Todd was born and where her mother lived, on a green slope above the water, with dark spruce woods still higher. There were crops in the fields, which we presently distinguished from one another. Mrs. Todd examined them while we were still far at sea. "Mother's late potatoes looks backward; ain't had rain enough so far," she pronounced her opinion. "They look weedier than what they call Front Street down to Cowper Centre. I expect brother William is so occupied with his herrin' weirs an' servin' out bait to the schooners that he don't think once a day of the land."

"What's the flag for, up above the spruces there behind the house?" I inquired, with eagerness.

"Oh, that's the sign for herrin'," she explained kindly, while Johnny Bowden regarded me with contemptuous surprise. "When they get enough for schooners they raise that flag; an' when 't is a poor catch in the weir pocket they just fly a little signal down by the shore, an' then the small b'ots comes and get enough an' over for their trawls. There, look! there she is: mother sees us; she's wavin' somethin' out o' the fore door! She'll be to the landin'-place quick's we are."

I looked, and could see a tiny flutter in the doorway, but a quicker signal had made its way from the heart on shore to the heart on the sea.

"How do you suppose she knows it's me?" said Mrs. Todd, with a tender smile on her broad face. "There, you never get over bein' a child long's you have a mother to go to. Look at the chimney, now; she's gone right in an' brightened up the fire. Well, there, I'm glad mother's well; you'll enjoy seein' her very much."

Mrs. Todd leaned back into her proper position, and the boat trimmed again. She took a firmer grasp of the sheet, and gave an impatient look up at the gaff and the leech of the little sail, and twitched the sheet as if she urged the wind like a horse. There came at once a fresh gust, and we seemed to have doubled our speed. Soon we were near enough to see a tiny figure with handkerchiefed head come down across the field and stand waiting for us at the cove above a curve of pebble beach.

Presently the dory grated on the pebbles, and Johnny Bowden, who had been kept in abeyance during the voyage, sprang out and used manful exertions to haul us up with the next wave, so that Mrs. Todd could make a dry landing.

"You done that very well," she said, mounting to her feet, and coming ashore somewhat stiffly, but with great dignity, refusing our outstretched hands, and returning to possess herself of a bag which had lain at her feet.

"Well, mother, here I be!" she announced with indifference; but they stood and beamed in each other's faces.

"Lookin' pretty well for an old lady, ain't she?" said Mrs. Todd's mother, turning away from her daughter to speak to me. She was a delightful little person herself, with bright eyes and an affectionate air of expectation like a child on a holiday. You felt as if Mrs. Blackett were an old and dear friend before you let go her cordial hand. We all started together up the hill.

"Now don't you haste too fast, mother," said Mrs. Todd warningly; " 't is a far reach o' risin' ground to the fore door, and you won't set an' get your breath when you're once there, but go trotting about. Now don't you go a mite faster than we proceed with this bag an' basket. Johnny, there, 'll fetch up the haddock. I just made one stop to underrun William's trawl till I come to jes' such a fish's I thought you'd want to make one o' your nice chowders of. I've brought an onion with me that was layin' about on the window-sill at home."

"That's just what I was wantin'," said the hostess. "I give a sigh when you spoke o' chowder, knowin' my onions was out. William forgot to replenish us last time he was to the Landin'. Don't you haste so yourself, Almiry, up this risin' ground. I hear you commencin' to wheeze a'ready."

This mild revenge seemed to afford great pleasure to both giver and receiver. They laughed a little, and looked at each other affectionately, and then at me. Mrs. Todd considerately paused, and faced about to regard the wide sea view. I was glad to stop, being more out of breath than either of my companions, and I prolonged the halt by asking the names of the neighboring islands. There was a fine breeze blowing, which we felt more there on the high land than when we were running before it in the dory.

"Why, this ain't that kitten I saw when I was out last, the one that I said didn't appear likely?" exclaimed Mrs. Todd as we went our way.

"That's the one, Almiry," said her mother. "She always had a likely look to me, an' she's right after her business. I never see such a mouser for one of her age. If 't wan't for William, I never should have housed that other dronin' old thing so long; but he sets by her on account of her havin' a bob tail. I don't deem it advisable to maintain cats just on account of their havin' bob tails; they're like all other curiosities, good for them that wants to see 'em twice. This kitten catches mice for both, an' keeps me respectable as I ain't been for a year. She's a real understandin' little help, this kitten is. I picked her from among five Miss Augusta Pennell had over to Burnt Island," said the old woman, trudging along with the kitten close at her skirts. "Augusta, she says to me, 'Why, Mis' Blackett, you've took the homeliest;' an' says I, I've got the smartest; I'm satisfied.' "

"I'd trust nobody sooner'n you to pick out a kitten, mother," said the daughter handsomely, and we went on in peace and harmony.

The house was just before us now, on a green level that looked as if a huge hand had scooped it out of the long green field we had been ascending. A little way above, the dark spruce woods began to climb the top of the hill and cover the seaward slopes of the island. There was just room for the small farm and the forest; we looked down at the fish-house and its rough sheds, and the weirs stretching far out into the water. As we looked upward, the tops of the firs came sharp against the blue sky. There was a great stretch of rough pasture-land round the shoulder of the island to the eastward, and here were all the thick-scattered gray rocks that kept their places, and the gray backs of many sheep that forever wandered and fed on the thin sweet pasturage that fringed the ledges and made soft hollows and strips of green turf like growing velvet. I could see the rich green of bayberry bushes here and there, where the rocks made room. The air was very sweet; one could not help wishing to be a citizen of such a complete and tiny continent and home of fisherfolk.

The house was broad and clean, with a roof that looked heavy on its low walls. It was one of the houses that seem firm-rooted in the ground, as if they were two-thirds below the surface, like icebergs. The front door stood hospitably open in expectation of company, and an orderly vine grew at each side; but our path led to the kitchen door at the house-end, and there grew a mass of gay flowers and greenery, as if they had been swept together by some diligent garden broom into a tangled heap: there were portulacas all along under the lower step and straggling off into the grass, and clustering mallows that crept as near as they dared, like poor relations. I saw the bright eyes and brainless little heads of two half-grown chickens who were snuggled down among the mallows as if they had been chased away from the door more than once, and expected to be again.

"It seems kind o' formal comin' in this way," said Mrs. Todd impulsively, as we passed the flowers and came to the front doorstep; but she was mindful of the proprieties, and walked before us into the best room on the left.

"Why, mother, if you haven't gone an' turned the carpet!" she exclaimed, with something in her voice that spoke of awe and admiration. "When 'd you get to it? I s'pose Mis' Addicks come over an' helped you, from White Island Landing?"

"No, she didn't," answered the old woman, standing proudly erect, and making the most of a great moment. "I done it all myself with William's help. He had a spare day, an' took right holt with me; an' 't was all well beat on the grass, an' turned, an' put down again afore we went to bed. I ripped an' sewed over two o' them long breadths. I ain't had such a good night's sleep for two years."

"There, what do you think o' havin' such a mother as that for eighty-six year old?" said Mrs. Todd, standing before us like a large figure of Victory.

As for the mother, she took on a sudden look of youth; you felt as if she promised a great future, and was beginning, not ending, her summers and their happy toils.

"My, my!" exclaimed Mrs. Todd. "I couldn't ha' done it myself, I've got to own it."

"I was much pleased to have it off my mind," said Mrs. Blackett, humbly; "the more so because along at the first of the next week I wasn't very well. I suppose it may have been the change of weather."

Mrs. Todd could not resist a significant glance at me, but, with charming sympathy, she forbore to point the lesson or to connect this illness with its apparent cause. She loomed larger than ever in the little old-fashioned best room, with its few pieces of good furniture and pictures of national interest. The green paper curtains were stamped with conventional landscapes of a foreign order,—castles on inaccessible crags, and lovely lakes with steep wooded shores; under-foot the treasured carpet was covered thick with home-made rugs. There were empty glass lamps and crystallized bouquets of grass and some fine shells on the narrow mantelpiece.

"I was married in this room," said Mrs. Todd unexpectedly; and I heard her give a sigh after she had spoken, as if she could not help the touch of regret that would forever come with all her thoughts of happiness.

"We stood right there between the windows," she added, "and the minister stood here. William wouldn't come in. He was always odd about seein' folks, just 's he is now. I run to meet 'em from a child, an' William, he'd take an' run away."

"I've been the gainer," said the old mother cheerfully. "William has been son an' daughter both since you was married off the island. He's been 'most too satisfied to stop at home 'long o' his old mother, but I always tell 'em I'm the gainer."

We were all moving toward the kitchen as if by common

instinct. The best room was too suggestive of serious occasions, and the shades were all pulled down to shut out the summer light and air. It was indeed a tribute to Society to find a room set apart for her behests out there on so apparently neighborless and remote an island. Afternoon visits and evening festivals must be few in such a bleak situation at certain seasons of the year, but Mrs. Blackett was of those who do not live to themselves, and who have long since passed the line that divides mere self-concern from a valued share in whatever Society can give and take. There were those of her neighbors who never had taken the trouble to furnish a best room, but Mrs. Blackett was one who knew the uses of a parlor.

"Yes, do come right out into the old kitchen; I shan't make any stranger of you," she invited us pleasantly, after we had been properly received in the room appointed to formality. "I expect Almiry, here,'ll be driftin' out'mongst the pasture-weeds quick's she can find a good excuse. 'T is hot now. You'd better content yourselves till you get nice an' rested, an' 'long after dinner the sea-breeze 'll spring up, an' then you can take your walks, an' go up an' see the prospect from the big ledge. Almiry'll want to show off everything there is. Then I'll get you a good cup o' tea before you start to go home. The days are plenty long now."

While we were talking in the best room the selected fish had been mysteriously brought up from the shore, and lay all cleaned and ready in an earthen crock on the table.

"I think William might have just stopped an' said a word," remarked Mrs. Todd, pouting with high affront as she caught sight of it. "He's friendly enough when he comes ashore, an' was remarkable social the last time, for him."

"He ain't disposed to be very social with the ladies," explained William's mother, with a delightful glance at me, as if she counted upon my friendship and tolerance. "He's very particular, and he's all in his old fishin'-clothes to-day. He'll want me to tell him everything you said and done, after you've gone. William has very deep affections. He'll want to see you, Almiry. Yes, I guess he'll be in by an' by."

"I'll search for him by 'n' by, if he don't," proclaimed Mrs. Todd, with an air of unalterable resolution. "I know all of his burrows down 'long the shore. I'll catch him by hand 'fore he knows it. I've got some business with William, anyway. I brought forty-two cents with me that was due him for them last lobsters he brought in."

"You can leave it with me," suggested the little old mother, who was already stepping about among her pots and pans in the pantry, and preparing to make the chowder.

I became possessed of a sudden unwonted curiosity in regard to William, and felt that half the pleasure of my visit would be lost if I could not make his interesting acquaintance.

Mrs. Todd had taken the onion out of her basket and laid it down upon the kitchen table. "There's Johnny Bowden come with us, you know," she reminded her mother. "He'll be hungry enough to eat his size."

"I've got new doughnuts, dear," said the little old lady. "You don't often catch William 'n' me out o' provisions. I expect you might have chose a somewhat larger fish, but I'll try an' make it do. I shall have to have a few extra potatoes, but there's a field full out there, an' the hoe's leanin' against the well-house, in 'mongst the climbin'-beans." She smiled, and gave her daughter a commanding nod.

"Land sakes alive! Le' 's blow the horn for William," insisted Mrs. Todd, with some excitement. "He needn't break his spirit so far's to come in. He'll know you need him for something particular, an' then we can call to him as he comes up the path. I won't put him to no pain."

Mrs. Blackett's old face, for the first time, wore a look of trouble, and I found it necessary to counteract the teasing spirit of Almira. It was too pleasant to stay indoors altogether, even in such rewarding companionship; besides, I might meet William; and, straying out presently, I found the hoe by the well-house and an old splint basket at the wood-shed door, and also found my way down to the field where there was a great square patch of rough, weedy potato-tops and tall ragweed. One corner was already dug, and I chose a fat-looking hill where the tops were well withered. There is all the pleasure that one can have in gold-digging in finding one's hopes satisfied in the riches of a good hill of potatoes. I longed to go on; but it did not seem frugal to dig any longer after my basket was full, and at last I took my hoe by the middle and lifted the basket to go back up the hill. I was sure that Mrs. Blackett must be waiting impatiently to slice the potatoes into the chowder, layer after layer, with the fish.

"You let me take holt o' that basket, ma'am," said a pleasant, anxious voice behind me.

I turned, startled in the silence of the wide field, and saw an elderly man, bent in the shoulders as fishermen often are, gray-headed and clean-shaven, and with a timid air. It was William. He looked just like his mother, and I had been imagining that he was large and stout like his sister, Almira Todd; and, strange to say, my fancy had led me to picture him not far from thirty and a little loutish. It was necessary instead to pay William the respect due to age.

I accustomed myself to plain facts on the instant, and we said good-morning like old friends. The basket was really heavy, and I put the hoe through its handle and offered him one end; then we moved easily toward the house together, speaking of the fine weather and of mackerel which were reported to be striking in all about the bay. William had been out since three o'clock, and had taken an extra fare of fish. I could feel that Mrs. Todd's eyes were upon us as we approached the house, and although I fell behind in the narrow path, and let William take the basket alone and precede me at some little distance the rest of the way, I could plainly hear her greet him.

"Got round to comin' in, didn't you?" she inquired, with amusement. "Well, now, that's clever. Didn't know's I should see you to-day, William, an' I wanted to settle an account."

I felt somewhat disturbed and responsible, but when I joined them they were on most simple and friendly terms. It became evident that, with William, it was the first step that cost, and that, having once joined in social interests, he was able to pursue them with more or less pleasure. He was about sixty, and not young-looking for his years, yet so undying is the spirit of youth, and bashfulness has such a power of survival, that I felt all the time as if one must try to make the occasion easy for some one who was young and new to the affairs of social life. He asked politely if I would like to go up to the great ledge while dinner was getting ready; so, not without a deep sense of pleasure and a delighted look of surprise from the two hostesses, we started, William and I, as if both of us felt much younger than we looked. Such was the innocence and simplicity of the moment that when I heard Mrs. Todd laughing behind us in the kitchen I laughed too, but William did not even blush. I think he was a little deaf, and he stepped along before me most businesslike and intent upon his errand.

We went from the upper edge of the field above the house into a smooth, brown path among the dark spruces. The hot sun brought out the fragrance of the pitchy bark, and the shade was pleasant as we climbed the hill. William stopped once or twice to show me a great wasps'-nest close by, or some fishhawks'-nests below in a bit of swamp. He picked a few sprigs of late-blooming linnæa as we came out upon an open bit of pasture at the top of the island, and gave them to me without speaking, but he knew as well as I that one could not say half he wished about linnæa. Through this piece of rough pasture ran a huge shape of stone like the great backbone of an enormous creature. At the end, near the woods, we could climb up on it and walk along to the highest point; there above the circle of pointed firs we could look down over all the island, and could see the ocean that circled this and a hundred other bits of island-ground, the mainland shore and all the far horizons. It gave a sudden sense of space, for nothing stopped the eye or hedged one in—that sense of liberty in space and time which great prospects always give.

"There ain't no such view in the world, I expect," said William proudly, and I hastened to speak my heartfelt tribute of praise; it was impossible not to feel as if an untraveled boy had spoken, and yet one loved to have him value his native heath.

X.

WHERE PENNYROYAL GREW

✦

We were a little late to dinner, but Mrs. Blackett and Mrs. Todd were lenient, and we all took our places after William had paused to wash his hands, like a pious Brahmin, at the well, and put on a neat blue coat which he took from a peg behind the kitchen door. Then he resolutely asked a blessing in words that I could not hear, and we ate the chowder and were thankful. The kitten went round and round the table, quite erect, and, holding on by her fierce young claws, she stopped to mew with pathos at each elbow, or darted off to the open door when a song sparrow forgot himself and lit in the grass too near. William did not talk much, but his sister Todd occupied the time and told all the news there was to tell of Dunnet Landing and its coasts, while the old mother listened with delight. Her hospitality was something exquisite; she had the gift which so many women lack, of being able to make themselves and their houses belong entirely to a guest's pleasure,—that charming surrender for the moment of themselves and whatever belongs to them, so that they make a part of one's own life that can never be forgotten. Tact is after all a kind of mindreading, and my hostess held the golden gift. Sympathy is of the mind as well as the heart, and Mrs. Blackett's world and mine were one from the moment we met. Besides, she had that final, that highest gift of heaven, a perfect self-forgetfulness. Sometimes, as I watched her eager, sweet old face, I wondered why she had been set to shine on this lonely island of the northern coast. It must have been to keep the balance true, and make up to all her scattered and depending neighbors for other things which they may have lacked.

When we had finished clearing away the old blue plates, and the kitten had taken care of her share of the fresh haddock, just as we were putting back the kitchen chairs in their places, Mrs. Todd said briskly that she must go up into the pasture now to gather the desired herbs.

"You can stop here an' rest, or you can accompany me," she announced. "Mother ought to have her nap, and when we come back she an' William'll sing for you. She admires music," said Mrs. Todd, turning to speak to her mother.

But Mrs. Blackett tried to say that she couldn't sing as she used, and perhaps William wouldn't feel like it. She looked tired, the good old soul, or I should have liked to sit in the peaceful little house while she slept; I had had much pleasant experience of pastures already in her daughter's company. But it seemed best to go with Mrs. Todd, and off we went.

Mrs. Todd carried the gingham bag which she had brought from home, and a small heavy burden in the bottom made it hang straight and slender from her hand. The way was steep, and she soon grew breathless, so that we sat down to rest awhile on a convenient large stone among the bayberry.

"There, I wanted you to see this—'t is mother's picture," said Mrs. Todd; " 't was taken once when she was up to Portland, soon after she was married. That's me," she added, opening another worn case, and displaying the full face of the cheerful child she looked like still in spite of being past sixty. "And here's William an' father together. I take after father, large and heavy, an' William is like mother's folks, short an' thin. He ought to have made something o' himself, bein' a man an' so like mother; but though he's been very steady to work, an' kept up the farm, an' done his fishin' too right along, he never had mother's snap an' power o' seein' things just as they be. He's got excellent judgment, too," meditated William's sister, but she could not arrive at any satisfactory decision upon what she evidently thought his failure in life. "I think it is well to see anyone so happy an' makin' the most of life just as it falls to hand," she said as she began to put the daguerreotypes away again; but I reached out my hand to see her mother's once more, a most flower-like face of a lovely young woman in quaint dress. There was in the eyes a look of anticipation and joy, a far-off look that sought the horizon; one often sees it in seafaring families, inherited by girls and boys alike from men who spend their lives at sea, and are always watching for distant sails or the first loom of the land. At sea there is nothing to be seen close by, and this has its counterpart in a sailor's character, in the large and brave and patient traits that are developed, the hopeful pleasantness that one loves so in a seafarer.

When the family pictures were wrapped again in a big handkerchief, we set forward in a narrow footpath and made our way to a lonely place that faced northward, where there was more pasturage and fewer bushes, and we went down to the edge of short grass above some rocky cliffs where the deep sea broke with a great noise, though the wind was down and the water looked quiet a little way from shore. Among the grass grew such pennyroyal as the rest of the world could not provide. There was a fine fragrance in the air as we gathered it sprig by sprig and stepped along carefully, and Mrs. Todd pressed her aromatic nosegay between her hands and offered it to me again and again.

"There's nothin' like it," she said; "oh no, there's no such pennyr'yal as this in the State of Maine. It's the right pattern of the plant, and all the rest I ever see is but an imitation. Don't it do you good?" And I answered with enthusiasm.

"There, dear, I never showed nobody else but mother where to find this place; 't is kind of sainted to me. Nathan, my husband, an' I used to love this place when we was courtin', and"—she hesitated, and then spoke softly—"when he was lost, 't was just off shore tryin' to get in by the short channel out there between Squaw Islands, right in sight o' this headland where we'd set an' made our plans all summer long."

I had never heard her speak of her husband before, but I felt that we were friends now since she had brought me to this place.

"'T was but a dream with us," Mrs. Todd said. "I knew it when he was gone. I knew it"—and she whispered as if she were at confession—"I knew it afore he started to go to sea. My heart was gone out o' my keepin' before I ever saw Nathan; but he loved me well, and he made me real happy, and he died before he ever knew what he'd had to know if we'd lived long together. 'T is very strange about love. No, Nathan never found out, but my heart was troubled when I knew him first. There's more women likes to be loved than there is of those that loves. I spent some happy hours right here. I always liked Nathan, and he never knew. But this pennyr'yal always reminded me, as I'd sit and gather it and hear him talkin'—it always would remind me of—the other one."

She looked away from me, and presently rose and went on by herself. There was something lonely and solitary about her great determined shape. She might have been Antigone alone on the Theban plain. It is not often given in a noisy world to come to the places of great grief and silence. An absolute, archaic grief possessed this countrywoman; she seemed like a renewal of some historic soul, with her sorrows and the remoteness of a daily life busied with rustic simplicities and the scents of primeval herbs.

I was not incompetent at herb-gathering, and after a while, when I had sat long enough waking myself to new thoughts, and reading a page of remembrance with new pleasure, I gathered some bunches, as I was bound to do, and at last we met again higher up the shore, in the plain every-day world we had left behind when we went down to the pennyroyal plot. As we walked together along the high edge of the field we saw a hundred sails about the bay and farther seaward; it was mid-afternoon or after, and the day was coming to an end.

"Yes, they're all makin' towards the shore—the small craft an' the lobster smacks an' all," said my companion. "We must spend a little time with mother now, just to have our tea, an' then put for home."

"No matter if we lose the wind at sundown; I can row in with Johnny," said I; and Mrs. Todd nodded reassuringly and kept to her steady plod, not quickening her gait even when we saw William come round the corner of the house as if to look for us, and wave his hand and disappear.

"Why, William's right on deck; I didn't know's we should see any more of him!" exclaimed Mrs. Todd. "Now mother'll put the kettle right on; she's got a good fire goin'." I too could see the blue smoke thicken, and then we both walked a little faster, while Mrs. Todd groped in her full bag of herbs to find the daguerreotypes and be ready to put them in their places.

XI

THE OLD SINGERS

❦

William was sitting on the side door step, and the old mother was busy making her tea; she gave into my hand an old flowered-glass tea-caddy.

"William thought you'd like to see this, when he was settin' the table. My father brought it to my mother from the island of Tobago; an' here's a pair of beautiful mugs that came with it." She opened the glass door of a little cupboard beside the chimney. "These I call my best things, dear," she said. "You'd laugh to see how we enjoy 'em Sunday nights in winter: we have a real company tea 'stead o' livin' right along just the same, an' I make somethin' good for a s'prise an' put on some o' my preserves, an' we get a-talkin' together an' have real pleasant times."

Mrs. Todd laughed indulgently, and looked to see what I thought of such childishness.

"I wish I could be here some Sunday evening," said I.

"William an' me 'll be talkin' about you an' thinkin' o' this nice day," said Mrs. Blackett affectionately, and she glanced at William, and he looked up bravely and nodded. I began to discover that he and his sister could not speak their deeper feelings before each other.

"Now I want you an' mother to sing," said Mrs. Todd abruptly, with an air of command, and I gave William much sympathy in his evident distress.

"After I've had my cup o' tea, dear," answered the old hostess cheerfully; and so we sat down and took our cups and made merry while they lasted. It was impossible not to wish to stay on forever at Green Island, and I could not help saying so.

"I'm very happy here, both winter an' summer," said old Mrs. Blackett. "William an' I never wish for any other home, do we, William? I'm glad you find it pleasant; I wish you'd come an' stay, dear, whenever you feel inclined. But here's Almiry; I always think Providence was kind to plot an' have her husband leave her a good house where she really belonged. She'd been very restless if she'd had to continue here on Green Island. You wanted more scope, didn't you, Almiry, an' to live in a large place where more things grew? Sometimes folks wonders that we don't live together; perhaps we shall some time," and a shadow of sadness and apprehension flitted across her face. "The time o' sickness an' failin' has got to come to all. But Almiry's got an herb that's good for everything." She smiled as she spoke, and looked bright again.

"There's some herb that's good for everybody, except for them that thinks they're sick when they ain't," announced Mrs. Todd with a truly professional air of finality. "Come, William, let's have Sweet Home, an' then mother'll sing Cupid an' the Bee for us."

Then followed a most charming surprise. William mastered his timidity and began to sing. His voice was a little faint and frail, like the family daguerreotypes, but it was a tenor voice, and perfectly true and sweet. I have never heard Home, Sweet Home sung as touchingly and seriously as he sang it; he seemed to make it quite new; and when he paused for a moment at the end of the first line and began the next, the old mother joined him and they sang together, she missing only the higher notes, where he seemed to lend his voice to hers for the moment and carry on her very note and air. It was the silent man's real and only means of expression, and one could have listened forever, and have asked for more and more songs of old Scotch and English inheritance and the best that have lived from the ballad music of the war. Mrs. Todd kept time visibly, and sometimes audibly, with her ample foot. I saw the tears in her eyes sometimes, when I could see beyond the tears in mine. But at last the songs ended and the time came to say good-by; it was the end of a great pleasure.

Mrs. Blackett, the dear old lady, opened the door of her bedroom while Mrs. Todd was tying up the herb bag, and William had gone down to get the boat ready and to blow the horn for Johnny Bowden, who had joined a roving boat party who were off the shore lobstering.

I went to the door of the bedroom, and thought how pleasant it looked, with its pink-and-white patchwork quilt and the brown unpainted paneling of its woodwork.

"Come right in, dear," she said. "I want you to set down in my old quilted rockin'-chair there by the window; you'll say it's the prettiest view in the house. I set there a good deal to rest me and when I want to read."

There was a worn red Bible on the lightstand, and Mrs. Blackett's heavy silver-bowed glasses; her thimble was on the narrow window-ledge, and folded carefully on the table was a thick striped-cotton shirt that she was making for her son. Those dear old fingers and their loving stitches, that heart which had made the most of everything that needed love! Here was the real home, the heart of the old house on Green Island! I sat in the rocking-chair, and felt that it was a place of peace, the little brown bedroom, and the quiet outlook upon field and sea and sky.

I looked up, and we understood each other without speaking. "I shall like to think o' your settin' here to-day," said Mrs. Blackett. "I want you to come again. It has been so pleasant for William."

The wind served us all the way home, and did not fall or let the sail slacken until we were close to the shore. We had a generous freight of lobsters in the boat, and new potatoes which William had put aboard, and what Mrs. Todd proudly called a full "kag" of prime number one salted mackerel; and when we landed we had to make business arrangements to have these conveyed to her house in a wheelbarrow.

I never shall forget the day at Green Island. The town of Dunnet Landing seemed large and noisy and oppressive as we came ashore. Such is the power of contrast; for the village was so still that I could hear the shy whippoorwills singing that night as I lay awake in my downstairs bedroom, and the scent of Mrs. Todd's herb garden under the window blew in again and again with every gentle rising of the sea-breeze.

XII.

A STRANGE SAIL

❧

Except for a few stray guests, islanders or from the inland
country, to whom Mrs. Todd offered the hospitalities of a
single meal, we were quite by ourselves all summer; and
when there were signs of invasion, late in July, and a certain
Mrs. Fosdick appeared like a strange sail on the far horizon,
I suffered much from apprehension. I had been living in the
quaint little house with as much comfort and unconsciousness
as if it were a larger body, or a double shell, in whose simple
convolutions Mrs. Todd and I had secreted ourselves, until
some wandering hermit crab of a visitor marked the little
spare room for her own. Perhaps now and then a castaway
on a lonely desert island dreads the thought of being rescued.
I heard of Mrs. Fosdick for the first time with a selfish sense
of objection; but after all, I was still vacation-tenant of the
schoolhouse, where I could always be alone, and it was impossible not to sympathize with Mrs. Todd, who, in spite of
some preliminary grumbling, was really delighted with the
prospect of entertaining an old friend.

For nearly a month we received occasional news of Mrs.
Fosdick, who seemed to be making a royal progress from
house to house in the inland neighborhood, after the fashion
of Queen Elizabeth. One Sunday after another came and
went, disappointing Mrs. Todd in the hope of seeing her
guest at church and fixing the day for the great visit to begin;
but Mrs. Fosdick was not ready to commit herself to a date.
An assurance of "some time this week" was not sufficiently
definite from a free-footed housekeeper's point of view, and
Mrs. Todd put aside all herb-gathering plans, and went
through the various stages of expectation, provocation, and
despair. At last she was ready to believe that Mrs. Fosdick
must have forgotten her promise and returned to her home,
which was vaguely said to be over Thomaston way. But one
evening, just as the supper-table was cleared and "readied
up," and Mrs. Todd had put her large apron over her head

and stepped forth for an evening stroll in the garden, the unexpected happened. She heard the sound of wheels, and gave an excited cry to me, as I sat by the window, that Mrs. Fosdick was coming right up the street.

"She may not be considerate, but she's dreadful good company," said Mrs. Todd hastily, coming back a few steps from the neighborhood of the gate. "No, she ain't a mite considerate, but there's a small lobster left over from your tea; yes, it's a real mercy there's a lobster. Susan Fosdick might just as well have passed the compliment o' comin' an hour ago."

"Perhaps she has had her supper," I ventured to suggest, sharing the housekeeper's anxiety, and meekly conscious of an inconsiderate appetite for my own supper after a long expedition up the bay. There were so few emergencies of any sort at Dunnet Landing that this one appeared overwhelming.

"No, she's rode 'way over from Nahum Brayton's place. I expect they were busy on the farm, and couldn't spare the horse in proper season. You just sly out an' set the teakittle on again, dear, an' drop in a good han'ful o' chips; the fire's all alive. I'll take her right up to lay off her things, an' she'll be occupied with explanations an' gettin' her bunnit off, so you'll have plenty o' time. She's one I shouldn't like to have find me unprepared."

Mrs. Fosdick was already at the gate, and Mrs. Todd now turned with an air of complete surprise and delight to welcome her.

"Why, Susan Fosdick," I heard her exclaim in a fine unhindered voice, as if she were calling across a field, "I come near giving of you up! I was afraid you'd gone an' 'portioned out my visit to somebody else. I s'pose you've been to supper?"

"Lor', no, I ain't, Almiry Todd," said Mrs. Fosdick cheerfully, as she turned, laden with bags and bundles, from making her adieux to the boy driver. "I ain't had a mite o' supper, dear. I've been lottin' all the way on a cup o' that best tea o' yourn—some o' that Oolong you keep in the little chist. I don't want none o' your useful herbs."

"I keep that tea for ministers' folks," gayly responded Mrs. Todd. "Come right along in, Susan Fosdick. I declare if you ain't the same old sixpence!"

As they came up the walk together, laughing like girls, I fled, full of cares, to the kitchen, to brighten the fire and be sure that the lobster, sole dependence of a late supper, was well out of reach of the cat. There proved to be fine reserves of wild raspberries and bread and butter, so that I regained my composure, and waited impatiently for my own share of this illustrious visit to begin. There was an instant sense of high festivity in the evening air from the moment when our guest had so frankly demanded the Oolong tea.

The great moment arrived. I was formally presented at the stair-foot, and the two friends passed on to the kitchen, where I soon heard a hospitable clink of crockery and the brisk stirring of a tea-cup. I sat in my high-backed rocking-chair by the window in the front room with an unreasonable feeling of being left out, like the child who stood at the gate in Hans Andersen's story. Mrs. Fosdick did not look, at first sight, like a person of great social gifts. She was a serious-looking little bit of an old woman, with a birdlike nod of the head. I had often been told that she was the "best hand in the world to make a visit"—as if to visit were the highest of vocations; that everybody wished for her, while few could get her; and I saw that Mrs. Todd felt a comfortable sense of distinction in being favored with the company of this eminent person who "knew just how." It was certainly true that Mrs. Fosdick gave both her hostess and me a warm feeling of enjoyment and expectation, as if she had the power of social suggestion to all neighboring minds.

The two friends did not reappear for at least an hour. I could hear their busy voices, loud and low by turns, as they ranged from public to confidential topics. At last Mrs. Todd kindly remembered me and returned, giving my door a ceremonious knock before she stepped in, with the small visitor in her wake. She reached behind her and took Mrs. Fosdick's hand as if she were young and bashful, and gave her a gentle pull forward.

"There, I don't know whether you're goin' to take to each other or not; no, nobody can't tell whether you'll suit each other, but I expect you'll get along some way, both having seen the world," said our affectionate hostess. "You can inform Mis' Fosdick how we found the folks out to Green Island the other day. She's always been well acquainted with mother. I'll slip out now an' put away the supper things an' set my bread to rise, if you'll both excuse me. You can come out an' keep me company when you get ready, either or both." And Mrs. Todd, large and amiable, disappeared and left us.

Being furnished not only with a subject of conversation, but with a safe refuge in the kitchen in case of incompatibil-

ity, Mrs. Fosdick and I sat down, prepared to make the best
of each other. I soon discovered that she, like many of the
elder women of that coast, had spent a part of her life at sea,
and was full of a good traveler's curiosity and enlightenment.
By the time we thought it discreet to join our hostess we were
already sincere friends.

You may speak of a visit's setting in as well as a tide's, and
it was impossible, as Mrs. Todd whispered to me, not to be
pleased at the way this visit was setting in; a new impulse and
refreshing of the social currents and seldom visited bays of
memory appeared to have begun. Mrs. Fosdick had been the
mother of a large family of sons and daughters—sailors and
sailors' wives—and most of them had died before her. I soon
grew more or less acquainted with the histories of all their
fortunes and misfortunes, and subjects of an intimate nature
were no more withheld from my ears than if I had been a
shell on the mantelpiece. Mrs. Fosdick was not without a
touch of dignity and elegance; she was fashionable in her
dress, but it was a curiously well-preserved provincial fashion
of some years back. In a wider sphere one might have called
her a woman of the world, with her unexpected bits of modern knowledge, but Mrs. Todd's wisdom was an intimation of
truth itself. She might belong to any age, like an idyl of The-
ocritus; but while she always understood Mrs. Fosdick, that
entertaining pilgrim could not always understand Mrs. Todd.

That very first evening my friends plunged into a border-
less sea of reminiscences and personal news. Mrs. Fosdick
had been staying with a family who owned the farm where
she was born, and she had visited every sunny knoll and
shady field corner; but when she said that it might be for the
last time, I detected in her tone something expectant of the
contradiction which Mrs. Todd promptly offered.

"Almiry," said Mrs. Fosdick, with sadness, "you may say
what you like, but I am one of nine brothers and sisters,
brought up on the old place, and we're all dead but me."

"Your sister Dailey ain't gone, is she? Why, no, Louisa ain't
gone!" exclaimed Mrs. Todd, with surprise. "Why, I never
heard of that occurrence!"

"Yes 'm; she passed away last October, in Lynn. She had
made her distant home in Vermont State, but she was making
a visit to her youngest daughter. Louisa was the only one of
my family whose funeral I wasn't able to attend, but 't was a
mere accident. All the rest of us were settled right about

home. I thought it was very slack of 'em in Lynn not to fetch her to the old place; but when I came to hear about it, I learned that they 'd recently put up a very elegant monument, and my sister Dailey was always great for show. She'd just been out to see the monument the week before she was taken down, and admired it so much that they felt sure of her wishes."

"So she's really gone, and the funeral was up to Lynn!" repeated Mrs. Todd, as if to impress the sad fact upon her mind. "She was some years younger than we be, too. I recollect the first day she ever came to school; 't was that first year mother sent me inshore to stay with aunt Topham's folks and get my schooling. You fetched little Louisa to school one Monday mornin' in a pink dress an' her long curls, and she set between you an' me, and got cryin' after a while, so the teacher sent us home with her at recess."

"She was scared of seeing so many children about her; there was only her and me and brother John at home then; the older boys were to sea with father, an' the rest of us wa'n't born," explained Mrs. Fosdick. "That next fall we all went to sea together. Mother was uncertain till the last minute, as one may say. The ship was waiting orders, but the baby that then was, was born just in time, and there was a long spell of extra bad weather, so mother got about again before they had to sail, an' we all went. I remember my clothes were all left ashore in the east chamber in a basket where mother'd took them out o' my chist o' drawers an' left 'em ready to carry aboard. She didn't have nothing aboard, of her own, that she wanted to cut up for me, so when my dress wore out she just put me into a spare suit o' John's, jacket and trousers. I wasn't but eight years old an' he was most seven and large of his age. Quick as we made a port she went right ashore an' fitted me out pretty, but we was bound for the East Indies and didn't put in anywhere for a good while. So I had quite a spell o' freedom. Mother made my new skirt long because I was growing, and I poked about the deck after that, real discouraged, feeling the hem at my heels every minute, and as if youth was past and gone. I liked the trousers best; I used to climb the riggin' with 'em and frighten mother till she said an' vowed she'd never take me to sea again.

I thought by the polite absent-minded smile on Mrs. Todd's face this was no new story.

"Little Louisa was a beautiful child; yes, I always thought

Louisa was very pretty," Mrs. Todd said. "She was a dear little girl in those days. She favored your mother; the rest of you took after your father's folks."

"We did certain," agreed Mrs. Fosdick, rocking steadily. "There, it does seem so pleasant to talk with an old acquaintance that knows what you know. I see so many of these new folks nowadays, that seem to have neither past nor future. Conversation's got to have some root in the past, or else you've got to explain every remark you make, an' it wears a person out."

Mrs. Todd gave a funny little laugh. "Yes'm, old friends is always best, 'less you can catch a new one that's fit to make an old one out of," she said, and we gave an affectionate glance at each other which Mrs. Fosdick could not have understood, being the latest comer to the house.

XIII.

POOR JOANNA

One evening my ears caught a mysterious allusion which Mrs. Todd made to Shell-heap Island. It was a chilly night of cold northeasterly rain, and I made a fire for the first time in the Franklin stove in my room, and begged my two house-mates to come in and keep me company. The weather had convinced Mrs. Todd that it was time to make a supply of cough-drops, and she had been bringing forth herbs from dark and dry hiding places, until now the pungent dust and odor of them had resolved themselves into one mighty flavor of spearmint that came from a simmering caldron of syrup in the kitchen. She called it done, and well done, and had osten-tatiously left it to cool, and taken her knitting-work because Mrs. Fosdick was busy with hers. They sat in the two rock-ing-chairs, the small woman and the large one, but now and then I could see that Mrs. Todd's thoughts remained with the cough-drops. The time of gathering herbs was nearly over, but the time of syrups and cordials had begun.

The heat of the open fire made us a little drowsy, but something in the way Mrs. Todd spoke of Shell-heap Island waked my interest. I waited to see if she would say any more, and then took a roundabout way back to the subject by say-ing what was first in my mind: that I wished the Green Is-land family were there to spend the evening with us—Mrs. Todd's mother and her brother William.

Mrs. Todd smiled, and drummed on the arm of the rock-ing-chair. "Might scare William to death," she warned me; and Mrs. Fosdick mentioned her intention of going out to Green Island to stay two or three days, if this wind didn't make too much sea.

"Where is Shell-heap Island?" I ventured to ask, seizing the opportunity.

"Bears nor'east somewheres about three miles from Green Island; right off-shore, I should call it about eight miles out," said Mrs. Todd. "You never was there, dear; 't is off the thoroughfares, and a very bad place to land at best."

"I should think 't was," agreed Mrs. Fosdick, smoothing down her black silk apron. " 'T is a place worth visitin' when you once get there. Some o' the old folks was kind o' fearful about it. 'T was 'counted a great place in Old Indian times; you can pick up their stone tools 'most any time if you hunt about. There's a beautiful spring o' water, too. Yes, I remember when they used to tell queer stories about Shell-heap Island. Some said 't was a great bangeing-place for the Indians, and an old chief resided there once that ruled the winds; and others said they'd always heard that once the Indians come down from up country an' left a captive there without any bo't, an' 't was too far to swim across to Black Island, so called, an' he lived there till he perished."

"I've heard say he walked the island after that, and sharp-sighted folks could see him an' lose him like one o' them citizens Cap'n Littlepage was acquainted with up to the north pole," announced Mrs. Todd grimly. "Anyway, there was Indians—you can see their shell-heap that named the island; and I've heard myself that 't was one o' their cannibal places, but I never could believe it. There never was no cannibals on the coast o' Maine. All the Indians o' these regions are tame-looking folks."

"Sakes alive, yes!" exclaimed Mrs. Fosdick. "Ought to see them painted savages I've seen when I was young out in the South Sea Islands! That was the time for folks to travel, 'way back in the old whalin' days!"

"Whalin' must have been dull for a lady, hardly ever makin' a lively port, and not takin' in any mixed cargoes," said Mrs. Todd. "I never desired to go a whalin' v'y'ge myself."

"I used to return feelin' very slack an' behind the times, 't is true," explained Mrs. Fosdick, "but 't was excitin', an' we always done extra well, and felt rich when we did get ashore. I liked the variety. There, how times have changed; how few seafarin' families there are left! What a lot o' queer folks there used to be about here, anyway, when we was young, Almiry. Everybody's just like everybody else, now; nobody to laugh about, and nobody to cry about."

It seemed to me that there were peculiarities of character in the region of Dunnet Landing yet, but I did not like to interrupt.

"Yes," said Mrs. Todd after a moment of meditation,

"there was certain a good many curiosities of human natur' in this neighborhood years ago. There was more energy then, and in some the energy took a singular turn. In these days the young folks is all copy-cats, 'fraid to death they won't be all just alike; as for the old folks, they pray for the advantage o' bein' a little different."

"I ain't heard of a copy-cat this great many years," said Mrs. Fosdick, laughing; " 't was a favorite term o' my grandmother's. No, I wa'n't thinking o' those things, but of them strange straying creatur's that used to rove the country. You don't see them now, or the ones that used to hive away in their own houses with some strange notion or other."

I thought again of Captain Littlepage, but my companions were not reminded of his name; and there was brother William at Green Island, whom we all three knew.

"I was talking o' poor Joanna the other day. I hadn't thought of her for a great while," said Mrs. Fosdick abruptly. "Mis' Brayton an' I recalled her as we sat together sewing. She was one o' your peculiar persons, wa'n't she? Speaking of such persons," she turned to explain to me, "there was a sort of a nun or hermit person lived out there for years all alone on Shell-heap Island. Miss Joanna Todd, her name was—a cousin o' Almiry's late husband."

I expressed my interest, but as I glanced at Mrs. Todd I saw that she was confused by sudden affectionate feeling and unmistakable desire for reticence.

"I never want to hear Joanna laughed about," she said anxiously.

"Nor I," answered Mrs. Fosdick reassuringly. "She was crossed in love—that was all the matter to begin with; but as I look back, I can see that Joanna was one doomed from the first to fall into a melancholy. She retired from the world for good an' all, though she was a well-off woman. All she wanted was to get away from folks; she thought she wasn't fit to live with anybody, and wanted to be free. Shell-heap Island come to her from her father, and first thing folks knew she'd gone off out there to live, and left word she didn't want no company. 'T was a bad place to get to, unless the wind an' tide were just right; 't was hard work to make a landing."

"What time of year was this?" I asked.

"Very late in the summer," said Mrs. Fosdick. "No, I never could laugh at Joanna, as some did. She set everything by the young man, an' they were going to marry in about a month, when he got bewitched with a girl 'way up the bay,

and married her, and went off to Massachusetts. He wasn't
well thought of—there were those who thought Joanna's
money was what had tempted him; but she'd given him her
whole heart, an' she wa'n't so young as she had been. All her
hopes were built on marryin', an' havin' a real home and
somebody to look to; she acted just like a bird when its nest
is spoilt. The day after she heard the news she was in dreadful woe, but the next she came to herself very quiet, and took
the horse and wagon, and drove fourteen miles to the lawyer's, and signed a paper givin' her half of the farm to her
brother. They never had got along very well together, but he
didn't want to sign it, till she acted so distressed that he gave
in. Edward Todd's wife was a good woman, who felt very
bad indeed, and used every argument with Joanna; but
Joanna took a poor old boat that had been her father's and
lo'ded in a few things, and off she put all alone, with a good
land breeze, right out to sea. Edward Todd ran down to the
beach, an' stood there cryin' like a boy to see her go, but she
was out o' hearin'. She never stepped foot on the mainland
again long as she lived."

"How large an island is it? How did she manage in winter?" I asked.

"Perhaps thirty acres, rocks and all," answered Mrs. Todd,
taking up the story gravely. "There can't be much of it that
the salt spray don't fly over in storms. No, 't is a dreadful
small place to make a world of; it has a different look from
any of the other islands, but there's a sheltered cove on the
south side, with mud-flats across one end of it at low water
where there's excellent clams, and the big shell-heap keeps
some o' the wind off a little house her father took the trouble
to build when he was a young man. They said there was an
old house built o' logs there before that, with a kind of
natural cellar in the rock under it. He used to stay out there
days to a time, and anchor a little sloop he had, and dig
clams to fill it, and sail up to Portland. They said the dealers
always gave him an extra price, the clams were so noted.
Joanna used to go out and stay with him. They were always
great companions, so she knew just what 't was out there.
There was a few sheep that belonged to her brother an' her,
but she bargained for him to come and get them on the edge
o' cold weather. Yes, she desired him to come for the sheep;
an' his wife thought perhaps Joanna'd return, but he said no,
an' lo'ded the bo't with warm things an' what he thought sh'd
need through the winter. He come home with the sheep an'

left the other things by the house, but she never so much as looked out o' the window. She done it for a penance. She must have wanted to see Edward by that time."

Mrs. Fosdick was fidgeting with eagerness to speak.

"Some thought the first cold snap would set her ashore, but she always remained," concluded Mrs. Todd soberly.

"Talk about the men not having any curiosity!" exclaimed Mrs. Fosdick scornfully. "Why, the waters round Shell-heap Island were white with sails all that fall. 'T was never called no great of a fishin'-ground before. Many of 'em made excuse to go ashore to get water at the spring; but at last she spoke to a bo't-load, very dignified and calm, and said that she'd like it better if they'd make a practice of getting water to Black Island or somewheres else and leave her alone, except in case of accident or trouble. But there was one man who had always set everything by her from a boy. He'd have married her if the other hadn't come about an' spoilt his chance, and he used to get close to the island, before light, on his way out fishin', and throw a little bundle 'way up the green slope front o' the house. His sister told me she happened to see, the first time, what a pretty choice he made o' useful things that a woman would feel lost without. He stood off fishin', and could see them in the grass all day, though sometimes she'd come out and walk right by them. There was other bo'ts near, out after mackerel. But early next morning his present was gone. He didn't presume too much, but once he took her a nice firkin o' things he got up to Portland, and when spring come he landed her a hen and chickens in a nice little coop. There was a good many old friends had Joanna on their minds."

"Yes," said Mrs. Todd, losing her sad reserve in the growing sympathy of these reminiscences. "How everybody used to notice whether there was smoke out of the chimney! The Black Island folks could see her with their spy-glass, and if they'd ever missed getting some sign o' life they'd have sent notice to her folks. But after the first year or two Joanna was more and more forgotten as an every-day charge. Folks lived very simple in those days, you know," she continued, as Mrs. Fosdick's knitting was taking much thought at the moment. "I expect there was always plenty of driftwood thrown up, and a poor failin' patch of spruces covered all the north side of the island, so she always had something to burn. She was very fond of workin' in the garden ashore, and that first summer she began to till the little field out there, and raised a

nice parcel o' potatoes. She could fish, o' course, and there
was all her clams an' lobsters. You can always live well in
any wild place by the sea when you'd starve to death up
country, except 't was berry time. Joanna had berries out
there, blackberries at least, and there was a few herbs in case
she needed them. Mullein in great quantities and a plant o'
wormwood I remember seeing once when I stayed there, long
before she fled out to Shell-heap. Yes, I recall the wormwood,
which is always a planted herb, so there must have been folks
there before the Todds' day. A growin' bush makes the best
gravestone; I expect that wormwood always stood for somebody's solemn monument. Catnip, too, is a very endurin' herb
about an old place."

"But what I want to know is what she did for other
things," interrupted Mrs. Fosdick. "Almiry, what did she do
for clothin' when she needed to replenish, or risin' for her
bread, or the piece-bag that no woman can live long without?"

"Or company," suggested Mrs. Todd. "Joanna was one that
loved her friends. There must have been a terrible sight o'
long winter evenin's that first year."

"There was her hens," suggested Mrs. Fosdick, after re-
viewing the melancholy situation. "She never wanted the
sheep after that first season. There wa'n't no proper pasture
for sheep after the June grass was past, and she ascertained
the fact and couldn't bear to see them suffer; but the chickens
done well. I remember sailin' by one spring afternoon, an'
seein' the coops out front o' the house in the sun. How long
was it before you went out with the minister? You were the
first ones that ever really got ashore to see Joanna."

I had been reflecting upon a state of society which admitted such personal freedom and a voluntary hermitage. There
was something mediæval in the behavior of poor Joanna
Todd under a disappointment of the heart. The two women
had drawn closer together, and were talking on, quite unconscious of a listener.

"Poor Joanna!" said Mrs. Todd again, and sadly shook her
head as if there were things one could not speak about.

"I called her a great fool," declared Mrs. Fosdick, with
spirit, "but I pitied her then, and I pity her far more now.
Some other minister would have been a great help to her—
one that preached self-forgetfulness and doin' for others to
cure our own ills; but Parson Dimmick was a vague person,
well meanin', but very numb in his feelin's. I don't suppose at

that troubled time Joanna could think of any way to mend her troubles except to run off and hide."

"Mother used to say she didn't see how Joanna lived without having nobody to do for, getting her own meals and tending her own poor self day in an' day out," said Mrs. Todd sorrowfully.

"There was the hens," repeated Mrs. Fosdick kindly. "I expect she soon came to makin' folks o' them. No, I never went to work to blame Joanna, as some did. She was full o' feeling, and her troubles hurt her more than she could bear. I see it all now as I couldn't when I was young."

"I suppose in old times they had their shut-up convents for just such folks," said Mrs. Todd, as if she and her friend had disagreed about Joanna once, and were now in happy harmony. She semed to speak with new openness and freedom. "Oh yes, I was only too pleased when the Reverend Mr. Dimmick invited me to go out with him. He hadn't been very long in the place when Joanna left home and friends 'T was one day that next summer after she went, and I had been married early in the spring. He felt that he ought to go out and visit her. She was a member of the church, and might wish to have him consider her spiritual state. I wa'n't so sure o' that, but I always liked Joanna, and I'd come to be her cousin by marriage. Nathan an' I had conversed about goin' out to pay her a visit, but he got his chance to sail sooner'n he expected. He always thought everything of her, and last time he come home, knowing nothing of her change. he brought her a beautiful coral pin from a port he'd touched at somewheres up the Mediterranean. So I wrapped the little box in a nice piece of paper and put it in my pocket, and picked her a bunch of fresh lemon balm, and off we started."

Mrs. Fosdick laughed. "I remember hearin' about your trials on the v'y'ge," she said.

"Why, yes," continued Mrs. Todd in her company manner. "I picked her the balm, an' we started. Why, yes, Susan the minister liked to have cost me my life that day. He would fasten the sheet, though I advised against it. He said the rope was rough an' cut his hand. There was a fresh breeze, an' he went on talking rather high flown, an' I felt some interested. All of a sudden there come up a gust, and he give a screech and stood right up and called for help, 'way out there to sea. I knocked him right over into the bottom o' the bo't, getting by to catch hold of the sheet an' untie it. He wasn't but a little man; I helped him right up after the squall passed, and made a handsome apology to him, but he did act kind o' offended."

"I do think they ought not to settle them landlocked folks in parishes where they're liable to be on the water," insisted Mrs. Fosdick. "Think of the families in our parish that was scattered all about the bay, and what a sight o' sails you used to see, in Mr. Dimmick's day, standing across to the mainland on a pleasant Sunday morning, filled with church-going folks, all sure to want him some time or other! You couldn't find no doctor that would stand up in the boat and screech if a flaw struck her."

"Old Dr. Bennett had a beautiful sailboat, didn't he?" responded Mrs. Todd. "And how well he used to brave the weather! Mother always said that in time o' trouble that tall white sail used to look like an angel's wing comin' over the sea to them that was in pain. Well, there's a difference in gifts. Mr. Dimmick was not without light."

" 'T was light o' the moon, then," snapped Mrs. Fosdick; "he was pompous enough, but I never could remember a single word he said. There, go on, Mis' Todd; I forget a great deal about that day you went to see poor Joanna."

"I felt she saw us coming, and knew us a great way off; yes, I seemed to feel it within me," said our friend, laying down her knitting. "I kept my seat, and took the bo't inshore without saying a word; there was a short channel that I was sure Mr. Dimmick wasn't acquainted with, and the tide was very low. She never came out to warn us off nor anything, and I thought, as I hauled the bo't up on a wave and let the Reverend Mr. Dimmick step out, that it was somethin' gained to be safe ashore. There was a little smoke out o' the chimney o' Joanna's house, and it did look sort of homelike and pleasant with wild mornin'-glory vines trained up; an' there was a plot o' flowers under the front window, portulacas and things. I believe she'd made a garden once, when she was stopping there with her father, and some things must have seeded in. It looked as if she might have gone over to the other side of the island. 'T was neat and pretty all about the house, and a lovely day in July. We walked up from the beach together very sedate, and I felt for poor Nathan's little pin to see if 't was safe in my dress pocket. All of a sudden Joanna come right to the fore door and stood there, not sayin' a word.

XIV.

THE HERMITAGE

❧

My companions and I had been so intent upon the subject of the conversation that we had not heard anyone open the gate, but at this moment, above the noise of the rain, we heard a loud knocking. We were all startled as we sat by the fire, and Mrs. Todd rose hastily and went to answer the call, leaving her rocking-chair in violent motion. Mrs. Fosdick and I heard an anxious voice at the door speaking of a sick child, and Mrs. Todd's kind, motherly voice inviting the messenger in: then we waited in silence. There was a sound of heavy dropping of rain from the eaves, and the distant roar and undertone of the sea. My thoughts flew back to the lonely woman on her outer island; what separation from humankind she must have felt, what terror and sadness, even in a summer storm like this!

"You send right after the doctor if she ain't better in half an hour," said Mrs. Todd to her worried customer as they parted; and I felt a warm sense of comfort in the evident resources of even so small a neighborhood, but for the poor hermit Joanna there was no neighbor on a winter night.

"How did she look?" demanded Mrs. Fosdick, without preface, as our large hostess returned to the little room with a mist about her from standing long in the wet doorway, and the sudden draught of her coming beat out the smoke and flame from the Franklin stove. "How did poor Joanna look?"

"She was the same as ever, except I thought she looked smaller," answered Mrs. Todd after thinking a moment; perhaps it was only a last considering thought about her patient. "Yes, she was just the same, and looked very nice, Joanna did. I had been married since she left home, an' she treated me like her own folks. I expected she'd look strange, with her hair turned gray in a night or somethin', but she wore a pretty gingham dress I'd often seen her wear before she went away; she must have kept it nice for best in the afternoons.

She always had beautiful, quiet manners. I remember she
waited till we were close to her, and then kissed me real affectionate, and inquired for Nathan before she shook hands
with the minister, and then she invited us both in. 'T was the
same little house her father had built him when he was a
bachelor, with one livin'-room, and a little mite of a bedroom
out of it where she slept, but 't was neat as a ship's cabin.
There was some old chairs, an' a seat made of a long box
that might have held boat tackle an' things to lock up in his
fishin' days, and a good enough stove so anybody could cook
and keep warm in cold weather. I went over once from home
and stayed 'most a week with Joanna when we was girls, and
those young happy days rose up before me. Her father was
busy all day fishin' or clammin'; he was one o' the pleasantest
men in the world, but Joanna's mother had the grim streak,
and never knew what 't was to be happy. The first minute my
eyes fell upon Joanna's face that day I saw how she had
grown to look like Mis' Todd. 'T was the mother right over
again."

"Oh dear me!" said Mrs. Fosdick.

"Joanna had done one thing very pretty. There was a little
piece o' swamp on the island where good rushes grew plenty,
and she'd gathered 'em, and braided some beautiful mats for
the floor and a thick cushion for the long bunk. She'd showed
a good deal of invention; you see there was a nice chance to
pick up pieces o' wood and boards that drove ashore, and
she'd made good use o' what she found. There wasn't no
clock, but she had a few dishes on a shelf, and flowers set
about in shells fixed to the walls, so it did look sort of home-
like, though so lonely and poor. I couldn't keep the tears out
o' my eyes, I felt so sad. I said to myself, I must get mother
to come over an' see Joanna; the love in mother's heart
would warm her, an' she might be able to advise."

"Oh no, Joanna was dreadful stern," said Mrs. Fosdick.

"We were all settin' down very proper, but Joanna would
keep stealin' glances at me as if she was glad I come. She had
but little to say; she was real polite an' gentle, and yet forbid-
din'. The minister found it hard," confessed Mrs. Todd; "he
got embarrassed, an' when he put on his authority and asked
her if she felt to enjoy religion in her present situation, an'
she replied that she must be excused from answerin', I
thought I should fly. She might have made it easier for him;
after all, he was the minister and had taken some trouble to
come out, though 't was kind of cold an' unfeelin' the way he

inquired. I thought he might have seen the little old Bible a-
layin' on the shelf close by him, an' I wished he knew enough
to just lay his hand on it an' read somethin' kind an' fatherly
'stead of accusin' her, an' then given poor Joanna his blessin'
with the hope she might be led to comfort. He did offer
prayer, but 't was all about hearin' the voice o' God out o' the
whirlwind; and I thought while he was goin' on that anybody
that had spent the long cold winter all alone out on Shell-
heap Island knew a good deal more about those things than
he did. I got so provoked I opened my eyes and stared right
at him.

"She didn't take no notice, she kep' a nice respectful manner towards him, and when there come a pause she asked if
he had any interest about the old Indian remains, and took
down some queer stone gouges and hammers off of one of
her shelves and showed them to him same's if he was a boy.
He remarked that he'd like to walk over an' see the shell-
heap; so she went right to the door and pointed him the way.
I see then that she'd made her some kind o' sandal-shoes out
o' the fine rushes to wear on her feet; she stepped light an'
nice in 'em as shoes."

Mrs. Fosdick leaned back in her rocking-chair and gave a
heavy sigh.

"I didn't move at first, but I'd held out just as long as I
could," said Mrs. Todd, whose voice trembled a little. "When
Joanna returned from the door, an' I could see that man's
stupid back departin' among the wild rose bushes, I just ran
to her an' caught her in my arms. I wasn't so big as I be
now, and she was older than me, but I hugged her tight, just
as if she was a child. 'Oh, Joanna dear,' I says, 'won't you
come ashore an' live 'long o' me at the Landin', or go over to
Green Island to mother's when winter comes? Nobody shall
trouble you, an' mother finds it hard bein' alone. I can't bear
to leave you here'—and I burst right out crying. I'd had my
own trials, young as I was, an' she knew it. Oh, I did entreat
her; yes, I entreated Joanna."

"What did she say then?" asked Mrs. Fosdick, much
moved.

"She looked the same way, sad an' remote through it all,"
said Mrs. Todd mournfully. "She took hold of my hand, and
we sat down close together; 't was as if she turned round an'
made a child of me. 'I haven't got no right to live with folks
no more,' she said. 'You must never ask me again, Almiry:
I've done the only thing I could do, and I've made my

choice. I feel a great comfort in your kindness, but I don't deserve it. I have committed the unpardonable sin; you don't understand,' says she humbly. 'I was in great wrath and trouble, and my thoughts was so wicked towards God that I can't expect ever to be forgiven. I have come to know what it is to have patience, but I have lost my hope. You must tell those that ask how 't is with me,' she said, 'an' tell them I want to be alone.' I couldn't speak; no, there wa'n't anything I could say, she seemed so above everything common. I was a good deal younger then than I be now, and I got Nathan's little coral pin out o' my pocket and put it into her hand; and when she saw it and I told her where it come from, her face did really light up for a minute, sort of bright an' pleasant. 'Nathan an' I was always good friends; I'm glad he don't think hard of me,' says she. 'I want you to have it, Almiry, an' wear it for love o' both o' us,' and she handed it back to me. 'You give my love to Nathan—he's a dear good man,' she said; 'an' tell your mother, if I should be sick she mustn't wish I could get well, but I want her to be the one to come.' Then she seemed to have said all she wanted to, as if she was done with the world, and we sat there a few minutes longer together. It was real sweet and quiet except for a good many birds and the sea rollin' up on the beach; but at last she rose, an' I did too, and she kissed me and held my hand in hers a minute, as if to say good-by; then she turned and went right away out o' the door and disappeared.

"The minister come back pretty soon, and I told him I was all ready, and we started down to the bo't. He had picked up some round stones and things and was carrying them in his pocket-handkerchief; an' he sat down amidships without making any question, and let me take the rudder an' work the bo't, an' made no remarks for some time, until we sort of eased it off speaking of the weather, an' subjects that arose as we skirted Black Island, where two or three families lived belongin' to the parish. He preached next Sabbath as usual, somethin' high soundin' about the creation, and I couldn't help thinkin' he might never get no further; he seemed to know no remedies, but he had a great use of words."

Mrs. Fosdick sighed again. "Hearin' you tell about Joanna brings the time right back as if 't was yesterday," said she. "Yes, she was one o' them poor things that talked about the great sin; we don't seem to hear nothing about the unpardonable sin now, but you may say 't was not uncommon then."

"I expect that if it had been in these days, such a person would be plagued to death with idle folks," continued Mrs. Todd, after a long pause. "As it was, nobody trespassed on her; all the folks about the bay respected her an' her feelings; but as time wore on, after you left here, one after another ventured to make occasion to put somethin' ashore for her if they went that way. I know mother used to go to see her sometimes, and send William over now and then with something fresh an' nice from the farm. There is a point on the sheltered side where you can lay a boat close to shore an' land anything safe on the turf out o' reach o' the water. There were one or two others, old folks, that she would see, and now an' then she'd hail a passin' boat an' ask for somethin'; and mother got her to promise that she would make some sign to the Black Island folks if she wanted help. I never saw her myself to speak to after that day."

"I expect nowadays, if such a thing happened, she'd have gone out West to her uncle's folks or up to Massachusetts and had a change, an' come home good as new. The world's bigger an' freer than it used to be," urged Mrs. Fosdick.

"No," said her friend. " 'T is like bad eyesight, the mind of such a person: if your eyes don't see right there may be a remedy, but there's no kind of glasses to remedy the mind. No, Joanna was Joanna, and there she lays on her island where she lived and did her poor penance. She told mother the day she was dyin' that she always used to want to be fetched inshore when it come to the last; but she'd thought it over, and desired to be laid on the island, if 't was thought right. So the funeral was out there, a Saturday afternoon in September. 'T was a pretty day, and there wa'n't hardly a boat on the coast within twenty miles that didn't head for Shell-heap cram-full o' folks, an' all real respectful, same's if she'd always stayed ashore and held her friends. Some went out o' mere curiosity, I don't doubt—there's always such to every funeral; but most had real feelin', and went purpose to show it. She'd got most o' the wild sparrows as tame as could be, livin' out there so long among 'em, and one flew right in and lit on the coffin an' begun to sing while Mr. Dimmick was speakin'. He was put out by it, an' acted as if he didn't know whether to stop or go on. I may have been prejudiced, but I wa'n't the only one thought the poor little bird done the best of the two."

"What became o' the man that treated her so, did you ever hear?" asked Mrs. Fosdick. "I know he lived up to Massachusetts for a while. Somebody who came from the same place told me that he was in trade there an' doin very well, but that was years ago."

"I never heard anything more than that; he went to the war in one o' the early rigiments. No, I never heard any more of him," answered Mrs. Todd. "Joanna was another sort of person, and perhaps he showed good judgment in marryin' somebody else, if only he'd behaved straightforward and manly. He was a shifty-eyed, coaxin' sort of man, that got what he wanted out o' folks, an' only gave when he wanted to buy, made friends easy and lost 'em without knowin' the difference. She'd had a piece o' work tryin' to make him walk accordin' to her right ideas, but she'd have had too much variety ever to fall into a melancholy. Some is meant to be the Joannas in this world, an' 't was her poor lot."

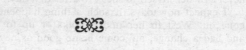

XV.

ON SHELL-HEAP ISLAND

Some time after Mrs. Fosdick's visit was over and we had returned to our former quietness, I was out sailing alone with Captain Bowden in his large boat. We were taking the crooked northeasterly channel seaward, and were well out from shore while it was still early in the afternoon. I found myself presently among some unfamiliar islands, and suddenly remembered the story of poor Joanna. There is something in the fact of a hermitage that cannot fail to touch the imagination; the recluses are sad kindred, but they are never commonplace. Mrs. Todd had truly said that Joanna was like one of the saints in the desert; the loneliness of sorrow will forever keep alive their sad succession.

"Where is Shell-heap Island!" I asked eagerly.

"You see Shell-heap now, layin' 'way out beyond Black Island there," answered the captain, pointing with outstretched arm as he stood, and holding the rudder with his knee.

"I should like very much to go there," said I, and the captain, without comment, changed his course a little more to the eastward and let the reef out of his mainsail.

"I don't know's we can make an easy landin' for ye," he remarked doubtfully. "May get your feet wet; bad place to land. Trouble is I ought to have brought a tag-boat; but they clutch on to the water so, an' I do love to sail free. This gre't boat gets easy bothered with anything trailin'. 'T ain't breakin' much on the meetin'-house ledges; guess I can fetch in to Shell-heap."

"How long is it since Miss Joanna Todd died?" I asked, partly by way of explanation.

"Twenty-two years come September," answered the captain, after reflection. "She died the same year my oldest boy was born, an' the town house was burnt over to the Port. I didn't know but you merely wanted to hunt for some o' them Indian relics. Long's you want to see where Joanna lived— No, 't ain't breakin' over the ledges; we'll manage to fetch across the shoals somehow, 't is such a distance to go 'way round, and tide's a-risin'," he ended hopefully, and we sailed steadily on, the captain speechless with intent watching of a difficult course, until the small island with its low whitish promontory lay in full view before us under the bright afternoon sun.

The month was August, and I had seen the color of the islands change from the fresh green of June to a sunburnt brown that made them look like stone, except where the dark green of the spruces and fir balsam kept the tint that even winter storms might deepen, but not fade. The few wind-bent trees on Shell-heap Island were mostly dead and gray, but there were some low-growing bushes, and a stripe of light green ran along just above the shore, which I knew to be wild morning-glories. As we came close I could see the high stone walls of a small square field, though there were no sheep left to assail it; and below, there was a little harbor-like cove where Captain Bowden was boldly running the great boat in to seek a landing-place. There was a crooked channel of deep water which led close up against the shore.

"There, you hold fast for'ard there, an' wait for her to lift on the wave. You'll make a good landin' if you're smart; right on the port-hand side!" the captain called excitedly; and I, standing ready with high ambition, seized my chance and leaped over to the grassy bank.

"I'm beat if I ain't aground after all!" mourned the captain despondently.

But I could reach the bowsprit, and he pushed with the boat-hook, while the wind veered round a little as if on purpose and helped with the sail; so presently the boat was free and began to drift out from shore.

"Used to call this p'int Joanna's wharf privilege, but 't has worn away in the weather since her time. I thought one or two bumps wouldn't hurt us none—paint's got to be renewed, anyway—but I never thought she'd tetch. I figured on shyin' by," the captain apologized. "She's too gre't a boat to handle well in here; but I used to sort of shy by in Joanna's day, an' cast a little somethin' ashore—some apples or a couple o' pears if I had 'em—on the grass, where she'd be sure to see."

I stood watching while Captain Bowden cleverly found his way back to deeper water. "You needn't make no haste," he called to me; "I'll keep within call. Joanna lays right up there in the far corner o' the field. There used to be a path led to the place. I always knew her well. I was out here to the funeral."

I found the path; it was touching to discover that this lonely spot was not without pilgrims. Later generations will know less and less of Joanna herself, but there are paths trodden to the shrines of solitude the world over—the world cannot forget them, try as it may; the feet of the young find them out because of curiosity and dim foreboding, while the old bring hearts full of remembrance. This plain anchorite had been one of those whom sorrow made too lonely to brave the sight of men, too timid to front the simple world she knew, yet valiant enough to live alone with her poor insistent human nature and the calms and passions of the sea and sky.

The birds were flying all about the field; they fluttered up out of the grass at my feet as I walked along, so tame that I liked to think they kept some happy tradition from summer to summer of the safety of nests and good fellowship of mankind. Poor Joanna's house was gone except the stones of its foundations, and there was little trace of her flower garden except a single faded sprig of much-enduring French pinks, which a great bee and a yellow butterfly were befriending together. I drank at the spring, and thought that now and then some one would follow me from the busy, hard-worked, and simple-thoughted countryside of the mainland, which lay dim and dreamlike in the August haze, as Joanna must have watched it many a day. There was the world, and here was she with eternity well begun. In the life of each of us, I said to myself, there is a place remote and islanded, and given to endless regret or secret happiness; we are each the uncompanioned hermit and recluse of an hour or a day; we understand our fellows of the cell to whatever age of history they may belong.

But as I stood alone on the island, in the sea-breeze, suddenly there came a sound of distant voices; gay voices and laughter from a pleasure-boat that was going seaward full of boys and girls. I knew, as if she had told me, that poor Joanna must have heard the like on many and many a summer afternoon, and must have welcomed the good cheer in spite of hopelessness and winter weather, and all the sorrow and disappointment in the world.

XVI.
THE GREAT EXPEDITION

Mrs. Todd never by any chance gave warning over night of her great projects and adventures by sea and land. She first came to an understanding with the primal forces of nature, and never trusted to any preliminary promise of good weather, but examined the day for herself in its infancy. Then, if the stars were propitious, and the wind blew from a quarter of good inheritance whence no surprises of sea-turns or southwest sultriness might be feared, long before I was fairly awake I used to hear a rustle and knocking like a great mouse in the walls, and an impatient tread on the steep garret stairs that led to Mrs. Todd's chief place of storage. She went and came as if she had already started on her expedition with utmost haste and kept returning for something that was forgotten. When I appeared in quest of my breakfast, she would be absent-minded and sparing of speech, as if I had displeased her, and she was now, by main force of principle, holding herself back from altercation and strife of tongues.

These signs of a change became familiar to me in the course of time, and Mrs. Todd hardly noticed some plain proofs of divination one August morning when I said, without preface, that I had just seen the Beggs' best chaise go by, and that we should have to take the grocery. Mrs. Todd was alert in a moment.

"There! I might have known!" she exclaimed. "It's the fifteenth of August, when he goes and gets his money. He heired an annuity from an uncle o' his on his mother's side. I understood the uncle said none o' Sam Begg's wife's folks should make free with it, so after Sam's gone it'll all be past an' spent, like last summer. That's what Sam prospers on now, if you can call it prosperin'. Yes, I might have known. 'T is the fifteenth o' August with him, an' he gener'ly stops to dinner with a cousin's widow on the way home. Feb'uary an' August is the times. Takes him 'bout all day to go an' come."

I heard this explanation with interest. The tone of Mrs. Todd's voice was complaining at the last.

"I like the grocery just as well as the chaise," I hastened to say, referring to a long-bodied high wagon with a canopy-top, like an attenuated four-posted bedstead on wheels, in which we sometimes journeyed. "We can put things in behind—roots and flowers and raspberries, or anything you are going after—much better than if we had the chaise."

Mrs. Todd looked stony and unwilling. "I counted upon the chaise," she said, turning her back to me, and roughly pushing back all the quiet tumblers on the cupboard shelf as if they had been impertinent. "Yes, I desired the chaise for once. I ain't goin' berryin' nor to fetch home no more wilted vegetation this year. Season's about past, except for a poor few o' late things," she added in a milder tone. "I'm goin' up country. No, I ain't intendin' to go berryin'. I've been plottin' for it for it the past fortnight and hopin' for a good day."

"Would you like to have me go too?" I asked frankly, but not without a humble fear that I might have mistaken the purpose of this latest plan.

"Oh certain, dear!" answered my friend affectionately. "Oh no, I never thought o' anyone else for comp'ny, it it's convenient for you, long 's poor mother ain't come. I ain't nothin' like so handy with a conveyance as I be with a good bo't. Comes o' my early bringing-up. I expect we've got to make that great high wagon do. The tires want settin' and 't is all loose-jointed, so I can hear it shackle the other side o' the ridge. We'll put the basket in front. I ain't goin' to have it bouncin' an' twirlin' all the way. Why, I've been makin' some nice hearts and rounds to carry."

These were signs of high festivity, and my interest deepened moment by moment.

"I'll go down to the Beggs' and get the horse just as soon as I finish my breakfast," said I. "Then we can start whenever you are ready."

Mrs. Todd looked cloudy again. "I don't know but you look nice enough to go just as you be," she suggested doubtfully. "No, you wouldn't want to wear that pretty blue dress o' yourn 'way up country. 'T ain't dusty now, but it may be comin' home. No, I expect you'd rather not wear that and the other hat."

"Oh yes. I should n't think of wearing these clothes," said I, with sudden illumination. "Why, if we're going up country and are likely to see some of your friends, I'll put on my blue dress, and you must wear your watch; I am not going at all if you mean to wear the big hat."

"Now you're behavin' pretty," responded Mrs. Todd, with a gay toss of her head and a cheerful smile, as she came across the room, bringing a saucerful of wild raspberries, a pretty piece of salvage from supper-time. "I was cast down when I see you come to breakfast. I didn't think 't was just what you'd select to wear to the reunion, where you're goin' to meet everybody."

"What reunion do you mean?" I asked, not without amazement. "Not the Bowden Family's? I thought that was going to take place in September."

"To-day's the day. They sent word the middle o' the week. I thought you might have heard of it. Yes, they changed the day. I been thinkin' we'd talk it over, but you never can tell beforehand how it's goin' to be, and 't ain't worth while to wear a day all out before it comes." Mrs. Todd gave no place to the pleasures of anticipation, but she spoke like the oracle that she was. "I wish mother was here to go," she continued sadly. "I did look for her last night, and I couldn't keep back the tears when the dark really fell and she wa'n't here, she does so enjoy a great occasion. If William had a mite o' snap an' ambition, he'd take the lead at such a time. Mother likes variety, and there ain't but a few nice opportunities 'round here, an' them she has to miss 'less she contrives to get ashore to me. I do re'lly hate to go to the reunion without mother, an' 't is a beautiful day; everybody'll be asking where she is. Once she'd have got here anyway. Poor mother's beginnin' to feel her age."

"Why, there's your mother now!" I exclaimed with joy, I was so glad to see the dear old soul again. "I hear her voice at the gate." But Mrs. Todd was out of the door before me.

There, sure enough, stood Mrs. Blackett, who must have left Green Island before daylight. She had climbed the steep road from the water-side so eagerly that she was out of breath, and was standing by the garden fence to rest. She held an old-fashioned brown wicker cap-basket in her hand, as if visiting were a thing of every day, and looked up at us as pleased and triumphant as a child.

"Oh, what a poor, plain garden! Hardly a flower in it except your bush o' balm!" she said. "But you do keep your garden neat, Almiry. Are you both well, an' goin' up country with me?" She came a step or two closer to meet us, with quaint politeness and quite as delightful as if she were at home. She dropped a quick little curtsey before Mrs. Todd.

"There, mother, what a girl you be! I am so pleased! I was

just bewailin' you," said the daughter, with unwonted feeling. "I was just bewailin' you, I was so disappointed, an' I kep' myself awake a good piece o' the night scoldin' poor William. I watched for the boat till I was ready to shed tears yesterday, and when 't was comin' dark I kep' making errands out to the gate an' down the road to see if you wa'n't in the doldrums somewhere down the bay."

"There was a head wind, as you know," said Mrs. Blackett, giving me the cap-basket, and holding my hand affectionately as we walked up the clean-swept path to the door. "I was partly ready to come, but dear William said I should be all tired out and might get cold, havin' to beat all the way in. So we give it up, and set down and spent the evenin' together. It was a little rough and windy outside, and I guess 't was better judgment; we went to bed very early and made a good start just at daylight. It's been a lovely mornin' on the water. William thought he'd better fetch across beyond Bird Rocks, rowin' the greater part o' the way; then we sailed from there right over to the Landin', makin' only one tack. William'll be in again for me to-morrow, so I can come back here an' rest me over night, an' go to meetin' to-morrow, and a have a nice, good visit."

"She was just havin' her breakfast," said Mrs. Todd, who had listened eagerly to the long explanation without a word of disapproval, while her face shone more and more with joy. "You just sit right down an' have a cup of tea and rest you while we make our preparations. Oh, I am so gratified to think you've come! Yes, she was just havin' her breakfast, and we were speakin' of you. Where's William?"

"He went right back; he said he expected some schooners in about noon after bait, but he'll come an' have his dinner with us to-morrow, unless it rains; then next day. I laid his best things out all ready," explained Mrs. Blackett, a little anxiously. "This wind will serve him nice all the way home. Yes, I will take a cup of tea, dear—a cup of tea is always good; and then I'll rest a minute and be all ready to start."

"I do feel condemned for havin' such hard thoughts o' William," openly confessed Mrs. Todd. She stood before us so large and serious that we both laughed and could not find it in our hearts to convict so rueful a culprit. "He shall have a good dinner to-morrow, if it can be got, and I shall be real glad to see William," the confession ended handsomely, while Mrs. Blackett smiled approval and made haste to praise the tea. Then I hurried away to make sure of the grocery wagon.

Whatever might be the good of the reunion, I was going to
have the pleasure and delight of a day in Mrs. Blackett's
company, not to speak of Mrs. Todd's.

The early morning breeze was still blowing, and the warm,
sunshiny air was of some ethereal northern sort, with a cool
freshness as if it came over new-fallen snow. The world was
filled with a fragrance of fir-balsam and the faintest flavor of
seaweed from the ledges, bare and brown at low tide in the
little harbor. It was so still and so early that the village was
but half awake. I could hear no voices but those of the birds,
small and great—the constant song sparrows, the clink of a
yellow-hammer over in the woods, and the far conversation
of some deliberate crows. I saw William Blackett's escaping
sail already far from land, and Captain Littlepage was sitting
behind his closed window as I passed by, watching for some
one who never came. I tried to speak to him, but he did not
see me. There was a patient look on the old man's face, as if
the world were a great mistake and he had nobody with
whom to speak his own language or find companionship.

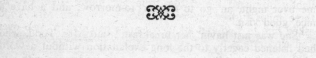

XVII.

A COUNTRY ROAD

Whatever doubts and anxieties I may have had about the inconvenience of the Begg's high wagon for a person of Mrs. Blackett's age and shortness, they were happily overcome by the aid of a chair and her own valiant spirit. Mrs. Todd bestowed great care upon seating us as if we were taking passage by boat, but she finally pronounced that we were properly trimmed. When we had gone only a little way up the hill she remembered that she had left the house door wide open, though the large key was safe in her pocket. I offered to run back, but my offer was met with lofty scorn, and we lightly dismissed the matter from our minds, until two or three miles further on we met the doctor, and Mrs. Todd asked him to stop and ask her nearest neighbor to step over and close the door if the dust seemed to blow in the afternoon.

"She'll be there in her kitchen; she'll hear you the minute you call; 't wont give you no delay," said Mrs. Todd to the doctor. "Yes, Mis' Dennett's right there, with the windows all open. It isn't as if my fore door opened right on the road, anyway." At which proof of composure Mrs. Blackett smiled wisely at me.

The doctor seemed delighted to see our guest; they were evidently the warmest friends, and I saw a look of affectionate confidence in their eyes. The good man left his carriage to speak to us, but as he took Mrs. Blackett's hand he held it a moment, and, as if merely from force of habit, felt her pulse as they talked; then to my delight he gave the firm old wrist a commending pat.

"You're wearing well: good for another ten years at this rate," he assured her cheerfully, and smiled back. "I like to keep a strict account of my old stand-bys," and he turned to me. "Don't you let Mrs. Todd overdo to-day—old folks like her are apt to be thoughtless;" and then we all laughed, and, parting, went our ways gayly.

"I suppose he puts up with your rivalry the same as ever?" asked Mrs. Blackett. "You and he are as friendly as ever, I see, Almiry," and Almira sagely nodded.

"He's got too many long routes now to stop to 'tend to all his door patients," she said, "especially them that takes pleasure in talkin' themselves over. The doctor and me have got to be kind of partners; he's gone a good deal, far an' wide. Looked tired, didn't he? I shall have to advise with him an' get him off for a good rest. He'll take the big boat from Rockland an' go off up to Boston an' mouse round among the other doctors, once in two or three years, and come home fresh as a boy. I guess they think consider'ble of him up there." Mrs. Todd shook the reins and reached determinedly for the whip, as if she were compelling public opinion.

Whatever energy and spirit the white horse had to begin with were soon exhausted by the steep hills and his discernment of a long expedition ahead. We toiled slowly along. Mrs. Blackett and I sat together, and Mrs. Todd sat alone in front with much majesty and the large basket of provisions. Part of the way the road was shaded by thick woods, but we also passed one farmhouse after another on the high uplands, which we all three regarded with deep interest, the house itself and the barns and garden-spots and poultry all having to suffer an inspection of the shrewdest sort. This was a highway quite new to me; in fact, most of my journeys with Mrs. Todd had been made afoot and between the roads, in open pasture-lands. My friends stopped several times for brief dooryard visits, and made so many promises of stopping again on the way home that I began to wonder how long the expedition would last. I had often noticed how warmly Mrs. Todd was greeted by her friends, but it was hardly to be compared to the feelings now shown toward Mrs. Blackett. A look of delight came to the faces of those who recognized the plain, dear old figure beside me; one revelation after another was made of the constant interest and intercourse that had linked the far island and these scattered farms into a golden chain of love and dependence.

"Now, we mustn't stop again if we can help it," insisted Mrs. Todd at last. "You'll get tired, mother, and you'll think the less o' reunions. We can visit along here any day. There, if they ain't frying doughnuts in this next house, too! These are new folks, you know, from over St. George way; they took this old Talcot farm last year. 'T is the best water on the road, and the checkrain's come undone—yes, we'd best delay a little and water the horse."

We stopped, and seeing a party of pleasure-seekers in holiday attire, the thin, anxious mistress of the farmhouse came out with wistful sympathy to hear what news we might have to give. Mrs. Blackett first spied her at the half-closed door, and asked with such cheerful directness if we were trespassing that, after a few words, she went back to her kitchen and reappeared with a plateful of doughnuts.

"Entertainment for man and beast," announced Mrs. Todd with satisfaction. "Why, we've perceived there was new doughnuts all along the road, but you're the first that has treated us."

Our new acquaintance flushed with pleasure, but said nothing.

"They're very nice; you've had good luck with 'em," pronounced Mrs. Todd. "Yes, we've observed there was doughnuts all the way along; if one house is frying all the rest is; 't is so with a great many things."

"I don't suppose likely you're goin' up to the Bowden reunion?" asked the hostess as the white horse lifted his head and we were saying good-by.

"Why, yes," said Mrs. Blackett and Mrs. Todd and I, all together.

"I am connected with the family. Yes, I expect to be there this afternoon. I've been lookin' forward to it," she told us eagerly.

"We shall see you there. Come and sit with us if it's convenient," said dear Mrs. Blackett, and we drove away.

"I wonder who she was before she was married?" said Mrs. Todd, who was usually unerring in matters of genealogy. "She must have been one of that remote branch that lived down beyond Thomaston. We can find out this afternoon. I expect that the families'll march together, or be sorted out some way. I'm willing to own a relation that has such proper ideas of doughnuts."

"I seem to see the family looks," said Mrs. Blackett. "I wish we'd asked her name. She's a stranger, and I want to help make it pleasant for all such."

"She resembles Cousin Pa'lina Bowden about the forehead," said Mrs. Todd with decision.

We had just passed a piece of woodland that shaded the road, and come out to some open fields beyond, when Mrs. Todd suddenly reined in the horse as if somebody had stood on the roadside and stopped her. She even gave that quick reassuring nod of her head which was usually made to answer for a bow, but I discovered that she was looking eagerly at a tall ash-tree that grew just inside the field fence.

"I thought 't was goin' to do well," she said complacently as we went on again. "Last time I was up this way that tree was kind of drooping and discouraged. Grown trees act that way sometimes, same's folks; then they'll put right to it and strike their roots off into new ground and start all over again with real good courage. Ash-trees is very likely to have poor spells; they ain't got the resolution of other trees."

I listened hopefully for more; it was this peculiar wisdom that made one value Mrs. Todd's pleasant company.

"There's sometimes a good hearty tree growin' right out of the bare rock, out o' some crack that just holds the roots;" she went on to say, "right on the pitch o' one o' them bare stony hills where you can't seem to see a wheel-barrowful o' good earth in a place, but that tree'll keep a green top in the driest summer. You lay your ear down to the ground an' you'll hear a little stream runnin'. Every such tree has got its own livin' spring; there's folks made to match 'em."

I could not help turning to look at Mrs. Blackett, close beside me. Her hands were clasped placidly in their thin black woolen gloves, and she was looking at the flowery wayside as we went slowly along, with a pleased, expectant smile. I do not think she had heard a word about the trees.

"I just saw a nice plant o' elecampane growin' back there," she said presently to her daughter.

"I haven't got my mind on herbs today," responded Mrs. Todd, in the most matter-of-fact way. "I'm bent on seeing folks," and she shook the reins again.

I for one had no wish to hurry, it was so pleasant in the shady roads. The woods stood close to the road on the right; on the left were narrow fields and pastures where there were as many acres of spruces and pines as there were acres of bay and juniper and huckleberry, with a little turf between. When I thought we were in the heart of the inland country, we reached the top of a hill, and suddenly there lay spread out before us a wonderful great view of well-cleared fields that swept down to the wide water of a bay. Beyond this were distant shores like another country in the midday haze which half hid the hills beyond, and the far-away pale blue mountains on the northern horizon. There was a schooner with all sails set coming down the bay from a white village that was sprinkled on the shore, and there were many sail-boats flitting about. It was a noble landscape, and my eyes, which had grown used to the narrow inspection of a shaded roadside, could hardly take it in.

"Why, it's the upper bay," said Mrs. Todd. "You can see 'way over into the town of Fessenden. Those farms 'way over there are all in Fessenden. Mother used to have a sister that lived up that shore. If we started as early's we could on a summer mornin', we couldn't get to her place from Green Island till late afternoon, even with a fair, steady breeze, and you had to strike the time just right so as to fetch up 'long o' the tide and land near the flood. 'T was ticklish business, an' we didn't visit back an' forth as much as mother desired. You have to go 'way down the co'st to Cold Spring Light an' round that long point—up here's what they call the Back Shore."

"No, we were 'most always separated, my dear sister and me, after the first year she was married," said Mrs. Blackett. "We had our little families an' plenty o' cares. We were always lookin' forward to the time we could see each other more. Now and then she'd get out to the island for a few days while her husband'd go fishin'; and once he stopped with her an' two children, and made him some flakes right there and cured all his fish for winter. We did have a beautiful time together, sister an' me; she used to look back to it long's she lived."

"I do love to look over there where she used to live," Mrs. Blackett went on as we began to go down the hill. "It seems as if she must still be there, though she's long been gone. She loved their farm—she didn't see how I got so used to our island; but somehow I was always happy from the first."

"Yes, it's very dull to me up among those slow farms," declared Mrs. Todd. "The snow troubles 'em in winter. They're all besieged by winter, as you may say; 't is far better by the shore than up among such places. I never thought I should like to live up country."

"Why, just see the carriages ahead of us on the next rise!" exclaimed Mrs. Blackett. "There's going to be a great gathering, don't you believe there is, Almiry? It hasn't seemed up to now as if anybody was going but us. An' 't is such a beautiful day, with yesterday cool and pleasant to work an' get ready, I shouldn't wonder if everybody was there, even the slow ones like Phebe Ann Brock."

Mrs. Blackett's eyes were bright with excitement, and even

Mrs. Todd showed remarkable enthusiasm. She hurried the horse and caught up with the holiday-makers ahead. "There's all the Dep'fords goin', six in the wagon," she told us joyfully; "an' Mis' Alva Tilley's folks are now risin' the hill in their new carryall."

Mrs. Blackett pulled at the neat bow of her black bonnet-strings, and tied them again with careful precision. "I believe your bonnet's on a little bit sideways, dear," she advised Mrs. Todd as if she were a child; but Mrs. Todd was too much occupied to pay proper heed. We began to feel a new sense of gayety and of taking part in the great occasion as we joined the little train.

XVIII.

THE BOWDEN REUNION

It is very rare in country life, where high days and holidays are few, that any occasion of general interest proves to be less than great. Such is the hidden fire of enthusiasm in the New England nature that, once given an outlet, it shines forth with almost volcanic light and heat. In quiet neighborhoods such inward force does not waste itself upon those petty excitements of every day that belong to cities, but when, at long intervals, the altars to patriotism, to friendship, to the ties of kindred, are reared in our familiar fields, then the fires glow, the flames come up as if from the inexhaustible burning heart of the earth; the primal fires break through the granite dust in which our souls are set. Each heart is warm and every face shines with the ancient light. Such a day as this has transfiguring powers, and easily makes friends of those who have been cold-hearted, and gives to those who are dumb their chance to speak, and lends some beauty to the plainest face.

"Oh, I expect I shall meet friends today that I haven't seen in a long while," said Mrs. Blackett with deep satisfaction. "'T will bring out a good many of the old folks, 't is such a lovely day. I'm always glad not to have them disappointed."

"I guess likely the best of 'em'll be there," answered Mrs. Todd with gentle humor, stealing a glance at me. "There's one thing certain: there's nothing takes in this whole neighborhood like anything related to the Bowdens. Yes, I do feel that when you call upon the Bowdens you may expect most families to rise up between the Landing and the far end of the Back Cove. Those that are n't kin by blood are kin by marriage."

"There used to be an old story goin' about when I was a girl," said Mrs. Blackett, with much amusement. "There was a great many more Bowdens then than there are now, and the folks was all setting in meeting a dreadful hot Sunday afternoon, and a scatter-witted little bound girl came running to the meetin'-house door all out o' breath from somewheres in the neighborhood. 'Mis' Bowden, Mis' Bowden!' says she. 'Your baby's in a fit!' They used to tell that the whole congregation was up on its feet in a minute and right out into the aisles. All the Mis' Bowdens was setting right out for home; the minister stood there in the pulpit trying' to keep sober, an' all at once he burst right out laughin'. He was a very nice man, they said, and he said he'd better give 'em the benediction, and they could hear the sermon next Sunday, so he kept it over. My mother was there, and she thought certain 't was me."

"None of our family was ever subject to fits," interrupted Mrs. Todd severely. "No, we never had fits, none of us, and 't was lucky we didn't 'way out there to Green Island. Now these folks right in front: dear sakes knows the bunches o' soothing catnip an' yarrow I've had to favor old Mis' Evins with dryin'! You can see it right in their expressions, all them Evins folks. There, just you look up to the cross-roads, mother," she suddenly exclaimed. "See all the teams ahead of us. And oh, look down on the bay; yes, look down on the bay! See what a sight o' boats, all headin' for the Bowden place cove!"

"Oh, ain't it beautiful!" said Mrs. Blackett, with all the delight of a girl. She stood up in the high wagon to see everything, and when she sat down again she took fast hold of my hand.

"Hadn't you better urge the horse a little, Almiry?" she asked. "He's had it easy as we came along, and he can rest when we get there. The others are some little ways ahead, and I don't want to lose a minute."

We watched the boats drop their sails one by one in the cove as we drove along the high land. The old Bowden house stood, low-storied and broad-roofed, in its green fields, as if it were a motherly brown hen waiting for the flock that came straying toward it from every direction. The first Bowden settler had made his home there, and it was still the Bowden farm; five generations of sailors and farmers and soldiers had been its children. And presently Mrs. Blackett showed me the stone-walled burying-ground that stood like a little fort on a knoll overlooking the bay, but, as she said, there were plenty of scattered Bowdens who were not laid there—some lost at sea, and some out West, and some who died in the war; most of the home graves were those of women.

We could see now that there were different footpaths from along shore and across country. In all these there were straggling processions walking in single file, like old illustrations of the Pilgrim's Progress. There was a crowd about the house as if huge bees were swarming in the lilac bushes. Beyond the fields and cove a higher point of land ran out into the bay, covered with woods which must have kept away much of the northwest wind in winter. Now there was a pleasant look of shade and shelter there for the great family meeting.

We hurried on our way, beginning to feel as if we were very late, and it was a great satisfaction at last to turn out of the stony highroad into a green lane shaded with old apple-trees. Mrs. Todd encouraged the horse until he fairly pranced with gayety as we drove round to the front of the house on the soft turf. There was an instant cry of rejoicing, and two or three persons ran toward us from the busy group.

"Why, dear Mis' Blackett!—here's Mis' Blackett!" I heard them say, as if it were pleasure enough for one day to have a sight of her. Mrs. Todd turned to me with a lovely look of triumph and self-forgetfulness. An elderly man who wore the look of a prosperous sea-captain put up both arms and lifted Mrs. Blackett down from the high wagon like a child, and kissed her with hearty affection. "I was master afraid she wouldn't be here," he said, looking at Mrs. Todd with a face like a happy sunburnt schoolboy, while everybody crowded round to give their welcome.

"Mother's always the queen," said Mrs. Todd. "Yes, they'll all make everything of mother; she'll have a lovely time to-day. I wouldn't have had her miss it, and there won't be a thing she'll ever regret, except to mourn because William wa'n't here."

Mrs. Blackett having been properly escorted to the house, Mrs. Todd received her own full share of honor, and some of the men, with a simple kindness that was the soul of chivalry, waited upon us and our baskets and led away the white horse. I already knew some of Mrs. Todd's friends and kindred, and felt like an adopted Bowden in this happy moment. It seemed to be enough for anyone to have arrived by the same conveyance as Mrs. Blackett, who presently had her court inside the house, while Mrs. Todd, large, hospitable, and preeminent, was the centre of a rapidly increasing crowd about the lilac bushes. Small companies were continually coming up the long green slope from the water, and nearly all the boats had come to shore. I counted three or four that were baffled by the light breeze, but before long all the Bow-

dens, small and great, seemed to have assembled, and we
started to go up to the grove across the field.

Out of the chattering crowd of noisy children, and large-
waisted women whose best black dresses fell straight to the
ground in generous folds, and sunburnt men who looked as
serious as if it were town-meeting day, there suddenly came
silence and order. I saw the straight, soldierly little figure of a
man who bore a fine resemblance to Mrs. Blackett, and who
appeared to marshal us with perfect ease. He was imperative
enough, but with a grand military sort of courtesy, and bore
himself with solemn dignity of importance. We were sorted
out according to some clear design of his own, and stood as
speechless as a troop to await his orders. Even the children
were ready to march together, a pretty flock, and at the last
moment Mrs. Blackett and a few distinguished companions,
the ministers and those who were very old, came out of the
house together and took their places. We ranked by fours,
and even then we made a long procession.

There was a wide path mowed for us across the field, and,
as we moved along, the birds flew up out of the thick second
crop of clover, and the bees hummed as if it still were June.
There was a flashing of white gulls over the water where the
fleet of boats rode the low waves together in the cove, swaying their small masts as if they kept time to our steps. The
plash of the water could be heard faintly, yet still be heard;
we might have been a company of ancient Greeks going to
celebrate a victory, or to worship the god of harvests in the
grove above. It was strangely moving to see this and to make
part of it. The sky, the sea, have watched poor humanity at
its rites so long; we were no more a New England family cel-
ebrating its own existence and simple progress; we carried the
tokens and inheritance of all such households from which this
had descended, and were only the latest of our line. We
possessed the instincts of a far, forgotten childhood; I found
myself thinking that we ought to be carrying green branches
and singing as we went. So we came to the thick shaded
grove still silent, and were set in our places by the straight
trees that swayed together and let sunshine through here and
there like a single golden leaf that flickered down, vanishing
in the cool shade.

The grove was so large that the great family looked far
smaller than it had in the open field; there was a thick growth
of dark pines and firs with an occasional maple or oak that
gave a gleam of color like a bright window in the great roof.

On three sides we could see the water, shining behind the tree-trunks, and feel the cool salt breeze that began to come up with the tide just as the day reached its highest point of heat. We could see the green sunlit field we had just crossed as if we looked out at it from a dark room, and the old house and its lilacs standing placidly in the sun, and the great barn with a stockade of carriages from which two or three care-taking men who had lingered were coming across the field together. Mrs. Todd had taken off her warm gloves and looked the picture of content.

"There!" she exclaimed. "I've always meant to have you see this place, but I never looked for such a beautiful opportunity—weather an' occasion both made to match. Yes, it suits me: I don't ask no more. I want to know if you saw mother walkin' at the head! It choked me right up to see mother at the head, walkin' with the ministers," and Mrs. Todd turned away to hide the feelings she could not instantly control.

"Who was the marshal?" I hastened to ask. "Was he an old soldier?"

"Don't he do well?" answered Mrs. Todd with satisfaction.

"He don't often have such a chance to show off his gifts," said Mrs. Caplin, a friend from the Landing who had joined us. "That's Sant Bowden; he always takes the lead, such days. Good for nothing else most o' his time; trouble is, he"—

I turned with interest to hear the worst. Mrs. Caplin's tone was both zealous and impressive.

"Stim'lates," she explained scornfully.

"No, Santin never was in the war," said Mrs. Todd with lofty indifference. "It was a cause of real distress to him. He kep' enlistin', and traveled far an' wide about here, an' even took the bo't and went to Boston to volunteer; but he ain't a sound man, an' they wouldn't have him. They say he knows all their tactics, an' can tell all about the battle o' Waterloo well's he can Bunker Hill. I told him once the country'd lost a great general, an' I meant it, too."

"I expect you're near right," said Mrs. Caplin, a little crest-fallen and apologetic.

"I be right," insisted Mrs. Todd with much amiability. " 'T was most too bad to cramp him down to his peaceful trade, but he's a most excellent shoemaker at his best, an' he always says it's a trade that gives him time to think an' plan his manœuvres. Over to the Port they always invite him to march

Decoration Day, same as the rest, an' he does look noble; he comes of soldier stock."

I had been noticing with great interest the curiously French type of face which prevailed in this rustic company. I had said to myself before that Mrs. Blackett was plainly of French descent, in both her appearance and her charming gifts, but this is not surprising when one has learned how large a proportion of the early settlers on this northern coast of New England were of Huguenot blood, and that it is the Norman Englishman, not the Saxon, who goes adventuring to a new world.

"They used to say in old times," said Mrs. Todd modestly, "that our family came of very high folks in France, and one of 'em was a great general in some o' the old wars. I sometimes think that Santin's ability has come 'way down from then. 'T ain't nothin' he's ever acquired; 't was born in him. I don't know's he ever saw a fine parade, or met with those that studied up such things. He's figured it all out an' got his papers so he knows how to aim a cannon right for William's fish-house five miles out on Green Island, or up there on Burnt Island where the signal is. He had it all over to me one day, an' I tried hard to appear interested. His life's all in it, but he will have those poor gloomy spells come over him now an' then, an' then he has to drink."

Mrs. Caplin gave a heavy sigh.

"There's a great many such strayaway folks, just as there is plants," continued Mrs. Todd, who was nothing if not botanical. "I know of just one sprig of laurel that grows over back here in a wild spot, an' I never could hear of no other on this coast. I had a large bunch brought me once from Massachusetts way, so I know it. This piece grows in an open spot where you'd think 't would do well, but it's sort o' poor-lookin'. I've visited it time an' again, just to notice its poor blooms. 'T is a real Sant Bowden, out of its own place."

Mrs. Caplin looked bewildered and blank. "Well, all I know is, last year he worked out some kind of a plan so's to parade the county conference in platoons, and got 'em all flustered up tryin' to sense his ideas of a holler square," she burst forth, "They was holler enough anyway after ridin' 'way down from up country into the salt air, and they'd been treated to a sermon on faith an' works from old Fayther Harlow that never knows when to cease. 'T wa'n't no time for tactics then—they wa'n't a-thinkin' of the church military. Sant, he couldn't do nothin' with 'em. All he thinks of, when he sees a crowd, is how to march 'em. 'T is all very well when he don't 'tempt too much. He never did act like other folks."

"Ain't I just been maintainin' that he ain't like 'em?" urged Mrs. Todd decidedly. "Strange folks has got to have strange ways, for what I see."

"Somebody observed once that you could pick out the likeness of 'most every sort of a foreigner when you looked about you in our parish," said Sister Caplin, her face brightening with sudden illumination. "I didn't see the bearin' of it then quite so plain. I always did think Mari' Harris resembled a Chinee."

"Mari' Harris was pretty as a child, I remember," said the pleasant voice of Mrs. Blackett, who, after receiving the affectionate greetings of nearly the whole company, came to join us—to see, as she insisted, that we were out of mischief.

"Yes, Mari' was one o' them pretty little lambs that make dreadful homely old sheep," replied Mrs. Todd with energy. "Cap'n Littlepage never'd look so disconsolate if she was any sort of a proper person to direct things. She might divert him; yes, she might divert the old gentleman, an' let him think he had his own way, 'stead o' arguing everything down to the bare bone. 'T wouldn't hurt her to sit down an' hear his great stories once in a while."

"The stories are very interesting," I ventured to say.

"Yes, you always catch yourself a-thinkin' what if they was all true, and he had the right of it," answered Mrs. Todd. "He's a good sight better company, though dreamy, than such sordid creatur's as Mari' Harris."

"Live and let live," said dear old Mrs. Blackett gently. "I haven't seen the captain for a good while, now that I ain't so constant to meetin'," she added wistfully. "We always have known each other."

"Why, if it is a good pleasant day tomorrow, I'll get William to call an' invite the capt'in to dinner. William'll be in early so's to pass up the street without meetin' anybody."

"There, they're callin' out it's time to set the tables," said Mrs. Caplin, with great excitement.

"Here's Cousin Sarah Jane Blackett! Well, I am pleased, certain!" exclaimed Mrs. Todd, with unaffected delight; and these kindred spirits met and parted with the promise of a good talk later on. After this there was no more time for conversation until we were seated in order at the long tables.

"I'm one that always dreads seeing some o' the folks that I

don't like, at such a time as this," announced Mrs. Todd privately to me after a season of reflection. We were just waiting for the feast to begin. "You wouldn't think such a great creatur' 's I be could feel all over pins an' needles. I remember, the day I promised to Nathan, how it come over me, just 's I was feelin' happy 's I could, that I'd got to have an own cousin o' his for my near relation all the rest o' my life, an' it seemed as if die I should. Poor Nathan saw somethin' had crossed me—he had very nice feelings—and when he asked me what 't was, I told him. 'I never could like her myself,' said he. 'You sha'n't be bothered, dear,' he says; an' 't was one o' the things that made me set a good deal by Nathan, he didn't make a habit of always opposin', like some men. 'Yes,' says I, 'but think o' Thanksgivin' times an' funerals; she's our relation, an' we've got to own her.' Young folks don't think o' those things. There she goes now, do let's pray her by!" said Mrs. Todd, with an alarming transition from general opinions to particular animosities. "I hate her just the same as I always did; but she's got on a real pretty dress. I do try to remember that she's Nathan's cousin. Oh dear, well; she's gone by after all, an' ain't seen me. I expected she'd come pleasantin' round just to show off an' say afterwards she was acquainted."

This was so different from Mrs. Todd's usual largeness of mind that I had a moment's uneasiness; but the cloud passed quickly over her spirit, and was gone with the offender.

There never was a more generous out-of-door feast along the coast than the Bowden family set forth that day. To call it a picnic would make it seem trivial. The great tables were edged with pretty oak-leaf trimming, which the boys and girls made. We brought flowers from the fence-thickets of the great field; and out of the disorder of flowers and provisions suddenly appeared as orderly a scheme for the feast as the marshal had shaped for the procession. I began to respect the Bowdens for their inheritance of good taste and skill and a certain pleasing gift of formality. Something made them do all these things in a finer way than most country people would have done them. As I looked up and down the tables there was a good cheer, a grave soberness that shone with pleasure, a humble dignity of bearing. There were some who should have sat below the salt for lack of this good breeding; but they were not many. So, I said to myself, their ancestors may have sat in the great hall of some old French house in the Middle Ages, when battles and sieges and processions and feasts were familiar things. The ministers and Mrs. Blackett, with a few of their rank and age, were put in places of honor, and for once that I looked any other way I looked twice at Mrs. Blackett's face, serene and mindful of privilege and responsibility, the mistress by simple fitness of this great day.

Mrs. Todd looked up at the roof of green trees, and then carefully surveyed the company. "I see 'em better now they're all settin' down," she said with satisfaction. "There's old Mr. Gilbraith and his sister. I wish they were settin' with us; they're not among folks they can parley with, an' they look disappointed."

As the feast went on, the spirits of my companion steadily rose. The excitement of an unexpectedly great occasion was a subtle stimulant to her disposition, and I could see that sometimes when Mrs. Todd had seemed limited and heavily domestic, she had simply grown sluggish for lack of proper surroundings. She was not so much reminiscent now as expectant, and as alert and gay as a girl. We who were her neighbors were full of gayety, which was but the reflected light from her beaming countenance. It was not the first time that I was full of wonder at the waste of human ability in this world, as a botanist wonders at the wastefulness of nature, the thousand seeds that die, the unused provision of every sort. The reserve force of society grows more and more amazing to one's thought. More than one face among the Bowdens showed that only opportunity and stimulus were lacking,—a narrow set of circumstances had caged a fine able character and held it captive. One sees exactly the same types in a country gathering as in the most brilliant city company. You are safe to be understood if the spirit of your speech is the same for one neighbor as for the other.

XIX.

THE FEAST'S END

❧❧

The feast was a noble feast, as has already been said. There was an elegant ingenuity displayed in the form of pies which delighted my heart. Once acknowledge that an American pie is far to be preferred to its humble ancestor, the English tart, and it is joyful to be reassured at a Bowden reunion that invention has not yet failed. Beside a delightful variety of material the decorations went beyond all my former experience; dates and names were wrought in lines of pastry and frosting on the tops. There was even more elaborate reading matter on an excellent early-apple pie which we began to share and eat, precept upon precept. Mrs. Todd helped me generously to the whole word *Bowden*, and consumed *Reunion* herself, save an undecipherable fragment; but the most renowned essay in cookery on the tables was a model of the old Bowden house made of durable gingerbread, with all the windows and doors in the right places, and sprigs of genuine lilac set at the front. It must have been baked in sections, in one of the last of the great brick ovens, and fastened together on the morning of the day. There was a general sigh when this fell into ruin at the feast's end, and it was shared by a great part of the assembly, not without seriousness, and as if it were a pledge and token of loyalty. I met the maker of the gingerbread house, which had called up lively remembrances of a childish story. She had the gleaming eye of an enthusiast and a look of high ideals.

"I could just as well have made it all of frosted cake," she said, "but 't wouldn't have been the right shade; the old house, as you observe, was never painted, and I concluded that plain gingerbread would represent it best. It wasn't all I expected it would be," she said sadly, as many an artist had said before her of his work.

There were speeches by the ministers; and there proved to be a historian among the Bowdens, who gave some fine anecdotes of the family history; and then appeared a poetess, whom Mrs. Todd regarded with wistful compassion and indulgence, and when the long faded garland of verses came to an appealing end, she turned to me with words of praise.

"Sounded pretty," said the generous listener. "Yes, I thought she did very well. We went to school together, an' Mary Anna had a very hard time; trouble was, her mother thought she'd given birth to a genius, an' Mary Anna's come to believe it herself. There, I don't know what we should have done without her; there ain't nobody else that can write poetry between here and 'way up towards Rockland; it adds a great deal at such a time. When she speaks o' those that are gone, she feels it all, and so does everybody else, but she harps too much. I'd laid half of that away for next time, if I was Mary Anna. There comes mother to speak to her, an' old Mr. Gilbraith's sister; now she'll be heartened right up. Mother'll say just the right thing."

The leave-takings were as affecting as the meetings of these old friends had been. There were enough young persons at the reunion, but it is the old who really value such opportunities; as for the young, it is the habit of every day to meet their comrades—the time of separation has not come. To see the joy with which these elder kinsfolk and acquaintances had looked in one another's faces, and the lingering touch of their friendly hands; to see these affectionate meetings and then the reluctant partings, gave one a new idea of the isolation in which it was possible to live in that after all thinly settled region. They did not expect to see one another again very soon; the steady, hard work on the farms, the difficulty of getting from place to place, especially in winter when boats were laid up, gave double value to any occasion which could bring a large number of families together. Even funerals in this country of the pointed firs were not without their social advantages and satisfactions. I heard the words "next summer" repeated many times, though summer was still ours and all the leaves were green.

The boats began to put out from shore, and the wagons to drive away. Mrs. Blackett took me into the old house when we came back from the grove: it was her father's birthplace and early home, and she had spent much of her own childhood there with her grandmother. She spoke of those days as if they had but lately passed; in fact, I could imagine that the house looked almost exactly the same to her. I could see the brown rafters of the unfinished roof as I looked up the steep staircase, though the best room was as handsome with its

good wainscoting and touch of ornament on the cornice as
any old room of its day in a town.

Some of the guests who came from a distance were still sitting in the best room when we went in to take leave of the
master and mistress of the house. We all said eagerly what a
pleasant day it had been, and how swiftly the time had
passed. Perhaps it is the great national anniversaries which
our country has lately kept, and the soldiers' meetings that
take place everywhere, which have made reunions of every
sort the fashion. This one, at least, had been very interesting.
I fancied that old feuds had been overlooked, and the old
saying that blood is thicker than water had again proved itself true, though from the variety of names one argued a certain adulteration of the Bowden traits and belongings.
Clannishness is an instinct of the heart,—it is more than a
birthright, or a custom; and lesser rights were forgotten in the
claim to a common inheritance.

We were among the very last to return to our proper lives
and lodgings. I came near to feeling like a true Bowden, and
parted from certain new friends as if they were old friends;
we were rich with the treasure of a new remembrance.

At last we were in the high wagon again; the old white
horse had been well fed in the Bowden barn, and we drove
away and soon began to climb the long hill toward the
wooded ridge. The road was new to me, as roads always are,
going back. Most of our companions had been full of anxious
thoughts of home—of the cows, or of young children likely
to fall into disaster—but we had no reasons for haste, and
drove slowly along, talking and resting by the way. Mrs.
Todd said once that she really hoped her front door had been
shut on account of the dust blowing in, but added that nothing made any weight on her mind except not to forget to turn
a few late mullein leaves that were drying on a newspaper in
the little loft. Mrs. Blackett and I gave our word of honor
that we would remind her of this heavy responsibility. The
way seemed short, we had so much to talk about. We
climbed hills where we could see the great bay and the islands, and then went down into shady valleys where the air
began to feel like evening, cool and damp with a fragrance of
wet ferns. Mrs. Todd alighted once or twice, refusing all assistance in securing some boughs of a rare shrub which she
valued for its bark, though she proved incommunicative as to
her reasons. We passed the house where we had been so

kindly entertained with doughnuts earlier in the day, and found it closed and deserted, which was a disappointment.

"They must have stopped to tea somewheres and thought they'd finish up the day," said Mrs. Todd. "Those that enjoyed it best'll want to get right home so's to think it over."

"I didn't see the woman there after all, did you?" asked Mrs. Blackett as the horse stopped to drink at the trough.

"Oh yes, I spoke with her," answered Mrs. Todd, with but scant interest or approval. "She ain't a member o' our family."

"I thought you said she resembled Cousin Pa'lina Bowden about the forehead," suggested Mrs. Blackett.

"Well, she don't," answered Mrs. Todd impatiently. "I ain't one that's ord'narily mistaken about family likenesses, and she didn't seem to meet with friends, so I went square up to her. 'I expect you're a Bowden by your looks,' says I. 'Yes, I take it you're one o' the Bowdens.' 'Lor', no,' says she. 'Dennett was my maiden name, but I married a Bowden for my first husband. I thought I'd come an' just see what was a-goin' on'!"

Mrs. Blackett laughed heartily. "I'm goin' to remember to tell William o' that," she said. "There, Almiry, the only thing that's troubled me all this day is to think how William would have enjoyed it. I do so wish William had been there."

"I sort of wish he had, myself," said Mrs. Todd frankly.

"There wa'n't many old folks there, somehow," said Mrs. Blackett, with a touch of sadness in her voice. "There ain't so many to come as there used to be, I'm aware, but I expected to see more."

"I thought they turned out pretty well, when you come to think of it; why, everybody was sayin' so an' feelin' gratified," answered Mrs. Todd hastily with pleasing unconsciousness; then I saw the quick color flash into her cheek, and presently she made some excuse to turn and steal an anxious look at her mother. Mrs. Blackett was smiling and thinking about her happy day, though she began to look a little tired. Neither of my companions was troubled by her burden of years. I hoped in my heart that I might be like them as I lived on into age, and then smiled to think that I too was no longer very young. So we always keep the same hearts, though our outer framework fails and shows the touch of time.

" 'T was pretty when they sang the hymn, wasn't it?" asked Mrs. Blackett at suppertime, with real enthusiasm. "There was such a plenty o' men's voices; where I sat it did sound beautiful. I had to stop and listen when they came to the last verse."

I saw that Mrs. Todd's broad shoulders began to shake. "There was good singers there; yes, there was excellent singers," she agreed heartily, putting down her teacup, "but I chanced to drift alongside Mis' Peter Bowden o' Great Bay, an' I couldn't help thinkin' if she was as far out o' town as she was out o' tune, she wouldn't get back in a day."

XX.

ALONG SHORE

❦

One day as I went along the shore beyond the old wharves and the newer, high-stepped fabric of the steamer landing, I saw that all the boats were beached, and the slack water period of the early afternoon prevailed. Nothing was going on, not even the most leisurely of occupations, like baiting trawls or mending nets, or repairing lobster pots; the very boats seemed to be taking an afternoon nap in the sun. I could harldy discover a distant sail as I looked seaward, except a weather-beaten lobster smack, which seemed to have been taken for a plaything by the light airs that blew about the bay. It drifted and turned about so aimlessly in the wide reach off Burnt Island, that I suspected there was nobody at the wheel, or that she might have parted her rusty anchor chain while all the crew were asleep.

I watched her for a minute or two; she was the old Miranda, owned by some of the Caplins, and I knew her by an odd shaped patch of newish duck that was set into the peak of her dingy mainsail. Her vagaries offered such an exciting subject for conversation that my heart rejoiced at the sound of a hoarse voice behind me. At that moment, before I had time to answer, I saw something large and shapeless flung from the Miranda's deck that splashed the water high against her black side, and my companion gave a satisfied chuckle. The old lobster smack's sail caught the breeze again at this moment, and she moved off down the bay. Turning, I found Old Elijah Tilley, who had come softly out of his dark fish house, as if it were a burrow.

"Boy got kind o' drowsy steerin' of her; Monroe he hove him right overboard; 'wake now fast enough," explained Mr. Tilley, and we laughed together.

I was delighted, for my part, that the vicissitudes and dangers of the Miranda, in a rocky channel, should have given me this opportunity to make acquaintance with an old fisherman to whom I had never spoken. At first he had seemed to

137

be one of those evasive and uncomfortable persons who are
so suspicious of you that they make you almost suspicious of
yourself. Mr. Elijah Tilley appeared to regard a stranger with
scornful indifference. You might see him standing on the
pebble beach or in a fishhouse doorway, but when you came
nearer he was gone. He was one of the small company of
elderly, gaunt-shaped great fishermen whom I used to like to
see leading up a deep-laden boat by the head, as if it were a
horse, from the water's edge to the steep slope of the pebble
beach. There were four of these large old men at the Landing, who were the survivors of an earlier and more vigorous
generation. There was an alliance and understanding between
them, so close that it was apparently speechless. They gave
much time to watching one another's boats go out or come
in; they lent a ready hand at tending one another's lobster
traps in rough weather; they helped to clean the fish, or to
sliver porgies for the trawls, as if they were in close partnership; and when a boat came in from deep-sea fishing they
were never far out of the way, and hastened to help carry it
ashore, two by two, splashing alongside, or holding its steady
head, as if it were a willful sea colt. As a matter of fact no
boat could help being steady and way-wise under their instant
direction and companionship. Abel's boat and Jonathan Bowden's boat were as distinct and experienced personalities as
the men themselves, and as inexpressive. Arguments and
opinions were unknown to the conversation of these ancient
friends; you would as soon have expected to hear small talk
in a company of elephants as to hear old Mr. Bowden or Elijah Tilley and their two mates waste breath upon any form of
trivial gossip. They made brief statements to one another
from time to time. As you came to know them you wondered
more and more that they should talk at all. Speech seemed to
be a light and elegant accomplishment, and their unexpected
acquaintance with its arts made them of new value to the listener. You felt almost as if a landmark pine should suddenly
address you in regard to the weather, or a lofty-minded old
camel make a remark as you stood respectfully near him under the circus tent.

I often wondered a great deal about the inner life and
thought of these self-contained old fishermen; their minds
seemed to be fixed upon nature and the elements rather than
upon any contrivances of man, like politics or theology. My
friend, Captain Bowden, who was the nephew of the eldest of
this group, regarded them with deference; but he did not be-

long to their secret companionship, though he was neither young nor talkative.

"They've gone together ever since they were boys, they know most everything about the sea amon'st them," he told me once. "They was always just as you see 'em now since the memory of man."

These ancient seafarers had houses and lands not outwardly different from other Dunnet Landing dwellings, and two of them were fathers of families, but their true dwelling places were the sea, and the stony beach that edged its familiar shore, and the fishhouses, where much salt brine from the mackerel kits had soaked the very timbers into a state of brown permanence and petrifaction. It had also affected the old fishermen's hard complexions, until one fancied that when Death claimed them it could only be with the aid, not of any slender modern dart, but the good serviceable harpoon of a seventeenth century woodcut.

Elijah Tilley was such an evasive, discouraged-looking person, heavy-headed, and stooping so that one could never look him in the face, that even after his friendly exclamation about Monroe Pennell, the lobster smack's skipper, and the sleepy boy, I did not venture at once to speak again. Mr. Tilley was carrying a small haddock in one hand, and presently shifted it to the other hand lest it might touch my skirt. I knew that my company was accepted, and we walked together a little way.

"You mean to have a good supper," I ventured to say, by way of friendliness.

"Goin' to have this 'ere haddock an' some o' my good baked potatoes; must eat to live," responded my companion with great pleasantness and open approval. I found that I had suddenly left the forbidding coast and come into a smooth little harbor of friendship.

"You ain't never been up to my place," said the old man. "Folks don't come now as they used to; no, 't ain't no use to ask folks now. My poor dear she was a great hand to draw young company."

I remembered that Mrs. Todd had once said that this old fisherman had been sore stricken and unconsoled at the death of his wife.

"I should like very much to come," said I. "Perhaps you are going to be at home later on?"

Mr. Tilley agreed, by a sober nod, and went his way bent-shouldered and with a rolling gait. There was a new patch high on the shoulder of his old waistcoat, which corresponded to the renewing of the Miranda's mainsail down the bay, and I wondered if his own fingers, clumsy with much deep-sea fishing, had set it in.

"Was there a good catch to-day?" I asked, stopping a moment. "I didn't happen to be on the shore when the boats came in."

"No; all come in pretty light," answered Mr. Tilley. "Addicks an' Bowden they done the best; Abel an' me we had but a slim fare. We went out 'arly, but not so 'arly as sometimes; looked like a poor mornin'. I got nine haddick, all small, and seven fish; the rest on 'em got more fish than haddick. Well, I don't expect they feel like bitin' every day; we l'arn to humor 'em a little, an' let 'em have their way 'bout it. These plaguey dog-fish kind of worry 'em." Mr. Tilley pronounced the last sentence with much sympathy, as if he looked upon himself as a true friend of all the haddock and codfish that lived on the fishing grounds, and so we parted.

Later in the afternoon I went along the beach again until I came to the foot of Mr. Tilley's land, and found his rough track across the cobble-stones and rocks to the field edge, where there was a heavy piece of old wreck timber, like a ship's bone, full of treenails. From this a little footpath, narrow with one man's treading, led up across the small green field that made Mr. Tilley's whole estate, except a straggling pasture that tilted on edge up the steep hillside beyond the house and road. I could hear the tinkle-tankle of a cow-bell somewhere among the spruces by which the pasture was being walked over and forested from every side; it was likely to be called the wood lot before long, but the field was unmolested. I could not see a bush or a brier anywhere within its walls, and hardly a stray pebble showed itself. This was most surprising in that country of firm ledges, and scattered stones which all the walls that industry could devise had hardly begun to clear away off the land. In the narrow field I noticed some stout stakes, apparently planted at random in the grass and among the hills of potatoes, but carefully painted yellow and white to match the house, a neat sharp-edged little dwelling, which looked strangely modern for its owner. I should have much sooner believed that the smart young wholesale egg merchant of the Landing was its occupant than Mr. Tilley, since a man's house is really but his larger body, and expresses in a way his nature and character.

I went up the field, following the smooth little path to the side door. As for using the front door, that was a matter of great ceremony; the long grass grew close against the high stone step, and a snowberry bush leaned over it, top-heavy with the weight of a morning-glory vine that had managed to take what the fishermen might call a half hitch about the door-knob. Elijah Tilley came to the side door to receive me; he was knitting a blue yarn stocking without looking on, and was warmly dressed for the season in a thick blue flannel shirt with white crockery buttons, a faded waistcoat and trousers heavily patched at the knees. These were not his fishing clothes. There was something delightful in the grasp of his hand, warm and clean, as if it never touched anything but the comfortable woolen yarn, instead of cold sea water and slippery fish.

"What are the painted stakes for, down in the field?" I hastened to ask, and he came out a step or two along the path to see; and looked at the stakes as if his attention were called to them for the first time.

"Folks laughed at me when I first bought this place an' come here to live," he explained. "They said 't wa'n't no kind of a field privilege at all; no place to raise anything, all full o' stones. I was aware 't was good land, an' I worked some on it—odd times when I didn't have nothin' else on hand—till I cleared them loose stones all out. You never see a prettier piece than 't is now; now did ye? Well, as for them painted marks, them's my buoys. I struck on to some heavy rocks that didn't show none, but a plow'd be liable to ground on 'em, an' so I ketched holt an' buoyed 'em same's you see. They don't trouble me no more'n if they wa'n't there."

"You haven't been to sea for nothing," I said, laughing.

"One trade helps another," said Elijah with an amiable smile. "Come right in an' set down. Come in an' rest ye," he exclaimed, and led the way into his comfortable kitchen. The sunshine poured in at the two further windows, and a cat was curled up sound asleep on the table that stood between them. There was a new-looking light oilcloth of a tiled pattern on the floor, and a crockery teapot, large for a household of only one person, stood on the bright stove. I ventured to say that somebody must be a very good housekeeper.

"That's me," acknowledged the old fisherman with frankness. "There ain't nobody here but me. I try to keep things looking right, same's poor dear left 'em. You set down here in this chair, then you can look off an' see the water.

None on 'em thought I was goin' to get along alone, no way, but I wa'n't goin' to have my house turned upsi' down an' all changed about; no, not to please nobody. I was the only one knew just how she liked to have things set, poor dear, an' I said I was goin' to make shift, and I have made shift. I'd rather tough it out alone." And he sighed heavily, as if to sigh were his familiar consolation.

We were both silent for a minute; the old man looked out of the window, as if he had forgotten I was there.

"You must miss her very much?" I said at last.

"I do miss her," he answered, and sighed again. "Folks all kep' repeatin' that time would ease me, but I can't find it does. No, I miss her just the same every day."

"How long is it since she died?" I asked.

"Eight year now, come the first of October. It don't seem near so long. I've got a sister that comes and stops 'long o' me a little spell, spring an' fall, an' odd times if I send after her. I ain't near so good a hand to sew as I be to knit, and she's very quick to set everything to rights. She's a married woman with a family; her son's folks lives at home, an' I can't make no great claim on her time. But it makes me a kind' o good excuse, when I do send, to help her a little; she ain't none too well off. Poor dear always liked her, and we used to contrive our ways together. 'T is full as easy to be alone. I set here an' think it all over, an' think considerable when the weather's bad to go outside. I get so some days it feels as if poor dear might step right back into this kitchen. I keep a watchin' them doors as if she might step in to ary one. Yes, ma'am, I keep a-lookin' off an' droppin' o' my stitches; that's just how it seems. I can't git over losin' of her no way nor no how. Yes, ma'am, that's just how it seems to me."

I did not say anything, and he did not look up.

"I git feelin' so sometimes I have to lay everything by an' go out door. She was a sweet pretty creatur' long's she lived," the old man added mournfully. "There's that little rockin' chair o' her'n, I set an' notice it an' think how strange 't is a creatur' like her should be gone an' that chair be here right in its old place."

"I wish I had known her; Mrs. Todd told me about your wife one day," I said.

"You'd have liked to come and see her; all the folks did," said poor Elijah. "She'd been so pleased to hear everything and see somebody new that took such an int'rest. She had a kind o' gift to make it pleasant for folks. I guess likely Almiry Todd told you she was a pretty woman, especially in her young days; late years, too, she kep' her looks and come to be so pleasant lookin'." There, 't ain't so much matter, I shall be done afore a great while. No; I sha'n't trouble the fish a great sight more."

The old widower sat with his head bowed over his knitting, as if he were hastily shortening the very thread of time. The minutes went slowly by. He stopped his work and clasped his hands firmly together. I saw he had forgotten his guest, and I kept the afternoon watch with him. At last he looked up as if but a moment had passed of his continual loneliness.

"Yes, ma'am, I'm one that has seen trouble," he said, and began to knit again.

The visible tribute of his careful housekeeping, and the clean bright room which had once enshrined his wife, and now enshrined her memory, was very moving to me; he had no thought for any one else or for any other place. I began to see her myself in her home—a delicate-looking, faded little woman, who leaned upon his rough strength and affectionate heart, who was always watching for his boat out of this very window, and who always opened the door and welcomed him when he came home.

"I used to laugh at her, poor dear," said Elijah, as if he read my thought. "I used to make light of her timid notions. She used to be fearful when I was out in bad weather or baffled about gettin' ashore. She used to say the time seemed long to her, but I've found out all about it now. I used to be dreadful thoughtless when I was a young man and the fish was bitin' well. I'd stay out late some o' them days, an' I expect she'd watch an' watch an' lose heart a-waitin'. My heart alive! what a supper she'd git, an' be right there watchin' from the door, with somethin' over her head if 't was cold, waitin' to hear all about it as I come up the field. Lord, how I think o' all them little things!"

"This was what she called the best room; in this way," he said presently, laying his knitting on the table, and leading the way across the front entry and unlocking a door, which he threw open with an air of pride. The best room seemed to me a much sadder and more empty place than the kitchen; its conventionalities lacked the simple perfection of the humbler room and failed on the side of poor ambition; it was only when one remembered what patient saving, and what high respect for society in the abstract go to such furnishing that the little parlor was interesting at all. I could imagine the great day of certain purchases, the bewildering shops of the next large town, the aspiring anxious woman, the clumsy sea-tanned man in his best clothes, so eager to be pleased, but at ease only when they were safe back in the sail-boat again, going down the bay with their precious freight, the hoarded money all spent and nothing to think of but tiller and sail. I looked at the unworn carpet, the glass vases on the mantelpiece with their prim bunches of bleached swamp grass and dusty marsh rosemary, and I could read the history of Mrs. Tilley's best room from its very beginning.

"You see for yourself what beautiful rugs she could make; now I'm going to show you her best tea things she thought so much of," said the master of the house, opening the door of a shallow cupboard. "That's real chiny, all of it on those two shelves," he told me proudly. "I bought it all myself, when we was first married, in the port of Bordeaux. There never was one single piece of it broke until— Well, I used to say, long as she lived, there never was a piece broke, but long at the last I noticed she'd look kind o' distressed, an' I thought 't was 'count o' me boastin'. When they asked if they should use it when the folks was here to supper, time o' her funeral, I knew she'd want to have everything nice, and I said 'certain.' Some o' the women they come runnin' to me an' called me, while they was takin' of the chiny down, an' showed me there was one o' the cups broke an' the pieces wropped in paper and pushed way back here, corner o' the shelf. They didn't want me to go an' think they done it. Poor dear! I had to put right out o' the house when I see that. I knowed in one minute how 't was. We'd got so used to sayin' 't was all there just's I fetched it home, an' so when she broke that cup somehow or 'nother she couldn't frame no words to come an' tell me. She couldn't think 't would vex me, 't was her own hurt pride. I guess there wa'n't no other secret ever lay between us."

The French cups with their gay sprigs of pink and blue, the best tumblers, an old flowered bowl and tea caddy, and a japanned waiter or two adorned the shelves. These, with a few daguerreotypes in a little square pile, had the closet to themselves, and I was conscious of much pleasure in seeing them. One is shown over many a house in these days where the interest may be more complex, but not more definite.

"Those were her best things, poor dear," said Elijah as he locked the door again. "She told me that last summer before she was taken away that she couldn't think o' anything more she wanted, there was everything in the house, an' all her rooms was furnished pretty. I was goin' over to the Port, an' inquired for errands. I used to ask her to say what she wanted, cost or no cost—she was a very reasonable woman, an' 't was the place where she done all but her extra shopping. It kind o' chilled me up when she spoke so satisfied."

"You don't go out fishing after Christmas?" I asked, as we came back to the bright kitchen.

"No; I take stiddy to my knitting after January sets in," said the old seafarer. " 'T ain't worth while, fish make off into deeper water an' you can't stand no such perishin' for the sake o' what you get. I leave out a few traps in sheltered coves an' do a little lobsterin' on fair days. The young fellows braves it out, some on 'em; but, for me, I lay in my winter's yarn an' set here where 't is warm, an' knit an' take my comfort. Mother learnt me once when I was a lad; she was a beautiful knitter herself. I was laid up with a bad knee, an' she said 't would take up my time an' help her; we was a large family. They'll buy all the folks can do down here to Addicks' store. They say our Dunnet stockin's is gettin' to be celebrated up to Boston—good quality o' wool an' even knittin' or somethin'. I've always been called a pretty hand to do nettin', but seines is master cheap to what they used to be when they was all hand worked. I change off to nettin' long towards spring, and I piece up my trawls and lines and get my fishin' stuff to rights. Lobster pots they require attention, but I make 'em up in spring weather when it's warm there in the barn. No; I ain't one o' them that likes to set an' do nothin'."

"You see the rugs, poor dear did them; she wa'n't very partial to knittin'," old Elijah went on, after he had counted his stitches. "Our rugs is beginnin' to show wear, but I can't master none o' them womanish tricks. My sister, she tinkers 'em up. She said last time she was here that she guessed they'd last my time."

"The old ones are always the prettiest," I said.

"You ain't referrin' to the braided ones now?" answered Mr. Tilley. "You see ours is braided for the most part, an' their good looks is all in the beginnin'. Poor dear used to say they made an easier floor. I go shufflin' round the house same's if 't was a bo't, and I always used to be stubbin' up the corners o' the hooked kind. Her an' me was always havin' our jokes together same's a boy an' girl. Outsiders never'd know nothin' about it to see us. She had nice manners with all, but to me there was nobody so entertainin'. She'd take off anybody's natural talk winter evenin's when we set here alone, so you'd think 't was them a-speakin'. There, there!"

I saw that he had dropped a stitch again, and was snarling the blue yarn round his clumsy fingers. He handled it and threw it off at arm's length as if it were a cod line; and frowned impatiently, but I saw a tear shining on his cheek.

I said that I must be going, it was growing late, and asked if I might come again, and if he would take me out to the fishing grounds some day.

"Yes, come any time you want to," said my host, " 't ain't so pleasant as when poor dear was here. Oh, I didn't want to lose her an' she didn't want to go, but it had to be. Such things ain't for us to say; there's no yes an' no to it."

"You find Almiry Todd one o' the best o' women?" said Mr. Tilley as we parted. He was standing in the doorway and I had started off down the narrow green field. "No, there ain't a better hearted woman in the State o' Maine. I've known her from a girl. She's had the best o' mothers. You tell her I'm liable to fetch her up a couple or three nice good mackerel early tomorrow," he said. "Now don't let it slip your mind. Poor dear, she always thought a sight o' Almiry, and she used to remind me there was nobody to fish for her; but I don't rec'lect it as I ought to. I see you drop a line yourself very handy now an' then."

We laughed together like the best of friends, and I spoke again about the fishing grounds, and confessed that I had no fancy for a southerly breeze and a ground swell.

"Nor me neither," said the old fisherman. "Nobody likes 'em, say what they may. Poor dear was disobliged by the mere sight of a bo't. Almiry's got the best o' mothers, I expect you know; Mis' Blackett out to Green Island; and we was always plannin' to go out when summer come; but there, I couldn't pick no day's weather that seemed to suit her just right. I never set out to worry her neither, 't wa'n't no kind o' use; she was so pleasant we couldn't have no fret nor trouble. 'T was never 'you dear an' you darlin' 'afore folks, an' 'you divil' behind the door!"

As I looked back from the lower end of the field I saw him still standing, a lonely figure in the doorway. "Poor dear," I repeated to myself half aloud; "I wonder where she is and what she knows of the little world she left. I wonder what she has been doing these eight years!"

I gave the message about the mackerel to Mrs. Todd.

"Been visitin' with 'Lijah?" she asked with interest. "I expect you had kind of a dull session; he ain't the talkin' kind; dwellin' so much long o' fish seems to make 'em lose the gift o' speech." But when I told her that Mr. Tilley had been talking to me that day, she interrupted me quickly.

"Then 't was all about his wife, an' he can't say nothin' too pleasant neither. She was modest with strangers, but there ain't one o' her old friends can ever make up her loss. For me, I don't want to go there no more. There's some folks you miss and some folks you don't, when they're gone, but there ain't hardly a day I don't think o' dear Sarah Tilley. She was always right there; yes, you knew just where to find her like a plain flower. 'Lijah's worthy enough; I do esteem 'Lijah, but he's a ploddin' man."

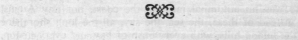

XXI.
THE BACKWARD VIEW

❧

At last it was the time of late summer, when the house was cool and damp in the morning, and all the light seemed to come through green leaves; but at the first step out of doors the sunshine always laid a warm hand on my shoulder, and the clear, high sky seemed to lift quickly as I looked at it. There was no autumnal mist on the coast, nor any August fog; instead of these, the sea, the sky, all the long shore line and the inland hills, with every bush of bay and every fir-top, gained a deeper color and a sharper clearness. There was something shining in the air, and a kind of lustre on the water and the pasture grass—a northern look that, except at this moment of the year, one must go far to seek. The sunshine of a northern summer was coming to its lovely end.

The days were few then at Dunnet Landing, and I let each of them slip away unwillingly as a miser spends his coins. I wished to have one of my first weeks back again, with those long hours when nothing happened except the growth of herbs and the course of the sun. Once I had not even known where to go for a walk; now there were many delightful things to be done and done again, as if I were in London. I felt hurried and full of pleasant engagements, and the days flew by like a handful of flowers flung to the sea wind.

At last I had to say good-by to all my Dunnet Landing friends, and my homelike place in the little house, and return to the world in which I feared to find myself a foreigner. There may be restrictions to such a summer's happiness, but the ease that belongs to simplicity is charming enough to make up for whatever a simple life may lack, and the gifts of peace are not for those who live in the thick of battle.

I was to take the small unpunctual steamer that went down the bay in the afternoon, and I sat for a while by my window looking out on the green herb garden, with regret for company. Mrs. Todd had hardly spoken all day except in the briefest and most disapproving way; it was as if we were on the edge of a quarrel. It seemed impossible to take my departure with anything like composure. At last I heard a footstep, and looked up to find that Mrs. Todd was standing at the door.

"I've seen to everything now," she told me in an unusually loud and business-like voice. "Your trunks are on the w'arf by this time. Cap'n Bowden he come and took 'em down himself, an' is going to see that they're safe aboard. Yes, I've seen to all your 'rangements," she repeated in a gentler tone. "These things I've left on the kitchen table you'll want to carry by hand; the basket needn't be returned. I guess I shall walk over towards the Port now an' inquire how old Mis' Edward Caplin is."

I glanced at my friend's face, and saw a look that touched me to the heart. I had been sorry enough before to go away.

"I guess you'll excuse me if I ain't down there to stand round on the w'arf and see you go," she said, still trying to be gruff. "Yes, I ought to go over and inquire for Mis' Edward Caplin; it's her third shock, and if mother gets in on Sunday she'll want to know just how the old lady is." With this last word Mrs. Todd turned and left me as if with sudden thought of something she had forgotten, so that I felt sure she was coming back, but presently I heard her go out of the kitchen door and walk down the path toward the gate. I could not part so; I ran after her to say good-by, but she shook her head and waved her hand without looking back when she heard my hurrying steps, and so went away down the street.

When I went in again the little house had suddenly grown lonely, and my room looked empty as it had the day I came. I and all my belongings had died out of it, and I knew how it would seem when Mrs. Todd came back and found her lodger gone. So we die before our own eyes; so we see some chapters of our lives come to their natural end.

I found the little packages on the kitchen table. There was a quaint West Indian basket which I knew its owner had valued, and which I had once admired; there was an affecting provision laid beside it for my seafaring supper, with a neatly tied bunch of southernwood and a twig of bay, and a little old leather box which held the coral pin that Nathan Todd brought home to give to poor Joanna.

There was still an hour to wait, and I went up to the hill just above the schoolhouse and sat there thinking of things, and looking off to sea, and watching for the boat to come in sight. I could see Green Island, small and darkly wooded at that distance; below me were the houses of the village with their apple-trees and bits of garden ground. Presently, as I looked at the pastures beyond, I caught a last glimpse of Mrs. Todd herself, walking slowly in the footpath that led along, following the shore toward the Port. At such a distance one can feel the large, positive qualities that control a character. Close at hand, Mrs. Todd seemed able and warm-hearted and quite absorbed in her bustling industries, but her distant figure looked mateless and appealing, with something about it that was strangely self-possessed and mysterious. Now and then she stooped to pick something—it might have been her favorite pennyroyal—and at last I lost sight of her as she slowly crossed an open space on one of the higher points of land, and disappeared again behind a dark clump of juniper and the pointed firs.

As I came away on the little coastwise steamer, there was an old sea running which made the surf leap high on all the rocky shores. I stood on deck, looking back, and watched the busy gulls agree and turn, and sway together down the long slopes of air, then separate hastily and plunge into the waves. The tide was setting in, and plenty of small fish were coming with it, unconscious of the silver flashing of the great birds overhead and the quickness of their fierce beaks. The sea was full of life and spirit, the tops of the waves flew back as if they were winged like the gulls themselves, and like them had the freedom of the wind. Out in the main channel we passed a bent-shouldered old fisherman bound for the evening round among his lobster traps. He was toiling along with short oars, and the dory tossed and sank and tossed again with the steamer's waves. I saw that it was old Elijah Tilley, and though we had so long been strangers we had come to be warm friends, and I wished that he had waited for one of his mates, it was such hard work to row along shore through rough seas and tend the traps alone. As we passed I waved my hand and tried to call to him, and he looked up and answered my farewells by a solemn nod. The little town, with the tall masts of its disabled schooners in the inner bay, stood high above the flat sea for a few minutes, then it sank back into the uniformity of the coast, and became indistinguishable from the other towns that looked as if they were crumbled on the furzy-green stoniness of the shore.

The small outer islands of the bay were covered among the ledges with turf that looked as fresh as the early grass; there had been some days of rain the week before, and the darker green of the sweet-fern was scattered on all the pasture heights. It looked like the beginning of summer ashore, though the sheep, round and warm in their winter wool, betrayed the season of the year as they went feeding along the slopes in the low afternoon sunshine. Presently the wind began to blow, and we struck out seaward to double the long sheltering headland of the cape, and when I looked back again, the islands and the headland had run together and Dunnet Landing and all its coasts were lost to sight.

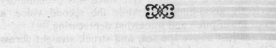

A Dunnet Shepherdess

I.

❈

Early one morning at Dunnet Landing, as if it were still night, I waked, suddenly startled by a spirited conversation beneath my window. It was not one of Mrs. Todd's morning soliloquies; she was not addressing her plants and flowers in words of either praise or blame. Her voice was declamatory though perfectly good-humored, while the second voice, a man's, was of lower pitch and somewhat deprecating.

The sun was just above the sea, and struck straight across my room through a crack in the blind. It was a strange hour for the arrival of a guest, and still too soon for the general run of business, even in that tiny eastern haven where daybreak fisheries and early tides must often rule the day.

The man's voice suddenly declared itself to my sleepy ears. It was Mr. William Blackett's.

"Why, sister Almiry," he protested gently, "I don't need none o' your nostrums!"

"Pick me a small han'ful," she commanded. "No, no, a *small* han'ful I said—o' them large pennyr'yal sprigs! I go to all the trouble an' cossetin' of 'em just so as to have you ready to meet such occasions, an' last year, you may remember, you never stopped here at all the day you went up country. An' the frost come at last an' blacked it. I never saw any herb that so objected to gardin ground; might as well try to flourish mayflowers in a common front yard. There, you can come in now, an' set and eat what breakfast you've got patience for. I've found everything I want, an' I'll mash 'em up an' be all ready to put 'em on."

I heard such a pleading note of appeal as the speakers went round the corner of the house, and my curiosity was so demanding, that I dressed in haste, and joined my friends a little later, with two unnoticed excuses of the beauty of the morning, and the early mail boat. William's breakfast had been slighted; he had taken his cup of tea and merely pushed back the rest on the kitchen table. He was now sitting in a helpless condition by the side window, with one of his sister's purple calico aprons pinned close about his neck. Poor William was meekly submitting to being smeared, as to his countenance, with a most pungent and unattractive lotion of pennyroyal and other green herbs which had been hastily pounded and mixed with cream in the little white stone mortar.

I had to cast two or three straightforward looks at William to reassure myself that he really looked happy and expectant in spite of his melancholy circumstances, and was not being overtaken by retribution. The brother and sister seemed to be on delightful terms with each other for once, and there was something of cheerful anticipation in their morning talk. I was reminded of Medea's anointing Jason before the great episode of the iron bulls, but to-day William really could not be going up country to see a railroad for the first time. I knew this to be one of his great schemes, but he was not fitted to appear in public, or to front an observing world of strangers. As I appeared he essayed to rise, but Mrs. Todd pushed him back into the chair.

"Set where you be till it dries on," she insisted. "Land sakes, you'd think he'd get over bein' a boy some time or 'nother, gettin' along in years as he is. An' you'd think he'd seen full enough o' fish, but once a year he has to break loose like this, an' travel off way up back o' the Bowden place—far out o' my beat, 't is—an' go a trout fishin'!"

Her tone of amused scorn was so full of challenge that William changed color even under the green streaks.

"I want some change," he said, looking at me and not at her. " 'Tis the prettiest little shady brook you ever saw."

"If he ever fetched home more 'n a couple o' minnies, 't would seem worth while," Mrs. Todd concluded, putting a last dab of the mysterious compound so perilously near her brother's mouth that William flushed again and was silent.

A little later I witnessed his escape, when Mrs. Todd had taken the foolish risk of going down cellar. There was a horse and wagon outside the garden fence, and presently we stood where we could see him driving up the hill with thoughtless speed. Mrs. Todd said nothing, but watched him affectionately out of sight.

"It serves to keep the mosquitoes off," she said, and a moment later it occurred to my slow mind that she spoke of the pennyroyal lotion. "I don't know sometimes but William's kind of poetical," she continued, in her gentlest voice. "You'd think if anything could cure him of it, 't would be the fish business."

It was only twenty minutes past six on a summer morning, but we both sat down to rest as if the activities of the day were over. Mrs. Todd rocked gently for a time, and seemed to be lost, though not poorly, like Macbeth, in her thoughts. At last she resumed relations with her actual surroundings. "I shall now put my lobsters on. They'll make us a good supper," she announced. "Then I can let the fire out for all day; give it a holiday, same's William. You can have a little one now, nice an' hot, if you ain't got all the breakfast you want. Yes, I'll put the lobsters on. William was very thoughtful to bring 'em over; William *is* thoughtful; if he only had a spark o' ambition, there be few could match him."

This unusual concession was afforded a sympathetic listener from the depths of the kitchen closet. Mrs. Todd was getting out her old iron lobster pot, and began to speak of prosaic affairs. I hoped that I should hear something more about her brother and their island life, and sat idly by the kitchen window looking at the morning glories that shaded it, believing that some flaw of wind might set Mrs. Todd's mind on its former course. Then it occurred to me that she had spoken about our supper rather than our dinner, and I guessed that she might have some great scheme before her for the day.

When I had loitered for some time and there was no further word about William, and at last I was conscious of receiving no attention whatever, I went away. It was something of a disappointment to find that she put no hindrance in the way of my usual morning affairs, of going up to the empty little white schoolhouse on the hill where I did my task of writing. I had been almost sure of a holiday when I discovered that Mrs. Todd was likely to take one herself; we had not been far afield to gather herbs and pleasures for many days now, but a little later she had silently vanished. I found my luncheon ready on the table in the little entry, wrapped in its shining old homespun napkin, and as if by way of special consolation, there was a stone bottle of Mrs. Todd's best spruce beer, with a long piece of cod line wound round it by which it could be lowered for coolness into the deep schoolhouse well.

I walked away with a dull supply of writing-paper and these provisions, feeling like a reluctant child who hopes to be called back at every step. There was no relenting voice to be heard, and when I reached the schoolhouse, I found that I had left an open window and a swinging shutter the day before, and the sea wind that blew at evening had fluttered my poor sheaf of papers all about the room.

So the day did not begin very well, and I began to recognize that it was one of the days when nothing could be done without company. The truth was that my heart had gone trouting with William, but it would have been too selfish to say a word even to one's self about spoiling his day. If there is one way above another of getting so close to nature that one simply is a piece of nature, following a primeval instinct with perfect self-forgetfulness and forgetting everything except the dreamy consciousness of pleasant freedom, it is to take the course of a shady trout brook. The dark pools and the sunny shallows beckon one on; the wedge of sky between the trees on either bank, the speaking, companioning noise of the water, the amazing importance of what one is doing, and the constant sense of life and beauty make a strange transformation of the quick hours. I had a sudden memory of all this, and another, and another. I could not get myself free from "fishing and wishing."

At that moment I heard the unusual sound of wheels, and I looked past the high-growing thicket of wild-roses and straggling sumach to see the white nose and meagre shape of the Caplin horse; then I saw William sitting in the open wagon, with a small expectant smile upon his face.

"I've got two lines," he said. "I was quite a piece up the road. I thought perhaps 't was so you'd feel like going."

There was enough excitement for most occasions in hearing William speak three sentences at once. Words seemed but vain to me at that bright moment. I stepped back from the schoolhouse window with a beating heart. The spruce-beer bottle was not yet in the well, and with that and my luncheon, and Pleasure at the helm, I went out into the happy world. The land breeze was blowing, and, as we turned away, I saw a flutter of white go past the window as I left the schoolhouse and my morning's work to their neglected fate.

II.

One seldom gave way to a cruel impulse to look at an ancient seafaring William, but one felt as if he were a growing boy; I only hope that he felt much the same about me. He did not wear the fishing clothes that belonged to his sea-going life, but a strangely shaped old suit of tea-colored linen garments that might have been brought home years ago from Canton or Bombay. William had a peculiar way of giving silent assent when one spoke, but of answering your unspoken thoughts as if they reached him better than words. "I find them very easy," he said, frankly referring to the clothes. "Father had them in his old sea-chest."

The antique fashion, a quaint touch of foreign grace and even imagination about the cut were very pleasing; if ever Mr. William Blackett had faintly resembled an old beau, it was upon that day. He now appeared to feel as if everything had been explained between us, as if everything were quite understood; and we drove for some distance without finding it necessary to speak again about anything. At last, when it must have been a little past nine o'clock, he stopped the horse beside a small farmhouse, and nodded when I asked if I should get down from the wagon. "You can steer about northeast right across the pasture," he said, looking from under the eaves of his hat with an expectant smile. "I always leave the team here."

I helped to unfasten the harness, and William led the horse away to the barn. It was a poor-looking little place, and a forlorn woman looked at us through the window before she appeared at the door. I told her that Mr. Blackett and I came up from the Landing to go fishing. "He keeps a-comin', don't he?" she answered, with a funny little laugh, to which I was at a loss to find answer. When he joined us, I could not see that he took notice of her presence in any way, except to take an armful of dried salt fish from a corded stack in the back of the wagon which had been carefully covered with a piece

of old sail. We had left a wake of their pungent flavor behind
us all the way. I wondered what was going to become of the
rest of them and some fresh lobsters which were also disclosed to view, but he laid the present gift on the doorstep
without a word, and a few minutes later, when I looked back
as we crossed the pasture, the fish were being carried into the
house.

I could not see any signs of a trout brook until I came
close upon it in the bushy pasture, and presently we struck
into the low woods of straggling spruce and fir mixed into a
tangle of swamp maples and alders which stretched away on
either hand up and down stream. We found an open place in
the pasture where some taller trees seemed to have been overlooked rather than spared. The sun was bright and hot by this
time, and I sat down in the shade while William produced his
lines and cut and trimmed us each a slender rod. I wondered
where Mrs. Todd was spending the morning, and if later she
would think that pirates had landed and captured me from
the schoolhouse.

III.

❦

The brook was giving that live, persistent call to a listener that trout brooks always make; it ran with a free, swift current even here, where it crossed an apparently level piece of land. I saw two unpromising, quick barbel chase each other upstream from bank to bank as we solemnly arranged our hooks and sinkers. I felt that William's glances changed from anxiety to relief when he found that I was used to such gear; perhaps he felt that we must stay together if I could not bait my own hook, but we parted happily, full of a pleasing sense of companionship.

William had pointed me up the brook, but I chose to go down, which was only fair because it was his day, though one likes as well to follow and see where a brook goes as to find one's way to the places it comes from, and its tiny springs and headwaters, and in this case trout were not to be considered. William's only real anxiety was lest I might suffer from mosquitoes. His own complexion was still strangely impaired by its defenses, but I kept forgetting it, and looking to see if we were treading fresh pennyroyal underfoot, so efficient was Mrs. Todd's remedy. I was conscious, after we parted, and I turned to see if he were already fishing, and saw him wave his hand gallantly as he went away, that our friendship had made a great gain.

The moment that I began to fish the brook, I had a sense of its emptiness; when my bait first touched the water and went lightly down the quick stream, I knew that there was nothing to lie in wait for it. It is the same certainty that comes when one knocks at the door of an empty house, a lack of answering consciousness and of possible response; it is quite different if there is any life within. But it was a lovely brook, and I went a long way through woods and breezy open pastures, and found a forsaken house and overgrown farm, and laid up many pleasures for future joy and remembrance. At the end of the morning I came back to our meeting-place hungry and without any fish. William was already waiting, and we did not mention the matter of trout. We ate our luncheons with good appetites, and William brought our two stone bottles of spruce beer from the deep place in the brook where he had left them to cool. Then we sat awhile longer in peace and quietness on the green banks.

As for William, he looked more boyish than ever, and kept a more remote and juvenile sort of silence. Once I wondered how he had come to be so curiously wrinkled, forgetting, absent-mindedly, to recognize the effects of time. He did not expect any one else to keep up a vain show of conversation, and so I was silent as well as he. I glanced at him now and then, but I watched the leaves tossing against the sky and the red cattle moving in the pasture. "I don't know 's we need head for home. It's early yet," he said at last, and I was as startled as if one of the gray firs had spoken.

"I guess I'll go up-along and ask after Thankful Hight's folks," he continued. "Mother 'd like to get word;" and I nodded a pleased assent.

IV.

William led the way across the pasture, and I followed with a deep sense of pleased anticipation. I do not believe that my companion had expected me to make any objection, but I knew that he was gratified by the easy way that his plans for the day were being seconded. He gave a look at the sky to see if there were any portents, but the sky was frankly blue; even the doubtful morning haze had disappeared.

We went northward along a rough, clayey road, across a bare-looking, sunburnt country full of tiresome long slopes where the sun was hot and bright, and I could not help observing the forlorn look of the farms. There was a great deal of pasture, but it looked deserted, and I wondered afresh why the people did not raise more sheep when that seemed the only possible use to make of their land. I said so to Mr. Blackett, who gave me a look of pleased surprise.

"That's what She always maintains," he said eagerly. "She's right about it, too; well, you'll see!" I was glad to find myself approved, but I had not the least idea whom he meant, and waited until he felt like speaking again.

A few minutes later we drove down a steep hill and entered a large tract of dark spruce woods. It was delightful to be sheltered from the afternoon sun, and when we had gone some distance in the shade, to my great pleasure William turned the horse's head toward some bars, which he let down, and I drove through into one of those narrow, still, sweet-scented by-ways which seem to be paths rather than roads. Often we had to put aside the heavy drooping branches which barred the way, and once, when a sharp twig struck William in the face, he announced with such spirit that somebody ought to go through there with an axe, that I felt unexpectedly guilty. So far as I now remember, this was William's only remark all the way through the woods to Thankful Hight's folks, but from time to time he pointed or nodded at something which I might have missed: a sleepy little owl

snuggled into the bend of a branch, or a tall stalk of cardinal
flowers where the sunlight came down at the edge of a small,
bright piece of marsh. Many times, being used to the company of Mrs. Todd and other friends who were in the habit
of talking, I came near making an idle remark to William,
but I was for the most part happily preserved; to be with him
only for a short time was to live on a different level, where
thoughts served best because they were thoughts in common;
the primary effect upon our minds of the simple things and
beauties that we saw. Once when I caught sight of a lovely
gay pigeon-woodpecker eyeing us curiously from a dead
branch, and instinctively turned toward William, he gave an
indulgent, comprehending nod which silenced me all the rest
of the way. The wood-road was not a place for common
noisy conversation; one would interrupt the birds and all the
still little beasts that belonged there. But it was mortifying to
find how strong the habit of idle speech may become in one's
self. One need not always be saying something in this noisy
world. I grew conscious of the difference between William's
usual fashion of life and mine; for him there were long days
of silence in a sea-going boat, and I could believe that he and
his mother usually spoke very little because they so perfectly
understood each other. There was something peculiarly unre-
sponding about their quiet island in the sea, solidly fixed into
the still foundations of the world, against whose rocky shores
the sea beats and calls and is unanswered.

We were quite half an hour going through the woods; the
horse's feet made no sound on the brown, soft track under
the dark evergreens. I thought that we should come out at
last into more pastures, but there was no half-wooded strip of
land at the end; the high woods grew squarely against an old
stone wall and a sunshiny open field, and we came out suddenly into broad daylight that startled us and even startled
the horse, who might have been napping as he walked, like
an old soldier. The field sloped up to a low unpainted house
that faced the east. Behind it were long, frost-whitened ledges
that made the hill, with strips of green turf and bushes between. It was the wildest, most Titanic sort of pasture country up there; there was a sort of daring in putting a frail
wooden house before it, though it might have the homely
field and honest woods to front against. You thought of the
elements and even of possible volcanoes as you looked up the
stony heights. Suddenly I saw that a region of what I had

thought gray stones was slowly moving, as if the sun was making my eyesight unsteady.

"There 's the sheep!" exclaimed William, pointing eagerly. "You see the sheep?" and sure enough, it was a great company of woolly backs, which seemed to have taken a mysterious protective resemblance to the ledges themselves. I could discover but little chance for pasturage on that high sunburnt ridge, but the sheep were moving steadily in a satisfied way as they fed along the slopes and hollows.

"I never have seen half so many sheep as these, all summer long!" I cried with admiration.

"There ain't so many," answered William soberly. "It's a great sight. They do so well because they're shepherded, but you can't beat sense into some folks."

"You mean that somebody stays and watches them?" I asked.

"She observed years ago in her readin' that they don't turn out their flocks without protection anywhere but in the State o' Maine," returned William. "First thing that put it into her mind was a little old book mother's got; she read it one time when she come out to the Island. They call it the 'Shepherd o' Salisbury Plain.' 'T wasn't the purpose o' the book to most, but when she read it, 'There, Mis' Blackett!' she said, 'that's where we've all lacked sense; our Bibles ought to have taught us that what sheep need is a shepherd.' You see most folks about here gave up sheep-raisin' years ago 'count o' the dogs. So she gave up school-teachin' and went out to tend her flock, and has shepherded ever since, an' done well."

For William, this approached an oration. He spoke with enthusiasm, and I shared the triumph of the moment. "There she is now!" he exclaimed, in a different tone, as the tall figure of a woman came following the flock and stood still on the ridge, looking toward us as if her eyes had been quick to see a strange object in the familiar emptiness of the field. William stood up in the wagon, and I thought he was going to call or wave his hand to her, but he sat down again more clumsily than if the wagon had made the familiar motion of a boat, and we drove on toward the house.

It was a most solitary place to live—a place where one might think that a life could hide itself. The thick woods were between the farm and the main road, and as one looked up and down the country, there was no other house in sight.

"Potatoes look well," announced William. "The old folks

used to say that there wa'n't no better land outdoors than the Hight field."

I found myself possessed of a surprising interest in the shepherdess, who stood far away in the hill pasture with her great flock, like a figure of Millet's, high against the sky.

V.

❦

Everything about the old farmhouse was clean and orderly, as if the green door-yard were not only swept, but dusted. I saw a flock of turkeys stepping off carefully at a distance, but there was not the usual untidy flock of hens about the place to make everything look in disarray. William helped me out of the wagon as carefully as if I had been his mother, and nodded toward the open door with a reassuring look at me; but I waited until he had tied the horse and could lead the way, himself. He took off his hat just as we were going in, and stopped for a moment to smooth his thin gray hair with his hand, by which I saw that we had an affair of some ceremony. We entered an old-fashioned country kitchen, the floor scrubbed into unevenness, and the doors well polished by the touch of hands. In a large chair facing the window there sat a masterful-looking old woman with the features of a warlike Roman emperor, emphasized by a bonnet-like black cap with a band of green ribbon. Her sceptre was a palm-leaf fan.

William crossed the room toward her, and bent his head close to her ear.

"Feelin' pretty well to-day, Mis' Hight?" he asked, with all the voice his narrow chest could muster.

"No, I ain't, William. Here I have to set," she answered coldly, but she gave an inquiring glance over his shoulder at me.

"This is the young lady who is stopping with Almiry this summer," he explained, and I approached as if to give the countersign. She offered her left hand with considerable dignity, but her expression never seemed to change for the better. A moment later she said that she was pleased to meet me, and I felt as if the worst were over. William must have felt some apprehension, while I was only ignorant, as we had come across the field. Our hostess was more than disapproving, she was forbidding; but I was not long in suspecting that she felt the natural resentment of a strong energy that has been defeated by illness and made the spoil of captivity.

"Mother well as usual since you was up last year?" and William replied by a series of cheerful nods. The mention of dear Mrs. Blackett was a help to any conversation.

"Been fishin', ashore," he explained, in a somewhat conciliatory voice. "Thought you'd like a few for winter," which explained at once the generous freight we had brought in the back of the wagon. I could see that the offering was no surprise, and that Mrs. Hight was interested.

"Well, I expect they're good as the last," she said, but did not even approach a smile. She kept a straight, discerning eye upon me.

"Give the lady a cheer," she admonished William, who hastened to place close by her side one of the straight-backed chairs that stood against the kitchen wall. Then he lingered for a moment like a timid boy. I could see that he wore a look of resolve, but he did not ask the permission for which he evidently waited.

"You can go search for Esther," she said, at the end of a long pause that became anxious for both her guests. "Esther'd like to see her;" and William in his pale nankeens disappeared with one light step and was off.

VI.

❧

"Don't speak too loud, it jars a person's head," directed Mrs. Hight plainly. "Clear an' distinct is what reaches me best. Any news to the Landin'?"

I was happily furnished with the particulars of a sudden death, and an engagement of marriage between a Caplin, a seafaring widower home from his voyage, and one of the younger Harrises; and now Mrs. Hight really smiled and settled herself in her chair. We exhausted one subject completely before we turned to the other. One of the returning turkeys took an unwarrantable liberty, and, mounting the doorstep, came in and walked about the kitchen without being observed by its strict owner; and the tin dipper slipped off its nail behind us and made an astonishing noise, and jar enough to reach Mrs. Hight's inner ear and make her turn her head to look at it; but we talked straight on. We came at last to understand each other upon such terms of friendship that she unbent her majestic port and complained to me as any poor old woman might of the hardships of her illness. She had already fixed various dates upon the sad certainty of the year when she had the shock, which had left her perfectly helpless except for a clumsy left hand which fanned and gestured, and settled and resettled the folds of her dress, but could do no comfortable time-shortening work.

"Yes'm, you can feel sure I use it what I can," she said severely. " 'T was a long spell before I could let Esther go forth in the mornin' till she'd got me up an' dressed me, but now she leaves things ready overnight and I get 'em as I want 'em with my light pair o' tongs, and I feel very able about helpin' myself to what I once did. Then when Esther returns, all she has to do is to push out here into the kitchen. Some parts o' the year Esther stays out all night, them moonlight nights when the dogs are apt to be after the sheep, but she don't use herself as hard as she once had to. She's well able to hire somebody, Esther is, but there, you can't find no hired man that wants to git up before five o'clock nowadays; 't ain't as 't was in my time. They're liable to fall asleep, too, and them moonlight nights she's so anxious she can't sleep, and out she goes. There's a kind of a fold, she calls it, up there in a sheltered spot, and she sleeps up in a little shed she's got—built it herself for lambin' time and when the poor foolish creatur's gets hurt or anything. I've never seen it, but she says it's in a lovely spot and always pleasant in any weather. You see off, other side of the ridge, to the south'ard, where there's houses. I used to think some time I'd get up to see it again, and all them spots she lives in, but I sha'n't now. I'm beginnin' to go back; an' 't ain't surprisin'. I've kind of got used to disappointments," and the poor soul drew a deep sigh.

VII.

✺

It was long before we noticed the lapse of time; I not only told every circumstance known to me of recent events among the households of Mrs. Todd's neighborhood at the shore, but Mrs. Hight became more and more communicative on her part, and went carefully into the genealogical descent and personal experience of many acquaintances, until between us we had pretty nearly circumnavigated the globe and reached Dunnet Landing from an opposite direction to that in which we had started. It was long before my own interest began to flag; there was a flavor of the best sort in her definite and descriptive fashion of speech. It may be only a fancy of my own that in the sound and value of many words, with their lengthened vowels and doubled cadences, there is some faint survival on the Maine coast of the sound of English speech of Chaucer's time.

At last Mrs. Thankful Hight gave a suspicious look through the window.

"Where do you suppose they be?" she asked me. "Esther must ha' been off to the far edge o' everything. I doubt William ain't been able to find her; can't he hear their bells? His hearin' all right?"

William had heard some herons that morning which were beyond the reach of my own ears, and almost beyond eyesight in the upper skies, and I told her so. I was luckily preserved by some unconscious instinct from saying that we had seen the shepherdess so near as we crossed the field. Unless she had fled faster than Atalanta, William must have been but a few minutes in reaching her immediate neighborhood. I now discovered with a quick leap of amusement and delight in my heart that I had fallen upon a serious chapter of romance. The old woman looked suspiciously at me, and I made a dash to cover with a new piece of information; but she listened with lofty indifference, and soon interrupted my eager statements.

"Ain't William been gone some considerable time?" she demanded, and then in a milder tone: "The time has re'lly flown; I do enjoy havin' company. I set here alone a sight o' long days. Sheep is dreadful fools; I expect they heard a strange step, and set right off through bush an' brier, spite of all she could do. But William might have the sense to return, 'stead o' searchin' about. I want to inquire of him about his mother. What was you goin' to say? I guess you'll have time to relate it."

My powers of entertainment were on the ebb, but I doubled my diligence and we went on for another half-hour at least with banners flying, but still William did not reappear. Mrs. Hight frankly began to show fatigue.

"Somethin' 's happened, an' he's stopped to help her," groaned the old lady, in the middle of what I had found to tell her about a rumor of disaffection with the minister of a town I merely knew by name in the weekly newspaper to which Mrs. Todd subscribed. "You step to the door, dear, an' look if you can't see 'em." I promptly stepped, and once outside the house I looked anxiously in the direction which William had taken.

To my astonishment I saw all the sheep so near that I wonder we had not been aware in the house of every bleat and tinkle. And there, within a stone's-throw, on the first long gray ledge that showed above the juniper, were William and the shepherdess engaged in pleasant conversation. At first I was provoked and then amused, and a thrill of sympathy warmed my whole heart. They had seen me and risen as if by magic; I had a sense of being the messenger of Fate. One could almost hear their sighs of regret as I appeared; they must have passed a lovely afternoon. I hurried into the house with the reassuring news that they were not only in sight but perfectly safe, with all the sheep.

VIII.

❦

Mrs. Hight, like myself, was spent with conversation, and had ceased even the one activity of fanning herself. I brought a desired drink of water, and happily remembered some fruit that was left from my luncheon. She revived with splendid vigor, and told me the simple history of her later years since she had been smitten in the prime of her life by the stroke of paralysis, and her husband had died and left her alone with Esther and a mortgage on their farm. There was only one field of good land, but they owned a great region of sheep pasture and a little woodland. Esther had always been laughed at for her belief in sheep-raising when one by one their neighbors were giving up their flocks, and when everything had come to the point of despair she had raised all the money and bought all the sheep she could, insisting that Maine lambs were as good as any, and that there was a straight path by sea to Boston market. And by tending her flock herself she had managed to succeed; she had made money enough to pay off the mortgage five years ago, and now what they did not spend was safe in the bank. "It has been stubborn work, day and night, summer and winter, an' now she's beginnin' to get along in years," said the old mother sadly. "She's tended me 'long o' the sheep, an' she's been a good girl right along, but she ought to have been a teacher;" and Mrs. Hight sighed heavily and plied the fan again.

We heard voices, and William and Esther entered; they did not know that it was so late in the afternoon. William looked almost bold, and oddly like a happy young man rather than an ancient boy. As for Esther, she might have been Jeanne d'Arc returned to her sheep, touched with age and gray with the ashes of a great remembrance. She wore the simple look of sainthood and unfeigned devotion. My heart was moved by the sight of her plain sweet face, weather-worn and gentle in its looks, her thin figure in its close dress, and the strong hand that clasped a shepherd's staff, and I could only hold

William in new reverence; this silent farmer-fisherman who knew, and he alone, the noble and patient heart that beat within her breast. I am not sure that they acknowledged even to themselves that they had always been lovers; they could not consent to anything so definite or pronounced; but they were happy in being together in the world. Esther was untouched by the fret and fury of life; she had lived in sunshine and rain among her silly sheep, and been refined instead of coarsened, while her touching patience with a ramping old mother, stung by the sense of defeat and mourning her lost activities, had given back a lovely self-possession, and habit of sweet temper. I had seen enough of old Mrs. Hight to know that nothing a sheep might do could vex a person who was used to the uncertainties and severities of her companionship.

❊

IX

Mrs. Hight told her daughter at once that she had enjoyed a beautiful call, and got a great many new things to think of. This was said so frankly in my hearing that it gave a consciousness of high reward, and I was indeed recompensed by the grateful look in Esther's eyes. We did not speak much together, but we understood each other. For the poor old woman did not read, and could not sew or knit with her helpless hand, and they were far from any neighbors, while her spirit was as eager in age as in youth, and expected even more from a disappointing world. She had lived to see the mortgage paid and money in the bank, and Esther's success acknowledged on every hand, and there were still a few pleasures left in life. William had his mother, and Esther had hers, and they had not seen each other for a year, though Mrs. Hight had spoken of a year's making no change in William even at his age. She must have been in the far eighties herself, but of a noble courage and persistence in the world she ruled from her stiff-backed rocking-chair.

William unloaded his gift of dried fish, each one chosen with perfect care, and Esther stood by, watching him, and then she walked across the field with us beside the wagon. I believed that I was the only one who knew their happy secret, and she blushed a little as we said good-by.

"I hope you ain't goin to feel too tired, mother's so deaf; no, I hope you won't be tired," she said kindly, speaking as if she well knew what tiredness was. We could hear the neglected sheep bleating on the hill in the next moment's silence. Then she smiled at me, a smile of noble patience, of uncomprehended sacrifice, which I can never forget. There was all the remembrance of disappointed hopes, the hardships of winter, the loneliness of single-handedness in her look, but I understood, and I love to remember her worn face and her young blue eyes.

"Good-by, William," she said gently, and William said

good-by, and gave her a quick glance, but he did not turn to look back, though I did, and waved my hand as she was putting up the bars behind us. Nor did he speak again until we had passed through the dark woods and were on our way homeward by the main road. The grave yearly visit had been changed from a hope into a happy memory.

"You can see the sea from the top of her pasture hill," said William at last.

"Can you?" I asked, with surprise.

"Yes, it's very high land; the ledges up there show very plain in clear weather from the top of our island, and there's a high upstandin' tree that makes a landmark for the fishin' grounds." And William gave a happy sigh.

When we had nearly reached the Landing, my companion looked over into the back of the wagon and saw that the piece of sailcloth was safe, with which he had covered the dried fish. "I wish we had got some trout," he said wistfully. "They always appease Almiry, and make her feel 't was worth while to go."

I stole a glance at William Blackett. We had not seen a solitary mosquito, but there was a dark stripe across his mild face, which might have been an old scar won long ago in battle.

The Foreigner

I.

One evening, at the end of August, in Dunnet Landing, I heard Mrs. Todd's firm footstep crossing the small front entry outside my door, and her conventional cough which served as a herald's trumpet, or a plain New England knock, in the harmony of our fellowship.

"Oh, please come in!" I cried, for it had been so still in the house that I supposed my friend and hostess had gone to see one of her neighbors. The first cold northeasterly storm of the season was blowing hard outside. Now and then there was a dash of great rain-drops and a flick of wet lilac leaves against the window, but I could hear that the sea was already stirred to its dark depths, and the great rollers were coming in heavily against the shore. One might well believe that Summer was coming to a sad end that night, in the darkness and rain and sudden access of autumnal cold. It seemed as if there must be danger offshore among the outer islands.

"Oh, there!" exclaimed Mrs. Todd, as she entered. "I know nothing ain't ever happened out to Green Island since the world began, but I always do worry about mother in these great gales. You know those tidal waves occur sometimes down to the West Indies, and I get dwellin' on 'em so I can't set still in my chair, nor knit a common row to a stocking. William might get mooning, out in his small bo't, and not observe how the sea was making, an' meet with some accident. Yes, I thought I'd come in and set with you if you wa'n't busy. No, I never feel any concern about 'em in winter 'cause then they're prepared, and all ashore and everything snug. William ought to keep help, as I tell him; yes, he ought to keep help."

I hastened to reassure my anxious guest by saying that Elijah Tilley had told me in the afternoon, when I came along the shore past the fish houses, that Johnny Bowden and the Captain were out at Green Island; he had seen them beating up the bay, and thought they must have put into Burnt Island cove, but one of the lobstermen brought word later that he saw them hauling out at Green Island as he came by, and Captain Bowden pointed ashore and shook his head to say that he did not mean to try to get in. "The old Miranda just managed it, but she will have to stay at home a day or two and put new patches in her sail," I ended, not without pride in so much circumstantial evidence.

Mrs. Todd was alert in a moment. "Then they'll all have a very pleasant evening," she assured me, apparently dismissing all fears of tidal waves and other sea-going disasters. "I was urging Alick Bowden to go ashore some day and see mother before cold weather. He's her own nephew; she sets a great deal by him. And Johnny's a great chum o' William's; don't you know the first day we had Johnny out 'long of us, he took an' give William his money to keep for him that he'd been a-savin', and William showed it to me an' was so affected I thought he was goin' to shed tears? 'T was a dollar an' eighty cents; yes, they'll have a beautiful evenin' all together, and like's not the sea'll be flat as a doorstep come morning."

I had drawn a large wooden rocking-chair before the fire, and Mrs. Todd was sitting there jogging herself a little, knitting fast, and wonderfully placid of countenance. There came a fresh gust of wind and rain, and we could feel the small wooden house rock and hear it creak as if it were a ship at sea.

"Lord, hear the great breakers!" exclaimed Mrs. Todd. "How they pound!—there, there! I always run of an idea that the sea knows anger these nights and gets full o' fight. I can hear the rote o' them old black ledges way down the thoroughfare. Calls up all those stormy verses in the Book o' Psalms; David he knew how old sea-goin' folks have to quake at the heart."

I thought as I had never thought before of such anxieties. The families of sailors and coastwise adventurers by sea must always be worrying about somebody, this side of the world or the other. There was hardly one of Mrs. Todd's elder acquaintances, men or women, who had not at some time or other made a sea voyage, and there was often no news until the voyagers themselves came back to bring it.

"There's a roaring high overhead, and a roaring in the deep sea," said Mrs. Todd solemnly, "and they battle together nights like this. No, I couldn't sleep; some women folks always goes right to bed an' to sleep, so's to forget, but 't ain't my way. Well, it's a blessin' we don't feel alike; there's hardly any of our folks at sea to worry about, nowadays, but I can't help my feelin's, an' I got thinking of mother all alone, if William had happened to be out lobsterin' and couldn't make the cove gettin' back."

"They will have a pleasant evening," I repeated. "Captain Bowden is the best of good company."

"Mother'll make him some pancakes for his supper, like's not," said Mrs. Todd, clicking her knitting needles and giving a pull at her yarn. Just then the old cat pushed open the un-latched door and came straight toward her mistress's lap. She was regarded severely as she stepped about and turned on the broad expanse, and then made herself into a round cushion of fur, but was not openly admonished. There was another great blast of wind overhead, and a puff of smoke came down the chimney.

"This makes me think o' the night Mis' Cap'n Tolland died," said Mrs. Todd, half to herself. "Folks used to say these gales only blew when somebody's a-dyin', or the devil was a-comin' for his own, but the worst man I ever knew died a real pretty mornin' in June."

"You have never told me any ghost stories," said I; and such was the gloomy weather and the influence of the night that I was instantly filled with reluctance to have this sugges-tion followed. I had not chosen the best of moments; just be-fore I spoke we had begun to feel as cheerful as possible. Mrs. Todd glanced doubtfully at the cat and then at me, with a strange absent look, and I was really afraid that she was going to tell me something that would haunt my thoughts on every dark stormy night as long as I lived.

"Never mind now; tell me to-morrow by daylight, Mrs. Todd," I hastened to say, but she still looked at me full of doubt and deliberation.

"Ghost stories!" she answered. "Yes, I don't know but I've heard a plenty of 'em first an' last. I was just sayin' to myself that this is like the night Mis' Cap'n Tolland died. 'T was the great line storm in September all of thirty, or maybe forty, year ago. I ain't one that keeps much account o' time."

"Tolland? That's a name I have never heard in Dunnet," I said.

"Then you haven't looked well about the old part o' the buryin' ground, no'theast corner," replied Mrs. Todd. "All their women folks lies there; the sea's got most o' the men. They were a known family o' shipmasters in early times.

Mother had a mate, Ellen Tolland, that she mourns to this day; died right in her bloom with quick consumption, but the rest o' that family was all boys but one, and older than she, an' they lived hard seafarin' lives an' all died hard. They were called very smart seamen. I've heard that when the youngest went into one o' the old shippin' houses in Boston, the head o' the firm called out to him: 'Did you say Tolland from Dunnet? That's recommendation enough for any vessel!' There was some o' them old shipmasters as tough as iron, an' they had the name o' usin' their crews very severe, but there wa'n't a man that wouldn't rather sign with 'em an' take his chances, than with the slack ones that didn't know how to meet accidents."

II.

❦

There was so long a pause, and Mrs. Todd still looked so absent-minded, that I was afraid she and the cat were growing drowsy together before the fire, and I should have no reminiscences at all. The wind struck the house again, so that we both started in our chairs and Mrs. Todd gave a curious, startled look at me. The cat lifted her head and listened too, in the silence that followed, while after the wind sank we were more conscious than ever of the awful roar of the sea. The house jarred now and then, in a strange, disturbing way.

"Yes, they'll have a beautiful evening out to the island," said Mrs. Todd again; but she did not say it gayly. I had not seen her before in her weaker moments.

"Who was Mrs. Captain Tolland?" I asked eagerly, to change the current of our thoughts.

"I never knew her maiden name; if I ever heard it, I've gone an' forgot; 't would mean nothing to me," answered Mrs. Todd.

"She was a foreigner, an' he met with her out in the Island o' Jamaica. They said she'd been left a widow with property. Land knows what become of it; she was French born, an' her first husband was a Portugee, or somethin'."

I kept silence now, a poor and insufficient question being worse than none.

"Cap'n John Tolland was the least smartest of any of 'em, but he was full smart enough, an' commanded a good brig at the time, in the sugar trade; he'd taken out a cargo o' pine lumber to the islands from somewheres up the river, an' had been loadin' for home in the port o' Kingston, an' had gone ashore that afternoon for his papers, an' remained afterwards 'long of three friends o' his, all shipmasters. They was havin' their suppers together in a tavern; 't was late in the evenin' an' they was more lively than usual, an' felt boyish; and over opposite was another house full o' company, real bright and pleasant lookin', with a lot o' lights, an' they heard somebody singin' very pretty to a guitar. They wa'n't in no go-to-meetin' condition, an' one of 'em, he slapped the table an' said, 'Le' 's go over an' hear that lady sing!' an' over they all went, good honest sailors, but three sheets in the wind, and stepped in as if they was invited, an' made their bows inside the door, an' asked if they could hear the music; they were all respectable well-dressed men. They saw the woman that had the guitar, an' there was a company a-listenin', regular highbinders all of 'em; an' there was a long table all spread out with big candlesticks like little trees o' light, and a sight o' glass an' silver ware; an' part o' the men was young officers in uniform, an' the colored folks was steppin' round servin' 'em, an' they had the lady singin'. 'T was a wasteful scene, an' a loud talkin' company, an' though they was three sheets in the wind themselves there wa'n't one o' them cap'ns but had sense to perceive it. The others had pushed back their chairs, an' their decanters an' glasses was standin' thick about, an' they was teasin' the one that was singin' as if they'd just got her in to amuse 'em. But they quieted down; one o' the young officers had beautiful manners, an' invited the four cap'ns to join 'em, very polite; 't was a kind of public house, and after they'd all heard another song, he come to consult with 'em whether they wouldn't git up and dance a hornpipe or somethin' to the lady's music.

"They was all elderly men an' shipmasters, and owned property; two of 'em was church members in good standin'," continued Mrs. Todd loftily, "an' they wouldn't lend theirselves to no such kick-shows as that, an' spite o' bein' three sheets in the wind, as I have once observed; they waved aside the tumblers of wine the young officer was pourin' out for 'em so freehanded, and said they should rather be excused. An' when they all rose, still very dignified, as I've been well informed, and made their partin' bows and was goin' out, them young sports got round 'em an' tried to prevent 'em, and they had to push an' strive considerable, but out they come. There was this Cap'n Tolland and two Cap'n Bowdens, and the fourth was my own father." (Mrs. Todd spoke slowly, as if to impress the value of her authority.) "Two of them was very religious, upright men, but they would have their night off sometimes, all o' them old-fashioned cap'ns, when they was free of business and ready to leave port.

"An' they went back to their tavern an' got their bills paid, an' set down kind o' mad with everybody by the front windows, mistrusting some o' their tavern charges, like's not, by that time, an' when they got tempered down, they watched the house over across, where the party was.

"There was a kind of a grove o' trees between the house an' the road, an' they heard the guitar a-goin' an' a-stoppin' short by turns, and pretty soon somebody began to screech, an' they saw a white dress come runnin' out through the bushes, an' tumbled over each other in their haste to offer help; an' out she come, with the guitar, cryin' into the street, and they just walked off four square with her amongst 'em, down toward the wharves where they felt more to home. They couldn't make out at first what 't was she spoke—Cap'n Lorenzo Bowden was well acquainted in Havre an' Bordeaux, an' spoke a poor quality o' French, an' she knew a little mite o' English, but not much; and they come somehow or other to discern that she was in real distress. Her husband and her children had died o' yellow fever; they'd all come up to Kingston from one o' the far Wind'ard Islands to get passage on a steamer to France, an' a negro had stole their money off her husband while he lay sick o' the fever, an' she had been befriended some, but the folks that knew about her had died too; it had been a dreadful run o' the fever that season, an' she fell at last to playin' an' singin' for hire, and for what money they'd throw to her round them harbor houses.

" 'T was a real hard case, an' when them cap'ns made out about it, there wa'n't one that meant to take leave without helpin' of her. They was pretty mellow, an' whatever they might lack o' prudence they more'n made up with charity: they didn't want to see nobody abused, an' she was sort of a pretty woman, an' they stopped in the street then an' there an' drew lots who should take her aboard, bein' all bound home. An' the lot fell to Cap'n Jonathan Bowden who did act discouraged; his vessel had but small accommodations, though he could stow a big freight, an' she was a dreadful slow sailer through bein' square as a box, an' his first wife, that was livin' then, was a dreadful jealous woman. He threw himself right onto the mercy o' Cap'n Tolland."

Mrs. Todd indulged herself for a short time in a season of calm reflection.

"I always thought they'd have done better, and more reasonable, to give her some money to pay her passage home to France, or wherever she may have wanted to go," she continued.

I nodded and looked for the rest of the story.

"Father told mother," said Mrs. Todd confidentially, "that

Cap'n Jonathan Bowden an' Cap'n John Tolland had both taken a little more than usual; I wouldn't have you think, either, that they both wasn't the best o' men, an' they was solemn as owls, and argued the matter between 'em, an' waved aside the other two when they tried to put their oars in. An' spite o' Cap'n Tolland's bein' a settled old bachelor they fixed it that he was to take the prize on his brig; she was a fast sailer, and there was a good spare cabin or two where he'd sometimes carried passengers, but he'd filled 'em with bags o' sugar on his own account an' was loaded very heavy beside. He said he'd shift the sugar an' get along somehow, an' the last the other three cap'ns saw of the party was Cap'n John handing the lady into his bo't, guitar and all, an' off they all set tow'ds their ships with their men rowin' 'em in the bright moonlight down to Port Royal where the anchorage was, an' where they all lay, goin' out with the tide an mornin' wind at break o' day. An' the others thought they heard music of the guitar, two o' the bo'ts kept well together, but it may have come from another source."

"Well; and then?" I asked eagerly after a pause. Mrs. Todd was almost laughing aloud over her knitting and nodding emphatically. We had forgotten all about the noise of the wind and sea.

"Lord bless you! he come sailing into Portland with his sugar, all in good time, an' they stepped right afore a justice o' the peace, and Cap'n John Tolland come paradin' home to Dunnet Landin' a married man. He owned one o' them thin, narrow-lookin' houses with one room each side o' the front door, and two slim black spruce spindlin' up against the front windows to make it gloomy inside. There was no horse nor cattle of course, though he owned pasture land, an' you could see rifts o' light right through the barn as you drove by. And there was a good excellent kitchen, but his sister reigned over that; she had a right to two rooms, and took the kitchen an' a bedroom that led out of it; an' bein' given no rights in the kitchen had angered the cap'n so they weren't on no kind o' speakin' terms. He preferred his old brig for comfort, but now and then, between voyages, he'd come home for a few days, just to show he was master over his part o' the house, and show Eliza she couldn't commit no trespass.

"They stayed a little while; 't was pretty spring weather, an' I used to see Cap'n John rollin' by with his arms full o' bundles from the store, lookin' as pleased and important as a boy; an' then they went right off to sea again, an' was gone a good many months. Next time he left her to live there alone, after they'd stopped at home together some weeks, an' they said she suffered from bein' at sea, but some said that the owners wouldn't have a woman aboard. 'T was before father was lost on that last voyage of his, an' he and mother went up once or twice to see them. Father said there wa'n't a mite o' harm in her, but somehow or other a sight o' prejudice arose; it may have been caused by the remarks of Eliza an' her feelin's tow'ds her brother. Even my mother had no regard for Eliza Tolland. But mother asked the cap'n's wife to come with her one evenin' to a social circle that was down to the meetin'-house vestry, so she'd get acquainted a little, an' she appeared very pretty until they started to have some singin' to the melodeon. Mari' Harris an' one o' the younger Caplin girls undertook to sing a duet, an' they sort o' flatted, an' she put her hands right up to her ears, and give a little squeal, an' went quick as could be an' give 'em the right notes, for she could read the music like plain print, an' made 'em try it over again. She was real willin' an' pleasant, but that didn't suit, an' she made faces when they got it wrong. An' then there fell a dead calm, an' we was all settin' round prim as dishes, an' my mother, that never expects ill feelin', asked her if she wouldn't sing somethin', an' up she got— poor creatur', it all seems so different to me now—an' sung a lovey little song standin' in the floor; it seemed to have something gay about it that kept a-repeatin', an' nobody could help keepin' time, an' all of a sudden she looked round at the tables and caught up a tin plate that somebody'd fetched a Washin'ton pie in, an' she begun to drum on it with her fingers like one o' them tambourines, an' went right on singin' faster an' faster, and next minute she began to dance a little pretty dance between the verses, just as light and pleasant as a child. You couldn't help seein' how pretty 't was; we all got to trottin' a foot, an' some o' the men clapped their hands quite loud, a-keepin' time, 't was so catchin', an' seemed so natural to her. There wa'n't one of 'em but enjoyed it; she just tried to do her part, an' some urged her on, till she stopped with a little twirl of her skirts an' went to her place again by mother. And I can see mother now, reachin' over an' smilin' an' pattin' her hand.

"But next day there was an awful scandal goin' in the parish, an' Mari' Harris reproached my mother to her face, an' I never wanted to see her since, but I've had to a good many times. I said Mis' Tolland didn't intend no impropriety—I reminded her of David's dancin' before the Lord; but she said such a man as David never would have thought o' dancin' right there in the Orthodox vestry, and she felt I spoke with irreverence.

"And next Sunday Mis' Tolland come walkin' into our meeting, but I must say she acted like a cat in a strange garret, and went right out down the aisle with her head in the air, from the pew Deacon Caplin had showed her into. 'T was just in the beginning of the long prayer. I wished she'd stayed through, whatever her reasons were. Whether she'd expected somethin' different, or misunderstood some o' the pastor's remarks, or what 't was, I don't really feel able to explain, but she kind o' declared war, at least folks thought so, an' war 't was from that time. I see she was cryin', or had been, as she passed by me; perhaps bein' in meetin' was what had power to make her feel homesick and strange.

"Cap'n John Tolland was away fittin' out; that next week he come home to see her and say farewell. He was lost with his ship in the Straits of Malacca, and she lived there alone in the old house a few months longer till she died. He left her well off; 't was said he hid his money about the house and she knew where 't was. Oh, I expect you've heard that story told over an' over twenty times, since you've been here at the Landin'?"

"Never one word," I insisted.

"It was a good while ago," explained Mrs. Todd, with reassurance. "Yes, it all happened a great while ago."

III.

At this moment, with a sudden flaw of the wind, some wet twigs outside blew against the window panes and made a noise like a distressed creature trying to get in. I started with sudden fear, and so did the cat, but Mrs. Todd knitted away and did not even look over her shoulder.

"She was a good-looking woman; yes, I always thought Mis' Tolland was good-looking, though she had, as was reasonable, a sort of foreign cast, and she spoke very broken English, no better than a child. She was always at work about her house, or settin' at a front window with her sewing; she was a beautiful hand to embroider. Sometimes, summer evenings, when the windows was open, she'd set an' drum on her guitar, but I don't know as I ever heard her sing but once after the cap'n went away. She appeared very happy about havin' him, and took on dreadful at partin' when he was down here on the wharf, going back to Portland by boat to take ship for that last v'y'ge. He acted kind of ashamed, Cap'n John did; folks about here ain't so much accustomed to show their feelings. The whistle had blown an' they was waitin' for him to get aboard, an' he was put to it to know what to do and treated her very affectionate in spite of all impatience; but mother happened to be there and she went an' spoke, and I remember what a comfort she seemed to be. Mis' Tolland clung to her then, and she wouldn't give a glance after the boat when it started, though the captain was very eager a-wavin' to her. She wanted mother to come home with her an' wouldn't let go her hand, and mother had just come in to stop all night with me an' had plenty o' time ashore, which didn't always happen, so they walked off together, an' 't was some considerable time before she got back.

"'I want you to neighbor with that poor lonesome creatur',' says mother to me, lookin' reproachful. 'She's a stranger in a strange land,' says mother. 'I want you to make her have a sense that somebody feels kind to her.'

" 'Why, since that time she flaunted out o' meetin', folks have felt she liked other ways better'n our'n,' says I. I was provoked, because I'd had a nice supper ready, an' mother'd let it wait so long 't was spoiled. 'I hope you'll like your supper!' I told her. I was dreadful ashamed afterward of speakin' so to mother.

" 'What consequence is my supper?' says she to me; mother can be very stern—'or your comfort or mine, beside letting a foreign person an' a stranger feel so desolate; she's done the best a woman could do in her lonesome place, and she asks nothing of anybody except a little common kindness. Think if 't was you in a foreign land!'

"And mother set down to drink her tea, an' I set down humbled enough over by the wall to wait till she finished. An' I did think it all over, an' next day I never said nothin', but I put on my bonnet, and went to see Mis' Cap'n Tolland, if 't was only for mother's sake. 'T was about three quarters of a mile up the road here, beyond the school-house. I forgot to tell you that the cap'n had bought out his sister's right at three or four times what 't was worth, to save trouble, so they'd got clear o' her, an' I went round into the side yard sort o' friendly an' sociable, rather than stop an' deal with the knocker an' the front door. It looked so pleasant an pretty I was glad I come; she had set a little table for supper, though 't was still early, with a white cloth on it, right out under an old apple tree close by the house. I noticed 't was same as with me at home, there was only one plate. She was just coming out with a dish; you couldn't see the door nor the table from the road.

"In the few weeks she'd been there she'd got some bloomin' pinks an' other flowers next the doorstep. Somehow it looked as if she'd known how to make it homelike for the cap'n. She asked me to set down; she was very polite, but she looked very mournful, and I spoke of mother, an' she put down her dish and caught holt o' me with both hands an' said my mother was an angel. When I see the tears in her eyes 't was all right between us, and we were always friendly after that, and mother had us come out and make a little visit that summer; but she come a foreigner and she went a foreigner, and never was anything but a stranger among our folks. She taught me a sight o' things about herbs I never knew before nor since; she was well acquainted with the virtues o' plants. She'd act awful secret about some things too, an' used to work charms for herself sometimes, an' some o' the neighbors

told to an' fro after she died that they knew enough not to
provoke her, but 't was all nonsense; 't is the believin' in such
things that causes 'em to be any harm, an' so I told 'em,"
confided Mrs. Todd contemptuously. "That first night I
stopped to tea with her she'd cooked some eggs with some
herb or other sprinkled all through, and 't was she that first
led me to discern mushrooms; an' she went right down on her
knees in my garden here when she saw I had my different officious herbs. Yes, 't was she that learned me the proper use
o' parsley too; she was a beautiful cook."

Mrs. Todd stopped talking, and rose, putting the cat gently
in the chair, while she went away to get another stick of
apple-tree wood. It was not an evening when one wished to
let the fire go down, and we had a splendid bank of bright
coals. I had always wondered where Mrs. Todd had got such
an unusual knowledge of cookery, of the varieties of
mushrooms, and the use of sorrel as a vegetable, and other
blessings of that sort. I had long ago learned that she could
vary her omelettes like a child of France, which was indeed a
surprise in Dunnet Landing.

IV.

❈

All these revelations were of the deepest interest, and I was ready with a question as soon as Mrs. Todd came in and had well settled the fire and herself and the cat again.

"I wonder why she never went back to France, after she was left alone?"

"She come here from the French islands," explained Mrs. Todd. "I asked her once about her folks, an' she said they were all dead; 't was the fever took 'em. She made this her home, lonesome as 't was; she told me she hadn't been in France since she was 'so small,' and measured me off a child o' six. She'd lived right out in the country before, so that part wa'n't unusual to her. Oh yes, there was something very strange about her, and she hadn't been brought up in high circles nor nothing o' that kind. I think she'd been really pleased to have the cap'n marry her an' give her a good home, after all she'd passed through, and leave her free with his money an' all that. An' she got over bein' so strange-looking to me after a while, but 't was a very singular expression: she wore a fixed smile that wa'n't a smile; there wa'n't no light behind it, same's a lamp can't shine if it ain't lit. I don't know just how to express it, 't was a sort of made countenance."

One could not help thinking of Sir Philip Sidney's phrase, "A made countenance, between simpering and smiling."

"She took it hard, havin' the captain go off on that last voyage," Mrs. Todd went on. "She said somethin' told her when they was partin' that he would never come back. He was lucky to speak a home-bound ship this side o' the Cape o' Good Hope, an' got a chance to send her a letter, an' that cheered her up. You often felt as if you was dealin' with a child's mind, for all she had so much information that other folks hadn't. I was a sight younger than I be now, and she made me imagine new things, and I got interested watchin' her an' findin' out what she had to say, but you couldn't get

to no affectionateness with her. I used to blame me sometimes; we used to be real good comrades goin' off for an afternoon, but I never gave her a kiss till the day she laid in
her coffin and it come to my heart there wa'n't no one else to
do it."

"And Captain Tolland died," I suggested after a while.

"Yes, the cap'n was lost," said Mrs. Todd, "and of course
word didn't come for a good while after it happened. The letter come from the owners to my uncle, Cap'n Lorenzo Bowden, who was in charge of Cap'n Tolland's affairs at home,
and he come right up for me an' said I must go with him to
the house. I had known what it was to be a widow, myself,
for near a year, an' there was plenty o' widow women along
this coast that the sea had made desolate, but I never saw a
heart break as I did then.

" 'T was this way: we walked together along the road, me
an' uncle Lorenzo. You know how it leads straight from just
above the schoolhouse to the brook bridge, and their house
was just this side o' the brook bridge on the left hand; the
cellar's there now, and a couple or three good-sized gray
birches growin' in it. And when we come near enough I saw
that the best room, this way, where she most never set, was
all lighted up, and the curtains up so that the light shone
bright down the road, and as we walked, those lights would
dazzle and dazzle in my eyes, and I could hear the guitar
a-goin', an' she was singin'. She heard our steps with her quick
ears and come running to the door with her eyes a-shinin',
an' all that set look gone out of her face, an' begun to talk
French, gay as a bird, an' shook hands and behaved very
pretty an' girlish, sayin' 't was her fête day. I didn't know
what she meant then. And she had gone an' put a wreath o'
flowers on her hair an' wore a handsome gold chain that the
cap'n had given her; an' there she was, poor creatur', makin'
believe have a party all alone in her best room; 't was prim
enough to discourage a person, with too many chairs set close
to the walls, just as the cap'n's mother had left it, but she had
put sort o' long garlands on the walls, droopin' very graceful,
and a sight of green boughs in the corners, till it looked
lovely, and all lit up with a lot o' candles."

"Oh dear!" I sighed. "Oh, Mrs. Todd, what did you do?"

"She beheld our countenances," answered Mrs. Todd
solemnly. "I expect they was telling everything plain enough,
but Cap'n Lorenzo spoke the sad words to her as if he had
been her father; and she wavered a minute and then over she

went on the floor before we could catch hold of her, and then we tried to bring her to herself and failed, and at last we carried her upstairs, an' I told uncle to run down and put out the lights, and then go fast as he could for Mrs. Begg, being very experienced in sickness, an' he so did. I got off her clothes and her poor wreath, and cried as I done it. We both stayed there that night and the doctor said 't was a shock when he come in the morning; he'd been over to Black Island an' had to stay all night with a very sick child."

"You said that she lived alone some time after the news came," I reminded Mrs. Todd then.

"Oh yes, dear," answered my friend sadly, "but it wa'n't what you'd call livin'; no, it was only dyin', though at a snail's pace. She never went out again those few months, but for a while she could manage to get about the house a little, and do what was needed, an' I never let two days go by without seein' her or hearin' from her. She never took much notice as I came an' went except to answer if I asked her anything. Mother was the one who gave her the only comfort."

"What was that?" I asked softly.

"She said that anybody in such trouble ought to see their minister, mother did, and one day she spoke to Mis' Tolland, and found that the poor soul had been believin' all the time that there weren't any priests here. We'd come to know she was a Catholic by her beads and all, and that had set some narrow minds against her. And mother explained it just as she would to a child: and uncle Lorenzo sent word right off somewheres up river by a packet that was bound up the bay, and the first o' the week a priest come by the boat, an' uncle Lorenzo was on the wharf 'tendin' to some business; so they just come up for me, and I walked with him to show him the house. He was a kind-hearted old man; he looked so benevolent an' fatherly I could ha' stopped an' told him my own troubles; yes, I was satisfied when I first saw his face, an' when poor Mis' Tolland beheld him enter the room, she went right down on her knees and clasped her hands together to him as if he'd come to save her life, and he lifted her up and blessed her, an' I left 'em together, and slipped out into the open field and walked there in sight so if they needed to call me, and I had my own thoughts. At last I saw him at the door; he had to catch the return boat. I meant to walk back with him and offer him some supper, but he said no, and said he was comin' again if needed, and signed me to go into the house to her, and shook his head in a way that meant he understood everything. I can see him now; he walked with a cane, rather tired and feeble; I wished somebody would come along, so's to carry him down to the shore.

"Mis' Tolland looked up at me with a new look when I went in, an' she even took hold o' my hand and kept it. He had put some oil on her forehead, but nothing anybody could do would keep her alive very long; 't was his medicine for the soul rather 'n the body. I helped her to bed, and next morning she couldn't get up to dress her, and that was Monday, and she began to fail, and 't was Friday night she died." (Mrs. Todd spoke with unusual haste and lack of detail.) "Mrs. Begg and I watched with her, and made everything nice and proper, and after all the ill will there was a good number gathered to the funeral. 'T was in Reverend Mr. Bascom's day, and he done very well in his prayer, considering he couldn't fill in with mentioning all the near connections by name as was his habit. He spoke very feeling about her being a stranger and twice widowed, and all he said about her being reared among the heathen was to observe that there might be roads leadin' up to the New Jerusalem from various points. I says to myself that I guessed quite a number must ha' reached there that wa'n't able to set out from Dunnet Landin'!"

Mrs. Todd gave an odd little laugh as she bent toward the firelight to pick up a dropped stitch in her knitting, and then I heard a heartfelt sigh.

"'T was most forty years ago," she said; "most everybody's gone a'ready that was there that day."

V.

Suddenly Mrs. Todd gave an energetic shrug of her shoulders, and a quick look at me, and I saw that the sails of her narrative were filled with a fresh breeze.

"Uncle Lorenzo, Cap'n Bowden that I have referred to"—

"Certainly!" I agreed with eager expectation.

"He was the one that had been left in charge of Cap'n John Tolland's affairs, and had now come to be of unforeseen importance.

"Mrs. Begg an' I had stayed in the house both before an' after Mis' Tolland's decease, and she was now in haste to be done, having affairs to call her home; but uncle come to me as the exercises was beginning, and said he thought I'd better remain at the house while they went to the buryin' ground. I couldn't understand his reasons, an' I felt disappointed, bein' as near to her as most anybody; 't was rough weather, so mother couldn't get in, and didn't even hear Mis' Tolland was gone till next day. I just nodded to satisfy him, 't wa'n't no time to discuss anything. Uncle seemed flustered; he'd gone out deep-sea fishin' the day she died, and the storm I told you of rose very sudden, so they got blown off way down the coast beyond Monhegan, and he'd just got back in time to dress himself and come.

"I set there in the house after I'd watched her away down the straight road far's I could see from the door; 't was a little short walkin' funeral an' a cloudy sky, so everything looked dull an' gray, an' it crawled along all in one piece, same's walking funerals do, an' I wondered how it ever come to the Lord's mind to let her begin down among them gay islands all heat and sun, and end up here among the rocks with a north wind blowin'. 'T was a gale that begun the afternoon before she died, and had kept blowin' off an' on ever since. I'd thought more than once how glad I should be to get home an' out o' sound o' them black spruces a-beatin' an' scratchin' at the front windows.

"I set to work pretty soon to put the chairs back, an' set outdoors some that was borrowed, an' I went out in the kitchen, an' I made up a good fire in case somebody come an' wanted a cup o' tea; but I didn't expect anyone to travel way back to the house unless 't was uncle Lorenzo. 'T was growin' so chilly that I fetched some kindlin' wood and made fires in both the fore rooms. Then I set down an' begun to feel as usual, and I got my knittin' out of a drawer. You can't be sorry for a poor creatur' that's come to the end o' all her troubles; my only discomfort was I thought I'd ought to feel worse at losin' her than I did; I was younger then than I be now. And as I set there, I begun to hear some long notes o' dronin' music from upstairs that chilled me to the bone."

Mrs. Todd gave a hasty glance at me.

"Quick's I could gather me, I went right upstairs to see what 't was," she added eagerly, "an' 't was just what I might ha' known. She'd always kept her guitar hangin' right against the wall in her room; 't was tied by a blue ribbon, and there was a window left wide open; the wind was veerin' a good deal, an' it slanted in and searched the room. The strings was jarrin' yet.

" 'T was growin' pretty late in the afternoon, an' I begun to feel lonesome as I shouldn't now, and I was disappointed at having to stay there, the more I thought it over, but after a while I saw Cap'n Lorenzo polin' back up the road all alone, and when he come nearer I could see he had a bundle under his arm and had shifted his best black clothes for his every-day ones. I ran out and put some tea into the teapot and set it back on the stove to draw, an' when he come in I reached down a little jug o' spirits—Cap'n Tolland had left his house well provisioned as if his wife was goin' to put to sea same's himself, an' then she'd gone an' left it. There was some cake that Mis' Begg an' I had made the day before. I thought that uncle an' me had a good right to the funeral supper, even if there wa'n't anyone to join us. I was lookin' forward to my cup o' tea; 't was beautiful tea out of a green lacquered chest that I've got now."

"You must have felt very tired," said I, eagerly listening.

"I was 'most beat out, with watchin' an' tendin' and all," answered Mrs. Todd, with as much sympathy in her voice as if she were speaking of another person. "But I called out to uncle as he came in, 'Well, I expect it's all over now, an' we've all done what we could. I thought we'd better have some tea or somethin' before we go home. Come right out in the kitchen, sir,' says I, never thinking but we only had to let the fires out and lock up everything safe an' eat our refreshment, an' go home.

" 'I want both of us to stop here tonight,' says uncle, looking at me very important.

" 'Oh, what for?' says I, kind o' fretful.

" 'I've got my proper reasons,' says uncle. 'I'll see you well satisfied, Almira. Your tongue ain't so easy-goin' as some o' the women folks, an' there's property here to take charge of that you don't know nothin' at all about.'

" 'What do you mean?' says I.

" 'Cap'n Tolland acquainted me with his affairs; he hadn't no sort o' confidence in nobody but me an' his wife, after he was tricked into signin' that Portland note, an' lost money. An' she didn't know nothin' about business; but what he didn't take to sea to be sunk with him he's hid somewhere in this house. I expect Mis' Tolland may have told you where she kept things?' said uncle.

"I see he was dependin' a good deal on my answer," said Mrs. Todd, "but I had to disappoint him; no, she had never said nothin' to me.

" 'Well, then, we've got to make a search, says he, with considerable relish; but he was all tired and worked up, and we set down to the table, an' he had somethin', an' I took my desired cup o' tea, and then I begun to feel more interested.

" 'Where you goin' to look first?' says I, but he give me a short look an' made no answer, an begun to mix me a very small portion out of the jug, in another glass. I took it to please him; he said I looked tired, speakin' real fatherly, and I did feel better for it, and we set talkin' a few minutes, an' then he started for the cellar, carrying an old ship's lantern he fetched out o' the stairway an' lit.

" 'What are you lookin' for, some kind of a chist?' I inqured, and he said yes. All of a sudden it come to me to ask who was the heirs; Eliza Tolland, Cap'n John's own sister, had never demeaned herself to come near the funeral, and uncle Lorenzo faced right about and begun to laugh, sort o' pleased. I thought queer of it; 't wa'n't what he'd taken, which would be nothin' to an old weathered sailor like him.

" 'Who's the heir?' says I the second time.

" 'Why, it's *you*, Almiry,' says he; and I was so took aback I set right down on the turn o' the cellar stairs.

" 'Yes 't is,' said Uncle Lorenzo. 'I'm glad of it too. Some thought she didn't have no sense but foreign sense, an' a poor stock o' that, but she said you was friendly to her, an' one day after she got news of Tolland's death, an' I had fetched up his will that left everything to her, she said she was goin' to make a writin', so's you could have things after she was gone, an' she give five hundred to me for bein' executor. Square Pease fixed up the paper, an' she signed it; it's all accordin' to law.' "There, I begun to cry," said Mrs. Todd; "I couldn't help it. I wished I had her back again to do somethin' for, an' to make her know I felt sisterly to her more'n I'd ever showed, an' it come over me 't was all too late, an' I cried the more, till uncle showed impatience, an' I got up an' stumbled along down cellar with my apern to my eyes the greater part of the time.

" 'I'm goin' to have a clean search,' says he; 'you hold the light.' An' I held it and he rummaged in the arches an' under the stairs, an' over in some old closet where he reached out bottles an' stone jugs an' canted some kags an' one or two casks, an' chuckled well when he heard there was somethin' inside—but there wa'n't nothin' to find but things usual in a cellar, an' then the old lantern was givin' out an' we come away.

" 'He spoke to me of a chist, Cap'n Tolland did,' says uncle in a whisper. 'He said a good sound chist was as safe a bank as there was, an' I beat him out of such nonsense, 'count o' fire an' other risks.' 'There's no chist in the rooms above,' says I; 'no, uncle, there ain't no sea-chist, for I've been here long enough to see what there was to be seen. Yet he wouldn't feel contented till he'd mounted up into the top-loft; 't was one o' them single, hip-roofed houses that don't give proper accommodation for a real garret, like Cap'n Little-page's down here at the Landin'. There was broken furniture and rubbish, an' he let down a terrible sight o' dust into the front entry, but sure enough there wasn't no chist. I had it all to sweep up next day.

" 'He must have took it away to sea,' says I to the cap'n, an' even then he didn't want to agree, but we was both beat out. I told him where I'd always seen Mis' Tolland get her money from, and we found much as a hundred dollars there in an old red morocco wallet. Cap'n John had been gone a good while a'ready, and she had spent what she needed. 'T was in an old desk o' his in the settin' room that we found the wallet."

"At the last minute he may have taken his money to sea," I suggested.

"Oh yes," agreed Mrs. Todd. "He did take considerable to make his venture to bring home, as was customary, an' that was drowned with him as uncle agreed; but he had other property in shipping, and a thousand dollars invested in Portland in a cordage shop, but 't was about the time shipping begun to decay, and the cordage shop failed, and in the end I wa'n't so rich as I thought I was goin' to be for those few minutes on the cellar stairs. There was an auction that accumulated something. Old Mis' Tolland, the cap'n's mother, had heired some good furniture from a sister: there was above thirty chairs in all, and they're apt to sell well. I got over a thousand dollars when we come to settle up, and I made uncle take his five hundred; he was getting along in years and had met with losses in navigation, and he left it back to me when he died, so I had a real good lift. It all lays in the bank over to Rockland, and I draw my interest fall an' spring, with the little Mr. Todd was able to leave me; but that's kind o' sacred money; 't was earnt and saved with the hope o' youth, an' I'm very particular what I spend it for. Oh yes, what with ownin' my house, I've been enabled to get along very well, with prudence!" said Mrs. Todd contentedly.

"But there was the house and land," I asked—"what became of that part of the property?"

Mrs. Todd looked into the fire, and a shadow of disapproval flitted over her face.

"Poor old uncle!" she said, "he got childish about the matter. I was hoping to sell at first, and I had an offer, but he always run of an idea that there was more money hid away, and kept wanting me to delay; an' he used to go up there all alone and search, and dig in the cellar, empty an' bleak as 't was in winter weather or any time. An' he'd come and tell me he'd dreamed he found gold behind a stone in the cellar wall, or somethin.' And one night we all see the light o' fire up that way, an' the whole Landin' took the road, and run to look, and the Tolland property was all in a light blaze. I expect the old gentleman had dropped fire about; he said he'd been up there to see if everything was safe in the afternoon. As for the land, 't was so poor that everybody used to have a joke that the Tolland boys preferred to farm the sea instead. It's 'most all grown up to bushes now where it ain't poor water grass in the low places. There's some upland that has a pretty view, after you cross the brook bridge. Years an' years after she died, there was some o' her flowers used to come up an' bloom in the door garden. I brought two or three that

was unusual down here; they always come up and remind me
of her, constant as the spring. But I never did want to fetch
home that guitar, some way or 'nother; I wouldn't let it go at
the auction, either. It was hangin' right there in the house
when the fire took place. I've got some o' her other little
things scattered about the house: that picture on the mantelpiece belonged to her."

I had often wondered where such a picture had come
from, and why Mrs. Todd had chosen it; it was a French
print of the statue of the Empress Josephine in the Savane at
old Fort Royal, in Martinique.

VI.

Mrs. Todd drew her chair closer to mine; she held the cat and her knitting with one hand as she moved, but the cat was so warm and so sound asleep that she only stretched a lazy paw in spite of what must have felt like a slight earthquake. Mrs. Todd began to speak almost in a whisper.

"I ain't told you all," she continued; "no, I haven't spoken of all to but very few. The way it came was this," she said solemnly, and then stopped to listen to the wind, and sat for a moment in deferential silence, as if she waited for the wind to speak first. The cat suddenly lifted her head with quick excitement and gleaming eyes, and her mistress was leaning forward toward the fire with an arm laid on either knee, as if they were consulting the glowing coals for some augury. Mrs. Todd looked like an old prophetess as she sat there with the firelight shining on her strong face; she was posed for some great painter. The woman with the cat was as unconscious and as mysterious as any sibyl of the Sistine Chapel.

"There, that's the last struggle o' the gale," said Mrs. Todd, nodding her head with impressive certainty and still looking into the bright embers of the fire. "You'll see!" She gave me another quick glance, and spoke in a low tone as if we might be overheard.

" 'T was such a gale as this the night Mis' Tolland died. She appeared more comfortable the first o' the evenin'; and Mrs. Begg was more spent than I, bein' older, and a beautiful nurse that was the first to see and think of everything, but perfectly quiet an' never asked a useless question. You remember her funeral when you first come to the Landing? And she consented to goin' an' havin' a good sleep while she could, and left me one o' those good little pewter lamps that burnt whale oil an' made plenty o' light in the room, but not too bright to be disturbin'.'

"Poor Mis' Tolland had been distressed the night before, an' all that day, but as night come on she grew more and more easy, an' was layin' there asleep; 't was like settin' by any sleepin' person, and I had none but usual thoughts. When the wind lulled and the rain, I could hear the seas, though more distant than this, and I don' know's I observed any other sound than what the weather made; 't was a very solemn feelin' night. I set close by the bed; there was times she looked to find somebody when she was awake. The light was on her face, so I could see her plain; there was always times when she wore a look that made her seem a stranger you'd never set eyes on before. I did think what a world it was that her an' me should have come together so, and she have nobody but Dunnet Landin' folks about her in her extremity. 'You're one o' the stray ones, poor creatur',' I said. I remember those very words passin' through my mind, but I saw reason to be glad she had some comforts, and didn't lack friends at the last, though she'd seen misery an' pain. I was glad she was quiet; all day she'd been restless, and we couldn't understand what she wanted from her French speech. We had the window open to give her air, an' now an' then a gust would strike that guitar that was on the wall and set it swinging by the blue ribbon, and soundin' as if somebody begun to play it. I come near takin' it down, but you never know what'll fret a sick person an' put 'em on the rack, an' that guitar was one o' the few things she'd brought with her."

I nodded assent, and Mrs. Todd spoke still lower.

"I set there close by the bed; I'd been through a good deal for some days back, and I thought I might's well be droppin' asleep too, bein' a quick person to wake. She looked to me as if she might last a day longer, certain, now she'd got more comfortable, but I was real tired, an' sort o' cramped as watchers will get, an' a fretful feeling begun to creep over me such as they often do have. If you give way, there ain't no support for the sick person; they can't count on no composure o' their own. Mis' Tolland moved then, a little restless, an' I forgot me quick enough, an' begun to hum out a little part of a hymn tune just to make her feel everything was as usual an' not wake up into a poor uncertainty. All of a sudden she set right up in bed with her eyes wide open, an' I stood an' put my arm behind her; she hadn't moved like that for days. And she reached out both her arms toward the door, an' I looked the way she was lookin', an' I see someone was standin' there against the dark. No, 't wa'n't Mis' Begg; 't was somebody a good deal shorter than Mis' Begg. The lamplight struck across the room between us. I couldn't tell the shape, but 't was a woman's dark face lookin' right at us; 't wa'n't but an instant I could see. I felt dreadful cold, and my head begun to swim; I thought the light went out; 't wa'n't but an instant, as I say, an' when my sight come back I couldn't see nothing there. I was one that didn't know what it was to faint away, no matter what happened; time was I felt above it in others, but 't was somethin' that made poor human natur' quail. I saw very plain while I could see; 't was a pleasant enough face, shaped somethin' like Mis' Tolland's, and a kind of expectin' look.

"No, I don't expect I was asleep," Mrs. Todd assured me quietly, after a moment's pause, though I had not spoken. She gave a heavy sigh before she went on. I could see that the recollection moved her in the deepest way.

"I suppose if I hadn't been so spent an' quavery with long watchin', I might have kept my head an' observed much better," she added humbly; "but I see all I could bear. I did try to act calm, an' I laid Mis' Tolland down on her pillow, an' I was a-shakin' as I done it. All she did was to look up to me so satisfied and sort o' questioning, an' I looked back to her.

" 'You saw her, didn't you?' she says to me, speakin' perfectly reasonable. ' 'T is my mother,' she says again, very feeble, but lookin' straight up at me, kind of surprised with the pleasure, and smiling as if she saw I was overcome, an' would have said more if she could, but we had hold of hands. I see then her change was comin', but I didn't call Mis' Begg, nor make no uproar. I felt calm then, an' lifted to somethin' different as I never was since. She opened her eyes just as she was goin'—

" 'You saw her, didn't you?' she said the second time, an' I says, 'Yes, dear, I did; you ain't never goin' to feel strange an' lonesome no more.' An' then in a few quiet minutes 't was all over. I felt they'd gone away together. No, I wa'n't alarmed afterward; 't was just that one moment I couldn't live under, but I never called it beyond reason I should see the other watcher. I saw plain enough there was somebody there with me in the room.

VII.

"'T was just such a night as this Mis' Tolland died," repeated Mrs. Todd, returning to her usual tone and leaning back comfortably in her chair as she took up her knitting. "'T was just such a night as this. I've told the circumstances to but very few; but I don't call it beyond reason. When folks is goin' 't is all natural, and only common things can jar upon the mind. You know plain enough there's somethin' beyond this world; the doors stand wide open. There's somethin' of us that must still live on; we've got to join both worlds together an' live in one but for the other. The doctor said that to me one day, an' I never could forget it; he said 't was in one o' his old doctor's books."

We sat together in silence in the warm little room; the rain dropped heavily from the eaves, and the sea still roared, but the high wind had done blowing. We heard the far complaining fog horn of a steamer up the Bay.

"There goes the Boston boat out, pretty near on time," said Mrs. Todd with satisfaction. "Sometimes these late August storms'll sound a good deal worse than they really be. I do hate to hear the poor steamers callin' when they're bewildered in thick nights in winter, comin' on the coast. Yes, there goes the boat; they'll find it rough at sea, but the storm's all over."

The Queen's Twin

I.

❀

The coast of Maine was in former years brought so near to foreign shores by its busy fleet of ships that among the older men and women one still finds a surprising proportion of travelers. Each seaward-stretching headland with its high-set houses, each island of a single farm, has sent its spies to view many a Land of Eshcol; one may see plain, contented old faces at the windows, whose eyes have looked at far-away ports and known the splendors of the Eastern world. They shame the easy voyager of the North Atlantic and the Mediterranean; they have rounded the Cape of Good Hope and braved the angry seas of Cape Horn in small wooden ships; they have brought up their hardy boys and girls on narrow decks; they were among the last of the Northmen's children to go adventuring to unknown shores. More than this one cannot give to a young State for its enlightenment; the sea captains and the captains' wives of Maine knew something of the wide world, and never mistook their native parishes for the whole instead of a part thereof; they knew not only Thomaston and Castine and Portland, but London and Bristol and Bordeaux, and the strange-mannered harbors of the China Sea.

One September day, when I was nearly at the end of a summer spent in a village called Dunnet Landing, on the Maine coast, my friend Mrs. Todd, in whose house I lived, came home from a long, solitary stroll in the wild pastures, with an eager look as if she were just starting on a hopeful quest instead of returning. She brought a little basket with blackberries enough for supper, and held it towards me so that I could see that there were also some late and surprising raspberries sprinkled on top, but she made no comment upon her wayfaring. I could tell plainly that she had something very important to say.

"You haven't brought home a leaf of anything," I ventured

to this practiced herb-gatherer. "You were saying yesterday that the witch hazel might be in bloom."

"I dare say, dear," she answered in a'lofty manner; "I ain't goin' to say it wasn't; I ain't much concerned either way 'bout the facts o' witch hazel. Truth is, I've been off visitin'; there's an old Indian footpath leadin' over towards the Back Shore through the great heron swamp that anybody can't travel over all summer. You have to seize your time some day just now, while the low ground's summer-dried as it is to-day, and before the fall rains set in. I never thought of it till I was out o' sight o' home, and I says to myself, 'To-day's the day, certain!' and stepped along smart as I could. Yes, I've been visitin'. I did get into one spot that was wet under-foot before I noticed; you wait till I get me a pair o' dry woolen stockings, in case of cold, and I'll come an' tell ye."

Mrs. Todd disappeared. I could see that something had deeply interested her. She might have fallen in with either the sea-serpent or the lost tribes of Israel, such was her air of mystery and satisfaction. She had been away since just before mid-morning, and as I sat waiting by my window I saw the last red glow of autumn sunshine flare along the gray rocks of the shore and leave them cold again, and touch the far sails of some coast-wise schooners so that they stood like golden houses on the sea.

I was left to wonder longer than I liked. Mrs. Todd was making an evening fire and putting things in train for supper; presently she returned, still looking warm and cheerful after her long walk.

"There's a beautiful view from a hill over where I've been," she told me; "yes, there's a beautiful prospect of land and sea. You wouldn't discern the hill from any distance, but 't is the pretty situation of it that counts. I sat there a long spell, and I did wish for you. No, I didn't know a word about goin' when I set out this morning" (as if I had openly reproached her!); "I only felt one o' them travelin' fits comin' on, an' I ketched up my little basket; I didn't know but I might turn and come back time for dinner. I thought it wise to set out your luncheon for you in case I didn't. Hope you had all you wanted; yes, I hope you had enough."

"Oh, yes, indeed," said I. My landlady was always pecu-liarly bountiful in her supplies when she left me to fare for myself, as if she made a sort of peace-offering or affectionate apology.

"You know that hill with the old house right on top, over

beyond the heron swamp? You'll excuse me for explainin'," Mrs. Todd began, "but you ain't so apt to strike inland as you be to go right along shore. You know that hill; there's a path leadin' right over to it that you have to look sharp to find nowaways; it belonged to the up-country Indians when they had to make a carry to the landing here to get to the out' islands. I've heard the old folks say that there used to be a place across a ledge where they'd worn a deep track with their moccasin feet, but I never could find it. 'T is so overgrown in some places that you keep losin' the path in the bushes and findin' it as you can; but it runs pretty straight considerin' the lay o' the land, and I keep my eye on the sun and the moss that grows one side o' the tree trunks. Some brook's been choked up and the swamp's bigger than it used to be. Yes; I did get in deep enough, one place!"

I showed the solicitude that I felt. Mrs. Todd was no longer young, and in spite of her strong, great frame and spirited behavior, I knew that certain ills were apt to seize upon her, and would end some day by leaving her lame and ailing.

"Don't you go to worryin' about me," she insisted, "settin' still's the only way the Evil One'll ever get the upper hand o' me. Keep me movin' enough, an' I'm twenty year old summer an' winter both. I don't know why 't is, but I've never happened to mention the one I've been to see. I don't know why I never happened to speak the name of Abby Martin, for I often give her a thought, but 't is a dreadful out-o'-the-way place where she lives, and I haven't seen her myself for three or four years. She's a real good interesting woman, and we're well acquainted; she's nigher mother's age than mine, but she's very young feeling. She made me a nice cup o' tea, and I don't know but I should have stopped all night if I could have got word to you not to worry."

Then there was a serious silence before Mrs. Todd spoke again to make a formal announcement.

"She is the Queen's Twin," and Mrs. Todd looked steadily to see how I might bear the great surprise.

"The Queen's Twin?" I repeated.

"Yes, she's come to feel a real interest in the Queen, and anybody can see how natural 't is. They were born the very same day, and you would be astonished to see what a number o' other things have corresponded. She was speaking o' some o' the facts to me to-day, an' you'd think she'd never done nothing but read history. I see how earnest she was about it as I never did before. I've often and often heard her allude to the facts, but now she's got to be old and the hurry's over with her work, she's come to live a good deal in her thoughts, as folks often do, and I tell you 't is a sight o' company for her. If you want to hear about Queen Victoria, why Mis' Abby Martin 'll tell you everything. And the prospect from that hill I spoke of is as beautiful as anything in this world; 't is worth while your goin' over to see her just for that."

"When can you go again?" I demanded eagerly.

"I should say to-morrow," answered Mrs. Todd; "yes, I should say to-morrow; but I expect 't would be better to take one day to rest, in between. I considered that question as I was comin' home, but I hurried so that there wa'n't much time to think. It's a dreadful long way to go with a horse; you have to go 'most as far as the old Bowden place an' turn off to the left, a master long, rough road, and then you have to turn right round as soon as you get there if you mean to get home before nine o'clock at night. But to strike across country from here, there's plenty o' time in the shortest day, and you can have a good hour or two's visit beside; 't ain't but a very few miles, and it's pretty all the way along. There used to be a few good families over there, but they've died and scattered, so now she's far from neighbors. There, she really cried, she was so glad to see anybody comin'. You'll be amused to hear her talk about the Queen, but I thought twice or three times as I set there 't was about all the company she'd got."

"Could we go day after to-morrow?" I asked eagerly.

" 'T would suit me exactly," said Mrs. Todd.

II.

One can never be so certain of good New England weather as in the days when a long easterly storm has blown away the warm late-summer mists, and cooled the air so that however bright the sunshine is by day, the nights come nearer and nearer to frostiness. There was a cold freshness in the morning air when Mrs. Todd and I locked the house-door behind us; we took the key of the fields into our own hands that day, and put out across country as one puts out to sea. When we reached the top of the ridge behind the town it seemed as if we had anxiously passed the harbor bar and were comfortably in open sea at last.

"There, now!" proclaimed Mrs. Todd, taking a long breath, "now I do feel safe. It's just the weather that's liable to bring somebody to spend the day; I've had a feeling of Mis' Elder Caplin from North Point bein' close upon me ever since I waked up this mornin', an' I didn't want to be hampered with our present plans. She's a great hand to visit; she'll be spendin' the day somewhere from now till Thanksgivin', but there's plenty o' places at the Landin' where she goes, an' if I ain't there she'll just select another. I thought mother might be in, too, 't is so pleasant; but I run up the road to look off this mornin' before you was awake, and there was no sign o' the boat. If they hadn't started by that time they wouldn't start, just as the tide is now; besides, I see a lot o' mackerel-men headin' Green Island way, and they'll detain William. No, we're safe now, an' if mother should be comin' in to-morrow we'll have all this to tell her. She an' Mis' Abby Martin's very old friends."

We were walking down the long pasture slopes towards the dark woods and thickets of the low ground. They stretched away northward like an unbroken wilderness; the early mists still dulled much of the color and made the uplands beyond look like a very far-off country.

"It ain't so far as it looks from here," said my companion

reassuringly, "but we've got no time to spare either," and she
hurried on, leading the way with a fine sort of spirit in her
step; and presently we struck into the old Indian footpath,
which could be plainly seen across the long-unploughed turf
of the pastures, and followed it among the thick, low-growing
spruces. There the ground was smooth and brown under foot,
and the thin-stemmed trees held a dark and shadowy roof
overhead. We walked a long way without speaking; sometimes we had to push aside the branches, and sometimes we
walked in a broad aisle where the trees were larger. It was a
solitary woods, birdless and beastless; there was not even a
rabbit to be seen, or a crow high in air to break the silence.

"I don't believe the Queen ever saw such a lonesome trail
as this," said Mrs. Todd, as if she followed the thoughts that
were in my mind. Our visit to Mrs. Abby Martin seemed in
some strange way to concern the high affairs of royalty. I had
just been thinking of English landscapes, and of the solemn
hills of Scotland with their lonely cottages and stone-walled
sheepfolds, and the wandering flocks on high cloudy pastures.
I had often been struck by the quick interest and familiar allusion to certain members of the royal house which one
found in distant neighborhoods of New England; whether
some old instincts of personal loyalty have survived all
changes of time and national vicissitudes, or whether it is
only that the Queen's own character and disposition have
won friends for her so far away, it is impossible to tell. But
to hear of a twin sister was the most surprising proof of inti-
macy of all, and I must confess that there was something re-
markably exciting to the imagination in my morning walk.
To think of being presented at Court in the usual way was
for the moment quite commonplace.

III.

꧁꧂

Mrs. Todd was swinging her basket to and fro like a schoolgirl as she walked, and at this moment it slipped from her hand and rolled lightly along the ground as if there were nothing in it. I picked it up and gave it to her, whereupon she lifted the cover and looked in with anxiety.

" 'T is only a few little things, but I don't want to lose 'em," she explained humbly. " 'T was lucky you took the other basket if I was goin' to roll it round. Mis' Abby Martin complained o' lacking some pretty pink silk to finish one o' her little frames, an' I thought I'd carry her some, and I had a bunch o' gold thread that had been in a box o' mine this twenty year. I never was one to do much fancy work, but we're all liable to be swept away by fashion. And then there's a small packet o' very choice herbs that I gave a good deal of attention to; they'll smarten her up and give her the best of appetites, come spring. She was tellin' me that spring weather is very wiltin' an' tryin' to her, and she was beginnin' to dread it already. Mother's just the same way; if I could prevail on mother to take some o' these remedies in good season 't would make a world o' difference, but she gets all down hill before I have a chance to hear of it, and then William comes in to tell me, sighin' and bewailin', how feeble mother is. 'Why can't you remember 'bout them good herbs that I never let her be without?' I say to him—he does provoke me so; and then off he goes, sulky enough, down to his boat. Next thing I know, she comes in to go to meetin', wantin' to speak to everybody and feelin' like a girl. Mis' Martin's case is very very much the same; but she's nobody to watch her. William's kind o' slow-moulded; but there, any William's better than none when you get to be Mis' Martin's age."

"Hadn't she any children?" I asked.

"Quite a number," replied Mrs. Todd grandly, "but some are gone and the rest are married and settled. She never was a great hand to go about visitin'. I don't know but Mis' Mar-

tin might be called a little peculiar. Even her own folks has
to make company of her; she never slips in and lives right
along with the rest as if 't was at home, even in her own children's houses. I heard one o' her sons' wives say once she'd
much rather have the Queen to spend the day if she could
choose between the two, but I never thought Abby was so
difficult as that. I used to love to have her come; she may
have been sort o' ceremonious, but very pleasant and
sprightly if you had sense enough to treat her her own way. I
always think she'd know just how to live with great folks, and
feel easier 'long of them an' their ways. Her son's wife's a
great driver with farm-work, boards a great tableful o' men
in hayin' time, an' feels right in her element. I don't say but
she's a good woman an' smart, but sort o' rough. Anybody
that's gentle-mannered an' precise like Mis' Martin would be
a sort o' restraint.

"There's all sorts o' folks in the country, same's there is in
the city," concluded Mrs. Todd gravely, and I as gravely
agreed. The thick woods were behind us now, and the sun
was shining clear overhead, the morning mists were gone, and
a faint blue haze softened the distance; as we climbed the hill
where we were to see the view, it seemed like a summer day.
There was an old house on the height, facing southward—a
mere forsaken shell of an old house, with empty windows
that looked like blind eyes. The frost-bitten grass grew close
about it like brown fur, and there was a single crooked bough
of lilac holding its green leaves close by the door.

"We'll just have a good piece of bread-an'-butter now,"
said the commander of the expedition, "and then we'll hang
up the basket on some peg inside the house out o' the way o'
the sheep, and have a han'some entertainment as we're
comin' back. She'll be all through her little dinner when we
get there, Mis' Martin will; but she'll want to make us some
tea, an' we must have our visit an' be startin' back pretty
soon after two. I don't want to cross all that low ground
again after it's begun to grow chilly. An' it looks to me as if
the clouds might begin to gather late in the afternoon."

Before us lay a splendid world of sea and shore. The autumn colors already brightened the landscape; and here and
there at the edge of a dark tract of pointed firs stood a row
of bright swamp-maples like scarlet flowers. The blue sea and
the great tide inlets were untroubled by the lightest winds.

"Poor land, this is!" sighed Mrs. Todd as we sat down to
rest on the worn doorstep. "I've known three good hard-

workin' families that come here full o' hope an' pride and tried to make something o' this farm, but it beat 'em all. There's one small field that's excellent for potatoes if you let half of it rest every year; but the land's always hungry. Now, you see them little peakéd-topped spruces an' fir balsams comin' up over the hill all green an' hearty; they've got it all their own way! Seems sometimes as if wild Natur' got jealous over a certain spot, and wanted to do just as she'd a mind to. You'll see here; she'll do her own ploughin' an' harrowin' with frost an' wet, an' plant just what she wants and wait for her own crops. Man can't do nothin' with it, try as he may. I tell you those little trees means business!"

I looked down the slope, and felt as if we ourselves were likely to be surrounded and overcome if we lingered too long. There was a vigor of growth, a persistence and savagery about the sturdy little trees that put weak human nature at complete defiance. One felt a sudden pity for the men and women who had been worsted after a long fight in that lonely place; one felt a sudden fear of the unconquerable, immediate forces of Nature, as in the irresistible moment of a thunderstorm.

"I can recollect the time when folks were shy o' these woods we just come through," said Mrs. Todd seriously. "The men-folks themselves never'd venture into 'em alone; if their cattle got strayed they'd collect whoever they could get, and start off all together. They said a person was liable to get bewildered in there alone, and in old times folks had been lost. I expect there was considerable fear left over from the old Indian times, and the poor days o' witchcraft; anyway, I've seen bold men act kind o' timid. Some women o' the Asa Bowden family went out one afternoon berryin' when I was a girl, and got lost and was out all night; they found 'em middle o' the mornin' next day, not half a mile from home, scared most to death, an' sayin' they'd heard wolves and other beasts sufficient for a caravan. Poor creatur's! they'd strayed at last into a kind of low place amongst some alders, an' one of 'em was so overset she never got over it, an' went off in a sort o' slow decline. 'T was like them victims that drowns in a foot o' water; but their minds did suffer dreadful. Some folks is born afraid of the woods and all wild places, but I must say they've always been like home to me."

I glanced at the resolute, confident face of my companion. Life was very strong in her, as if some force of Nature were personified in this simple-hearted woman and gave her cousinship to the ancient deities. She might have walked the primeval fields of Sicily; her strong gingham skirts might at that very moment bend the slender stalks of asphodel and be fragrant with trodden thyme, instead of the brown wind-brushed grass of New England and frost-bitten goldenrod. She was a great soul, was Mrs. Todd, and I her humble follower, as we went our way to visit the Queen's Twin, leaving the bright view of the sea behind us, and descending to a lower country-side through the dry pastures and fields.

The farms all wore a look of gathering age, though the settlement was, after all, so young. The fences were already fragile, and it seemed as if the first impulse of agriculture had soon spent itself without hope of renewal. The better houses were always those that had some hold upon the riches of the sea; a house that could not harbor a fishing-boat in some neighboring inlet was far from being sure of every-day comforts. The land alone was not enough to live upon in that stony region; it belonged by right to the forest, and to the forest it fast returned. From the top of the hill where we had been sitting we had seen prosperity in the dim distance, where the land was good and the sun shone upon fat barns, and where warm-looking houses with three or four chimneys apiece stood high on their solid ridge above the bay.

As we drew nearer to Mrs. Martin's it was sad to see what poor bushy fields, what thin and empty dwelling-places had been left by those who had chosen this disappointing part of the northern country for their home. We crossed the last field and came into a narrow rain-washed road, and Mrs. Todd looked eager and expectant and said that we were almost at our journey's end. "I do hope Mis' Martin 'll ask you into her best room where she keeps all the Queen's pictures. Yes, I think likely she will ask you; but 't ain't everybody she deems worthy to visit 'em, I can tell you," said Mrs. Todd warningly. "She's been collectin' 'em an' cuttin' 'em out o' newspapers an' magazines time out o' mind, and if she heard of anybody sailin' for an English port she'd contrive to get a little money to 'em and ask to have the last likeness there was. She's most covered her best-room wall now; she keeps that room shut up sacred as a meetin'-house! 'I won't say but I have my favorites amongst 'em,' she told me t' other day, 'but they're all beautiful to me as they can be!' And she's made some kind o' pretty little frames for 'em all—you know there's always a new fashion o' frames comin' round; first 't was shell-work, and then 't was pine-cones, and bead-work's had its day, and now she's much concerned with perforated cardboard worked with silk. I tell you that best room's a sight to see! But you mustn't look for anything elegant," continued Mrs. Todd, after a moment's reflection. "Mis' Martin's always been in very poor, strugglin' circumstances. She had ambition for her children, though they took right after their father an' had little for themselves; she wa'n't over an' above well married, however kind she may see fit to speak. She's been patient an' hard-workin' all her life, and always high above makin' mean complaints of other folks. I expect all this business about the Queen has buoyed her over many a shoal place in life. Yes, you might say that Abby'd been a slave, but there ain't any slave but has some freedom."

IV.

Presently I saw a low gray house standing on a grassy bank close to the road. The door was at the side, facing us, and a tangle of snowberry bushes and cinnamon roses grew to the level of the window-sills. On the doorstep stood a bent-shouldered, little old woman; there was an air of welcome and of unmistakable dignity about her.

"She sees us coming," exclaimed Mrs. Todd in an excited whisper. "There, I told her I might be over this way again if the weather held good, and if I came I'd bring you. She said right off she'd take great pleasure in havin' a visit from you; I was surprised, she's usually so retirin'."

Even this reassurance did not quell a faint apprehension on our part; there was something distinctly formal in the occasion, and one felt that consciousness of inadequacy which is never easy for the humblest pride to bear. On the way I had torn my dress in an unexpected encounter with a little thorn-bush, and I could now imagine how it felt to be going to Court and forgetting one's feathers or her Court train.

The Queen's Twin was oblivious of such trifles; she stood waiting with a calm look until we came near enough to take her kind hand. She was a beautiful old woman, with clear eyes and a lovely quietness and genuineness of manner; there was not a trace of anything pretentious about her, or high-flown, as Mrs. Todd would say comprehensively. Beauty in age is rare enough in women who have spent their lives in the hard work of a farmhouse; but autumn-like and withered as this woman may have looked, her features had kept, or rather gained, a great refinement. She led us into her old kitchen and gave us seats, and took one of the little straight-backed chairs herself and sat a short distance away, as if she were giving audience to an ambassador. It seemed as if we should all be standing; you could not help feeling that the habits of her life were more ceremonious, but that for the moment she assumed the simplicities of the occasion.

Mrs. Todd was always Mrs. Todd, too great and self-possessed a soul for any occasion to ruffle. I admired her calmness, and presently the slow current of neighborhood talk carried one easily along; we spoke of the weather and the small adventures of the way, and then, as if I were after all not a stranger, our hostess turned almost affectionately to speak to me.

"The weather will be growing dark in London now. I expect that you've been in London, dear?" she said.

"Oh, yes," I answered. "Only last year."

"It is a great many years since I was there, along in the forties," said Mrs. Martin. " 'T was the only voyage I ever made; most of my neighbors have been great travelers. My brother was master of a vessel, and his wife usually sailed with him; but that year she had a young child more frail than the others, and she dreaded the care of it at sea. It happened that my brother got a chance for my husband to go as supercargo, being a good accountant, and came one day to urge him to take it; he was very ill-disposed to the sea, but he had met with losses, and I saw my own opportunity and persuaded them both to let me go too. In those days they didn't object to a woman's being aboard to wash and mend, the voyages were sometimes very long. And that was the way I come to see the Queen."

Mrs. Martin was looking straight in my eyes to see if I showed any genuine interest in the most interesting person in the world.

"Oh, I am very glad you saw the Queen," I hastened to say. "Mrs. Todd has told me that you and she were born the very same day."

"We were indeed, dear!" said Mrs. Martin, and she leaned back comfortably and smiled as she had not smiled before. Mrs. Todd gave a satisfied nod and glance, as if to say that things were going on as well as possible in this anxious moment.

"Yes," said Mrs. Martin again, drawing her chair a little nearer, " 't was a very remarkable thing; we were born the same day, and at exactly the same hour, after you allowed for all the difference in time. My father figured it out sea-fashion. Her Royal Majesty and I opened our eyes upon this world together; say what you may 't is a bond between us."

Mrs. Todd assented with an air of triumph, and untied her hat-strings and threw them back over her shoulders with a gallant air.

"And I married a man by the name of Albert, just the same as she did, and all by chance, for I didn't get the news that she had an Albert too till a fortnight afterward; news was slower coming then than it is now. My first baby was a girl, and I called her Victoria after my mate; but the next one was a boy, and my husband wanted the right to name him, and took his own name and his brother Edward's, and pretty soon I saw in the paper that the little Prince o' Wales had been christened just the same. After that I made excuse to wait till I knew what she'd named her children. I didn't want to break the chain, so I had an Alfred, and my darling Alice that I lost long before she lost hers, and there I stopped. If I'd only had a dear daughter to stay at home with me, same's her youngest one, I should have been so thankful! But if only one of us could have a little Beatrice, I'm glad 't was the Queen; we've both seen trouble, but she's had the most care."

I asked Mrs. Martin if she lived alone all the year, and was told that she did except for a visit now and then from one of her grandchildren, "the only one that really likes to come an' stay quiet 'long o' grandma. She always says quick as she's through her schoolin' she's goin' to live with me all the time, but she's very pretty an' has taking ways," said Mrs. Martin, looking both proud and wistful, "so I can tell nothing at all about it! Yes, I've been alone most o' the time since my Albert was taken away, and that's a great many years; he had a long time o' failing and sickness first." (Mrs. Todd's foot gave an impatient scuff on the floor.) "An' I've always lived right here. I ain't like the Queen's Majesty, for this is the only palace I've got," said the dear old thing, smiling again. "I'm glad of it too, I don't like changing about, an' our stations in life are set very different. I don't require what the Queen does, but sometimes I've thought 't was left to me to do the plain things she don't have time for. I expect she's a beautiful housekeeper, nobody couldn't have done better in her high place, and she's been as good a mother as she's been a queen."

"I guess she has, Abby," agreed Mrs. Todd instantly. "How was it you happened to get such a good look at her? I meant to ask you again when I was here t' other day."

"Our ship was layin' in the Thames, right there above Wapping. We was dischargin' cargo, and under orders to clear as quick as we could for Bordeaux to take on an excellent freight o' French goods," explained Mrs. Martin eagerly.

"I heard that the Queen was goin' to a great review of her army, and would drive out o' her Buckin'ham Palace about ten o'clock in the mornin', and I ran aft to Albert, my husband, and brother Horace where they was standin' together by the hatchway, and told 'em they must one of 'em take me. They laughed, I was in such a hurry, and said they couldn't go; and I found they meant it and got sort of impatient when I began to talk, and I was 'most broken-hearted; 't was all the reason I had for makin' that hard voyage. Albert couldn't help often reproachin' me, for he did so resent the sea, an' I'd known how 't would be before we sailed; but I'd minded nothing all the way till then, and I just crep' back to my cabin an' begun to cry. They was disappointed about their ship's cook, an' I'd cooked for fo'c's'le an' cabin myself all the way over; 't was dreadful hard work, specially in rough weather; we'd had head winds an' a six weeks' voyage. They'd acted sort of ashamed o' me when I pled so to go ashore, an' that hurt my feelin's most of all. But Albert come below pretty soon; I'd never given way so in my life, an' he begun to act frightened, and treated me gentle just as he did when we was goin' to be married, an' when I got over sobbin' he went on deck and saw Horace an' talked it over what they could do; they really had their duty to the vessel, and couldn't be spared that day. Horace was real good when he understood everything, and he come an' told me I'd more than worked my passage an' was goin' to do just as I liked now we was in port. He'd engaged a cook, too, that was comin' aboard that mornin', and he was goin' to send the ship's carpenter with me—a nice fellow from up Thomaston way; he'd gone to put on his ashore clothes as quick's he could. So then I got ready, and we started off in the small boat and rowed up river. I was afraid we were too late, but the tide was setting up very strong, and we landed an' left the boat to a keeper, and I run all the way up those great streets and across a park. 'T was a great day, with sights o' folks everywhere, but 't was just as if they was nothin' but wax images to me. I kep' askin' my way an' runnin' on, with the carpenter comin' after as best he could, and just as I worked to the front o' the crowd by the palace, the gates was flung open and out she came; all prancin' horses and shinin' gold, and in a beautiful carriage there she sat; 't was a moment o' heaven to me. I saw her plain, and she looked right at me so pleasant and happy, just as if she knew there was somethin' different between us from other folks."

There was a moment when the Queen's Twin could not go on and neither of her listeners could ask a question.

"Prince Albert was sitting right beside her in the carriage," she continued. "Oh, he was a beautiful man! Yes, dear, I saw 'em both together just as I see you now, and then she was gone out o' sight in another minute, and the common crowd was all spread over the place pushin' an' cheerin'. 'T was some kind o' holiday, an' the carpenter and I got separated, an' then I found him again after I didn't think I should, an' he was all for makin' a day of it, and goin' to show me all the sights; he'd been in London before, but I didn't want nothin' else, an' we went back through the streets down to the waterside an' took the boat. I remember I mended an old coat o' my Albert's as good as I could, sittin' on the quarter-deck in the sun all that afternoon, and 't was all as if I was livin' in a lovely dream. I don't know how to explain it, but there hasn't been no friend I've felt so near to me ever since."

One could not say much—only listen. Mrs. Todd put in a discerning question now and then, and Mrs. Martin's eyes shone brighter and brighter as she talked. What a lovely gift of imagination and true affection was in this fond old heart! I looked about the plain New England kitchen, with its wood-smoked walls and homely braided rugs on the worn floor, and all its simple furnishings. The loud-ticking clock seemed to encourage us to speak; at the other side of the room was an early newspaper portrait of Her Majesty the Queen of Great Britain and Ireland. On a shelf below were some flowers in a little dish, as if they were put before a shrine.

"If I could have had more to read, I should have known 'most everything about her," said Mrs. Martin wistfully. "I've made the most of what I did have, and thought it over and over till it came clear. I sometimes seem to have her all my own, as if we'd lived right together. I've often walked out into the woods alone and told her what my troubles was, and it always seemed as if she told me 't was all right, an' we must have patience. I've got her beautiful book about the Highlands; 't was dear Mis' Todd here that found out about her printing it and got a copy for me, and it's been a treasure to my heart, just as if 't was written right to me. I always read it Sundays now, for my Sunday treat. Before that I used to have to imagine a good deal, but when I come to read her book, I knew what I expected was all true. We do think alike about so many things," said the Queen's Twin with affectionate certainty. "You see, there is something between us, being born just at the same time; 't is what they call a birthright. She's had great tasks put upon her, being the Queen, an' mine has been the humble lot; but she's done the best she could, nobody can say to the contrary, and there's something between us; she's been the great lesson I've had to live by. She's been everything to me. An' when she had her Jubilee, oh, how my heart was with her!"

"There, 't wouldn't play the part in her life it has in mine," said Mrs. Martin generously, in answer to something one of her listeners had said. "Sometimes I think, now she's older, she might like to know about us. When I think how few old friends anybody has left at our age, I suppose it may be just the same with her as it is with me; perhaps she would like to know how we came into life together. But I've had a great advantage in seeing her, an' I can always fancy her goin' on, while she don't know nothin' yet about me, except she may feel my love stayin' her heart sometimes an' not know just where it comes from. An' I dream about our being together out in some pretty fields, young as ever we was, and holdin' hands as we walk along. I'd like to know if she ever has that dream too. I used to have days when I made believe she did know, an' was comin' to see me," confessed the speaker shyly, with a little flush on her cheeks; "and I'd plan what I could have nice for supper, and I wasn't goin' to let anybody know she was here havin' a good rest, except I'd wish you, Almira Todd, or dear Mis' Blackett would happen in, for you'd know just how to talk with her. You see, she likes to be up in Scotland, right out in the wild country, better than she does anywhere else."

"I'd really love to take her out to see mother at Green Island," said Mrs. Todd with a sudden impulse.

"Oh, yes! I should love to have you," exclaimed Mrs. Martin, and then she began to speak in a lower tone. "One day I got thinkin' so about my dear Queen," she said, "an' livin' so in my thoughts, that I went to work an got all ready for her, just as if she was really comin'. I never told this to a livin' soul before, but I feel you'll understand. I put my best fine sheets and blankets I spun an' wove myself on the bed, and I picked some pretty flowers and put 'em all round the house, an' I worked as hard an' happy as I could all day, and had as nice a supper ready as I could get, sort of telling myself a story all the time. She was comin' an' I was goin' to see her again, an' I kep' it up until nightfall; an' when I see the dark an' it come to me I was all alone, the dream left me, an' I sat down on the doorstep an' felt all foolish an' tired. An', if you'll believe it, I heard steps comin', an' an old cousin o' mine come wanderin' along, one I was apt to be shy of. She wasn't all there, as folks used to say, but harmless enough and a kind of poor old talking body. And I went right to meet her when I first heard her call, 'stead o' hidin' as I sometimes did, an' she come in dreadful willin', an' we sat down to supper together; 't was a supper I should have had no heart to eat alone."

"I don't believe she ever had such a splendid time in her life as she did then. I heard her tell all about it afterwards," exclaimed Mrs. Todd compassionately. "There, now I hear all this it seems just as if the Queen might have known and couldn't come herself, so she sent that poor old creatur' that was always in need!"

Mrs. Martin looked timidly at Mrs. Todd and then at me. " 'T was childish o' me to go an' get supper," she confessed.

"I guess you wa'n't the first one to do that," said Mrs. Todd. "No, I guess you wa'n't the first one who got supper that way, Abby," and then for a moment she could say no more.

Mrs. Todd and Mrs. Martin had moved their chairs a little so that they faced each other, and I, at one side, could see them both.

"No, you never told me o' that before, Abby," said Mrs. Todd gently. "Don't it show that for folks that have any fancy in 'em, such beautiful dreams is the real part o' life? But to most folks the common things that happens outside 'em is all in all."

Mrs. Martin did not appear to understand at first, strange to say, when the secret of her heart was put into words; then a glow of pleasure and comprehension shone upon her face. "Why, I believe you're right, Almira!" she said, and turned to me.

"Wouldn't you like to look at my pictures of the Queen?" she asked, and we rose and went into the best room.

V.

The mid-day visit seemed very short; September hours are brief to match the shortening days. The great subject was dismissed for a while after our visit to the Queen's pictures, and my companions spoke much of lesser persons until we drank the cup of tea which Mrs. Todd had foreseen. I happily remembered that the Queen herself is said to like a proper cup of tea, and this at once seemed to make her Majesty kindly join so remote and reverent a company. Mrs. Martin's thin cheeks took on a pretty color like a girl's. "Somehow I always have thought of her when I made it extra good," she said. "I've got a real china cup that belonged to my grandmother, and I believe I shall call it hers now."

"Why don't you?" responded Mrs. Todd warmly, with a delightful smile.

Later they spoke of a promised visit which was to be made in the Indian summer to the Landing and Green Island, but I observed that Mrs. Todd presented the little parcel of dried herbs, with full directions, for a cure-all in the spring, as if there were no real chance of their meeting again first. As we looked back from the turn of the road the Queen's Twin was still standing on the doorstep watching us away, and Mrs. Todd stopped, and stood still for a moment before she waved her hand again.

"There's one thing certain, dear," she said to me with great discernment; "it ain't as if we left her all alone!"

Then we set out upon our long way home over the hill, where we lingered in the afternoon sunshine, and through the dark woods across the heron-swamp.

William's Wedding

I.

✥

The hurry of life in a large town, the constant putting aside of preference to yield to a most unsatisfactory activity, began to vex me, and one day I took the train, and only left it for the eastward-bound boat. Carlyle says somewhere that the only happiness a man ought to ask for is happiness enough to get his work done; and against this the complexity and futile ingenuity of social life seems a conspiracy. But the first salt wind from the east, the first sight of a lighthouse set boldly on its outer rock, the flash of a gull, the waiting procession of seaward-bound firs on an island, made me feel solid and definite again, instead of a poor, incoherent being. Life was resumed, and anxious living blew away as if it had not been. I could not breathe deep enough or long enough. It was a return to happiness.

The coast had still a wintry look; it was far on in May, but all the shore looked cold and sterile. One was conscious of going north as well as east and as the day went on the sea grew colder, and all the warmer air and bracing strength and stimulus of the autumn weather, and storage of the heat of summer, were quite gone. I was very cold and very tired when I came at evening up the lower bay, and saw the white houses of Dunnet Landing climbing the hill. They had a friendly look; these little houses, not as if they were climbing up the shore, but as if they were rather all coming down to meet a fond and weary traveler, and I could hardly wait with patience to step off the boat. It was not the usual eager company on the wharf. The coming-in of the mailboat was the one large public event of a summer day, and I was disappointed at seeing none of my intimate friends but Johnny Bowden, who had evidently done nothing all winter but grow, so that his short sea-smitten clothes gave him a look of poverty.

Johnny's expression did not change as we greeted each other, but I suddenly felt that I had shown indifference and inconvenient delay by not coming sooner; before I could make an apology he took my small portmanteau, and walking before me in his old fashion he made straight up the hilly road toward Mrs. Todd's. Yes, he was much grown—it had never occurred to me the summer before that Johnny was likely, with the help of time and other forces, to grow into a young man; he was such a well-framed and well-settled chunk of a boy that nature seemed to have set him aside as something finished, quite satisfactory, and entirely completed.

The wonderful little green garden had been enchanted away by winter. There were a few frost-bitten twigs and some thin shrubbery against the fence, but it was a most unpromising small piece of ground. My heart was beating like a lover's as I passed it on the way to the door of Mrs. Todd's house, which seemed to have become much smaller under the influence of winter weather.

"She hasn't gone away?" I asked Johnny Bowden with a sudden anxiety just as we reached the doorstep.

"Gone away!" he faced me with blank astonishment—"I see her settin' by Mis' Caplin's window, the one nighest the road, about four o'clock!" And eager with suppressed news of my coming he made his entrance as if the house were a burrow.

Then on my homesick heart fell the voice of Mrs. Todd. She stopped, through what I knew to be excess of feeling, to rebuke Johnny for bringing in so much mud, and I dallied without for one moment during the ceremony; then we met again face to face.

II.

✦

"I dare say you can advise me what shapes they are goin'
to wear. My meetin'-bunnit ain't goin' to do me again this
year; no! I can't expect 't would do me forever," said Mrs.
Todd, as soon as she could say anything. "There! do set down
and tell me how you have been! We've got a weddin' in the
family, I s'pose you know?"

"A wedding!" said I, still full of excitement.

"Yes; I expect if the tide serves and the line storm don't
overtake him they'll come in and appear out on Sunday, I
shouldn't have concerned me about the bunnit for a month
yet, nobody would notice, but havin' an occasion like this I
shall show consider'ble. 'Twill be an ordeal for William!"

"For *William!*" I exclaimed. "What do you mean, Mrs.
Todd?"

She gave a comfortable little laugh. "Well, the Lord's seen
reason at last an' removed Mis' Cap'n Hight up to the farm,
an' I don't know but the weddin's goin' to be this week. Esther's had a great deal of business disposin' of her flock, but
she's done extra well—the folks that owns the next place
goin' up country are well off. 'Tis elegant land north side o'
that bleak ridge, an' one o' the boys has been Esther's right-
hand man of late. She instructed him in all matters, and after
she markets the early lambs he's goin' to take the farm on
halves, an' she's give the refusal to him to buy her out within
two years. She's reserved the buryin' lot, an' the right o' way
in, an'—"

I couldn't stop for details. I demanded reassurance of the
central fact.

"William going to be married?" I repeated; whereat Mrs.
Todd gave me a searching look that was not without scorn.

"Old Mis' Hight's funeral was a week ago Wednesday, and
'twas very well attended," she assured me after a moment's
pause.

"Poor thing!" said I, with a sudden vision of her helplessness and angry battle against the fate of illness; "it was very hard for her."

"I thought it was hard for Esther!" said Mrs. Todd without sentiment.

III.

❦

I had an odd feeling of strangeness: I missed the garden, and the little rooms, to which I had added a few things of my own the summer before, seemed oddly unfamiliar. It was like the hermit crab in a cold new shell—and with the windows shut against the raw May air, and a strange silence and grayness of the sea all that first night and day of my visit, I felt as if I had after all lost my hold of that quiet life.

Mrs. Todd made the apt suggestion that city persons were prone to run themselves to death, and advised me to stay and get properly rested now that I had taken the trouble to come. She did not know how long I had been homesick for the conditions of life at the Landing the autumn before—it was natural enough to feel a little unsupported by compelling incidents on my return.

Some one has said that one never leaves a place, or arrives at one, until the next day! But on the second morning I woke with the familiar feeling of interest and ease, and the bright May sun was streaming in, while I could hear Mrs. Todd's heavy footsteps pounding about in the other part of the house as if something were going to happen. There was the first golden robin singing somewhere close to the house, and a lovely aspect of spring now, and I looked at the garden to see that in the warm night some of its treasures had grown a hand's breadth; the determined spikes of yellow daffies stood tall against the doorsteps, and the blood-root was unfolding leaf and flower. The belated spring which I had left behind farther south had overtaken me on this northern coast. I even saw a presumptuous dandelion in the garden border.

It is difficult to report the great events of New England; expression is so slight, and those few words which escape us in moments of deep feeling look but meagre on the printed page. One has to assume too much of the dramatic fervor as one reads; but as I came out of my room at breakfast-time I met Mrs. Todd face to face, and when she said to me, "This weather'll bring William in after her; 'tis their happy day!" I felt something take possession of me which ought to communicate itself to the least sympathetic reader of this cold page. It is written for those who have a Dunnet Landing of their own: who either kindly share this with the writer, or possess another.

"I ain't seen his comin' sail yet; he'll be likely to dodge round among the islands so he'll be the less observed," continued Mrs. Todd. "You can get a dory up the bay, even a clean new painted one, if you know as how, keepin' it against the high land." She stepped to the door and looked off to sea as she spoke. I could see her eye follow the gray shores to and fro, and then a bright light spread over her calm face. "There he comes, and he's strikin' right in across the open bay like a man!" she said with splendid approval. "See, there he comes! Yes, there's William, and he's bent his new sail."

I looked too, and saw the fleck of white no larger than a gull's wing yet, but present to her eager vision.

I was going to France for the whole long summer that year, and the more I thought of such an absence from these simple scenes the more dear and delightful they became. Santa Teresa says that the true proficiency of the soul is not in much thinking, but in much loving, and sometimes I believed that I had never found love in its simplicity as I had found it at Dunnet Landing in the various hearts of Mrs. Blackett and Mrs. Todd and William. It is only because one came to know them, these three, loving and wise and true, in their own habitations. Their counterparts are in every village in the world, thank heaven, and the gift to one's life is only in its discernment. I had only lived in Dunnet until the usual distractions and artifices of the world were no longer in control, and I saw these simple natures clear. "The happiness of life is in its recognitions. It seems that we are not ignorant of these truths, and even that we believe them; but we are so little accustomed to think of them, they are so strange to us—"

"Well now, deary me!" said Mrs. Todd, breaking into exclamation: "I've got to fly round—I thought he'd have to beat; he can't sail far on that tack, and he won't be in for a good hour yet—I expect he's made every arrangement, but he said he shouldn't go up after Esther unless the weather was good, and I declare it did look doubtful this morning."

I remembered Esther's weather-worn face. She was like a Frenchwoman who had spent her life in the fields. I remembered her pleasant look, her childlike eyes, and thought of the astonishment of joy she would feel now in being taken care of and tenderly sheltered from wind and weather after all these years. They were going to be young again now, she and William, to forget work and care in the spring weather. I could hardly wait for the boat to come to land, I was so eager to see his happy face.

"Cake an' wine I'm goin' to set 'em out!" said Mrs. Todd. "They won't stop to set down for an ordered meal, they'll want to get right out home quick's they can. Yes, I'll give 'em some cake an' wine—I've got a rare plum-cake from my best receipt, and a bottle o' wine that the old Cap'n Denton of all give me, one of two, the day I was married, one we had and one we saved, and I've never touched it till now. He said there wa'n't none like it in the State o' Maine."

It was a day of waiting, that day of spring; the May weather was as expectant as our fond hearts, and one could see the grass grow green hour by hour. The warm air was full of birds, there was a glow of light on the sea instead of the cold shining of chilly weather which had lingered late. There was a look on Mrs. Todd's face which I saw once and could not meet again. She was in her highest mood. Then I went out early for a walk, and when I came back we sat in different rooms for the most part. There was such a thrill in the air that our only conversation was in her most abrupt and incisive manner. She was knitting, I believe, and as for me I dallied with a book. I heard her walking to and fro, and the door being wide open now, she went out and paced the front walk to the gate as if she walked a quarter-deck.

It is very solemn to sit waiting for the great events of life—most of us have done it again and again—to be expectant of life or expectant of death gives one the same feeling.

But at the last Mrs. Todd came quickly back from the gate, and standing in the sunshine of the door, she beckoned me as if she were a sibyl.

"I thought you comprehended everything the day you was up there," she added with a little more patience in her tone, but I felt that she thought I had lost instead of gained since we parted the autumn before.

"William's made this pretext o' goin' fishin' for the last time. 'T wouldn't done to take notice, 't would 'a scared him to death! but there never was nobody took less comfort out o' forty years courtin'. No, he won't have to make no further pretexts," said Mrs. Todd, with an air of triumph.

"Did you know where he was going that day?" I asked, with a sudden burst of admiration at such discernment.

"I did!" replied Mrs. Todd grandly.

"Oh! but that pennyroyal lotion," I indignantly protested, remembering that under pretext of mosquitoes she had be-smeared the poor lover in an awful way—why, it was outrageous! Medea could not have been more conscious of high ultimate purposes.

"Darlin'," said Mrs. Todd, in the excitement of my arrival and the great concerns of marriage, "he's got a beautiful shaped face and they pison him very unusual—you wouldn't have had him present himself to his lady all lop-sided with a mosquito-bite? Once when he was young I rode up with him, and they set upon him in concert the minute we entered the woods." She stood before me reproachfully, and I was conscious of deserved rebuke. "Yes, you've come just in the nick of time to advise me about a bunnit. They say large bows on top is liable to be worn."

IV.

❧

The period of waiting was one of direct contrast to these high moments of recognition. The very slowness of the morning hours wasted that sense of excitement with which we had begun the day. Mrs. Todd came down from the mount where her face had shone so bright, to the cares of common life, and some acquaintances from Black Island for whom she had little natural preference or liking came, bringing a poor, sickly child to get medical advice. They were noisy women, with harsh, clamorous voices, and they stayed a long time. I heard the clink of teacups, however, and could detect no impatience in the tones of Mrs. Todd's voice; but when they were at last going away, she did not linger unduly over her leave-taking, and returned to me to explain that they were people she had never liked, and they had made an excuse of a friendly visit to save their doctor's bill; but she pitied the poor little child, and knew beside that the doctor was away.

"I had to give 'em the remedies right out," she told me; "they wouldn't have bought a cent's worth o' drugs down to the store for that dwindlin' thing. She needed feedin' up, and I don't expect she gets milk enough; they're great butter-makers down to Black Island, 't is excellent pasturage, but they use no milk themselves, and their butter is heavy laden with salt to make weight, so that you'd think all their ideas come down from Sodom."

She was very indignant and very wistful about the pale little girl. "I wish they'd let me kept her," she said. "I kind of advised it, and her eyes was so wishful in that pinched face when she heard me, so that I could see what was the matter with her, but they said she wa'n't prepared. Prepared!" And Mrs. Todd snuffed like an offended war-horse and departed; but I could hear her still grumbling and talking to herself in high dudgeon an hour afterward.

At the end of that time her arch enemy, Mari' Harris, appeared at the side-door with gingham handkerchief over her head. She was always on hand for the news, and made some formal excuse for her presence—she wished to borrow the weekly paper. Captain Littlepage, whose housekeeper she was, had taken it from the post-office in the morning, but had forgotten, being of failing memory, what he had done with it.

"How is the poor old gentlemen?" asked Mrs. Todd with solicitude, ignoring the present errand of Maria and all her concerns.

I had spoken the evening before of intended visits to Captain Littlepage and Elijah Tilley, and I now heard Mrs. Todd repeating my inquiries and intentions, and fending off with unusual volubility of her own the curious questions that were sure to come. But at last Maria Harris secured an opportunity and boldly inquired if she had not seen William ashore early that morning.

"I don't say he wasn't," replied Mrs. Todd; "Thu'sday's a very usual day with him to come ashore."

"He was all dressed up," insisted Maria—she really had no sense of propriety. "I didn't know but they was going to be married?"

Mrs. Todd did not reply. I recognized from the sounds that reached me that she had retired to the fastnesses of the kitchen-closet and was clattering the tins.

"I expect they'll marry soon anyway," continued the visitor.

"I expect they will if they want to," answered Mrs. Todd. "I don't know nothin' 't all about it; that's what folks say." And presently the gingham handkerchief retreated past my window.

"I routed her, horse and foot," said Mrs. Todd proudly, coming at once to stand at my door. "Who's comin' now?" as two figures passed inward bound to the kitchen.

They were Mrs. Begg and Johnny Bowden's mother, who were favorites, and were received with Mrs. Todd's usual civilities. Then one of the Mrs. Caplins came with a cup in hand to borrow yeast. On one pretext or another nearly all our acquaintances came to satisfy themselves of the facts, and see what Mrs. Todd would impart about the wedding. But she firmly avoided the subject through the length of every call and errand, and answered the final leading question of each curious guest with her noncommittal phrase, "I don't know nothin' 't all about it; that's what folks say!"

She had just repeated this for the fourth or fifth time and shut the door upon the last comers, when we met in the little front entry. Mrs. Todd was not in a bad temper, but highly amused. "I've been havin' all sorts o' social privileges, you may have observed. They didn't seem to consider that if they could only hold out till afternoon they'd know as much as I did. There wa'n't but one o' the whole sixteen that showed real interest, the rest demeaned themselves to ask out o' cheap curiosity; no, there wa'n't but one showed any real feelin'."

"Miss Maria Harris, you mean?" and Mrs. Todd laughed.

"Certain, dear," she agreed, "how you do understand poor human natur'!"

A short distance down the hilly street stood a narrow house that was newly painted white. It blinded one's eyes to catch the reflection of the sun. It was the house of the minister, and a wagon had just stopped before it; a man was helping a woman to alight, and they stood side by side for a moment, while Johnny Bowden appeared as if by magic, and climbed to the wagon-seat. Then they went into the house and shut the door. Mrs. Todd and I stood close together and watched; the tears were running down her cheeks. I watched Johnny Bowden, who made light of so great a moment by so handling the whip that the old white Caplin horse started up from time to time and was inexorably stopped as if he had some idea of running away. There was something in the back of the wagon which now and then claimed the boy's attention; he leaned over as if there were something very precious left in his charge; perhaps it was only Esther's little trunk going to its new home.

At last the door of the parsonage opened, and two figures came out. The minister followed them and stood in the doorway, delaying them with parting words; he could not have thought it was a time for admonition.

"He's all alone; his wife's up to Portland to her sister's," said Mrs. Todd aloud, in a matter-of-fact voice. "She's a nice woman, but she might ha' talked too much. There! see, they're comin' here. I didn't know how 't would be. Yes, they're comin' up to see us before they go home. I declare, if William ain't lookin' just like a king!"

Mrs. Todd took one step forward, and we stood and waited. The happy pair came walking up the street, Johnny Bowden driving ahead. I heard a plaintive little cry from time to time to which in the excitement of the moment I had not stopped to listen; but when William and Esther had come and shaken hands with Mrs. Todd and then with me, all in silence, Esther stepped quickly to the back of the wagon, and unfastening some cords returned to us carrying a little white lamb. She gave a shy glance at William as she fondled it and held it to her heart, and then, still silent, we went into the house together. The lamb had stopped bleating. It was lovely to see Esther carry it in her arms.

When we got into the house, all the repression of Mrs. Todd's usual manner was swept away by her flood of feeling. She took Esther's thin figure, lamb and all, to her heart and held her there, kissing her as she might have kissed a child, and then held out her hand to William and they gave each other the kiss of peace. This was so moving, so tender, so free from their usual fetters of self-consciousness, that Esther and I could not help giving each other a happy glance of comprehension. I never saw a young bride half so touching in her happiness as Esther was that day of her wedding. We took the cake and wine of the marriage feast together, always in silence, like a true sacrament, and then to my astonishment I found that sympathy and public interest in so great an occasion were going to have their way. I shrank from the thought of William's possible sufferings, but he welcomed both the first group of neighbors and the last with heartiness; and when at last they had gone, for there were thoughtless loiterers in Dunnet Landing, I made ready with eager zeal and walked with William and Esther to the water-side. It was only a little way, and kind faces nodded reassuringly from the windows, while kind voices spoke from the doors. Esther carried the lamb on one arm; she had found time to tell me that its mother had died that morning and she could not bring herself to the thought of leaving it behind. She kept the other hand on William's arm until we reached the landing. Then he shook hands with me, and looked me full in the face to be sure I understood how happy he was, and stepping into the boat held out his arms to Esther—at last she was his own.

I watched him make a nest for the lamb out of an old sea-cloak at Esther's feet, and then he wrapped her own shawl round her shoulders, and finding a pin in the lapel of his Sunday coat he pinned it for her. She looked at him fondly while he did this, and then glanced up at us, a pretty, girlish color brightening her cheeks.

We stood there together and watched them go far out into the bay. The sunshine of the May day was low now, but there was a steady breeze, and the boat moved well.

"Mother'll be watching for them," said Mrs. Todd. "Yes,

mother'll be watching all day, and waiting. She'll be so happy
to have Esther come."

We went home together up the hill, and Mrs. Todd said
nothing more; but we held each other's hands all the way.

Miss Peck's Promotion

❧

Miss Peck had spent a lonely day in her old farm-house, high on a long Vermont hillside that sloped toward the west. She was able for an hour at noon to overlook the fog in the valley below, and pitied the people in the village whose location she could distinguish only by means of the church steeple which pricked through the gray mist, like a buoy set over a dangerous reef. During this brief time, when the sun was apparently shining for her benefit alone, she reflected proudly upon the advantage of living on high land, but in the early afternoon, when the fog began to rise slowly, and at last shut her in, as well as the rest of the world, she was conscious of uncommon depression of spirits.

"I might as well face it now as any time," she said aloud, as she lighted her clean kerosene lamp and put it on the table. "Eliza Peck! just set down and make it blazing clear how things stand with you, and what you're going to do in regard to 'em! 'T ain't no use matching your feelin's to the weather, without you've got reason for it." And she twitched the short curtains across the windows so that their brass rings squeaked on the wires, opened the door for the impatient cat that was mewing outside, and then seated herself in the old rocking-chair at the table end.

It is quite a mistake to believe that people who live by themselves find every day a lonely one. Miss Peck and many other solitary persons could assure us that it is very seldom that they feel their lack of companionship. As the habit of living alone grows more fixed, it becomes confusing to have other people about, and seems more or less bewildering to be interfered with by other people's plans and suggestions. Only once in a while does the feeling of solitariness become burdensome, or a creeping dread and sense of defenselessness assail one's comfort. But when Miss Peck was aware of the approach of such a mood she feared it, and was prepared to fight it with her best weapon of common-sense.

She was much given to talking aloud, as many solitary persons are; not merely talking to herself in the usual half-conscious way, but making her weaker self listen to severe comment and pointed instruction. Miss Peck the less was frequently brought to trial in this way by Miss Peck the greater, and when it was once announced that justice must be done, no amount of quailing or excuse averted the process of definite conviction.

This evening she turned the light up to its full brightness, reached for her knitting-work, lifted it high above her lap for a moment, as her favorite cat jumped up to its evening quarters; then she began to rock to and fro with regularity and decision. " 'T is all nonsense," she said, as if she were addressing some one greatly her inferior—" 't is all nonsense for you to go on this way, Elizy Peck! you're better off than you've been this six year, if you only had sense to feel so."

There was no audible reply, and the speaker evidently mistook the silence for unconvinced stubbornness.

"If ever there was a woman who was determined to live by other folks' wits, and to eat other folks' dinners, 't was and is your lamented brother's widder, Harri't Peck—Harri't White that was. She's claimed the town's compassion till it's good as run dry, and she's thought that you, Elizy Peck, a hard-workin' and self-supportin' woman, was made for nothin' but her use and comfort. Ever since your father died and you've been left alone you've had her for a clog to your upward way. Six years you've been at her beck an' call, and now that a respectable man, able an' willing to do for her, has been an' fell in love with her, and shouldered her and all her whims, and promised to do for the children as if they was his own, you've been grumpin' all day, an' *I'd* like to know what there is to grump about!"

There was a lack of response even to this appeal to reason, and the knitting-needles clicked in dangerous nearness to the old cat's ears, so that they twitched now and then, and one soft paw unexpectedly revealed its white curving claws.

"Yes," said Miss Peck, presently, in a more lenient tone, "I s'pose 't is the children you're thinking of most. I declare I should like to see that Tom's little red head, and feel it warm with my two hands this minute! There's always somethin' hopeful in havin' to do with children, 'less they come of *too* bad a stock. Grown folks—well, you can make out to grin an' bear 'em if you must; but like's not young ones'll turn out to be somebody, and what you do for 'em may count towards it. There's that Tom, he looks just as his father used to, and there ain't a day he won't say somethin' real pleasant, and never sees the difference betwixt you an' somebody handsome. I expect they'll spile him—you don't know what kind o' young ones they'll let him play with, nor how they'll let him murder the king's English, and never think o' boxin' his ears. Them big factory towns is all for eatin' and clothes. I'm glad you was raised in a good old academy town, if 't was the Lord's will to plant you in the far outskirts. Land, how Harri't did smirk at that man! I will say she looked pretty—'t is hard work and worry makes folks plain like me—I believe she's fared better to be left a widder with three child'n, and everybody saying how hard it was, an' takin' holt, than she would if brother had lived and she'd had to stir herself to keep house and do for him. You've been the real widder that Tom left—you've mourned him, and had your way to go alone—not she! The colonel's lady," repeated Miss Peck, scornfully—"that's what sp'ilt her. She never could come down to common things, Mis' Colonel Peck! Well, she may have noble means now, but she's got to be spoke of as Mis' Noah Pigley all the rest of her days. Not that I'm goin' to fling at any man's accident of name," said the just Eliza, in an apologetic tone. "I did want to adopt little Tom, but 't was to be expected he'd object—a boy's goin' to be useful in his business, and poor Tommy's the likeliest. I would have 'dopted him out an' out, and he shall have the old farm anyway. But oh dear me, he's all spoilt for farming now, is little Tom, unless I can make sure of him now and then for a good long visit in summer time.

"Summer an' winter; I s'pose you're likely to live a great many years, Elizy," sighed the good woman. "All sole alone, too! There, I've landed right at the startin' point"—and the kitchen was very still while some dropped stitches in a belated stocking for the favorite nephew were obscured by a mist of tears like the fog outside. There was no more talking aloud, for Miss Peck fell into a revery about old days and the only brother who had left his little household in her care and marched to the war whence for him there was to be no return. She had remembered very often, with a great sense of comfort, a message in one of his very last letters. "Tell Eliza that she's more likely to be promoted than I am," he said (when he had just got his step of Major); "she's my superior officer, however high I get, and now I've heard what luck she's had with the haying, I appoint her Brigadier-General for gallantry in the field." How poor Tom's jokes had kept their courage up even when they were most anxious! Yes, she had made many sacrifices of personal gain, as every good soldier must. She had meant to be a school-teacher. She had the gift for it, and had studied hard in her girlhood. One thing after another had kept her at home, and now she must stay here—her ambitions were at an end. She would do what good she could among her neighbors, and stand in her lot and place. It was the first time she had found to think soberly about her life, for her sister-in-law and the children had gone to their new home within a few days, and since then she had stifled all power of proper reflection by hard work at setting the house in order and getting in her winter supplies. "Thank Heaven the house and place belong to me," she said in a decisive tone. " 'T was wise o' father to leave it so—and let her have the money. She'd left me no peace till I moved off if I'd only been half-owner; she's always meant to get to a larger place—but what I want is real promotion."

The Peck farm-house was not only on a by-road that wandered among the slopes of the hills, but it was at the end of a long lane of its own. There was rarely any sound at night except from the winds of heaven or the soughing of the neighboring pine-trees. By day, there was a beautiful inspiriting outlook over the wide country from the farm-house windows, but on such a night as this the darkness made an impenetrable wall. Miss Peck was not afraid of it; on the contrary, she had a sense of security in being shut safe into the very heart of the night. By day she might be vexed by intruders, by night they could scarcely find her—her bright light could not be seen from the road. If she were to wither away in the old gray house like an unplanted kernel in its shell, she would at least wither undisturbed. Her sorrow of loneliness was not the fear of molestation. She was fearless enough at the thought of physical dangers.

The evening did not seem so long as she expected—a glance at her reliable timekeeper told her at last that it was already past eight o'clock, and her eyes began to feel heavy. The fire was low, the fog was making its presence felt even in the house, for the autumn night was chilly, and Miss Peck decided that when she came to the end of the stitches on a certain needle she would go to bed. To-morrow, she meant to cut her apples for drying, a duty too long delayed. She had sent away some of her best fruit that day to make the annual barrel of cider with which she provided herself, more from habit than from real need of either the wholesome beverage or its resultant vinegar. "If this fog lasts, I've got to dry my apples by the stove," she thought, doubtfully, and was conscious of a desire to survey the weather from the outer doorway before she slept. How she missed Harriet and the children!—though they had been living with her only for a short time before the wedding, and since the half-house they had occupied in the village had been let. The thought of bright-eyed, red-headed little Tom still brought the warm tears very near to falling. He had cried bitterly when he went away. So had his mother—at least, she held up her pocket-handkerchief. Miss Peck never had believed in Harriet's tears.

Out of the silence of the great hillslope came the dull sound of a voice, and as Miss Peck sprang from her chair to the window, dropping the sleeping cat in a solid mass on the floor, she recognized the noise of a carriage. Her heart was beating provokingly; she was tired by the excitement of the last few days. She did not remember this, but was conscious of being startled in an unusual way. It must be some strange crisis in her life; she turned and looked about the familiar kitchen as if it were going to be altogether swept away. "Now, you needn't be afraid that Pigley's comin' to bring her back, Elizy Peck!" she assured herself with grim humor in that minute's apprehension of disaster.

A man outside spoke sternly to his horse, Eliza stepped quickly to the door and opened it wide. She was not afraid of the messenger, only of the message.

"Hold the light so's I can see to tie this colt," said a familiar voice; "it's as dark as a pocket, 'Liza. I'll be right in. You must put on a good warm shawl; 't is as bad as rain, this fog is. The minister wants you to come down to his house; he's at his wits' end, and there was nobody we could think of that's free an' able except you. His wife's gone, died at quarter to six, and left a mis'able baby; but the doctor expects 't will live. The nurse they bargained with's failed 'em, and 't is an awful state o' things as you ever see. Half the women in town are there, and the minister's overcome; he's sort of fainted away two or three times, and they don't know who else to get, till the doctor said your name, and he groaned right out you was the one. 'T ain't right to refuse, as I view it. Mis' Spence and Mis' Corbell is going to watch with the dead, but there needs a head."

Eliza Peck felt for once as if she lacked that useful possession herself, and sat down, with amazing appearance of calmness, in one of her splint-bottomed chairs to collect her thoughts. The messenger was a good deal excited; so was she; but in a few moments she rose, cutting short his inconsequent description of affairs at the parsonage.

"You just put out the fire as best you can," she said. "We'll talk as we go along. There's plenty o' ashes there, I'm sure; I let the stove cool off considerable, for I was meanin' to go to bed in another five minutes. The cat'll do well enough. I'll leave her plenty for to-morrow, and she's got a place where she can crep in an' out of the wood-shed. I'll just slip on another dress and put the nails over the windows, an' we'll be right off." She was quite herself again now; and, true to her promise, it was not many minutes before the door was locked, the house left in darkness, and Ezra Weston and Miss Peck were driving comfortably down the lane. The fog had all blown away, suddenly the stars were out, and the air was sweet with the smell of the wet bark of black birches and cherry and apple-trees that grew by the fences. The leaves had fallen fast through the day, weighted by the dampness until their feeble stems could keep them in place no longer; for the bright colors of the foliage there had come at night sweet odors and a richness of fragrance in the soft air.

" 'T is an unwholesome streak o' weather, ain't it?" asked Ezra Weston. "Feels like a dog-day evenin' now, don't it? Come this time o' year we want bracin' up."

Miss Peck did not respond; her sympathetic heart was dwelling on the thought that she was going, not only to a house of mourning, but to a bereft parsonage. She would not have felt so unequal to soothing the sorrows of her every-day acquaintances, but she could hardly face the duty of consoling the new minister. But she never once wished that she had not consented so easily to respond to his piteous summons.

There was a strangely festive look in the village, for the exciting news of Mrs. Elbury's death had flown from house to house—lights were bright everywhere, and in the parsonage brightest of all. It looked as if the hostess were receiving her friends, and helping them to make merry, instead of being white and still, and done with this world, while the busy women of the parish were pulling open her closets and bureau drawers in search of household possessions. Nobody stopped to sentimentalize over the poor soul's delicate orderliness, or the simple, loving preparations she had made for the coming of the baby which fretfully wailed in the next room.

"Here's a nice black silk that never was touched with the scissors!" said one good dame, as if a kind Providence ought to have arranged for the use of such a treasure in setting the bounds of the dead woman's life.

"Does seem too bad, don't it? I always heard her folks was well off," replied somebody in a loud whisper; "she had everything to live for." There was great eagerness to be of service to the stricken pastor, and the kind neighbors did their best to prove the extent of their sympathy. One after another went to the room where he was, armed with various excuses, and the story of his sad looks and distress was repeated again and again to a grieved audience.

When Miss Peck came in she had to listen to a full description of the day's events, and was decorously slow in assuming her authority; but at last the house was nearly empty again, and only the watchers and one patient little mother of many children, who held this motherless child in loving arms, were left with Miss Peck in the parsonage. It seemed a year since she had sat in her quiet kitchen, a solitary woman whose occupations seemed too few and too trivial for her eager capacities and ambitions.

The autumn days went by, winter set in early, and Miss Peck was still mistress of the parsonage housekeeping. Her own cider was brought to the parsonage, and so were the potatoes and the apples; even the cat was transferred to a dull village existence, far removed in every way from her happy hunting-grounds among the snow-birds and plump squirrels. The minister's pale little baby loved Miss Peck and submitted to her rule already. She clung fast to the good woman with her little arms, and Miss Peck, who had always imagined that she did not care for infants, found herself watching the growth of this spark of human intelligence and affection with intense interest. After all, it was good to be spared the long winter at the farm; it had never occurred to her to dread it, but she saw now that it was a season to be dreaded, and one by one forgot the duties which at first beckoned her homeward and seemed so unavoidable. The farm-house seemed cold and empty when she paid it an occasional visit. She would not have believed that she could content herself so well away from the dear old home. If she could have had her favorite little Tom within reach, life would have been perfectly happy.

The minister proved at first very disappointing to her imaginary estimate and knowledge of him. If it had not been for her sturdy loyalty to him as pastor and employer, she could sometimes have joined more or less heartily in the expressions of the disaffected faction which forms a difficult element in every parish. Her sense of humor was deeply gratified when the leader of the opposition remarked that the minister was beginning to take notice a little, and was wearing his best hat every day, like every other widower since the world was made. Miss Peck's shrewd mind had already made sure that Mr. Elbury's loss was not so great as she had at first sympathetically believed; she knew that his romantic, ease-loving, self-absorbed, and self-admiring nature had been curbed and held in check by the literal, prosaic, faithful-in-little-things disposition of his dead wife. She was self-denying, he was self-indulgent; she was dutiful, while he was given to indolence—and the unfounded plea of ill-health made his only excuse. Miss Peck soon fell into the way of putting her shoulder to the wheel, and unobtrusively, even secretly, led the affairs of the parish. She never was deaf to the explanation of the wearing effect of brain-work, but accepted the weakness as well as the power of the ministerial character; and nobody listened more respectfully to his somewhat flowery and inconsequent discourses on Sunday than Miss Peck. The first Sunday they went to church together Eliza slipped into her own pew, half-way up the side aisle, and thought well of herself for her prompt decision afterward, though she regretted the act for a moment as she saw the minister stop to let her into the empty pew of the parsonage. He had been sure she was just behind him, and gained much sympathy from the congregation as he sighed and went his lonely way up the pulpitstairs. Even Mrs. Corbell, who had been averse to settling the Rev. Mr. Elbury, was moved by this incident, but directly afterward whispered to her next neighbor that "Lizy Peck would be sitting there before the year was out if she had the business-head they had all given her credit for."

It gives rise to melancholy reflections when one sees how quickly those who have suffered most cruel and disturbing bereavements learn to go their way alone. The great plan of our lives is never really broken nor suffers accidents. However stunning the shock, one can almost always understand gratefully that it was best for the vanished friend to vanish just when he did; that this world held no more duties or satisfactions for him; that his earthly life was in fact done and ended. Our relations with him must be lifted to a new plane.

Miss Peck thought often of the minister's loss, and always with tender sympathy, yet she could not help seeing that he was far from being unresigned or miserable in his grief. She was ready to overlook the fact that he depended upon his calling rather than upon his own character and efforts. The only way in which she made herself uncongenial to the minister was by persistent suggestions that he should take more exercise and "stir about out-doors a little." Once, when she had gone so far as to briskly inform him that he was getting logy, Mr. Elbury showed entire displeasure; and a little later, in the privacy of the kitchen, she voiced the opinion that Elizy Peck knew very well that she never did think ministers were angels—only human beings, like herself, in great danger of being made fools of. But the two good friends made up their little quarrel at supper-time.

"I have been looking up the derivation of that severe word you applied to me this noon," said the Reverend Mr. Elbury, pleasantly. "It is a localism; but it comes from the Dutch word *log,* which means heavy or unwieldy."

These words were pronounced plaintively, with evident consciousness that they hardly applied to his somewhat lank figure; and Miss Peck felt confused and rebuked, and went on pouring tea until both cup and saucer were full, and she scalded the end of her thumb. She was very weak in the hands of such a scholar as this, but later she had a reassuring sense of not having applied the epithet unjustly. With a feminine reverence for his profession, and for his attainments she had a keen sense of his human fallibility; and neither his grief, nor his ecclesiastical halo, nor his considerate idea of his own value, could blind her sharp eyes to certain shortcomings. She forgave them readily, but she knew them all by sight and name.

If there were any gift of Mr. Elbury's which could be sincerely called perfectly delightful by many people, it was his voice. When he was in a hurry, and gave hasty directions to his housekeeper about some mislaid possession, or called her down-stairs to stop the baby's vexatious crying, the tones were entirely different from those best known to the parish. Nature had gifted him with a power of carrying his voice into the depths of his sympathetic being and recovering it again gallantly. He had been considered the superior, in some respects, of that teacher of elocution who led the students of the theological seminary toward the glorious paths of oratory. There was a mellow middle-tone, most suggestive of tender feeling; but though it sounded sweet to other feminine ears, Miss Peck was always annoyed by it and impatient of a certain artificial quality in its cadences. To hear Mr. Elbury talk to his child in this tone, and address her as "my motherless babe," however affecting to other ears, was always unpleasant to Miss Peck. But she thought very well of his preaching; and the more he let all the decisions and responsibilities of everyday life fall to her share, the more she enjoyed life and told her friends that Mr. Elbury was a most amiable man to live with. And when spring was come the hillside farm was let on shares to one of Miss Peck's neighbors whom she could entirely trust. It was not the best of bargains for its owner, who had the reputation of being an excellent farmer, and the agreement cost her many sighs and not a little wakefulness. She felt too much shut in by this village life; but the minister pleaded his hapless lot, the little child was even more appealing in her babyhood, and so the long visit from little Tom and his sisters, the familiar garden, the three beehives, and the glory of the sunsets in the great, unbroken, western sky were all given up together for that year.

It was not so hard as it might have been. There was one most rewarding condition of life—the feast of books, which was new and bewilderingly delightful to the minister's housekeeper. She had made the most of the few well-chosen volumes of the farmhouse, but she never had known the joy of having more books than she could read, or their exquisite power of temptation, the delight of their friendly company. She was oftenest the student, the brain-wearied member, of the parsonage-family, but she never made it an excuse, or really recognized the new stimulus either. Life had never seemed so full to her; she was working with both hands earnestly, and no half-heartedness. She was filled with reverence in the presence of the minister's books; to her his calling, his character, and his influence were all made positive and respectable by this foundation of learning on his library-shelves. He was to her a man of letters, a critic, and a philosopher, besides being an experienced theologian from the very nature of his profession. Indeed, he had an honest liking for books, and was fond of reading aloud or being read to; and many an evening went joyfully by in the presence of the great English writers, whose best thoughts were rolled out in Mr. Elbury's best tones, and Miss Peck listened with delight, and cast many an affectionate glance at the sleeping child in the cradle at her feet, filled with gratitude as she was for all her privileges.

Mr. Elbury was most generous in his appreciation of Miss Peck's devotion, and never hesitated to give expression to sincere praise of her uncommon power of mind. He was led into paths of literature, otherwise untrod, by her delight; and sometimes, to rest his brain and make him ready for a good night's sleep, he asked his companion to read him a clever story. It was all a new world to the good woman whose schooling and reading had been sound, but restricted; and if ever a mind waked up with joy to its possession of the world of books, it was hers. She became ambitious for the increase of her own little library; and it was in reply to her outspoken plan for larger crops and more money from the farm another year, for the sake of bookbuying, that Mr. Elbury once said, earnestly, that his books were hers now. This careless expression was the spark which lit a new light for Miss Peck's imagination. For the first time a thrill of personal interest in the man made itself felt, through her devoted capacity for service and appreciation. He had ceased to be simply himself; he stood now for a widened life, a suggestion of added good and growth, a larger circle of human interests; in fact, his existence had made all the difference between her limited rural home and that connection with the great world which even the most contracted parsonage is sure to hold.

And that very night, while Mr. Elbury had gone, somewhat ruefully and ill-prepared, to his Bible class, Miss Peck's conscience set her womanly weakness before it for a famous arraigning. It was so far successful that words failed the defendant completely, and the session was dissolved in tears. For some days Miss Peck was not only stern with herself, but even with the minister, and was entirely devoted to her domestic affairs.

The very next Sunday it happened that Mr. Elbury exchanged pulpits with a brother-clergyman in the next large town, a thriving manufacturing centre, and he came home afterward in the best of spirits. He never had seemed so appreciative of his comfortable home, or Miss Peck's motherly desire to shield his weak nature from these practical cares of life to which he was entirely inadequate. He was unusually gay and amusing, and described, not with the best taste, the efforts of two of his unmarried lady-parishioners to make themselves agreeable. He had met them on the short journey, and did not hesitate to speak of himself lightly as a widower;

in fact, he recognized his own popularity and attractions in a way that was not pleasing to Miss Peck, yet she was used to his way of speaking and unaffectedly glad to have him at home again. She had been much disturbed and grieved by her own thoughts in his absence. She could not be sure whether she was wise in drifting toward a nearer relation to the minister. She was not exactly shocked at finding herself interested in him, but, with her usual sense of propriety and justice, she insisted upon taking everybody's view of the question before the weaker Miss Peck was accorded a hearing. She was enraged with herself for feeling abashed and liking to avoid the direct scrutiny of her fellow-parishioners. Mrs. Corbell and she had always been the best of friends, but for the first time Miss Peck was annoyed by such freedom of comment and opinion. And Sister Corbell had never been so forward about spending the afternoon at the parsonage, or running in for half-hours of gossip in the morning, as in these latter days. At last she began to ask the coy Eliza about her plans for the wedding, in a half-joking, half-serious tone which was hard to bear.

"You're a sight too good for him," was the usual conclusion, "and so I tell everybody. The whole parish has got it settled for you; and there's as many as six think hard of you, because you've given 'em no chance, bein' right here on the spot."

It seemed as if a resistless torrent of fate were sweeping our independent friend toward the brink of a great change. She insisted to the quailing side of her nature that she did not care for the minister himself, that she was likely to age much sooner than he, with his round, boyish face and plump cheeks. "They'll be takin' you for his mother, Lizy, when you go amongst strangers, little and dried up as you're gettin' to be a'ready; you're three years older anyway, and look as if 't was nine." Yet the capable, clear-headed woman was greatly enticed by the high position and requirements of mistress of the parsonage. She liked the new excitement and authority, and grew more and more happy in the exercise of powers which a solitary life at the farm would hardly arouse or engage. There was a vigorous growth of independence and determination in Miss Peck's character, and she had not lived alone so many years for nothing. But there was no outward sign yet of capitulation. She was firmly convinced that the minister could not get on without her, and that she would rather not get on without him and the pleasure of her new activities. If possible, she grew a little more self-contained and reserved in manner and speech, while carefully anticipating his wants and putting better and better dinners on the parochial table.

As for Mr. Elbury himself, he became more cheerful every day, and was almost demonstrative in his affectionate gratitude. He spoke always as if they were one in their desire to interest and benefit the parish; he had fallen into a pleasant home-like habit of saying "we" whenever household or parish affairs were under discussion. Once, when somebody had been remarking the too-evident efforts of one of her sister-parishioners to gain Mr. Elbury's affection, he had laughed leniently; but when this gossiping caller had gone away the minister said, gently, "We know better, don't we, Miss Peck?" and Eliza could not help feeling that his tone meant a great deal. Yet she took no special notice of him, and grew much more taciturn than was natural. Her heart beat warmly under her prim alpacca-dress; she already looked younger and a great deal happier than when she first came to live at the parsonage. Her executive ability was made glad by the many duties that fell upon her, and those who knew her and Mr. Elbury best thought nothing could be wiser than their impending marriage. Did not the little child need Miss Peck's motherly care? did not the helpless minister need the assistance of a clear-sighted business-woman and good housekeeper? did not Eliza herself need and deserve a husband? But even with increasing certainty she still gave no outward sign of their secret understanding. It was likely that Mr. Elbury thought best to wait a year after his wife's death, and when he spoke right out was the time to show what her answer would be. But somehow the thought of the dear old threadbare farm in the autumn weather was always a sorrowful thought; and on the days when Mr. Elbury hired a horse and wagon, and invited her and the baby to accompany him on a series of parochial visitations, she could not bear to look at the home-fields and the pasture-slopes. She was thankful that the house itself was not in sight from the main road. The crops that summer had been unusually good; something called her thoughts back continually to the old home, and accused her of disloyalty. Yet she consoled herself by thinking it was very natural to have such regrets, and to consider the importance of such a step at her sensible time of life. So it drew near winter again, and she grew more and more unrelenting and scornful whenever her acquaintances suggested the idea that her wedding ought to be drawing near.

Mr. Elbury seemed to have taken a new lease of youthful hope and ardor. He was busy in the parish and very popular, particularly among his women-parishioners. Miss Peck urged him on with his good works, and it seemed as if they expressed their interest in each other by their friendliness to the parish in general. Mr. Elbury had joined a ministers' club in the large town already spoken of, and spent a day there now and then, besides his regular Monday-night attendance on the club-meeting. He was preparing a series of sermons on the history of the Jews, and was glad to avail himself of a good free-library, the lack of which he frequently lamented in his own village. Once he said, eagerly, that he had no idea of ending his days here, and this gave Miss Peck a sharp pang. She could not bear to think of leaving her old home, and the tears filled her eyes. When she had reached the shelter of the kitchen, she retorted to the too-easily ruffled element of her character that there was no need of crossing that bridge till she came to it; and, after an appealing glance at the academy-steeple above the maple-trees, she returned to the study to finish dusting. She saw, without apprehension, that the minister quickly pushed something under the leaves of his blotting-paper and frowned a little. It was not his usual time for writing—she had a new proof of her admiring certainty that Mr. Elbury wrote for the papers at times under an assumed name.

One Monday evening he had not returned from the ministers' meeting until later than usual, and she began to be slightly anxious. The baby had not been very well all day, and she particularly wished to have an errand done before night, but did not dare to leave the child alone, while, for a wonder, nobody had been in. Mr. Elbury had shown a great deal of feeling before he went away in the morning, and as she was admiringly looking at his well-fitting clothes and neat clerical attire, a thrill of pride and affection had made her eyes shine unwontedly. She was really beginning to like him very much. For the first and last time in his life the minister stepped quickly forward and kissed her on the forehead. "My good, kind friend!" he exclaimed, in that deep tone which the whole parish loved; then he hurried away. Miss Peck felt a strange dismay, and stood by the breakfast-table like a statue. She even touched her forehead with trembling fingers. Somehow she inwardly rebelled, but kissing meant more to her

than to some people. She never had been used to it, except
with little Tom—though the last brotherly kiss his father gave
her before he went to the war had been one of the treasures
of her memory. All that day she was often reminded of the
responsible and darker side, the inspected and criticised side,
of the high position of minister's wife. It was clearly time for
proper rebuke when evening came; and as she sat by the
light, mending Mr. Elbury's stockings, she said over and over
again that she had walked into this with her eyes wide open,
and if the experience of forty years hadn't put any sense into
her it was too late to help it now.

Suddenly she heard the noise of wheels in the side yard.
Could anything have happened to Mr. Elbury? were they
bringing him home hurt, or dead even? He never drove up
from the station unless it were bad weather. She rushed to the
door with a flaring light, and was bewildered at the sight of
trunks and, most of all, at the approach of Mr. Elbury, for
he wore a most sentimental expression, and led a young person by the hand.

"Dear friend," he said, in that mellow tone of his, "I hope
you, too, will love my little wife."

Almost any other woman would have dropped the kerosene
lamp on the doorstep, but not Miss Eliza Peck. Luckily a
gust of autumn wind blew it out, and the bride had to fumble
her way into her new home. Miss Peck quickly procured one
of her own crinkly lamplighters, and bent toward the open
fire to kindle a new light.

"You've taken me by surprise," she managed to say, in her
usual tone of voice, though she felt herself shaking with excitement.

At that moemnt the ailing step-daughter gave a forlorn
little wail from the wide sofa, where she had been put to
sleep with difficulty. Miss Peck's kind heart felt the pathos of
the situation; she lifted the little child and stilled it, then she
held out a kindly hand to the minister's new wife, while Mr.
Elbury stood beaming by.

"I wish you may be very happy here, as I have been," said
the good woman, earnestly. "But Mr. Elbury, you ought to
have let me know. I could have kept a secret"—and satisfaction filled Eliza Peck's heart that she never, to use her own
expression, had made a fool of herself before the First Parish.
She had kept her own secret, and in this earthquake of a moment was clearly conscious that she was hero enough to behave as if there had never been any secret to keep. And

indignation with the Reverend Mr. Elbury, who had so imprudently kept his own counsel, threw down the sham temple of Cupid which a faithless god called Propinquity had succeeded in rearing.

Miss Peck made a feast, and for the last time played the part of hostess at the minister's table. She had remorselessly inspected the conspicuous bad taste of the new Mrs. Elbury's dress, the waving, cheap-looking feather of her hat, the make-believe richness of her clothes, and saw, with dire compassion, how unused she was to young children. The brave Eliza tried to make the best of things—but one moment she found herself thinking how uncomfortable Mr. Elbury's home would be henceforth with this poor reed to lean upon, a townish, empty-faced, tiresomely pretty girl; the next moment she pitied the girl herself, who would have the hard task before her of being the wife of an indolent preacher in a country town. Miss Peck had generously allowed her farm to supplement the limited salary of the First Parish; in fact, she had been a silent partner in the parsonage establishment rather than a dependent. Would the First Parish laugh at her now? It was a stinging thought; but she honestly believed that the minister himself would be most commiserated when the parish opinion had found time to simmer down.

The next day our heroine, whose face was singularly free from disappointment, told the minister that she would like to leave at once, for she was belated about many things, not having had notice in season of his change of plan.

"I've been telling your wife all about the house and parish interests the best I can, and it's likely she wants to take everything into her own hands right away," added the uncommon housekeeper, with a spice of malice; but Mr. Elbury flushed, and looked down at the short, capable Eliza appealingly. He knew her virtues so well that this announcement gave him a crushing blow.

"Why, I thought of course you would continue here as usual," he said, in a strange, harsh voice that would have been perfectly surprising in the pulpit. "Mrs. Elbury has never known any care. We count upon your remaining."

Whereupon Miss Peck looked him disdainfully in the face, and, for a moment, mistook him for that self so often reproved and now sunk into depths of ignominy.

"If you thought that, you ought to have known better," she said. "You can't expect a woman who has property and relations of her own to give up her interests for yours altogether.

I got a letter this morning from my brother's boy, little Tom, and he's got leave from his mother and her husband to come and stop with me a good while—he says all winter. He's been sick, and they've had to take him out o' school. I never supposed that such stived-up air would agree with him," concluded Miss Peck, triumphantly. She was full of joy and hope at this new turn of affairs, and the minister was correspondingly hopeless. "I'll take the baby home for a while, if 't would be a convenience for you," she added, more leniently. "That is, after I get my house well warmed, and there's something in it to eat. I wish you could have spoken to me a fortnight ago; but I saw Joe Farley to-day—that boy that lived with me quite a while—he's glad to come back. He only engaged to stop till after cider time where he's been this summer, and he's promised to look about for a good cow for me. I always thought well of Joe."

The minister turned away ruefully, and Miss Peck went about her work. She meant to leave the house in the best of order; but the whole congregation came trooping in that day and the next, and she hardly had time to build a fire in her own kitchen before Joe Farley followed her from the station with the beloved little Tom. He looked tall and thin and pale, and largely freckled under his topknot of red hair. Bless his heart! how his lonely aunt hugged him and kissed him, and how thankful he was to get back to her, though she never would have suspected it if she had not known him so well. A shy boy-fashion of reserve and stolidity had replaced his early demonstrations, but he promptly went to the shelf of books to find the familiar old "Robinson Crusoe." Miss Peck's heart leaped for joy as she remembered how much more she could teach the child about books. She felt a great wave of gratitude fill her cheerful soul as she remembered the pleasure and gain of those evenings when she and Mr. Elbury had read together.

There was a great deal of eager discussion in the village; and much amused scrutiny of Eliza's countenance, as she walked up the side aisle that first Sunday after the minister was married. She led little Tom by the hand, but he opened the pew-door and ushered her in handsomely, and she looked smilingly at her neighbors and nodded her head sideways at the boy in a way that made them suspect that she was much more in love with him, freckles and all, than she had ever been with Mr. Elbury. A few minutes later she frowned at Tom sternly for greeting his old acquaintances over the pew-

rail in a way that did not fit the day or place. There was no
chance to laugh at her disappointment; for nobody could help
understanding that her experience at the parsonage had been
merely incidental in her life, and that she had returned
willingly to her old associations. The dream of being a minister's wife had been only a dream, and she was surprised to
find herself waking from it with such resignation to her lot.

"I'd just like to know what sort of a breakfast they had,"
she said to herself, as the bride's topknot went waving and
bobbing up to the parsonage pew. "If ever there was a man
who was fussy about his cup o' coffee, 't is Reverend Wilbur
Elbury! There now, Elizy Peck, don't you wish 't was you a-
setting there up front and feeling the eyes of the whole parish
sticking in your back? You could have had him, you know, if
you'd set right about it. I never did think you had proper
ideas of what gettin' promoted is; but if you ain't discovered
a new world for yourself like C'lumbus, I miss my guess. If
you'd stayed on the farm all alone last year you'd had no
thoughts but hens and rutabagys, and as 't is you've been
livin' amon'st books. There's nothin' to regret if you did just
miss makin' a fool o' yourself."

At this moment Mr. Elbury's voice gently sounded from
the pulpit, and Miss Peck sprang to her feet with the agility
of a jack-in-the-box—she had forgotten her surroundings in
the vividness of her revery. She hardly knew what the minister said in that first prayer; for many reasons this was an exciting day.

A little later our heroine accepted the invitation of her second cousin, Mrs. Corbell, to spend the hour or two between
morning and afternoon services. They had agreed that it
seemed like old times, and took pleasure in renewing this custom of the Sunday visit. Little Tom was commented upon as
to health and growth and freckles and family resemblance;
and when he strayed out-of-doors, after such an early dinner
as only a growing boy can make vanish with the enchanter's
wand of his appetite, the two women indulged in a good talk.

"I don't know how you viewed it, this morning," began
Cousin Corbell; "but, to my eyes, the minister looked as if he
felt cheap as a broom. There, I never was one o' his wor-
shipers, you well know. To speak plain, Elizy, I was really
concerned at one time for fear you would be over-persuaded.
I never said one word to warp your judgment, but I did feel
as if 't would be a shame. I—"

But Miss Peck was not ready yet to join the opposition,

and she interrupted at once in an amiable but decided tone. "We'll let by-gones be by-gones; it's just as well, and a good deal better. Mr. Elbury always treated me the best he knew how; and I knew he wa'n't perfect, but 't was full as much his misfortune as his fault. I declare I don't know what else there was he could ha' done if he hadn't taken to preaching; and he has very kind feelings, specially if any one's in trouble. Talk of 'leading about captive silly women,' there are some cases where we've got to turn round and say it right the other way—'t is the silly women that do the leadin' themselves. And I tell you," concluded Miss Peck, with apparent irrelevancy, "I was glad last night to have a good honest look at a yellow sunset. If ever I do go and set my mind on a minister, I'm going to hunt for one that's well settled in a hill parish. I used to feel as if I was shut right in, there at the parsonage; it's a good house enough, if it only stood where you could see anything out of the windows. I can't carry out my plans o' life in any such situation."

"I expect to hear that you've blown right off the top o' your hill some o' these windy days," said Mrs. Corbell, without resentment, though she was very dependent, herself, upon seeing the passing.

The church bell began to ring, and our friends rose to put on their bonnets and answer its summons. Miss Peck's practical mind revolved the possibility of there having been a decent noonday meal at the parsonage. "Maria Corbell!" she said, with dramatic intensity, "mark what I'm goin' to say—it ain't I that's goin' to reap the whirlwind; it's your pastor, the Reverend Mr. Elbury, of the First Parish!"

The Town Poor

❧

Mrs. William Trimble and Miss Rebecca Wright were driving along Hampden east road, one afternoon in early spring. Their progress was slow. Mrs. Trimble's sorrel horse was old and stiff, and the wheels were clogged by clay mud. The frost was not yet out of the ground, although the snow was nearly gone, except in a few places on the north side of the woods, or where it had drifted all winter against a length of fence.

"There must be a good deal o' snow to the nor'ard of us yet," said weather-wise Mrs. Trimble. "I feel it in the air; 't is more than the ground-damp. We ain't goin' to have real nice weather till the up-country snow's all gone."

"I heard say yesterday that there was good sleddin' yet, all up through Parsley," responded Miss Wright. "I shouldn't like to live in them northern places. My cousin Ellen's husband was a Parsley man, an' he was obliged, as you may have heard, to go up north to his father's second wife's funeral; got back day before yesterday. 'T was about twenty-one miles, an' they started on wheels; but when they'd gone nine or ten miles, they found 't was no sort o' use, an' left their wagon an' took a sleigh. The man that owned it charged 'em four an' six, too. I shouldn't have thought he would; they told him they was goin' to a funeral; an' they had their own buffaloes an' everything."

"Well, I expect it's a good deal harder scratchin', up that way; they have to git money where they can; the farms is very poor as you go north," suggested Mrs. Trimble kindly. " 'T ain't none too rich a country where we be, but I've always been grateful I wa'n't born up to Parsley."

The old horse plodded along, and the sun, coming out from the heavy spring clouds, sent a sudden shine of light along the muddy road. Sister Wright drew her large veil forward over the high brim of her bonnet. She was not used to driving, or to being much in the open air; but Mrs. Trimble was an active business woman, and looked after her own affairs herself, in all weathers. The late Mr. Trimble had left her a good farm, but not much ready money, and it was often said that she was better off in the end than if he had lived. She regretted his loss deeply, however; it was impossible for her to speak of him, even to intimate friends, without emotion, and nobody had ever hinted that this emotion was insincere. She was most warm-hearted and generous, and in her limited way played the part of Lady Bountiful in the town of Hampden.

"Why, there's where the Bray girls lives, ain't it?" she exclaimed, as, beyond a thicket of witch-hazel and scrub-oak, they came in sight of a weather-beaten, solitary farmhouse. The barn was too far away for thrift or comfort, and they could see long lines of light between the shrunken boards as they came nearer. The fields looked both stony and sodden. Somehow, even Parsley itself could be hardly more forlorn.

"Yes'm," said Miss Wright, "that's where they live now, poor things. I know the place, though I ain't been up here for years. You don't suppose, Mis' Trimble—I ain't seen the girls out to meetin' all winter. I've re'lly been covetin' "—

"Why, yes, Rebecca, of course we could stop," answered Mrs. Trimble heartily. "The exercises was over earlier'n I expected, an' you're goin' to remain over night long o' me, you know. There won't be no tea till we git there, so we can't be late. I'm in the habit o' sendin' a basket to the Bray girls when any o' our folks is comin' this way, but I ain't been to see 'em since they moved up here. Why, it must be a good deal over a year ago. I know 't was in the late winter they had to make the move. 'T was cruel hard, I must say, an' if I hadn't been down with my pleurisy fever I'd have stirred round an' done somethin' about it. There was a good deal o' sickness at the time, an'—well, 't was kind o' rushed through, breakin' of 'em up, an' lots o' folks blamed the selec'*men;* but when 't was done, 't was done, an' nobody took holt to undo it. Ann an' Mandy looked same's ever when they come to meetin', 'long in the summer—kind o' wishful, perhaps. They've always sent me word they was gittin' on pretty comfortable."

"That would be their way," said Rebecca Wright. "They never was any hand to complain, though Mandy's less cheerful than Ann. If Mandy'd been spared such poor eyesight, an' Ann hadn't got her lame wrist that wa'n't set right, they'd kep' off the town fast enough. They both shed tears when they talked to me about havin' to break up, when I went to see 'em before I went over to brother Asa's. You see we was brought up neighbors, an' we went to school together, the Brays an' me. 'T was a special Providence brought us home this road, I've been so covetin' a chance to git to see 'em. My lameness hampers me."

"I'm glad we come this way, myself," said Mrs. Trimble.

"I'd like to see just how they fare," Miss Rebecca Wright continued. "They give their consent to goin' on the town because they knew they'd got to be dependent, an' so they felt 't would come easier for all than for a few to help 'em. They acted real dignified an' right-minded, contrary to what most do in such cases, but they was dreadful anxious to see who would bid 'em off, town-meeting day; they did so hope 't would be somebody right in the village. I just sat down an' cried good when I found Abel Janes's folks had got hold of 'em. They always had the name of bein' slack an' poor-spirited, an' they did it just for what they got out o' the town. The selectmen this last year ain't what we have had. I hope they've been considerate about the Bray girls."

"I should have be'n more considerate about fetchin' of you over," apologized Mrs. Trimble. "I've got my horse, an' you're lame-footed; 't is too far for you to come. But time does slip away with busy folks, an' I forgit a good deal I ought to remember."

"There's nobody more considerate than you be," protested Miss Rebecca Wright.

Mrs. Trimble made no answer, but took out her whip and gently touched the sorrel horse, who walked considerably faster, but did not think it worth while to trot. It was a long, round-about way to the house, farther down the road and up a lane.

"I never had any opinion of the Bray girls' father, leavin' 'em as he did," said Mrs. Trimble.

"He was much praised in his time, though there was always some said his early life hadn't been up to the mark," explained her companion. "He was a great favorite of our then preacher, the Reverend Daniel Longbrother. They did a good deal for the parish, but they did it their own way. Bray was one that did his part in the repairs without urging. You know 't was in his time the first repairs was made, when they got out the old soundin'-board an' them handsome square pews. It cost an awful sight o' money, too. They hadn't done payin' up that debt when they set to alter it again an' git the walls frescoed. My grandmother was one that always spoke her mind right out, an' she was dreadful

opposed to breakin' up the square pews where she'd always
set. They was countin' up what 't would cost in parish
meetin', and she riz right up an' said 't wouldn't cost nothin'
to let 'em stay, an' there wa'n't a house carpenter left in the
parish that could do such nice work, an' time would come
when the great-grandchildren would give their eye-teeth to
have the old meetin'-house look just as it did then. But haul
the inside to pieces they would and did."

"There come to be a real fight over it, didn't there?"
agreed Mrs. Trimble soothingly. "Well, 't wa'n't good taste. I
remember the old house well. I come here as a child to visit a
cousin o' mother's, an' Mr. Trimble's folks was neighbors, an'
we was drawed to each other then, young's we was. Mr.
Trimble spoke of it many's the time—that first time he ever see
me, in a leghorn hat with a feather; 't was one that mother
had, an' pressed over."

"When I think of them old sermons that used to be
preached in that old meetin'-house of all, I'm glad it's altered over, so's not to remind folks," said Miss Rebecca
Wright, after a suitable pause. "Them old brimstone discourses, you know, Mis' Trimble. Preachers is far more reasonable, nowadays. Why, I set an' thought, last Sabbath, as I
listened, that if old Mr. Longbrother an' Deacon Bray could
hear the difference they'd crack the ground over 'em like pole
beans, an' come right up 'long side their headstones."

Mrs. Trimble laughed heartily, and shook the reins three or
four times by way of emphasis. "There's no gitting round
you," she said, much pleased. "I should think Deacon Bray
would want to rise, any way, if 't was so he could, an' knew
how his poor girls was farin'. A man ought to provide for his
folks he's got to leave behind him, specially if they're women.
To be sure, they had their little home; but we've seen how,
with all their industrious ways, they hadn't means to keep it.
I s'pose he thought he'd got time enough to lay by, when he
give so generous in collections; but he didn't lay by, an' there
they be. He might have took lessons from the squirrels: even
them little wild creatur's makes them their winter hoards, an'
menfolks ought to know enough if squirrels does. 'Be just before you are generous:' that's what was always set for the B's
in the copy-books, when I was to school, and it often runs
through my mind."

" 'As for man, his days are as grass'—that was for A; the
two go well together," added Miss Rebecca Wright soberly.
"My good gracious, ain't this a starved-lookin' place? It

makes me ache to think them nice Bray girls has to brook it here."

The sorrel horse, though somewhat puzzled by an unexpected deviation from his homeward way, willingly came to a stand by the gnawed corner of the door-yard fence, which evidently served as hitching-place. Two or three ragged old hens were picking about the yard, and at last a face appeared at the kitchen window, tied up in a handkerchief, as if it were a case of toothache. By the time our friends reached the side door next this window, Mrs. Janes came disconsolately to open it for them, shutting it again as soon as possible, though the air felt more chilly inside the house.

"Take seats," said Mrs. Janes briefly. "You'll have to see me just as I be. I have been suffering these four days with the ague, and everything to do. Mr. Janes is to court, on the jury. 'T was inconvenient to spare him. I should be pleased to have you lay off your things."

Comfortable Mrs. Trimble looked about the cheerless kitchen, and could not think of anything to say; so she smiled blandly and shook her head in answer to the invitation. "We'll just set a few minutes with you, to pass the time o' day, an' then we must go in an' have a word with the Miss Brays, bein' old acquaintance. It ain't been so we could git to call on 'em before. I don't know's you're acquainted with Miss R'becca Wright. She's been out of town a good deal."

"I heard she was stopping over to Plainfields with her brother's folks," replied Mrs. Janes, rocking herself with irregular motion, as she sat close to the stove. "Got back some time in the fall, I believe?"

"Yes'm," said Miss Rebecca, with an undue sense of guilt and conviction. "We've been to the installation over to the East Parish, an' thought we'd stop in; we took this road home to see if 't was any better. How is the Miss Brays gettin' on?"

"They're well's common," answered Mrs. Janes grudgingly. "I was put out with Mr. Janes for fetchin' of 'em here, with all I've got to do, an' I own I was kind o' surly to 'em 'long to the first of it. He gits the money from the town, an' it helps him out; but he bid 'em off for five dollars a month, an' we can't do much for 'em at no such price as that. I went an' dealt with the selec'men, an' made 'em promise to find their firewood an' some other things extra. They was glad to get rid o' the matter the fourth time I went, an' would ha' promised 'most anything. But Mr. Janes don't keep me half the time in oven-wood, he's off so much, an' we was cramped o' room, any way. I have to store things up garrit a good deal, an' that keeps me trampin' right through their room. I do the best for 'em I can, Mis' Trimble, but 't ain't so easy for me as 't is for you, with all your means to do with."

The poor woman looked pinched and miserable herself, though it was evident that she had no gift at house or home keeping. Mrs. Trimble's heart was wrung with pain, as she thought of the unwelcome inmates of such a place; but she held her peace bravely, while Miss Rebecca again gave some brief information in regard to the installation.

"You go right up them back stairs," the hostess directed at last. "I'm glad some o' you church folks has seen fit to come an' visit 'em. There ain't been nobody here this long spell, an' they've aged a sight since they come. They always send down a taste out of your baskets, Mis' Trimble, an' I relish it, I tell you. I'll shut the door after you, if you don't object. I feel every draught o' cold air."

"I've always heard she was a great hand to make a poor mouth. Wa'n't she from somewheres up Parsley way?" whispered Miss Rebecca, as they stumbled in the half-light.

"Poor meechin' body, wherever she come from," replied Mrs. Trimble, as she knocked at the door.

There was silence for a moment after this unusual sound; then one of the Bray sisters opened the door. The eager guests stared into a small, low room, brown with age, and gray, too, as if former dust and cobwebs could not be made wholly to disappear. The two elderly women who stood there looked like captives. Their withered faces wore a look of apprehension, and the room itself was more bare and plain than was fitting to their evident refinement of character and self-respect. There was an uncovered small table in the middle of the floor, with some crackers on a plate; and, for some reason or other, this added a great deal to the general desolation.

But Miss Ann Bray, the elder sister, who carried her right arm in a sling, with piteously drooping fingers, gazed at the visitors with radiant joy. She had not seen them arrive.

The one window gave only the view at the back of the house, across the fields, and their coming was indeed a surprise. The next minute she was laughing and crying together. "Oh, sister!" she said, "if here ain't our dear Mis' Trimble!—an' my heart o' goodness, 't is 'Becca Wright, too! What dear good creatur's you be! I've felt all day as if something good was goin' to happen, an' was just sayin' to myself 't was most sundown now, but I wouldn't let on to Mandany

I'd give up hope quite yet. You see, the scissors stuck in the floor this very mornin' an' it's always a reliable sign. There, I've got to kiss ye both again!"

"I don't know where we can all set," lamented sister Mandana. "There ain't but the one chair an' the bed; t' other chair's too rickety; an' we've been promised another these ten days; but first they've forgot it, an' next Mis' Janes can't spare it—one excuse an' another. I am goin' to git a stump o' wood an' nail a board on to it, when I can git outdoor again," said Mandana, in a plaintive voice. "There, I ain't goin' to complain o' nothin', now you've come," she added; and the guests sat down, Mrs. Trimble, as was proper, in the one chair.

"We've sat on the bed many's the time with you, 'Becca, an' talked over our girl nonsense, ain't we? You know where 't was—in the little back bedroom we had when we was girls, an' used to peek out at our beaux through the strings o' mornin'-glories," laughed Ann Bray delightedly, her thin face shining more and more with joy. "I brought some o' them mornin'-glory seeds along when we come away, we'd raised 'em so many years; an' we got 'em started all right, but the hens found 'em out. I declare I chased them poor hens, foolish as 't was; but the mornin'-glories I'd counted on a sight to remind me o' home. You see, our debts was so large, after my long sickness an' all, that we didn't feel 't was right to keep back anything we could help from the auction."

It was impossible for anyone to speak for a moment or two; the sisters felt their own uprooted condition afresh, and their guests for the first time really comprehended the piteous contrast between that neat little village house, which now seemed a palace of comfort, and this cold, unpainted upper room in the remote Janes farmhouse. It was an unwelcome thought to Mrs. Trimble that the well-to-do town of Hampden could provide no better for its poor than this, and her round face flushed with resentment and the shame of personal responsibility. "The girls shall be well settled in the village before another winter, if I pay their board myself," she made an inward resolution, and took another almost tearful look at the broken stove, the miserable bed, and the sisters' one hair-covered trunk, on which Mandana was sitting. But the poor place was filled with a golden spirit of hospitality.

Rebecca was again discoursing eloquently of the installation; it was so much easier to speak of general subjects, and the sisters had evidently been longing to hear some news.

Since the late summer they had not been to church, and presently Mrs. Trimble asked the reason.

"Now, don't you go to pouring out our woes, Mandy!" begged little old Ann, looking shy and almost girlish, and as if she insisted upon playing that life was still all before them and all pleasure. "Don't you go to spoilin' their visit with our complaints! They know well 's we do that changes must come, an' we'd been so wonted to our home things that this come hard at first; but then they felt for us, I know just as well 's can be. 'T will soon be summer again, an' 't is real pleasant right out in the fields here, when there ain't too hot a spell. I've got to know a sight o' singing' birds since we come."

"Give me the folks I've always known," sighed the younger sister, who looked older than Miss Ann, and less even-tempered. "You may have your birds, if you want 'em. I do re'lly long to go to meetin' an' see folks go by up the aisle. Now, I will speak of it, Ann, whatever you say. We need, each of us, a pair o' good stout shoes an' rubbers—ours are all wore out; an' we've asked an' asked, an' they never think to bring 'em, an'—"

Poor old Mandana, on the trunk, covered her face with her arms and sobbed aloud. The elder sister stood over her, and patted her on the thin shoulder like a child, and tried to comfort her. It crossed Mrs. Trimble's mind that it was not the first time one had wept and the other had comforted. The sad scene must have been repeated many times in that long, drear winter. She would see them forever after in her mind as fixed as a picture, and her own tears fell fast.

"You didn't see Mis' Janes's cunning little boy, the next one to the baby, did you?" asked Ann Bray, turning round quickly at last, and going cheerfully on with the conversation. "Now, hush, Mandy, dear; they'll think you're childish! He's a dear, friendly little creatur', an' likes to stay with us a good deal, though we feel 's if it 't was too cold for him, now we are waitin' to get us more wood."

"When I think of the acres o' woodland in this town!" groaned Rebecca Wright. "I believe I'm goin' to preach next Sunday, 'stead o' the minister, an' I'll make the sparks fly. I've always heard the saying, 'What's everybody's business is nobody's business,' an' I've come to believe it."

"Now, don't you, 'Becca. You've happened on a kind of a poor time with us, but we've got more belongings than you see here, an' a good large cluset, where we can store those things there ain't room to have about. You an' Miss Trimble have happened on a kind of poor day, you know. Soon's I git me some stout shoes an' rubbers, as Mandy says, I can fetch home plenty o' little dry boughs o' pine; you remember I was always a great hand to roam in the woods? If we could only have a front room, so 't we could look out on the road an' see passin', an' was shod for meetin', I don' know 's we should complain. Now we're just goin' to give you what we've got, an' make out with a good welcome. We make more tea'n we want in the mornin', an' then let the fire go down, since 't has been so mild. We've got a *good* cluset" (disappearing as she spoke), "an' I know this to be good tea, 'cause it's some o' yourn, Mis' Trimble. An' here's our sprigged chiny cups that R'becca knows by sight, if Mis' Trimble don't. We kep' out four o' 'em, an' put the even half dozen with the rest of the auction stuff. I've often wondered who'd got 'em, but I never asked, for fear 't would be somebody that would distress us. They was mother's, you know."

The four cups were poured, and the little table pushed to the bed, where Rebecca Wright still sat, and Mandana, wiping her eyes, came and joined her. Mrs. Trimble sat in her chair at the end, and Ann trotted about the room in pleased content for a while, and in and out of the closet, as if she still had much to do; then she came and stood opposite Mrs. Trimble. She was very short and small, and there was no painful sense of her being obliged to stand. The four cups were not quite full of cold tea, but there was a clean old tablecloth folded double, and a plate with three pairs of crackers neatly piled, and a small—it must be owned, a very small—piece of hard white cheese. Then, for a treat, in a glass dish, there was a little preserved peach, the last—Miss Rebecca knew it instinctively—of the household stores brought from their old home. It was very sugary, this bit of peach; and as she helped her guests and sister Mandy, Miss Ann Bray said, half unconsciously, as she often had said with less reason in the old days, "Our preserves ain't so good as usual this year; this is beginning to candy." Both the guests protested, while Rebecca added that the taste of it carried her back, and made her feel young again. The Brays had always managed to keep one or two peach-trees alive in their corner of a garden. "I've been keeping this preserve for a treat," said her friend. "I'm glad to have you eat some, 'Becca. Last summer I often wished you was home an' could come an' see us, 'stead o' being away off to Plainfields."

The crackers did not taste too dry. Miss Ann took the last of the peach on her own cracker; there could not have been quite a small spoonful, after the others were helped, but she asked them first if they would not have some more. Then there was a silence, and in the silence a wave of tender feeling rose high in the hearts of the four elderly women. At this moment the setting sun flooded the poor plain room with light; the unpainted wood was all of a golden-brown, and Ann Bray, with her gray hair and aged face, stood at the head of the table in a kind of aureole. Mrs. Trimble's face was all aquiver as she looked at her; she thought of the text about two or three being gathered together, and was half afraid.

"I believe we ought to 've asked Mis' Janes if she wouldn't come up," said Ann. "She's real good feelin', but she's had it very hard, an' gits discouraged. I can't find that she's ever had anything real pleasant to look back to, as we have. There, next time we'll make a good heartenin' time for her too."

The sorrel horse had taken a long nap by the gnawed fence-rail, and the cool air after sundown made him impatient to be gone. The two friends jolted homeward in the gathering darkness, through the stiffening mud, and neither Mrs. Trimble nor Rebecca Wright said a word until they were out of sight as well as out of sound of the Janes house. Time must elapse before they could reach a more familiar part of the road and resume conversation on its natural level.

"I consider myself to blame," insisted Mrs. Trimble at last. "I haven't no words of accusation for nobody else, an' I ain't one to take comfort in calling names to the board o' selec'*men*. I make no reproaches, an' I take it all on my own shoulders; but I'm goin' to stir about me, I tell you! I shall begin early to-morrow. They're goin' back to their own house —it's been standin' empty all winter—an' the town's goin' to give 'em the rent an' what firewood they need; it won't come to more than the board's payin' out now. An' you an' me'll take this same horse an' wagon, an' ride an go afoot by turns, an' git means enough together to buy back their furniture an' whatever was sold at that plaguey auction; an' then we'll put it all back, an' tell 'em they've got to move to a new place, an' just carry 'em right back again where they come from. An' don't you never tell, R'becca, but here I be a widow woman, layin' up what I make from my farm for nobody knows who, an' I'm goin' to do for them Bray girls all

I'm a mind to. I should be sca't to wake up in heaven, an'
hear anybody there ask how the Bray girls was. Don't talk to
me about the town o' Hampden, an' don't ever let me hear
the name o' town poor! I'm ashamed to go home an' see
what's set out for supper. I wish I'd brought 'em right along."

"I was goin' to ask if we couldn't git the new doctor to go
up an' do somethin' for poor Ann's arm," said Miss Rebecca.
"They say he's very smart. If she could get so's to braid straw
or hook rugs again, she'd soon be earnin' a little somethin'.
An' maybe he could do somethin' for Mandy's eyes. They did
use to live so neat an' ladylike. Somehow I couldn't speak to
tell 'em there that 't was I bought them six best cups an' saucers, time of the auction; they went very low, as everything
else did, an' I thought I could save it some other way. They
shall have 'em back an' welcome. You're real whole-hearted,
Mis' Trimble. I expect Ann'll be sayin' that her father's
child'n wa'n't goin' to be left desolate, an' that all the bread
he cast on the water's comin' back through you."

"I don't care what she says, dear creatur'!" exclaimed Mrs.
Trimble. "I'm full o' regrets I took time for that installation,
an' set there seepin' in a lot o' talk this whole day long, except for its kind of bringin' us to the Bray girls. I wish to my
heart 't was to-morrow mornin' a'ready, an' I a-startin' for
the selec'*men*."

The Passing of Sister Barsett

❦

Mrs. Mercy Crane was of such firm persuasion that a house is meant to be lived in, that during many years she was never known to leave her own neat two-storied dwelling-place on the Ridge road. Yet being very fond of company, in pleasant weather she often sat in the side doorway looking out on her green yard, where the grass grew short and thick and was undisfigured even by a path toward the steps. All her faded green blinds were securely tied together and knotted on the inside by pieces of white tape; but now and then, when the sun was not too hot for her carpets, she opened one window at a time for a few hours, having pronounced views upon the necessity of light and air. Although Mrs. Crane was acknowledged by her best friends to be a peculiar person and very set in her ways, she was much respected, and one acquaintance vied with another in making up for her melancholy seclusion by bringing her all the news they could gather. She had been left alone many years before by the sudden death of her husband from sunstroke, and though she was by no means poor, she had, as some one said, "such a pretty way of taking a little present that you couldn't help being pleased when you gave her anything.

For a lover of society, such a life must have had its difficulties at times, except that the Ridge road was more traveled than any other in the township, and Mrs. Crane had invented a system of signals, to which she always resorted in case of wishing to speak to some one of her neighbors.

The afternoon was wearing late, one day toward the end of summer, and Mercy Crane sat in her doorway dressed in a favorite old-fashioned light calico and a small shoulder shawl figured with large palm leaves. She was making some tatting of a somewhat intricate pattern; she believed it to be the prettiest and most durable of trimmings, and having decorated her own wardrobe in the course of unlimited leisure, she was now making a few yards apiece for each of her more inti-

263

mate friends, so that they might have something to remember her by. She kept glancing up the road as if she expected some one, but the time went slowly by, until at last a woman appeared to view, walking fast, and carrying a large bundle in a checked handkerchief.

Then Mercy Crane worked steadily for a short time without looking up, until the desired friend was crossing the grass between the dusty road and the steps. The visitor was out of breath, and did not respond to the polite greeting of her hostess until she had recovered herself to her satisfaction. Mrs. Crane made her the kind offer of a glass of water or a few peppermints, but was answered only by a shake of the head, so she resumed her work for a time until the silence should be broken.

"I have come from the house of mourning," said Sarah Ellen Dow at last, unexpectedly.

"You don't tell me that Sister Barsett—"

"She's left us this time, she's really gone," and the excited news-bringer burst into tears. The poor soul was completely overwrought; she looked tired and wan, as if she had spent her forces in sympathy as well as hard work. She felt in her great bundle for a pocket handkerchief, but was not successful in the search, and finally produced a faded gingham apron with long, narrow strings, with which she hastily dried her tears. The sad news appealed also to Mercy Crane, who looked across to the apple-trees, and could not see them for a dazzle of tears in her own eyes. The spectacle of Sarah Ellen Dow going home with her humble workaday possessions, from the house where she had gone in haste only a few days before to care for a sick person well known to them both, was a very sad sight.

"You sent word yesterday that you should be returnin' early this afternoon, and would stop. I presume I received the message as you gave it?" asked Mrs. Crane, who was tenacious in such matters; "but I do declare I never looked to hear she was gone."

"She's been failin' right along since yisterday about this time," said the nurse. "She's taken no notice to speak of, an' been eatin' the vally o' nothin', I may say, since I went there a-Tuesday. Her sisters both come back yesterday, an' of course I was expected to give up charge to them. They're used to sickness, an' both havin' such a name for bein' great housekeepers!"

Sarah Ellen spoke with bitterness, but Mrs. Crane was reminded instantly of her own affairs. "I feel condemned that I ain't begun my own fall cleanin' yet," she said, with an ostentatious sigh.

"Plenty o' time to worry about that," her friend hastened to console her.

"I do desire to have everything decent about my house," resumed Mrs. Crane. "There's nobody to do anything but me. If I was to be taken away sudden myself, I shouldn't want to have it said afterwards that there was wisps under my sofy or—There! I can't dwell on my own troubles with Sister Barsett's loss right before me. I can't seem to believe she's really passed away; she always was saying she should go in some o' these spells, but I deemed her to be troubled with narves."

Sarah Ellen Dow shook her head. "I'm all nerved up myself," she said brokenly. "I made light of her sickness when I went there first, I'd seen her what she called dreadful low so many times; but I saw her looks this morning, an' I begun to believe her at last. Them sisters o' hers is the master for unfeelin' hearts. Sister Barsett was a-layin' there yisterday, an' one of 'em was a-settin' right by her tellin' how difficult 't was for her to leave home, her niece was goin' to graduate to the high school, an' they was goin' to have a time in the evening, an' all the exercises promised to be extry interesting. Poor Sister Barsett knew what she said an' looked at her with contempt, an' then she give a glance at me an' closed up her eyes as if 't was for the last time. I know she felt it."

Sarah Ellen Dow was more and more excited by a sense of bitter grievance. Her rule of the afflicted household had evidently been interfered with; she was not accustomed to be ignored and set aside at such times. Her simple nature and uncommon ability found satisfaction in the exercise of authority, but she had now left her post feeling hurt and wronged, besides knowing something of the pain of honest affliction.

"If it hadn't been for esteemin' Sister Barsett as I always have done, I should have told 'em no, an' held to it, when they asked me to come back an' watch to-night. 'T ain't for none o' their sakes, but Sister Barsett was a good friend to me in her way." Sarah Ellen broke down once more, and felt in her bundle again hastily, but the handkerchief was again elusive, while a small object fell out upon the doorstep with a bounce.

" 'T ain't nothin' but a little taste-cake I spared out o' the loaf I baked this mornin'," she explained, with a blush. "I was so shoved out that I seemed to want to turn my hand to somethin' useful an' feel I was still doin' for Sister Barsett. Try a little piece, won't you, Mis' Crane? I thought it seemed light an' good."

They shared the taste-cake with serious enjoyment, and pronounced it very good indeed when they had finished and shaken the crumbs out of their laps. "There's nobody but you shall come an' do for me at the last, if I can have my way about things," said Mercy Crane impulsively. She meant it for a tribute to Miss Dow's character and general ability, and as such it was meekly accepted.

"You're a younger person than I be, an' less wore," said Sarah Ellen, but she felt better now that she had rested, and her conversational powers seemed to be refreshed by her share of the little cake. "Doctor Bangs has behaved real pretty, I can say that," she continued presently in a mournful tone.

"Heretofore, in the sickness of Sister Barsett, I have always felt to hope certain that she would survive; she's recovered from a sight o' things in her day. She has been the first to have all the new diseases that's visited this region. I know she had the spinal mergeetis months before there was any other case about," observed Mrs. Crane with satisfaction.

"An' the new throat troubles, all of 'em," agreed Sarah Ellen; "an' has made trial of all the best patent medicines, an' could tell you their merits as no one else could in this vicinity. She never was one that depended on herbs alone, though she considered 'em extremely useful in some cases. Everybody has their herb, as we know, but I'm free to say that Sister Barsett sometimes done everything she could to kill herself with such rovin' ways o' dosin'. She must see it now she's gone an' can't stuff down no more invigorators." Sarah Ellen Dow burst out suddenly with this, as if she could no longer contain her honest opinion.

"There, there! you're all worked up," answered placid Mercy Crane, looking more interested than ever.

"An' she was dreadful handy to talk religion to other folks, but I've come to a realizin' sense that religion is somethin' besides opinions. She an' Elder French has been mostly of one mind, but I don't know's they've got hold of all the religion there is."

"Why, why, Sarah Ellen!" exclaimed Mrs. Crane, but there was still something in her tone that urged the speaker to further expression of her feelings. The good creature was much excited, her face was clouded with disapproval.

"I ain't forgettin' nothin' about their good points either," she went on in a more subdued tone, and suddenly stopped.

"Preachin' 'll be done away with soon or late—preachin' o' Elder French's kind," announced Mercy Crane, after waiting to see if her guest did not mean to say anything more. "I should like to read 'em out that verse another fashion: 'Be ye doers o' the word, not preachers only,' would hit it about right; but there, it's easy for all of us to talk. In my early days I used to like to get out to meetin' regular, because sure as I didn't I had bad luck all the week. I didn't feel pacified 'less I'd been half a day, but I was out all day the Sabbath before Mr. Barlow died as he did. So you mean to say that Sister Barsett's really gone?"

Mrs. Crane's tone changed to one of real concern, and her manner indicated that she had put the preceding conversation behind her with decision.

"She was herself to the last," instantly responded Miss Dow. "I see her put out a thumb an' finger from under the spread an' pinch up a fold of her sister Deckett's dress, to try an' see if 't was all wool. I thought 't wa'n't all wool, myself, an' I know it now by the way she looked. She was a very knowin' person about materials; we shall miss poor Mis' Barsett in many ways, she was always the one to consult with about matters o' dress."

"She passed away easy at the last, I hope?" asked Mrs. Crane with interest.

"Why, I wa'n't there, if you'll believe it!" exclaimed Sarah Ellen, flushing, and looking at her friend for sympathy. "Sister Barsett revived up the first o' the afternoon, an' they sent for Elder French. She took notice of him, an' he exhorted quite a spell, an' then he spoke o' there being need of air in the room, Mis' Deckett havin' closed every window, an' she asked me of all folks if I hadn't better step out; but Elder French come too, an' he was very reasonable, an' had a word with me about Mis' Deckett an' Mis' Peak an' the way they was workin' things. I told him right out how they never come near when the rest of us was havin' it so hard with her along in the spring, but now they thought she was re'lly goin' to die, they come settlin' down like a pair o' old crows in a field to pick for what they could get. I just made up my mind they should have all the care if they wanted it. It didn't seem as if there was anything more I could do for Sister Barsett, an' I set there in the kitchen within call an' waited, an' when I heard 'em sayin', 'There, she's gone, she's gone!' and Mis' Deckett a-weepin', I put on my bunnit and stepped myself out into the road. I felt to repent after I had gone but a rod, but I was so worked up, an' I thought they'd call me back, an' then I was put out because they didn't, an' so here I be. I can't help it now." Sarah Ellen was crying again; she and Mrs. Crane could not look at each other.

"Well, you set an' rest," said Mrs. Crane kindly, and with the merest shadow of disapproval. "You set an' rest, an' by an' by, if you'd feel better, you could go back an' just make a little stop an' inquire about the arrangements. I wouldn't harbor no feelin's, if they be inconsiderate folks. Sister Barsett has often deplored their actions in my hearing an' wished she had sisters like other folks. With all her faults she was a useful person an' a good neighbor," mourned Mercy Crane sincerely. "She was one that always had somethin' interestin' to tell, an' if it wa'n't for her dyin' spells an' all that sort o' nonsense, she'd make a figger in the world, she would so. She walked with an air always, Mis' Barsett did; you'd ask who she was if you hadn't known, as she passed you by. How quick we forget the outs about anybody that's gone! but I always feel grateful to anybody that's friendly, situated as I be. I shall miss her runnin' over. I can seem to see her now, coming over the rise in the road. But don't you get in a way of takin' things too hard, Sarah Ellen! You've worked yourself all to pieces since I saw you last; you're gettin' to be as lean as a meetin'-house fly. Now, you're comin' in to have a cup o' tea with me, an' then you'll feel better. I've got some new molasses gingerbread that I baked this mornin'."

"I do feel beat out, Mis' Crane," acknowledged the poor little soul, glad of a chance to speak, but touched by this unexpected mark of consideration. "If I could ha' done as I wanted to I should be feelin' well enough, but to be set aside an' ordered about, where I'd taken the lead in sickness so much, an' knew how to deal with Sister Barsett so well! She might be livin' now, perhaps—"

"Come; we'd better go in, 't is gettin' damp," and the mistress of the house rose so hurriedly as to seem bustling. "Don't dwell on Sister Barsett an' her foolish folks no more; I wouldn't, if I was you."

They went into the front room, which was dim with the twilight of the half-closed blinds and two great syringa bushes that grew against them. Sarah Ellen put down her bundle and bestowed herself in the large, cane-seated rocking-chair. Mrs. Crane directed her to stay there awhile and rest, and then come out into the kitchen when she got ready.

A cheerful clatter of dishes was heard at once upon Mrs. Crane's disappearance. "I hope she's goin' to make one o' her nice short-cakes, but I don't know's she'll think it quite worth while," thought the guest humbly. She desired to go out into the kitchen, but it was proper behavior to wait until she should be called. Mercy Crane was not a person with whom one could venture to take liberties. Presently Sarah Ellen began to feel better. She did not often find such a quiet place, or the quarter of an hour of idleness in which to enjoy it, and was glad to make the most of this opportunity. Just now she felt tired and lonely. She was a busy, unselfish, eager-minded creature by nature, but now, while grief was sometimes uppermost in her mind and sometimes a sense of wrong, every moment found her more peaceful, and the great excitement little by little faded away.

"What a person poor Sister Barsett was to dread growing old so she couldn't get about. I'm sure I shall miss her as much as anybody," said Mrs. Crane, suddenly opening the kitchen door, and letting in an unmistakable and delicious odor of shortcake that revived still more the drooping spirits of her guest. "An' a good deal of knowledge has died with her," she added, coming into the room and seeming to make it lighter.

"There, she knew a good deal, but she didn't know all, especially o' doctorin'," insisted Sarah Ellen from the rocking-chair, with an unexpected little laugh. "She used to lay down the law to me as if I had neither sense nor experience, but when it came to her bad spells she'd always send for me. It takes everybody to know everything, but Sister Barsett was of an opinion that her information was sufficient for the town. She was tellin' me the day I went there how she disliked to have old Mis' Doubleday come an' visit with her, an' remarked that she called Mis' Doubleday very officious. 'Went right down on her knees an' prayed,' says she. 'Anybody would have thought I was a heathen!' But I kind of pacified her feelin's, an' told her I supposed the old lady meant well."

"Did she give away any of her things?—Mis' Barsett, I mean," inquired Mrs. Crane.

"Not in my hearin'," replied Sarah Ellen Dow. "Except one day, the first of the week, she told her oldest sister, Mis' Deckett—'t was that first day she rode over—that she might have her green quilted petticoat; you see it was a rainy day, an' Mis' Deckett had complained o' feelin' thin. She went right up an' got it, and put it on an' wore it off, an' I'm sure I thought no more about it, until I heard Sister Barsett groanin' dreadful in the night. I got right up to see what the matter was, an' what do you think but she was wantin' that petticoat back, and not thinking any too well o' Nancy Deckett for takin' it when 't was offered. 'Nancy never showed no sense o' propriety,' says Sister Barsett; I just wish you'd heard her go on!

"If she had felt to remember me," continued Sarah Ellen, after they had laughed a little, "I'd full as soon have some of her nice crockery-ware. She told me once, years ago, when I was stoppin' to tea with her an' we were havin' it real friendly, that she should leave me her Britannia tea-set, but I ain't got it in writin', and I can't say she's ever referred to the matter since. It ain't as if I had a home o' my own to keep it in, but I should have thought a great deal of it for her sake," and the speaker's voice faltered. "I must say that with all her virtues she never was a first-class housekeeper, but I wouldn't say it to any but a friend. You never eat no preserves o' hers that wa'n't commencin' to work, an' you know as well as I how little forethought she had about putting away her woolens. I sat behind her once in meetin' when I was stoppin' with the Tremletts and so occupied a seat in their pew, an' I see between ten an' a dozen moth millers come workin' out o' her fitch-fur tippet. They was flutterin' round her bonnet same's 't was a lamp. I should be mortified to death to have such a thing happen to me."

"Every housekeeper has her weak point; I've got mine as much as anybody else," acknowledged Mercy Crane with spirit, "but you never see no moth millers come workin' out o' me in a public place."

"Ain't your oven beginning to get over-het?" anxiously inquired Sarah Ellen Dow, who was sitting more in the draught, and could not bear to have any accident happen to the supper. Mrs. Crane flew to a shortcake's rescue, and presently called her guest to the table.

The two women sat down to deep and brimming cups of tea. Sarah Ellen noticed with great gratification that her hostess had put on two of the best tea-cups and some citron-melon preserves. It was not an every-day supper. She was used to hard fare, poor, hard-working Sarah Ellen, and this handsome social attention did her good. Sister Crane rarely entertained a friend, and it would be a pleasure to speak of the tea-drinking for weeks to come.

"You've put yourself out quite a consid'able for me," she acknowledged. "How pretty these cups is! You oughtn't to use 'em so common as for me. I wish I had a home I could really call my own to ask you to, but 't ain't never been so I could. Sometimes I wonder what's goin' to become o' me when I get so I'm past work. Takin' care o' sick folks an' bein' in houses where there's a sight goin' on an' everybody in a hurry kind of wears on me now I'm most a-gittin' in years. I was wishin' the other day that I could get with some comfortable kind of a sick person, where I could live right along quiet as other folks do, but folks never sends for me 'less they're drove to it. I ain't laid up anything to really depend upon."

The situation appealed to Mercy Crane, well to do as she was and not burdened with responsibilities. She stirred uneasily in her chair, but could not bring herself to the point of offering Sarah Ellen the home she coveted.

"Have some hot tea," she insisted, in a matter of fact tone, and Sarah Ellen's face, which had been lighted by a sudden eager hopefulness, grew dull and narrow again.

"Plenty, plenty, Mis' Crane," she said sadly, " 't is beautiful tea—you always have good tea"; but she could not turn her thoughts from her own uncertain future. "None of our folks has ever lived to be a burden," she said presently, in a pathetic tone, putting down her cup. "My mother was thought to be doing well until four o'clock an' was dead at ten. My Aunt Nancy came to our house well at twelve o'clock an' died that afternoon; my father was sick but ten days. There was dear sister Betsy, she did go in consumption, but 't wa'n't an expensive sickness."

"I've thought sometimes about you, how you'd get past rovin' from house to house one o' these days. I guess your friends will stand by you." Mrs. Crane spoke with unwonted sympathy, and Sarah Ellen's heart leaped with joy.

"You're real kind," she said simply. "There's nobody I set so much by. But I shall miss Sister Barsett, when all's said an' done. She's asked me many a time to stop with her when I wasn't doin' nothin'. We all have our failin's, but she was a friendly creatur'. I sha'n't want to see her laid away."

"Yes, I was thinkin' a few minutes ago that I shouldn't want to look out an' see the funeral go by. She's one o' the old neighbors. I s'pose I shall have to look, or I shouldn't feel right afterward," said Mrs. Crane mournfully. "If I hadn't got so kind of housebound," she added with touching frankness, "I'd just as soon go over with you an' offer to watch this night."

" 'T would astonish Sister Barsett so I don't know but she'd return." Sarah Ellen's eyes danced with amusement; she could not resist her own joke, and Mercy Crane herself had to smile.

"Now I must be goin', or 't will be dark," said the guest, rising and sighing after she had eaten her last crumb of gingerbread. "Yes, thank ye, you're real good, I will come back if I find I ain't wanted. Look what a pretty sky there is!" and the two friends went to the side door and stood together in a moment of affectionate silence, looking out toward the sunset across the wide fields. The country was still with that deep rural stillness which seems to mean the absence of humanity. Only the thrushes were singing far away in the walnut woods beyond the orchard, and some crows were flying over and cawed once loudly, as if they were speaking to the women at the door.

Just as the friends were parting, after most grateful acknowledgments from Sarah Ellen Dow, some one came driving along the road in a hurry and stopped.

"Who's that with you, Mis' Crane?" called one of their near neighbors.

"It's Sarah Ellen Dow," answered Mrs. Crane. "What's the matter?"

"I thought so, but I couldn't rightly see. Come, they are in a peck o' trouble up to Sister Barsett's, wonderin' where you be," grumbled the man. "They can't do nothin' with her; she's drove off everybody an' keeps a-screechin' for you. Come, step along, Sarah Ellen, do!"

"Sister Barsett!" exclaimed both the women. Mercy Crane sank down upon the doorstep, but Sarah Ellen stepped out upon the grass all of a tremble, and went toward the wagon. "They said this afternoon that Sister Barsett was gone," she managed to say. "What did they mean?"

"Gone where?" asked the impatient neighbor. "I expect 't was one of her spells. She's come to; they say she wants somethin' hearty for her tea. Nobody can't take one step till you get there, neither."

Sarah Ellen was still dazed; she returned to the doorway, where Mercy Crane sat shaking with laughter. "I don't know but we might as well laugh as cry," she said in an aimless sort of way. "I know you too well to think you're going to repeat a single word. Well, I'll get my bonnet an' start; I expect I've got considerable to cope with, but I'm well rested. Good-night, Mis' Crane, I certain did have a beautiful tea, whatever the future may have in store."

She wore a solemn expression as she mounted into the wagon in haste and departed, but she was far out of sight when Mercy Crane stopped laughing and went into the house.

Miss Esther's Guest

I.

Old Miss Porley put on her silk shawl, and arranged it carefully over her thin shoulders, and pinned it with a hand that shook a little as if she were much excited. She bent forward to examine the shawl in the mahogany-framed mirror, for there was a frayed and tender spot in the silk where she had pinned it so many years. The shawl was very old; it had been her mother's, and she disliked to wear it too often, but she never could make up her mind to go out into the street in summer, as some of her neighbors did, with nothing over her shoulders at all. Next she put on her bonnet and tried to set it straight, allowing for a wave in the looking-glass that made one side of her face appear much longer than the other; then she drew on a pair of well-darned silk gloves; one had a wide crack all the way up the back of the hand, but they were still neat and decent for every-day wear, if she were careful to keep her left hand under the edge of the shawl. She had discussed the propriety of drawing the raveled silk together, but a thick seam would look very ugly, and there was something accidental about the crack.

Then, after hesitating a few moments, she took a small piece of folded white letter-paper from the table and went out of the house, locking the door and trying it, and stepped away bravely down the village street. Everybody said, "How do you do, Miss Porley?" or "Good-mornin', Esther." Every one in Daleham knew the good woman; she was one of the unchanging persons, always to be found in her place, and always pleased and friendly and ready to take an interest in old and young. She and her mother, who had early been left a widow, had been for many years the village tailoresses and makers of little boys' clothes. Mrs. Porley had been dead three years, however, and her daughter "Easter," as old friends called our heroine, had lived quite alone. She was made very sorrowful by her loneliness, but she never could be persuaded to take anybody to board: she could not bear to think of any one's taking her mother's place.

It was a warm summer morning, and Miss Porley had not very far to walk, but she was still more shaky and excited by the time she reached the First Church parsonage. She stood at the gate undecidedly, and, after she pushed it open a little way, she drew back again, and felt a curious beating at her heart and a general reluctance of mind and body. At that moment the minister's wife, a pleasant young woman with a smiling, eager face, looked out of the window and asked the tremulous visitor to come in. Miss Esther straightened herself and went briskly up the walk; she was very fond of the minister's wife, who had only been in Daleham a few months.

"Won't you take off your shawl?" asked Mrs. Wayton affectionately; "I have just been making gingerbread, and you shall have a piece as soon as it cools."

"I don't know's I ought to stop," answered Miss Esther, flushing quickly. "I came on business; I won't keep you long."

"Oh, please stay a little while," urged the hostess. "I'll take my sewing, if you don't mind; there are two or three things that I want to ask you about."

"I've thought and flustered a sight over taking this step," said good old Esther abruptly. "I had to conquer a sight o' reluctance, I must say. I've got so used to livin' by myself that I sha'n't know how to consider another. But I see I ain't got common feelin' for others unless I can set my own comfort aside once in a while. I've brought you my name as one of those that will take one o' them city folks that needs a spell o' change. It come straight home to me how I should be feeling it by this time, if my lot had been cast in one o' them city garrets that the minister described so affecting. If 't hadn't been for kind consideration somewheres, mother an' me might have sewed all them pleasant years away in the city that we enjoyed so in our own home, and our garding to step right out into when our sides set in to ache. And I ain't rich, but we was able to save a little something, and now I'm eatin' of it all up alone. It come to me I should like to have somebody take a taste out o' mother's part. Now, don't you let 'em send me no rampin' boys like them Barnard's folks had come last year, that vexed dumb creatur's so; and I don't know how to cope with no kind o' men-folks or strange girls, but I should know how to do for a woman that's getting well along in years, an' has come to feel kind o' spent. P'raps we ain't no right to pick an' choose, but I should know best how to make that sort comfortable on 'count of doin' for mother and studying what she preferred."

Miss Esther rose with quaint formality and put the folded paper, on which she had neatly written her name and address, into Mrs. Wayton's hand. Mrs. Wayton rose soberly to receive it, and then they both sat down again.

"I'm sure that you will feel more than repaid for your kindness, dear Miss Esther," said the minister's wife. "I know one of the ladies who have charge of the arrangements for the Country Week, and I will explain as well as I can the kind of guest you have in mind. I quite envy her: I have often thought, when I was busy and tired, how much I should like to run along the street and make you a visit in your dear old-fashioned little house."

"I should be more than pleased to have you, I'm sure," said Miss Esther, startled into a bright smile and forgetting her anxiety. "Come any day, and take me just as I am. We used to have a good deal o' company years ago, when there was a number o' mother's folks still livin' over Ashfield way. Sure as we had a pile o' work on hand and was hurrying for dear life an' limb, a wagon-load would light down at the front gate to spend the day an' have an early tea. Mother never was one to get flustered same's I do 'bout everything. She was a lovely cook, and she'd fill 'em up an' cheer 'em, and git 'em off early as she could, an' then we'd be kind o' waked up an' spirited ourselves, and would set up late sewin' and talkin' the company over, an' I 'd have things saved to tell her that had been said while she was out o' the room. I make such a towse over everything myself, but mother was waked right up and felt pleased an' smart, if anything unexpected happened. I miss her more every year," and Miss Esther gave a great sigh. "I s'pose 't wa'n't reasonable to expect that I could have her to help me through with old age, but I'm a poor tool, alone."

"Oh, no, you mustn't say that!" exclaimed the minister's wife. "Why, nobody could get along without you. I wish I had come to Daleham in time to know your mother too."

Miss Esther shook her head sadly. "She would have set everything by you and Mr. Wayton. Now I must be getting back in case I'm wanted, but you let 'em send me somebody right away, while my bush beans is so nice. An' if any o' your little boy's clothes wants repairin', just give 'em to me; 't will be a real pleasant thing to set a few stitches. Or the minister's; ain't there something needed for him?"

Mrs. Wayton was about to say no, when she became conscious of the pleading old face before her. "I'm sure you are most kind, dear friend," she answered, "and I do have a great deal to do. I'll bring you two or three things to-night that are beyond my art, as I go to evening meeting. Mr. Wayton frayed out his best coat sleeve yesterday, and I was disheartened, for we had counted upon his not having a new one before the fall."

" 'T would be mere play to me," said Miss Esther, and presently she went smiling down the street.

II.

The Committee for the Country Week in a certain ward of
Boston were considering the long list of children, and mothers with babies, and sewing-women, who were looking forward, some of them for the first time in many years, to a
country holiday. Some were to go as guests to hospitable,
generous farmhouses that opened their doors willingly now
and then to tired city people; for some persons board could
be paid.

The immediate arrangements of that time were settled at
last, except that Mrs. Belton, the chairman, suddenly took a
letter from her pocket. "I had almost forgotten this," she
said; "it is another place offered in dear quiet old Daleham.
My friend, the minister's wife there, writes me a word about
it: 'The applicant desires especially an old person, being used
to the care of an aged parent and sure of her power of making such a one comfortable, and she would like to have her
guest come as soon as possible.' My friend asks me to choose
a person of some refinement—'one who would appreciate the
delicate simplicity and quaint ways of the hostess.'"

Mrs. Belton glanced hurriedly down the page. "I believe
that's all," she said. "How about that nice old sewing-woman,
Mrs. Connolly, in Bantry Street?"

"Oh, no!" someone entreated, looking up from her writing.
"Why isn't it just the place for my old Mr. Rill, the dear old
Englishman who lives alone up four flights in Town Court
and has the bullfinch? He used to engrave seals, and his eyes
gave out, and he is so thrifty with his own bit of savings and
an atom of a pension. Someone pays his expenses to the
country, and this sounds like a place he would be sure to like.
I've been watching for the right chance."

"Take it, then," said the busy chairman, and there was a
little more writing and talking, and then the committee meeting was over which settled Miss Esther Porley's fate.

III.

❊

The journey to Daleham was a great experience to Mr. Rill. He was a sensible old person, who knew well that he was getting stiffer and clumsier than need be in his garret, and that, as certain friends had said, a short time spent in the country would cheer and invigorate him. There had been occasional propositions that he should leave his garret altogether and go to the country to live, or at least to the suburbs of the city. He could not see things close at hand so well as he could take a wide outlook, and as his outlook from the one garret window was a still higher brick wall and many chimneys, he was losing a great deal that he might have had. But so long as he was expected to take an interest in the unseen and unknown he failed to accede to any plans about the country home, and declared that he was well enough in his high abode. He had lost a sister a few years before who had been his mainstay, but with his hands so well used to delicate work he had been less bungling in his simple household affairs than many another man might have been. But he was very lonely and was growing anxious; as he was rattled along in the train toward Daleham he held the chirping bullfinch's cage fast with both hands, and said to himself now and then, "This may lead to something: the country air smells very good to me."

The Daleham station was not very far out of the village, so that Miss Esther Porley put on her silk shawl and bonnet and everyday gloves just before four o'clock that afternoon, and went to meet her Country Week guest. Word had come the day before that the person for Miss Porley's would start two days in advance of the little company of children and helpless women, and since this message had come from the parsonage Miss Esther had worked diligently, late and early, to have her house in proper order. Whatever her mother had liked was thought of and provided. There were going to be rye shortcakes for tea, and there were some sprigs of thyme and sweet-balm in an old-fashioned wine-glass on the keeping-room table; mother always said they were so freshening. And Miss Esther had taken out a little shoulder-shawl and folded it over the arm of the rocking-chair by the window that looked out into the small garden where the London-pride was in full bloom, and the morning-glories had just begun to climb. Miss Esther was sixty-four herself, but still looked upon age as well in the distance.

She was always a prompt person, and had some minutes to wait at the station; then the time passed and the train was late. At last she saw the smoke far in the distance, and her heart began to sink. Perhaps she would not find it easy to get on with the old lady, and—well it was only for a week, and she had thought it right and best to take such a step, and now it would soon be over.

The train stopped, and there was no old lady at all.

Miss Esther had stood far back to get away from the smoke and roar—she was always as afraid of the cars as she could be—but as she moved away she took a few steps forward to scan the platform. There was no black bonnet with a worn lace veil, and no old lady with a burden of bundles; there were only the station master and two or three men, and an idle boy or two, and one clean-faced, bent old man with a bird-cage in one hand and an old carpet-bag in the other. She thought of the rye short-cakes for supper and all that she had done to make her small home pleasant, and her fire of excitement suddenly fell into ashes.

The old man with the bird-cage suddenly turned toward her. "Can you direct me to Miss Esther Porley's?" said he.

"I can," replied Miss Esther, looking at him with curiosity.

"I was directed to her house," said the pleasant old fellow, "by Mrs. Belton, of the Country Week Committee. My eyesight is poor. I should be glad if anybody would help me to find the place."

"You step this way with me, sir," said Miss Esther. She was afraid that the men on the platform heard every word they said, but nobody took particular notice, and off they walked down the road together. Miss Esther was enraged with the Country Week Committee.

"*You* were sent to—Miss Porley's?" she asked grimly, turning to look at him.

"I was, indeed," said Mr. Rill.

"I am Miss Porley, and I expected an old lady," she man-

aged to say, and they both stopped and looked at each other
with apprehension.

"I do declare!" faltered the old seal-cutter anxiously.
"What had I better do, ma'am? They most certain give me
your name. May be you could recommend me somewheres
else, an' I can get home to-morrow if 't ain't convenient."

They were standing under a willow-tree in the shade; Mr.
Rill took off his heavy hat—it was a silk hat of by-gone
shape; a golden robin began to sing, high in the willow, and
the old bullfinch twittered and chirped in the cage. Miss Esther heard some footsteps coming behind them along the
road. She changed color; she tried to remember that she was
a woman of mature years and considerable experience.

" 'T ain't a mite o' matter, sir," she said cheerfully. "I guess
you 'll find everything comfortable for you;" and they turned,
much relieved, and walked along together.

"That's Lawyer Barstow's house," she said calmly, a
minute afterward, "the handsomest place in town, we think
't is," and Mr. Rill answered politely that Daleham was a
pretty place; he had not been out of the city for so many
years that everything looked beautiful as a picture.

IV.

❧

Miss Porley rapidly recovered her composure, and bent her energies to the preparing of an early tea. She showed her guest to the snug bedroom under the low gambrel roof, and when she apologized for his having to go upstairs, he begged her to remember that it was nothing but a step to a man who was used to four long flights. They were both excited at finding a proper nail for the birdcage outside the window, though Miss Esther said that she should love to have the pretty bird downstairs where she could see it and hear it sing. She said to herself over and over that if she could have her long-lost brother come home from sea, she should like to have him look and behave as gentle and kind as Mr. Rill. Somehow she found herself singing a cheerful hymn as she mixed and stirred the short-cakes. She could not help wishing that her mother were there to enjoy this surprise, but it did seem very odd, after so many years, to have a man in the house. It had not happened for fifteen years, at least, when they had entertained Deacon Sparks and wife, delegates from the neighboring town of East Wilby to the County Conference.

The neighbors did not laugh at Miss Esther openly or cause her to blush with self-consciousness, however much they may have discussed the situation and smiled behind her back. She took the presence of her guest with delighted simplicity, and the country week was extended to a fortnight, and then to a month. At last, one day Miss Esther and Mr. Rill were seen on their way to the railroad station, with a large bundle apiece beside the carpet-bag, though someone noticed that the bullfinch was left behind. Miss Esther came back alone, looking very woebegone and lonely, and if the truth must be known, she found her house too solitary. She looked into the woodhouse where there was a great store of kindlings, neatly piled, and her water-pail was filled to the brim, her garden-paths were clean of weeds and swept, and yet everywhere she looked it seemed more lonely than ever.

She pinned on her shawl again and went along the street to the parsonage.

"My old lady's just gone," she said to the minister's wife. "I was so lonesome I could not stay in the house."

"You found him a very pleasant visitor, didn't you, Miss Esther?" asked Mrs. Wayton, laughing a little.

"I did so; he wa'n't like other men—kind and friendly and fatherly, and never stayed round when I was occupied, but entertained himself down street considerable, an' was as industrious as a bee, always asking me if there wa'n't something he could do about house. He and a sister some years older used to keep house together, and it was her long sickness used up what they'd saved, and yet he's got a little somethin', and there are friends he used to work for, jewelers, a big firm, that gives him somethin' regular. He's goin' to see"—and Miss Esther blushed crimson—"he's goin' to see if they'd be willin' to pay it just the same if he come to reside in Daleham. He thinks the air agrees with him here."

"Does he indeed?" inquired the minister's wife, with deep interest and a look of amusement.

"Yes 'm," said Miss Esther simply; "but don't you go an' say nothin' yet. I don't want folks to make a joke of it. Seems to me if he does feel to come back, and remains of the same mind he went away, we might be judicious to take the step—"

"Why, Miss Esther!" exclaimed the listener.

"Not till fall—not till fall," said Miss Esther hastily. "I ain't going to count on it too much anyway. I expect we could get along; there 's considerable goodness left in me, and you can always work better when you've got somebody beside yourself to work for. There, now I've told you I feel as if I was blown away in a gale."

"Why, I don't know what to say at such a piece of news!" exclaimed Mrs. Wayton again.

"I don't know's there's anything *to* say," gravely answered Miss Esther. "But I did laugh just now coming in the gate to think what a twitter I got into the day I fetched you that piece of paper."

"Why, I must go right and tell Mr. Wayton!" said the minister's wife.

"Oh, don't you, Mis' Wayton; no, no!" begged Miss Esther, looking quite coy and girlish. "I really don't know's it's quite settled—it don't seem's if it could be. I'm going to hear from him in the course of a week. But I suppose *he* thinks it's settled; he's left the bird."

Aunt Cynthy Dallett

I.

❦

"No," said Mrs. Hand, speaking wistfully—"no, we never were in the habit of keeping Christmas at our house. Mother died when we were all young; she would have been the one to keep up with all new ideas, but father and grandmother were old-fashioned folks, and—well, you know how 't was then, Miss Pendexter: nobody took much notice of the day except to a wish you a Merry Christmas."

"They didn't do much to make it merry, certain," answered Miss Pendexter. "Sometimes nowadays I hear folks complainin' o' bein' overtaxed with all the Christmas work they have to do."

"Well, others think that it makes a lovely chance for all that really enjoys givin'; you get an opportunity to speak your kind feelin' right out," answered Mrs. Hand, with a bright smile. "But there! I shall always keep New Year's Day, too; it won't do no hurt to have an extra day kept an' made pleasant. And there's many of the real old folks have got pretty things to remember about New Year's Day."

"Aunt Cynthy Dallett's just one of 'em," said Miss Pendexter. "She's always very reproachful if I don't get up to see her. Last year I missed it, on account of a light fall o' snow that seemed to make the walkin' too bad, an' she sent a neighbor's boy 'way down from the mount'in to see if I was sick. Her lameness confines her to the house altogether now, an' I have her on my mind a good deal. How anybody does get thinkin' of those that lives alone, as they get older! I waked up only last night with a start, thinkin' if Aunt Cynthy's house should get afire or anything, what she would do, 'way up there all alone. I was half dreamin', I s'pose, but I couldn't seem to settle down until I got up an' went upstairs to the north garret window to see if I could see any light; but the mountains was all dark an' safe, same's usual. I remember noticin' last time I was there that her chimney needed pointin', and I spoke to her about it—the bricks looked poor in some places."

"Can you see the house from your north gable window?" asked Mrs. Hand, a little absently.

"Yes'm; it's a great comfort that I can," answered her companion. "I have often wished we were near enough to have her make me some sort o' signal in case she needed help. I used to plead with her to come down and spend the winters with me, but she told me one day I might as well try to fetch down one o' the old hemlocks, an' I believe 't was true."

"Your aunt Dallett is a very self-contained person," observed Mrs. Hand.

"Oh, very!" exclaimed the elderly niece, with a pleased look. "Aunt Cynthy laughs, an' says she expects the time will come when age'll compel her to have me move up an' take care of her; and last time I was there she looked up real funny, an' says, 'I do' know, Abby; I'm most afeard sometimes that I feel myself beginnin' to look for'ard to it!' 'T was a good deal, comin' from Aunt Cynthy, an' I so esteemed it."

"She ought to have you there now," said Mrs. Hand. "You'd both make a savin' by doin' it; but I don't expect she needs to save as much as some. There! I know just how you both feel. I like to have my own home an' do everything just my way too." And the friends laughed, and looked at each other affectionately.

"There was old Mr. Nathan Dunn—left no debts an' no money when he died," said Mrs. Hand. " 'T was over to his niece's last summer. He had a little money in his wallet, an' when the bill for funeral expenses come in there was just exactly enough; some item or other made it come to so many dollars an' eighty-four cents, and, lo an' behold! there was eighty-four cents in a little separate pocket beside the neat fold o' bills, as if the old gentleman had known beforehand. His niece couldn't help laughin', to save her; she said the old gentleman died as methodical as he lived. She didn't expect he had any money, an' was prepared to pay for everything herself; she's very well off."

" 'T was funny, certain," said Miss Pendexter. "I expect he felt comfortable, knowin' he had that money by him. 'T is a comfort, when all's said and done, 'specially to folks that's gettin' old."

A sad look shadowed her face for an instant, and then she

smiled and rose to take leave, looking expectantly at her hostess to see if there were anything more to be said.

"I hope to come out square myself," she said, by way of farewell pleasantry; "but there are times when I feel doubtful."

Mrs. Hand was evidently considering something, and waited a moment or two before she spoke. "Suppose we both walk up to see your aunt Dallett, New Year's Day, if it ain't too windy and the snow keeps off?" she proposed. "I couldn't rise the hill if 't was a windy day. We could take a hearty breakfast an' start in good season; I'd rather walk than ride, the road's so rough this time o' year."

"Oh, what a person you are to think o' things! I did so dread goin' 'way up there all alone," said Abby Pendexter. "I'm no hand to go off alone, an' I had it before me, so I really got to dread it. I do so enjoy it after I get there, seein' Aunt Cynthy, an' she's always so much better than I expect to find her."

"Well, we'll start early," said Mrs. Hand cheerfully; and so they parted. As Miss Pendexter went down the foot-path to the gate, she sent grateful thoughts back to the little sitting-room she had just left.

"How doors are opened!" she exclaimed to herself. "Here I've been so poor an' distressed at beginnin' the year with nothin', as it were, that I couldn't think o' even goin' to make poor old Aunt Cynthy a friendly call. I'll manage to make some kind of a little pleasure too, an' somethin' for dear Mis' Hand. 'Use what you've got,' mother always used to say when every sort of an emergency come up, an' I may only have wishes to give, but I'll make 'em good ones!"

II.

❧

The first day of the year was clear and bright, as if it were a New Year's pattern of what winter can be at its very best. The two friends were prepared for changes of weather, and met each other well wrapped in their winter cloaks and shawls, with sufficient brown barége veils tied securely over their bonnets. They ignored for some time the plain truth that each carried something under her arm; the shawls were rounded out suspiciously, especially Miss Pendexter's, but each respected the other's air of secrecy. The narrow road was frozen in deep ruts, but a smooth-trodden little foot-path that ran along its edge was very inviting to the wayfarers. Mrs. Hand walked first and Miss Pendexter followed, and they were talking busily nearly all the way, so that they had to stop for breath now and then at the tops of the little hills. It was not a hard walk; there were a good many almost level stretches through the woods, in spite of the fact that they should be a very great deal higher when they reached Mrs. Dallett's door.

"I do declare, what a nice day 't is, an' such pretty footin'!" said Mrs. Hand, with satisfaction. "Seems to me as if my feet went o' themselves; gener'lly I have to toil so when I walk that I can't enjoy nothin' when I get to a place."

"It's partly this beautiful bracin' air," said Abby Pendexter. "Sometimes such nice air comes just before a fall of snow. Don't it seem to make anybody feel young again and to take all your troubles away?"

Mrs. Hand was a comfortable, well-to-do soul, who seldom worried about anything, but something in her companion's tone touched her heart, and she glanced sidewise and saw a pained look in Abby Pendexter's thin face. It was a moment for confidence.

"Why, you speak as if something distressed your mind, Abby," said the elder woman kindly.

"I ain't one that has myself on my mind as a usual thing,

but it does seem now as if I was goin' to have it very hard," said Abby. "Well, I've been anxious before."

"Is it anything wrong about your property?" Mrs. Hand ventured to ask.

"Only that I ain't got any," answered Abby, trying to speak gayly, " 'T was all I could do to pay my last quarter's rent, twelve dollars. I sold my hens, all but this one that had run away at the time, an' now I'm carryin' her up to Aunt Cynthy, roasted just as nice as I know how."

"I thought you was carrying somethin'," said Mrs. Hand, in her usual tone. "For me, I've got a couple o' my mince pies. I thought the old lady might like 'em; one we can eat for our dinner, and one she shall have to keep. But were n't you unwise to sacrifice your poultry, Abby? You always need eggs, and hens don't cost much to keep."

"Why, yes, I shall miss 'em," said Abby; "but, you see, I had to do every way to get my rent-money. Now the shop's shut down I haven't got any way of earnin' anything, and I spent what little I've saved through the summer."

"Your aunt Cynthy ought to know it an' ought to help you," said Mrs. Hand. "You're a real foolish person, I must say. I expect you do for her when she ought to do for you."

"She's old, an' she's all the near relation I've got," said the little woman. "I've always felt the time would come when she'd need me, but it's been her great pleasure to live alone an' feel free. I shall get along somehow, but I shall have it hard. Somebody may want help for a spell this winter, but I'm afraid I shall have to give up my house. 'T ain't as if I owned it. I don't know just what to do, but there'll be a way."

Mrs. Hand shifted her two pies to the other arm, and stepped across to the other side of the road where the ground looked a little smoother.

"No, I wouldn't worry if I was you, Abby," she said. "There, I suppose if 't was me I should worry a good deal more! I expect I should lay awake nights." But Abby answered nothing, and they came to a steep place in the road and found another subject for conversation at the top.

"Your aunt don't know we're coming?" asked the chief guest of the occasion.

"Oh, no, I never send her word," said Miss Pendexter. "She'd be so desirous to get everything ready, just as she used to."

"She never seemed to make any trouble o' havin' company; she always appeared so easy and pleasant, and let you set with her while she made her preparations," said Mrs. Hand, with great approval. "Some has such a dreadful way of making you feel inopportune, and you can't always send word you're comin'. I did have a visit once that's always been a lesson to me; 't was years ago; I don't know's I ever told you?"

"I don't believe you ever did," responded the listener to this somewhat indefinite prelude.

"Well, 't was one hot summer afternoon. I set forth an' took a great long walk 'way over to Mis' Eben Fulham's, on the crossroad between the cranberry ma'sh and Staples's Corner. The doctor was driven' that way, an' he give me a lift that shortened it some at the last; but I never should have started, if I'd known 't was so far. I had been promisin' all summer to go, and every time I saw Mis' Fulham, Sundays, she'd say somethin' about it. We wa'n't very well acquainted, but always friendly. She moved here from Bedford Hill."

"Oh, yes; I used to know her," said Abby, with interest.

"Well, now, she did give me a beautiful welcome when I got there," continued Mrs. Hand. " 'T was about four o'clock in the afternoon, an' I told her I'd come to accept her invitation if 't was convenient, an' the doctor had been called several miles beyond and expected to be detained, but he was goin' to pick me up as he returned about seven; 't was very kind of him. She took me right in, and she did appear so pleased, an' I must go right into the best room where 't was cool, and then she said she'd have tea early, and I should have to excuse her a short time. I asked her not to make any difference, and if I couldn't assist her; but she said no, I must just take her as I found her; and she give me a large fan, and off she went.

"There. I was glad to be still and rest where 't was cool, an' I set there in the rockin'-chair an' enjoyed it for a while, an' I heard her clacking at the oven door out beyond, an' gittin' out some dishes. She was a brisk-actin' little woman, an' I thought I'd caution her when she come back not to make up a great fire, only for a cup o' tea, perhaps. I started to go right out in the kitchen, an' then somethin' told me I'd better not, we never'd been so free together as that; I didn't know how she'd take it, an' there I set an' set. 'T was sort of a greenish light in the best room, an' it begun to feel a little damp to me—the s'rubs outside grew close up to the windows. Oh, it did seem dreadful long! I could hear her busy with the dishes an' beatin' eggs an' stirrin', an' I knew she was puttin' herself out to get up a great supper, and I kind o' fidgeted about a little an' even stepped to the door, but I thought she'd expect me to remain where I was. I saw everything in that room forty times over, an' I did divert myself killin' off a brood o' moths that was in a worsted-work mat on the table. It all fell to pieces. I never saw such a sight o' moths to once. But occupation failed after that, an' I begun to feel sort o' tired an' numb. There was one o' them late crickets got into the room an' begun to chirp, an' it sounded kind o' fallish. I couldn't help sayin' to myself that Mis' Fulham had forgot all about my bein' there. I thought of all the beauties of hospitality that ever I see!"

"Didn't she ever come back at all, not whilst things was in the oven, nor nothin'?" inquired Miss Pendexter, with awe.

"I never see her again till she come beamin' to the parlor door an' invited me to walk out to tea," said Mrs. Hand. "'T was 'most a quarter past six by the clock; I thought 't was seven. I'd thought o' everything, an' I'd counted, an' I'd trotted my foot, an' I'd looked more 'n twenty times to see if there was any more moth-millers."

"I s'pose you did have a very nice tea?" suggested Abby, with interest.

"Oh, a beautiful tea! She couldn't have done more if I'd been the Queen," said Mrs. Hand. "I don't know how she could ever have done it all in the time, I'm sure. The table was loaded down; there was cup-custards and custard pie, an' cream pie, an' two kinds o' hot biscuits, an' black tea as well as green, an' elegant cake—one kind she'd just made new, and called it quick cake; I've often made it since—an' she'd opened her best preserves, two kinds. We set down together, an' I'm sure I appreciated what she'd done; but 't wa'n't no time for real conversation whilst we was to the table, an' before we got quite through the doctor come hurryin' along, an' I had to leave. He asked us if we'd had a good talk, as we come out, an' I couldn't help laughing to myself; but she said quite hearty that she'd had a nice visit from me. She appeared well satisfied, Mis' Fulham did; but for me, I was disappointed; an' early that fall she died."

Abby Pendexter was laughing like a girl; the speaker's tone had grown more and more complaining. "I do call that a funny experience," she said. "'Better a dinner o' herbs.' I guess that text must ha' risen to your mind in connection. You must tell that to Aunt Cynthy, if conversation seems to fail." And she laughed again, but Mrs. Hand still looked solemn and reproachful.

"Here we are; there's Aunt Cynthy's lane right ahead, there by the great yellow birch," said Abby. "I must say, you've made the way seem very short, Mis' Hand."

III.

Old Aunt Cynthia Dallett sat in her high-backed rocking-chair by the little north window, which was her favorite dwelling-place.

"New Year's Day again!" she said, aloud—"New Year's Day again!" And she folded her old bent hands, and looked out at the great woodland view and the hills without really seeing them, she was lost in so deep a reverie. "I'm gittin' to be very old," she added, after a little while.

It was perfectly still in the small gray house. Outside in the apple-trees there were some blue-jays flitting about and calling noisily, like schoolboys fighting at their games. The kitchen was full of pale winter sunshine. It was more like late October than the first of January, and the plain little room seemed to smile back into the sun's face. The outer door was standing open into the green dooryard, and a fat small dog lay asleep on the step. A capacious cupboard stood behind Mrs. Dallett's chair and kept the wind away from her corner. Its doors and drawers were painted a clean lead-color, and there were places round the knobs and buttons where the touch of hands had worn deep into the wood. Every braided rug was straight on the floor. The square clock on its shelf between the front windows looked as if it had just had its face washed and been wound up for a whole year to come. If Mrs. Dallett turned her head she could look into the bedroom, where her plump feather bed was covered with its dark blue homespun winter quilt. It was all very peaceful and comfortable, but it was very lonely. By her side, on a lightstand, lay the religious newspaper of her denomination, and a pair of spectacles whose jointed silver bows looked like a funny two-legged beetle cast helplessly upon its back.

"New Year's Day again," said old Cynthia Dallett. Time had left nobody in her house to wish her a Happy New Year—she was the last one left in the old nest. "I'm gittin' to be very old," she said for the second time; it seemed to be all there was to say.

She was keeping a careful eye on her friendly clock, but it was hardly past the middle of the morning, and there was no excuse for moving; it was the long hour between the end of her slow morning work and the appointed time for beginning to get dinner. She was so stiff and lame that this hour's rest was usually most welcome, but to-day she sat as if it were Sunday, and did not take up her old shallow splint basket of braiding-rags from the side of her footstool.

"I do hope Abby Pendexter 'll make out to git up to see me this afternoon as usual," she continued. "I know 't ain't so easy for her to get up the hill as it used to be, but I do seem to want to see some o' my own folks. I wish 't I'd thought to send her word I expected her when Jabez Hooper went back after he came up here with the flour. I'd like to have had her come prepared to stop two or three days."

A little chickadee perched on the windowsill outside and bobbed his head sideways to look in, and then pecked impatiently at the glass. The old woman laughed at him with childish pleasure and felt companioned; it was pleasant at that moment to see the life in even a bird's bright eye.

"Sign of a stranger," she said, as he whisked his wings and flew away in a hurry. "I must throw out some crumbs for 'em; it's getting to be hard pickin' for the stayin'-birds." She looked past the trees of her little orchard now with seeing eyes, and followed the long forest slopes that led downward to the lowland country. She could see the two white steeples of Fairfield Village, and the map of fields and pastures along the valley beyond, and the great hills across the valley to the westward. The scattered houses looked like toys that had been scattered by children. She knew their lights by night, and watched the smoke of their chimneys by day. Far to the northward were higher mountains, and these were already white with snow. Winter was already in sight, but to-day the wind was in the south, and the snow seemed only part of a great picture.

"I do hope the cold 'll keep off a while longer," thought Mrs. Dallett. "I don't know how I'm going to get along after the deep snow comes."

The little dog suddenly waked, as if he had had a bad dream, and after giving a few anxious whines he began to bark outrageously. His mistress tried, as usual, to appeal to his better feelings.

" 'T ain't nobody, Tiger," she said. "Can't you have some patience? Maybe it's some foolish boys that's rangin' about with their guns." But Tiger kept on, and even took the trouble to waddle in on his short legs, barking all the way. He looked warningly at her, and then turned and ran out again. Then she saw him go hurrying down to the bars, as if it were an occasion of unusual interest.

"I guess somebody is comin'; he don't act as if 't were a vagrant kind o' noise; must really be somebody in our lane." And Mrs. Dallett smothed her apron and gave an anxious housekeeper's glance round the kitchen. None of her state visitors, the minister or the deacons, ever came in the morning. Country people are usually too busy to go visiting in the forenoons.

Presently two figures appeared where the road came out of the woods—the two women already known to the story, but very surprising to Mrs. Dallett; the short, thin one was easily recognized as Abby Pendexter, and the taller, stout one was soon discovered to be Mrs. Hand. Their old friend's heart was in a glow. As the guests approached they could see her pale face with its thin white hair framed under the close black silk handkerchief.

"There she is at her window smilin' away!" exclaimed Mrs. Hand; but by the time they reached the doorstep she stood waiting to meet them.

"Why, you two dear creatur's!" she said, with a beaming smile. "I don't know when I've ever been so glad to see folks comin'. I had a kind of left-all-alone feelin' this mornin', an' I didn't even make bold to be certain o' you, Abby, though it looked so pleasant. Come right in an' set down. You're all out o' breath, ain't you, Mis' Hand?"

Mrs. Dallett led the way with eager hospitality. She was the tiniest little bent old creature, her handkerchiefed head was quick and alert, and her eyes were bright with excitement and feeling, but the rest of her was much the worse for age; she could hardly move, poor soul, as if she had only a make-believe framework of a body under a shoulder-shawl and thick petticoats. She got back to her chair again, and the guests took off their bonnets in the bedroom, and returned discreet and sedate in their black woolen dresses. The lonely kitchen was blest with society at last, to its mistress's heart's content. They talked as fast as possible about the weather, and how warm it had been walking up the mountain, and how cold it had been a year ago, that day when Abby Pendexter had been kept at home by a snowstorm and missed her visit. "And I ain't seen you now, aunt, since the twenty-eighth of September, but I've thought of you a great deal, and looked forward to comin' more 'n usual," she ended, with an affectionate glance at the pleased old face by the window.

"I've been wantin' to see you, dear, and wonderin' how you was gettin' on," said Aunt Cynthy kindly. "And I take it as a great attention to have you come to-day, Mis' Hand," she added, turning again towards the more distinguished guest. "We have to put one thing against another. I should hate dreadfully to live anywhere except on a high hill farm, 'cordin' as I was born an' raised. But there ain't the chance to neighbor that townfolks has, an' I do seem to have more lonely hours than I used to when I was younger. I don't know but I shall soon be gittin' too old to live alone." And she turned to her niece with an expectant, lovely look, and Abby smiled back.

"I often wish I could run in an' see you every day, aunt," she answered. "I have been sayin' so to Mrs. Hand."

"There, how anybody does relish company when they don't have but a little of it!" exclaimed Aunt Cynthia. "I am all alone to-day; there is going to be a shootin'-match somewhere the other side o' the mountain, an' Johnny Foss, that does my chores, begged off to go when he brought the milk unusual early this mornin'. Gener'lly he's about here all the fore part of the day; but he don't go off with the boys very often, and I like to have him have a little sport; 't was New Year's Day, anyway; he's a good, stiddy boy for my wants."

"Why, I wish you Happy New Year, aunt!" said Abby, springing up with unusual spirit. "Why, that's just what we come to say, and we like to have forgot all about it!" She kissed her aunt, and stood a minute holding her hand with a soft, affectionate touch. Mrs. Hand rose and kissed Mrs. Dallett too, and it was a moment of ceremony and deep feeling.

"I always like to keep the day," said the old hostess, as they seated themselves and drew their splint-bottomed chairs a little nearer together than before. "You see, I was brought up to it, and father made a good deal of it; he said he liked to make it pleasant and give the year a fair start. I can see him now, how he used to be standing there by the fireplace when we came out o' the two bedrooms early in the morning, an' he always made out, poor's he was, to give us some little present, and he'd heap 'em up on the corner o' the mantel-piece, an' we'd stand front of him in a row, and mother be

bustling about gettin' breakfast. One year he give me a beautiful copy o' the 'Life o' General Lafayette,' in a green
cover—I've got it now, but we child'n 'bout read it to
pieces—an' one year a nice piece o' blue ribbon, an' Abby—
that was your mother, Abby—had a pink one. Father was
real kind to his child'n. I thought o' them early days when I
first waked up this mornin', and I couldn't help lookin' up
then to the corner o' the shelf just as I used to look."

"There's nothin' so beautiful as to have a bright childhood
to look back to," said Mrs. Hand. "Sometimes I think child'n
has too hard a time now—all the responsibility is put on to
'em, since they take the lead o' what to do an' what they
want, and get to be so toppin' an' knowin'. 'T was happier in
the old days, when the fathers an' mothers done the rulin'."

"They say things have changed," said Aunt Cynthy; "but
staying right here, I don't know much of any world but my
own world."

Abby Pendexter did not join in this conversation, but sat in
her straight-backed chair with folded hands and the air of a
good child. The little old dog had followed her in, and now
lay sound asleep again at her feet. The front breadth of her
black dress looked rusty and old in the sunshine that slanted
across it, and the aunt's sharp eyes saw this and saw the careful darns. Abby was as neat as wax, but she looked as if the
frost had struck her. "I declare, she's gittin along in years,"
thought Aunt Cynthia compassionately. "She begins to look
sort o' set and dried up, Abby does. She oughtn't to live all
alone; she's one that needs company."

At this moment Abby looked up with new interest. "Now,
aunt," she said, in her pleasant voice, "I don't want you to
forget to tell me if there ain't some sewin' or mendin' I can
do whilst I'm here. I know your hands trouble you some, an'
I may's well tell you we're bent on stayin' all day an' makin'
a good visit, Mis' Hand an' me."

"Thank ye kindly," said the old woman; "I do want a little
sewin' done before long, but 't ain't no use to spile a good
holiday." Her face took a resolved expression. "I'm goin' to
make other arrangements," she said. "No, you needn't come
up here to pass New Year's Day an' be put right down to sewin'. I make out to do what mendin' I need, an' to sew on
my hooks an' eyes. I get Johnny Ross to thread me up a good
lot o' needles every little while, an' that helps me a good deal.
Abby, why can't you step into the best room an' bring out
the rockin'-chair? I seem to want Mis' Hand to have it."

"I opened the window to let the sun in awhile," said the niece, as she returned. "It felt cool in there an' shut up."

"I thought of doin' it not long before you come," said Mrs. Dallett, looking gratified. Once the taking of such a liberty would have been very provoking to her. "Why, it does seem good to have somebody think o' things an' take right hold like that!"

"I'm sure you would, if you were down at my house," said Abby, blushing. "Aunt Cynthy, I don't suppose you could feel as if 't would be best to come down an' pass the winter with me—just durin' the cold weather, I mean. You'd see more folks to amuse you, an'—I do think of you so anxious these long winter nights."

There was a terrible silence in the room, and Miss Pendexter felt her heart begin to beat very fast. She did not dare to look at her aunt at first.

Presently the silence was broken. Aunt Cynthia had been gazing out of the window, and she turned towards them a little paler and older than before, and smiling sadly.

"Well, dear, I'll do just as you say," she answered. "I'm beat by age at last, but I've had my own way for eighty-five years, come the month o' March, an' last winter I did use to lay awake an' worry in the long storms. I'm kind o' humble now about livin' alone to what I was once." At this moment a new light shone in her face. "I don't expect you'd be willin' to come up here an' stay till spring—not if I had Foss's folks stop for you to ride to meetin' every pleasant Sunday, an' take you down to the Corners plenty o' other times besides?" she said beseechingly. "No, Abby, I'm too old to move now; I should be homesick down to the village. If you'll come an' stay with me, all I have shall be yours. Mis' Hand hears me say it."

"Oh, don't you think o' that; you're all I've got near to me in the world, an' I'll come an' welcome," said Abby, though the thought of her own little home gave a hard tug at her heart. "Yes, Aunt Cynthy, I'll come, an' we'll be real comfortable together. I've been lonesome sometimes—"

" 'T will be best for both," said Mrs. Hand judicially. And so the great question was settled, and suddenly, without too much excitement, it became a thing of the past.

"We must be thinkin' o' dinner," said Aunt Cynthia gayly. "I wish I was better prepared; but there's nice eggs an' pork an' potatoes, an' you girls can take hold an' help." At this moment the roast chicken and the best mince pies were offered and kindly accepted, and before another hour had gone they were sitting at their New Year feast, which Mrs. Dallett decided to be quite proper for the Queen.

Before the guests departed, when the sun was getting low, Aunt Cynthia called her niece to her side and took hold of her hand.

"Don't you make it too long now, Abby," said she. "I shall be wantin' ye every day till you come; but you mustn't forgit what a set old thing I be."

Abby had the kindest of hearts, and was always longing for somebody to love and care for; her aunt's very age and helplessness seemed to beg for pity.

Mary
Wilkins Freeman

A Mistaken Charity

❧

There were in a green field a little, low, weather-stained cottage, with a foot-path leading to it from the highway several rods distant, and two old women—one with a tin pan and old knife searching for dandelion greens among the short young grass, and the other sitting on the door-step watching her, or, rather, having the appearance of watching her.

"Air there enough for a mess, Harriét?" asked the old woman on the door-step. She accented oddly the last syllable of the Harriet, and there was a curious quality in her feeble, cracked old voice. Besides the question denoted by the arrangement of her words and the rising inflection, there was another, broader and subtler, the very essence of all questioning, in the tone of her voice itself; the cracked, quavering notes that she used reached out of themselves, and asked, and groped like fingers in the dark. One would have known by the voice that the old woman was blind.

The old woman on her knees in the grass searching for dandelions did not reply; she evidently had not heard the question. So the old woman on the door-step, after waiting a few minutes with her head turned expectantly, asked again, varying her question slightly, and speaking louder:

"Air there enough for a mess, do ye s'pose, Harriét?"

The old woman in the grass heard this time. She rose slowly and laboriously; the effort of straightening out the rheumatic old muscles was evidently a painful one; then she eyed the greens heaped up in the tin pan, and pressed them down with her hand.

"Wa'al, I don't know, Charlotte," she replied, hoarsely. "There's plenty on 'em here, but I 'ain't got near enough for a mess; they do bile down so when you get 'em in the pot; an' it's all I can do to bend my j'ints enough to dig 'em."

"I'd give consider'ble to help ye, Harriét," said the old woman on the door-step.

But the other did not hear her; she was down on her knees in the grass again, anxiously spying out the dandelions.

So the old woman on the door-step crossed her little shrivelled hands over her calico knees, and sat quite still, with the soft spring wind blowing over her.

The old wooden door-step was sunk low down among the grasses, and the whole house to which it belonged had an air of settling down and mouldering into the grass as into its own grave.

When Harriet Shattuck grew deaf and rheumatic, and had to give up her work as tailoress, and Charlotte Shattuck lost her eyesight, and was unable to do any more sewing for her livelihood, it was a small and trifling charity for the rich man who held a mortgage on the little house in which they had been born and lived all their lives to give them the use of it, rent and interest free. He might as well have taken credit to himself for not charging a squirrel for his tenement in some old decaying tree in his woods.

So ancient was the little habitation, so wavering and mouldering, the hands that had fashioned it had lain still so long in their graves, that it almost seemed to have fallen below its distinctive rank as a house. Rain and snow had filtered through its roof, mosses had grown over it, worms had eaten it, and birds built their nests under its eaves; nature had almost completely overrun and obliterated the work of man, and taken her own to herself again, till the house seemed as much a natural ruin as an old tree-stump.

The Shattucks had always been poor people and common people; no especial grace and refinement or fine ambition had ever characterized any of them; they had always been poor and coarse and common. The father and his father before him had simply lived in the poor little house, grubbed for their living, and then unquestioningly died. The mother had been of no rarer stamp, and the two daughters were cast in the same mould.

After their parents' death Harriet and Charlotte had lived along in the old place from youth to old age, with the one hope of ability to keep a roof over their heads, covering on their backs, and victuals in their mouths—an all-sufficient one with them.

Neither of them had ever had a lover; they had always seemed to repel rather than attract the opposite sex. It was not merely because they were poor, ordinary, and homely; there were plenty of men in the place who would have

matched them well in that respect; the fault lay deeper—in
their characters. Harriet, even in her girlhood, had a blunt,
defiant manner that almost amounted to surliness, and was
well calculated to alarm timid adorers, and Charlotte had always had the reputation of not being any too strong in her
mind.

Harriet had gone about from house to house doing tailor-
work after the primitive country fashion, and Charlotte had
done plain sewing and mending for the neighbors. They had
been, in the main, except when pressed by some temporary
anxiety about their work or the payment thereof, happy and
contented, with that negative kind of happiness and content-
ment which comes not from gratified ambition, but a lack of
ambition itself. All that they cared for they had had in toler-
able abundance, for Harriet at least had been swift and capable about her work. The patched, mossy old roof had been
kept over their heads, the coarse, hearty food that they loved
had been set on their table, and their cheap clothes had been
warm and strong.

After Charlotte's eyes failed her, and Harriet had the rheumatic fever, and the little hoard of earnings went to the doctors, times were harder with them, though still it could not be
said that they actually suffered.

When they could not pay the interest on the mortgage they
were allowed to keep the place interest free; there was as
much fitness in a mortgage on the little house, anyway, as
there would have been on a rotten old apple-tree; and the
people about, who were mostly farmers, and good friendly
folk, helped them out with their living. One would donate a
barrel of apples from his abundant harvest to the two poor
old women, one a barrel of potatoes, another a load of wood
for the winter fuel, and many a farmer's wife had bustled up
the narrow foot-path with a pound of butter, or a dozen fresh
eggs, or a nice bit of pork. Besides all this, there was a tiny
garden patch behind the house, with a straggling row of currant bushes in it, and one of gooseberries, where Harriet con-
trived every year to raise a few pumpkins, which were the
pride of her life. On the right of the garden were two old
apple-trees, a Baldwin and a Porter, both yet in a tolerably
good fruit-bearing state.

The delight which the two poor old souls took in their own
pumpkins, their apples and currants, was indescribable. It was
not merely that they contributed largely towards their living;
they were their own, their private share of the great wealth of

nature, the little taste set apart for them alone out of her bounty, and worth more to them on that account, though they were not conscious of it, than all the richer fruits which they received from their neighbors' gardens.

This morning the two apple-trees were brave with flowers, the currant bushes looked alive, and the pumpkin seeds were in the ground. Harriet cast complacent glances in their direction from time to time, as she painfully dug her dandelion greens. She was a short, stoutly built old woman, with a large face coarsely wrinkled, with a suspicion of a stubble of beard on the square chin.

When her tin pan was filled to her satisfaction with the sprawling, spidery greens, and she was hobbling stiffly towards her sister on the door-step, she saw another woman standing before her with a basket in her hand.

"Good-morning, Harriet," she said, in a loud, strident voice, as she drew near. "I've been frying some doughnuts, and I brought you over some warm."

"I've been tellin' her it was real good in her," piped Charlotte from the door-step, with an anxious turn of her sightless face towards the sound of her sister's footstep.

Harriet said nothing but a hoarse "Good-mornin', Mis' Simonds." Then she took the basket in her hand, lifted the towel off the top, selected a doughnut, and deliberately tasted it.

"Tough," said she. "I s'posed so. If there is anything I 'spise on this airth it's a tough doughnut."

"Oh, Harriét!" said Charlotte, with a frightened look.

"They air tough," said Harriet, with hoarse defiance, "and if there is anything I 'spise on this airth it's a tough doughnut."

The woman whose benevolence and cookery were being thus ungratefully received only laughed. She was quite fleshy, and had a round, rosy, determined face.

"Well, Harriet," said she, "I am sorry they are tough, but perhaps you had better take them out on a plate, and give me my basket. You may be able to eat two or three of them if they are tough."

"They air tough—turrible tough," said Harriet, stubbornly; but she took the basket into the house and emptied it of its contents nevertheless.

"I suppose your roof leaked as bad as ever in that heavy rain day before yesterday?" said the visitor to Harriet, with an inquiring squint towards the mossy shingles, as she was about to leave with her empty basket.

"It was turrible," replied Harriet, with crusty acquiescence—"turrible. We had to set pails an' pans everywheres, an' move the bed out."

"Mr. Upton ought to fix it."

"There ain't any fix to it; the old ruff ain't fit to nail new shingles on to; the hammerin' would bring the whole thing down on our heads," said Harriet, grimly.

"Well, I don't know as it can be fixed, it's so old. I suppose the wind comes in bad around the windows and doors too?"

"It's like livin' with a piece of paper, or mebbe a sieve, 'twixt you an' the wind an' the rain," quoth Harriet, with a jerk of her head.

"You ought to have a more comfortable home in your old age," said the visitor, thoughtfully.

"Oh, it's well enough," cried Harriet, in quick alarm, and with a complete change of tone; the woman's remark had brought an old dread over her. "The old house'll last as long as Charlotte an' me do. The rain ain't so bad, nuther is the wind; there's room enough for us in the dry places, an' out of the way of the doors an' windows. It's enough sight better than goin' on the town." Her square, defiant old face actually looked pale as she uttered the last words and stared apprehensively at the woman.

"Oh, I did not think of your doing that," she said, hastily and kindly. "We all know how you feel about that, Harriet, and not one of us neighbors will see you and Charlotte go to the poorhouse while we've got a crust of bread to share with you."

Harriet's face brightened. "Thank ye, Mis' Simonds," she said, with reluctant courtesy. "I'm much obleeged to you an' the neighbors. I think mebbe we'll be able to eat some of them doughnuts if they air tough," she added, mollifyingly, as her caller turned down the foot-path.

"My, Harriét," said Charlotte, lifting up a weakly, wondering, peaked old face, "what did you tell her them doughnuts was tough fur?"

"Charlotte, do you want everybody to look down on us, an' think we ain't no account at all, just like any beggars, 'cause they bring us in vittles?" said Harriet, with a grim glance at her sister's meek, unconscious face.

"No, Harriét," she whispered.

"Do you want *to go to the poor-house?*"

"No, Harriét." The poor little old woman on the door-step fairly cowered before her aggressive old sister.

"Then don't hender me agin when I tell folks their dough-nuts is tough an' their pertaters is poor. If I don't kinder keep up an' show some sperrit, I sha'n't think nothing of myself, an' other folks won't nuther, and fust thing we know they'll kerry us to the poorhouse. You'd 'a been there before now if it hadn't been for me, Charlotte."

Charlotte looked meekly convinced, and her sister sat down on a chair in the doorway to scrape her dandelions.

"Did you git a good mess, Harriét?" asked Charlotte, in a humble tone.

"Toler'ble."

"They'll be proper relishin' with that piece of pork Mis' Mann brought in yesterday. O Lord, Harriét, it's a chink!"

Harriet sniffed.

Her sister caught with her sensitive ear the little contemp-tuous sound. "I guess," she said, querulously, and with more pertinacity than she had shown in the matter of the dough-nuts, "that if you was in the dark, as I am, Harriét, you wouldn't make fun an' turn up your nose at chinks. If you had seen the light streamin' in all of a sudden through some little hole that you hadn't known of before when you set down on the door-step this mornin', and the wind with the smell of the apple blows in it came in your face, an' when Mis' Simonds brought them hot doughnuts, an' when I thought of the pork an' greens jest now— O Lord, how it did shine in! An' it does now. If you was me, Harriét, you would know there was chinks."

Tears began starting from the sightless eyes, and streaming pitifully down the pale old cheeks.

Harriet looked at her sister, and her grim face softened. "Why, Charlotte, hev it that thar *is* chinks if you want to. Who cares?"

"Thar *is* chinks, Harriét."

"Wa'al, thar *is* chinks, then. If I don't hurry, I sha'n't get these greens in in time for dinner."

When the two old women sat down complacently to their meal of pork and dandelion greens in their little kitchen they did not dream how destiny slowly and surely was introducing some new colors into their web of life, even when it was al-most completed, and that this was one of the last meals they would eat in their old home for many a day. In about a week from that day they were established in the "Old Ladies'

Home" in a neighboring city. It came about in this wise: Mrs. Simonds, the woman who had brought the gift of hot doughnuts, was a smart, energetic person, bent on doing good, and she did a great deal. To be sure, she always did it in her own way. If she chose to give hot doughnuts, she gave hot doughnuts; it made not the slightest difference to her if the recipients of her charity would infinitely have preferred ginger cookies. Still, a great many would like hot doughnuts, and she did unquestionably a great deal of good.

She had a worthy coadjutor in the person of a rich and childless elderly widow in the place. They had fairly entered into a partnership in good works, with about an equal capital on both sides, the widow furnishing the money, and Mrs. Simonds, who had much the better head of the two, furnishing the active schemes of benevolence.

The afternoon after the doughnut episode she had gone to the widow with a new project, and the result was that entrance fees had been paid, and old Harriet and Charlotte made sure of a comfortable home for the rest of their lives. The widow was hand in glove with officers of missionary boards and trustees of charitable institutions. There had been an unusual mortality among the inmates of the "Home" this spring, there were several vacancies, and the matter of the admission of Harriet and Charlotte was very quickly and easily arranged. But the matter which would have seemed the least difficult—inducing the two old women to accept the bounty which Providence, the widow, and Mrs. Simonds were ready to bestow on them—proved the most so. The struggle to persuade them to abandon their tottering old home for a better was a terrible one. The widow had pleaded with mild surprise, and Mrs. Simonds with benevolent determination; the counsel and reverend eloquence of the minister had been called in; and when they yielded at last it was with a sad grace for the recipients of a worthy charity.

It had been hard to convince them that the "Home" was not an almshouse under another name, and their yielding at length to anything short of actual force was only due probably to the plea, which was advanced most eloquently to Harriet, that Charlotte would be so much more comfortable.

The morning they came away, Charlotte cried pitifully, and trembled all over her little shrivelled body. Harriet did not cry. But when her sister had passed out the low, sagging door she turned the key in the lock, then took it out and thrust it slyly into her pocket, shaking her head to herself with an air of fierce determination.

Mrs. Simonds's husband, who was to take them to the depot, said to himself, with disloyal defiance of his wife's active charity, that it was a shame, as he helped the two distressed old souls into his light wagon, and put the poor little box, with their homely clothes in it, in behind.

Mrs. Simonds, the widow, the minister, and the gentleman from the "Home" who was to take charge of them, were all at the depot, their faces beaming with the delight of successful benevolence. But the two poor old women looked like two forlorn prisoners in their midst. It was an impressive illustration of the truth of the saying "that it is more blessed to give than to receive."

Well, Harriet and Charlotte Shattuck went to the "Old Ladies' Home" with reluctance and distress. They stayed two months, and then—they ran away.

The "Home" was comfortable, and in some respects even luxurious; but nothing suited those two unhappy, unreasonable old women.

The fare was of a finer, more delicately served variety than they had been accustomed to; those finely flavored nourishing soups for which the "Home" took great credit to itself failed to please palates used to common, coarser food.

"O Lord, Harriét, when I set down to the table here there ain't no chinks," Charlotte used to say. "If we could hev some cabbage, or some pork an' greens, how the light would stream in!"

Then they had to be more particular about their dress. They had always been tidy enough, but now it had to be something more; the widow, in the kindness of her heart, had made it possible, and the good folks in charge of the "Home," in the kindness of their hearts, tried to carry out the widow's designs.

But nothing could transform these two unpolished old women into two nice old ladies. They did not take kindly to white lace caps and delicate neckerchiefs. They liked their new black cashmere dresses well enough, but they felt as if they broke a commandment when they put them on every afternoon. They had always worn calico with long aprons at home, and they wanted to now; and they wanted to twist up their scanty gray locks into little knots at the back of their heads, and go without caps, just as they always had done.

Charlotte in a dainty white cap was pitiful, but Harriet was both pitiful and comical. They were totally at variance with their surroundings, and they felt it keenly, as people of their stamp always do. No amount of kindness and attention—and they had enough of both—sufficed to reconcile them to their new abode. Charlotte pleaded continually with her sister to go back to their home.

"O Lord, Harriét, she would exclaim (by the way, Charlotte's "O Lord," which, as she used it, was innocent enough, had been heard with much disfavor in the "Home," and she, not knowing at all why, had been remonstrated with concerning it), "let us go home. I can't stay here no ways in this world. I don't like their vittles, an' I don't like to wear a cap; I want to go home and do different. The currants will be ripe, Harriét. O Lord, thar was almost a chink, thinking about 'em. I want some of 'em; an' the Porter apples will be gittin' ripe, an' we could have some apple-pie. This here ain't good; I want merlasses fur sweeting. Can't we get back no ways, Harriét? It ain't far, an' we could walk, an' they don't lock us in, nor nothin'. I don't want to die here; it ain't so straight up to heaven from here. O Lord, I've felt as if I was slantendicular from heaven ever since I've been here, an' it's been so awful dark. I ain't had any chinks. I want to go home, Harriét."

"We'll go to-morrow mornin'," said Harriet, finally; "we'll pack up our things an' go; we'll put on our old dresses, an' we'll do up the new ones in bundles, an' we'll just shy out the back way to-morrow mornin'; an' we'll go. I kin find the way, an' I reckon we kin git thar, if it is fourteen mile. Mebbe somebody will give us a lift."

And they went. With a grim humor Harriet hung the new white lace caps with which she and Charlotte had been so pestered, one on each post at the head of the bedstead, so they would meet the eyes of the first person who opened the door. Then they took their bundles, stole slyly out, and were soon on the high-road, hobbling along, holding each other's hands, as jubilant as two children, and chuckling to themselves over their escape, and the probable astonishment there would be in the "Home" over it.

"O Lord, Harriét, what do you s'pose they will say to them caps?" cried Charlotte, with a gleeful cackle.

"I guess they'll see as folks ain't goin' to be made to wear caps agin their will in a free kentry," returned Harriet, with an echoing cackle, as they sped feebly and bravely along.

The "Home" stood on the very outskirts of the city, luckily for them. They would have found it a difficult undertaking to traverse the crowded streets. As it was, a short walk brought them into the free country road—free comparatively, for even here at ten o'clock in the morning there was considerable travelling to and from the city on business or pleasure.

People whom they met on the road did not stare at them as curiously as might have been expected. Harriet held her bristling chin high in air, and hobbled along with an appearance of being well aware of what she was about, that led folks to doubt their own first opinion that there was something unusual about the two old women.

Still their evident feebleness now and then occasioned from one and another more particular scrutiny. When they had been on the road a half-hour or so, a man in a covered wagon drove up behind them. After he had passed them, he poked his head around the front of the vehicle and looked back. Finally he stopped, and waited for them to come up to him.

"Like a ride, ma'am?" said he, looking at once bewildered and compassionate.

"Thankee," said Harriet, "we'd be much obleeged."

After the man had lifted the old women into the wagon, and established them on the back seat, he turned around, as he drove slowly along, and gazed at them curiously.

"Seems to me you look pretty feeble to be walking far," said he. "Where were you going?"

Harriet told him with an air of defiance.

"Why," he exclaimed, "it is fourteen miles out. You could never walk it in the world. Well, I am going within three miles of there, and I can go on a little farther as well as not. But I don't see— Have you been in the city?"

"I have been visitin' my married darter in the city," said Harriet, calmly.

Charlotte started, and swallowed convulsively.

Harriet had never told a deliberate falsehood before in her life, but this seemed to her one of the tremendous exigencies of life which justify a lie. She felt desperate. If she could not contrive to deceive him in some way, the man might turn directly around and carry Charlotte and her back to the "Home" and the white caps.

"I should not have thought your daughter would have let you start for such a walk as that," said the man. "Is this lady your sister? She is blind, isn't she? She does not look fit to walk a mile."

"Yes, she's my sister," replied Harriet, stubbornly: "an'

she's blind; an' my darter didn't want us to walk. She felt reel bad about it. But she couldn't help it. She's poor, and her husband's dead, an' she's got four leetle children."

Harriet recounted the hardships of her imaginary daughter with a glibness that was astonishing. Charlotte swallowed again.

"Well," said the man, "I am glad I overtook you, for I don't think you would ever have reached home alive."

About six miles from the city an open buggy passed them swiftly. In it were seated the matron and one of the gentlemen in charge of the "Home." They never thought of looking into the covered wagon—and indeed one can travel in one of those vehicles, so popular in some parts of New England, with as much privacy as he could in his tomb. The two in the buggy were seriously alarmed, and anxious for the safety of the old women, who were chuckling maliciously in the wagon they soon left far behind. Harriet had watched them breathlessly until they disappeared on a curve of the road; then she whispered to Charlotte.

A little after noon the two old women crept slowly up the foot-path across the field to their old home.

"The clover is up to our knees," said Harriet; "an' the sorrel and the white-weed; an' there's lots of yaller butterflies."

"O Lord, Harriét, thar's a chink, an' I do believe I saw one of them yaller butterflies go past it," cried Charlotte, trembling all over, and nodding her gray head violently.

Harriet stood on the old sunken door-step and fitted the key, which she drew triumphantly from her pocket, in the lock, while Charlotte stood waiting and shaking behind her.

Then they went in. Everything was there just as they had left it. Charlotte sank down on a chair and began to cry. Harriet hurried across to the window that looked out on the garden.

"The currants air ripe," said she, "*an'* them pumpkins hev run all over everything."

"O Lord, Harriét," sobbed Charlotte, "thar is so many chinks that they air all runnin' together!"

❊❊❊

Gentian

❦

It had been raining hard all night; when the morning dawned clear everything looked vivid and unnatural. The wet leaves on the trees and hedges seemed to emit a real green light of their own; the tree trunks were black and dank, and the spots of moss on them stood out distinctly.

A tall old woman was coming quickly up the street. She had on a stiffly starched calico gown, which sprang and rattled as she walked. She kept smoothing it anxiously. "Gittin' every mite of the stiff'nin' out," she muttered to herself.

She stopped at a long cottage house, whose unpainted walls, with white window-facings, and wide sweep of shingled roof, looked dark and startling through being sodden with rain.

There was a low stone wall by way of fence, with a gap in it for a gate.

She had just passed through this gap when the house door opened, and a woman put out her head.

"Is that you, Hannah?" said she.

"Yes, it's me." She laid a hard emphasis on the last word; then she sighed heavily.

"Hadn't you better hold your dress up comin' through that wet grass, Hannah? You'll git it all bedraggled."

"I know it. I'm a-gittin' every mite of the stiff'nin' out on't. I worked half the forenoon ironin' on't yesterday, too. Well, I thought I'd got to git over here an' fetch a few of these fried cakes. I thought mebbe Alferd would relish 'em fur his breakfast; an' he'd got to have 'em while they was hot; they ain't good fur nothin' cold; an' I didn't hev a soul to send—never do. How is Alferd this mornin', Lucy?"

"'Bout the same, I guess."

"'Ain't had the doctor yit?"

"No." She had a little, patient, pleasant smile on her face, looking up at her questioner.

312

The women were sisters. Hannah was Hannah Orton, unmarried. Lucy was Mrs. Tollet. Alfred was her sick husband.

Hannah's long, sallow face was deeply wrinkled. Her wide mouth twisted emphatically as she talked.

"Well, I know one thing; ef he was my husband he'd *hev* a doctor."

Mrs. Tollet's voice was old, but there was a childish tone in it, a sweet, uncertain pipe.

"No; you couldn't make him, Hannah; you couldn't, no more'n me. Alferd was allers jest so. He ain't never thought nothin' of doctors, nor doctors' stuff."

"Well, I'd make him take somethin'. In my opinion he needs somethin' bitter." She screwed her mouth as if the bitter morsel were on her own tongue.

"Lor'! he wouldn't take it, you know, Hannah."

"He'd hev to. Gentian would be good fur him."

"He wouldn't tech it."

"I'd make him, ef I put it in his tea unbeknownst to him."

"O, I wouldn't dare to."

"Land! I guess I'd dare to. Ef folks don't know enough to take what's good fur 'em, they'd orter be made to by hook or crook. I don't believe in deceivin' generally, but I don't believe the Lord would hev let folks hed the faculty fur deceivin' in 'em ef it wa'n't to be used fur good sometimes. It's my opinion Alferd won't last long ef he don't hev somethin' pretty soon to strengthen of him up an' give him a start. Well, it ain't no use talkin'. I've got to git home an' put this dress in the wash-tub agin, I s'pose. I never see such a sight—just look at that! You'd better give Alferd those cakes afore they git cold."

"I shouldn't wonder ef he relished 'em. You was real good to think of it, Hannah."

"Well, I'm a-goin'. Every mite of the stiff'nin's out. Sometimes it seems as ef thar wa'n't no end to the work. I didn't know how to git out this mornin', anyway."

When Mrs. Tollet entered the house she found her husband in a wooden rocking-chair with a calico cushion, by the kitchen window. He was a short, large-framed old man, but he was very thin. There were great hollows in his yellow cheeks.

"What you got thar, Lucy?"

"Some griddle-cakes Hannah brought."

"Griddle-cakes!"

"They're real nice-lookin' ones. Don't you think you'd relish one or two, Alferd?"

"Ef you an' Hannah want griddle-cakes, you kin hev griddle-cakes."

"Then you don't want to hev one, with some maple merlasses on it? They've kept hit; she hed 'em kivered up."

"Take 'em away!"

She set them meekly on the pantry shelf; then she came back and stood before her husband, gentle deprecation in her soft old face and in the whole poise of her little slender body.

"What will you hev fur breakfast, Alferd?"

"I don' know. Well, you might as well fry a little slice of bacon, an' git a cup of tea."

"Ain't you 'most afeard of—bacon, Alferd?"

"No, I ain't. Ef anybody's sick, they kin tell what they want themselves 'bout as well's anybody kin tell 'em. They don't hev any hankerin' arter anythin' unless it's good for 'em. When they need anythin', natur gives 'em a longin' arter it. I wish you'd hurry up an' cook that bacon, Lucy. I'm awful faint at my stomach."

She cooked the bacon and made the tea with no more words. Indeed, it was seldom that she used as many as she had now. Alfred Tollet, ever since she had married him, had been the sole autocrat of all her little Russias; her very thoughts had followed after him, like sheep.

After breakfast she went about putting her house in order for the day. When that was done, and she was ready to sit down with her sewing, she found that her husband had fallen asleep in his chair. She stood over him a minute, looking at his pale old face with the sincerest love and reverence. Then she sat down by the window and sewed, but not long. She got her bonnet and shawl stealthily, and stole out of the house. She sped quickly down the village street. She was light-footed for an old woman. She slackened her pace when she reached the village store, and crept hesitatingly into the great lumbering, rank-smelling room, with its dark, newly-sprinkled floor. She bought a bar of soap; then she stood irresolute.

"Anything else this mornin', Mis' Tollet?" The proprietor himself, a narrow-shouldered, irritable man, was waiting on her. His tone was impatient. Mrs. Tollet was too absorbed to notice it. She stood hesitating.

"*Is* there anything else you want?"

"Well—I don' know; but—p'rhaps I'd better—hev—ten cents' wuth of gentian." Her very lips were white; she had an expression of frightened, guilty resolution. If she had asked for strychnine, with a view to her own bodily destruction, she would not have had a different look.

The man mistook it, and his conscience smote him. He thought his manner had frightened her, but she had never noticed it.

"Goin' to give your husband some bitters?" he asked, affably, as he handed her the package.

She started and blushed. "No—I—thought some would be good fur—me."

"Well, gentian is a first-rate bitter. Good-morning, Mis' Tollet."

"Good-morning, Mr. Gill."

She was trembling all over when she reached her house door. There is a subtle, easily raised wind which blows spirits about like leaves, and she had come into it with her little paper of gentian. She had hidden the parcel in her pocket before she entered the kitchen. Her husband was awake. He turned his wondering, half-resentful eyes towards her without moving his head.

"Where hev you been, Lucy?"

"I—jest went down to the store a minit, Alferd, while you was asleep."

"What fur?"

"A bar of soap."

Alfred Tollet had always been a very healthy man until this spring. Some people thought that his illness was alarming now, more from its unwontedness and consequent effect on his mind, than from anything serious in its nature. However that may have been, he had complained of great depression and languor all the spring, and had not attempted to do any work.

It was the beginning of May now.

"Ef Alferd kin only git up May hill," Mrs. Tollet's sister had said to her, "he'll git along all right through the summer. It's a dretful tryin' time."

So up May hill, under the white apple and plum boughs, over the dandelions and the young grass, Alfred Tollet climbed, pushed and led faithfully by his loving old wife. At last he stood triumphantly on the summit of that fair hill, with its sweet, wearisome ascent. When the first of June came, people said, "Alfred Tollet's a good deal better."

He began to plant a little and bestir himself.

"Alfred's out workin' in the garden," Mrs. Tollet told her

sister one afternoon. She had strolled over to her house with
her knitting after dinner.

"You don't say so! Well, I thought when I see him Sunday
that he was lookin' better. He's got through May, an' I guess
he'll pull through. I did feel kinder worried 'bout him one
spell —Why, Lucy, what's the matter?"

"Nothin'. Why?"

"You looked at me dretful kind of queer an' distressed, I
thought."

"I guess you must hev imagined it, Hannah. Thar ain't
nothin' the matter." She tried to look unconcernedly at her sister, but her lips were trembling.

"Well, I don't know 'bout it. You look kinder queer now. I
guess you walked too fast comin' over here. You allers did
race."

"Mebbe I did."

"For the land's sake, jest see that dust you tracked in! I've
got to git the dust-pan an' brush now, an' sweep it up."

"I'll do it."

"No; set still. I'd rather see to it myself."

As the summer went on Alfred Tollet continued to im-
prove. He was as hearty as ever by September. But his wife
seemed to lose as he gained. She grew thin, and her small face
had a solemn, anxious look. She went out very little. She did
not go to church at all, and she had been a devout church-
goer. Occasionally she went over to her sister's, that was all.
Hannah watched her shrewdly. She was a woman who arrived
at conclusions slowly; but she never turned aside from the
road to them.

"Look-a here, Lucy," she said one day, "I know what's the
matter with you; thar's somethin' on your mind; an' I think
you'd better out with it."

The woods seemed propelled like bullets by her vehemence. Lucy shrank down and away from them, her pitiful
eyes turned up towards her sister.

"Oh, Hannah, you scare me; I don't know what you
mean."

"Yes, you do. Do you s'pose I'm blind? You're worrying
yourself to death, an' I want to know the reason why. Is it
anything 'bout Alferd?"

"Yes—don't, Hannah."

"Well, I'll go over an' give him a piece of my mind! I'll
see—"

"Oh, Hannah, don't! It ain't him. It's me—it's me."

"What on airth hev you done?"

Mrs. Tollet began to sob.

"For the land sake, stop cryin' an' tell me."

"Oh, I—give him—gentian."

"Lucy Ann Tollet, air you crazy? What ef you did give him gentian? I don't see nothin' to take on so about."

"I—deceived him, an' it's been 'most killin' me to think on't ever since."

"What do you mean?"

"I put it in his tea, the way you said."

"An' he never knew it?"

"He kinder complained 'bout its tastin' bitter, an' I told him 'twas his mouth. He asked me ef it didn't taste bitter to me, an' I said, 'No.' I don' know nothin' what's goin' to become of me. Then I had to be so keerful 'bout putting too much on't in his tea, that I was afraid he wouldn't get enough. So I put little sprinklin's on't in the bread an' pies an' everythin' I cooked. An' when he'd say nothin' tasted right nowadays, an' somehow everything was kinder bitterish, I's tell him it must be his mouth."

"Look here, Lucy, you didn't eat everythin' with gentian in it yourself?"

"Course I did."

"Fur the land sake!"

"I s'pose the stuff must hev done him good; he's picked right up ever since he begun takin' it. But I can't git over my deceivin' of him so. I've 'bout made up my mind to tell him."

"Well, all I've got to say is you're a big fool if you do. I declare, Lucy Ann Tollet, I never saw sech a woman! The idee of your worryin' over such a thing as that, when it's done Alferd good, too! P'rhaps you'd ruther he'd died?"

"Sometimes I think I hed 'most ruther."

"Well!"

In the course of a few days Mrs. Tollet did tell her husband. He received her disclosure in precisely the way she had known that he would. Her nerves received just the shock which they were braced to meet.

They had come home from meeting on a Sunday night. Mrs. Tollet stood before him; she had not even taken off her shawl and little black bonnet.

"Alferd," said she, "I've got somethin' to tell you; it's been on my mind a long time. I meant it all fur the best; but I've been doin' somethin' wrong. I've been deceivin' of you. I give you gentian last spring when you was so poorly. I put little sprinklin's on't into everything you ate. An' I didn't tell the truth when I said 'twas your mouth, an' it didn't taste bitter to me."

The old man half closed his eyes, and looked at her intently; his mouth widened out rigidly. "You put a little gentian into everything I ate unbeknownst to me, did you?" said he. "H'm!"

"Oh, Alferd, don't look at me so! I meant it all fur the best. I was afeard you wouldn't git well without you hed it, Alferd. I was dretful worried about you; you didn't know nothin' about it, but I was. I laid awake nights a-worryin' an' prayin. I know I did wrong; it wa'n't right to deceive you, but it was all along of my worryin' an' my thinkin' so much of you, Alferd. I was afeard you'd die an' leave me all alone; an'—it 'most killed me to think on't."

Mr. Tollet pulled off his boots, then pattered heavily about the house, locking the doors and making preparations for retiring. He would not speak another word to his wife about the matter, though she kept on with her piteous little protestations.

Next morning, while she was getting breakfast, he went down to the store. The meal, a nice one—she had taken unusual pains with it—was on the table when he returned; but he never glanced at it. His hands were full of bundles, which he opened with painstaking deliberation. His wife watched apprehensively. There was a new teapot, a pound of tea, and some bread and cheese, also a salt mackerel.

Mrs. Tollet's eyes shone round and big; her lips were white. Her husband put a pinch of tea in the new teapot, and filled it with boiling water from the kettle.

"What air you a-doin' on, Alferd?" she asked, feebly.

"I'm jest a-goin' to make sure I hev some tea, an' somethin' to eat without any gentian in it."

"Oh, Alferd, I made these corn-cakes on purpose, an' they air real light. They 'ain't got no gentian on 'em, Alferd."

He sliced his bread and cheese clumsily, and sat down to eat them in stubborn silence.

Mrs. Tollet, motionless at her end of the table, stared at him with an appalled look. She never thought of eating anything herself.

After breakfast, when her husband started out to work, he pointed at the mackerel. "Don't you tech that," said he.

"But, Alferd—"

"I ain't got nothin' more to say. Don't you tech it."

Never a morning had passed before but Lucy Tollet had set her house in order; to-day she remained there at the kitchen-table till noon, and did not put away the breakfast dishes.

Alfred came home, kindled up the fire, cooked and ate his salt mackerel imperturbably; and she did not move or speak till he was about to go away again. Then she said, in a voice which seemed to shrink of itself, "Alferd!"

He did not turn his head.

"Alferd, you must answer me; I'm in airnest. Don't you want me to do nothin' fur you any more? Don't you never want me to cook anything fur you agin?"

"No; I'm afeard of gittin' things that's bitter."

"I won't never put any gentian in anything again, Alferd. Won't you let me git supper?"

"No, I won't. I don't want to talk no more about it. In futur I'm a-goin' to cook my vittles myself, an' that's all thar is about it."

"Alferd, if you don't want me to do nothin' fur you, mebbe—you'll think I ain't airnin' my own vittles; mebbe—you'd rather I go over to Hannah's—"

She sobbed aloud when she said that. He looked startled, and eyed her sharply for a minute. The other performer in the little melodrama which this thwarted, arbitrary old man had arranged was adopting a *rôle* that he had not anticipated, but he was still going to abide by his own.

"Mebbe 'twould be jest as well," said he. Then he went out of the door.

Hannah Orton was in her kitchen sewing when her sister entered.

"Fur the land sake, Lucy, what is the matter?"

"I've left him—I've left Alferd! Oh! oh!"

Lucy Tollet gasped for breath; she sank into a chair, and leaned her head against the wall. Hannah got some water.

"Don't, Lucy—there, there! Drink this, poor lamb!"

She did not quite faint. She could speak in a few minutes. "He bought him a new tea-pot this mornin', Hannah, an' some bread an' cheese and salt mackerel. He's goin' to do his own cookin'; he don't want me to do nothin' more fur him; he's afeard I'll put gentian in it. I've left him! I've come to stay with you!"

"You told him, then?"

"I hed to; I couldn't go on so no longer. He wouldn't let

me tech that mackerel, an' it orter hev been soaked. It was salt enough to kill him."

"Serve him right ef it did."

"Hannah Orton, I ain't a-goin' to hev a thing said agin Alferd."

"Well, ef you want to stan' up fur Alferd Tollet, you kin. You allers would stan' up fur him agin your own folks. Ef you want to keep on carin' fur sech a miserable, set, unfeelin'—"

"Don't you say another word, Hannah—not another one; I won't hear it."

"I ain't a-goin' to say nothin'; thar ain't any need of your bein' so fierce. Now don't cry so, Lucy. We shell git along real nice here together. You'll get used to it arter a little while, an' you'll see you air a good deal better off without him; you've been nothin' but jest a slave ever since you was married. Don't you s'pose I've seen it? I've pitied you so, I didn't know what to do. I've seen the time when I'd like to ha' shook Alferd."

"Don't, Hannah."

"I ain't a-goin' to say nothin' more. You jest stop cryin', an' try an' be calm, or you'll be sick. Hev you hed any dinner?"

"I don't want none."

"You've got to eat somethin', Lucy Ann Tollet. Thar ain't no sense in your givin' up so. I've got a nice little piece of lamb, an' some pease an' string-beans, left over, an' I'm a-goin' to get 'em. You've got to eat 'em, an' then you'll feel better. Look-a here, I want to know ef Alferd drove you out of the house 'cause you give him gentian? I ain't got it through my head yet."

"I asked him ef he'd ruther hev me go, an' he said mebbe 'twould be jest as well. I thought I shouldn't hev no right to stay ef I couldn't git his meals for him."

"Right to stay! Lucy Ann Tollet, ef it wa'n't fur the grace of the Lord, I believe you'd be a simpleton. I don't understand no sech goodness; I allers thought it would run into foolishness some time, an' I believe it has with you. Well, don't worry no more about it; set up an' eat your dinner. Jest smooth out that mat under your feet a little; you've got it all scrolled up."

No bitter herb could have added anything to the bitterness of that first dinner which poor Lucy Tollet ate after she had left her own home. Time and custom lessened, but not much, the bitterness of the subsequent ones. Hannah had sewed for her living all her narrow, single life; Lucy shared her work now. They had to live frugally; still they had enough. Hannah owned the little house in which she lived.

Lucy Tollet lived with her through the fall and winter. Her leaving her husband started a great whirlpool of excitement in this little village. Hannah's custom doubled: people came ostensibly for work, but really for information. They quizzed her about her sister, but Hannah could be taciturn. She did their work and divulged nothing, except occasionally when she was surprised. Then she would let fall a few little hints, which were not at Lucy's expense.

They never saw Mrs. Tollet; she always ran when she heard any one coming. She never went out to church nor on the street. She grew to have a morbid dread of meeting her husband or seeing him. She would never sit at the window, lest he might go past. Hannah could not understand this; neither could Lucy herself.

Hannah thought she was suffering less, and was becoming weaned from her affection, because she did so. But in reality she was suffering more, and her faithful love for her imperious old husband was strengthening.

All the autumn and winter she stayed and worked quietly; in the spring she grew restless, though not perceptibly. She had never bewailed herself much after the first; she dreaded her sister's attacks on Alfred. Silence as to her own grief was her best way of defending him.

Towards spring she often let her work fall in her lap, and thought. Then she would glance timidly at Hannah, as if she could know what her thoughts were; but Hannah was no mind-reader. Hannah, when she set out for meeting one evening in May, had no conception whatever of the plan which was all matured in her sister's mind.

Lucy watched her out of sight; then she got herself ready quickly. She smoothed her hair, put on her bonnet and shawl, and started up the road towards her old home.

There was no moon, but it was clear and starry. The blooming trees stood beside the road like sweet, white, spring angels; there was a whippoorwill calling somewhere across the fields. Lucy Tollet saw neither stars nor blooming trees; she did not hear the whippoorwill. That hard, whimsical old man in the little weather-beaten house ahead towered up like a grand giant between the white trees and this one living old woman; his voice in her ears drowned out all the sweet notes of the spring birds.

When she came in sight of the house there was a light in the kitchen window. She crept up to it softly and looked in. Alfred was standing there with his hat on. He was looking straight at the window, and he saw her the minute her little pale face came up above the sill.

He opened the door quickly and came out. "Lucy, is that you?"

"Oh, Alferd, let me come home! I'll never deceive you agin!"

"You jest go straight back to Hannah's this minute."

She caught hold of his coat. "Oh, Alferd, don't—don't drive me away agin! It'll kill me this time; it will! it will!"

"You go right back."

She sank right down at his feet then, and clung to them. "Alferd, I won't go; I won't! I won't! You sha'n't drive me away agin. Oh, Alferd, don't drive me away from home! I've lived here with you for fifty year a'most. Let me come home an' cook fur you, an' do fur you agin. Oh, Alferd, Alferd!"

"See here, Lucy—git up; stop takin' on so. I want to tell you somethin'. You jest go right back to Hannah's, an' don't you worry. You set down an' wait a minute. Thar!"

Lucy looked at him. "What do you mean, Alferd?"

"Never you mind; you jist go right along."

Lucy Tollet sped back along the road to Hannah's, hardly knowing what she was about. It is doubtful if she realized anything but a blind obedience to her husband's will, and a hope of something roused by a new tone in his voice. She sat down on the door-step and waited, she did not know for what. In a few minutes she heard the creak of heavy boots, and her husband came in sight. He walked straight up to her.

"I've come to ask you to come home, Lucy. I'm a-feelin' kinder poorly this spring, an'—I want you ter stew me up a little gentian. That you give me afore did me a sight of good."

"Oh, Alferd!"

"That's what I'd got laid out to do when I see you at the winder, Lucy, an' I was a-goin' to do it."

❀

An Independent Thinker

❧❧❧

Esther Gay's house was little and square, and mounted on posts like stilts. A stair led up to the door on the left side. Morning-glories climbed up the stair-railing, the front of the house and the other side were covered with them, all the windows but one were curtained with the matted green vines. Esther sat at the uncurtained window, and knitted. She perked her thin, pale nose up in the air, her pointed chin tilted upward too; she held her knitting high, and the needles clicked loud, and shone in the sun. The bell was ringing for church, and a good many people were passing. They could look in on her, and see very plainly what she was doing. Every time a group went by she pursed her thin old lips tighter, and pointed up her nose higher, and knitted more fiercely. Her skinny shoulders jerked. She cast a sharp glance at every one who passed, but no one caught her looking. She knew them all. This was a little village. By and by the bell had stopped tolling, and even the late church-goers had creaked briskly out of sight. The street, which was narrow here, was still and vacant.

Presently a woman appeared in a little flower-garden in front of the opposite house. She was picking a nosegay. She was little and spare, and she bent over the flowers with a stiffness as of stiff wires. It seemed as if it would take mechanical force to spring her up again.

Esther watched her. "It's dretful hard work for her to git around," she muttered to herself.

Finally, she laid down her knitting and called across to her. "Laviny!" said she.

The woman came out to the gate with some marigolds and candytuft in her hand. Her dim blue eyes blinked in the light. She looked over and smiled with a sort of helpless inquiry.

"Come over here a minute."

"I—guess I—can't."

Esther was very deaf. She could not hear a word, but she

323

saw the deprecating shake of the head, and she knew well
enough.

"I'd like to know why you can't, a minute. You kin hear
your mother the minute she speaks."

The woman glanced back at the house, then she looked
over at Esther. Her streaked light hair hung in half-curls over
her wide crocheted collar, she had a little, narrow, wrinkled
face, but her cheeks were as red as roses.

"I guess I'd better not. It's Sunday, you know," said she.
Her soft, timid voice could by no possibility reach those deaf
ears across the way.

"What?"

"I--guess I'd better not—as long as it's *Sunday*."

Esther's strained attention caught the last word, and
guessed at the rest from a knowledge of the speaker.

"Stuff," said she, with a sniff through her delicate, uptilted
nostrils. "I'd like to know how much worse 't is for you to
step over here a minute, an' tell me how *she* is when I can't
hear across the road, than to stop an' talk comin' out o'
meetin'; you'd do that quick enough. You're strainin', Laviny
Dodge."

Lavinia, as if overwhelmed by the argument, cast one anxious glance back at the house, and came through the gate.

Just then a feeble, tremulous voice, with a wonderful quality of fine sharpness in it, broke forth behind her,

"Laviny, Laviny, where be you goin'? Come back here."

Lavinia, wheeling with such precipitate vigor that it suggested a creak, went up the path.

"I wa'n't goin' anywhere, mother," she called out. "What's
the matter?"

"You can't pull the wool over my eyes. I *seed* you a-goin'
out the gate."

Lavinia's mother was over ninety and bedridden. That infinitesimal face which had passed through the stages of
beauty, commonplaceness, and hideousness, and now arrived
at that of the fine grotesqueness which has, as well as beauty,
a certain charm of its own, peered out from its great feather
pillows. The skin on the pinched face was of a dark-yellow
color, the eyes were like black points, the tiny, sunken mouth
had a sardonic pucker.

"Esther jest wanted me to come over there a minute. She
wanted to ask after you," said Lavinia, standing beside the
bed, holding her flowers.

"Hey?"

"She *jest* wanted me to come over an' tell her how you was."

"How I was?"

"Yes."

"Did you tell her I was miser'ble?"

"I didn't go, mother."

"I *seed* you a-goin' out the gate."

"I came back. She couldn't hear 'thout I went way over."

"Hey?"

"It's all right, mother," screamed Lavinia. Then she went about putting the flowers in water.

The old woman's little eyes followed her, with a sharp light like steel.

"I ain't goin' to hev you goin' over to Esther Gay's, Sabbath day," she went on, her thin voice rasping out from her pillows like a file. "She ain't no kind of a girl. Wa'n't she knittin'?"

"Yes."

"Hey?"

"Yes, she was knittin', mother."

"Wa'n't knittin'?"

"Y-e-s, she was."

"I knowed it. Stayin' home from meetin' an' knittin'. I ain't goin' to hev you over thar, Laviny."

Esther Gay, over in her window, held her knitting up higher, and knitted with fury. "H'm, the old lady called her back," said she. "If they want to show out they kin, I'm goin' to do what I think's right."

The morning-glories on the house were beautiful this morning, the purple and white and rosy ones stood out with a soft crispness. Esther Gay's house was not so pretty in winter— there was no paint on it, and some crooked outlines showed. It was a poor little structure, but Esther owned it free of encumbrances. She had also a pension of ninety-six dollars which served her for support. She considered herself well to do. There was not enough for anything besides necessaries, but Esther was one who had always looked upon necessaries as luxuries. Her sharp eyes saw the farthest worth of things. When she bought a half-cord of pine wood with an allotment of her pension-money, she saw in a vision all the warmth and utility which could ever come from it. When it was heaped up in the space under the house which she used for a woodshed, she used to go and look at it.

"Esther Gay does think so much of her own things," people said.

That little house, which, with its precipitous stair and festoons of morning-glories, had something of a foreign picturesqueness, looked to her like a real palace. She paid a higher tax upon it than she should have done. A lesser one had been levied, and regarded by her as an insult. "My house is worth more'n that," she had told the assessor with an indignant bridle. She paid the increased tax with cheerful pride, and frequently spoke of it. To-day she often glanced from her knitting around the room. There was a certain beauty in it, although it was hardly the one which she recognized. It was full of a lovely, wavering, gold-green light, and there was a fine order and cleanness which gave a sense of peace. But Esther saw mainly her striped rag-carpet, her formally set chairs, her lounge covered with Brussels, and her shining cooking-stove.

Still she looked at nothing with the delight with which she surveyed her granddaughter Hatty, when she returned from church.

"Well, you've got home, ain't you?" she said, when the young, slim girl, with her pale, sharp face, which was like her grandmother's, stood before her. Hatty in her meeting-gown of light-brown delaine, and her white meeting-hat trimmed with light-brown ribbons and blue flowers was not pretty, but the old woman admired her.

"Yes," said Hatty. Then she went into her little bedroom to take off her things. There was a slow shyness about her. She never talked much, even to her grandmother.

"You kin git you somethin' to eat, if you want it," said the old woman. "I don't want to stop myself till I git this heel done. Was Henry to meetin'?"

"Yes."

"His father an' mother?"

"Yes."

Henry was the young man who had been paying attention to Hatty. Her grandmother was proud and pleased; she liked him.

Hatty generally went to church Sunday evenings, and the young man escorted her home, and came in and made a call. To-night the girl did not go to church as usual. Esther was astonished.

"Why, ain't you goin' to meetin'?" said she.

"No; I guess not."

"Why? why not?"

"I thought I wouldn't."

The old woman looked at her sharply. The tea-things were cleared away, and she was at her knitting again, a little lamp at her elbow.

Presently Hatty went out, and sat at the head of the stairs, in the twilight. She sat there by herself until meeting was over, and the people had been straggling by for some time. Then she went down-stairs, and joined a young man who passed at the foot of them. She was gone half an hour.

"Where hev you been?" asked her grandmother, when she returned.

"I went out a little way."

"Who with?"

"Henry."

"Why didn't he come in?"

"He thought he wouldn't."

"I don't see why."

Hatty said nothing. she lit her candle to go to bed. Her little thin face was imperturbable.

She worked in a shop, and earned a little money. Her grandmother would not touch a dollar of it; what she did not need to spend for herself, she made her save. Lately the old woman had been considering the advisability of her taking a sum from the saving's bank to buy a silk dress. She thought she might need it soon.

Monday, she opened upon the subject. "Hatty," said she, "I've been thinkin'—don't you believe it would be a good plan for you to take a little of your money out of the bank an' buy you a nice dress?"

Hatty never answered quickly. She looked at her grandmother, then she kept on with her sewing. It was after supper, her shop-work was done, and she was sitting at the table with her needle. She seemed to be considering her grandmother's remark.

The old woman waited a moment, then she proceeded: "I've been thinkin'—you ain't never had any real nice dress, you know—that it would be a real good plan for you to take some money, now you've got it, an' buy you a silk one. You ain't never had one, an' you're old enough to."

Still Hatty sewed, and said nothing.

"You might want to go somewhar," continued Esther, "an'—well, of course, if anythin' should happen, if Henry— It's jest as well not to hev' to do everythin' all to once, an' it's consider'ble work to make a silk dress— Why don't you say somethin'?"

"I don't want any silk dress."

"I'd like to know why not?"

Hatty made no reply.

"Look here, Hatty, you an' Henry Little ain't had no trouble, hev' you?"

"I don't know as we have."

"What?"

"I don't know as we have."

"Hatty Gay, I know there's somethin' the matter. Now you jest tell me what 'tis. Ain't he comin' here no more?"

Suddenly the girl curved her arm around on the table, and laid her face down on it. She would not speak another word. She did not seem to be crying, but she sat there, hiding her little plain, uncommunicative face.

"Hatty Gay, ain't he comin'? *Why* ain't he comin'?"

Hatty would give the old woman no information. All she got was that obtained from ensuing events. Henry Little did not come; she ascertained that. The weeks went on, and he had never once climbed those vine-wreathed stairs to see Hatty.

Esther fretted and questioned. One day, in the midst of her nervous conjectures, she struck the chord in Hatty which vibrated with information.

"I hope you want too forrard with Henry, Hatty," said the old woman. "You didn't act too anxious arter him, did you? That's apt to turn fellows."

Then Hatty spoke. Some pink spots flared out on her quiet, pale cheeks.

"Grandma," said she, "I'll tell you, if you want to know, what the trouble is. I wasn't goin' to, because I didn't want to make you feel bad; but, if you're goin' to throw out such things as that to me, I don't care. Henry's mother don't like you, there!"

"What?"

"Henry's mother don't like you."

"Don't like me?"

"No."

"Why, what hev I done? I don't see what you mean, Hatty Gay."

"Grace Porter told me. Mrs. Little told her mother. Then I asked him, an' he owned up it was so."

"I'd like to know what she said."

Hatty went on, pitilessly, "She told Grace's mother she didn't want her son to marry into the Gay tribe anyhow. She didn't think much of 'em. She said any girl whose folks didn't keep Sunday, an' stayed away from meetin' an' worked, wouldn't amount to much."

"I don't believe she said it."

"She did. Henry said his mother took on so he was afraid she'd die, if he didn't give it up."

Esther sat up straight. She seemed to bristle out suddenly with points, from her knitting-needles to her sharp elbows and thin chin and nose. "Well, he kin give it up then, if he wants to, for all me. I ain't goin' to give up my principles fir him, nor any of his folks, an' they'll find it out. You kin git somebody else jest as good as he is."

"I don't want anybody else."

"H'm, you needn't have 'em then, ef you ain't got no more sperit. I shouldn't think you'd want your grandmother to give up doin' what's right yourself, Hatty Gay."

"I ain't sure it is right."

"Ain't sure it's right. Then I s'pose you think it would be better for an old woman that's stone deaf, an' can't hear a word of the preachin', to go to meetin' an' set there, doin' nothin' two hours, instead of stayin' to home an' knittin', to airn a leetle money to give to the Lord. All I've got to say is, you kin think so, then. I'm a-goin' to do what's right, no matter what happens."

Hatty said nothing more. She took up her sewing again; her grandmother kept glancing at her. Finally she said, in a mollifying voice, "Why don't you go an' git you a leetle piece of that cake in the cupboard; you didn't eat no supper hardly."

"I don't want any."

"Well, if you want to make yourself sick, an' go without eatin, you kin."

Hatty did go without eating much through the following weeks. She laid awake nights, too, staring pitifully into the darkness, but she did not make herself ill. There was an un-flinching strength in that little, meagre body, which lay even back of her own will. It would take long for her lack of spirit to break her down entirely; but her grandmother did not know that. She watched her and worried. Still she had not the least idea of giving in. She knitted more zealously than ever Sundays; indeed, there was, to her possibly distorted percep-tions, a religious zeal in it.

She knitted on week-days too. She reeled off a good many pairs of those reliable blue-yarn stockings, and sold them to a dealer in the city. She gave away every cent which she earned, and carefully concealed the direction of her giving. Even Hatty did not know of it.

Six weeks after Hatty's lover left, the old woman across the way died. After the funeral, when measures were taken for the settlement of the estate, it was discovered that all the little property was gone, eaten up by a mortgage and the interest. The two old women had lived upon the small house and the few acres of land for the last ten years, ever since Lavinia's father had died. He had grubbed away in a boot-shop, and earned enough for their frugal support as long as he lived. Lavinia had never been able to work for her own living; she was not now. "Laviny Dodge will have to go to the poor-house," everybody said.

One noon Hatty spoke of it to her grandmother. She rarely spoke of anything now, but this was uncommon news.

"They say Laviny Dodge has got to go to the poorhouse," said she.

"What?"

"They say Laviny Dodge has got to go to the poorhouse."

"I don't believe a word on't."

"They say it's so."

That afternoon Esther went over to ascertain the truth of the report for herself. She found Lavinia sitting alone in the kitchen crying. Esther went right in, and stood looking at her.

"It's so, ain't it?" said she.

Lavinia started. There was a momentary glimpse of a red, distorted face; then she hid it again, and went on rocking herself to and fro and sobbing. She had seated herself in the rocking-chair to weep. "Yes," she wailed, "it's so! I've got to go. Mr. Barnes come in, an' said I had this mornin'; there ain't no other way. I've—got—to go. Oh, what would mother have said!"

Esther stood still, looking. "A place gits run out afore you know it," she remarked.

"Oh, I didn't s'pose it was quite so near gone. I thought mebbe I could stay—as long as I lived."

"You'd oughter hev kept account."

"I s'pose I hed, but I never knew much 'bout money-matters, an' poor mother, she was too old. Father was real sharp, ef he'd lived. Oh, I've got to go! I never thought it would come to this!"

"I don't think you're fit to do any work."

"No; they say I ain't. My rheumatism has been worse lately. It's been hard work for me to crawl round an' wait on mother. I've got to go. Oh, Esther, it's awful to think I can't die in my own home. Now I've got—to die in the poorhouse! I've—got—to die in the poorhouse!"

"I've go to go now," said Esther.

"Don't go. You ain't but jest come. I ain't got a soul to speak to."

"I'll come in agin arter supper," said Esther, and went out resolutely, with Lavinia wailing after her to come back. At home, she sat down and deliberated. She had a long talk with Hatty when she returned. "I don't care," was all she could get out of the girl, who was more silent than usual. She ate very little supper.

It was eight o'clock when Esther went over to the Dodge house. The windows were dark. "Land, I believe she's gone to bed," said the old woman, fumbling along through the yard. The door was fast, so she knocked. "Laviny, Laviny, be you gone to bed? Laviny Dodge!"

"Who is it?" said a quavering voice on the other side, presently.

"It's me. You gone to bed?"

"It's you, Mis' Gay, ain't it?"

"Yes. Let me in. I want to see you a minute."

Then Lavinia opened the door and stood there, her old knees knocking together with cold and nervousness. She had got out of bed and put a plaid shawl over her shoulders when she heard Esther.

"I want to come in jest a minute," said Esther. "I hadn't any idee you'd be gone to bed."

The fire had gone out, and it was chilly in the kitchen, where the two women sat down.

"You'll ketch your death of cold in your night-gown," said Esther. "You'd better git somethin' more to put over you."

"I don't keer if I do ketch cold," said Lavinia, with an air of feeble recklessness, which sat oddly upon her.

"Laviny Dodge, don't talk so."

"I don't keer. I'd ruther ketch my death of cold than not; then I shouldn't have to die in the poorhouse." The old head, in its little cotton night-cap, cocked itself sideways, with pitiful bravado.

Esther rose, went into the bedroom, got a quilt and put it over Lavinia's knees. "There," said she, "you hev that over you. There ain't no sense in your talkin' that way. You're jest a-flyin' in the face of Providence, an' Providence don't mind the little flappin' you kin make, any more than a barn does a swaller."

"I can't help it."

"What?"

"I—can't help it."

"Yes, you kin help it, too. Now, I'll tell you what I've come over here for. I've been thinkin' on't all the afternoon, an' I've made up my mind. I want you to come over and live with me."

Lavinia sat feebly staring at her. "Live with you!"

"Yes. I've got my house an' my pension, an' I pick up some with my knittin'. Two won't cost much more'n one. I reckon we kin git along well enough."

Lavinia said nothing, she still sat staring. She looked scared.

Esther began to feel hurt. "Mebbe you don't want to come," she said, stiffly, at last.

Lavinia shivered. "There's jest—one thing—" she commenced.

"What?"

"There's jest one thing—"

"What's that?"

"I dunno what— Mother— You're real good; but— Oh, I don't see how I kin come, Esther!"

"Why not? If there's any reason why you don't want to live with me, I want to know what 'tis."

Lavinia was crying. "I can't tell you," she sobbed; "but, mother— If—you didn't work Sundays. Oh!"

"Then you mean to say you'd ruther go to the poorhouse than come to live with me, Lavinia Dodge?"

"I—can't help it."

"Then, all I've got to say is, you kin go."

Esther went home, and said no more. In a few days she, peering around her curtain, saw poor Lavinia Dodge, a little, trembling, shivering figure, hoisted into the poorhouse covered wagon, and driven off. After the wagon was out of sight, she sat down and cried.

It was early in the afternoon. Hatty had just gone to her work, having scarcely tasted her dinner. Her grandmother had worked hard to get an extra one to-day, too, but she had no heart to eat. Her mournful silence, which seemed almost obstinate, made the old woman at once angry and wretched.

Now she wept over Lavinia Dodge and Hatty, and the two causes combined made bitter tears.

"I wish to the land" she cried out loud once—"I wish to the land I could find some excuse; but I ain't goin' to give up what I think's right."

Esther Gay had never been so miserable in her life as she was for the three months after Lavinia Dodge left her home. She thought of her, she watched Hatty, and she knitted. Hatty was at last beginning to show the effects of her long worry. She looked badly, and the neighbors began speaking about it to her grandmother. The old woman seemed to resent it when they did. At times she scolded the girl, at times she tried to pet her, and she knitted constantly, week-days and Sundays.

Lavinia had been in the almshouse three months, when one of the neighbors came in one day and told Esther that she was confined to her bed. Her rheumatism was worse, and she was helpless. Esther dropped her knitting, and stared radiantly at the neighbor. "You said she was an awful sight of trouble, didn't you?" said she.

"Yes; Mis' Marvin said it was worse than takin' care of a baby."

"I should think it would take about all of anybody's time."

"I should. Why, Esther Gay, you look real tickled 'cause she's sick!" cried the woman, bluntly.

Esther colored. "You talk pretty," said she.

"Well, I don't care; you looked so. I don't s'pose you was," said the other, apologetically.

That afternoon Esther Gay made two visits: one at the selectmen's room, in the town-hall, the other at Henry Little's. One of her errands at the selectmen's room was concerning the reduction of her taxes.

"I'm a-payin' too much on that leetle house," said she, standing up, alert and defiant. "It ain't wuth it." There was some dickering, but she gained her point. Poor Esther Gay would never make again her foolish little boast about her large tax. More than all her patient, toilsome knitting was the sacrifice of this bit of harmless vanity.

When she arrived at the Littles', Henry was out in the yard. He was very young; his innocent, awkward face flushed when he saw Esther coming up the path.

"Good afternoon," said she. Henry jerked his head.

"Your mother to home?"

"Ye—s."

Esther advanced and knocked, while Henry stood staring.

Presently Mrs. Little answered the knock. She was a large woman. The astonished young man saw his mother turn red, in the face, and rear herself in order of battle, as it were, when she saw who her caller was; then he heard Esther speak.

"I'm a-comin' right to the p'int afore I come in," said she. "I've heard you said you didn't want your son to marry my granddaughter because you didn't like some things about me. Now, I want to know if you said it."

"Yes; I did," replied Mrs. Little, tremulous with agitation, red, and perspiring, but not weakening.

"Then you didn't have nothin' again' Hatty, you nor Henry? 'Twa'n't an excuse?"

"I ain't never had anything against the girl."

"Then I want to come in a minute. I've got somethin' I want to say to you, Mrs. Little."

"Well, you can come in—if you want to."

After Esther had entered, Henry stood looking wistfully at the windows. It seemed to him that he could not wait to know the reason of Esther's visit. He took things more soberly than Hatty; he had not lost his meals nor his sleep; still he had suffered. He was very fond of the girl, and he had a heart which was not easily diverted. It was hardly possible that he would ever die of grief, but it was quite possible that he might live long with a memory, young as he was.

When his mother escorted Esther to the door, as she took leave, there was a marked difference in her manner. "Come again soon, Mis' Gay," he heard her say; "run up any time you feel like it, an' stay to tea. I'd really like to have you."

"Thank ye," said Esther, as she went down the steps. She had an aspect of sweetness about her which did not seem to mix well with herself.

When she reached home she found Hatty lying on the lounge. "How do you feel to-night?" said she, unpinning her shawl.

"Pretty well."

"You'd better go an' brush your hair an' change your dress. I've been over to Henry's an' seen his mother, an' I shouldn't wonder if he was over here to-night."

Hatty sat bolt upright and looked at her grandmother. "What do you mean?"

"What I say. I've been over to Mrs. Little's, an' we've had a talk. I guess she thought she'd been kind of silly to make such a fuss. I reasoned with her, an' I guess she saw I'd been more right about some things than she'd thought for. An' as far as goin' to meetin' an' knittin' Sundays is concerned— Well, I don't s'pose I kin knit any more if I want to. I've been to see about it, an' Laviny Dodge is comin' here Saturday, an' she's so bad with her rheumatiz that she can't move, an' I guess it'll be all I kin do to wait on her, without doin' much knittin'. Mebbe I kin git a few minutes evenin's, but I reckon 't won't amount to much. Of course I couldn't go to meetin' if I wanted to. I couldn't leave Laviny."

"Did she say he—was coming?"

"Yes; she said she shouldn't wonder if he was up."

The young man did come that evening, and Esther retired to her little bedroom early, and lay listening happily to the soft murmur of voices outside. Lavinia Dodge arrived Saturday. The next morning, when Hatty had gone to church, she called Esther. "I want to speak to you a minute," said she. "I want to know if— Mr. Winter brought me over, and he married the Ball girl that's been in the post-office, you know, and somethin' he said—Esther Gay, I want to know if you're the one that's been sendin' that money to me and mother all along?"

Esther colored, and turned to go. "I don't see why you think it's me."

"Esther, don't you go. I know 'twas; you can't say 'twa'n't."

"It wa'n't much, anyhow."

"'Twas to us. It kept us goin' a good while longer. We never said anythin' about it. Mother was awful proud, you know, but I dunno what we should have done. Esther, how could you do it?"

"Oh, it wa'n't anythin'. It was extra money. I airn'd it."

"Knittin'?"

Esther jerked her head defiantly. The sick woman began to cry. "If I'd ha' known, I would ha' come. I wouldn't have said a word."

"Yes, you would, too. You was bound to stan' up for what you thought was right, jest as much as I was. Now, we've both stood up, an' it's right. Don't you fret no more about it."

"To think—"

"Land sakes, don't cry. The tea's all steeped, and I'm goin' to bring you in a cup now."

Henry came that evening. About nine o'clock Esther got a

pitcher and went down to the well to draw some water for the invalid. Her old joints were so tired and stiff that she could scarcely move. She had had a hard day. After she had filled her pitcher she stood resting for a moment, staring up at the bright sitting-room windows. Henry and Hatty were in there: just a simple, awkward young pair, with nothing beautiful about them, save the spark of eternal nature, which had its own light. But they sat up stiffly and timidly in their two chairs, looking at each other with full content. They had glanced solemnly and bashfully at Esther when she passed through the room; she appeared not to see them.

Standing at the well, looking up at the windows, she chuckled softly to herself. "It's all settled right," said she, "an' there don't none of 'em suspect that I'm a-carryin' out my p'int arter all."

A Conflict Ended

❧❧

In Acton there were two churches, a Congregational and a
Baptist. They stood on opposite sides of the road, and the
Baptist edifice was a little farther down than the other. On
Sunday morning both bells were ringing. The Baptist bell was
much larger, and followed quickly on the soft peal of the
Congregational with a heavy brazen clang which vibrated a
good while. The people went flocking through the street to
the irregular jangle of the bells. It was a very hot day, and
the sun beat down heavily; parasols were bobbing over all the
ladies' heads.

More people went into the Baptist church, whose society
was much the larger of the two. It had been for the last ten
years—ever since the Congregational had settled a new minister. His advent had divided the church, and a good third of
the congregation had gone over to the Baptist brethren, with
whom they still remained.

It is probable that many of them passed their old sanctuary
to-day with the original stubborn animosity as active as ever
in their hearts, and led their families up the Baptist steps with
the same strong spiritual pull of indignation.

One old lady, who had made herself prominent on the opposition, trotted by this morning with the identical wiry vehemence which she had manifested ten years ago. She wore a
full black silk skirt, which she held up inanely in front, and
allowed to trail in the dust in the rear.

Some of the staunch Congregational people glanced at her
amusedly. One fleshy, fair-faced girl in blue muslin said to
her companion, with a laugh: "See that old lady trailing her
best black silk by to the Baptist. Ain't it ridiculous how she
keeps on showing out? I heard someone talking about it yesterday."

"Yes."

The girl colored up confusedly. "Oh dear!" she thought to
herself. The lady with her had an unpleasant history connected

with this old church quarrel. She was a small, bony woman in a shiny purple silk, which was strained very tightly across her sharp shoulder-blades. Her bonnet was quite elaborate with flowers and plumes, as was also her companion's. In fact, she was the village milliner, and the girl was her apprentice.

When the two went up the church steps, they passed a man of about fifty, who was sitting thereon well to one side. He had a singular face—a mild forehead, a gently curving mouth, and a terrible chin, with a look of strength in it that might have abashed mountains. He held his straw hat in his hand, and the sun was shining full on his bald head.

The milliner half stopped, and gave an anxious glance at him; then passed on. In the vestibule she stopped again.

"You go right in, Margy," she said to the girl. "I'll be along in a minute."

"Where be you going, Miss Barney?"

"You'll go right in. I'll be there in a minute."

Margy entered the audience-room then, as if fairly brushed in by the imperious wave of a little knotty hand, and Esther Barney stood waiting until the rush of entering people was over. Then she stepped swiftly back to the side of the man seated on the steps. She spread her large black parasol deliberately, and extended the handle towards him.

"No, no, Esther; I don't want it—I don't want it."

"If you're determined on setting out in this broiling sun, Marcus Woodman, you jest take this parasol of mine an' use it."

"I don't want your parasol, Esther. I—"

"Don't you say it over again. Take it."

"I won't—not if I don't want to."

"You'll get a sun-stroke."

"That's my own lookout."

"Marcus Woodman, you take it."

She threw all the force there was in her intense, nervous nature into her tone and look; but she failed in her attempt, because of the utter difference in quality between her own will and that with which she had to deal. They were on such different planes that hers slid by his with its own momentum; there could be no contact even of antagonism between them. He sat there rigid, every line of his face stiffened into an icy obstinacy. She held out the parasol towards him like a weapon.

Finally she let it drop at her side, her whole expression changed.

"Marcus," said she, "how's your mother?"

He started. "Pretty well, thank you, Esther."

"She's out to meeting, then?"

"Yes."

"I've been a-thinking—I ain't drove jest now—that maybe I'd come over an' see her some day this week."

He rose politely then. "Wish you would, Esther. Mother'd be real pleased, I know."

"Well, I'll see—Wednesday, p'rhaps, if I ain't too busy. I must go in now; they're 'most through singing."

"Esther—"

"I don't believe I can stop any longer, Marcus."

"About the parasol—thank you jest the same if I don't take it. Of course you know I can't set out here holding a parasol; folks would laugh. But I'm obliged to you all the same. Hope I didn't say anything to hurt your feelings?"

"Oh no; why, no, Marcus. Of course I don't want to make you take it if you don't want it. I don't know but it would look kinder queer, come to think of it. Oh dear! they are through singing."

"Say, Esther, I don't know but I might as well take that parasol, if you'd jest as soon. The sun is pretty hot, an' I might get a headache. I forgot my umbrella, to tell the truth."

"I might have known better than to have gone at him the way I did," thought Esther to herself, when she was seated at last in the cool church beside Margy. "Seems as if I might have got used to Marcus Woodman by this time."

She did not see him when she came out of church; but a little boy in the vestibule handed her the parasol, with the remark, "Mr. Woodman said for me to give this to you."

She and Margy passed down the street towards home. Going by the Baptist church, they noticed a young man standing by the entrance. He stared hard at Margy.

She began to laugh after they had passed him. "Did you see that fellow stare?" said she. "Hope he'll know me next time."

"That's George Elliot; he's that old lady's son you was speaking about this morning."

"Well, that's enough for me."

"He's a real good, steady young man."

Margy sniffed.

"P'rhaps you'll change your mind some day."

She did, and speedily, too. That glimpse of Margy Wilson's

pretty, new face—for she was a stranger in the town—had
been too much for George Elliot. He obtained an introduction, and soon was a steady visitor at Esther Barney's house.
Margy fell in love with him easily. She had never had much
attention from the young men, and he was an engaging
young fellow, small and bright-eyed, though with a nervous
persistency like his mother's in his manner.

"I'm going to have it an understood thing," Margy told Esther, after her lover had become constant in his attentions,
"that I'm going with George, and I ain't going with his
mother. I can't bear that old woman."

But poor Margy found that it was not so easy to thrust determined old age off the stage, even when young Love was
flying about so fast on his butterfly wings that he seemed to
multiply himself, and there was no room for anything else,
because the air was so full of Loves. That old mother, with
her trailing black skirt and her wiry obstinacy, trotted as un-
waveringly through the sweet stir as a ghost through a door.

One Monday morning Margy could not eat any breakfast,
and there were tear stains around her blue eyes.

"Why, what's the matter, Margy?" asked Esther, eying her
across the little kitchen-table.

"Nothing's the matter. I ain't hungry any to speak of,
that's all. I guess I'll go right to work on Mis' Fuller's bonnet."

"I'd try an' eat something if I was you. Be sure you cut
that velvet straight, if you go to work on it."

When the two were sitting together at their work in the
little room back of the shop, Margy suddenly threw her scissors down. "There!" said she, "I've done it; I knew I should. I
cut this velvet bias. I knew I should cut everything bias I
touched to-day."

There was a droll pucker on her mouth; then it began to
quiver. She hid her face in her hands and sobbed. "Oh, dear,
dear, dear!"

"Margy Wilson, what is the matter?"

"George and I—had a talk last night. We've broke the engagement, an' it's killing me. An' now I've cut this velvet
bias. Oh, dear, dear, *dear*, dear!"

"For the land's sake, don't mind anything about the velvet.
What's come betwixt you an' George?"

"His mother—horrid old thing! He said she'd got to live
with us, and I said she shouldn't. Then he said he wouldn't
marry any girl that wasn't willing to live with his mother, and

I said he wouldn't ever marry me, then. If George Elliot thinks more of his mother than he does of me, he can have her. I don't care. I'll show him I can get along without him."

"Well, I don't know, Margy. I'm real sorry about it. George Elliot's a good, likely young man; but if you didn't want to live with his mother, it was better to say so right in the beginning. And I don't know as I blame you much: she's pretty set in her ways."

"I guess she is. I never could bear her. I guess he'll find out—"

Margy dried her eyes defiantly, and took up the velvet again. "I've spoilt this velvet. I don't see why being disappointed in love should affect a girl so's to make her cut bias."

There was a whimsical element in Margy which seemed to roll uppermost along with her grief.

Esther looked a little puzzled. "Never mind the velvet, child: it ain't much, anyway." She began tossing over some ribbons to cover her departure from her usual reticence. "I'm real sorry about it, Margy. Such things are hard to bear, but they can be lived through. I know something about it myself. You knew I'd had some of this kind of touble, didn't you?"

"About Mr. Woodman, you mean?"

"Yes, about Marcus Woodman. I'll tell you what 'tis, Margy Wilson, you've got one thing to be thankful for, and that is that there ain't anything ridickerlous about this affair of yourn. That makes it the hardest of anything, according to my mind—when you know that everybody's laughing, and you can hardly help laughing yourself, though you feel 'most ready to die."

"Ain't that Mr. Woodman crazy?"

"No, he ain't crazy; he's got too much will for his common-sense, that's all, and the will teeters the sense a little too far into the air. I see all through it from the beginning. I could read Marcus Woodman jest like a book."

"I don't see how in the world you ever come to like such a man."

"Well, I s'pose love's the strongest when there ain't any good reason for it. They say it is. I can't say as I ever really admired Marcus Woodman much. I always see right through him; but that didn't hinder my thinking so much of him that I never felt as if I could marry any other man. And I've had chances, though I shouldn't want you to say so."

"You turned him off because he went to sitting on the church steps?"

"Course I did. Do you s'pose I was going to marry a man who made a laughing-stock of himself that way?"

"I don't see how he ever come to do it. It's the funniest thing I ever heard of."

"I know it. It seems so silly nobody'd believe it. Well, all there is about it, Marcus Woodman's got so much mulishness in him it makes him almost miraculous. You see, he got up an' spoke in that church meeting when they had such a row about Mr. Morton's being settled here—Marcus was awful set again' him. I never could see any reason why, and I don't think he could. He said Mr. Morton wa'n't doctrinal; that was what they all said; but I don't believe half of 'em knew what doctrinal was. I never could see why Mr. Morton wa'n't as good as most ministers—enough sight better than them that treated him so, anyway. I always felt that they was really setting him in a pulpit high over their heads by using him the way they did, though they didn't know it.

"Well, Marcus spoke in that church meeting, an' he kept getting more and more set every word he said. He always had a way of saying things over and over, as if he was making steps out of 'em, an' raising of himself up on 'em, till there was no moving him at all. And he did that night. Finally, when he was up real high, he said, as for him, if Mr. Morton was settled over that church, he'd never go inside the door himself as long as he lived. Somebody spoke out then—I never quite knew who 'twas, though I suspected—an' says, 'You'll have to set on the steps, then, Brother Woodman.'

"Everybody laughed at that but Marcus. He didn't see nothing to laugh at. He spoke out awful set, kinder gritting his teeth, 'I will set on the steps fifty years before I'll go into this house if that man's settled here.'

"I couldn't believe he'd really do it. We were going to be married that spring, an' it did seem as if he might listen to me; but he wouldn't. The Sunday Mr. Morton begun to preach, he begun to set on them steps, an' he's set there ever since, in all kinds of weather. It's a wonder it 'ain't killed him; but I guess it's made him tough."

"Why, didn't he feel bad when you wouldn't marry him?"

"Feel bad? Of course he did. He took on terribly. But it didn't make any difference; he wouldn't give in a hair's breadth. I declare it did seem as if I should die. His mother felt awfully too—she's a real good woman. I don't know what Marcus would have done without her. He wants a sight of tending and waiting on; he's dreadful babyish in some ways, though you wouldn't think it.

"Well, it's all over now, as far as I'm concerned. I've got over it a good deal, though sometimes it makes me jest as mad as ever to see him setting there. But I try to be reconciled, and I get along jest as well, mebbe, as if I'd had him— I don't know. I fretted more at first than there was any sense in, and I hope you won't."

"I ain't going to fret at all, Miss Barney. I may cut bias for a while, but I sha'n't do anything worse."

"How you do talk, child!"

A good deal of it was talk with Margy; she had not as much courage as her words proclaimed. She was capable of a strong temporary resolution, but of no enduring one. She gradually weakened as the days without her lover went on, and one Saturday night she succumbed entirely. There was quite a rush of business, but through it all she caught a conversation between some customers—two pretty young girls.

"Who was that with you last night at the concert?"

"That—oh, that was George Elliot. Didn't you know him?"

"He's got another girl," thought Margy, with a great throb.

The next Sunday night, coming out of meeting with Miss Barney, she left her suddenly. George Elliot was one of a waiting line of young men in the vestibule. She went straight up to him. He looked at her in bewilderment, his dark face turning red.

"Good-evening, Miss Wilson," he stammered out, finally.

"Good-evening," she whispered, and stood looking up at him piteously. She was white and trembling.

At last he stepped forward suddenly and offered her his arm. In spite of his resentment, he could not put her to open shame before all his mates, who were staring curiously.

When they were out in the dark, cool street, he bent over her. "Why, Margy, what does all this mean?"

"Oh, George, let her live with us, please. I want her to. I know I can get along with her if I try. I'll do everything I can. Please let her live with us."

"Who's *her*?"

"Your mother."

"And I suppose *us* is you and I? I thought that was all over, Margy; ain't it?"

"Oh, George, I am sorry I treated you so."

"And you are willing to let mother live with us now?"

"I'll do anything. Oh, George!"

"Don't cry, Margy. There—nobody's looking—give us a kiss. It's been a long time; ain't it dear? So you've made up your mind that you're willing to let mother live with us?"

"Yes."

"Well, I don't believe she ever will, Margy. She's about made up her mind to go and live with my brother Edward, whether or no. So you won't be troubled with her. I dare say she might have been a little trial as she grew older."

"You didn't tell me."

"I thought it was your place to give in, dear."

"Yes, it was, George."

"I'm mighty glad you did. I tell you what it is, dear, I don't know how you've felt, but I've been pretty miserable lately."

"Poor George!"

They passed Esther Barney's house, and strolled along half a mile farther. When they returned, and Margy stole softly into the house and up-stairs, it was quite late, and Esther had gone to bed. Margy saw the light was not out in her room, so she peeped in. She could not wait till morning to tell her.

"Where have you been?" said Esther, looking up at her out of her pillows.

"Oh, I went to walk a little way with George."

"Then you've made up?"

"Yes."

"Is his mother going to live with you?"

"No; I guess not. She's going to live with Edward. But I told him I was willing she should. I've about made up my mind it's a woman's place to give in mostly. I s'pose you think I'm an awful fool."

"No, I don't; no, I don't, Margy. I'm real glad it's all right betwixt you and George. I've seen you weren't very happy lately."

They talked a little longer; then Margy said "Good-night," going over to Esther and kissing her. Being so rich in love made her generous with it. She looked down sweetly into the older woman's thin, red-cheeked face. "I wish you were as happy as I," said she. "I wish you and Mr. Woodman could make up too."

"That's an entirely different matter. I couldn't give in in such a thing as that."

Margy looked at her; she was not subtle, but she had just come out triumphant through innocent love and submission, and used the wisdom she had gained thereby.

"Don't you believe," said she, "if you was to give in the way I did, that he would?"

Esther started up with an astonished air. That had never occurred to her before. "Oh, I don't believe he would. You don't know him; he's awful set. Besides, I don't know but I'm better off the way it is."

In spite of herself, however, she could not help thinking of Margy's suggestion. Would he give in? She was hardly disposed to run the risk. With her peculiar cast of mind, her feeling for the ludicrous so keen that it almost amounted to a special sense, and her sensitiveness to ridicule, it would have been easier for her to have married a man under the shadow of a crime than one who was the deserving target of gibes and jests. Besides, she told herself, it was possible that he had changed his mind, that he no longer cared for her. How could she make the first overtures? She had not Margy's impulsiveness and innocence of youth to excuse her.

Also, she was partly influenced by the reason which she had given Margy: she was not so very sure that it would be best for her to take any such step. She was more fixed in the peace and pride of her old maidenhood than she had realized, and was more shy of disturbing it. Her comfortable meals, her tidy housekeeping, and her prosperous work had become such sources of satisfaction to her that she was almost wedded to them, and jealous of any interference.

So it is doubtful if there would have been any change in the state of affairs if Marcus Woodman's mother had not died towards spring. Esther was greatly distressed about it.

"I don't see what Marcus is going to do," she told Margy. "He ain't any fitter to take care of himself than a baby, and he won't have any housekeeper, they say."

One evening, after Marcus's mother had been dead about three weeks, Esther went over there. Margy had gone out to walk with George, so nobody knew. When she reached the house—a white cottage on a hill—she saw a light in the kitchen window.

"He's there," said she. She knocked on the door softly. Marcus shuffled over to it—he was in his stocking feet—and opened it.

"Good-evening, Marcus," said she, speaking first.

"Good-evening."

"I hadn't anything special to do this evening, so I thought I'd look in a minute and see how you was getting along."

"I ain't getting along very well; but I'm glad to see you. Come right in."

When she was seated opposite him by the kitchen fire, she surveyed him and his surroundings pityingly. Everything had an abject air of forlornness; there was neither tidiness nor comfort. After a few words she rose energetically. "See here, Marcus," said she, "you jest fill up that tea-kettle, and I'm going to slick up here a little for you while I stay."

"No, Esther, I don't feel as if—"

"Don't you say nothing. Here's the tea-kettle. I might jest as well be doing that as setting still."

He watched her, in a way that made her nervous, as she flew about putting things to rights; but she said to herself that this was easier than sitting still, and gradually leading up to the object for which she had come. She kept wondering if she could ever accomplish it. When the room was in order, finally, she sat down again, with a strained-up look in her face.

"Marcus," said she, "I might as well begin. There was something I wanted to say to you to-night."

He looked at her, and she went on:

"I've been thinking some lately about how matters used to be betwixt you an' me, and it's jest possible—I don't know—but I might have been a little more patient than I was. I don't know as I'd feel the same way now if—"

"Oh, Esther, what do you mean?"

"I ain't going to tell you, Marcus Woodman, if you can't find out. I've said full enough; more'n I ever thought I should."

He was an awkward man, but he rose and threw himself on his knees at her feet with all the grace of complete unconsciousness of action. "Oh, Esther, you don't mean, do you?—you don't mean that you'd be willing to—marry me?"

"No; not if you don't get up. You look ridickerlous."

"Esther, do you mean it?"

"Yes. Now get up."

"You ain't thinking—I can't give up what we had the trouble about, any more now than I could then."

"Ain't I said once that wouldn't make any difference?"

At that he put his head down on her knees and sobbed.

"Do, for mercy sake, stop. Somebody'll be coming in. 'T ain't as if we was a young couple."

"I ain't going to till I've told you about it, Esther. You ain't never really understood. In the first of it, we was both mad; but we ain't now, and we can talk it over. Oh, Esther,

I've had such an awful life! I've looked at you, and— Oh, dear, dear, dear!"

"Marcus, you scare me to death crying so."

"I won't. Esther, look here—it's the gospel truth: I ain't a thing again' Mr. Morton now."

"Then why on earth don't you go into the meeting-house and behave yourself?"

"Don't you suppose I would if I could? I can't, Esther—I can't."

"I don't know what you mean by can't."

"Do you s'pose I took any comfort sitting there on them steps in the winter snows an' the summer suns? Do you s'pose I've took any comfort not marrying you? Don't you s'pose I'd given all I was worth any time the last ten years to have got up an' walked into the church with the rest of the folks?"

"Well, I'll own, Marcus, I don't see why you couldn't if you wanted to."

"I ain't sure as I see myself, Esther. All I know is I can't make myself give it up. I can't. I ain't made strong enough to."

"As near as I can make out, you've taken to sitting on the church steps the way other men take to smoking and drinking."

"I don't know but you're right, Esther, though I hadn't thought of it in that way before."

"Well, you must try to overcome it."

"I never can, Esther. It ain't right for me to let you think I can."

"Well, we won't talk about it any more to-night. It's time I was going home."

"Esther—did you mean it?"

"Mean what?"

"That you'd marry me anyway?"

"Yes, I did. Now do get up. I do hate to see you looking so silly."

Esther had a new pearl-colored silk gown, and a little mantle like it, and a bonnet trimmed with roses and plumes, and she and Marcus were married in June.

The Sunday on which she came out a bride they were late at church; but late as it was, curious people were lingering by the steps to watch them. What would they do? Would Marcus Woodman enter that church door which his awful will had guarded for him so long?

They walked slowly up the steps between the watching

people. When they came to the place where he was accustomed to sit, Marcus stopped short and looked down at his wife with an agonized face.

"Oh, Esther, I've—got—to stop."

"Well, we'll both sit down here, then."

"*You?*"

"Yes; I'm willing."

"No; you go in."

"No, Marcus; I sit with you on our wedding Sunday."

Her sharp, middle-aged face as she looked up at him was fairly heroic. This was all that she could do; her last weapon was used. If this failed, she would accept the chances with which she married, and before the eyes of all these tittering people she would sit down at his side on these church steps. She was determined, and she would not weaken.

He stood for a moment staring into her face. He trembled so that the bystanders noticed it. He actually leaned over towards his old seat as if wire ropes were pulling him down upon it. Then he stood up straight, like a man, and walked through the church door with his wife.

The people followed. Not one of them even smiled. They had felt the pathos in the comedy.

The sitters in the pews watched Marcus wonderingly as he went up the aisle with Esther. He looked strange to them; he had almost the grand mien of a conqueror.

A New England Nun

It was late in the afternoon, and the light was waning. There was a difference in the look of the tree shadows out in the yard. Somewhere in the distance cows were lowing and a little bell was tinkling; now and then a farm-wagon tilted by, and the dust flew; some blue-shirted laborers with shovels over their shoulders plodded past; little swarms of flies were dancing up and down before the peoples' faces in the soft air. There seemed to be a gentle stir arising over everything for the mere sake of subsidence—a very premonition of rest and hush and night.

This soft diurnal commotion was over Louisa Ellis also. She had been peacefully sewing at her sitting-room window all the afternoon. Now she quilted her needle carefully into her work, which she folded precisely, and laid in a basket with her thimble and thread and scissors. Louisa Ellis could not remember that ever in her life she had mislaid one of these little feminine appurtenances, which had become, from long use and constant association, a very part of her personality.

Louisa tied a green apron round her waist, and got out a flat straw hat with a green ribbon. Then she went into the garden with a little blue crockery bowl, to pick some currants for her tea. After the currants were picked she sat on the back door-step and stemmed them, collecting the stems carefully in her apron, and afterwards throwing them into the hen-coop. She looked sharply at the grass beside the step to see if any had fallen there.

Louisa was slow and still in her movements; it took her a long time to prepare her tea; but when ready it was set forth with as much grace as if she had been a veritable guest to her own self. The little square table stood exactly in the centre of the kitchen, and was covered with a starched linen cloth whose border pattern of flowers glistened. Louisa had a damask napkin on her tea-tray, where were arranged a cut-glass tumbler full of teaspoons, a silver cream-pitcher, a china sugar-bowl, and one pink china cup and saucer. Louisa used china every day—something which none of her neighbors did. They whispered about it among themselves. Their daily tables were laid with common crockery, their sets of best china stayed in the parlor closet, and Louisa Ellis was no richer nor better bred than they. Still she would use the china. She had for her supper a glass dish full of sugared currants, a plate of little cakes, and one of light white biscuits. Also a leaf or two of lettuce, which she cut up daintily. Louisa was very fond of lettuce, which she raised to perfection in her little garden. She ate quite heartily, though in a delicate, pecking way; it seemed almost surprising that any considerable bulk of the food should vanish.

After tea she filled a plate with nicely baked thin corn-cakes, and carried them out into the back-yard.

"Cæsar!" she called. "Cæsar! Cæsar!"

There was a little rush, and the clank of a chain, and a large yellow-and-white dog appeared at the door of his tiny hut, which was half hidden among the tall grasses and flowers. Louisa patted him and gave him the corn-cakes. Then she returned to the house and washed the tea-things, polishing the china carefully. The twilight had deepened; the chorus of the frogs floated in at the open window wonderfully loud and shrill, and once in a while a long sharp drone from a tree-toad pierced it. Louisa took off her green gingham apron, disclosing a shorter one of pink and white print. She lighted her lamp, and sat down again with her sewing.

In about half an hour Joe Dagget came. She heard his heavy step on the walk, and rose and took off her pink-and-white apron. Under that was still another—white linen with a little cambric edging on the bottom; that was Louisa's company apron. She never wore it without her calico sewing apron over it unless she had a guest. She had barely folded the pink and white one with methodical haste and laid it in a table-drawer when the door opened and Joe Dagget entered.

He seemed to fill up the whole room. A little yellow canary that had been asleep in his green cage at the south window woke up and fluttered wildly, beating his little yellow wings against the wires. He always did so when Joe Dagget came into the room.

"Good-evening," said Louisa. She extended her hand with a kind of solemn cordiality.

"Good-evening, Louisa," returned the man, in a loud voice.

She placed a chair for him, and they sat facing each other, with the table between them. He sat bolt-upright, toeing out his heavy feet squarely, glancing with a good-humored uneasiness around the room. She sat gently erect, folding her slender hands in her white-linen lap.

"Been a pleasant day," remarked Dagget.

"Real pleasant," Louisa assented, softly. "Have you been haying?" she asked, after a little while.

"Yes, I've been haying all day, down in the ten-acre lot. Pretty hot work."

"It must be."

"Yes, it's pretty hot work in the sun."

"Is your mother well to-day?"

"Yes, mother's pretty well."

"I suppose Lily Dyer's with her now?"

Dagget colored. "Yes, she's with her," he answered, slowly.

He was not very young, but there was a boyish look about his large face. Louisa was not quite as old as he, her face was fairer and smoother, but she gave people the impression of being older.

"I suppose she's a good deal of help to your mother," she said, further.

"I guess she is; I don't know how mother'd get along without her," said Dagget, with a sort of embarrassed warmth.

"She looks like a real capable girl. She's pretty-looking too," remarked Louisa.

"Yes, she is pretty fair looking."

Presently Dagget began fingering the books on the table. There was a square red autograph album, and a Young Lady's Gift-Book which had belonged to Louisa's mother. He took them up one after the other and opened them; then laid them down again, the album on the Gift-Book.

Louisa kept eying them with mild uneasiness. Finally she rose and changed the position of the books, putting the album underneath. That was the way they had been arranged in the first place.

Dagget gave an awkward little laugh. "Now what difference did it make which book was on top?" said he.

Louisa looked at him with a deprecating smile. "I always keep them that way," murmured she.

"You do beat everything," said Dagget, trying to laugh again. His large face was flushed.

He remained about an hour longer, then rose to take leave. Going out, he stumbled over a rug, and trying to recover himself, hit Louisa's work-basket on the table, and knocked it on the floor.

He looked at Louisa, then at the rolling spools; he ducked himself awkwardly toward them, but she stopped him. "Never mind," said she; "I'll pick them up after you're gone."

She spoke with a mild stiffness. Either she was a little disturbed, or his nervousness affected her, and made her seem constrained in her effort to reassure him.

When Joe Dagget was outside he drew in the sweet evening air with a sigh, and felt much as an innocent and perfectly well-intentioned bear might after his exit from a china shop.

Louisa, on her part, felt much as the kind-hearted, long-suffering owner of the china shop might have done after the exit of the bear.

She tied on the pink, then the green apron, picked up all the scattered treasures and replaced them in her work-basket, and straightened the rug. Then she set the lamp on the floor, and began sharply examining the carpet. She even rubbed her fingers over it, and looked at them.

"He's tracked in a good deal of dust," she murmured. "I thought he must have."

Louisa got a dust-pan and brush, and swept Joe Dagget's track carefully.

If he could have known it, it would have increased his perplexity and uneasiness, although it would not have disturbed his loyalty in the least. He came twice a week to see Louisa Ellis, and every time, sitting there in her delicately sweet room, he felt as if surrounded by a hedge of lace. He was afraid to stir lest he should put a clumsy foot or hand through the fairy web, and he had always the consciousness that Louisa was watching fearfully lest he should.

Still the lace and Louisa commanded perforce his perfect respect and patience and loyalty. They were to be married in a month, after a singular courtship which had lasted for a matter of fifteen years. For fourteen out of the fifteen years the two had not once seen each other, and they had seldom exchanged letters. Joe had been all those years in Australia, where he had gone to make his fortune, and where he had stayed until he made it. He would have stayed fifty years if it had taken so long, and come home feeble and tottering, or never come home at all, to marry Louisa.

But the fortune had been made in the fourteen years, and he had come home now to marry the woman who had been patiently and unquestioningly waiting for him all that time.

Shortly after they were engaged he had announced to Louisa his determination to strike out into new fields, and secure a competency before they should be married. She had listened and assented with the sweet serenity which never failed her, not even when her lover set forth on that long and uncertain journey. Joe, buoyed up as he was by his sturdy determination, broke down a little at the last, but Louisa kissed him with a mild blush, and said good-by.

"It won't be for long," poor Joe had said, huskily; but it was for fourteen years.

In that length of time much had happened. Louisa's mother and brother had died, and she was all alone in the world. But greatest happening of all—a subtle happening which both were too simple to understand—Louisa's feet had turned into a path, smooth maybe under a calm, serene sky, but so straight and unswerving that it could only meet a check at her grave, and so narrow that there was no room for any one at her side.

Louisa's first emotion when Joe Dagget came home (he had not apprised her of his coming) was consternation, although she would not admit it to herself, and he never dreamed of it. Fifteen years ago she had been in love with him—at least she considered herself to be. Just at that time, gently acquiescing with and falling into the natural drift of girlhood, she had seen marriage ahead as a reasonable feature and a probable desirability of life. She had listened with calm docility to her mother's views upon the subject. Her mother was remarkable for her cool sense and sweet, even temperament. She talked wisely to her daughter when Joe Dagget presented himself, and Louisa accepted him with no hesitation. He was the first lover she had ever had.

She had been faithful to him all these years. She had never dreamed of the possibility of marrying any one else. Her life, especially for the last seven years, had been full of a pleasant peace, she had never felt discontented nor impatient over her lover's absence; still she had always looked forward to his return and their marriage as the inevitable conclusion of things. However, she had fallen into a way of placing it so far in the future that it was almost equal to placing it over the boundaries of another life.

When Joe came she had been expecting him, and expecting to be married for fourteen years, but she was as much surprised and taken aback as if she had never thought of it.

Joe's consternation came later. He eyed Louisa with an in-

stant confirmation of his old admiration. She had changed
but little. She still kept her pretty manner and soft grace, and
was, he considered, every whit as attractive as ever. As for
himself, his stent was done; he had turned his face away
from fortune-seeking, and the old winds of romance whistled
as loud and sweet as ever through his ears. All the song
which he had been wont to hear in them was Louisa; he had
for a long time a loyal belief that he heard it still, but finally
it seemed to him that although the winds sang always that
one song, it had another name. But for Louisa the wind had
never more than murmured; now it had gone down, and everything was still. She listened for a little while with half-wist-
ful attention; then she turned quietly away and went to work
on her wedding clothes.

Joe had made some extensive and quite magnificent alterations in his house. It was the old homestead; the newly-mar-
ried couple would live there, for Joe could not desert his
mother, who refused to leave her old home. So Louisa must
leave hers. Every morning, rising and going about among her
neat maidenly possessions, she felt as one looking her last
upon the faces of dear friends. It was true that in a measure
she could take them with her, but, robbed of her old environments, they would appear in such new guises that they would
almost cease to be themselves. Then there were some peculiar
features of her happy solitary life which she would probably
be obliged to relinquish altogether. Sterner tasks than these
graceful but half-needless ones would probably devolve upon
her. There would be a large house to care for; there would be
company to entertain; there would be Joe's rigorous and
feeble old mother to wait upon; and it would be contrary to
all thrifty village traditions for her to keep more than one
servant. Louisa had a little still, and she used to occupy herself pleasantly in summer weather with distilling the sweet
and aromatic essences from rose and peppermint and spearmint. By-and-by her still must be laid away. Her store of
essences was already considerable, and there would be no
time for her to distil for the mere pleasure of it. Then Joe's
mother would think it foolishness; she had already hinted her
opinion in the matter. Louisa dearly loved to sew a linen
seam, not always for use, but for the simple, mild pleasure
which she took in it. She would have been loath to confess
how more than once she had ripped a seam for the mere delight of sewing it together again. Sitting at her window during
long sweet afternoons, drawing her needle gently through the

dainty fabric, she was peace itself. But there was small chance of such foolish comfort in the future. Joe's mother, domineering, shrewd old matron that she was even in her old age, and very likely even Joe himself, with his honest masculine rudeness, would laugh and frown down all these pretty but senseless old maiden ways.

Louisa had almost the enthusiasm of an artist over the mere order and cleanliness of her solitary home. She had throbs of genuine triumph at the sight of the window-panes which she had polished until they shone like jewels. She gloated gently over her orderly bureau-drawers, with their exquisitely folded contents redolent with lavender and sweet clover and very purity. Could she be sure of the endurance of even this? She had visions, so startling that she half repudiated them as indelicate, of coarse masculine belongings strewn about in endless litter; of dust and disorder arising necessarily from a coarse masculine presence in the midst of all this delicate harmony.

Among her forebodings of disturbance, not the least was with regard to Cæsar. Cæsar was a veritable hermit of a dog. For the greater part of his life he had dwelt in his secluded hut, shut out from the society of his kind and all innocent canine joys. Never had Cæsar since his early youth watched at a woodchuck's hole; never had he known the delights of a stray bone at a neighbor's kitchen door. And it was all on account of a sin committed when hardly out of his puppyhood. No one knew the possible depth of remorse of which this mild-visaged, altogether innocent looking old dog might be capable; but whether or not he had encountered remorse, he had encountered a full measure of righteous retribution. Old Cæsar seldom lifted up his voice in a growl or a bark; he was fat and sleepy; there were yellow rings which looked like spectacles around his dim old eyes; but there was a neighbor who bore on his hand the imprint of several of Cæsar's sharp white youthful teeth, and for that he had lived at the end of a chain, all alone in a little hut, for fourteen years. The neighbor, who was choleric and smarting with the pain of his wound, had demanded either Cæsar's death or complete ostracism. So Louisa's brother, to whom the dog had belonged, had built him his little kennel and tied him up. It was now fourteen years since, in a flood of youthful spirits, he had inflicted that memorable bite, and with the exception of short excursions, always at the end of the chain, under the strict guardianship of his master or Louisa, the old dog had re-

mained a close prisoner. It is doubtful if, with his limited ambition, he took much pride in the fact, but it is certain that
he was possessed of considerable cheap fame. He was regarded by all the children in the village and by many adults
as a very monster of ferocity. St. George's dragon could
hardly have surpassed in evil repute Louisa Ellis's old yellow
dog. Mothers charged their children with solemn emphasis
not to go too near to him, and the children listened and believed greedily, with a fascinated appetite for terror, and ran
by Louisa's house stealthily, with many sidelong and backward glances at the terrible dog. If perchance he sounded a
hoarse bark, there was a panic. Wayfarers chancing into
Louisa's yard eyed him with respect, and inquired if the
chain were stout. Cæsar at large might have seemed an ordinary dog, and excited no comment whatever; chained, his
reputation overshadowed him, so that he lost his own proper
outlines and looked darkly vague and enormous. Joe Dagget,
however, with his good-humored sense and shrewdness, saw
him as he was. He strode valiantly up to him and patted him
on the head, in spite of Louisa's soft clamor of warning, and
even attempted to set him loose. Louisa grew so alarmed that
he desisted, but kept announcing his opinion in the matter
quite forcibly at intervals. "There ain't a better-natured dog
in town," he would say, "and it's downright cruel to keep him
tied up there. Some day I'm going to take him out."

Louisa had very little hope that he would not, one of these
days, when their interests and possessions should be more
completely fused in one. She pictured to herself Cæsar on the
rampage through the quiet and unguarded village. She saw
innocent children bleeding in his path. She was herself very
fond of the old dog, because he had belonged to her dead
brother, and he was always very gentle with her; still she had
great faith in his ferocity. She always warned people not to
go too near him. She fed him an ascetic fare of corn-mush
and cakes, and never fired his dangerous temper with heating
and sanguinary diet of flesh and bones. Louisa looked at the
old dog munching his simple fare, and thought of her approaching marriage and trembled. Still no anticipation of
disorder and confusion in lieu of sweet peace and harmony,
no forebodings of Cæsar on the rampage, no wild fluttering of
her little yellow canary, were sufficient to turn her a
hair's-breadth. Joe Dagget had been fond of her and working
for her all these years. It was not for her, whatever came to
pass, to prove untrue and break his heart. She put the exquisite

little stitches into her wedding-garments, and the time went
on until it was only a week before her wedding-day. It was a
Tuesday evening, and the wedding was to be a week from
Wednesday.

There was a full moon that night. About nine o'clock
Louisa strolled down the road a little way. There were har-
vest-fields on either hand, bordered by low stone walls. Luxuriant clumps of bushes grew beside the wall, and trees—wild
cherry and old apple-trees—at intervals. Presently Louisa sat
down on the wall and looked about her with mildly sorrowful
reflectiveness. Tall shrubs of blueberry and meadow-sweet, all
woven together and tangled with blackberry vines and horse-
briers, shut her in on either side. She had a little clear space
between them. Opposite her, on the other side of the road,
was a spreading tree; the moon shone between its boughs,
and the leaves twinkled like silver. The road was bespread
with a beautiful shifting dapple of silver and shadow; the air
was full of a mysterious sweetness. "I wonder if it's wild
grapes?" muttered Louisa. She sat there some time. She was
just thinking of rising, when she heard footsteps and low
voices, and remained quiet. It was a lonely place, and she felt
a little timid. She thought she would keep still in the shadow
and let the persons, whoever they might be, pass her.

But just before they reached her the voices ceased, and the
footsteps. She understood that their owners had also found
seats upon the stone wall. She was wondering if she could not
steal away unobserved, when the voice broke the stillness. It
was Joe Dagget's. She sat still and listened.

The voice was announced by a loud sigh, which was as
familiar as itself. "Well," said Dagget, "you've made up your
mind, then, I suppose?"

"Yes," returned another voice; "I'm going day after to-
morrow."

"That's Lily Dyer," thought Louisa to herself. The voice
embodied itself in her mind. She saw a girl tall and full-fig-
ured, with a firm, fair face, looking fairer and firmer in the
moonlight, her strong yellow hair braided in a close knot. A
girl full of a calm rustic strength and bloom, with a masterful
way which might have beseemed a princess. Lily Dyer was a
favorite with the village folk; she had just the qualities to
arouse the admiration. She was good and handsome and
smart. Louisa had often heard her praises sounded.

"Well," said Joe Dagget, "I ain't got a word to say."

"I don't know what you could say," returned Lily Dyer.

"Not a word to say," repeated Joe, drawing out the words heavily. Then there was a silence. "I ain't sorry," he began at last, "that that happened yesterday—that we kind of let on how we felt to each other. I guess it's just as well we knew. Of course I can't do anything any different. I'm going right on an' get married next week. I ain't going back on a woman that's waited for me fourteen years, an' break her heart."

"If you should jilt her to-morrow, I wouldn't have you," spoke up the girl, with sudden vehemence.

"Well, I ain't going to give you the chance," said he; "but I don't believe you would, either."

"You'd see I wouldn't. Honor's honor, an' rights right. An' I'd never think anything of any man that went against 'em for me or any other girl; you'd find that out, Joe Dagget."

"Well, you'll find out fast enough that I ain't going against 'em for you or any other girl," returned he. Their voices sounded almost as if they were angry with each other. Louisa was listening eagerly.

"I'm sorry you feel as if you must go away," said Joe, "but I don't know but it's best."

"Of course it's best. I hope you and I have got common-sense."

"Well, I suppose you're right." Suddenly Joe's voice got an undertone of tenderness. "Say, Lily," said he, "I'll get along well enough myself, but I can't bear to think—You don't suppose you're going to fret much over it?"

"I guess you'll find out I sha'n't fret much over a married man."

"Well, I hope you won't—I hope you won't, Lily. God knows I do. And—I hope—one of these days—you'll—come across somebody else—"

"I don't see any reason why I shouldn't." Suddenly her tone changed. She spoke in a sweet, clear voice, so loud that she could have been heard across the street. "No, Joe Dagget," said she, "I'll never marry any other man as long as I live. I've got good sense, an' I ain't going to break my heart nor make a fool of myself; but I'm never going to be married, you can be sure of that. I ain't that sort of a girl to feel this way twice."

Louisa heard an exclamation and a soft commotion behind the bushes; then Lily spoke again—the voice sounded as if she had risen. "This must be put a stop to," said she. "We've stayed here long enough. I'm going home."

Louisa sat there in a daze, listening to their retreating steps.

After a while she got up and slunk softly home herself. The next day she did her housework methodically; that was as much a matter of course as breathing; but she did not sew on her wedding-clothes. She sat at her window and meditated. In the evening Joe came. Louisa Ellis had never known that she had any diplomacy in her, but when she came to look for it that night she found it, although meek of its kind, among her little feminine weapons. Even now she could hardly believe that she had heard aright, and that she would not do Joe a terrible injury should she break her troth-plight. She wanted to sound him without betraying too soon her own inclinations in the matter. She did it successfully, and they finally came to an understanding; but it was a difficult thing, for he was as afraid of betraying himself as she.

She never mentioned Lily Dyer. She simply said that while she had no cause of complaint against him, she had lived so long in one way that she shrank from making a change.

"Well, I never shrank, Louisa," said Dagget. "I'm going to be honest enough to say that I think maybe it's better this way; but if you'd wanted to keep on, I'd have stuck to you till my dying day. I hope you know that."

"Yes, I do," said she.

That night she and Joe parted more tenderly than they had done for a long time. Standing in the door, holding each other's hands, a last great wave of regretful memory swept over them.

"Well, this ain't the way we've thought it was all going to end, is it, Louisa?" said Joe.

She shook her head. There was a little quiver on her placid face.

"You let me know if there's ever anything I can do for you," said he. "I ain't ever going to forget you, Louisa." Then he kissed her, and went down the path.

Louisa, all alone by herself that night, wept a little, she hardly knew why; but the next morning, on waking, she felt like a queen who, after fearing lest her domain be wrested away from her, sees it firmly insured in her possession.

Now the tall weeds and grasses might cluster around Cæsar's little hermit hut, the snow might fall on its roof year in and year out, but he never would go on a rampage through the unguarded village. Now the little canary might turn itself into a peaceful yellow ball night after night, and have no need to wake and flutter with wild terror against its bars. Louisa could sew linen seams, and distil roses, and dust and polish and fold away in lavender, as long as she listed. That afternoon she sat with her needle-work at the window, and felt fairly steeped in peace. Lily Dyer, tall and erect and blooming, went past; but she felt no qualm. If Louisa Ellis had sold her birthright she did not know it, the taste of the pottage was so delicious, and had been her sole satisfaction for so long. Serenity and placid narrowness had become to her as the birthright itself. She gazed ahead through a long reach of future days strung together like pearls in a rosary, every one like the others, and all smooth and flawless and innocent, and her heart went up in thankfulness. Outside was the fervid summer afternoon; the air was filled with the sounds of the busy harvest of men and birds and bees; there were halloos, metallic clatterings, sweet calls, and long hummings. Louisa sat, prayerfully numbering her days, like an uncloistered nun.

A Village Singer

The trees were in full leaf, a heavy south wind was blowing, and there was a loud murmur among the new leaves. The people noticed it, for it was the first time that year that the trees had so murmured in the wind. The spring had come with a rush during the last few days.

The murmur of the trees sounded loud in the village church, where the people sat waiting for the service to begin. The windows were open; it was a very warm Sunday for May.

The church was already filled with this soft sylvan music—the tender harmony of the leaves and the south wind, and the sweet, desultory whistles of birds—when the choir arose and began to sing.

In the centre of the row of women singers stood Alma Way. All the people stared at her, and turned their ears critically. She was the new leading soprano. Candace Whitcomb, the old one, who had sung in the choir for forty years, had lately been given her dismissal. The audience considered that her voice had grown too cracked and uncertain on the upper notes. There had been much complaint, and after long deliberation the church-officers had made known their decision as mildly as possible to the old singer. She had sung for the last time the Sunday before, and Alma Way had been engaged to take her place. With the exception of the organist, the leading soprano was the only paid musician in the large choir. The salary was very modest, still the village people considered it large for a young woman. Alma was from the adjoining village of East Derby; she had quite a local reputation as a singer.

Now she fixed her large solemn blue eyes; her long, delicate face, which had been pretty, turned paler; the blue flowers on her bonnet trembled; her little thin gloved hands, clutching the singing-book, shook perceptibly; but she sang out bravely. That most formidable mountain-height of the world, self-distrust and timidity, arose before her, but her nerves were braced for its ascent. In the midst of the hymn she had a solo; her voice rang out piercingly sweet; the people nodded admiringly at each other; but suddenly there was a stir; all the faces turned toward the windows on the south side of the church. Above the din of the wind and the birds, above Alma Way's sweetly straining tones, arose another female voice, singing another hymn to another tune.

"It's her," the women whispered to each other; they were half aghast, half smiling.

Candace Whitcomb's cottage stood close to the south side of the church. She was playing on her parlor organ, and singing, to drown out the voice of her rival.

Alma caught her breath; she almost stopped; the hymnbook waved like a fan; then she went on. But the long husky drone of the parlor organ and the shrill clamor of the other voice seemed louder than anything else.

When the hymn was finished, Alma sat down. She felt faint; the woman next her slipped a peppermint into her hand. "It ain't worth minding," she whispered, vigorously. Alma tried to smile; down in the audience a young man was watching her with a kind of fierce pity.

In the last hymn Alma had another solo. Again the parlor organ droned above the carefully delicate accompaniment of the church organ, and again Candace Whitcomb's voice clamored forth in another tune.

After the benediction, the other singers pressed around Alma. She did not say much in return for their expressions of indignation and sympathy. She wiped her eyes furtively once or twice, and tried to smile. William Emmons, the choir leader, elderly, stout, and smooth-faced, stood over her, and raised his voice. He was the old musical dignitary of the village, the leader of the choral club and the singing-schools. "A most outrageous proceeding," he said. People had coupled his name with Candace Whitcomb's. The old bachelor tenor and old maiden soprano had been wont to walk together to her home next door after the Saturday night rehearsals, and they had sung duets to the parlor organ. People had watched sharply her old face, on which the blushes of youth sat pitifully, when William Emmons entered the singing-seats. They wondered if he would ever ask her to marry him.

And now he said further to Alma Way that Candace Whitcomb's voice had failed utterly of late, that she sang shockingly, and ought to have had sense enough to know it.

When Alma went down into the audience-room, in the midst of the chattering singers, who seemed to have descended, like birds, from song flights to chirps, the minister approached her. He had been waiting to speak to her. He was a steady-faced, fleshy old man, who had preached from that one pulpit over forty years. He told Alma, in his slow way, how much he regretted the annoyance to which she had been subjected, and intimated that he would endeavor to prevent a recurrence of it. "Miss Whitcomb—must be—reasoned with," said he; he had a slight hesitation of speech, not an impediment. It was as if his thoughts did not slide readily into his words, although both were present. He walked down the aisle with Alma, and bade her good-morning when he saw Wilson Ford waiting for her in the doorway. Everybody knew that Wilson Ford and Alma were lovers; they had been for the last ten years.

Alma colored softly, and made a little imperceptible motion with her head; her silk dress and the lace on her mantle fluttered, but she did not speak. Neither did Wilson, although they had not met before that day. They did not look at each other's faces—they seemed to see each other without that—and they walked along side by side.

They reached the gate before Candace Whitcomb's little house. Wilson looked past the front yard, full of pink and white spikes on flowering bushes, at the lace-curtained windows; a thin white profile, stiffly inclined, apparently over a book, was visible at one of them. Wilson gave his head a shake. He was a stout man, with features so strong that they overcame his flesh. "I'm going up home with you, Alma," said he; "and then—I'm just coming back, to give Aunt Candace one blowing up."

"Oh, don't, Wilson."

"Yes, I shall. If you want to stand this kind of thing you may; I sha'n't."

"There's no need of your talking to her. Mr. Pollard's going to."

"Did he say he was?"

"Yes. I think he's going in before the afternoon meeting, from what he said."

"Well, there's one thing about it, if she does that thing again this afternoon, I'll go in there and break that old organ up into kindling wood." Wilson set his mouth hard, and shook his head again.

Alma gave little side glances up at him, her tone was deprecatory, but her face was full of soft smiles. "I suppose she does feel dreadfully about it," said she. "I can't help feeling kind of guilty, taking her place."

"I don't see how you're to blame. It's outrageous, her acting so."

"The choir gave her a photograph album last week, didn't they?"

"Yes. They went there last Thursday night, and gave her an album and a surprise-party. She ought to behave herself."

"Well, she's sung there so long, I suppose it must be dreadful hard for her to give it up."

Other people going home from church were very near Wilson and Alma. She spoke softly that they might not hear; he did not lower his voice in the least. Presently Alma stopped before a gate.

"What are you stopping here for?" asked Wilson.

"Minnie Lansing wanted me to come and stay with her this noon."

"You're going home with me."

"I'm afraid I'll put your mother out."

"Put mother out! I told her you were coming, this morning. She's got all ready for you. Come along; don't stand here."

He did not tell Alma of the pugnacious spirit with which his mother had received the announcement of her coming, and how she had stayed at home to prepare the dinner, and make a parade of her hard work and her injury.

Wilson's mother was the reason why he did not marry Alma. He would not take his wife home to live with her, and was unable to support separate establishments. Alma was willing enough to be married and put up with Wilson's mother, but she did not complain of his decision. Her delicate blond features grew sharper, and her blue eyes more hollow. She had had a certain fine prettiness, but now she was losing it, and beginning to look old, and there was a prim, angular, old maiden carriage about her narrow shoulders.

Wilson never noticed it, and never thought of Alma as not possessed of eternal youth, or capable of losing or regretting it.

"Come along, Alma," said he; and she followed meekly after him down the street.

Soon after they passed Candace Whitcomb's house, the minister went up the front walk and rang the bell. The pale profile at the window had never stirred as he opened the gate and came up the walk. However, the door was promptly opened, in response to his ring. "Good-morning, Miss Whitcomb," said the minister.

"*Good*-morning." Candace gave a sweeping toss of her head as she spoke. There was a fierce upward curl to her thin nostrils and her lips, as if she scented an adversary. Her black eyes had two tiny cold sparks of fury in them, like an enraged bird's. She did not ask the minister to enter, but he stepped lumberingly into the entry, and she retreated rather than led the way into her little parlor. He settled into the great rocking-chair and wiped his face. Candace sat down again in her old place by the window. She was a tall woman, but very slender and full of pliable motions, like a blade of grass.

"It's a—very pleasant day," said the minister.

Candace made no reply. She sat still, with her head drooping. The wind stirred the looped lace-curtains; a tall rose-tree outside the window waved; soft shadows floated through the room. Candace's parlor organ stood in front of an open window that faced the church; on the corner was a pitcher with a bunch of white lilacs. The whole room was scented with them. Presently the minister looked over at them and sniffed pleasantly.

"You have—some beautiful—lilacs there."

Candace did not speak. Every line of her slender figure looked flexible, but it was a flexibility more resistant than rigor.

The minister looked at her. He filled up the great rocking-chair; his arms in his shiny black coat-sleeves rested squarely and comfortably upon the hair-cloth arms of the chair.

"Well, Miss Whitcomb, I suppose I—may as well come to—the point. There was—a little—matter I wished to speak to you about. I don't suppose you were—at least I can't suppose you were—aware of it, but—this morning, during the singing by the choir, you played and—sung a little too—loud. That is, with—the windows open. It—disturbed us—a little. I hope you won't feel hurt—my dear Miss Candace, but I knew you would rather I would speak of it, for I knew—you would be more disturbed than anybody else at the idea of such a thing."

Candace did not raise her eyes; she looked as if his words might sway her through the window. "I ain't disturbed at it," said she. "I did it on purpose; I meant to."

The minister looked at her.

"You needn't look at me. I know jest what I'm about. I sung the way I did on purpose, an' I'm goin' to do it again, an' I'd like to see you stop me. I guess I've got a right to set down to my own organ, an' sing a psalm tune on a Sabbath day, 'f I want to; an' there ain't no amount of talkin' an' palaverin' a-goin' to stop me. See there!" Candace swung aside her skirts a little. "Look at that!"

The minister looked. Candace's feet were resting on a large red-plush photograph album.

"Makes a nice footstool, don't it?" said she.

The minister looked at the album, then at her; there was a slowly gathering alarm in his face; he began to think she was losing her reason.

Candace had her eyes full upon him now, and her head up. She laughed, and her laugh was almost a snarl. "Yes; I thought it would make a beautiful footstool," said she. "I've been wantin' one for some time." Her tone was full of vicious irony.

"Why, miss—" began the minister; but she interrupted him:

"I know what you're a-goin' to say, Mr. Pollard, an' now I'm goin' to have my say; I'm a-goin' to speak. I want to know what you think of folks that pretend to be Christians treatin' anybody the way they've treated me? Here I've sung in those singin'-seats forty year. I 'ain't never missed a Sunday, except when I've been sick, an' I've gone an' sung a good many times when I'd better been in bed, an' now I'm turned out without a word of warnin'. My voice is jest as good as ever 'twas; there can't anybody say it ain't. It wa'n't ever quite so high-pitched as that Way girl's, mebbe; but she flats the whole durin' time. My voice is as good an' high to-day as it was twenty year ago; an' if it wa'n't, I'd like to know where the Christianity comes in. I'd like to know if it wouldn't be more to the credit of folks in a church to keep an old singer an' an old minister, if they didn't sing an' hold forth quite so smart as they used to, rather than turn 'em off an' hurt their feelin's. I guess it would be full as much to the glory of God. S'pose the singin' an' the preachin' wa'n't quite so good, what difference would it make? Salvation don't hang on anybody's hittin' a high note, that I ever heard of. Folks are gettin' as high-steppin' an' fussy in a meetin'-house as they are in a tavern, nowadays. S'pose they should turn you off, Mr. Pollard, come an' give you a photograph album, an' tell you to clear out, how'd you like it? I ain't findin' any fault with your preachin'; it was always good enough to suit me; but it don't stand to reason folks'll be as took up with your sermons as when you was a young man. You can't expect it. S'pose they should turn you out in your old age, an' call in some young bob squirt, how'd you feel? There's William Emmons, too; he's three years older'n I am, if he does lead the choir an' run all the singin' in town. If my voice has gi'en out, it stan's to reason his has. It ain't, though. William Emmons sings jest as well as he ever did. Why don't they turn him out the way they have me, an' give him a photograph album? I dun know but it would be a good idea to send everybody, as soon as they get a little old an' gone by, an' young folks begin to push, onto some desert island, an' give 'em each a photograph album. Then they can sit down an' look at pictures the rest of their days. Mebbe government'll take it up.

"There they come here last week Thursday, all the choir, jest about eight o'clock in the evenin', an' pretended they'd come to give me a nice little surprise. Surprise! h'm! Brought cake an' oranges, an' was jest as nice as they could be, an' I was real tickled. I never had a surprise-party before in my life. Jenny Carr she played, an' they wanted me to sing alone, an' I never suspected a thing. I've been mad ever since to think what a fool I was, an' how they must have laughed in their sleeves.

"When they'd gone I found this photograph album on the table, all done up as nice as you please, an' directed to Miss Candace Whitcomb from her many friends, an' I opened it, an' there was the letter inside givin' me notice to quit.

"If they'd gone about it any decent way, told me right out honest that they'd got tired of me, an' wanted Alma Way to sing instead of me, I wouldn't minded so much; I should have been hurt 'nough, for I'd felt as if some that had pretended to be my friends, wa'n't; but it wouldn't have been as bad as this. They said in the letter that they'd always set great value on my services, an' it wa'n't from any lack of appreciation that they turned me off, but they thought the duty was gettin' a little too arduous for me. H'm! I hadn't complained. If they'd turned me right out fair an' square, showed me the door, an' said, 'Here, you get out,' but to go an' spill molasses, as it were, all over the threshold, tryin' to make me think it's all nice an' sweet—

"I'd sent that photograph album back quick's I could pack it, but I didn't know who started it, so I've used it for a footstool. It's all it's good for, 'cordin' to my way of thinkin'. An' I ain't been particular to get the dust off my shoes before I used it neither."

Mr. Pollard, the minister, sat staring. He did not look at Candace; his eyes were fastened upon a point straight ahead. He had a look of helpless solidity, like a block of granite. This country minister, with his steady, even temperament, treading with heavy precision his own track for over forty years, having nothing new in his life except the new sameness of the seasons, and desiring nothing new, was incapable of understanding a woman like this, who had lived as quietly as he, and all the time held within herself the elements of revolution. He could not account for such violence, such extremes, except in a loss of reason. He had a conviction that Candace was getting beyond herself. He himself was not a typical New-Englander; the national elements of character were not pronounced in him. He was aghast and bewildered at this outbreak, which was tropical, and more than tropical, for a New England nature has a floodgate, and the power which it releases is an accumulation. Candace Whitcomb had been a quiet woman, so delicately resolute that the quality had been scarcely noticed in her, and her ambition had been unsuspected. Now the resolution and the ambition appeared raging over her whole self.

She began to talk again. "I've made up my mind that I'm goin' to sing Sundays the way I did this mornin', an' I don't care what folks say," said she. "I've made up my mind that I'm goin' to take matters into my own hands. I'm goin' to let folks see that I ain't trod down quite flat, that there's a little rise left in me. I ain't goin' to give up beat yet a while; an' I'd like to see anybody stop me. If I ain't got a right to play a psalm tune on my organ an' sing, I'd like to know. If you don't like it, you can move the meetin'-house."

Candace had had an inborn reverence for clergymen. She had always treated Mr. Pollard with the utmost deference. Indeed, her manner toward all men had been marked by a certain delicate stiffness and dignity. Now she was talking to the old minister with the homely freedom with which she might have addressed a female gossip over the back fence. He could not say much in return. He did not feel competent to make headway against any such tide of passion; all he could do was to let it beat against him. He made a few expostulations, which increased Candace's vehemence; he expressed his regret over the whole affair, and suggested that they should kneel and ask the guidance of the Lord in the matter, that she might be led to see it all in a different light.

Candace refused flatly. "I don't see any use prayin' about it," said she. "I don't think the Lord's got much to do with it, anyhow."

It was almost time for the afternoon service when the minister left. He had missed his comfortable noontide rest, through this encounter with his revolutionary parishioner. After the minister had gone, Candace sat by the window and waited. The bell rang, and she watched the people file past. When her nephew Wilson Ford with Alma appeared, she grunted to herself. "She's thin as a rail," said she; "guess there won't be much left by the time Wilson gets her. Little soft-spoken nippin' thing, she wouldn't make him no kind of a wife, anyway. Guess it's jest as well."

When the bell had stopped tolling, and all the people entered the church, Candace went over to her organ and seated herself. She arranged a singing-book before her, and sat still, waiting. Her thin, colorless neck and temples were full of beating pulses; her black eyes were bright and eager; she leaned stiffly over toward the music-rack, to hear better. When the church organ sounded out she straightened herself; her long skinny fingers pressed her own organ-keys with nervous energy. She worked the pedals with all her strength; all her slender body was in motion. When the first notes of Alma's solo began, Candace sang. She had really possessed a fine voice, and it was wonderful how little she had lost it. Straining her throat with jealous fury, her notes were still for the main part true. Her voice filled the whole room; she sang with wonderful fire and expression. That, at least, mild little Alma Way could never emulate. She was full of steadfastness and unquestioning constancy, but there were in her no smouldering fires of ambition and resolution. Music was not to her what it had been to her older rival. To this obscure woman, kept relentlessly by circumstances in a narrow track, singing in the village choir had been as much as Italy was to Napoleon—and now on her island of exile she was still showing fight.

After the church service was done, Candace left the organ and went over to her old chair by the window. Her knees felt weak, and shook under her. She sat down, and leaned back her head. There were red spots on her cheeks. Pretty soon she heard a quick slam of her gate, and an impetuous tread on the gravel-walk. She looked up, and there was her nephew

Wilson Ford hurrying up to the door. She cringed a little, then she settled herself more firmly in her chair.

Wilson came into the room with a rush. He left the door open, and the wind slammed it to after him.

"Aunt Candace, where are you?" he called out, in a loud voice.

She made no reply. He looked around fiercely, and his eyes seemed to pounce upon her.

"Look here, Aunt Candace," said he, "are you crazy?" Candace said nothing. "Aunt Candace!" She did not seem to see him. "If you don't answer me," said Wilson, "I'll just go over there and pitch that old organ out of the window!"

"Wilson Ford!" said Candace, in a voice that was almost a scream.

"Well, what say! What have you got to say for yourself, acting the way you have? I tell you what 'tis, Aunt Candace, I won't stand it."

"I'd like to see you help yourself."

"I will help myself. I'll pitch that old organ out of the window, and then I'll board up the window on that side of your house. Then we'll see."

"It ain't your house, and it won't never be."

"Who said it was my house? You're my aunt, and I've got a little lookout for the credit of the family. Aunt Candace, what are you doing this way for?"

"It don't make no odds what I'm doin' so for. I ain't bound to give my reasons to a young fellar like you, if you do act so mighty toppin'. But I'll tell you one thing, Wilson Ford, after the way you've spoke to-day, you sha'n't never have one cent of my money, an' you can't never marry that Way girl if you don't have it. You can't never take her home to live with your mother, an' this house would have been mighty nice an' convenient for you some day. Now you won't get it. I'm goin' to make another will. I'd made one, if you did but know it. Now you won't get a cent of my money, you nor your mother neither. An' I ain't goin' to live a dreadful while longer, neither. Now I wish you'd go home; I want to lay down. I'm 'bout sick."

Wilson could not get another word from his aunt. His indignation had not in the least cooled. Her threat of disinheriting him did not cow him at all; he had too much rough independence, and indeed his aunt Candace's house had always been too much of an air-castle for him to contemplate seriously. Wilson, with his burly frame and his headless common-sense, could have little to do with air-castles, had he been hard enough to build them over graves. Still, he had not admitted that he never could marry Alma. All his hopes were based upon a rise in his own fortunes, not by some sudden convulsion, but by his own long and steady labor. Some time, he thought, he should have saved enough for the two homes.

He went out of his aunt's house still storming. She arose after the door had shut behind him, and got out into the kitchen. She thought that she would start a fire and make a cup of tea. She had not eaten anything all day. She put some kindling-wood into the stove and touched a match to it; then she went back to the sitting-room, and settled down again into the chair by the window. The fire in the kitchen-stove roared, and the light wood was soon burned out. She thought no more about it. She had not put on the teakettle. Her head ached, and once in a while she shivered. She sat at the window while the afternoon waned and the dusk came on. At seven o'clock the meeting bell rang again, and the people flocked by. This time she did not stir. She had shut her parlor organ. She did not need to out-sing her rival this evening; there was only congregational singing at the Sunday-night prayer-meeting.

She sat still until it was nearly time for meeting to be done; her head ached harder and harder, and she shivered more. Finally she arose. "Guess I'll go to bed," she muttered. She went about the house, bent over and shaking, to lock the the doors. She stood a minute in the back door, looking over the fields to the woods. There was a red light over there. "The woods are on fire," said Candace. She watched with a dull interest the flames roll up, withering and destroying the tender green spring foliage. The air was full of smoke, although the fire was half a mile away.

Candace locked the door and went in. The trees with their delicate garlands of new leaves, with the new nests of song birds, might fall, she was in the roar of an intenser fire; the growths of all her springs and the delicate wontedness of her whole life were going down in it. Candace went to bed in her little room off the parlor, but she could not sleep. She lay awake all night. In the morning she crawled to the door and hailed a little boy who was passing. She bade him go for the doctor as quickly as he could, then to Mrs. Ford's, and ask her to come over. She held on to the door while she was talking. The boy stood staring wonderingly at her. The spring wind fanned her face. She had drawn on a dress skirt and put her shawl over her shoulders, and her gray hair was blowing over her red cheeks.

She shut the door and went back to her bed. She never arose from it again. The doctor and Mrs. Ford came and looked after her, and she lived a week. Nobody but herself thought until the very last that she would die; the doctor called her illness merely a light run of fever; she had her senses fully.

But Candace gave up at the first. "It's my last sickness," she said to Mrs. Ford that morning when she first entered; and Mrs. Ford had laughed at the notion; but the sick woman held to it. She did not seem to suffer much physical pain; she only grew weaker and weaker, but she was distressed mentally. She did not talk much, but her eyes followed everybody with an agonized expression.

On Wednesday William Emmons came to inquire for her. Candace heard him out in the parlor. She tried to raise herself on one elbow that she might listen better to his voice.

"William Emmons come in to ask how you was," Mrs. Ford said, after he was gone.

"I—heard him," replied Candace. Presently she spoke again. "Nancy," said she, "where's that photograph album?"

"On the table," replied her sister, hesitatingly.

"Mebbe—you'd better—brush it up a little."

"Well."

Sunday morning Candace wished that the minister should be asked to come in at the noon intermission. She had refused to see him before. He came and prayed with her, and she asked his forgiveness for the way she had spoken the Sunday before. "I—hadn't ought to—spoke so," said she. "I was—dreadful wrought up."

"Perhaps it was your sickness coming on," said the minister, soothingly.

Candace shook her head. "No—it wa'n't. I hope the Lord will—forgive me."

After the minister had gone, Candace still appeared unhappy. Her pitiful eyes followed her sister everywhere with the mechanical persistency of a portrait.

"What is it you want, Candace?" Mrs. Ford said at last. She had nursed her sister faithfully, but once in a while her impatience showed itself.

"Nancy!"

"What say?"

"I wish—you'd go out when—meetin's done, an'—head off

Alma an' Wilson, an'—ask 'em to come in. I feel as if—I'd like to—hear her sing."

Mrs. Ford stared. "Well," said she.

The meeting was now in session. The windows were all open, for it was another warm Sunday. Candace lay listening to the music when it began, and a look of peace came over her face. Her sister had smoothed her hair back, and put on a clean cap. The white curtain in the bedroom window waved in the wind like a white sail. Candace almost felt as if she were better, but the thought of death seemed easy.

Mrs. Ford at the parlor window watched for the meeting to be out. When the people appeared, she ran down the walk and waited for Alma and Wilson. When they came she told them what Candace wanted, and they all went in together.

"Here's Alma an' Wilson, Candace," said Mrs. Ford, leading them to the bedroom door.

Candace smiled. "Come in," she said, feebly. And Alma and Wilson entered and stood beside the bed. Candace continued to look at them, the smile straining her lips.

"Wilson!"

"What is it, Aunt Candace?"

"I ain't altered that—will. You an' Alma can—come here an'—live—when I'm—gone. Your mother won't mind livin' alone. Alma can have—all—my things."

"Don't, Aunt Candace." Tears were running over Wilson's cheeks, and Alma's delicate face was all of a quiver.

"I thought—maybe—Alma'd be willin' to—sing for me," said Candace.

"What do you want me to sing?" Alma asked, in a trembling voice.

" 'Jesus, lover of my soul.' "

Alma, standing there beside Wilson, began to sing. At first she could hardly control her voice, then she sang sweetly and clearly.

Candace lay and listened. Her face had a holy and radiant expression. When Alma stopped singing it did not disappear, but she looked up and spoke, and it was like a secondary glimpse of the old shape of a forest tree through the smoke and flame of the transfiguring fire the instant before it falls. "You flatted a little on—soul," said Candace.

A Poetess

❦

The garden-patch at the right of the house was all a gay spangle with sweet-peas and red-flowering beans, and flanked with feathery asparagus. A woman in blue was moving about there. Another woman, in a black bonnet, stood at the front door of the house. She knocked and waited. She could not see from where she stood the blue-clad woman in the garden. The house was very close to the road, from which a tall evergreen hedge separated it, and the view to the side was in a measure cut off.

The front door was open; the woman had to reach to knock on it, as it swung into the entry. She was a small woman and quite young, with a bright alertness about her which had almost the effect of prettiness. It was to her what greenness and crispness are to a plant. She poked her little face forward, and her sharp pretty eyes took in the entry and a room at the left, of which the door stood open. The entry was small and square and unfurnished, except for a well-rubbed old card-table against the back wall. The room was full of green light from the tall hedge, and bristling with grasses and flowers and asparagus stalks.

"Betsey, you there?" called the woman. When she spoke, a yellow canary, whose cage hung beside the front door, began to chirp and twitter.

"Betsey, you there?" the woman called again. The bird's chirps came in a quick volley; then he began to trill and sing.

"She ain't there," said the woman. She turned and went out of the yard through the gap in the hedge; then she looked around. She caught sight of the blue figure in the garden. "There she is," said she.

She went around the house to the garden. She wore a gay cashmere patterned calico dress with her mourning bonnet, and she held it carefully away from the dewy grass and vines.

The other woman did not notice her until she was close to

374

her and said, "Good mornin', Betsey." Then she started and turned around.

"Why, Mis' Caxton! That you?" said she.

"Yes. I've been standin' at your door for the last half-hour. I was jest goin' away when I caught sight of you out here."

In spite of her brisk speech her manner was subdued. She drew down the corners of her mouth sadly.

"I declare I'm dreadful sorry you had to stan' there so long!" said the other woman.

She set a pan partly filled with beans on the ground, wiped her hands, which were damp and green from the wet vines, on her apron, then extended her right one with a solemn and sympathetic air.

"It don't make much odds, Betsey," replied Mrs. Caxton. "I ain't got much to take up my time nowadays." She sighed heavily as she shook hands, and the other echoed her.

"We'll go right in now. I'm dreadful sorry you stood there so long," said Betsey.

"You'd better finish pickin' your beans."

"No; I wa'n't goin' to pick any more. I was jest goin' in."

"I declare, Betsey Dole, I shouldn't think you'd got enough for a cat!" said Mrs. Caxton, eying the pan.

"I've got pretty near all there is. I guess I've got more flowerin' beans than eatin' ones, anyway."

"I should think you had," said Mrs. Caxton, surveying the row of bean-poles topped with swarms of delicate red flowers. "I should think they were pretty near all flowerin' ones. Had any peas?"

"I didn't have more'n three or four messes. I guess I planted sweet-peas mostly. I don't know hardly how I happened to."

"Had any summer squash?"

"Two or three. There's some more set, if they ever get ripe. I planted some gourds. I think they look real pretty on the kitchen shelf in the winter."

"I should think you'd got a sage bed big enough for the whole town."

"Well, I have got a pretty good-sized one. I always liked them blue sage-blows. You'd better hold up your dress real careful goin' through here, Mis' Caxton, or you'll get it wet."

The two women picked their way through the dewy grass, around a corner of the hedge, and Betsey ushered her visitor into the house.

"Set right down in the rockin-chair," said she. "I'll jest carry these beans out into the kitchen."

"I should think you'd better get another pan and string 'em, or you won't get 'em done for dinner."

"Well, mebbe I will, if you'll excuse it, Mis' Caxton. The beans had ought to boil quite a while, they're pretty old."

Betsey went into the kitchen and returned with a pan and an old knife. She seated herself opposite Mrs. Caxton, and began to string and cut the beans.

"If I was in your place I shouldn't feel as if I'd got enough to boil a kettle for," said Mrs. Caxton, eying the beans. "I should 'most have thought when you didn't have any more room for a garden than you've got that you'd planted more real beans and peas instead of so many flowerin' ones. I'd rather have a good mess of green peas boiled with a piece of salt pork than all the sweet-peas you could give me. I like flowers well enough, but I never set up for a butterfly, an' I want something else to live on." She looked at Betsey with pensive superiority.

Betsey was near-sighted; she had to bend low over the beans in order to string them. She was fifty years old, but she wore her streaky light hair in curls like a young girl. The curls hung over her faded cheeks and almost concealed them. Once in a while she flung them back with a childish gesture which sat strangely upon her.

"I dare say you're in the right of it," she said, meekly.

"I know I am. You folks that write poetry wouldn't have a single thing to eat growin' if they were left alone. And that brings to mind what I come for. I've been thinkin' about it ever since—our—little Willie—left us." Mrs. Caxton's manner was suddenly full of shamefaced dramatic fervor, her eyes reddened with tears.

Betsey looked up inquiringly, throwing back her curls. Her face took on unconsciously lines of grief so like the other woman's that she looked like her for the minute.

"I thought maybe," Mrs. Caxton went on, tremulously, "you'd be willin' to—write a few lines."

"Of course I will, Mis' Caxton. I'll be glad to, if I can do 'em to suit you," Betsey said, tearfully.

"I thought jest a few—lines. You could mention how—handsome he was, and good, and I never had to punish him but once in his life, and how pleased he was with his little new suit, and what a sufferer he was, and—how we hope he is at rest—in a better land."

"I'll try, Mis' Caxton, I'll try," sobbed Betsey. The two women wept together for a few minutes.

"It seems as if—I couldn't have it so sometimes," Mrs. Caxton said, brokenly. "I keep thinkin' he's in the other— room. Every time I go back home when I've been away it's like—losin' him again. Oh, it don't seem as if I could go home and not find him there—it don't, it don't! Oh, you don't know anything about it, Betsey. You never had any children!"

"I don't s'pose I do, Mis' Caxton; I don't s'pose I do."

Presently Mrs. Caxton wiped her eyes. "I've been thinkin'," said she, keeping her mouth steady with an effort, "that it would be real pretty to have—some lines printed on some sheets of white paper with a neat black border. I'd like to send some to my folks, and one to the Perkinses in Brigham, and thre's a good many others I thought would value 'em."

"I'll do jest the best I can, Mis' Caxton, an' be glad to. It's little enough anybody can do at such times."

Mrs. Caxton broke out weeping again. "Oh, it's true, it's true, Betsey!" she sobbed. "Nobody can do anything, and nothin' amounts to anything—poetry or anything else—when he's *gone*. Nothin' can bring him back. Oh, what shall I do, what shall I do?"

Mrs. Caxton dried her tears again, and arose to take leave. "Well, I must be goin', or Wilson won't have any dinner," she said, with an effort at self-control.

"Well, I'll do jest the best I can with the poetry," said Betsey. "I'll write it this afternoon." She had set down her pan of beans and was standing beside Mrs. Caxton. She reached up and straightened her black bonnet, which had slipped backward.

"I've got to get a pin," said Mrs. Caxton, tearfully. "I can't keep it anywheres. It drags right off my head, the veil is so heavy."

Betsey went to the door with her visitor. "It's dreadful dusty, ain't it?" she remarked, in that sad, contemptuous tone with which one speaks of discomforts in the presence of affliction.

"Terrible," replied Mrs. Caxton. "I wouldn't wear my black dress in it nohow; a black bonnet is bad enough. This dress is 'most too good. It's enough to spoil everything. Well, I'm much obliged to you, Betsey, for bein' willin' to do that."

"I'll do jest the best I can, Mis' Caxton."

After Betsey had watched her visitor out of the yard she

returned to the sitting-room and took up the pan of beans. She looked doubtfully at the handful of beans all nicely strung and cut up. "I declare I don't know what to do," said she. "Seems as if I should kind of relish these, but it's goin' to take some time to cook 'em, tendin' the fire an' everything, an' I'd ought to go to work on that poetry. Then, there's another thing, if I have 'em to-day, I can't to-morrow. Mebbe I shall take more comfort thinkin' about 'em. I guess I'll leave 'em over till to-morrow."

Betsey carried the pan of beans out into the kitchen and set them away in the pantry. She stood scrutinizing the shelves like a veritable Mother Hubbard. There was a plate containing three or four potatoes and a slice of cold boiled pork, and a spoonful of red jelly in a tumbler; that was all the food in sight. Betsey stooped and lifted the lid from an earthen jar on the floor. She took out two slices of bread. "There!" said she. "I'll have this bread and that jelly this noon, an' to-night I'll have a kind of dinner-supper with them potatoes warmed up with the pork. An' then I can sit right down an' go to work on that poetry."

It was scarcely eleven o'clock, and not time for dinner. Betsey returned to the sitting room, got an old black portfolio and pen and ink out of the chimney cupboard, and seated herself to work. She meditated, and wrote one line, then another. Now and then she read aloud what she had written with a solemn intonation. She sat there thinking and writing, and the time went on. The twelve-o'clock bell rang, but she never noticed it; she had quite forgotten the bread and jelly. The long curls drooped over her cheeks; her thin yellow hand, cramped around the pen, moved slowly and fitfully over the paper. The light in the room was dim and green, like the light in an arbor, from the tall hedge before the windows. Great plumy bunches of asparagus waved over the tops of the looking-glass; a framed sampler, a steel engraving of a female head taken from some old magazine, and sheaves of dried grasses hung on or were fastened to the walls; vases and tumblers of flowers stood on the shelf and table. The air was heavy and sweet.

Betsey in this room, bending over her portfolio, looked like the very genius of gentle, old-fashioned, sentimental poetry. It seemed as if one, given the premises of herself and the room, could easily deduce what she would write, and read without seeing those lines wherein flowers rhymed sweetly with vernal bowers, home with beyond the tomb, and heaven with even.

The summer afternoon wore on. It grew warmer and closer; the air was full of the rasping babble of insects, with the cicadas shrilling over them; now and then a team passed, and a dust cloud floated over the top of the hedge; the canary at the door chirped and trilled, and Betsey wrote poor little Willie Caxton's obituary poetry.

Tears stood in her pale blue eyes; occasionally they rolled down her cheeks, and she wiped them away. She kept her handkerchief in her lap with her portfolio. When she looked away from the paper she seemed to see two childish forms in the room—one purely human, a boy clad in his little girl petticoats, with a fair chubby face; the other in a little straight white night-gown, with long, shining wings, and the same face. Betsey had not enough imagination to change the face. Little Willie Caxton's angel was still himself to her, although decked in the paraphernalia of the resurrection.

"I s'pose I can't feel about it nor write about it anything the way I could if I'd had any children of my own an' lost 'em. I s'pose it *would* have come home to be different," Betsey murmured once, sniffing. A soft color flamed up under her curls at the thought. For a second the room seemed all aslant with white wings, and smiling with the faces of children that had never been. Betsey straightened herself as if she were trying to be dignified to her inner consciousness. "That's one trouble I've been clear of, anyhow," said she; "an' I guess I can enter into her feelin's considerable."

She glanced at a great pink shell on the shelf, and remembered how she had often given it to the dead child to play with when he had been in with his mother, and how he had put it to his ear to hear the sea.

"Dear little fellow!" she sobbed, and sat awhile with her handkerchief at her face.

Betsey wrote her poem upon backs of old letters and odd scraps of paper. She found it difficult to procure enough paper for fair copies of her poems when composed; she was forced to be very economical with the first draft. Her portfolio was piled with a loose litter of written papers when she at length arose and stretched her stiff limbs. It was near sunset; men with dinner-pails were tramping past the gate, going home from their work.

Betsey laid the portfolio on the table. "There! I've wrote sixteen verses," said she, "an' I guess I've got everything in. I guess she'll think that's enough. I can copy it off nice to-morrow. I can't see to-night to do it, anyhow."

There were red spots on Betsey's cheeks; her knees were unsteady when she walked. She went into the kitchen and made a fire, and set on the tea-kettle. "I guess I won't warm up them potatoes to-night," said she; "I'll have the bread an' jelly, an' save 'em for breakfast. Somehow I don't seem to feel so much like 'em as I did, an' fried potatoes is apt to lay heavy at night."

When the kettle boiled, Betsey drank her cup of tea and soaked her slice of bread in it; then she put away her cup and saucer and plate, and went out to water her garden. The weather was so dry and hot it had to be watered every night. Betsey had to carry the water from a neighbor's well; her own was dry. Back and forth she went in the deepening twilight, her slender body strained to one side with the heavy water-pail, until the garden-mould looked dark and wet. Then she took in the canary-bird, locked up her house, and soon her light went out. Often on these summer nights Betsey went to bed without lighting a lamp at all. There was no moon, but it was a beautiful starlight night. She lay awake nearly all night, thinking of her poem. She altered several lines in her mind.

She arose early, made herself a cup of tea, and warmed over the potatoes, then sat down to copy the poem. She wrote it out on both sides of note-paper, in a neat, cramped hand. It was the middle of the afternoon before it was finished. She had been obliged to stop work and cook the beans for dinner, although she begrudged the time. When the poem was fairly copied, she rolled it neatly and tied it with a bit of black ribbon; then she made herself ready to carry it to Mrs. Caxton's.

It was a hot afternoon. Betsey went down the street in her thinnest dress—an old delaine, with delicate bunches of faded flowers on a faded green ground. There was a narrow green belt ribbon around her long waist. She wore a green barège bonnet, stiffened with rattans, scooping over her face, with her curls pushed forward over her thin cheeks in two bunches, and she carried a small green parasol with a jointed handle. Her costume was obsolete, even in the little country village where she lived. She had worn it every summer for the last twenty years. She made no more change in her attire than the old perennials in her garden. She had no money with which to buy new clothes, and the old satisfied her. She had come to regard them as being as unalterably a part of herself as her body.

Betsey went on, setting her slim, cloth-gaitered feet daintily in the hot sand of the road. She carried her roll of poetry in a black-mitted hand. She walked rather slowly. She was not very strong; there was a limp feeling in her knees; her face, under the green shade of her bonnet, was pale and moist with the heat.

She was glad to reach Mrs. Caxton's and sit down in her parlor, damp and cool and dark as twilight, for the blinds and curtains had been drawn all day. Not a breath of the fervid out-door air had penetrated it.

"Come right in this way; it's cooler than the sittin'-room," Mrs. Caxton said; and Betsey sank into the hair-cloth rocker and waved a palm-leaf fan.

Mrs. Caxton sat close to the window in the dim light, and read the poem. She took out her handkerchief and wiped her eyes as she read. "It's beautiful, beautiful," she said, tearfully, when she had finished. "It's jest as comfortin' as it can be, and you worked that in about his new suit so nice. I feel real obliged to you, Betsey, and you shall have one of the printed ones when they're done. I'm goin' to see to it right off."

Betsey flushed and smiled. It was to her as if her poem had been approved and accepted by one of the great magazines. She had the pride and self-wonderment of recognized genius. She went home buoyantly, under the wilting sun, after her call was done. When she reached home there was no one to whom she could tell her triumph, but the hot spicy breath of the evergreen hedge and the fervent sweetness of the sweet-peas seemd to greet her like the voices of friends.

She could scarcely wait for the printed poem. Mrs. Caxton brought it, and she inspected it, neatly printed in its black border. She was quite overcome with innocent pride.

"Well, I don't know but it does read pretty well," said she.

"It's beautiful," said Mrs. Caxton, fervently. "Mr. White said he never read anything any more touchin', when I carried it to him to print. I think folks are goin' to think a good deal of havin' it. I've had two dozen printed."

It was to Betsey like a large edition of a book. She had written obituary poems before, but never one had been printed in this sumptuous fashion. "I declare I think it would look pretty framed!" said she.

"Well, I don't know but it would," said Mrs. Caxton. "Anybody might have a neat little black frame, and it would look real appropriate."

"I wonder how much it would cost?" said Betsey.

After Mrs. Caxton had gone, she sat long, staring admiringly at the poem, and speculating as to the cost of a frame. "There ain't no use; I can't have it nohow, not if it don't cost mor'n a quarter of a dollar," said she.

Then she put the poem away and got her supper. Nobody knew how frugal Betsey Dole's suppers and breakfasts and dinners were. Nearly all her food in the summer came from the scanty vegetables which flourished between the flowers in her garden. She ate scarcely more than her canary-bird, and sang as assiduously. Her income was almost infinitesimal: the interest at a low percent, of a tiny sum in the village savings-bank, the remnant of her father's little hoard after his funeral expenses had been paid. Betsey had lived upon it for twenty years, and considered herself well-to-do. She had never received a cent for her poems; she had not thought of such a thing as possible. The appearance of this last in such shape was worth more to her than its words represented in as many dollars.

Betsey kept the poem pinned on the wall under the looking-glass; if any one came in, she tried with delicate hints to call attention to it. It was two weeks after she received it that the downfall of her innocent pride came.

One afternoon Mrs. Caxton called. It was raining hard. Betsey could scarcely believe it was she when she went to the door and found her standing there.

"Why, Mis' Caxton!" said she. "Ain't you wet to your skin?"

"Yes, I guess I be, pretty near. I s'pose I hadn't ought to come 'way down here in such a soak; but I went into Sarah Roger's a minute after dinner, and something she said made me so mad, I made up my mind I'd come down here and tell you about it if I got drowned." Mrs. Caxton was out of breath; rain-drops trickled from her hair over her face; she stood in the door and shut her umbrella with a vicious shake to scatter the water from it. "I don't know what you're goin' to do with this," said she; "it's drippin'."

"I'll take it out an' put it in the kitchen sink."

"Well, I'll take off my shawl here too, and you can hang it out in the kitchen. I spread this shawl out. I thought it would keep the rain off me some. I know one thing, I'm goin' to have a waterproof if I live."

When the two women were seated in the sitting-room, Mrs. Caxton was quiet for a moment. There was a hesitating look on her face, fresh with the moist wind, with strands of wet hair clinging to the temples.

"I don't know as I had ought to tell you," she said, doubt-fully.

"Why hadn't you ought to?"

"Well, I don't care; I'm goin' to, anyhow. I think you'd ought to know, an' it ain't so bad for you as it is for me. It don't begin to be. I put considerable money into 'em. I think Mr. White was pretty high, myself."

Betsey looked scared. "What is it?" she asked, in a weak voice.

"Sarah Rogers says that the minister told her Ida that that poetry you wrote was jest as poor as it could be, an' it was in dreadful bad taste to have it printed an' sent round that way. What do you think of that?" .

Betsey did not reply. She sat looking at Mrs. Caxton as a victim whom the first blow had not killed might look at her executioner. Her face was like a pale wedge of ice between her curls.

Mrs. Caxton went on. "Yes, she said that right to my face, word for word. An' there was something else. She said the minister said that you had never wrote anything that could be called poetry, an' it was a dreadful waste of time. I don't s'pose he thought 'twas comin' back to you. You know he goes with Ida Rogers, an' I s'pose he said it to her kind of confidential when she showed him the poetry. There! I gave Sarah Rogers one of them nice printed ones, an' she acted glad enough to have it. Bad taste! H'm! If anybody wants to say anything against that beautiful poetry, printed with that nice black border, they can. I don't care if it's the minister, or who it is. I don't care if he does write poetry himself, an' has had some printed in a magazine. Maybe his ain't quite so fine as he thinks 'tis. Maybe them magazine folks jest took his for lack of something better. I'd like to have you sent that poetry there. Bad taste! I jest got right up. 'Sarah Rogers,' says I, 'I hope you won't never do anything yourself in any worse taste.' I trembled so I could hardly speak, and I made up my mind I'd come right straight over here."

Mrs. Caxton went on and on. Betsey sat listening, and saying nothing. She looked ghastly. Just before Mrs. Caxton went home she noticed it. "Why, Betsey Dole," she cried, "you look as white as a sheet. You ain't takin' it to heart as much as all that comes to, I hope. Goodness, I wish I hadn't told you!"

"I'd a good deal ruther you told me," replied Betsey, with

a certain dignity. She looked at Mrs. Caxton. Her back was as stiff as if she were bound to a stake.

"Well, I thought you would," said Mrs. Caxton, uneasily; "and you're dreadful silly if you take it to heart, Betsey, that's all I've got to say. Goodness, I guess I don't, and it's full as hard on me as 'tis on you!"

Mrs. Caxton arose to go. Betsey brought her shawl and umbrella from the kitchen, and helped her off. Mrs. Caxton turned on the door-step and looked back at Betsey's white face. "Now don't go thinkin' about it any more," said she. "I ain't goin' to. It ain't worth mindin'. Everybody knows what Sarah Rogers is. Good-by."

"Good-by, Mis' Caxton," said Betsey. She went back into the sitting-room. It was a cold rain, and the room was gloomy and chilly. She stood looking out of the window, watching the rain pelt on the hedge. The bird-cage hung at the other window. The bird watched her with his head on one side; then he begun to chirp.

Suddenly Betsey faced about and began talking. It was not as if she were talking to herself; it seemed as if she recognized some other presence in the room. "I'd like to know if it's fair," said she. "I'd like to know if you think it's fair. Had I ought to have been born with the wantin' to write poetry if I couldn't write it—had I? Had I ought to have been let to write all my life, an' not know before there wa'n't any use in it? Would it be fair if that canary-bird there, that ain't never done anything but sing, should turn out not to be singin'? Would it, I'd like to know? S'pose them sweet-peas shouldn't be smellin' the right way? I ain't been dealt with as fair as they have, I'd like to know if I have."

The bird trilled and trilled. It was as if the golden down on his throat bubbled. Betsey went across the room to a cupboard beside the chimney. On the shelves were neatly stacked newspapers and little white rolls of writing-paper. Betsey began clearing the shelves. She took out the newspapers first, got the scissors, and cut a poem neatly out of the corner of each. Then she took up the clipped poems and the white rolls in her apron, and carried them into the kitchen. She cleaned out the stove carefully, removing every trace of ashes; then she put in the papers, and set them on fire. She stood watching them as their edges curled and blackened, then leaped into flame. Her face twisted as if the fire were curling over it also. Other women might have burned their lovers' letters in agony of heart. Betsey had never had any lover, but she was burning all the love-letters that had passed between her and life. When the flames died out she got a blue china sugar-bowl from the pantry and dipped the ashes into it with one of her thin silver teaspoons; then she put on the cover and set it away in the sitting-room cupboard.

The bird, who had been silent while she was out, began chirping again. Betsey went back to the pantry and got a lump of sugar, which she stuck between the cage wires. She looked at the clock on the kitchen shelf as she went by. It was after six. "I guess I don't want any supper to-night," she muttered.

She sat down by the window again. The bird pecked at his sugar. Betsey shivered and coughed. She had coughed more or less for years. People said she had the old-fashioned consumption. She sat at the window until it was quite dark; then she went to bed in her little bedroom out of the sitting-room. She shivered so she could not hold herself upright crossing the room. She coughed a great deal in the night.

Betsey was always an early riser. She was up at five the next morning. The sun shone, but it was very cold for the season. The leaves showed white in a north wind, and the flowers looked brighter than usual, though they were bent with the rain of the day before. Betsey went out in the garden to straighten her sweet-peas.

Coming back, a neighbor passing in the street eyed her curiously. "Why, Betsey, you sick?" said she.

"No; I'm kinder chilly, that's all," replied Betsey.

But the woman went home and reported that Betsey Dole looked dreadfully, and she didn't believe she'd ever see another summer.

It was now late August. Before October it was quite generally recognized that Betsey Dole's life was nearly over. She had no relatives, and hired nurses were rare in this little village. Mrs. Caxton came voluntarily and took care of her, only going home to prepare her husband's meals. Betsey's bed was moved into the sitting-room, and the neighbors came every day to see her, and brought little delicacies. Betsey had talked very little all her life; she talked less now, and there was a reticence about her which somewhat intimidated the other women. They would look pityingly and solemnly at her, and whisper in the entry when they went out.

Betsey never complained; but she kept asking if the minister had got home. He had been called away by his mother's illness, and returned only a week before Betsey died.

He came over at once to see her. Mrs. Caxton ushered him in one afternoon.

"Here's Mr. Lang come to see you, Betsey," said she, in the tone she would have used towards a little child. She placed the rocking-chair for the minister, and was about to seat herself, when Betsey spoke:

"Would you mind goin' out in the kitchen jest a few minutes, Mis' Caxton?" said she.

Mrs. Caxton arose, and went out with an embarrassed trot. Then there was silence. The minister was a young man—a country boy who had worked his way through a country college. He was gaunt and awkward, but sturdy in his loose clothes. He had a homely, impetuous face, with a good forehead.

He looked at Betsey's gentle, wasted face, sunken in the pillow, framed by its clusters of curls; finally he began to speak in the stilted fashion, yet with a certain force by reason of his unpolished honesty, about her spiritual welfare. Betsey listened quietly; now and then she assented. She had been a church member for years. It seemed now to the young man that this elderly maiden, drawing near the end of her simple, innocent life, had indeed her lamp, which no strong winds of temptation had ever met, well trimmed and burning.

When he paused, Betsey spoke. "Will you go to the cupboard side of the chimney and bring me the blue sugarbowl on the top shelf?" said she, feebly.

The young man stared at her a minute; then he went to the cupboard, and brought the sugar-bowl to her. He held it, and Betsey took off the lid with her weak hand. "Do you see what's in there?" said she.

"It looks like ashes."

"It's—the ashes of all—the poetry I—ever wrote."

"Why, what made you burn it, Miss Dole?"

"I found out it wa'n't worth nothin'."

The minister looked at her in a bewildered way. He began to question if she were not wandering in her mind. He did not once suspect his own connection with the matter.

Betsey fastened her eager, sunken eyes upon his face. "What I want to know is—if you'll 'tend to—havin' this—buried with me."

The minister recoiled. He thought to himself that she certainly was wandering.

"No, I ain't out of my head," said Betsey. "I know what I'm sayin'. Maybe it's queer soundin', but it's a notion I've took. If you'll—'tend to it, I shall be—much obliged. I don't know anybody else I can ask."

"Well, I'll attend to it, if you wish me to, Miss Dole," said the minister, in a serious, perplexed manner. She replaced the lid on the sugar-bowl, and left it in his hands.

"Well, I shall be much obliged if you will 'tend to it; an' now there's something else," said she.

"What is it, Miss Dole?"

She hesitated a moment. "You write poetry, don't you?"

The minister colored. "Why, yes; a little sometimes."

"It's good poetry, ain't it? They printed some in a magazine."

The minister laughed confusedly. "Well, Miss Dole. I don't know how good poetry it may be, but they did print some in a magazine."

Betsey lay looking at him. "I never wrote none that was—good," she whispered, presently; "but I've been thinkin'—if you would jest write a few—lines about me—afterward—I've been thinkin' that mebbe my—dyin' was goin' to make me—a good subject for—poetry, if I never wrote none. If you would jest write a few lines."

The minister stood holding the sugar-bowl; he was quite pale with bewilderment and sympathy. "I'll—do the best I can, Miss Dole," he stammered.

"I'll be much obliged," said Betsey, as if the sense of grateful obligation was immortal like herself. She smiled, and the sweetness of the smile was as evident through the drawn lines of her mouth as the old red in the leaves of a withered rose. The sun was setting; a red beam flashed softly over the top of the hedge and lay along the opposite wall; then the bird in his cage began to chirp. He chirped faster and faster until he thrilled into a triumphant song.

Louisa

"I don't see what kind of ideas you've got in your head for my part." Mrs. Britton looked sharply at her daughter Louisa, but she got no response.

Louisa sat in one of the kitchen chairs close to the door. She had dropped into it when she first entered. Her hands were all brown and grimy with garden-mould; it clung to the bottom of her old dress and her coarse shoes.

Mrs. Britton, sitting opposite by the window, waited, looking at her. Suddenly Louisa's silence seemed to strike her mother's will with an electric shock; she recoiled, with an angry jerk of her head. "You don't know nothin' about it. You'd like him well enough after you was married to him," said she, as if in answer to an argument.

Louisa's face looked fairly dull; her obstinacy seemed to cast a film over it. Her eyelids were cast down; she leaned her head back against the wall.

"Sit there like a stick if you want to!" cried her mother.

Louisa got up. As she stirred, a faint earthy odor diffused itself through the room. It was like a breath from a ploughed field.

Mrs. Britton's little sallow face contracted more forcibly. "I s'pose now you're goin' back to your potater patch." said she. "Plantin' potaters out there jest like a man, for all the neighbors to see. Pretty sight, I call it."

"If they don't like it, they needn't look," returned Louisa. She spoke quite evenly. Her young back was stiff with bending over the potatoes, but she straightened it rigorously. She pulled her old hat farther over her eyes.

There was a shuffling sound outside the door and a fumble at the latch. It opened, and an old man came in, scraping his feet heavily over the threshold. He carried an old basket.

"What you got in that basket, father?" asked Mrs. Britton.

The old man looked at her. His old face had the round outlines and naïve grin of a child.

388

"Father, what you got in that basket?"

Louisa peered apprehensively into the basket. "Where did you get those potatoes, grandfather?" said she.

"Digged 'em." The old man's grin deepened. He chuckled hoarsely.

"Well, I'll give up if he ain't been an' dug up all them potaters you've been plantin'!" said Mrs. Britton.

"Yes, he has," said Louisa. "Oh, grandfather, didn't you know I'd jest planted those potatoes?"

The old man fastened his bleared blue eyes on her face, and still grinned.

"Didn't you know better, grandfather?" she asked again.

But the old man only chuckled. He was so old that he had come back into the mystery of childhood. His motives were hidden and inscrutable; his amalgamation with the human race was so much weaker.

"Land sakes! don't waste no more time talkin' to him," said Mrs. Britton. "You can't make out whether he knows what he's doin' or not. I've give it up. Father, you jest set them pertaters down, an' you come over here an' set down in the rockin'-chair; you've done about 'nough work to-day."

The old man shook his head with slow mutiny.

"Come right over here."

Louisa pulled at the basket of potatoes. "Let me have 'em, grandfather," said she. "I've got to have 'em."

The old man resisted. His grin disappeared, and he set his mouth. Mrs. Britton got up, with a determined air, and went over to him. She was a sickly, frail-looking woman, but the voice came firm, with deep bass tones, from her little lean throat.

"Now, father," said she, "you jest give her that basket, an' you walk across the room, and you set down in that rockin'-chair."

The old man looked down into her little, pale, wedge-shaped face. His grasp on the basket weakened. Louisa pulled it away, and pushed past out of the door, and the old man followed his daughter sullenly across the room to the rocking-chair.

The Brittons did not have a large potato field; they had only an acre of land in all. Louisa had planted two thirds of her potatoes; now she had to plant them all over again. She had gone in the house for a drink of water; her mother had detained her, and in the meantime the old man had undone her work. She began putting the cut potatoes back in the ground. She was careful and laborious about it. A strong wind, full of moisture, was blowing from the east. The smell of the sea was in it, although this was some miles inland. Louisa's brown calico skirt blew out in it like a sail. It beat her in the face when she raised her head.

"I've got to get these in to-day somehow," she muttered. "It'll rain to-morrow."

She worked as fast as she could, and the afternoon wore on. About five o'clock she happened to glance at the road—the potato field lay beside it—and she saw Jonathan Nye driving past with his gray horse and buggy. She turned her back to the road quickly, and listened until the rattle of the wheels died away. At six o'clock her mother looked out of the kitchen window and called her to supper.

"I'm comin' in a minute," Louisa shouted back. Then she worked faster than ever. At half-past six she went into the house, and the potatoes were all in the ground.

"Why didn't you come when I called you?" asked her mother.

"I had to get the potatoes in."

"I guess you wa'n't bound to get 'em all in to-night. It's kind of discouragin' when you work, an' get supper all ready, to have it stan' an hour, I call it. An' you've worked 'bout long enough for one day out in this damp wind, I should say."

Louisa washed her hands and face at the kitchen sink, and smoothed her hair at the little glass over it. She had wet her hair too, and made it look darker: it was quite a light brown. She brushed it in smooth straight lines back from her temples. Her whole face had a clear bright look from being exposed to the moist wind. She noticed it herself, and gave her head a little conscious turn.

When she sat down to the table her mother looked at her with admiration, which she veiled with disapproval.

"Jest look at your face," said she; "red as a beet. You'll be a pretty-lookin' sight before the summer's out, at this rate."

Louisa thought to herself that the light was not very strong, and the glass must have flattered her. She could not look as well as she had imagined. She spread some butter on her bread very sparsely. There was nothing for supper but some bread and butter and weak tea, though the old man had his dish of Indian-meal porridge. He could not eat much solid food. The porridge was covered with milk and molasses. He bent low over it, and ate large spoonfuls with loud noises. His daughter had tied a towel around his neck as she would have tied a pinafore on a child. She had also spread a towel over the tablecloth in front of him, and she watched him sharply lest he should spill his food.

"I wish I could have somethin' to eat that I could relish the way he does that porridge and molasses," said she. She had scarcely tasted anything. She sipped her weak tea laboriously.

Louisa looked across at her mother's meagre little figure in its neat old dress, at her poor small head bending over the tea-cup, showing the wide parting in the thin hair.

"Why don't you toast your bread, mother?" said she. "I'll toast it for you."

"No, I don't want it. I'd jest as soon have it this way as any. I don't want no bread, nohow. I want somethin' to rel-ish—a herrin', or a little mite of cold meat, or somethin'. I s'pose I could eat as well as anybody if I had as much as some folks have. Mis' Mitchell was sayin' the other day that she didn't believe but what they had butcher's meat up to Mis' Nye's every day in the week. She said Jonathan he went to Wolfsborough and brought home great pieces in a market-basket every week. I guess they have everything."

Louisa was not eating much herself, but now she took an-other slice of bread with a resolute air. "I guess some folks would be thankful to get this," said she.

"Yes, I s'pose we'd ought to be thankful for enough to keep us alive, anybody takes so much comfort livin'," re-turned her mother, with a tragic bitterness that sat oddly upon her, as she was so small and feeble. Her face worked and strained under the stress of emotion; her eyes were full of tears; she sipped her tea fiercely.

"There's some sugar," said Louisa. "We might have had a little cake."

The old man caught the word. "Cake?" he mumbled, with pleased inquiry, looking up, and extending his grasping old hand.

"I guess we ain't got no sugar to waste in cake," returned Mrs. Britton. "Eat your porridge, father, an' stop teasin'. There ain't no cake."

After supper Louisa cleared away the dishes; then she put on her shawl and hat.

"Where you goin'?" asked her mother.

"Down to the store."

"What for?"

"The oil's out. There wasn't enough to fill the lamps this mornin'. I ain't had a chance to get it before."

It was nearly dark. The mist was so heavy it was almost rain. Louisa went swiftly down the road with the oil-can. It was a half-mile to the store where the few staples were kept that sufficed the simple folk in this little settlement. She was gone a half-hour. When she returned, she had besides the oil-can a package under her arm. She went into the kitchen and set them down. The old man was asleep in the rocking-chair. She heard voices in the adjoining room. She frowned, and stood still, listening.

"Louisa!" called her mother. Her voice was sweet, and higher pitched than usual. She sounded the *i* in Louisa long.

"What say?"

"Come in here after you've taken your things off."

Louisa knew that Jonathan Nye was in the sitting-room. She flung off her hat and shawl. Her old dress was damp, and had still some earth stains on it; her hair was roughened by the wind, but she would not look again in the glass; she went into the sitting room just as she was.

"It's Mr. Nye, Louisa," said her mother, with effusion.

"Good-evenin', Mr. Nye," said Louisa.

Jonathan Nye half rose and extended his hand, but she did not notice it. She sat down peremptorily in a chair at the other side of the room. Jonathan had the one rocking-chair; Mrs. Britton's frail little body was poised anxiously on the hard rounded top of the carpet-covered lounge. She looked at Louisa's dress and hair, and her eyes were stony with disapproval, but her lips still smirked, and she kept her voice sweet. She pointed to a glass dish on the table.

"See what Mr. Nye has brought us over, Louisa," said she.

Louisa looked indifferently at the dish.

"It's honey," said her mother; "some of his own bees made it. Don't you want to get a dish an' taste of it? One of them little glass sauce dishes."

"No, I guess not," replied Louisa. "I never cared much about honey. Grandfather'll like it."

The smile vanished momentarily from Mrs. Britton's lips, but she recovered herself. She arose and went across the room to the china closet. Her set of china dishes was on the top shelves, the lower were filled with books and papers. "I've got somethin' to show you, Mr. Nye," said she.

This was scarcely more than a hamlet, but it was incorporated, and had its town books. She brought forth a pile of them, and laid them on the table beside Jonathan Nye. "There," said she, "I thought mebbe you'd like to look at these." She opened one and pointed to the school report. This mother could not display her daughter's accomplishments to attract a suitor, for she had none. Louisa did not own a piano or organ; she could not paint; but she had taught school acceptably for eight years—ever since she was sixteen—and in every one of the town books was testimonial to that effect, intermixed with glowing eulogy. Jonathan Nye looked soberly through the books; he was a slow reader. He was a few years older than Louisa, tall and clumsy, long-featured and long-necked. His face was a deep red with embarrassment, and it contrasted oddly with his stiff dignity of demeanor.

Mrs. Britton drew a chair close to him while he read. "You see, Louisa taught that school for eight year," said she; "an' she'd be teachin' it now if Mr. Mosely's daughter hadn't grown up an' wanted somethin' to do, an' he put her in. He was committee, you know. I dun' know as I'd ought to say so, an' I wouldn't want you to repeat it, but they do say Ida Mosely don't give very good satisfaction, an' I guess she won't have no reports like these in the town books unless her father writes 'em. See this one."

Jonathan Nye pondered over the fulsome testimony to Louisa's capability, general worth, and amiability, while she sat in sulky silence at the farther corner of the room. Once in a while her mother, after a furtive glance at Jonathan, engrossed in a town book, would look at her and gesticulate fiercely for her to come over, but she did not stir. Her eyes were dull and quiet, her mouth closely shut; she looked homely. Louisa was very pretty when pleased and animated, at other times she had a look like a closed flower. One could see no prettiness in her.

Jonathan Nye read all the school reports; then he arose heavily. "They're real good," said he. He glanced at Louisa and tried to smile; his blushes deepened.

"Now don't be in a hurry," said Mrs. Britton.

"I guess I'd better be goin'; mother's alone."

"She won't be afraid; it's jest on the edge of the evenin'."

"I don't know as she will. But I guess I'd better be goin'." He looked hesitatingly at Louisa.

She arose and stood with an indifferent air.

"You'd better set down again," said Mrs. Britton.

"No; I guess I'd better be goin'." Jonathan turned towards Louisa. "Good-evenin'," said he.

"Good-evenin'."

Mrs. Britton followed him to the door. She looked back

and beckoned imperiously to Louisa, but she stood still. "Now come again, do," Mrs. Britton said to the departing caller. "Run in any time; we're real lonesome evenin's. Father he sets an' sleeps in his chair, an' Louisa an' me often wish somebody'd drop in; folks round here ain't none too neighborly. Come in any time you happen to feel like it, an' we'll both of us be glad to see you. Tell your mother I'll send home that dish to-morrer, an' we shall have a real feast off that beautiful honey."

When Mrs. Britton had fairly shut the outer door upon Jonathan Nye, she came back into the sitting room as if her anger had a propelling power like steam upon her body.

"Now, Louisa Britton," said she, "you'd ought to be ashamed of yourself—ashamed of yourself! You've treated him like a—hog!"

"I couldn't help it."

"Couldn't help it! I guess you could treat anybody decent if you tried. I never saw such actions! I guess you needn't be afraid of him. I guess he ain't so set on you that he means to ketch you up an' run off. There's other girls in town full as good as you an' better-lookin'. Why didn't you go an' put on your other dress? Comin' into the room with that old thing on, an' your hair all in a frowse! I guess he won't want to come again."

"I hope he won't," said Louisa, under her breath. She was trembling all over.

"What say?"

"Nothin'."

"I shouldn't think you'd want to say anything, treatin' him that way, when he came over and brought all that beautiful honey! He was all dressed up, too. He had on a real nice coat—cloth jest as fine as it could be, an' it was kinder damp when he come in. Then he dressed all up to come over here this rainy night an' bring this honey." Mrs. Britton snatched the dish of honey and scudded into the kitchen with it. "Sayin' you didn't like honey after he took all that **pains to** bring it over!" said she. "I'd said I liked it if I'd lied **up hill** and down." She set the dish in the pantry. "What in creation smells so kinder strong an' smoky in here?" said she, sharply.

"I guess it's the herrin'. I got two or three down to the store."

"I'd like to know what you got herrin' for?"

"I thought maybe you'd relish 'em."

"I don't want no herrin's, now we've got this honey. But I

don't know that you've got money to throw away." She shook the old man by the stove into partial wakefulness, and steered him into his little bedroom off the kitchen. She herself slept in one off the sitting-rooms; Louisa's room was up-stairs.

Louisa lighted her candle and went to bed, her mother's scolding voice pursuing her like a wrathful spirit. She cried when she was in bed in the dark, but she soon went to sleep. She was too healthfully tired with her out-door work not to. All her young bones ached with the strain of manual labor as they had ached many a time this last year since she had lost her school.

The Brittons had been and were in sore straits. All they had in the world was this little house with the acre of land. Louisa's meagre school money had bought their food and clothing since her father died. Now it was almost starvation for them. Louisa was struggling to wrest a little sustenance from their stony acre of land, toiling like a European peasant woman, sacrificing her New England dignity. Lately she had herself split up a cord of wood which she had bought of a neighbor, paying for it in instalments with work for his wife.

"Think of a school-teacher goin' into Mis' Mitchell's house to help clean!" said her mother.

She, although she had been of poor, hard-working people all her life, with the humblest surroundings, was a born aristocrat, with that fiercest and most bigoted aristocracy which sometimes arises from independent poverty. She had the feeling of a queen for a princess of the blood about her school-teacher daughter; her working in a neighbor's kitchen was as galling and terrible to her. The projected marriage with Jonathan Nye was like a royal alliance for the good of the state. Jonathan Nye was the only eligible young man in the place; he was the largest land-owner; he had the best house. There were only himself and his mother; after her death the property would all be his. Mrs. Nye was an older woman than Mrs. Britton, who forgot her own frailty in calculating their chances of life.

"Mis' Nye is considerable over seventy," she said often to herself; "an' then Jonathan will have it all."

She saw herself installed in that large white house as reigning dowager. All the obstacle was Louisa's obstinacy, which her mother could not understand. She could see no fault in Jonathan Nye. So far as absolute approval went, she herself was in love with him. There was no more sense, to her mind, in Louisa's refusing him than there would have been in a princess refusing the fairy prince and spoiling the story.

"I'd like to know what you've got against him," she said often to Louisa.

"I ain't got anything against him."

"Why don't you treat him different, then, I want to know?"

"I don't like him." Louisa said "like" shamefacedly, for she meant love, and dared not say it.

"*Like!* Well, I don't know nothin' about such likin's as some pretend to, an' I don't want to. If I see anybody is good an' worthy, I like 'em, an' that's all there is about it."

"I don't—believe that's the way you felt about—father," said Louisa, softly, her young face flushed red.

"Yes, it was. I had some common-sense about it."

And Mrs. Britton believed it. Many hard middle-aged years lay between her and her own love-time, and nothing is so changed by distance as the realities of youth. She believed herself to have been actuated by the same calm reason in marrying young John Britton, who had had fair prospects, which she thought should actuate her daughter in marrying Jonathan Nye.

Louisa got no sympathy from her, but she persisted in her refusal. She worked harder and harder. She did not spare herself in doors or out. As the summer wore on her face grew as sunburnt as a boy's, her hands were hard and brown. When she put on her white dress to go to meeting on a Sunday there was a white ring around her neck where the sun had not touched it. Above it her face and neck showed browner. Her sleeves were rather short, and there were also white rings above her brown wrists.

"You look as if you were turnin' Injun by inches," said her mother.

Louisa, when she sat in the meeting-house, tried slyly to pull her sleeves down to the brown on her wrists; she gave a little twitch to the ruffle around her neck. Then she glanced across, and Jonathan Nye was looking at her. She thrust her hands, in their short-wristed, loose cotton gloves, as far out of the sleeves as she could; her brown wrists showed conspicuously on her white lap. She had never heard of the princess who destroyed her beauty that she might not be forced to wed the man whom she did not love, but she had something of the same feeling, although she did not have it for the sake of any tangible lover. Louisa had never seen anybody whom she would have preferred to Jonathan Nye. There was no

other marriageable young man in the place. She had only her
dreams, which she had in common with other girls.

That Sunday evening before she went to meeting her
mother took some old wide lace out of her bureau drawer.
"There," said she, "I'm goin' to sew this in your neck an'
sleeves before you put your dress on. It'll cover up a little; it's
wider than the ruffle."

"I don't want it in," said Louisa.

"I'd like to know why not? You look a fright. I was
ashamed of you this mornin'."

Louisa thrust her arms into the white dress sleeves peremptorily. Her mother did not speak to her all the way to meeting. After meeting, Jonathan Nye walked home with them,
and Louisa kept on the other side of her mother. He went
into the house and stayed an hour. Mrs. Britton entertained
him, while Louisa sat silent. When he had gone, she looked at
her daughter as if she could have used bodily force, but she
said nothing. She shot the bolt of the kitchen door noisily.
Louisa lighted her candle. The old man's loud breathing
sounded from his room; he had been put to bed for safety before they went to meeting; through the open windows sounded the loud murmur of the summer night, as if that, too, slept
heavily.

"Good-night, mother," said Louisa, as she went up-stairs;
but her mother did not answer.

The next day was very warm. This was an exceptionally
hot summer. Louisa went out early; her mother would not
ask her where she was going. She did not come home until
noon. Her face was burning; her wet dress clung to her arms
and shoulders.

"Where have you been?" asked her mother.

"Oh, I've been out in the field."

"What field?"

"Mr. Mitchell's."

"What have you been doin' out there?"

"Rakin' hay."

"Rakin' hay with the men?"

"There wasn't anybody but Mr. Mitchell and Johnny.
Don't, mother!"

Mrs. Britton had turned white. She sank into a chair. "I
can't stan' it nohow," she moaned. "All the daughter I've got."

"Don't, mother! I ain't done any harm. What harm is it?
Why can't I rake hay as well as a man? Lots of women do
such things, if nobody round here does. He's goin' to pay me

right off, and we need the money. Don't, mother!" Louisa got
a tumbler of water. "Here, mother, drink this."

Mrs. Britton pushed it away. Louisa stood looking anxiously at her. Lately her mother had grown thinner than ever;
she looked scarcely bigger than a child. Presently she got up
and went to the stove.

"Don't try to do anything, mother; let me finish getting
dinner," pleaded Louisa. She tried to take the pan of biscuits
out of her mother's hands, but she jerked it away.

The old man was sitting on the door-step, huddled up
loosely in the sun, like an old dog.

"Come, father," Mrs. Britton called, in a dry voice, "dinner's ready—what there is of it!"

The old man shuffled in, smiling.

There was nothing for dinner but the hot biscuits and tea.
The fare was daily becoming more meagre. All Louisa's little
hoard of school money was gone, and her earnings were very
uncertain and slender. Their chief dependence for food
through the summer was their garden, but that had failed
them in some respects.

One day the old man had come in radiant, with his shaking hands full of potato blossoms; his old eyes twinkled over
them like a mischievous child's. Reproaches were useless; the
little potato crop was sadly damaged. Lately, in spite of close
watching, he had picked the squash blossoms, piling them in
a yellow mass beside the kitchen door. Still, it was nearly
time for the pease and beans and beets; they would keep
them from starvation while they lasted.

But when they came, and Louisa could pick plenty of
green food every morning, there was still a difficulty: Mrs.
Britton's appetite and digestion were poor; she could not live
upon a green-vegetable diet; and the old man missed his porridge, for the meal was all gone.

One morning in August he cried at the breakfast-table like
a baby, because he wanted his porridge, and Mrs. Britton
pushed away her own plate with a despairing gesture.

"There ain't no use," said she. "I can't eat no more
garden-sauce nohow. I don't blame poor father a mite. You
ain't got no feelin' at all."

"I don't know what I can do; I've worked as hard as I
can," said Louisa, miserably.

"I know what you can do, and so do you."

"No, I don't, mother," returned Louisa, with alacrity. "He
ain't been here for two weeks now, and I saw him with my

own eyes yesterday carryin' a dish into the Moselys', and I knew 'twas honey. I think he's after Ida."

"Carryin' honey into the Moselys'? I don't believe it."

"He was; I saw him."

"Well, I don't care if he was. If you're a mind to act decent now, you can bring him round again. He was dead set on you, an' I don't believe he's changed round to that Mosely girl as quick as this."

"You don't want me to ask him to come back here, do you?"

"I want you to act decent. You can go to meetin' tonight, if you're a mind to—I sha'n't go; I ain't got strength 'nough—an' 'twouldn't hurt you none to hang back a little after meetin', and kind of edge round his way. 'Twouldn't take more'n a look."

"Mother!"

"Well, I don't care. 'Twouldn't hurt you none. It's the way more'n one girl does, whether you believe it or not. Men don't do all the courtin'—not by a long shot. 'Twon't hurt you none. You needn't look so scart."

Mrs. Britton's own face was a burning red. She looked angrily away from her daughter's honest, indignant eyes.

"I wouldn't do such a thing as that for a man I liked," said Louisa; "and I certainly sh'an't for a man I don't like."

"Then me an' your grandfather'll starve," said her mother; "that's all there is about it. We can't neither of us stan' it much longer."

"We could—"

"Could what?"

"Put a—little mortgage on the house."

Mrs. Britton faced her daughter. She trembled in every inch of her weak frame. "Put a mortgage on this house, an' by-an'-by not have a roof to cover us! Are you crazy? I tell you what 'tis, Louisa Britton, we may starve, your grandfather an' me, an' you can follow us to the graveyard over there, but there's only one way I'll ever put a mortgage on this house. If you have Jonathan Nye, I'll ask him to take a little one to tide us along an' get your weddin' things."

"Mother, I'll tell you what I'm goin' to do."

"What?"

"I am goin' to ask Uncle Solomon."

"I guess when Solomon Mears does anythin' for us you'll know it. He never forgave your father about that wood lot, an' he's hated the whole of us ever since. When I went to his wife's funeral he never answered when I spoke to him. I guess if you go to him you'll take it out in goin'."

Louisa said nothing more. She began clearing away the breakfast dishes and setting the house to rights. Her mother was actually so weak that she could scarcely stand, and she recognized it. She had settled into the rocking-chair, and leaned her head back. Her face looked pale and sharp against the dark calico cover.

When the house was in order, Louisa stole up-stairs to her own chamber. She put on her clean old blue muslin and her hat, then she went slyly down and out the front way.

It was seven miles to her uncle Solomon Mears's, and she had made up her mind to walk them. She walked quite swiftly until the house windows were out of sight, then she slackened her pace a little. It was one of the fiercest dog-days. A damp heat settled heavily down upon the earth; the sun scalded.

At the foot of the hill Louisa passed a house where one of her girl acquaintances lived. She was going in the gate with a pan of early apples. "Hullo, Louisa," she called.

"Hullo, Vinnie."

"Where you goin'?"

"Oh, I'm goin' a little way."

"Ain't it awful hot? Say, Louisa, do you know Ida Mosely's cuttin' you out?"

"She's welcome."

The other girl, who was larger and stouter than Louisa, with a sallow, unhealthy face, looked at her curiously. "I don't see why you wouldn't have him," said she. "I should have thought you'd jumped at the chance."

"Should you if you didn't like him, I'd like to know?"

"I'd like him if he had such a nice house and as much money as Jonathan Nye," returned the other girl.

She offered Louisa some apples, and she went along the road eating them. She herself had scarcely tasted food that day.

It was about nine o'clock; she had risen early. She calculated how many hours it would take her to walk the seven miles. She walked as fast as she could to hold out. The heat seemed to increase as the sun stood higher. She had walked about three miles when she heard wheels behind her. Presently a team stopped at her side.

"Good-mornin'," said an embarrassed voice.

She looked around. It was Jonathan Nye, with his gray horse and light wagon.

"Good-mornin'," said she.

"Goin' far?"

"A little ways."

"Won't you—ride?"

"No, thank you. I guess I'd rather walk."

Jonathan Nye nodded, made an inarticulate noise in his throat, and drove on. Louisa watched the wagon bowling lightly along. The dust flew back. She took out her handkerchief and wiped her dripping face.

It was about noon when she came in sight of her uncle Solomon Mears's house in Wolfsborough. It stood far back from the road, behind a green expanse of untrodden yard. The blinds on the great square front were all closed; it looked as if everybody were away. Louisa went around to the side door. It stood wide open. There was a thin blue cloud of tobacco smoke issuing from it. Solomon Mears sat there in the large old kitchen smoking his pipe. On the table near him was an empty bowl; he had just eaten his dinner of bread and milk. He got his own dinner, for he had lived alone since his wife died. He looked at Louisa. Evidently he did not recognize her.

"How do you do, Uncle Solomon?" said Louisa.

"Oh, it's John Britton's daughter! How d'ye do?"

He took his pipe out of his mouth long enough to speak, then replaced it. His eyes, sharp under their shaggy brows, were fixed on Louisa; his broad bristling face had a look of stolid rebuff like an ox; his stout figure, in his soiled farmer dress, surged over his chair. He sat full in the doorway. Louisa standing before him, the perspiration trickling over her burning face, set forth her case with a certain dignity. This old man was her mother's nearest relative. He had property and to spare. Should she survive him, it would be hers, unless willed away. She, with her unsophisticated sense of justice, had a feeling that he ought to help her.

The old man listened. When she stopped speaking he took the pipe out of his mouth slowly, and stared gloomily past her at his hay field, where the grass was now a green stubble.

"I ain't got no money I can spare jest now," said he. "I s'pose you know your father cheated me out of consider'ble once?"

"We don't care so much about money, if you have got

something you could spare to—eat. We ain't got anything but garden-stuff."

Solomon Mears still frowned past her at the hay field. Presently he arose slowly and went across the kitchen. Louisa sat down on the door-step and waited. Her uncle was gone quite a while. She, too, stared over at the field, which seemed to undulate like a lake in the hot light.

"Here's some things you can take, if you want 'em," said her uncle, at her back.

She got up quickly. He pointed grimly to the kitchen table. He was a deacon, an orthodox believer; he recognized the claims of the poor, but he gave alms as a soldier might yield up his sword. Benevolence was the result of warfare with his own conscience.

On the table lay a ham, a bag of meal, one of flour, and a basket of eggs.

"I'm afraid I can't carry 'em all," said Louisa.

"Leave what you can't then." Solomon caught up his hat and went out. He muttered something about not spending any more time as he went.

Louisa stood looking at the packages. It was utterly impossible for her to carry them all at once. She heard her uncle shout to some oxen he was turning out of the barn. She took up the bag of meal and the basket of eggs and carried them out to the gate; then she returned, got the flour and ham, and went with them to a point beyond. Then she returned for the meal and eggs, and carried them past the others. In that way she traversed the seven miles home. The heat increased. She had eaten nothing since morning but the apples that her friend had given her. Her head was swimming, but she kept on. Her resolution was as immovable under the power of the sun as a rock. Once in a while she rested for a moment under a tree, but she soon arose and went on. It was like a pilgrimage, and the Mecca at the end of the burning, desert-like road was her own maiden independence.

It was after eight o'clock when she reached home. Her mother stood in the doorway watching for her, straining her eyes in the dusk.

"For goodness sake, Louisa Britton! where have you been?" she began; but Louisa laid the meal and eggs down on the step.

"I've got to go back a little ways," she panted.

When she returned with the flour and ham, she could hardly get into the house. She laid them on the kitcen table, where her mother had put the other parcels, and sank into a chair.

"Is this the way you've brought all these things home?" asked her mother.

Louisa nodded.

"All the way from Uncle Solomon's?"

"Yes."

Her mother went to her and took her hat off. "It's a mercy if you ain't got a sunstroke," said she, with a sharp tenderness. "I've got somethin' to tell you. What do you s'pose has happened? Mr. Mosely has been here, an' he wants you to take the school again when it opens next week. He says Ida ain't very well, but I guess that ain't it. They think she's goin' to get somebody. Mis' Mitchell says so. She's been in. She says he's carryin' things over there the whole time, but she don't b'lieve there's anything settled yet. She says they feel so sure of it they're goin' to have Ida give the school up. I told her I thought Ida would make him a good wife, an' she was easier suited than some girls. What do you s'pose Mis' Mitchell says? She says old Mis' Nye told her that there was one thing about it: if Jonathan had you, he wa'n't goin' to have me an' father hitched on to him; he'd look out for that. I told Mis' Mitchell that I guess there wa'n't none of us willin' to hitch, you nor anybody else. I hope she'll tell Mis' Nye. Now I'm a-goin' to turn you out a tumbler of milk— Mis' Mitchell she brought over a whole pitcherful; says she's got more'n they can use—they ain't got no pig now—an' then you go an' lay down on the sittin'-room lounge, an' cool off; an' I'll stir up some porridge for supper, an' boil some eggs. Father'll be tickled to death. Go right in there. I'm dreadful afraid you'll be sick. I never heard of anybody doin' such a thing as you have."

Louisa drank the milk and crept into the sitting-room. It was warm and close there, so she opened the front door and sat down on the step. The twilight was deep, but there was a clear yellow glow in the west. One great star had come out in the midst of it. A dewy coolness was spreading over everything. The air was full of bird calls and children's voices. Now and then there was a shout of laughter. Louisa leaned her head against the door-post.

The house was quite near the road. Some one passed—a man carrying a basket. Louisa glanced at him, and recognized Jonathan Nye by his gait. He kept on down the road toward the Moselys', and Louisa turned again from him to her sweet, mysterious, girlish dreams.

A Church Mouse

✠

"I never heard of a woman's bein' saxton."

"I dun' know what difference that makes; I don't see why they shouldn't have women saxtons as well as men saxtons, for my part, nor nobody else neither. They'd keep dusted 'nough sight cleaner. I've seen the dust layin' on my pew thick enough to write my name in a good many times, an' ain't said nothin' about it. An' I ain't goin' to say nothin' now again Joe Sowen, now he's dead an' gone. He did jest as well as most men do. Men git in a good many places where they don't belong, an' where they set as awkward as a cow on a hen-roost, jest because they push in ahead of women. I ain't blamin' 'em; I s'pose if I could push in I should, jest the same way. But there ain't no reason that I can see, nor nobody else neither, why a woman shouldn't be saxton."

Hetty Fifield stood in the rowen hay-field before Caleb Gale. He was a deacon, the chairman of the selectmen, and the rich and influential man of the village. One looking at him would not have guessed it. There was nothing imposing about his lumbering figure in his calico shirt and baggy trousers. However, his large face, red and moist with perspiration, scanned the distant horizon with a stiff and reserved air; he did not look at Hetty.

"How'd you go to work to ring the bell?" said he. "It would have to be tolled, too, if anybody died."

"I'd jest as lief ring that little meetin'-house bell as to stan' out here an' jingle a cow-bell," said Hetty; "an' as for tollin', I'd jest as soon toll the bell for Methusaleh, if he was livin' here! I'd laugh if I ain't got strength 'nough for that."

"It takes a kind of a knack."

"If I ain't got as much knack as old Joe Sowen ever had, I'll give up the ship."

"You couldn't tend the fires."

"Couldn't tend the fires—when I've cut an' carried in all

the wood I've burned for forty year! Couldn't keep the fires
a-goin' in them two little wood-stoves!"

"It's consider'ble work to sweep the meetin'-house."

"I guess I've done 'bout as much work as to sweep that
little meetin'-house, I ruther guess I have."

"There's one thing you ain't thought of."

"What's that?"

"Where'd you live? All old Sowen got for bein' saxton was
twenty dollar a year, an' we couldn't pay a woman so much
as that. You wouldn't have enough to pay for your livin' anywheres."

"Where am I goin' to live whether I'm saxton or not?"

Caleb Gale was silent.

There was a wind blowing, the rowen hay drifted round
Hetty like a brown-green sea touched with ripples of blue and
gold by the asters and golden-rod. She stood in the midst of it
like a May-weed that had gathered a slender toughness
through the long summer; her brown cotton gown clung
about her like a wilting leaf, outlining her harsh little form.
She was as sallow as a squaw, and she had pretty black eyes;
they were bright, although she was old. She kept them fixed
upon Caleb. Suddenly she raised herself upon her toes; the
wind caught her dress and made it blow out; her eyes flashed.
"I'll tell you where I'm goin' to live," said she. *"I'm goin' to
live in the meetin'-house."*

Caleb looked at her. *"Goin' to live in the meetin'-house!"*

"Yes, I be."

"Live in the meetin'-house!"

"I'd like to know why not."

"Why—you couldn't—live in the meetin'-house. You're
crazy."

Caleb flung out the rake which he was holding, and drew it
in full of rowen. Hetty moved around in front of him, he
raked imperturbably; she moved again right in the path of
the rake, then he stopped. "There ain't no sense in such talk."

"All I want is jest the east corner of the back gall'ry, where
the chimbly goes up. I'll set up my cookin'-stove there, an'
my bed, an' I'll curtain it off with my sunflower quilt, to keep
off the wind."

"A cookin'-stove an' a bed in the meetin'-house!"

"Mis' Grout she give me that cookin'-stove, an' that bed
I've allers slept on, before she died. She give 'em to me before Mary Anne Thomas, an' I moved 'em out. They air settin' out in the yard now, an' if it rains that stove an' that bed

will be spoilt. It looks some like rain now. I guess you'd better give me the meetin'-house key right off."

"You don't think you can move that cookin'-stove an' that bed into the meetin'-house—I ain't goin' to stop to hear such talk."

"My worsted-work, all my mottoes I've done, an' my wool flowers, air out there in the yard."

Caleb raked. Hetty kept standing herself about until he was forced to stop, or gather her in with the rowen hay. He looked straight at her, and scowled; the perspiration trickled down his cheeks. "If I go up to the house can Mis' Gale git me the key to the meetin'-house?" said Hetty.

"No, she can't."

"Be you goin' up before long?"

"No, I ain't." Suddenly Caleb's voice changed: it had been full of stubborn vexation, now it was blandly argumentative. "Don't you see it ain't no use talkin' such nonsense, Hetty? You'd better go right along, an' make up your mind it ain't to be thought of."

"Where be I goin' to-night, then?"

"To-night?"

"Yes; where be I a-goin'?"

"Ain't you got any place to go to?"

"Where do you s'pose I've got any place? Them folks air movin' into Mis' Grout's house, an' they as good as told me to clear out. I ain't got no folks to take me in. I dun' know where I'm goin'; mebbe I can go to your house?"

Caleb gave a start. "We've got company to home," said he, hastily. "I'm 'fraid Mis' Gale wouldn't think it was convenient."

Hetty laughed. "Most everybody in the town has got company," said she.

Caleb dug his rake into the ground as if it were a hoe, then he leaned on it, and stared at the horizon. There was a fringe of yellow birches on the edge of the hay-field; beyond them was a low range of misty blue hills. "You ain't got no place to go to, then?"

"I dun' know of any. There ain't no poor-house here, an' I ain't got no folks."

Caleb stood like a statue. Some crows flew cawing over the field. Hetty waited. "I s'pose that key is where Mis' Gale can find it?" she said, finally.

Caleb turned and threw out his rake with a jerk. "She knows where 'tis; it's hangin' up behind the settin'-room door.

I s'pose you can stay there to-night, as long as you ain't got no other place. We shall have to see what can be done."

Hetty scuttled off across the field. "You mustn't take no stove nor bed into the meetin'-house," Caleb called after her; "we can't have that, nohow."

Hetty went on as if she did not hear.

The golden-rod at the sides of the road was turning brown; the asters were in their prime, blue and white ones; here and there were rows of thistles with white tops. The dust was thick; Hetty, when she emerged from Caleb's house, trotted along in a cloud of it. She did not look to the right or left, she kept her small eager face fixed straight ahead, and moved forward like some little animal with the purpose to which it was born strong within it.

Presently she came to a large cottage-house on the right of the road; there she stopped. The front yard was full of furniture, tables and chairs standing among the dahlias and clumps of marigolds. Hetty leaned over the fence at one corner of the yard, and inspected a little knot of household goods set aside from the others. There were a small cooking-stove, a hair trunk, a yellow bedstead stacked up against the fence, and a pile of bedding. Some children in the yard stood in a group and eyed Hetty. A woman appeared in the door—she was small, there was a black smutch on her face, which was haggard with fatigue, and she scowled in the sun as she looked over at Hetty. "Well, got a place to stay in?" said she, in an unexpectedly deep voice.

"Yes, I guess so," replied Hetty.

"I dun' know how in the world I can have you. All the beds will be full—I expect his mother some to-night, an' I'm dreadful stirred up anyhow."

"Everybody's havin' company; I never see anything like it," Hetty's voice was inscrutable. The other woman looked sharply at her.

"You've got a place, ain't you?" she asked, doubtfully.

"Yes, I have."

At the left of this house, quite back from the road, was a little unpainted cottage, hardly more than a hut. There was smoke coming out of the chimney, and a tall youth lounged in the door. Hetty, with the woman and children staring after her, struck out across the field in the little footpath towards the cottage. "I wonder if she's goin' to stay there?" the woman muttered, meditating.

The youth did not see Hetty until she was quite near him,

then he aroused suddenly as if from sleep, and tried to slink off around the cottage. But Hetty called after him. "Sammy," she cried, "Sammy, come back here, I want you!"

"What d'ye want?"

"Come back here!"

The youth lounged back sulkily, and a tall woman came to the door. She bent out of it anxiously to hear Hetty.

"I want you to come an' help me move my stove an' things," said Hetty.

"Where to?"

"Into the meetin'-house."

"The meetin'-house?"

"Yes, the meetin'-house."

The woman in the door had sodden hands; behind her arose the steam of a wash-tub. She and the youth stared at Hetty, but surprise was too strong an emotion for them to grasp firmly.

"I want Sammy to come right over an' help me," said Hetty.

"He ain't strong enough to move a stove," said the woman.

"Ain't strong enough!"

"He's apt to git lame."

"Most folks are. Guess I've got lame. Come right along, Sammy!"

"He ain't able to lift much."

"I s'pose he's able to be lifted, ain't he?"

"I dun' know what you mean."

"The stove don't weigh nothin'," said Hetty; "I could carry it myself if I could git hold of it. Come, Sammy."

Hetty turned down the path, and the youth moved a little way after her, as if perforce. Then he stopped, and cast an appealing glance back at his mother. Her face was distressed. "Oh, Sammy, I'm afraid you'll git sick," said she.

"No, he ain't goin' to git sick," said Hetty. "Come, Sammy." And Sammy followed her down the path.

It was four o'clock then. At dusk Hetty had her gay sun-flower quilt curtaining off the chimney-corner of the church gallery; her stove and little bedstead were set up, and she had entered upon a life which endured successfully for three months. All that time a storm brewed; then it broke; but Hetty sailed in her own course for the three months.

It was on a Saturday that she took up her habitation in the meeting-house. The next morning, when the boy who had been supplying the dead sexton's place came and shook the door, Hetty was prompt on the other side. "Deacon Gale said for you to let me in so I could ring the bell," called the boy.

"Go away," responded Hetty. "I'm goin' to ring the bell; I'm saxton."

Hetty rang the bell with vigor, but she made a wild, irregular jangle at first; at the last it was better. The village people said to each other that a new hand was ringing. Only a few knew that Hetty was in the meeting-house. When the congregation had assembled, and saw that gaudy tent pitched in the house of the Lord, and the resolute little pilgrim at the door of it, there was a commotion. The farmers and their wives were stirred out of their Sabbath decorum. After the service was over, Hetty, sitting in a pew corner of the gallery, her little face dark and watchful against the flaming background of her quilt, saw the people below gathering in groups, whispering, and looking at her.

Presently the minister, Caleb Gale, and the other deacon came up the gallery stairs. Hetty sat stiffly erect. Caleb Gale went up to the sunflower quilt, slipped it aside, and looked in. He turned to Hetty with a frown. To-day his dignity was supported by important witnesses. "Did you bring that stove an' bedstead here?"

Hetty nodded.

"What made you do such a thing?"

"What was I goin' to do if I didn't? How's a woman as old as me goin' to sleep in a pew, an' go without a cup of tea?"

The men looked at each other. They withdrew to another corner of the gallery and conferred in low tones; then they went down-stairs and out of the church. Hetty smiled when she heard the door shut. When one is hard pressed, one, however simple, gets wisdom as to vantage-points. Hetty comprehended hers perfectly. She was the propounder of a problem; as long as it was unguessed, she was sure of her foothold as propounder. This little village in which she had lived all her life had removed the shelter from her head; she being penniless, it was beholden to provide her another; she asked it what. When the old woman with whom she had lived died, the town promptly seized the estate for taxes—none had been paid for years. Hetty had not laid up a cent; indeed, for the most of the time she had received no wages. There had been no money in the house; all she had gotten for her labor for a sickly, impecunious old woman was a frugal board. When the old woman died, Hetty gathered in the few household articles for which she had stipulated, and made no complaint.

She walked out of the house when the new tenants came in; all she asked was, "What are you going to do with me?" This little settlement of narrow-minded, prosperous farmers, however hard a task charity might be to them, could not turn an old woman out into the fields and highways to seek for food as they would a Jersey cow. They had their Puritan consciences, and her note of distress would sound louder in their ears than the Jersey's bell echoing down the valley in the stillest night. But the question as to Hetty Fifield's disposal was a hard one to answer. There was no almshouse in the village, and no private family was willing to take her in. Hetty was strong and capable; although she was old, she could well have paid for her food and shelter by her labor; but this could not secure her an entrance even among this hard-working and thrifty people, who would ordinarily grasp quickly enough at service without wage in dollars and cents. Hetty had somehow gotten for herself an unfortunate name in the village. She was held in the light of a long-thorned brier among the beanpoles, or a fierce little animal with claws and teeth bared. People were afraid to take her into their families; she had the reputation of always taking her own way, and never heeding the voice of authority. "I'd take her in an' have her give me a lift with the work," said one sickly farmer's wife; "but, near's I can find out, I couldn't never be sure that I'd get molasses in the beans, nor saleratus in my sour-milk cakes, if she took a notion not to put it in. I don't dare to risk it."

Stories were about concerning Hetty's authority over the old woman with whom she had lived. "Old Mis' Grout never dared to say her soul was her own," people said. Then Hetty's sharp, sarcastic sayings were repeated; the justice of them made them sting. People did not want a tongue like that in their homes.

Hetty as a church sexton was directly opposed to all their ideas of church decorum and propriety in general; her pitching her tent in the Lord's house was almost sacrilege; but what could they do? Hetty jangled the Sabbath bells for the three months; once she tolled the bell for an old man, and it seemed by the sound of the bell as if his long, calm years had swung by in a weak delirium; but people bore it. She swept and dusted the little meeting-house, and she garnished the walls with her treasures of worsted-work. The neatness and the garniture went far to quiet the dissatisfaction of the people. They had a crude taste. Hetty's skill in fancy-work was quite celebrated. Her wool flowers were much talked of, and young girls tried to copy them. So these wreaths and clusters of red and blue and yellow wool roses and lilies hung as acceptably between the meeting-house windows as pictures of saints in a cathedral.

Hetty hung a worsted motto over the pulpit; on it she set her chiefest treasure of art, a white wax cross with an ivy vine trailing over it, all covered with silver frost-work. Hetty always surveyed this cross with a species of awe; she felt the irresponsibility and amazement of a genius at his own work.

When she set it on the pulpit, no queen casting her rich robes and her jewels upon a shrine could have surpassed her in generous enthusiasm. "I guess when they see that they won't say no more," she said.

But the people, although they shared Hetty's admiration for the cross, were doubtful. They, looking at it, had a double vision of a little wax Virgin upon an altar. They wondered if it savored of popery. But the cross remained, and the minister was mindful not to jostle it in his gestures.

It was three months from the time Hetty took up her abode in the church, and a week before Christmas, when the problem was solved. Hetty herself precipitated the solution. She prepared a boiled dish in the meeting-house, upon a Saturday, and the next day the odors of turnip and cabbage were strong in the senses of the worshippers. They sniffed and looked at one another. This superseding the legitimate savor of the sanctuary, the fragrance of peppermint lozenges and wintergreen, the breath of Sunday clothes, by the homely week-day odors of kitchen vegetables, was too much for the sensibilities of the people. They looked indignantly around at Hetty, sitting before her sunflower hanging, comfortable from her good dinner of the day before, radiant with the consciousness of a great plateful of cold vegetables in her tent for her Sabbath dinner.

Poor Hetty had not many comfortable dinners. The selectmen doled out a small weekly sum to her, which she took with dignity as being her hire; then she had a mild forage in the neighbors' cellars and kitchens, of poor apples and stale bread and pie, paying for it in teaching her art of worsted-work to the daughters. Her Saturday's dinner had been a banquet to her: she had actually bought a piece of pork to boil with the vegetables; somebody had given her a nice little cabbage and some turnips, without a thought of the limitations of her housekeeping. Hetty herself had not a thought. She made the fires as usual that Sunday morning; the meeting-house was very clean, there was not a speck of dust any-where, the wax cross on the pulpit glistened in a sunbeam slanting through the house. Hetty, sitting in the gallery, thought innocently how nice it looked.

After the meeting, Caleb Gale approached the other deacon. "Somethin's got to be done," said he. And the other deacon nodded. He had not smelt the cabbage until his wife nudged him and mentioned it; neither had Caleb Gale.

In the afternoon of the next Thursday, Caleb and the other two selectmen waited upon Hetty in her tabernacle. They stumped up the gallery stairs, and Hetty emerged from be-hind the quilt and stood looking at them scared and defiant. The three men nodded stiffly; there was a pause; Caleb Gale motioned meaningly to one of the others, who shook his head; finally he himself had to speak. "I'm 'fraid you find it pretty cold here, don't you, Hetty?" said he.

"No, thank ye; it's very comfortable," replied Hetty, polite and wary.

"It ain't very convenient for you to do your cookin' here, I guess."

"It's jest as convenient as I want. I don't find no fault."

"I guess it's rayther lonesome here nights, ain't it?"

"I'd 'nough sight ruther be alone than have comp'ny, any day."

"It ain't fit for an old woman like you to be livin' alone here this way."

"Well, I dun' know of anything that's any fitter; mebbe you do."

Caleb looked appealingly at his companions; they stood stiff and irresponsive. Hetty's eyes were sharp and watchful upon them all.

"Well, Hetty," said Caleb, "we've found a nice, comfort-able place for you, an' I guess you'd better pack up your things, an' I'll carry you right over there." Caleb stepped back a little closer to the other men. Hetty, small and trem-bling and helpless before them, looked vicious. She was like a little animal driven from its cover, for whom there is nothing left but desperate warfare and death.

"Where to?" asked Hetty. Her voice shrilled up into a squeak.

Caleb hesitated. He looked again at the other selectmen. There was a solemn, far-away expression upon their faces. "Well," said he, "Mis' Radway wants to git somebody, an'—"

"You ain't goin' to take me to that woman's!"

"You'd be real comfortable—"

"I ain't goin'."

"Now, why not, I'd like to know?"

"I don't like Susan Radway, hain't never liked her, an' I ain't goin' to live with her."

"Mis' Radway's a good Christian woman. You hadn't ought to speak that way about her."

"You know what Susan Radway is, jest as well's I do; an' everybody else does too. I ain't goin' a step, an' you might jest as well make up your mind to it."

Then Hetty seated herself in the corner of the pew nearest her tent, and folded her hands in her lap. She looked over at the pulpit as if she were listening to preaching. She panted, and her eyes glittered, but she had an immovable air.

"Now, Hetty, you've got sense enough to know you can't stay here," said Caleb. "You'd better put on your bonnet, an' come right along before dark. You'll have a nice ride."

Hetty made no response.

The three men stood looking at her. "Come, Hetty," said Caleb, feebly; and another selectman spoke. "Yes, you'd better come," he said, in a mild voice.

Hetty continued to stare at the pulpit.

The three men withdrew a little and conferred. They did not know how to act. This was a new emergency in their simple, even lives. They were not constables; these three steady, sober old men did not want to drag an old woman by main force out of the meeting-house, and thrust her into Caleb Gale's buggy as if it were a police wagon.

Finally Caleb brightened. "I'll go over an' git mother," said he. He started with a brisk air, and went down the gallery stairs; the others followed. They took their stand in the meeting-house yard, and Caleb got into his buggy and gathered up the reins. The wind blew cold over the hill. "Hadn't you better go inside and wait out of the wind?" said Caleb.

"I guess we'll wait out here," replied one; and the other nodded.

"Well, I sha'n't be gone long," said Caleb. "Mother'll know how to manage her." He drove carefully down the hill; his buggy wings rattled in the wind. The other men pulled up their coat collars, and met the blast stubbornly.

"Pretty ticklish piece of business to tackle," said one, in a low grunt.

"That's so," assented the other. Then they were silent, and waited for Caleb. Once in a while they stamped their feet and slapped their mittened hands. They did not hear Hetty slip the bolt and turn the key of the meeting-house door, nor see her peeping at them from a gallery window.

Caleb returned in twenty minutes; he had not far to go. His wife, stout and handsome and full of vigor, sat beside him in the buggy. Her face was red with the cold wind; her thick cashmere shawl was pinned tightly over her broad bosom. "Has she come down yet?" she called out, in an imperious way.

The two selectmen shook their heads. Caleb kept the horse quiet while his wife got heavily and briskly out of the buggy. She went up the meeting-house steps, and reached out confidently to open the door. Then she drew back and looked around. "Why," said she, "the door's locked; she's locked the door. I call this pretty work!"

She turned again quite fiercely, and began beating on the door. "Hetty!" she called; "Hetty, Hetty Fifield! Let me in! What have you locked this door for?"

She stopped and turned to her husband.

"Don't you s'pose the barn key would unlock it?" she asked.

"I don't b'lieve 'twould."

"Well, you'd better go home and fetch it."

Caleb again drove down the hill, and the other men searched their pockets for keys. One had the key of his cornhouse, and produced it hopefully; but it would not unlock the meeting-house door.

A crowd seldom gathered in the little village for anything short of a fire; but to-day in a short time quite a number of people stood on the meeting-house hill, and more kept coming. When Caleb Gale returned with the barn key his daughter, a tall, pretty young girl, sat beside him, her little face alert and smiling in her red hood. The other selectmen's wives toiled eagerly up the hill, with a young daughter of one of them speeding on ahead. Then the two young girls stood close to each other and watched the proceedings. Key after key was tried; men brought all the large keys they could find, running importantly up the hill, but none would unlock the meeting-house door. After Caleb had tried the last available key, stooping and screwing it anxiously, he turned around. "There ain't no use in it, any way," said he; "most likely the door's bolted."

"You don't mean there's a bolt on that door?" cried his wife.

"Yes, there is."

"Then you might jest as well have tore 'round for hen's feathers as keys. Of course she's bolted it if she's got any wit, an' I guess she's got most as much as some of you men that have been bringin' keys. Try the windows."

But the windows were fast. Hetty had made her sacred castle impregnable except to violence. Either the door would have to be forced or a window broken to gain an entrance.

The people conferred with one another. Some were for retreating, and leaving Hetty in peaceful possession until time drove her to capitulate. "She'll open it to-morrow," they said. Others were for extreme measures, and their impetuosity gave them the lead. The project of forcing the door was urged; one man started for a crow-bar.

"They are a parcel of fools to do such a thing," said Caleb Gale's wife to another woman. "Spoil that good door! They'd better leave the poor thing alone till to-morrow. I dun' know what's goin' to be done with her when they git in. I ain't goin' to have father draggin' her over to Mis' Radway's by the hair of her head."

"That's jest what I say," returned the other woman.

Mrs. Gale went up to Caleb and nudged him. "Don't you let them break that door down, father," said she.

"Well, well, we'll see," Caleb replied. He moved away a little; his wife's voice had been drowned out lately by a masculine clamor, and he took advantage of it.

All the people talked at once; the wind was keen, and all their garments fluttered; the two young girls had their arms around each other under their shawls; the man with the crow-bar came stalking up the hill.

"Don't you let them break down that door, father," said Mrs. Gale.

"Well, well," grunted Caleb.

Regardless of remonstrances, the man set the crow-bar against the door; suddenly there was a cry, "There she is!" Everybody looked up. There was Hetty looking out of a gallery window.

Everybody was still. Hetty began to speak. Her dark old face, peering out of the window, looked ghastly; the wind blew her poor gray locks over it. She extended her little wrinkled hands. "Jest let me say one word," said she; "jest one word." Her voice shook. All her coolness was gone. The magnitude of her last act of defiance had caused it to react upon herself like an overloaded gun.

"Say all you want to, Hetty, an' don't be afraid," Mrs. Gale called out.

"I jest want to say a word," repeated Hetty. "Can't I stay here, nohow? It don't seem as if I could go to Mis' Radway's. I ain't nothin' again' her. I s'pose she's a good woman, but she's used to havin' her own way, and I've been livin' all my life with them that was, an' I've had to fight to keep a footin' on the earth, an' now I'm gittin' too old for't. If I can jest stay here in the meetin'-house, I won't ask for nothin' any better. I sha'n't need much to keep me, I wa'n't never a hefty eater; an' I'll keep the meetin'-house jest as clean as I know how. An' I'll make some more of them wool flowers. I'll make a wreath to go the whole length of the gallery, if I can git wool 'nough. Won't you let me stay? I ain't complainin', but I've always had a dretful hard time; seems as if now I might take a little comfort the last of it, if I could stay here. I can't go to Mis' Radway's nohow." Hetty covered her face with her hands; her words ended in a weak wail.

Mrs. Gale's voice rang out clear and strong and irrepressible. "Of course you can stay in the meetin'-house," said she; "I should laugh if you couldn't. Don't you worry another mite about it. You sha'n't go one step to Mis' Radway's; you couldn't live a day with her. You can stay jest where you are; you've kept the meetin'-house enough sight cleaner than I've ever seen it. Don't you worry another mite, Hetty."

Mrs. Gale stood majestically, and looked defiantly around; tears were in her eyes. Another woman edged up to her. "Why couldn't she have that little room side of the pulpit, where the minister hangs his hat?" she whispered. "He could hang it somewhere else."

"Course she could," responded Mrs. Gale, with alacrity, "jest as well as not. The minister can have a hook in the entry for his hat. She can have her stove an' her bed in there, an' be jest as comfortable as can be. I should laugh if she couldn't. Don't you worry, Hetty."

The crowd gradually dispersed, sending out stragglers down the hill until it was all gone. Mrs. Gale waited until the last, sitting in the buggy in state. When her husband gathered up the reins, she called back to Hetty: "Don't you worry one mite more about it, Hetty. I'm comin' up to see you in the mornin'!"

It was almost dusk when Caleb drove down the hill; he

was the last of the besiegers, and the feeble garrison was left triumphant.

The next day but one was Christmas, the next night Christmas Eve. On Christmas Eve Hetty had reached what to her was the flood-tide of peace and prosperity. Established in that small, lofty room, with her bed and her stove, with gifts of a rocking-chair and table, and a goodly store of food, with no one to molest or disturb her, she had nothing to wish for on earth. All her small desires were satisfied. No happy girl could have a merrier Christmas than this old woman with her little measure full of gifts. That Christmas Eve Hetty lay down under her sunflower quilt, and all her old hardships looked dim in the distance, like far-away hills, while her new joys came out like stars.

She was a light sleeper; the next morning she was up early. She opened the meeting-house door and stood looking out. The smoke from the village chimneys had not yet begun to rise blue and rosy in the clear frosty air. There was no snow, but over the hill there was a silver rime of frost; the bare branches of the trees glistened. Hetty stood looking. "Why, it's Christmas mornin'," she said, suddenly. Christmas had never been a gala-day to this old woman. Christmas had not been kept at all in this New England village when she was young. She was led to think of it now only in connection with the dinner Mrs. Gale had promised to bring her to-day.

Mrs. Gale had told her she should have some of her Christmas dinner, some turkey and plum-pudding. She called it to mind now with a thrill of delight. Her face grew momentarily more radiant. There was a certain beauty in it. A finer morning light than that which lit up the wintry earth seemed to shine over the furrows of her old face. "I'm goin' to have turkey an' plum-puddin' today," said she; "it's Christmas." Suddenly she started, and went into the meeting-house, straight up the gallery stairs. There in a clear space hung the bell-rope. Hetty grasped it. Never before had a Christmas bell been rung in this village; Hetty had probably never heard of Christmas bells. She was prompted by pure artless enthusiasm and grateful happiness. Her old arms pulled on the rope with a will, the bell sounded peal on peal. Down in the village, curtains rolled up, letting in the morning light, happy faces looked out of the windows. Hetty had awakened the whole village to Christmas Day.

The Revolt of "Mother"

✥

"Father!"

"What is it?"

"What are them men diggin' over there in the field for?"

There was a sudden dropping and enlarging of the lower part of the old man's face, as if some heavy weight had settled therein; he shut his mouth tight, and went on harnessing the great bay mare. He hustled the collar on to her neck with a jerk.

"Father!"

The old man slapped the saddle upon the mare's back.

"Look here, father, I want to know what them men are diggin' over in the field for, an' I'm goin' to know."

"I wish you'd go into the house, mother, an' 'tend to your own affairs," the old man said then. He ran his words together, and his speech was almost as inarticulate as a growl.

But the woman understood; it was her most native tongue. "I ain't goin' into the house till you tell me what them men are doin' over there in the field," said she.

Then she stood waiting. She was a small woman, short and straight-waisted like a child in her brown cotton gown. Her forehead was mild and benevolent between the smooth curves of gray hair; there were meek downward lines about her nose and mouth; but her eyes, fixed upon the old man, looked as if the meekness had been the result of her own will, never of the will of another.

They were in the barn, standing before the wide open doors. The spring air, full of the smell of growing grass and unseen blossoms, came in their faces. The deep yard in front was littered with farm wagons and piles of wood; on the edges, close to the fence and the house, the grass was a vivid green, and there were some dandelions.

The old man glanced doggedly at his wife as he tightened the last buckles on the harness. She looked as immovable to him as one of the rocks in his pasture-land, bound to the earth with generations of blackberry vines. He slapped the reins over the horse, and started forth from the barn.

"*Father!*" said she.

The old man pulled up. "What is it?"

"I want to know what them men are diggin' over there in that field for."

"They're diggin' a cellar, I s'pose, if you've got to know."

"A cellar for what?"

"A barn."

"A barn? You ain't goin' to build a barn over there where we was goin' to have a house, father?"

The old man said not another word. He hurried the horse into the farm wagon, and clattered out of the yard, jouncing as sturdily on his seat as a boy.

The woman stood a moment looking after him, then she went out of the barn across a corner of the yard to the house. The house, standing at right angles with the great barn and a long reach of sheds and out-buildings, was infinitesimal compared with them. It was scarcely as commodious for people as the little boxes under the barn eaves were for doves.

A pretty girl's face, pink and delicate as a flower, was looking out of one of the house windows. She was watching three men who were digging over in the field which bounded the yard near the road line. She turned quietly when the woman entered.

"What are they digging for, mother?" said she. "Did he tell you?"

"They're diggin' for—a cellar for a new barn."

"Oh, mother, he ain't going to build another barn?"

"That's what he says."

A boy stood before the kitchen glass combing his hair. He combed slowly and painstakingly, arranging his brown hair in a smooth hillock over his forehead. He did not seem to pay any attention to the conversation.

"Sammy, did you know father was going to build a new barn?" asked the girl.

The boy combed assiduously.

"Sammy!"

He turned, and showed a face like his father's under his smooth crest of hair. "Yes, I s'pose I did," he said, reluctantly.

"How long have you known it?" asked his mother.

"'Bout three months, I guess."

"Why didn't you tell of it?"

"Didn't think 'twould do no good."

"I don't see what father wants another barn for," said the girl, in her sweet, slow voice. She turned again to the window, and stared out at the digging men in the field. Her tender, sweet face was full of a gentle distress. Her forehead was as bald and innocent as a baby's, with the light hair strained back from it in a row of curl-papers. She was quite large, but her soft curves did not look as if they covered muscles.

Her mother looked sternly at the boy. "Is he goin' to buy more cows?" said she.

The boy did not reply; he was tying his shoes.

"Sammy, I want you to tell me if he's goin' to buy more cows."

"I s'pose he is."

"How many?"

"Four, I guess."

His mother said nothing more. She went into the pantry, and there was a clatter of dishes. The boy got his cap from a nail behind the door, took an old arithmetic from the shelf, and started for school. He was lightly built, but clumsy. He went out of the yard with a curious spring in the hips, that made his loose home-made jacket tilt up in the rear.

The girl went to the sink, and began to wash the dishes that were piled up there. Her mother came promptly out of the pantry, and shoved her aside. "You wipe 'em," said she; "I'll wash. There's a good many this mornin'."

The mother plunged her hands vigorously into the water, the girl wiped the plates slowly and dreamily. "Mother," said she, "don't you think it's too bad father's going to build that new barn, much as we need a decent house to live in?"

Her mother scrubbed a dish fiercely. "You ain't found out yet we're women-folks, Nanny Penn," said she. "You ain't seen enough of men-folks yet to. One of these days you'll find it out, an' then you'll know that we know only what men-folks think we do, so far as any use of it goes, an' how we'd ought to reckon men-folks in with Providence, an' not complain of what they do any more than we do of the weather."

"I don't care; I don't believe George is anything like that, anyhow," said Nanny. Her delicate face flushed pink, her lips pouted softly, as if she were going to cry.

"You wait an' see. I guess George Eastman ain't no better than other men. You hadn't ought to judge father, though. He can't help it, 'cause he don't look at things jest the way we do. An' we've been pretty comfortable here, after all. The roof don't leak—ain't never but once—that's one thing. Father's kept it shingled right up."

"I do wish we had a parlor."

"I guess it won't hurt George Eastman any to come to see you in a nice clean kitchen. I guess a good many girls don't have as good a place as this. Nobody's ever heard me complain."

"I ain't complained either, mother."

"Well, I don't think you'd better, a good father an' a good home as you've got. S'pose your father made you go out an' work for your livin'? Lots of girls have to that ain't no stronger an' better able to than you be."

Sarah Penn washed the frying-pan with a conclusive air. She scrubbed the outside of it as faithfully as the inside. She was a masterly keeper of her box of a house. Her one living-room never seemed to have in it any of the dust which the friction of life with inanimate matter produces. She swept, and there seemed to be no dirt to go before the broom; she cleaned, and one could see no difference. She was like an artist so perfect that he has apparently no art. To-day she got out a mixing bowl and a board, and rolled some pies, and there was no more flour upon her than upon her daughter who was doing finer work. Nanny was to be married in the fall, and she was sewing on some white cambric and embroidery. She sewed industriously while her mother cooked, her soft milk-white hands and wrists showed whiter than her delicate work.

"We must have the stove moved out in the shed before long," said Mrs. Penn. "Talk about not havin' things, it's been a real blessin' to be able to put a stove up in that shed in hot weather. Father did one good thing when he fixed that stove-pipe out there."

Sarah Penn's face as she rolled her pies had that expression of meek vigor which might have characterized one of the New Testament saints. She was making mince-pies. Her husband, Adoniram Penn, liked them better than any other kind. She baked twice a week. Adoniram often liked a piece of pie between meals. She hurried this morning. It had been later than usual when she began, and she wanted to have a pie baked for dinner. However deep a resentment she might be forced to hold against her husband, she would never fail in sedulous attention to his wants.

Nobility of character manifests itself at loop-holes when it is not provided with large doors. Sarah Penn's showed itself to-day in flaky dishes of pastry. So she made the pies faith-fully, while across the table she could see, when she glanced up from her work, the sight that rankled in her patient and steadfast soul—the digging of the cellar of the new barn in the place where Adoniram forty years ago had promised her their new house should stand.

The pies were done for dinner. Adoniram and Sammy were home a few minutes after twelve o'clock. The dinner was eaten with serious haste. There was never much conver-sation at the table in the Penn family. Adoniram asked a blessing, and they ate promptly, then rose up and went about their work.

Sammy went back to school, taking soft sly lopes out of the yard like a rabbit. He wanted a game of marbles before school, and feared his father would give him some chores to do. Adoniram hastened to the door and called after him, but he was out of sight.

"I don't see what you let him go for, mother," said he. "I wanted him to help me unload that wood."

Adoniram went to work out in the yard unloading wood from the wagon. Sarah put away the dinner dishes, while Nanny took down her curl-papers and changed her dress. She was going down to the store to buy some more embroidery and thread.

When Nanny was gone, Mrs. Penn went to the door. "Fa-ther!" she called.

"Well, what is it!"

"I want to see you jest a minute, father."

"I can't leave this wood nohow. I've got to git it unloaded an' go for a load of gravel afore two o'clock. Sammy had ought to helped me. You hadn't ought to let him go to school so early."

"I want to see you jest a minute."

"I tell ye I can't, nohow, mother."

"Father, you come here." Sarah Penn stood in the door like a queen; she held her head as if it bore a crown; there was that patience which makes authority royal in her voice. Adoniram went.

Mrs. Penn led the way into the kitchen, and pointed to a chair. "Sit down, father," said she; "I've got somethin' I want to say to you."

He sat down heavily; his face was quite stolid, but he looked at her with restive eyes. "Well, what is it, mother?"

"I want to know what you're buildin' that new barn for, father?"

"I ain't got nothin' to say about it."

"It can't be you think you need another barn?"

"I tell ye I ain't got nothin' to say about it, mother; an' I ain't goin' to say nothin'.'"

"Be you goin' to buy more cows?"

Adoniram did not reply; he shut his mouth tight.

"I know you be, as well as I want to. Now, father, look here"—Sarah Penn had not sat down; she stood before her husband in the humble fashion of a Scripture woman—"I'm goin' to talk real plain to you; I never have sence I married you, but I'm goin' to now. I ain't never complained, an' I ain't goin' to complain now, but I'm goin' to talk plain. You see this room here, father; you look at it well. You see there ain't no carpet on the floor, an' you see the paper is all dirty, an' droppin' off the walls. We ain't had no new paper on it for ten year, an' then I put it on myself, an' it didn't cost but ninepence a roll. You see this room, father; it's all the one I've had to work in an' eat in an' sit in sence we was married. There ain't another woman in the whole town whose husband ain't got half the means you have but what's got better. It's all the room Nanny's got to have her company in; an' there ain't one of her mates but what's got better, an' their fathers not so able as hers is. It's all the room she'll have to be married in. What would you have thought, father, if we had had our weddin' in a room no better than this? I was married in my mother's parlor, with a carpet on the floor, an' stuffed furniture, an' a mahogany card-table. An' this is all the room my daughter will have to be married in. Look here, father!"

Sarah Penn went across the room as though it were a tragic stage. She flung open a door and disclosed a tiny bedroom, only large enough for a bed and bureau, with a path between. "There, father," said she—"there's all the room I've had to sleep in forty year. All my children were born there—the two that died, an' the two that's livin'. I was sick with a fever there."

She stepped to another door and opened it. It led into the small, ill-lighted pantry. "Here," said she, "is all the buttery I've got—every place I've got for my dishes, to set away my victuals in, an' to keep my milk-pans in. Father, I've been takin' care of the milk of six cows in this place, an' now you're goin' to build a new barn, an' keep more cows, an' give me more to do in it."

She threw open another door. A narrow crooked flight of stairs wound upward from it. "There, father," said she, "I want you to look at the stairs that go up to them two unfinished chambers that are all the places our son an' daughter have had to sleep in all their lives. There ain't a prettier girl in town nor a more ladylike one than Nanny, an' that's the place she has to sleep in. It ain't so good as your horse's stall; it ain't so warm an' tight."

Sarah Penn went back and stood before her husband. "Now, father," said she, "I want to know if you think you're doin' right an' accordin' to what you profess. Here, when we was married, forty year ago, you promised me faithful that we should have a new house built in that lot over in the field before the year was out. You said you had money enough, an' you wouldn't ask me to live in no such place as this. It is forty year now, an' you've been makin' more money, an' I've been savin' of it for you ever since, an' you ain't built no house yet. You've built sheds an' cow-houses an' one new barn, an' now you're goin' to build another. Father, I want to know if you think it's right. You're lodgin' your dumb beasts better than you are your own flesh an' blood. I want to know if you think it's right."

"I ain't got nothin' to say."

"You can't say nothin' without ownin' it ain't right, father. An' there's another thing—I ain't complained; I've got along forty year, an' I s'pose I should forty more, if it wa'n't for that—if we don't have another house. Nanny she can't live with us after she's married. She'll have to go somewheres else to live away from us, an' it don't seem as if I could have it so, noways, father. She wa'n't ever strong. She's got considerable color, but there wa'n't never any backbone to her. I've always took the heft of everything off her, an' she ain't fit to keep house an' do everything herself. She'll be all worn out inside of a year. Think of her doin' all the washin' an' ironin' an' bakin' with them soft white hands an' arms, an' sweepin'! I can't have it so, noways, father."

Mrs. Penn's face was burning; her mild eyes gleamed. She had pleaded her little cause like a Webster; she had ranged from severity to pathos; but her opponent employed that obstinate silence which makes eloquence futile with mocking echoes. Adoniram arose clumsily.

"Father, ain't you got nothin' to say?" said Mrs. Penn.

"I've got to go off after that load of gravel. I can't stan' here talkin' all day."

"Father, won't you think it over, an' have a house built there instead of a barn?"

"I ain't got nothin' to say."

Adoniram shuffled out. Mrs. Penn went into her bedroom. When she came out, her eyes were red. She had a roll of unbleached cotton cloth. She spread it out on the kitchen table, and began cutting out some shirts for her husband. The men over in the field had a team to help them this afternoon; she could hear their halloos. She had a scanty pattern for the shirts; she had to plan and piece the sleeves.

Nanny came home with her embroidery, and sat down with her needlework. She had taken down her curl-papers, and there was a soft roll of fair hair like an aureole over her forehead; her face was as delicately fine and clear as porcelain. Suddenly she looked up, and the tender red flamed all over her face and neck. "Mother," said she.

"What say?"

"I've been thinking—I don't see how we're goin' to have any—wedding in this room. I'd be ashamed to have his folks come if we didn't have anybody else."

"Mebbe we can have some new paper before then; I can put it on. I guess you won't have no call to be ashamed of your belongin's."

"We might have the wedding in the new barn," said Nanny, with gentle pettishness. "Why, mother, what makes you look so?"

Mrs. Penn had started, and was staring at her with a curious expression. She turned again to her work, and spread out a pattern carefully on the cloth. "Nothin'," said she.

Presently Adoniram clattered out of the yard in his two-wheeled dump cart, standing as proudly upright as a Roman charioteer. Mrs. Penn opened the door and stood there a minute looking out; the halloos of the men sounded louder.

It seemed to her all through the spring months that she heard nothing but the halloos and the noises of saws and hammers. The new barn grew fast. It was a fine edifice for this little village. Men came on pleasant Sundays, in their meeting suits and clean shirt bosoms, and stood around it admiringly. Mrs. Penn did not speak of it, and Adoniram did not mention it to her, although sometimes, upon a return from inspecting it, he bore himself with injured dignity.

"It's a strange thing how your mother feels about the new barn," he said, confidentially, to Sammy one day.

Sammy only grunted after an odd fashion for a boy; he had learned it from his father.

The barn was all completed ready for use by the third week in July. Adoniram had planned to move his stock in on Wednesday, on Tuesday he received a letter which changed his plans. He came in with it early in the morning. "Sammy's been to the post-office," said he, "an' I've got a letter from Hiram." Hiram was Mrs. Penn's brother, who lived in Vermont.

"Well," said Mrs. Penn, "what does he say about the folks?"

"I guess they're all right. He says he thinks if I come up country right off there's a chance to buy jest the kind of a horse I want." He stared reflectively out of the window at the new barn.

Mrs. Penn was making pies. She went on clapping the rolling-pin into the crust, although she was very pale, and her heart beat loudly.

"I dun' know but what I'd better go," said Adoniram. "I hate to go off jest now, right in the midst of hayin', but the ten-acre lot's cut, an' I guess Rufus an' the others can git along without me three or four days. I can't get a horse round here to suit me, nohow, an' I've got to have another for all that wood-haulin' in the fall. I told Hiram to watch out, an' if he got wind of a good horse to let me know. I guess I'd better go."

"I'll get your clean shirt an' collar," said Mrs. Penn calmly.

She laid out Adoniram's Sunday suit and his clean clothes on the bed in the little bedroom. She got his shaving-water and razor ready. At last she buttoned on his collar and fastened his black cravat.

Adoniram never wore his collar and cravat except on extra occasions. He held his head high, with a rasped dignity. When he was all ready, with his coat and hat brushed, and a lunch of pie and cheese in a paper bag, he hesitated on the threshold of the door. He looked at his wife, and his manner was defiantly apologetic. "*If* them cows come to-day, Sammy can drive 'em into the new barn," said he; "an' when they bring the hay up, they can pitch it in there."

"Well," replied Mrs. Penn.

Adoniram set his shaven face ahead and started. When he had cleared the door-step, he turned and looked back with a kind of nervous solemnity. "I shall be back by Saturday if nothin' happens," said he.

"Do be careful, father," returned his wife.

She stood at the door with Nanny at her elbow and watched him out of sight. Her eyes had a strange, doubtful expression in them; her peaceful forehead was contracted. She went in, and about her baking again. Nanny sat sewing. Her wedding-day was drawing nearer, and she was getting pale and thin with her steady sewing. Her mother kept glancing at her.

"Have you got that pain in your side this mornin'?" she asked.

"A little."

Mrs. Penn's face, as she worked, changed, her perplexed forehead smoothed, her eyes were steady, her lips firmly set. She formed a maxim for herself, although incoherently with her unlettered thoughts. "Unsolicited opportunities are the guide-posts of the Lord to the new roads of life," she repeated in effect, and she made up her mind to her course of action.

"S'posin' I *had* wrote to Hiram," she muttered once, when she was in the pantry—"s'posin' I had wrote, an' asked him if he knew of any horse? But I didn't, an' father's goin' wa'n't none of my doin'. It looks like a providence." Her voice rang out quite loud at the last.

"What you talkin' about, mother?" called Nanny.

"Nothin'."

Mrs. Penn hurried her baking; at eleven o'clock it was all done. The load of hay from the west field came slowly down the cart track, and drew up at the new barn. Mrs. Penn ran out. "Stop!" she screamed—"stop!"

The men stopped and looked; Sammy upreared from the top of the load, and stared at his mother.

"Stop!" she cried out again. "Don't you put the hay in that barn; put it in the old one."

"Why, he said to put it in here," returned one of the hay-makers, wonderingly. He was a young man, a neighbor's son, whom Adoniram hired by the year to help on the farm.

"Don't you put the hay in the new barn; there's room enough in the old one, ain't there?" said Mrs. Penn.

"Room enough," returned the hired man, in his thick, rustic tones. "Didn't need the new barn, nohow, far as room's concerned. Well, I s'pose he changed his mind." He took hold of the horses' bridles.

Mrs. Penn went back to the house. Soon the kitchen windows were darkened, and a fragrance like warm honey came into the room.

Nanny laid down her work. "I thought father wanted them to put the hay into the new barn?" she said, wonderingly.

"It's all right," replied her mother.

Sammy slid down from the load of hay, and came in to see if dinner was ready.

"I ain't goin' to get a regular dinner to-day, as long as father's gone," said his mother. "I've let the fire go out. You can have some bread an' milk an' pie. I thought we could get along." She set out some bowls of milk, some bread, and a pie on the kitchen table. "You'd better eat your dinner now," said she. "You might jest as well get through with it. I want you to help me afterward."

Nanny and Sammy stared at each other. There was something strange in their mother's manner. Mrs. Penn did not eat anything herself. She went into the pantry, and they heard her moving dishes while they ate. Presently she came out with a pile of plates. She got the clothes-basket out of the shed, and packed them in it. Nanny and Sammy watched. She brought out cups and saucers, and put them in with the plates.

"What you goin' to do, mother?" inquired Nanny, in a timid voice. A sense of something unusual made her tremble, as if it were a ghost. Sammy rolled his eyes over his pie.

"You'll see what I'm goin' to do," replied Mrs. Penn. "If you're through, Nanny, I want you to go up-stairs an' pack up your things; an' I want you, Sammy, to help me take down the bed in the bedroom."

"Oh, mother, what for?" gasped Nanny.

"You'll see."

During the next few hours a feat was performed by this simple, pious New England mother which was equal in its way to Wolfe's storming of the Heights of Abraham. It took no more genius and audacity of bravery for Wolfe to cheer his wondering soldiers up those steep precipices, under the sleeping eyes of the enemy, than for Sarah Penn, at the head of her children, to move all their little household goods into the new barn while her husband was away.

Nanny and Sammy followed their mother's instructions without a murmur; indeed, they were overawed. There is a certain uncanny and superhuman quality about all such purely original undertakings as their mother's was to them. Nanny went back and forth with her light loads, and Sammy tugged with sober energy.

At five o'clock in the afternoon the little house in which the Penns had lived for forty years had emptied itself into the new barn.

Every builder builds somewhat for unknown purposes, and is in a measure a prophet. The architect of Adoniram Penn's barn, while he designed it for the comfort of four-footed animals, had planned better than he knew for the comfort of humans. Sarah Penn saw at a glance its possibilities. Those great box-stalls, with quilts hung before them, would make better bedrooms than the one she had occupied for forty years, and there was a tight carriage-room. The harness-room, with its chimney and shelves, would make a kitchen of her dreams. The great middle space would make a parlor, by-and-by, fit for a palace. Up stairs there was as much room as down. With partitions and windows, what a house would there be! Sarah looked at the row of stanchions before the allotted space for cows, and reflected that she would have her front entry there.

At six o'clock the stove was up in the harness-room, the kettle was boiling, and the table set for tea. It looked almost as home-like as the abandoned house across the yard had ever done. The young hired man milked, and Sarah directed him calmly to bring the milk to the new barn. He came gaping, dropping little blots of foam from the brimming pails on the grass. Before the next morning he had spread the story of Adoniram Penn's wife moving into the new barn all over the little village. Men assembled in the store and talked it over, women with shawls over their heads scuttled into each other's houses before their work was done. Any deviation from the ordinary course of life in this quiet town was enough to stop all progress in it. Everybody paused to look at the staid, independent figure on the side track. There was a difference of opinion with regard to her. Some held her to be insane; some, of a lawless and rebellious spirit.

Friday the minister went to see her. It was in the forenoon, and she was at the barn door shelling pease for dinner. She looked up and returned his salutation with dignity, then she went on with her work. She did not invite him in. The saintly expression of her face remained fixed, but there was an angry flush over it.

The minister stood awkwardly before her, and talked. She handled the pease as if they were bullets. At last she looked up, and her eyes showed the spirit that her meek front had covered for a lifetime.

"There ain't no use talkin', Mr. Hersey," said she. "I've thought it all over an' over, an' I believe I'm doin' what's right. I've made it the subject of prayer, an' it's betwixt me an' the Lord an' Adoniram. There ain't no call for nobody else to worry about it."

"Well, of course, if you have brought it to the Lord in prayer, and feel satisfied that you are doing right, Mrs. Penn," said the minister, helplessly. His thin gray-bearded face was pathetic. He was a sickly man; his youthful confidence had cooled; he had to scourge himself up to some of his pastoral duties as relentlessly as a Catholic ascetic, and then he was prostrated by the smart.

"I think it's right jest as much as I think it was right for our forefathers to come over from the old country 'cause they didn't have what belonged to 'em," said Mrs. Penn. She arose. The barn threshold might have been Plymouth Rock from her bearing. "I don't doubt you mean well, Mr. Hersey," said she, "but there are things people hadn't ought to interfere with. I've been a member of the church for over forty year. I've got my own mind an' my own feet, an' I'm goin' to think my own thoughts an' go my own ways, an' nobody but the Lord is goin' to dictate to me unless I've a mind to have him. Won't you come in an' set down? How is Mis' Hersey?"

"She is well, I thank you," replied the minister. He added some more perplexed apologetic remarks; then he retreated.

He could expound the intricacies of every character study in the Scriptures, he was competent to grasp the Pilgrim Fathers and all historical innovators, but Sarah Penn was beyond him. He could deal with primal cases, but parallel ones worsted him. But, after all, although it was aside from his province, he wondered more how Adoniram Penn would deal with his wife than how the Lord would. Everybody shared the wonder. When Adoniram's four new cows arrived, Sarah ordered three to be put in the old barn, the other in the house shed where the cooking-stove had stood. That added to the excitement. It was whispered that all four cows were domiciled in the house.

Towards sunset on Saturday, when Adoniram was expected home, there was a knot of men in the road near the new barn. The hired man had milked, but he still hung around the premises. Sarah Penn had supper all ready. There were brown-bread and baked beans and a custard pie; it was the supper that Adoniram loved on a Saturday night. She had on a clean calico, and she bore herself imperturbably. Nanny and Sammy kept close at her heels. Their eyes were large, and Nanny was full of nervous tremors. Still there was to them more pleasant excitement than anything else. An inborn confidence in their mother over their father asserted itself.

Sammy looked out of the harness-room window. "There he is," he announced, in an awed whisper. He and Nanny peeped around the casing. Mrs. Penn kept on about her work. The children watched Adoniram leave the new horse standing in the drive while he went to the house door. It was fastened. Then he went around to the shed. That door was seldom locked, even when the family was away. The thought how her father would be confronted by the cow flashed upon Nanny. There was a hysterical sob in her throat. Adoniram emerged from the shed and stood looking about in a dazed fashion. His lips moved; he was saying something, but they could not hear what it was. The hired man was peeping around a corner of the old barn, but nobody saw him.

Adoniram took the new horse by the bridle and led him across the yard to the new barn. Nanny and Sammy slunk close to their mother. The barn doors rolled back, and there stood Adoniram, with the long mild face of the great Canadian farm horse looking over his shoulder.

Nanny kept behind her mother, but Sammy stepped suddenly forward, and stood in front of her.

Adoniram stared at the group. "What on airth you all down here for?" said he. "What's the matter over to the house?"

"We've come here to live, father," said Sammy. His shrill voice quavered out bravely.

"What"—Adoniram sniffed—"what is it smells like cooking?" said he. He stepped forward and looked in the open door of the harness-room. Then he turned to his wife. His old bristling face was pale and frightened. "What on airth does this mean, mother?" he gasped.

"You come in here, father," said Sarah. She led the way into the harness-room and shut the door. "Now, father," said she, "you needn't be scared. I ain't crazy. There ain't nothin' to be upset over. But we've come here to live, an' we're goin' to live here. We've got jest as good a right here as new horses an' cows. The house wa'n't fit for us to live in any longer, an' I made up my mind I wa'n't goin' to stay there. I've done my duty by you forty year, an' I'm goin' to do it now; but I'm goin' to live here. You've got to put in some windows and partitions; an' you'll have to buy some furniture."

"Why, mother!" the old man gasped.

"You'd better take your coat off an' get washed—there's the wash-basin—an' then we'll have supper."

"Why, mother!"

Sammy went past the window, leading the new horse to the old barn. The old man saw him, and shook his head speechlessly. He tried to take off his coat, but his arms seemed to lack the power. His wife helped him. She poured some water into the tin basin, and put in a piece of soap. She got the comb and brush, and smoothed his thin gray hair after he had washed. Then she put the beans, hot bread, and tea on the table. Sammy came in, and the family drew up. Adoniram sat looking dazedly at his plate, and they waited.

"Ain't you goin' to ask a blessin', father?" said Sarah.

And the old man bent his head and mumbled.

All through the meal he stopped eating at intervals, and started furtively at his wife; but he ate well. The home food tasted good to him, and his old frame was too sturdily healthy to be affected by his mind. But after supper he went out, and sat down on the step of the smaller door at the right of the barn, through which he had meant his Jerseys to pass in stately file, but which Sarah designed for her front house door, and he leaned his head on his hands.

After the supper dishes were cleared away and the milk-pans washed, Sarah went out to him. The twilight was deepening. There was a clear green glow in the sky. Before them stretched the smooth level of field; in the distance was a cluster of hay-stacks like the huts of a village; the air was very cool and calm and sweet. The landscape might have been an ideal one of peace.

Sarah bent over and touched her husband on one of his thin, sinewy shoulders. "Father!"

The old man's shoulders heaved: he was weeping.

"Why, don't do so, father," said Sarah.

"I'll—put up the—partitions, an'—everything you—want, mother."

Sarah put her apron up to her face; she was overcome by her own triumph.

Adoniram was like a fortress whose walls had no active resistance, and went down the instant the right besieging tools were used. "Why, mother," he said, hoarsely, "I hadn't no idee you was so set on't as all this comes to."

THE END.

One Good Time

✳

Richard Stone was nearly seventy-five years old when he died, his wife was over sixty, and his daughter Narcissa past middle age. Narcissa Stone had been very pretty, and would have been pretty still had it not been for those lines, as distinctly garrulous of discontent and worry as any words of mouth, which come so easily in the face of a nervous, delicate-skinned woman. They were around Narcissa's blue eyes, her firmly closed lips, her thin nose; a frown like a crying repetition of some old anxiety and indecision was on her forehead; and she had turned her long neck so much to look over her shoulder for new troubles on her track that the lines of fearful expectation had settled there. Narcissa had yet her beautiful thick hair, which the people in the village had never quite liked because it was red, her cheeks were still pink, and she stooped only a little from her slender height when she walked. Some people said that Narcissa Stone would be quite good-looking now if she had a decent dress and bonnet. Neither she nor her mother had any clothes which were not deemed shabby, even by the humbly attired women in the little mountain village. "Mis' Richard Stone, she 'ain't had a new silk dress since Narcissa was born," they said; "and as for Narcissa, she 'ain't never had anything that looked fit to wear to meeting."

When Richard Stone died, people wondered if his widow and Narcissa would not have something new. Mrs. Nathan Wheat, who was a third cousin to Richard Stone, went, the day before the funeral, a half-mile down the brook road to see Hannah Turbin, the dressmaker. The road was little travelled; she walked through an undergrowth of late autumn flowers, and when she reached the Turbins' house her black thibet gown was gold-powdered and white-flecked to the knees with pollen and winged seeds of passed flowers.

Hannah Turbin's arm, brown and wrinkled like a monkey's, in its woollen sleeve, described arcs of jerky energy

433

past the window, and never ceased when Mrs. Wheat came up the path and entered the house. Hannah herself scarcely raised her seamy brown face from her work.

"Good-afternoon," said Mrs. Wheat.

Hannah nodded. "Good-afternoon," she responded then, as if words were an afterthought.

Mrs. Wheat shook her black skirts vigorously. "I'm all over dust from them yaller weeds," said she. "Well, I don't care about this old thibet." She pulled a rocking-chair forward and seated herself. "Warm for this time of year," said she.

Hannah drew her thread through her work. "Yes, 'tis," she returned, with a certain pucker of scorn, as if the utter fool-ishness of allusions to obvious conditions of nature struck her. Hannah Turbin was not a favorite in the village, but she was credited with having much common-sense, and people held her in somewhat distant respect.

"Guess it's Injun summer," remarked Mrs. Wheat.

Hannah Turbin said nothing at all to that. Mrs. Wheat cast furtive glances around the room as she swayed in her rock-ing-chair. Everything was very tidy, and there were few indi-cations of its owner's calling. A number of fashion papers were neatly piled on a bureau in the corner, and some nicely folded breadths of silk lay beside them. There was not a scrap or shred of cloth upon the floor; not a thread, even. Hannah was basting a brown silk basque. Mrs. Wheat could see nowhere the slightest evidence of what she had come to ascertain, so was finally driven to inquiry, still, however, by devious windings.

"Seems sad about Richard," she said.

"Yes," returned Hannah, with a sudden contraction of her brown face, which seemed to flash a light over a recollection in Mrs. Wheat's mind. She remembered that there was a time, years ago, when Richard Stone had paid some attention to Hannah Turbin, and people had thought he might marry her instead of Jane Basset. However, it had happened so long ago that she did not really believe that Hannah dwelt upon it, and it faded immediately from her own mind.

"Well," said she, with a sigh, "it is a happy release, after all, he's been such a sufferer so long. It's better for him, and it's better for Jane and Narcissa. He's left 'em comfortable; they've got the farm, and his life's insured, you know. Besides, I suppose Narcissa'll marry William Crane now. Most likely they'll rent the farm, and Jane will go and live with Narcissa when she's married. I want to know—"

Hannah Turbin sewed.

"I was wondering," continued Mrs. Wheat, "if Jane and Narcissa wasn't going to have some new black dresses for the funeral. They 'ain't got a thing that's fit to wear, I know. I don't suppose they've got much money on hand now except what little Richard saved up for his funeral expenses. I know he had a little for that because he told me so, but the life-insurance is coming in, and anybody would trust them. There's a nice piece of black cashmere down to the store, a dollar a yard. I didn't know but they'd get dresses off it; but Jane she never tells me anything—anybody'd think she might, seeing as I was poor Richard's cousin; and as for Narcissa, she's as close as her mother."

Hannah Turbin sewed.

"'Ain't Jane and Narcissa said anything to you about making them any new black dresses to wear to the funeral?" asked Mrs. Wheat, with desperate directness.

"No, they 'ain't," replied Hannah Turbin.

"Well, then, all I've got to say is they'd ought to be ashamed of themselves. There they've got fourteen if not fifteen hundred dollars coming in from poor Richard's insurance money, and they ain't even going to get decent clothes to wear to his funeral out of it. They 'ain't made any plans for new bonnets, I know. It ain't showing proper respect to the poor man. Don't you say so?"

"I suppose folks are their own best judges," said Hannah Turbin, in her conclusive, half-surly fashion, which intimidated most of her neighbors. Mrs. Wheat did not stay much longer. When she went home through the ghostly weeds and grasses of the country road she was almost as indignant with Hannah Turbin as with Jane Stone and Narcissa. "Never saw anybody so close in my life," said she to herself. "Needn't talk if she don't want to. Dun'no' as thar's any harm in my wanting to know if my own third cousin is going to have mourning wore for him."

Mrs. Wheat, when she reached home, got a black shawl which had belonged to her mother out of the chest, where it had lain in camphor, and hung it on the clothesline to air. She also removed a spray of bright velvet flowers from her bonnet, and sewed in its place a black ostrich feather. She found an old crape veil too, and steamed it into stiffness. "I'm going to go to that funeral looking decent, if his own wife and daughter ain't," she told her husband.

"If I wa'n't along, folks would take you for the widder,"

said Nathan Wheat, with a chuckle. Nathan Wheat was rather inclined to be facetious with his wife.

However, Mrs. Wheat was not the only person who attended poor Richard Stone's funeral in suitable attire. Hannah Turbin was black from head to foot; the material, it is true, was not of the conventional mourning kind, but the color was. She wore a black silk gown, a black ladies'-cloth mantle, a black velvet bonnet trimmed with black flowers, and a black lace veil.

"Hannah Turbin looked as if she was dressed in second mourning," Mrs. Wheat said to her husband after the funeral. "I should have thought she'd most have worn some color, seeing as some folks might remember she was disappointed about Richard Stone; but, anyway, it was better than to go looking the way Jane and Narcissa did. There was Jane in that old brown dress, and Narcissa in her green, with a blue flower in her bonnet. I think it was dreadful, and poor Richard leaving them all that money through his dying, too."

In truth, all the village was scandalized at the strange attire of the widow and daughter of Richard Stone at his funeral, except William Crane. He could not have told what Mrs. Stone wore, through scarcely admitting her in any guise into his inmost consciousness, and as for Narcissa, he admitted her so fully that he could not see her robes at all in such a dazzlement of vision.

"William Crane never took his eyes off Narcissa Stone all through the funeral; shouldn't be surprised if he married her in a month or six weeks," people said.

William Crane took Jane and Narcissa to the grave in his covered wagon, keeping his old white horse at a decorous jog behind the hearse in the little funeral procession, and people noted that. They wondered if he would go over to the Stones' that evening, and watched, but he did not. He left the mother and daughter to their closer communion of grief that night, but the next the neighbors saw him in his best suit going down the road before dark. "Must have done up his chores early to get started soon as this," they said.

William Crane was about Narcissa's age but he looked older. His gait was shuffling, his hair scanty and gray, and, moreover, he had that expression of patience which comes only from long abiding, both of body and soul. He went through the south yard to the side door of the house, stepping between the rocks. The yard abounded in mossy slopes of half-sunken rocks, as did the entire farm. Folks often remarked of Richard Stone's place, as well as himself, "Stone by name, and stone by nature." Underneath nearly all his fields, cropping plentifully to the surface, were rock ledges. The grass could be mown only by hand. As for this south yard, it required skilful manœuvering to drive a team through it. When William Crane knocked that evening, Narcissa opened the door. "Oh, it's you!" she said. "How do you do?"

"How do you do, Narcissa?" William responded, and walked in. He could have kissed his old love in the gloom of the little entry, but he did not think of that. He looked at her anxiously with his soft, patient eyes. "How are you gettin' on?" he asked.

"Well as can be expected," replied Narcissa.

"How's your mother?"

"She's well as can be expected."

William followed Narcissa, who led the way, not into the parlor, as he had hoped, but into the kitchen. The kitchen's great interior of smoky gloom was very familiar to him, but to-night it looked strange. For one thing, the arm-chair to which Richard Stone had been bound with his rheumatism for the last fifteen years was vacant, and pushed away into a corner. William looked at it, and it seemed to him that he must see the crooked, stern old figure in it, and hear again the peremptory tap of the stick which he kept always at his side to summon assistance. After his first involuntary glance at the dead man's chair, William saw his widow coming forward out of her bedroom with a great quilt over her arm.

"Good-evenin', William," she said, with faint melancholy, then lapsed into feeble weeping.

"Now, mother, you said you wouldn't; you know it don't do any good, and you'll be sick," Narcissa cried out, impatiently.

"I know it, Narcissa, but I can't help it, I can't, I'm dreadful upset! Oh, William, I'm dreadful upset! It ain't his death alone—it's—"

"Mother, I'd rather tell him myself," interrupted Narcissa. She took the quilt from her mother, and drew the rocking-chair towards her. "Do sit down and keep calm, mother," said she.

But it was not easy for the older woman, in her bewilderment of grief and change, to keep calm.

"Oh, William, do you know what we're goin' to do?" she wailed, yet seating herself obediently in the rocking-chair. "We're goin' to New York. Narcissa says so. We're goin' to take the insurance money, when we get it, and' we're goin' to

New York. I tell her we hadn't ought to, but she won't listen to it! There's the trunk. Look at there, William! She dragged it down from the garret this forenoon. Look at there, William!"

William's startled eyes followed the direction of Mrs. Stone's wavering index finger, and saw a great ancient trunk lined with blue and white wall-paper, standing open against the opposite wall.

"She dragged it down from the garret this forenoon," continued Mrs. Stone, in the same tone of unfaltering tragedy, while Narcissa, her delicate lips pursed tightly, folded up the bedquilt which her mother had brought. "It bumped so hard on those garret stairs I thought she'd break it, or fall herself, but she wouldn't let me help her. Then she cleaned it, an' made some paste, an' lined it with some of the parlor paper. There ain't any key to it—I never remember none. The trunk was in this house when I come here. Richard had it when he went West before we were married. Narcissa she says she is goin' to tie it up with the clothes-line. William, can't you talk to her? Seems to me I can't go to New York nohow."

William turned then to Narcissa, who was laying the folded bedquilt in the trunk. He looked pale and bewildered, and his voice trembled when he spoke. "This ain't true, is it, Narcissa?" he said.

"Yes, it is," she replied, shortly, still bending over the trunk.

"We ain't goin' for a month," interposed her mother again; "we can't get the insurance money before then, Lawyer Maxham says; but she says she's goin' to have the trunk standin' there, an' put things in when she thinks of it, so she won't forgit nothin'. She says we'd better take one bedquilt with us, in case they don't have 'nough clothes on the bed. We've got to stay to a hotel. Oh, William, can't you say anything to stop her?"

"This ain't true, Narcissa?" William repeated, helplessly.

Narcissa raised herself and faced him. Her cheeks were red, her blue eyes glowing, her hair tossing over her temples in loose waves. She looked as she had when he first courted her. "Yes, it is, William Crane," she cried. "Yes, it is."

William looked at her so strangely and piteously that she softened a little. "I've got my reasons," said she. "Maybe I owe it to you to tell them. I suppose you were expecting something different." She hesitated a minute, looking at her mother, who cried out again:

"Oh, William, say somethin' to stop her! Can't you say somethin' to stop her?"

Then Narcissa motioned to him resolutely. "Come into the parlor, William," said she, and he followed her out across the entry. The parlor was chilly; the chairs stood as they had done at the funeral, primly against the walls glimmering faintly in the dusk with blue and white paper like the trunk lining. Narcissa stood before William and talked with feverish haste. "I'm going," said she—"I'm going to take that money and go with mother to New York, and you mustn't try to stop me, William. I know what you've been expecting. I know, now father's gone, you think there ain't anything to hinder our getting married; you think we'll rent this house, and mother and me will settle down in yours for the rest of our lives. I know you ain't counting on that insurance money; it ain't like you."

"The Lord knows it ain't, Narcissa," William broke out with pathetic pride.

"I know that as well as you do. You thought we'd put it in the bank for a rainy day, in case mother got feeble, or anything, and that is all you did think. Maybe I'd ought to. I s'pose I had, but I ain't going to. I 'ain't never done anything my whole life that I thought I ought not to do, but now I'm going to. I'm going to if it's wicked. I've made up my mind. I 'ain't never had one good time in my whole life, and now I'm going to, even if I have to suffer for it afterwards.

"I 'ain't never had anything like other women. I've never had any clothes nor gone anywhere. I've just stayed at home here and drudged. I've done a man's work on the farm. I've milked and made butter and cheese; I've waited on father; I've got up early and gone to bed late. I've just drudged, drudged, ever since I can remember. I don't know anything about the world nor life. I don't know anything but my own old tracks, and—I'm going to get out of them for a while, whether or no."

"How long are you calculating to stay?"

"I don't know."

"I've been thinking," said William, "I'd have some new gilt paper on the sitting-room at my house, and a new stove in the kitchen. I thought—"

"I know what you thought," interrupted Narcissa, still trembling and glowing with nervous fervor. "And you're real good, William. It ain't many men would have waited for me as you've done, when father wouldn't let me get married as long as he lived. I know by good rights I hadn't ought to keep you waiting, but I'm going to, and it ain't because I don't think enough of you—it ain't that; I can't help it. If you give up having me at all, if you think you'd rather marry somebody else, I can't help it; I won't blame you—"

"Maybe you want me to, Narcissa," said William, with a sad dignity. "If you do, if you want to get rid of me, if that's it—"

Narcissa started. "That ain't it," said she. She hesitated, and added, with formal embarrassment—she had the usual reticence of a New England village woman about expressions of affection, and had never even told her lover in actual words that she loved him—"My feelings towards you are the same as they have always been, William."

It was almost dark in the parlor. They could see only each other's faces gleaming as with pale light. "It would be a blow to me if I thought they wa'n't, Narcissa," William returned, simply.

"They are."

William put his arm around her waist, and they stood close together for a moment. He stroked back her tumbled red hair with clumsy tenderness. "You have had a hard time, Narcissa," he whispered, brokenly. "If you want to go, I ain't going to say anything against it. I ain't going to deny I'm kind of disappointed. I've been living alone so long, and I feel kind of sore sometimes with waitin', but—"

"I shouldn't make you any kind of a wife if I married you now, without waiting," Narcissa said, in a voice at once stern and tender. She stood apart from him, and put up her hand with a sort of involuntary maiden primness to smooth her hair where his had stroked it awry. "If," she went on, "I had to settle down in your house, as I have done in father's, and see the years stretching ahead like a long road without any turn, and nothing but the same old dog-trot of washing and ironing and scrubbing and cooking and sewing and washing dishes till I drop into my grave, I should hate you, William Crane."

"I could fetch an' carry all the water for the washin', Narcissa, and I could wash the dishes," said William, with humble beseeching.

"It ain't that. I know you'd do all you could. It's— Oh, William! I've got to have a break; I've got to have one good time. I—like you, and—I liked father; but love ain't enough sometimes when it ties anybody. Everybody has got their own feet and their own wanting to use 'em, and sometimes when love comes in the way of that, it ain't anything but a dead wall. Once we had a black heifer that would jump all the walls; we had to sell her. She always made me think of myself. I tell you, William, I've got to jump my wall, and I've got to have one good time."

William Crane nodded his gray head in patient acquiescence. His forehead was knited helplessly; he could not in the least understand what his sweetheart meant; in her present mood she was in altogether a foreign language for him, but still the unintelligible sound of her was sweet as a song to his ears. This poor village lover had at least gained the crown of absolute faith through his weary years of waiting; the woman he loved was still a star, and her rays not yet resolved into human reachings and graspings.

"How long do you calculate to be gone, Narcissa?" he asked again.

"I don't know," she replied. "Fifteen hundred dollars is a good deal of money. I s'pose it'll take us quite a while to spend it, even if we ain't very saving."

"You ain't goin' to spend it all, Narcissa!" William gave a little dismayed gasp in spite of himself.

"Land, no! we couldn't, unless we stayed three years, an' I ain't calculating to be gone as long as that. I'm going to bring home what we don't want, and put it in the bank; but—I shouldn't be surprised if it took 'most a year to spend what I've laid out to."

" 'Most a year!"

"Yes; I've got to buy us both new clothes for one thing. We 'ain't neither of us got anything fit to wear, and 'ain't had for years. We didn't go to the funeral lookin' decent, and I know folks talked. Mother felt bad about it, but I couldn't help it. I wa'n't goin' to lay out money foolish and get things here when I was going to New York and could have others the way they ought to be. I'm going to buy us some jewelry too; I 'ain't never had a good breastpin even; and as for mother, father never even bought her a ring when they were married. I ain't saying anything against him; it wa'n't the fashion so much in those days."

"I was calculatin'—" William stammered, blushing. "I always meant to, Narcissa."

"Yes, I know you have; but you mustn't lay out too much on it, and I don't care anything about a stone ring—just a plain gold one. There's another thing I'm going to have, too, an' that's a gold watch. I've wanted one all my life."

"Mebbe—" began William, painfully.

"No!" cried Narcissa, peremptorily. "I don't want you to buy me one. I 'ain't ever thought of it. I'm going to buy it myself. I'm going to buy mother a real cashmere shawl, too, like the one that New York lady had that came to visit Lawyer Maxham's wife. I've got a list of things written down on paper. I guess I'll have to buy another trunk in New York to put them in."

"Well," said William, with a great sigh, "I guess I'd better be goin'. I hope you'll have as good a time as you're countin' on, Narcissa."

"It's the first good time I ever did count on, and I'd ought to," said Narcissa. "I'm going to take mother to the theatre, too. I don't know but it's wicked, but I'm going to." Narcissa fluttered out of the parlor and William shuffled after her. He would not go into the kitchen again.

"Well, good-night," said Narcissa, and William also said good-night, with another heavy sigh. "Look out for them rocks going out of the yard, an' don't tumble over 'em," she called after him.

"I'm used to 'em," he answered back, sadly, from the darkness.

Narcissa shut and bolted the door. "He don't like it; he feels real bad about it; but I can't help it—I'm going."

Through the next few weeks Narcissa Stone's face looked strange to those who had known her from childhood. While the features were the same, her soul informed them with a new purpose, which overlighted all the old ones of her life, and even the simple village folks saw the effect, though with no understanding. Soon the news that Narcissa and her mother were going to New York was abroad. On the morning they started, in the three-seated open wagon which served as stage to connect the little village with the railroad ten miles away, all the windows were set with furtively peering faces.

"There they go," the women told one another. "Narcissa an' her mother an' the trunk. Wonder if Narcissa's got that money put away safe? They're wearin' the same old clothes. S'pose we sha'n't know 'em when they get back. Heard they was goin' to stay a year. Guess old Mr. Stone would rise up in his grave if he knew it. Lizzy saw William Crane a-helpin' Narcissa h'ist the trunk out ready for the stage. I wouldn't stan' it if I was him. Ten chances to one Narcissa 'll pick up somebody down to New York, with all that money. She's good-lookin', and she looks better since her father died."

Narcissa, riding out of her native village to those unknown fields in which her imagination had laid the scene of the one good time of her life, regarded nothing around her. She sat straight, her slender body resisting stiffly the jolt of the stage. She said not a word, but looked ahead with shining eyes. Her mother wept, a fold of her old shawl before her face. Now and then she lamented aloud, but softly, lest the driver hear. "Goin' away from the place where I was born an' married, an' have lived ever since I knew anything, to stay a year. I can't stan' it, I can't."

"Hush, mother! You'll have a real good time."

"No, I sha'n't, I sha'n't. Goin'—to stay a whole—year. I—can't, nohow."

"S'pose we sha'n't see you back in these parts for some time," the stage-driver said, when he helped them out at the railroad station. He was an old man, and had known Narcissa since her childhood.

"Most likely not," she replied. Her mother's face was quite stiff with repressed emotion when the stage-driver lifted her out. She did not want him to report in the village that she was crying when she started for New York. She had some pride in spite of her distress.

"Well, I'll be on the lookout for ye a year from to-day," said the stage-driver, with a jocular twist of his face. There were no passengers for his village on the in-coming train, so he had to drive home alone through the melancholy autumn woods. The sky hung low with pale, freezing clouds; over everything was that strange hush which prevails before snow. The stage-driver, holding the reins loosely over his tramping team, settled forward with elbows on his knees, and old brows bent with aimless brooding. Over and over again his brain worked the thought, like a peaceful cud of contemplation. "They're goin' to be gone a year. Narcissa Stone an' her mother are goin' to be gone a year, afore I'll drive 'em home."

So little imagination had the routine of his life fostered that he speculated not, even upon the possible weather of that far-off day, or the chances of his living to see it. It was simply, "They're goin' to be gone a year afore I'll drive 'em home."

So fixed was his mind upon that one outcome of the situation that when Narcissa and her mother reappeared in less than one week—in six days—he could not for a moment bring his mind intelligently to bear upon it. The old stage-driver may have grown something like his own horses through his long sojourn in their company, and his intelligence, like theirs, been given to only the halts and gaits of its first breaking.

For a second he had a bewildered feeling that time had flown fast, that a week was a year. Everybody in the village had said the travellers would not return for a year. He hoisted the ancient paper-lined trunk into his stage, then a fine new one, nailed and clamped with shining brass, then a number of packages, all the time with puzzled eyes askant upon Narcissa and her mother. He would scarcely have known them, as far as their dress was concerned. Mrs. Stone wore a fine black satin gown; her perturbed old face looked out of luxurious environments of fur and lace and rich black plumage. As for Narcissa, she was almost regal. The old stage-driver backed and ducked awkwardly, as if she were a stranger, when she approached. Her fine skirts flared imposingly, and rustled with unseen silk; her slender shoulders were made shapely by the graceful spread of rich fur, her red hair shone under a hat fit for a princess, and there was about her a faint perfume of violets which made the stage-driver gaze confusedly at the snowy ground under the trees when they had started on the homeward road. "Seems as if I smelt posies, but I know there ain't none hereabouts this time of year," he remarked, finally, in a tone of mild ingratiation, as if more to himself than to his passengers.

"It's some perfumery Narcissa's got on her pocket-handkerchief that she bought in New York," said Mrs. Stone, with a sort of sad pride. She looked worn and bewildered, ready to weep at the sight of familiar things, and yet distinctly superior to all such weakness. As for Narcissa, she looked like a child thrilled with scared triumph at getting its own way, who rejoices even in the midst of correction at its own assertion of freedom.

"That so?" said the stage-driver, admiringly. Then he added, doubtfully, bringing one white-browed eye to bear over his shoulder, "Didn't stay quite so long as you calculated on?"

"No, we didn't," replied Narcissa, calmly. She nudged her mother with a stealthy, firm elbow, and her mother understood well that she was to maintain silence.

"I ain't going to tell a living soul about it but William

Crane; I owe it to him," Narcissa had said to her mother before they started on their homeward journey. "The other folks sha'n't know. They can guess and surmise all they want to, but they sha'n't know. I sha'n't tell; and William, he's as close-mouthed as a rock; and as for you, mother, you always did know enough to hold your tongue when you made up your mind to it."

Mrs. Stone had compressed her mouth until it looked like her daughter's. She nodded. "Yes," said she; "I know some things that I ain't never told you, Narcissa."

The stage passed William Crane's house. He was shuffling around to the side-door from the barn, with a milk-pail in each hand, when they reached it.

"Stop a minute," Narcissa said to the driver. She beckoned to William, who stared, standing stock-still, holding his pails. Narcissa beckoned again imperatively. Then William set the pails down on the snowy ground and came to the fence. He looked over it, quite pale, and gaping.

"We've got home," said Narcissa.

William nodded; he could not speak.

"Come over by-and-by," said Narcissa.

William nodded.

"I'm ready to go now," Narcissa said to the stage-driver. "That's all."

That evening, when William Crane reached his sweetheart's house, a bright light shone on the road from the parlor windows. Narcissa opened the door. He stared at her open-mouthed. She wore a gown the like of which he had never seen before—soft lengths of blue silk and lace trailed about her, blue ribbons fluttered.

"How do you do?" said she.

William nodded solemnly.

"Come in."

William followed her into the parlor, with a wary eye upon his feet, lest they trample her trailing draperies. Narcissa settled gracefully into the rocking chair; William sat opposite and looked at her. Narcissa was a little pale, still her face wore that look of insistent triumph.

"Home quicker 'n you expected," William said, at length.

"Yes," said Narcissa. There was a wonderful twist on her red hair, and she wore a high shell comb. William's dazzled eyes noted something sparkling in the laces at her throat; she moved her hand, and something on that flashed like a point of white flame. William remembered vaguely how, often in the summer-time when he had opened his house-door in the sunny morning, the dewdrops on the grass had flashed in his eyes. He had never seen diamonds.

"What started you home so much sooner than you expected?" he asked, after a little.

"I spent—all the money—"

"All—that money?"

"Yes."

"Fifteen hundred dollars in less 'n a week "

"I spent more'n that."

"More'n that?" William could scarcely bring out the words. He was very white.

"Yes," said Narcissa. She was paler than when he had entered, but she spoke quite decidedly. "I'm going to tell you all about it, William. I ain't going to make a long story of it. If after you've heard it you think you'd rather not marry me, I sha'n't blame you. I sha'n't have anything to say against it. I'm going to tell you just what I've been doing; then you can make up your mind.

"To-day's Tuesday, and we went away last Thursday. We've been gone just six days. Mother an' me got to New York Thursday night, an' when we got out of the cars the men come round hollering this hotel an' that hotel. I picked out a man that looked as if he didn't drink and would drive straight, an' he took us to an elegant carriage, an' mother an' me got in. Then we waited till he got the trunk an' put it up on the seat with him where he drove. Mother she hollered to him not to let it fall off.

"We went to a beautiful hotel. There was a parlor with a red velvet carpet and red stuffed furniture, and a green sitting-room, and a blue one. The ceilin' had pictures on it. There was a handsome young gentleman down-stairs at a counter in the room where we went first, and mother asked him, before I could stop her, if the folks in the hotel was all honest. She'd been worrying all the way for fear somebody 'd steal the money.

"The gentleman said—he was real polite—if we had any money or valuables, we had better leave them with him, and he would put them in the safe. So we did. Then a young man with brass buttons on his coat took us to the elevator and showed us our rooms. We had a parlor with a velvet carpet an' stuffed furniture and a gilt clock on the mantel-shelf, two bedrooms, and a bath-room. There ain't anything in town equal to it. Lawyer Maxham ain't got anything to come up to it. The young man offered to untie the rope on the trunk, so I let him. He seemed real kind about it.

"Soon 's the young man went I says to mother. 'We ain't going down to get any tea to-night.'

" 'Why not?' says she.

" 'I ain't going down a step in this old dress,' says I, 'an' you ain't going in yours.'

"Mother didn't like it very well. She said she was faint to her stomach, and wanted some tea, but I made her eat some gingerbread we'd brought from home, an' get along. The young man with the brass buttons come again after a while an' asked if there was anything we wanted, but I thanked him an' told him there wasn't.

"I would have asked him to bring up mother some tea and a hot biscuit, but I didn't know but what it would put 'em out; it was after seven o'clock then. So we got along till morning.

"The next morning mother an' me went out real early, an' went into a bakery an' bought some cookies. We ate 'em as we went down the street, just to stay our stomachs; then we went to buying. I'd taken some of the money in my purse, an' I got mother an' me, first of all, two handsome black silk dresses, and we put 'em on as soon as we got back to the hotel, and went down to breakfast.

"You never see anythin' like the dining-room, and the kinds of things to eat. We couldn't begin to eat 'em all. There were men standin' behind our chairs to wait on us all the time.

"Right after breakfast mother an' me put our rooms to rights; then we went out again and bought things at the stores. Everybody was buying Christmas presents, an' the stores were all trimmed with evergreen—you never see anything like it. Mother an' me never had any Christmas presents, an' I told her we'd begin, an' buy 'em for each other. When the money I'd taken with us was gone, I sent things to the hotel for the gentleman at the counter to pay, the way he'd told me to. That day we bought our breastpins and this ring, an' mother's and my gold watch, an'—I got one for you too, William. Don't you say anything—it's your Christmas present. That afternoon we went to Central Park, an' that evenin' we went to the theatre. The next day we went to the stores again, an' I bought mother a black satin dress, and me a green one. I got this I've got on, too. It's what they call a tea-gown. I always wore it to tea in the hotel after I got it. I got a hat, too, an' mother a bonnet; an' I got a fur cape, and mother a cloak with fur on the neck an' all around it. That evening mother an' me went to the opera; we sat in something they call a box. I wore my new green silk and breastpin, an' mother wore her black satin. We both of us took our bonnets off. The music was splendid; but I wouldn't have young folks go to it much.

"The next day was Sunday. Mother an' me went to meeting in a splendid church, and wore our new black silks. They gave us seats way up in front, an' there was a real good sermon, though mother thought it wa'n't very practical, an' folks got up an' sat down more'n we do. Mother an' me set still, for fear we'd get up an' down in the wrong place. That evening we went to a sacred concert. Everywhere we went we rode in a carriage. They invited us to at the hotel, an' I s'posed it was free, but it wa'n't, I found out afterwards.

"The next day was Monday—that's yesterday. Mother an' me went out to the stores again. I bought a silk bed-quilt, an' some handsome vases, an' some green an' gilt teacups setting in a tray to match. I've got 'em home without breaking. We got some silk stockings, too, an' some shoes, an' some gold-bowed spectacles for mother, an' two more silk dresses, an' mother a real cashmere shawl. Then we went to see some wax-works, and the pictures and curiosities in the Art Museum; then in the afternoon we went to ride again, and we were goin' to the theatre in the evening; but the gentleman at the counter called out to me when I was going past an' said he wanted to speak to me a minute.

"Then I found out we'd spent all that fifteen hundred dollars, an' more too. We owed 'em 'most ten dollars at the hotel; an' that wa'n't the worst of it—we didn't have enough money to take us home.

"Mother she broke right down an' cried, an' said it was all we had in the world besides the farm, an' it was poor father's insurance money, an' we couldn't get home, an' we'd have to go to prison.

"Folks come crowding round, an' I couldn't stop her. I don't know what I did do myself; I felt kind of dizzy, an' things looked dark. A lady come an' held a smelling-bottle to my nose, an' the gentleman at the counter sent a man with brass buttons for some wine.

"After I felt better an' could talk steady they questioned me up pretty sharp, an' I told 'em the whole story—about father an' his rheumatism, an' everything, just how I was situated, an' I must say they treated us like Christian folks, though, after all, I don't know as we were much beholden to 'em. We never begun to eat all there was on the list, an' we were real careful of the furniture; we didn't really get our money's worth after all was said. But they said the rest of our bill to them was no matter, an' they gave us our tickets to come home."

There was a pause. William looked at Narcissa in her blue gown as if she were a riddle whose answer was lost in his memory. His honest eyes were fairly pitiful from excess of questioning.

"Well," said Narcissa, "I've come back, an' I've spent all that money. I've been wasteful an' extravagant an'— There was a gentleman beautifully dressed who sat at our table, an' he talked real pleasant about the weather, an'—I got to thinking about him a little. Of course I didn't like him as well as you, William, for what comes first comes last with all our folks, but somehow he seemed to be kind of a part of the good time. I sha'n't never see him again, an' all there was betwixt us was his saying twice it was a pleasant day, an' once it was cold, an' me saying yes; but I'm going to tell you the whole. I've been an' wasted fifteen hundred dollars; I've let my thoughts wander from you; an' that ain't all. I've had a good time, an' I can't say I 'ain't. I've had one good time, an'—I ain't sorry. You can—do just what you think best, William, an'—I won't blame you."

William Crane went over to the window. When he turned round and looked at Narcissa his eyes were full of tears and his wide mouth was trembling. "Do you think you can be contented to—stay on my side of the wall now, Narcissa?" he said, with a sweet and pathetic dignity.

Narcissa in her blue robes went over to him, and put, for the first time of her own accord, an arm around his faithful neck. "I wouldn't go out again if the bars were down," said she.

❧

The Lombardy Poplar

❦

There had been five in the family of the Lombardy poplar. Formerly he had stood before the Dunn house in a lusty row of three brothers and a mighty father, from whose strong roots, extending far under the soil, they had all sprung.

Now they were all gone, except this one, the last of the sons of the tree. He alone remained, faithful as a sentinel before the onslaught of winter storms and summer suns; he yielded to neither. He was head and shoulders above the other trees—the cherry and horse-chestnuts in the square front yard behind him. Higher than the house, piercing the blue with his broad truncate of green, he stood silent, stiff, and immovable. He seldom made any sound with his closely massed foliage, and it required a mighty and concentrated gust of wind to sway him ever so little from his straight perpendicular.

As the tree was the last of his immediate family, so the woman who lived in the house was the last of hers. Sarah Dunn was the only survivor of a large family. No fewer than nine children had been born to her parents; now father, mother, and eight children were all dead, and this elderly woman was left alone in the old house. Consumption had been in the Dunn family. The last who had succumbed to it was Sarah's twin-sister Marah, and she had lived until both had gray hair.

After that last funeral, where she was the solitary real mourner, there being only distant relatives of the Dunn name, Sarah closed all the house except a few rooms, and resigned herself to living out her colorless life alone. She seldom went into any other house; she had few visitors, with the exception of one woman. She was a second cousin, of the same name, being also Sarah Dunn. She came regularly on Thursday afternoons, stayed to tea, and went to the evening prayer-meeting. Besides the sameness of name, there was a remarkable resemblance in personal appearance between the two women. They were of about the same age; they both had gray-blond hair, which was very thin, and strained painfully back from their ears and necks into tiny rosettes at the backs of their heads, below little, black lace caps trimmed with bows of purple ribbon. The cousin Sarah had not worn the black lace cap until the other Sarah's twin-sister Marah had died. Then all the dead woman's wardrobe had been given to her, since she was needy. Sarah and her twin had always dressed alike, and there were many in the village who never until the day of her death had been able to distinguish Marah from Sarah. They were alike not only in appearance, but in character. The resemblance was so absolute as to produce a feeling of something at fault in the beholder. It was difficult, when looking from one to the other, to believe that the second was a vital fact; it was like seeing double. After Marah was dead it was the same with the cousin, Sarah Dunn. The clothes of the deceased twin completed all that had been necessary to make the resemblance perfect. There was in the whole Dunn family a curious endurance of characteristics. It was said in the village that you could tell a Dunn if you met him at the ends of the earth. They were all described as little, and sloping-shouldered, and peak-chinned, and sharp-nosed, and light-livered. Sarah and Cousin Sarah were all these. The family tricks of color and form and feature were represented to their fullest extent in both. People said that they were Dunns from the soles of their feet to the crowns of their heads. They did not even use plurals in dealing with them. When they set out together for evening meeting in the summer twilight, both moving with the same gentle, mincing step, the same slight sway of shoulders, draped precisely alike with little, knitted, white wool shawls, the same deprecating cant of heads, identically bonneted, as if they were perpetually avoiding some low-hanging bough of life in their way of progress, the neighbors said, "There's Sarah Dunn goin' to meetin'."

When the twin was alive it was, "There's Sarah and Marah goin' to meetin'." Even the very similar names had served as a slight distinction, as formerly the different dress of the cousins had made it easier to distinguish between them. Now there was no difference between the outward characteristics of the two Sarah Dunns, even to a close observer. Name, appearance, dress, all were identical. And the minds of the two seemed to partake of this similarity. Their conversation consisted mainly of a peaceful monotony of agreement. "For the

Lord's sake, Sarah Dunn, 'ain't you got any mind of your own?" cried a neighbor of an energetic and independent turn, once when she had run in of a Thursday afternoon when the cousin was there. Sarah looked at the cousin before replying, and the two minds seemed to cogitate the problem through the medium of mild, pale eyes, set alike under faint levels of eyebrow. "For the Lord's sake, if you ain't lookin' at each other to find out!" cried the neighbor, with a high sniff, while the two other women stared at each other in a vain effort to understand.

The twin had been dead five years, and the cousin had come every Thursday afternoon to see Sarah before any point of difference in their mental attitudes was evident. They regarded the weather with identical emotions, they relished the same food, they felt the same degree of heat or cold, they had the same likes and dislikes for other people, but at last there came a disagreement. It was on a Thursday in summer, when the heat was intense. The cousin had come along the dusty road between the white-powdered weeds and flowers, holding above her head an umbrella small and ancient, covered with faded green silk, which had belonged to Marah, wearing an old purple muslin of the dead woman's, and her black lace mitts. Sarah was at home, rocking in the south parlor window, dressed in the mate to the purple muslin, fanning herself with a small black fan edged with feathers which gave out a curious odor of mouldy roses.

When the cousin entered, she laid aside her bonnet and mitts, and seated herself opposite Sarah, and fanned herself with the mate to the fan.

"It is dreadful warm," said the cousin.

"Dreadful!" said Sarah.

"Seems too me it 'ain't been so warm since that hot Sabbath the summer after Marah died," said the cousin, with gentle reminiscence.

"Just what I was thinking," said Sarah.

"An' it's dusty too, just as it was then."

"Yes, it was dreadful dusty then. I got my black silk so full of dust it was just about ruined, goin' to meetin' that Sabbath," said Sarah.

"An' I was dreadful afraid I had sp'ilt Marah's, an' she always kept it so nice."

"Yes, she had always kept it dreadful nice," assented Sarah.

"Yes, she had. I 'most wished, when I got home that after-

noon, and saw how dusty it was, that she'd kept it and been
laid away in it, instead of my havin' it, but I knew she'd said
to wear it, and get the good of it, and never mind."

"Yes, she would."

"And I got the dust all off it with a piece of her old black
velvet bunnit," said the cousin, with mild deprecation.

"That's the way I got the dust off mine, with a piece of my
old black velvet bunnit," said Sarah.

"It's better than anything else to take the dust off black
silk."

"Yes, 'tis."

"I saw Mis' Andrew Dunn as I was comin' past," said the
cousin.

"I saw her this mornin' down to the store," said Sarah.

"I thought she looked kind of pindlin', and she coughed
some."

"She did when I saw her. I thought she looked real miserable. Shouldn't wonder if she was goin in the same way as
the others."

"Just what I think."

"It was funny we didn't get the consumption, ain't it, when
all our folks died with it?"

"Yes, it is funny."

"I s'pose we wa'n't the kind to."

"Yes, I s'pose so."

Then the two women swayed peacefully back and forth in
their rocking-chairs, and fluttered their fans gently before
their calm faces.

"It is too hot to sew to-day," remarked Sarah Dunn.

"Yes, it is," assented her cousin.

"I thought I wouldn't bake biscuit for supper, long as it
was so dreadful hot."

"I was hopin' you wouldn't. It's too hot for hot biscuit.
They kind of go against you."

"That's what I said. Says I, now I ain't goin' to heat up the
house bakin' hot bread to-night. I know she won't want me
to."

"No, you was just right. I don't."

"Says I, I've got some good cold bread and butter, and
blackberries that I bought of the little Whitcomb boy this
mornin', and a nice custard-pie, and two kinds of cake
besides cookies, and I guess that'll do."

"That's just what I should have picked out for supper."

"And I thought we'd have it early, so as to get it cleared

away, and take our time walkin' to meetin', it's so dreadful hot."

"Yes, it's a good idea."

"I s'pose there won't be so many to meetin', it's so hot," said Sarah.

"Yes, I s'pose so."

"It's queer folks can stay away from meetin' on account of the weather."

"It don't mean much to them that do," said the cousin, with pious rancor.

"That's so," said Sarah. "I guess it don't. I guess it ain't the comfort to them that it is to me. I guess if some of them had lost as many folks as I have they'd go whether 'twas hot or cold."

"I guess they would. They don't know much about it."

Sarah gazed sadly and reflectively out of the window at the deep yard, with its front gravel walk bordered with wilting pinks and sprawling peonies, its horse-chestnut and cherry trees, and its solitary Lombardy poplar set in advance, straight and stiff as a sentinel of summer. "Speakin' of losin' folks," she said, "you 'ain't any idea what a blessin' that popple-tree out there has been to me, especially since Marah died."

Then, for the first time, the cousin stopped waving her fan in unison, and the shadow of a different opinion darkened her face. "That popple-tree?" she said, with harsh inquiry.

"Yes, that popple-tree." Sarah continued gazing at the tree, standing in majestic isolation, with its long streak of shadow athwart the grass.

The cousin looked, too; then she turned towards Sarah with a frown of puzzled dissent verging on irritability and scorn. "That popple-tree! Land! How you do talk!" said she. "What sort of a blessin' can an old tree be when your folks are gone, Sarah Dunn?"

Sarah faced her with stout affirmation: "I've seen that popple there ever since I can remember, and it's all I've got left that's anyways alive, and it seems like my own folks, and I can't help it."

The cousin sniffed audibly. She resumed fanning herself, with violent jerks. "Well," said she, "if you can feel as if an old popple-tree made up to you, in any fashion, for the loss of your own folks, and if you can feel as if it was them, all I've got to say is, I can't."

"I'm thankful I can," said Sarah Dunn.

"Well, I can't. It seems to me as if it was almost sacrilegious."

"I can't help how it seems to you." There was a flush of nervous indignation on Sarah Dunn's pale, flaccid cheeks; her voice rang sharp. The resemblance between the two faces, which had in reality been more marked in expression, as evincing a perfect accord of mental action, than in feature, had almost disappeared.

"An old popple-tree!" said the cousin, with a fury of sarcasm. "If it had been any other tree than a popple, it wouldn't strike anybody as quite so bad. I've always thought a popple was about the homeliest tree that grows. Much as ever as it does grow. It just stays, stiff and pointed, as if it was goin' to make a hole in the sky; don't give no shade worth anything; don't seem to have much to do with the earth and folks, anyhow. I was thankful when I got mine cut down. Them three that was in front of our house were always an eyesore to me, and I talked till I got father to cut them down. I always wondered why you hung on to this one so."

"I wouldn't have that popple-tree cut down for a hundred dollars," declared Sarah Dunn. She had closed her fan, and she held it up straight like a weapon.

"My land! Well, if I was goin' to make such a fuss over a tree I'd have taken something different from a popple. I'd have taken a pretty elm or a maple. They look something like trees. This don't look like anything on earth besides itself. It ain't a tree. It's a stick tryin' to look like one."

"That's why I like it," replied Sarah Dunn, with a high lift of her head. She gave a look of sharp resentment at her cousin. Then she gazed at the tree again, and her whole face changed indescribably. She seemed like another person. The tree seemed to cast a shadow of likeness over her. She appeared straighter, taller; all her lines of meek yielding, or scarcely even anything so strong as yielding, of utter passiveness, vanished. She looked stiff and uncompromising. Her mouth was firm, her chin high, her eyes steady, and, more than all, there was over her an expression of individuality which had not been there before. "That's why I like the popple," said she, in an incisive voice. "That's just why. I'm sick of things and folks that are just like everything and everybody else. I'm sick of trees that are just trees. I like one that ain't."

"My land!" ejaculated the cousin, in a tone of contempt not unmixed with timidity. She stared at the other woman with shrinking and aversion in her pale-blue eyes. "What has come over you, Sarah Dunn?" said she, at last, with a feeble attempt to assert herself.

"Nothin' has come over me. I always felt that way about that popple."

"Marah wa'n't such a fool about that old popple."

"No, she wa'n't, but maybe she would have been if I had been taken first instead of her. Everybody has got to have something to lean on."

"Well, I 'ain't got anything any more than you have, but I can stand up straight without an old popple."

"You 'ain't no call to talk that way," said Sarah.

"I hate to hear folks that I've always thought had common-sense talk like fools," said the cousin, with growing courage.

"If you don't like to hear me talk, it's always easy enough to get out of hearin' distance."

"I'd like to know what you mean by that, Sarah Dunn."

"I mean it just as you want to take it."

"Maybe you mean that my room is better than my company."

"Just as you are a mind to take it."

The cousin sat indeterminately for a few minutes. She thought of the bread and the blackberries, the pie and the two kinds of cake.

"What on earth do you mean goin' on so queer?" said she, in a hesitating and somewhat conciliatory voice.

"I mean just what I said. That tree is a blessin' to me, it's company, and I think it's the handsomest tree anywheres around. That's what I meant, and if you want to take me up for it, you can."

The cousin hesitated. She further reflected that she had in her solitary house no bread at all; she had not baked for two days. She would have to make a fire and bake biscuits in all that burning heat, and she had no cake nor berries. In fact, there was nothing whatever in her larder, except two cold potatoes, and a summer-squash pie, which she suspected was sour. She wanted to bury the hatchet, she wanted to stay, but her slow blood was up. All her strength of character lay in inertia. One inertia of acquiescence was over, the other of dissent was triumphant. She could scarcely yield for all the bread and blackberries and cake. She shut up her fan with a clap.

"That fan was Marah's," said Sarah, meaningly, with a glance of reproach and indignation.

"I know it was Marah's," returned the cousin, rising with a jerk. "I know it was Marah's. 'Most everything I've got was hers, and I know that too. I ought to know it; I've been twitted about it times enough. If you think I ain't careful enough with her things, you can take them back again. If presents ain't mine after they've been give me, I don't want 'em."

The cousin went out of the room with a flounce of her purple muslin skirts. She passed into Sarah's little room where her cape and bonnet lay carefully placed on the snowy hill of the feather bed. She put them on, snatched up her green silk parasol, and passed through the sitting-room to the front entry.

"If you are a mind to go off mad, for such a thing as that, you can," said Sarah, rocking violently.

"You can feel just the way you want to," returned the cousin, with a sniff, "but you can't expect anybody with a mite of common-sense to fall in with such crazy ideas." She was out of the room and the house then with a switch, and speeding down the road with the green parasol bobbing overhead.

Sarah gave a sigh; she stared after her cousin's retreating form, then at the poplar-tree, and nodded as in confirmation of some resolution within her own mind. Presently she got up, looked on the table, then on the bed and bureau in the bedroom. The cousin had taken the fan.

Sarah returned to her chair, and sat fanning herself absent-mindedly. She gazed out at the yard and the poplar-tree. She had not resumed her wonted expression; the shadow of the stately, concentrated tree seemed still over her. She held her faded blond head stiff and high, her pale-blue eyes were steady, her chin firm above the lace ruffle at her throat. But there was sorrow in her heart. She was a creature of as strong race-ties as the tree. All her kin were dear to her, and the cousin had been the dearest after the death of her sister. She felt as if part of herself had been cut away, leaving a bitter ache of vacancy, and yet a proud self-sufficiency was over her. She could exist and hold her head high in the world without her kindred, as well as the poplar. When it was teatime she did not stir. She forgot. She did not rouse herself until the meeting-bell began to ring. Then she rose hurriedly, put on her bonnet and cape, and hastened down the road.

When she came in sight of the church, with its open vestry windows, whence floated already singing voices, for she was somewhat late, she saw the cousin coming from the opposite direction. The two met at the vestry door, but neither spoke. They entered side by side; Sarah seated herself, and the cousin passed to the seat in front of her. The congregation, who were singing "Sweet Hour of Prayer," stared. There was quite a general turning of heads. Everybody seemed to notice that Sarah Dunn and her cousin Sarah Dunn were sitting in separate settees. Sarah opened her hymn-book and held it before her face. The cousin sang in a shrill tremolo. Sarah hesitated a moment, then she struck in and sang louder. Her voice was truer and better. Both had sung in the choir when young.

The singing ceased. The minister, who was old, offered prayer, and then requested a brother to make remarks, then another to offer prayer. Prayer and remarks alike were made in a low, inarticulate drone. Above it sounded the rustle of the trees outside in a rising wind, and the shrill reiteration of the locusts invisible in their tumult of sound. Sarah Dunn, sitting fanning, listening, yet scarcely comprehending the human speech any more than she comprehended the voices of the summer night outside, kept her eyes fastened on the straining surface of gray hair surmounted by the tiny black triangle of her cousin's bonnet. Now and then she gazed instead at the narrow black shoulders beneath. There was something rather pitiful as well as uncompromising about those narrow shoulders, suggesting as they did the narrowness of the life-path through which they moved, and also the stiff-neckedness in petty ends, if any, of their owner; but Sarah did not comprehend that. They were for her simply her cousin's shoulders, the cousin who had taken exception to her small assertion of her own individuality, and they bore for her an expression of arbitrary criticism as marked as if they had been the cousin's face. She felt an animosity distinctly vindictive towards the shoulders; she had an impulse to push and crowd in her own. The cousin sat fanning herself quite violently. Presently a short lock of hair on Sarah's forehead became disengaged from the rest, and blew wildly in the wind from the fan. Sarah put it back with an impatient motion, but it flew out again. Then Sarah shut up her own fan, and sat in stern resignation, holding to the recreant lock of hair to keep it in place, while the wind from the cousin's fan continued to smite her in the face. Sarah did not fan herself until the cousin laid down her fan for a moment, then she resumed hers with an angry sigh. When the cousin opened her fan again, Sarah dropped hers in her lap, and sat with one hand pressed against her hair, with an expression of bitter long-suffering drawing down the corners of her mouth.

After the service was over Sarah rose promptly and went out, almost crowding before the others in her effort to gain the door before her cousin. The cousin did the same; thus each defeated her own ends, and the two passed through the door shoulder to shoulder. Once out in the night air, they separated speedily, and each went her way to her solitary home.

Sarah, when she reached her house, stopped beside the poplar-tree and stood gazing up at its shaft of solitary vernal majesty. Its outlines were softened in the dim light. Sarah thought of the "pillar of cloud" in the Old Testament. As she gazed the feeling of righteous and justified indignation against the other Sarah Dunn grew and strengthened. She looked at the Lombardy poplar, one of a large race of trees, all with similar characteristics which determined kinship, yet there was this tree as separate and marked among its kind as if of another name and family. She could see from where she stood the pale tremulousness of a silver poplar in the corner of the next yard. "Them trees is both poplars," she reflected, "but each of 'em is its own tree." Then she reasoned by analogy. "There ain't any reason why if Sarah Dunn and I are both Dunns, and look alike, we should be just alike." She shook her head fiercely. "I ain't goin' to be Sarah Dunn, and she needn't try to make me," said she, quite aloud. Then she went into the house, and left the Lombardy poplar alone in the dark summer night.

It was not long before people began to talk about the quarrel between the two Sarah Dunns. Sarah Dunn proper said nothing, but the cousin told her story right and left: how Sarah had talked as if she didn't have common-sense, putting an old, stiff popple-tree on a par with the folks she'd lost, and she, the cousin, had told her she didn't have common-sense, and then Sarah had ordered her out of her house, and wouldn't speak to her comin' out of meetin'. People began to look askance at Sarah Dunn, but she was quite unaware of it. She had formed her own plan of action, and was engaged in carrying it out. The day succeeding that of the dispute with the cousin was the hottest of a hot trio, memorable long after in that vicinity, but Sarah dressed herself in one of her cool old muslins, took her parasol and fan, and started to walk to Atkins, five miles distant, where all the stores were. She had to pass the cousin's house. The cousin, peering between the slats of a blind in the sitting-room, watched her pass, and wondered with angry curiosity where she could be going. She watched all the forenoon for her to return, but it was high noon before Sarah came in sight. She was walking at a good pace, her face was composed and unflushed. She held her head high, and walked past, her starched white petticoat rattling and her purple muslin held up daintily in front, but trailing in the back in a cloud of dust. Her white-stockinged ankles and black cloth shoes were quite visible as she advanced, stepping swiftly and precisely. She had a number of large parcels pressed closely to her sides under her arms and dangling by the strings from her hands. The cousin wondered unhappily what she had bought in Atkins. Sarah, passing, knew that she wondered, and was filled with childish triumph and delight. "I'd like to know what she'd say if she knew what I'd got," she said to herself.

The next morning the neighbors saw Annie Doane, who went out dressmaking by the day, enter Sarah Dunn's yard with her bag of patterns. It was the first time for years that she had been seen to enter there, for Sarah and Marah had worn their clothes with delicate care, and they had seldom needed replenishing, since the fashions had been ignored by them.

The neighbors wondered. They lay in wait for Annie Doane on her way home that night, but she was very close. They discovered nothing, and could not even guess with the wildest imagination what Sarah Dunn was having made. But the next Sunday a shimmer of red silk and a toss of pink flowers were seen at the Dunn gate, and Sarah Dunn, clad in a gown of dark-red silk and a bonnet tufted with pink roses, holding aloft a red parasol, passed down the street to meeting. No Dunn had ever worn, within the memory of man, any colors save purple and black and faded green or drab, never any but purple or white or black flowers in her bonnet. No woman of half her years, and seldom a young girl, was ever seen in the village clad in red. Even the old minister hesitated a second in his discourse, and recovered himself with a hem of embarrassment when Sarah entered the meeting-house. She had waited until the sermon was begun before she sailed up the aisle. There were many of her name in the church. The pale, small, delicate faces in the neutral-colored bonnets stared at her as if a bird of another feather had gotten into their nest; but the cousin, who sat across the aisle from Sarah, caught her breath with an audible gasp.

After the service Sarah Dunn walked with her down the aisle, pressing close to her side. "Good-mornin'," said she, affably. The cousin in Marah's old black silk, which was matched by the one which Sarah would naturally have worn that Sunday, looked at her, and said, feebly, "Good-mornin'." There seemed no likeness whatever between the two women as they went down the aisle. Sarah was a Dunn apart. She held up her dress as she had seen young girls, drawing it tightly over her back and hips, elevating it on one side.

When they emerged from the meeting-house, Sarah spoke. "I should be happy to have you come over and spend the day to-morrow," said she, "and have a chicken dinner. I'm goin' to have the Plymouth Rock crower killed. I've got too many crowers. He'll weigh near five pounds, and I'm goin' to roast him."

"I'll be happy to come," replied the cousin, feebly. She was vanquished.

"And I'm goin' to give you my clothes like Marah's," said Sarah, calmly. "I'm goin' to dress different."

"Thank you," said the cousin.

"I'll have dinner ready about twelve. I want it early, so as to get it out of the way," said Sarah.

"I'll be there in time," said the cousin.

Then they went their ways. Sarah, when she reached home, paused at the front gate, and stood gazing up at the poplar. Then she nodded affirmatively and entered the house, and the door closed after her in her red silk dress. And the Lombardy poplar-tree stood in its green majesty before the house, and its shadow lengthened athwart the yard to the very walls.

The Selfishness of
Amelia Lamkin

❈

It was a morning in late February. The day before there had been a storm of unusually damp, clogging snow, which had lodged upon everything in strange, shapeless masses. The trees bore big blobs of snow, caught here and there in forks or upon extremities. They looked as if the northwester had pelted them with snowballs. Below the rise of ground on which the Lamkin house stood there was a low growth of trees, and they resembled snowball-bushes in full bloom. Amelia Lamkin at her breakfast-table could see them. There were seven persons at the breakfast-table: Josiah Lamkin and his wife Amelia; Annie Sears, the eldest daughter, who was married and lived at home; Addie Lamkin, the second daughter, a pretty girl of eighteen; Tommy Lamkin, aged thirteen; little Johnny Field, a child of four, an orphan grandchild of Amelia Lamkin; and Jane Strong, Amelia's unmarried sister, who was visiting her. Annie Sears was eating, with dainty little bites, toast and eggs prepared in a particular way. She was delicate, and careful about her diet. The one maid in the household was not trusted to prepare Annie's eggs. Amelia did that. She was obliged to rise early in any case. Harry Sears, Annie's husband, left for the city at seven o'clock, and he was also particular about his eggs, although he was not delicate. Addie loathed eggs in any form except an omelet, and Hannah, the maid, could not achieve one. Therefore, Amelia cooked Addie's nice, fluffy omelet. Tommy was not particular about quality, but about quantity, and Amelia had that very much upon her mind. Johnny's rice was cooked in a special way which Hannah had not mastered, and Amelia prepared that. Josiah liked porterhouse beefsteak broiled to an exact degree of rareness, and Hannah could not be trusted with that. Hannah's coffee was always muddy, and the Lamkins detested muddy coffee; therefore, Amelia made the coffee.

Hannah's morning duties resolved themselves into standing heavily about, resting her weight first upon one large flat

foot, then upon the other, while her mistress prepared breakfast, then waiting upon the table in an absent, desultory fashion. There was a theory in the Lamkin household that poor
Hannah worked very hard, since she was the only maid in a
family of seven. The neighbors also acquiesced in that opinion, and Hannah herself felt pleasantly and comfortably injured. Nobody pitied Amelia Lamkin, least of all her own
family. She had always waited upon them and obliterated
herself to that extent that she seemed scarcely to have a
foothold at all upon the earth, but to balance timidly upon
the extreme edge of existence. Now and then Amelia's unmarried sister, Jane Strong, visited the Lamkins, and always
expressed her unsolicited opinion. The Lamkins were justly
incensed, and even Amelia herself bristled her soft plumage
of indignation. She would say privately to her sister that she
realized that she meant well, but she did wish that she would
let her live her own way without interference; that she, Amelia, got her happiness in ways that Jane could not understand.
Amelia would be quite disagreeable, and her references to
Jane's single condition would be obvious; then later, being
gentle to the very core, she would beg Jane's pardon, which
would be granted stiffly, without the slightest retreat from the
position of attack. "Of course I don't mind a straw about
what you threw out about my not being married," said Jane.
"You know as well as I do that it was my own choice."

"Of course," responded Amelia, meekly, but she looked
reminiscent. She was trying to remember what serious suitors
Jane had really had. Jane saw the expression and understood.
She was nothing if not honest.

"Land! I don't mean to say there was a line of men on
their knees to marry me," she said, brusquely. "There wasn't
a run as there was on that New York bank, and men hanging
round from dawn till dark. Most of them got married afterward, and I guess they were pretty well satisfied, and I don't
believe one of them lost a meal of victuals or a night's sleep.
But you know as well as I do that there were chances I might
have followed up if I wanted to."

"Yes, I know," returned Amelia, with more assurance.
Really she had no doubt that if her sister had chosen to follow up any man, even her own husband Josiah, he might
have capitulated. There had always been something fascinat-
ing about Jane, and she had been and was still handsome.
She was much handsomer than Amelia, although she was ten
years older. Amelia was faded almost out as to color, and in-

tense solicitude for others and perfect meekness had crossed
her little face with deep lines, and bowed her slender figure
like that of a patient old horse, accustomed to having his
lameness ignored, and standing before doors in harness through
all kinds of weather. Amelia's neck, which was long and slender, had the same curve of utter submission which one sees in
the neck of a weary old beast of burden. She would slightly
raise that drooping neck to expostulate with Jane. There
would be a faint suggestion of ancient spirit; then it would
disappear. Jane, her own chin raised splendidly, eyed her sister with a sort of tender resentment and contempt.

"Of course you know," said Jane, "that I'm enough sight
better off the way I am. I'm freer than any married woman
in the world. Then I've kept my looks. My figure is just as
good as it ever was, and my hair's just as thick and not a
thread of gray. I suppose the time's got to come, if I live long
enough, that I shall look in my glass, and see my skin yellow
and flabby; but now the only change is that I'm settled *past*
change. I know that means I'm not young, and some may
think not as good-looking, but I *am*." Jane regarded her sister
with a sort of defiance. What she said was true. Her face was
quite as handsome as in her youth; all the change lay in the
fact of its impregnability to the shift and play of emotions. A
laugh no longer transformed her features. These reigned triumphant over mirth and joy, even grief. She was handsome,
but she was not young. She was immovably Jane Strong.

"I think you are just as good-looking as you ever were,"
replied Amelia. As she spoke she gave a gentle sigh. Amelia,
after all, was human. As a girl she had loved the soft, sweet
face, suffused with bloom like an apple blossom, which she
had seen in her looking-glass. She had enjoyed arranging the
pretty, fair hair around it. Now that enjoyment was quite
gone out of her life. The other face had been so dear and
pleasant to see. She could not feel the same toward this little
seamed countenance, with its shade of grayish hair over the
lined temples, and its meek, downward arc of thin lips. However, she told herself, with a little feeling of self-scorn, that
she, Josiah Lamkin's wife, and mother and grandmother,
could not possibly be so foolish as to regret the loss of her
beauty when she could see it renewed so many-fold in the
faces of her loved ones. She told herself that she was so
thankful that her husband had kept his looks so well. Josiah,
although older than she, was still fresh-colored and full-faced,
and he had not a gray hair. Amelia knew that it would have

been harder for her to see her husband's face grown old and worn in the faithful mirror of her heart than to view her own altered face in her looking-glass.

When Amelia sighed, Jane looked at her with a sort of angry pity: "You might be just as good-looking as you ever were if you had taken decent care of yourself, and not worn yourself out for other folks," said she. "There was no real need of your getting all bent over, no older than you were, and no need of your hair getting so thin and gray. You ought to have taken the time to put a tonic on it, and you ought to have stretched yourself out on the bed a good hour every afternoon, and remembered to hold your shoulders back."

"I haven't had much time to lie down every afternoon."

"You might have had if you had set others to doing what they ought, instead of doing it yourself."

Amelia bristled again, this time with more vigor. "You know," said she, "that Hannah can't cook. It isn't in her."

"I'd get a girl who could cook," returned Jane, setting her lips hard and doubling her chin in an obstinate fashion.

"I can't discharge Hannah after all the years she has been with me. She is honest and faithful."

"Faithful nothing!"

"She is faithful," said Amelia, with decision. "She is cranky, too, and I doubt if she could stay long with anybody except me. I know just how to manage her."

"She knows just how to manage you. They all do."

"Jane Strong. I won't hear you talk so about my family and poor Hannah."

"I should think it was poor Amelia."

"I have everything to be thankful for," said Amelia. "I have the best husband and children that ever a woman had, and Hannah is just as faithful as she can be; and as for the cooking, you know I always liked to do it, Jane."

"Yes, you always liked to do everything that everybody else didn't; no doubt about that. And you always pretended you liked to eat everything that everybody else didn't."

"I have everything I want to eat."

"What did you make your breakfast of this morning?" demanded Jane.

Amelia reflected. She colored a little, then she looked defiantly at her sister. "Beefsteak, and omelet, and biscuit, and coffee," said she.

Jane sniffed. "Yes, a little scraggy bit of steak that Josiah didn't want, and that little burnt corner of Addie's omelet, and that under crust of Tommy's biscuit, and a muddy cup of watered coffee, after all the others had had two cups apiece. You needn't think I didn't see. Amelia Lamkin, you are a fool! You are killing yourself, and you are hurting your whole family and that good-for-nothing Hannah thrown in."

Then Amelia looked at Jane with sudden distress. "What do you mean, Jane?" she quavered.

"Just what I say. You are simply making your whole family a set of pigs, and Hannah too, and you know you have an awful responsibility toward an ignorant person like that, and you are ruining your own health."

"I am very well, indeed, Jane," said Amelia, but she spoke with a slight hesitation.

"You are not well. No mortal woman who has lived her whole life on the fag ends of food and rest and happiness that nobody else had any use for can be well. You hear about dogs feeding on crumbs, and I suppose they may thrive on them, though I never saw a dog yet that didn't seem to me to get along better on bones with considerable meat sticking to them; but you don't hear about human beings living in such a fashion, and it isn't required of them. You've been doing your duty all your life so hard that you haven't given other people a chance to do theirs. You've been a very selfish woman as far as duty is concerned, Amelia Lamkin, and you have made other people selfish. If Addie marries Arthur Henderson, what kind of a wife will she make after the way you have brought her up? He's a poor man, and Addie has no more idea of waiting on herself than if she were a millionairess."

"I don't know that they have come to an understanding yet," said Amelia, and as she spoke she blushed softly. She was as delicate over her daughter's romance as over her own.

"Oh, they will," said Jane, with a sniff, "though I don't see, for my part, what Addie Lamkin, with her looks, is in such a hurry for. I don't mean that Arthur Henderson isn't well enough, but Addie might do better when it comes to money."

"Money isn't everything."

"It is a good deal," responded Jane, sententiously, "and I guess Addie Lamkin will find it is if she marries Arthur Henderson and has to live on next to nothing a year, with everything going up the way it is now, when you have to stretch on your tiptoes and reach your arms up as if you were hanging for dear life to a strap on a universe trolley-car to keep going at all."

"Oh, I don't think they have even thought of marriage yet," said Amelia.

"*Lord!*" said Jane, with infinite scorn. After a little she continued: "I don't care. You *are* miserable. You can't hide it from me. You have lost flesh. You needn't pretend you haven't. You don't weigh nearly as much as you did when I was here last fall."

"I haven't been weighed lately."

"You don't need to get weighed. You can tell by your clothes. That gray silk dress you wore last night fairly hung on you."

"I always went up and down in my weight; you know I did, Jane."

"One of these days you will go down and never come up," retorted Jane, with grim assurance. Then Addie Lamkin, young and vigorous and instinct with beauty and health, marched into the room, and in her wake trailed Annie, sweet and dainty in a pale blue cashmere wrapper.

Addie, with her young cheeks full of roses, with her young yellow hair standing up crispy above her full temples, with her blue eyes blazing, with her red mouth pouting, opened fire. "Now, Aunt Jane," said Addie, "you know we always like to have you visit us, but Annie and I couldn't help over-hearing—the door has been open all the time—and we have made up our minds to speak right out and tell you what we think. We love to have you here, don't we, Annie?"

"Yes, indeed, we love to have you, Aunt Jane," assented Annie, in her soft voice, which was very like her mother's.

Amelia made a little distressed noise.

"Don't you say a word, mother," said Addie. "We are going to say just what we think. We have made up our minds." Addie's face had the expression of one who dives. "We simply can't have you making mother miserable, Aunt Jane," said she, "and you might just as well understand. Don't you agree with me, Annie?"

"Yes," said Annie.

"Don't, dear," said Amelia.

"I must," Addie replied, firmly. "We both feel that it is our duty. We both love Aunt Jane, and we are not lacking in respect to her as to an older woman, but we must do our duty. We must speak. Aunt Jane, you simply must not interfere with mother. We will not have it."

Jane's face wore a curious expression. "How do I interfere?" asked she.

"You interfere with mother's having her own way and doing exactly what she likes," said Addie.

"And you never do?"

"No," replied Addie, "we never do. None of us do."

"No, we really don't," said Annie. She spoke apologetically. She was not as direct as Addie.

"You are quite right," said Jane Strong. "I don't think any of you ever do interfere with your mother. You let her have her own way about slaving for you and waiting upon you. Your father has, ever since he was married, and all you children have, ever since you were born; not the slightest doubt of it."

Addie looked fairly afire with righteous wrath. "Really, Aunt Jane," said she, "I don't feel that, as long as it makes mother's whole happiness to live as she does, you are called upon to hinder her."

Amelia in her turn was full of wrath. "I am sure I don't want to be hindered," said she.

"We know you don't, mother dear," said Addie, "and you shall not be."

"You need not worry," Jane said, slowly. "I shall not hinder your mother, but I miss my guess if she isn't hindered." Then she went out of the room, her head up, her carriage as majestic as that of a queen.

"Aunt Jane is hopping," said Addie, "but I don't care; as for having poor mother teased and made miserable every time she comes here, I won't, for one!"

"Your aunt has never had a family and she doesn't understand, dear," said Amelia. She was a trifle bewildered by her daughter's partisanship. She was not well, and had had visions of Addie's offering to assist about luncheon. Now she realized that Addie would consider that such an offer would make her unhappy.

"No, mother dear, you shall have your own way," Annie said, caressingly. "Your own family knows what makes you happy, and you shall do just what you like." Annie put her arm around her mother's poor little waist and kissed her softly. "I am feeling wretchedly this morning," said Annie. "I think I will follow Doctor Emerson's advice to wrap myself up and sit out on the piazza an hour. I can finish that new book."

"Mind you wrap up well," Amelia said, anxiously.

"I think I will finish embroidering my silk waist," said Addie. "I want to wear it to the Simpsons' party Saturday night."

Then the daughters went away, and Amelia Lamkin went into the kitchen and prepared some scalloped fish and a cake for luncheon. She attended to some soup stock, and had consultations with the butcher and grocer. She also assisted Hannah about the breakfast dishes.

Amelia worked all the morning. She did not sit down for a moment until lunch-time. Then suddenly the hindrance which Jane Strong had foretold that morning came without a moment's warning. There had not been enough fish left from the dinner of the day before to prepare the ramekins for the family and allow Tommy two, unless Amelia went without. She was patiently eating a slice of bread and butter and drinking tea when she fell over in a faint. The little, thin creature slid gently into her swoon, not even upsetting her teacup. She fainted considerately, as she had always done everything else. Jane, who sat next her sister, caught her before she had fallen from her chair. Josiah sprang up, and stood looking intensely shocked and perfectly helpless. Addie ran for a smelling-bottle, and Annie leaped back and gasped, as if she were about to faint herself. Tommy stared, with a spoon half-way to his mouth. Then he swallowed the contents of the spoon from force of habit. Then he stared again, and turned pale under his freckles. The baby cried and pounded the table with his fists.

Amelia's face, under its thin film of gray hair, was very ghastly. Jane, supporting that poor head, looked impatiently at Josiah standing inert, with his fresh contenance fixed in that stare of helpless, almost angry, astonishment. "For goodness' sake, Josiah Lamkin," said his sister-in-law, "don't stand there gaping like a nincompoop, but go for Doctor Emerson, if you've got sense enough!" Jane came from New England, and in moments of excitement she showed plainly the influence of the land of her birth. She spoke with forcible, almost vulgar, inelegance, but she spoke with the effect of an Ethan Allen or a Stark.

Josiah moved. He made one stride for the door. Then he shot past the window on his way for the doctor.

"Stop fainting away, Annie Sears," said Jane, "and hand me that glass of water for your mother, then spank that bawling young one. You are no more faint than I am. Tommy, tell Hannah to march up-stairs lively and get your mother's bed ready." Hannah at that moment appeared in the doorway, and she promptly dropped a cup of coffee, which crashed and broke into fragments with a gush of brown liquid. At the sound of that crash there was a slight flicker of poor Amelia Lamkin's eyelids, but they immediately closed. "Let that coffee and that cup be, now you have smashed it," said Jane Strong to Hannah, "and, for goodness' sake, stop staring, and get up-stairs lively and get Mrs. Lamkin's bed ready. Why don't you move?"

Hannah moved, and the house shook with the trembling thud of her steps on the stairs. Annie came falteringly around with the glass of water. Tommy, who, once awakened to the situation, showed remarkable sense, caught up the morning paper, and fanned his mother, while the tears rolled over his hard, boyish cheeks, and he gulped convulsively.

"Oh, what ails her?" gasped Annie, holding the glass of water to her mother's white lips.

"Jane was pitiless. "She's dead, for all I know," said she. "She's an awful time coming to. For the land's sake, don't spill that water all over her! Dip your fingers in and sprinkle some on her forehead. Haven't you got any sense at all?"

Annie sprinkled her mother's forehead as if she were baptizing her. "Oh, what is it?" she moaned again.

"She's dead if she ain't fainted away," said Jane. "How do I know? But I can tell you what the matter is, Annie Sears, and you too, Addie Lamkin" (for Addie was just returning with the little green smelling-bottle): "your mother is worn out with hard work because you've all been so afraid to cross her in slaving for everybody else and having nothing for herself. She's worked out and starved out."

Addie, holding the green bottle to her mother's little pinched nostrils, aroused at that, although her pretty, healthy young face retained a pale, shocked expression. "Mother isn't starved," she whispered.

"Yes, she is, too, living on odds and ends. She hasn't eaten a good square meal since I've been here. Hens can live on such truck, but your mother can't. She ain't a hen. Here, for goodness' sake, set down that old smelling-bottle, and, Tommy, you come here and help hold her head, and, Annie, you stop sniffing and shaking and help Addie, and we'll lay her down on the floor. She'll never come to, sitting up."

"I knew that all the time," volunteered Tommy, in a shaking voice. "Teacher said to lay Jim Addison down that time when he bumped his nose against his desk reaching down for a marble he dropped."

Between them they lowered the little inanimate form to the floor, and Tommy got a sofa cushion from the sitting-room and put it under his mother's head. Then Jane broke down completely. She became hysterical.

"Oh, Amelia, Amelia!" she wailed, in a dreadful voice of ascending notes, "my sister, the only sister I've got! Amelia, speak to me! Amelia, can't you hear? Speak to me!"

Annie sank down on the floor beside her unconscious mother and wept weakly. Addie, with her lips firmly set, rubbed her mother's hands. Tommy fanned with all his might! The morning paper made a steady breeze above the still, white face. The baby had succeeded in reaching the sugar-bowl and had stopped crying. He was eating the lumps in the bowl, with one wary eye of mischief on the group.

Amelia did not revive. Those around her became more and more alarmed. Hannah stood in the door. She stammered out that the bed was ready; then she, too, wailed the wail of her sort, lifting high a voice of uncouth animal woe.

"She's dead, she's dead!" at last sobbed Jane. "She'll never speak to any of us again. Oh, Amelia, Amelia, to think it should come to this!"

Addie, with one furious glance at her aunt, stopped rubbing her mother's hands. She stood back. She looked very stiff and straight. Her face was still, but tears rolled over her cheeks as if they had been marble. Annie wept with gentle grief. Jane continued to lament, as did Hannah. The baby steadily ate sugar. Tommy was the only one who held steadfast. He never whimpered, and he fanned as if life depended upon the newspaper gale.

Then there was a quick rattle of wheels, and Jane rushed to the door and shrieked out, as the doctor was fumbling for his medicine-chest:

"You're too late, doctor, you're too late!"

Poor Josiah, who had driven back with the doctor and was already out of the buggy, turned ghastly white.

"Oh, my God, doctor, she's gone!" he gasped.

The doctor, who was young and optimistic, clapped him on the shoulder. "Brace up, man!" he said, in a loud voice. Then he entered the house and the dining-room where poor Amelia lay. He pushed rather rudely past Jane and Hannah and Addie and Annie. He knelt down beside the prostrate woman, looked at her keenly, felt her wrist, and held his head to her breast. Then he addressed Tommy. "How long has your mother been unconscious?" he asked.

Tommy glanced up at the clock. "Most half an hour," he replied. His mouth and eyes and nose twitched, but he spoke quite firmly. There was the making of a man in Tommy.

"Oh, she's dead!" wailed Jane. "Oh, Amelia! Oh, my sister, my sister!"

Doctor Emerson rose and looked at Jane Strong with cool hostility. "She is not dead unless you make her so by your lack of self-control," said he. "You must all be as quiet as you can."

Jane stopped wailing and regarded him with awed eyes, the eyes of a feminine thing cowed by the superior coolness in adversity of a male. She was afraid of that clear, pink-and-white, young masculine face, with its steady outlook of rather cold blue eyes and its firm mouth. All became quiet and obeyed Doctor Emerson's orders. Josiah, Hannah, and the doctor carried Amelia to her room, and laid her, still unconscious, upon her bed. Then, after a while, she awakened, but she was a broken creature. They hardly recognized her as Amelia. Amelia without her ready hand for them all, her ready step for their comfort, seemed hardly credible. She lay sunken among her pillows in a curious, inert fashion. She was very small and slight, but she gave an impression of great weight, so complete was her abandonment to exhaustion, so entirely her bed sustained her, without any effort upon her part.

Addie cornered the doctor in the front hall on his way out. "What do you think is the matter with mother?" she whispered. The doctor looked at Addie's pretty, pale face. He was unmarried, and had had dreams about Addie Lamkin. He had dismissed those dreams upon the advent of Arthur Henderson. Still, the girl had almost the interest of an old love for him.

"Your mother is simply worn out, Miss Lamkin," said Doctor Emerson, curtly; yet his eyes, regarding that pretty face, were pitying.

"Worn out?" repeated Addie.

"Yes. To put it plainly, she has worked too hard for everybody else, and not hard enough for herself."

Soft rose suffused Addie's face and neck. She looked piteously at the doctor, with round eyes like a baby's, pleading not to be hurt. The doctor's tone softened a little.

"Of course I realize how almost impossible it is to prevent self-sacrificing women like your mother from offering themselves up," he said.

Tears stood in Addie's eyes. "Mother never complained, and she seemed to want—" she returned, brokenly.

"Yes, she seemed to want to do everything and not let anybody else do anything, and everybody indulged her."

"I don't think any of us realized," said Addie.

"Of course you didn't," said Doctor Emerson, and his voice, while slightly sarcastic, was still almost caressing.

"Of course now we shall see that mother does not overdo," said Addie.

"She can't—now."

Addie turned very white. "You don't mean—"

"I don't know. I shall do everything I can, but she is very weak. I never saw a case of more complete exhaustion."

After Doctor Emerson had driven out of the yard, Addie and Annie talked together, Jane Strong made gruel, and Tommy sat beside his mother. Josiah paced up and down the front walk. He had a feeling as if the solid ground was cut from under his feet. He had not known for so many years what it was to live without the sense of Amelia's sustaining care that he felt at once unreasoning anger with her, a monstrous self-pity, and an agony of anxious love. The one clear thing in his mind was that Amelia ever since their marriage had put in his sleeve-buttons and shirt-studs. Always he saw those little, nervous, frail hands struggling with the stiff linen and the studs and buttons. It seemed to him that of all her wrongs, that was the one which he should definitely grasp. He felt that she was worn out, maybe come to her death, through putting in those buttons and studs. Josiah was a great, lumbering masculine creature, full of helpless tenderness. He paced up and down the walk. He looked at his thick fingers, and he saw always those little, slender, nervous ones struggling with his linen and buttons, and he knew what remorse was. Finally he could bear it no longer, and he entered the house and the kitchen where Jane was making the gruel.

"Doctor Emerson says she is all worn out," he said, thickly.

Jane looked at him viciously. "Of course she is worn out."

"Jane, do you think putting in my sleeve-buttons and studs hurt her?"

Jane stared at him. "Everything has hurt her together, I suppose," she replied, grimly.

Josiah went into the dining-room, where Addie and Annie stood talking together in low voices, and sobbing softly between the words. The baby was asleep in his chair, his curly head hanging sidewise. "Your mother seems to be all worn out," Josiah said to his daughters.

"Yes, she is, I am afraid," Annie said, tearfully. "If *I* had only been stronger."

"If mother had only known *she* wasn't strong," Addie said, fiercely, and Annie did not resent it. "Here I've been saying mother must be let alone to do things because it worried her not to," said Addie. "Great fool, great hypocrite!" She gave a sob of fury at herself.

"I have been thinking how she has always put in my sleeve-buttons and shirt-studs," said Josiah.

Neither Annie nor Addie seemed to hear what he said.

"If only *I* had been stronger," repeated Annie.

Addie turned on her. "You have always been enough sight stronger than mother, Annie Sears," said she. "You fairly enjoy thinking you are delicate. You think it is a feather in your cap; you know you do!"

Annie was so astonished she fairly gaped at her sister. She could not speak. Addie made a dart toward Johnny and caught him up in her arms. "Here we are letting mother's baby break his neck," said she, furiously, "standing here like great gumps. Next thing he would have tumbled out of his chair." Johnny began to wail, and Addie kissed him, then shook him. "Johnny, hush up for mercy's sake," said she. "Grandma's very sick. Here, don't cry, and auntie will give you a lump of sugar." With that Addie poked a lump of sugar into the little, soft, red mouth, and Johnny was appeased and began sucking it.

"She's always put in my sleeve-buttons and studs," said Josiah, in his miserable monotone. Then he returned to the front walk, and began pacing up and down.

Addie turned to Annie. "Annie Sears," said she, "do you know mother is up there all alone with Tommy? Why don't you go up there?"

"Let me take Johnny, and you go, Addie," Annie said, faintly.

Addie thrust Johnny upon Annie, and turned and went up-stairs. Tommy looked up as she entered the room and gave an inaudible "hush!" "Mother is asleep," he motioned with his lips. Amelia, indeed, lay as if asleep, with her eyes partly open, and a ghastly line of white eyeball showing. Addie sat beside the bed and looked at her mother. Tommy broke down, and curved his arm in its rough sleeve around his freckled face and wept bitterly. Addie did not weep.

Gradually the expression of those who renunciate stole over her face. She was making up her mind to relinquish all thoughts of marriage, to live at home single, and devote her life to her mother. Addie's face, which had been pretty with a rather hard prettiness, grew beautiful. She looked as her mother had done as a girl. The possibilities of entire self-renunciation lit it with spiritual glory. She realized that she was very unhappy; she thought of Arthur Henderson, but she said to herself that he was a man and young, and men could forget. She knew quite well that his character was not one capable of going through life without snatching at one sweet if he could not obtain another. She felt glad that it was so. She had never been so mierable and so blissful in her whole life as she was, sitting beside her mother's bed; for she, for the first time, saw beyond her own self, and realized the unspeakable glory there. She reached out a hand and patted Tommy's heaving shoulder.

"We'll all take care of her, and she'll get well; don't cry, dear," she whispered, very softly.

But Tommy gave his shoulder an impatient shrug and wept on. He was remembering how he had worn so many holes in his mittens and his mother had mended them, and it seemed to him as if mending those mittens was the one thing which had tired her out. He made up his mind, whether she lived or died, that he would never get holes in his mittens again for anybody to mend. He would start to school with mittens on his hands, and when once out of sight of home, into his pockets they would go, and he would use his bare hands if they did get frost-bitten.

Down-stairs Annie Sears sat beside little Johnny and told him a story. She never knew what the story was about. Johnny had eaten all the sugar in the bowl, and he nestled his little curly head against Annie's shoulder while she talked in her unhappy voice. After a while Johnny's eyes closed, and Annie lifted him and carried him up-stairs and laid him on her own bed. He was a heavy child, and she bent painfully beneath his weight, and reflected, the while she did so, how many times she had seen her mother toil up-stairs with him—her little mother, whose shoulders were narrower than her own.

Jane finished the bowl of gruel, while Hannah stood looking on. Jane turned upon the girl with sudden fury.

"For the land's sake, get to work, can't you?" she said.

"What are you standing there for? Clear off the table, and wash the dishes, and sweep up the kitchen!"

Hannah did not resent the angry voice. She began to weep without covering her face, bawling aloud like a baby. "Oh, Lord! oh, Lord!" she wailed. "Here's that poor blessed soul all wore out doing my work while I've been standing watching her!"

"Well, you haven't got her to watch now," said Jane. "Get to work!" Hannah paddled into the dining-room, and the clatter of dishes accompanied her loud sobs. Jane carried the bowl of gruel to her sister, but poor Amelia was too spent to take more than a spoonful or two, for all her gentle willingness. "There's no use," said Jane, grimly. "She's got to have something to put some life in her. There's that bottle of port wine down cellar that the doctor ordered for Annie, and she didn't like. I'm going to put some in this gruel."

"Won't it be an awful mess?" whispered Addie.

"Mess or not, she's got to take it. She's got to have something to put some life in her."

The cellar in the Lamkin house was approached by a trap-door in a pantry opening out of the parlor. It was a strange arrangement, but there were many strange arrangements in the Lamkin house, which was very old, had suffered many alterations, and had been built originally by an eccentric man. Nobody saw Jane Strong enter the parlor and the pantry, raise the trap-door, and descend the main stairs. Jane knew just where the port wine was kept. It was standing by itself, giving out a dusky red glow like a carbuncle, in the southwest corner of the very neat cellar. Jane had her hand on the bottle when she heard a thud, and realized that the trap-door had fallen. She did not feel at all dismayed, but when she had climbed the stairs with her wine-bottle she found herself in difficulty. The trap-door was very heavy, and there was nothing whatever to take hold of on the under side. Jane raised herself as near the top of the stairs as she could and pushed in vain with her hands, then she butted the door with her little head banded with sleek black hair. Jane's neck was very slender, and her head was very small. She could not make the slightest impression upon the door. She descended the stairs and found a clean, empty stone jar in the northwest corner of the cellar. Jane took the lid of the jar, and with the wine-bottle still under her arm, she climbed the stairs again. Then she pounded upon the door viciously with the lid of the jar, until it suddenly broke in halves, and she, taken by surprise, fell down the stairs, with the wine-bottle, which broke. Jane Strong sat on the cellar floor and felt faint. Then came the consciousness of extreme pain in her foot and ankle. "I have spilled all that wine over my dress, I am soaked to my skin with wine, and I've sprained my ankle, maybe I've broken it; and there's Amelia up-stairs the way she is," said Jane Strong aloud, in a curiously cool, reflective voice. She had a judicial turn of mind, and she pulled herself together and considered the whole situation. "I've got to make somebody hear somehow," she said, also aloud. Jane had a very thin, reedy voice which did not carry far. She raised it as loud as she possibly could, and she called by name, each in turn, the members of the family. She thought that possibly Tommy had the most acute hearing, and she called, "Tommy! Tommy!" oftener than any other name. Nobody came. After a while she got incensed. "Might as well give it up," said she. She wore cloth shoes with elastic at the sides, and succeeded in pulling the one on the injured foot off, although it caused her agony. She eyed the swollen foot and ankle sternly. She felt of the ankle, and became almost sure that a bone was broken. She sat still, thinking. It seemed to her that she had never really thought in all her life before. Jane Strong had kept all the commandments from her youth up. She had always been considered a most exemplary woman by other people, and she had acquiesced in their opinion. Now suddenly she differed with other people and with her own previous estimation of herself. She had blamed her sister Amelia Lamkin for her sweet, subtle selfishness, which possibly loved the happiness of other people rather than their own spiritual gain; she had blamed all the Lamkin family for allowing a martyr to live among them, with no effort to save her from the flame of her own self-sacrifice. Now suddenly she blamed herself. She pictured to herself her easy, unhampered life in her nice little apartment, and was convicted of enormous selfishness in her own righteous person. "Lord!" she said, "what on earth have I been thinking about? I knew Amelia was overworked. What was to hinder my coming here at least half the year and taking some of the burden off her? I knew Addie was young, and Annie none too strong, and Josiah fussy, like all men. Why didn't I come? And now here she is flat on her back, and maybe she'll never get up; and here I am with a broken ankle, and can't do a thing. You've made a nice mess of it, Jane Strong! Instead of snooping around to find the sins of other folks, you'd better have looked at home. Good land!" Tears rolled

down Jane's cheeks. Then she wiped them away with a hand
wet with port wine, and she raised her voice and called again.
She sat there vainly calling until the light began to wane;
then it was Josiah who heard. Josiah, who had been in the
house, gazing at his prostrate wife, and going to his daughters
for comfort, and then returned to his miserable promenade
on the front walk, heard her through the cellar window. He
hurried into the house and met Addie.

"Somebody's calling me, and it sounds like it came from
the cellar," he stammered. His nerves were so unstrung that
he felt a shiver of superstition.

Addie also felt an answering thrill of horror. "What do you
think it is, father?" she whispered, fearfully.

"Don't know. Sounds like a cat calling 'Josiah!' as near as
anything else."

The two stood looking at each other.

"Where is Aunt Jane?" asked Addie.

"I don't know."

"Annie and I have been looking for her, and she doesn't
seem to be in the house."

"If she were here she would go down cellar and see what it
was," said Josiah, with open weakness.

Addie straightened herself. "Nonsense, father! We will go
together," said she.

When they had opened the trap-door in the parlor pantry,
and peered down into the gloom, and heard the faint voice
from below, Addie gave a cry and hurried down the stairs.

"Goodness, Aunt Jane!" said she, "is that you?"

"Yes, it's me." groaned Jane. Then she began to weep.
"Oh, Lord, it's a judgment on me!" said she.

"Are you hurt? How did you come down here?"

"Fell down. Oh, Lord, it's a judgment on me!"

"What did you come here for? How came the trap-door
shut?"

"It fell down. I came for that bottle of port wine for your
poor mother. It broke when I fell. I was trying to knock on
the trap-door with the lid of that jar, and I fell. I'm all wine
from head to foot."

"Are you hurt?"

"Guess my ankle is broken. It pains me something dreadful, but I don't care. It's a judgment on me! I've been terrible
selfish about your mother. It's a judgment on me!"

"Seems to me there's judgments on all of us," said Addie,
rather sharply, although there was pity in her voice as she

stooped over her aunt, but she was wondering what could be done, with her mother so ill and her aunt crippled.

Josiah stood over his sister-in-law, a helpless bulk of a man, drooping in every muscle before this new calamity.

"Can't you get up, Jane?" he inquired, quaveringly.

"For the land's sake, Josiah Lamkin, do you suppose I'd sit here catching my death of cold on this cellar floor if I could get up?" responded Jane.

"Father, you had better run as fast as you can and get Doctor Emerson. He said he would come again to see mother, but he may not until after his office hour," said Addie. "I'll get some pillows and a shawl, and Hannah can make some hot tea. Then I think you and Doctor Emerson can get her up-stairs. Hannah and I will have everything ready in her room."

Josiah, for the second time that day, raced for the doctor. Annie came and sat on the cellar stairs, while poor Jane drank her tea, and wept softly at this disaster.

Jane gulped down the tea in a sort of fury. "I don't deserve this tea," said she, "and I wouldn't touch it, but I've got to make trouble enough as it is without getting pneumonia. I don't know whether it is as dangerous to set soaked through with wine as it is with water, but I'm wet to the skin, anyhow, and all of a shake. How is she?"

"She just lies there, and she looks like death," moaned Annie.

"We've all been killing her, and now she's *killed*, I guess," said Jane.

"We didn't realize," said Annie. "If only I had been stronger!"

"For the Lord's sake, don't talk any more about being strong," said Jane. "You'd better hustle round and *get* strong. You've been as strong as your mother right along, and she has never said a word."

"I know it," Annie said. She bent over, and her whole slender body shook with sobs.

"For the land's sake," said Jane, "stop crying! You don't want to make yourself sick and have another to take care of. There's enough as it is. If Harry comes home and finds you've been crying, there'll be an awful to-do. He acts like a pox fool about you, and always did. I believe he's put it into your head about not being strong, anyhow. He's seen your mother getting up and getting his early breakfast for him, and he hasn't thought it was anything."

"I'm going to get Harry's breakfast now."

"You'd better. If a woman has married a man who has to gulp his breakfast and race for an early train, it's her place to get it for him, and not her poor old mother's."

"I am going to," said Annie. Then she wept again.

Meanwhile, Amelia Lamkin was lying in her peaceful bed up-stairs in a very trance of happiness. She was quite conscious. She had not a pain. She realized an enormous weakness and sheer inability to move, but along with it came the blessed sense of release from hard duties. Almost for the first time in her life Amelia Lamkin's conscience did not sting her because she was not up and doing for others. She knew that it was impossible. She felt like one who has received absolution. The weight of her life had slipped from her shoulders. She regarded Tommy's pale, disturbed face, but even that did not trouble her, so sunken was she in the peace of weakness and sweet irresponsibility. She made one effort to speak to him, to comfort him; then she gave it up, and lay smiling the ghost of a smile. It did not seem to her that he could be really distressed when she was not suffering and was relieved of the weight of existence under which she had staggered so long. The faces of the other members of her family came before her mental vision, and she beheld them with immense love and no anxiety. The sense of being herself so entirely in the arms of Providence, of being undriven by any lash of duty, filled her with peace concerning them. She was beatifically happy, while the others were bemoaning her condition, and while Jane was being attended to in another room for her badly sprained ankle, which would disable her for weeks, perhaps for life. They worried lest Amelia should hear some noise which would awaken her suspicion, lest she should ask for her sister, and be alarmed at her absence, but they had no occasion to worry. Amelia, for the time being, was past alarm. She missed nobody. She wanted nothing except to lie there in her clean white bed and feel that she need not move. The days went on, and her condition did not change.

She lay still day after day, opening her mouth obediently for the spoonfuls of sustenance which were given her, half dozing, half waking, and wholly happy. All her life she had done what she could, and all her life she had been anxious lest she should not do what she could. Now that she knew that she could do no more there came upon her a perfect peace. She did not know that Jane was confined to her bed with her injured foot. She did not know that Addie had turned a cold shoulder to Arthur Henderson, and that he was already engaged to Eliza Loomis. She did not know of the harrowing anxiety concerning her. She knew naught but her conviction that nothing was required of her except to lie still, that other people required nothing except that, that God required nothing except that. Addie always wore a cheerful face when with her mother. Indeed, the readiness with which Arthur Henderson had given her up had caused her pride to act as a tonic, and her eyes had been opened. She knew that she had never cared for a man who could relinquish her without more effort, and whose loss had caused her no more pain. At first she thought that her love and anxiety for her mother had made her callous, but after a little she knew. She even laughed at herself because she had once thought it possible for her to marry Arthur Henderson. She could not yet laugh at the prospect of the life of self-immolation which she ordered for herself since the day her mother had been taken ill, but she was schooling herself to contemplate it cheerfully, although the doctor, with his daily visits to her mother, was now making it hard. Addie began to realize that this man, had she allowed herself to think of him, might have been more difficult to relinquish than the other. After a while she saw him as little as possible, and received his directions through Annie. Addie and Annie had their days full. They were glad when Tommy's spring vacation came. Tommy was of much assistance, and he developed a curious aptitude for making Hannah work. "Now, Hannah, if you are any girl at all, if you ever mean to get married yourself and not have your fellow light out the first week, it's time for you to brace up and hustle," said Tommy; and the next morning Hannah achieved surprising biscuits and well-cooked eggs. Addie ate her eggs cooked any way now, and so did Annie, and Josiah Lamkin never said a word if his steak were not quite as rare as usual, and Johnny ate his rice half-cooked, and survived.

Amelia's window-shades were up all day, for the doctor said she should have all the light and sun possible; and as spring advanced she could see, with those patient eyes which apparently saw nothing, the blue sky crossed with tree branches deepening in color before they burst into leaf and flower. Amelia saw not only those branches, but beyond them, as though they were transparent, other branches, but those other branches grew on the trees of God, and were full of wonderful blooms; and beyond the trees she saw the far-away slope of mountains, and through them in turn the curves of beauty of the Delectable Hills. When Amelia closed her eyes, the picture of those trees beyond trees, those mountains beyond mountains, was still with her, and she saw also heavenly landscapes, rich green meadows, and pearly floods, and gardens of lilies, and her vision, which had been content for years with only the dear simple beauties of her little village, was fed to her soul's delight and surfeit. But she was too weak to speak more than a word at a time, and she scarcely seemed to know one of her dear ones. Poor Amelia Lamkin was so tired out in their service that she had gone almost out of their reach for her rest.

At last came a warm day during the first of May, when people said about the village that Mrs. Amelia Lamkin was very low indeed. The air was very soft and full of sweet languor, and those partly opened eyes of Amelia's saw blossoms through blossoms on the tree branches. In the afternoon Doctor Emerson came, and Addie did not shun him. Her mind was too full of her mother for a thought of any human soul beside. She and the young man stood in Amelia's room over the prostrate little figure, and the doctor took up the slender hand and felt for the pulse in the blue-veined wrist. Then he went over by the window, and stood there with Addie, and Amelia's eyes, which had been closed, opened slowly, and she saw the blooming boughs of the trees of heaven through *them* also. Addie was weeping softly, but her mother did not know it, at first, in her rapt contemplation. She did not see Doctor Emerson put an arm around the girl's waist, she did not hear what he said to her, but suddenly she *did* hear what the girl said. She heard it more clearly than anything since she had been taken ill. "I can't think of such things with mother lying there the way she is," Addie said, in a whisper. "I wonder at you."

"She can't hear a word; she does not know," said the young man; and Amelia, listening, was surprised to learn how little a physician really knows himself, when she was hearing and understanding every word, and presently seeing. "I would not speak now," Doctor Emerson continued. "I know it must seem untimely to you, but you have been through so much all these weeks, and it is possible that more still is before you soon, and I feel that if you can consent to lean upon me as one who loves you more than anybody else in the world, I may take it all easier. You know I love you, dear."

"You can't love me. I have been an unworthy daughter," Addie sobbed.

"An unworthy daughter? I have never seen such devotion."

"The devotion came too late," Addie replied, bitterly. "If mother had had a little more devotion years ago, she would be up and about now. There is no use talking, Doctor Emerson; you don't know me as I know myself or you wouldn't once think of me; but, anyway, it is out of the question."

"Why?"

"Because," said Addie, firmly, "I have resolved never to marry, never to allow any other love or interest to come between me and my own family. If mother—" Addie could not finish the sentence. She went on, with a word omitted: "I must make all the restitution to her in my power by devoting my whole life to her dear ones, to Tommy and the baby and father. Annie is delicate, although now she tries to think she isn't, and is doing so much, and Aunt Jane will never be able to walk as well as before she sprained her ankle falling down those cellar stairs. You know that."

Amelia heard. It was the first she had known of Jane's accident.

"She is getting on very well," Doctor Emerson said, rather evasively.

"Yes, but she is lame. That is the reason she won't come in here, though I have told her poor mother wouldn't notice. Aunt Jane has said that if it were not for her lameness she would come here and keep house, but she is a woman older than mother, and she *is* lame. There is nobody except myself to keep up the home here, and any other arrangement is out of the question."

"We could live here, dear," said the young man, and his voice sounded young and pleasing and pitiful. Amelia herself loved him as he spoke. But Addie turned upon him with a sort of fierceness.

"Don't talk to me any more," she said. "Haven't you eyes? Don't you see I can't bear it? We *could* live here, but you— and maybe others—would come between me and my sacred trust. It can't be, Edward. If mother had lived—" (she spoke of her mother as already dead). "Of course with Aunt Jane—I think she will live here now, anyway, and she *can* do a good deal—and with Annie, they could have got along, and I don't say I would not have. Of course it must cost me something to give up the sort of life a girl naturally expects. Don't talk to me any more."

Then Amelia sat up in bed. Her eyes were opened wide; they had seen her last of heavenly visions until the time when they should close forever. In a flash she saw how selfish it was for her, this patient, loving woman, who had thought of others all her life, to be happy in giving up her life. She realized, too, what she had never felt when in the midst of them, the torture and the fires of martyrdom in which her life had been spent. Now that the unselfishness of others had quenched those fires, she knew what had been, and saw how fair the world might yet be for her. She reached back her loving, longing, willing hands to her loved ones of earth and her earthly home. Amelia spoke in quite a clear, strong voice. Addie turned with a great start, and screamed, "Mother!" and Doctor Emerson was by her side in an instant. Amelia looked at them and smiled the smile of a happy, awakening infant.

"I am better," said she; "I am going to get well now. I have lain here long enough."

Old Woman Magoun

The hamlet of Barry's Ford is situated in a sort of high valley among the mountains. Below it the hills lie in moveless curves like a petrified ocean; above it they rise in green-cresting waves which never break. It is *Barry's* Ford because at one time the Barry family was the most important in the place; and *Ford* because just at the beginning of the hamlet the little turbulent Barry River is fordable. There is, however, now a rude bridge across the river.

Old Woman Magoun was largely instrumental in bringing the bridge to pass. She haunted the miserable little grocery, wherein whiskey and hands of tobacco were the most salient features of the stock in trade, and she talked much. She would elbow herself into the midst of a knot of idlers and talk.

"That bridge ought to be built this very summer," said Old Woman Magoun. She spread her strong arms like wings, and sent the loafers, half laughing, half angry, flying in every direction. "If I were a *man*," said she, "I'd go out this very minute and lay the fust log. If I were a passel of lazy men layin' round, I'd start up for once in my life, I would." The men cowered visibly—all except Nelson Barry; he swore under his breath and strode over to the counter.

Old Woman Magoun looked after him majestically. "You can cuss all you want to, Nelson Barry," said she; "I ain't afraid of you. I don't expect you to lay ary log of the bridge, but I'm goin' to have it built this very summer." She did. The weakness of the masculine element in Barry's Ford was laid low before such strenuous feminine assertion.

Old Woman Magoun and some other women planned a treat—two sucking pigs, and pies, and sweet cake—for a re-ward after the bridge should be finished. They even viewed leniently the increased consumption of ardent spirits.

"It seems queer to me," Old Woman Magoun said to Sally Jinks, "that men can't do nothin' without havin' to drink and chew to keep their sperits up. Lord! I've worked all my life and never done nuther."

"Men is different," said Sally Jinks.

"Yes, they be," assented Old Woman Magoun, with open contempt.

The two women sat on a bench in front of Old Woman Magoun's house, and little Lily Barry, her granddaughter, sat holding her doll on a small mossy stone near by. From where they sat they could see the men at work on the new bridge. It was the last day of the work.

Lily clasped her doll—a poor old rag thing—close to her childish bosom, like a little mother, and her face, round which curled her long yellow hair, was fixed upon the men at work. Little Lily had never been allowed to run with the other children of Barry's Ford. Her grandmother had taught her everything she knew—which was not much, but tending at least to a certain measure of spiritual growth—for she, as it were, poured the goodness of her own soul into this little receptive vase of another. Lily was firmly grounded in her knowledge that it was wrong to lie or steal or disobey her grandmother. She had also learned that one should be very industrious. It was seldom that Lily sat idly holding her doll-baby, but this was a holiday because of the bridge. She looked only a child, although she was nearly fourteen; her mother had been married at sixteen. That is, Old Woman Magoun said that her daughter, Lily's mother, had married at sixteen; there had been rumors, but no one had dared openly gainsay the old woman. She said that her daughter had married Nelson Barry, and he had deserted her. She had lived in her mother's house, and Lily had been born there, and she had died when the baby was only a week old. Lily's father, Nelson Barry, was the fairly dangerous degenerate of a good old family. Nelson's father before him had been bad. He was now the last of the family, with the exception of a sister of feeble intellect, with whom he lived in the old Barry house. He was a middle-aged man, still handsome. The shiftless population of Barry's Ford looked up to him as to an evil deity. They wondered how Old Woman Magoun dared brave him as she did. But Old Woman Magoun had within her a mighty sense of reliance upon herself as being on the right track in the midst of a maze of evil, which gave her courage. Nelson Barry had manifested no interest whatever in his daughter. Lily seldom saw her father. She did not often go to the store which was his favorite haunt. Her grandmother took care that she should not do so.

However, that afternoon she departed from her usual custom and sent Lily to the store.

She came in from the kitchen, whither she had been to baste the roasting pig. "There's no use talkin'," said she, "I've got to have some more salt. I've jest used the very last I had to dredge over that pig. I've got to go to the store."

Sally Jinks looked at Lily. "Why don't you send her?" she asked.

Old Woman Magoun gazed irresolutely at the girl. She was herself very tired. It did not seem to her that she could drag herself up the dusty hill to the store. She glanced with covert resentment at Sally Jinks. She thought that she might offer to go. But Sally Jinks said again, "Why don't you let her go?" and looked with a languid eye at Lily holding her doll on the stone.

Lily was watching the men at work on the bridge, with her childish delight in a spectacle of any kind, when her grandmother addressed her.

"Guess I'll let you go down to the store an' git some salt, Lily," said she.

The girl turned uncomprehending eyes upon her grandmother at the sound of her voice. She had been filled with one of the innocent reveries of childhood. Lily had in her the making of an artist or a poet. Her prolonged childhood went to prove it, and also her retrospective eyes, as clear and blue as blue light itself, which seemed to see past all that she looked upon. She had not come of the old Barry family for nothing. The best of the strain was in her, along with the splendid stanchness in humble lines which she had acquired from her grandmother.

"Put on your hat," said Old Woman Magoun; "the sun is hot, and you might git a headache." She called the girl to her, and put back the shower of fair curls under the rubber band which confined the hat. She gave Lily some money, and watched her knot it into a corner of her little cotton handkerchief. "Be careful you don't lose it," said she, "and don't stop to talk to anybody, for I am in a hurry for that salt. Of course, if anybody speaks to you answer them polite, and then come right along."

Lily started, her pocket-handkerchief weighted with the small silver dangling from one hand, and her rag doll carried over her shoulder like a baby. The absurd travesty of a face peeped forth from Lily's yellow curls. Sally Jinks looked after her with a sniff.

"She ain't goin' to carry that rag doll to the store?" said she.

"She likes to," replied Old Woman Magoun, in a half-shamed yet defiantly extenuating voice.

"Some girls at her age is thinkin' about beaux instead of rag dolls," said Sally Jinks.

The grandmother bristled, "Lily ain't big nor old for her age," said she. "I ain't in any hurry to have her git married. She ain't none too strong."

"She's got a good color," said Sally Jinks. She was crocheting white cotton lace, making her thick fingers fly. She really knew how to do scarcely anything except to crochet that coarse lace; somehow her heavy brain or her fingers had mastered that.

"I know she's got a beautiful color," replied Old Woman Magoun, with an odd mixture of pride and anxiety, "but it comes an' goes."

"I've heard that was a bad sign," remarked Sally Jinks, loosening some thread from her spool.

"Yes, it is," said the grandmother. "She's nothin' but a baby, though she's quicker than most to learn."

Lily Barry went on her way to the store. She was clad in a scanty short frock of blue cotton; her hat was tipped back, forming an oval frame for her innocent face. She was very small, and walked like a child, with the clap-clap of little feet of babyhood. She might have been considered, from her looks, under ten.

Presently she heard footsteps behind her; she turned around a little timidly to see who was coming. When she saw a handsome, well-dressed man, she felt reassured. The man came alongside and glanced down carelessly at first, then his look deepened. He smiled, and Lily saw he was very handsome indeed, and that his smile was not only reassuring but wonderfully sweet and compelling.

"Well, little one," said the man, "where are you bound, you and your dolly?"

"I am going to the store to buy some salt for grandma," replied Lily, in her sweet treble. She looked up in the man's face, and he fairly started at the revelation of its innocent beauty. He regulated his pace by hers, and the two went on together. The man did not speak again at once. Lily kept glancing timidly up at him, and every time that she did so the man smiled and her confidence increased. Presently when the man's hand grasped her little childish one hanging by her side, she felt a complete trust in him. Then she smiled up at him. She felt glad that this nice man had come along, for just here the road was lonely.

After a while the man spoke. "What is your name, little one?" he asked, caressingly.

"Lily Barry."

The man started. "What is your father's name?"

"Nelson Barry," replied Lily.

The man whistled. "Is your mother dead?"

"Yes, sir."

"How old are you, my dear?"

"Fourteen," replied Lily.

The man looked at her with surprise. "As old as that?"

Lily suddenly shrank from the man. She could not have told why. She pulled her little hand from his, and he let it go with no remonstrance. She clasped both her arms around her rag doll, in order that her hand should not be free for him to grasp again.

She walked a little farther away from the man, and he looked amused.

"You still play with your doll?" he said, in a soft voice.

"Yes, sir," replied Lily. She quickened her pace and reached the store.

When Lily entered the store, Hiram Gates, the owner, was behind the counter. The only man besides in the store was Nelson Barry. He sat tipping his chair back against the wall; he was half asleep, and his handsome face was bristling with a beard of several days' growth and darkly flushed. He opened his eyes when Lily entered, the strange man following. He brought his chair down on all fours, and he looked at the man—not noticing Lily at all—with a look compounded of defiance and uneasiness.

"Hullo, Jim!" he said.

"Hullo, old man!" returned the stranger.

Lily went over to the counter and asked for the salt, in her pretty little voice. When she had paid for it and was crossing the store, Nelson Barry was on his feet.

"Well, how are you, Lily? It is Lily, isn't it?" he said.

"Yes, sir," replied Lily, faintly.

Her father bent down and, for the first time in her life, kissed her, and the whiskey odor of his breath came into her face.

Lily involuntarily started, and shrank away from him.
Then she rubbed her mouth violently with her little cotton
handkerchief, which she held gathered up with the rag doll.

"Damn it all! I believe she is afraid of me," said Nelson
Barry, in a thick voice.

"Looks a little like it," said the other man, laughing.

"It's that damned old woman," said Nelson Barry. Then he
smiled again at Lily. "I didn't know what a pretty little
daughter I was blessed with," said he, and he softly stroked
Lily's pink cheek under her hat.

Now Lily did not shrink from him. Hereditary instincts
and nature itself were asserting themselves in the child's innocent, receptive breast.

Nelson Barry looked curiously at Lily. "How old are you,
anyway, child?" he asked.

"I'll be fourteen in September," replied Lily.

"But you still play with your doll?" said Barry, laughing
kindly down at her.

Lily hugged her doll more tightly, in spite of her father's
kind voice. "Yes, sir," she replied.

Nelson glanced across at some glass jars filled with sticks
of candy. "See here, little Lily, do you like candy?" said he.

"Yes, sir."

"Wait a minute."

Lily waited while her father went over to the counter. Soon
he returned with a package of the candy.

"I don't see how you are going to carry so much," he said,
smiling. "Suppose you throw away your doll?"

Lily gazed at her father and hugged the doll tightly, and
there was all at once in the child's expression something mature. It became the reproach of a woman. Nelson's face so-
bered.

"Oh, it's all right, Lily," he said; "keep your doll. Here, I
guess you can carry this candy under your arm."

Lily could not resist the candy. She obeyed Nelson's instructions for carrying it, and left the store laden. The two
men also left, and walked in the opposite direction, talking
busily.

When Lily reached home, her grandmother, who was
watching for her, spied at once the package of candy.

"What's that?" she asked, sharply.

"My father gave it to me," answered Lily, in a faltering
voice. Sally regarded her with something like alertness.

"Your father?"

"Yes, ma'am."

"Where did you see him?"

"In the store."

"He gave you this candy?"

"Yes, ma'am."

"What did he say?"

"He asked me how old I was, and——"

"And what?"

"I don't know," replied Lily; and it really seemed to her that she did not know, she was so frightened and bewildered by it all, and, more than anything else, by her grandmother's face as she questioned her.

Old Woman Magoun's face was that of one upon whom a long-anticipated blow had fallen. Sally Jinks gazed at her with a sort of stupid alarm.

Old Woman Magoun continued to gaze at her grandchild with that look of terrible solicitude, as if she saw the girl in the clutch of a tiger. "You can't remember what else he said?" she asked, fiercely, and the child began to whimper softly.

"No, ma'am," she sobbed. "I—don't know, and——"

"And what? Answer me."

"There was another man there. A real handsome man."

"Did he speak to you?" asked Old Woman Magoun.

"Yes ma'am; he walked along with me a piece," confessed Lily, with a sob of terror and bewilderment.

"What did *he* say to you?" asked Old Woman Magoun, with a sort of despair.

Lily told, in her little, faltering, frightened voice, all of the conversation which she could recall. It sounded harmless enough, but the look of the realization of a long-expected blow never left her grandmother's face.

The sun was getting low, and the bridge was nearing completion. Soon the workmen would be crowding into the cabin for their promised supper. There became visible in the distance, far up the road, the heavily plodding figure of another woman who had agreed to come and help. Old Woman Magoun turned again to Lily.

"You go right up-stairs to your own chamber now," said she.

"Good land! ain't you goin' to let that poor child stay up and see the fun?" said Sally Jinks.

"You jest mind your own business," said Old Woman Magoun, forcibly, and Sally Jinks shrank. "You go right up there now, Lily," said the grandmother, in a softer tone, "and grandma will bring you up a nice plate of supper."

"When be you goin' to let that girl grow up?" asked Sally Jinks, when Lily had disappeared.

"She'll grow up in the Lord's good time," replied Old Woman Magoun, and there was in her voice something both sad and threatening. Sally Jinks again shrank a little.

Soon the workmen came flocking noisily into the house. Old Woman Magoun and her two helpers served the bountiful supper. Most of the men had drunk as much as, and more than, was good for them, and Old Woman Magoun had stipulated that there was to be no drinking of anything except coffee during supper.

"I'll git you as good a meal as I know how," she said, "but if I see ary one of you drinkin' a drop, I'll run you all out. If you want anything to drink, you can go up to the store afterward. That's the place for you to to go, if you've got to make hogs of yourselves. I ain't goin' to have no hogs in my house."

Old Woman Magoun was implicitly obeyed. She had a curious authority over most people when she chose to exercise it. When the supper was in full swing, she quietly stole up-stairs and carried some food to Lily. She found the girl, with the rag doll in her arms, crouching by the window in her little rocking-chair—a relic of her infancy, which she still used.

"What a noise they are makin', grandma!" she said, in a terrified whisper, as her grandmother placed the plate before her on a chair."

"They've 'most all of 'em been drinkin'. They air a passel of hogs," replied the old woman.

"Is the man that was with—with my father down there?" asked Lily, in a timid fashion. Then she fairly cowered before the look in her grandmother's eyes.

"No, he ain't; and what's more, he never will be down there if I can help it," said Old Woman Magoun, in a fierce whisper. "I know who he is. They can't cheat me. He's one of them Willises—that family the Barrys married into. They're worse than the Barrys, ef they *have* got money. Eat your supper, and put him out of your mind, child."

It was after Lily was asleep, when Old Woman Magoun was alone, clearing away her supper dishes, that Lily's father came. The door was closed, and he knocked, and the old woman knew at once who was there. The sound of that knock meant as much to her as the whir of a bomb to the defender of a fortress. She opened the door, and Nelson Barry stood there.

"Good-evening, Mrs. Magoun," he said.

Old Woman Magoun stood before him, filling up the doorway with her firm bulk.

"Good-evening, Mrs. Magoun," said Nelson Barry again.

"I ain't got no time to waste," replied the old woman, harshly. "I've got my supper dishes to clean up after them men."

She stood there and looked at him as she might have looked at a rebellious animal which she was trying to tame. The man laughed.

"It's no use," said he. "You know me of old. No human being can turn me from my way when I am once started in it. You may as well let me come in."

Old Woman Magoun entered the house, and Barry followed her.

Barry began without any preface. "Where is the child?" asked he.

"Up-stairs. She has gone to bed."

"She goes to bed early."

"Children ought to," returned the old woman, polishing a plate.

Barry laughed. "You are keeping her a child a long while," he remarked, in a soft voice which had a sting in it.

"She *is* a child," returned the old woman, defiantly.

"Her mother was only three years older when Lily was born."

The old woman made a sudden motion toward the man which seemed fairly menacing. Then she turned again to her dish-washing.

"I want her," said Barry.

"You can't have her," replied the old woman, in a still stern voice.

"I don't see how you can help yourself. You have always acknowledged that she was my child."

The old woman continued her task, but her strong back heaved. Barry regarded her with an entirely pitiless expression.

"I am going to have the girl, that is the long and short of it," he said, "and it is for her best good, too. You are a fool, or you would see it."

"Her best good?" muttered the old woman.

"Yes, her best good. What are you going to do with her, anyway? The girl is a beauty, and almost a woman grown, although you try to make out that she is a baby. You can't live forever."

"The Lord will take care of her," replied the old woman, and again she turned and faced him, and her expression was that of a prophetess.

"Very well, let Him," said Barry, easily. "All the same I'm going to have her, and I tell you it is for her best good. Jim Willis saw her this afternoon, and—"

Old Woman Magoun looked at him. "Jim Willis!" she fairly shrieked.

"Well, what of it?"

"One of them Willises!" repeated the old woman, and this time her voice was thick. It seemed almost as if she were stricken with paralysis. She did not enunciate clearly.

The man shrank a little. "Now what is the need of your making such a fuss?" he said. "I will take her, and Isabel will look out for her."

"Your half-witted sister?" said Old Woman Magoun.

"Yes, my half-witted sister. She knows more than you think."

"More wickedness."

"Perhaps. Well, a knowledge of evil is a useful thing. How are you going to avoid evil if you don't know what it is like? My sister and I will take care of my daughter."

The old woman continued to look at the man, but his eyes never fell. Suddenly her gaze grew inconceivably keen. It was as if she saw through all externals.

"I know what it is!" she cried. "You have been playing cards and you lost, and this is the way you will pay him."

Then the man's face reddened, and he swore under his breath.

"Oh, my God!" said the old woman; and she really spoke with her eyes aloft as if addressing something outside of them both. Then she turned again to her dish-washing.

The man cast a dogged look at her back. "Well, there is no use talking. I have made up my mind," said he, "and you know me and what that means. I am going to have the girl."

"When?" said the old woman, without turning around.

"Well, I am willing to give you a week. Put her clothes in good order before she comes."

The old woman made no reply. She continued washing

dishes. She even handled them so carefully that they did not rattle.

"You understand," said Barry. "Have her ready a week from to-day."

"Yes," said Old Woman Magoun, "I understand."

Nelson Barry, going up the mountain road, reflected that Old Woman Magoun had a strong character, that she understood much better than her sex in general the futility of withstanding the inevitable.

"Well," he said to Jim Willis when he reached home, "the old woman did not make such a fuss as I expected."

"Are you going to have the girl?"

"Yes; a week from to-day. Look here, Jim; you've got to stick to your promise."

"All right," said Willis. "Go you one better."

The two were playing at cards in the old parlor, once magnificent, now squalid, of the Barry house. Isabel, the half-witted sister, entered, bringing some glasses on a tray. She had learned with her feeble intellect some tricks, like a dog. One of them was the mixing of sundry drinks. She set the tray on a little stand near the two men, and watched them with her silly simper.

"Clear out now and go to bed," her brother said to her, and she obeyed.

Early the next morning Old Woman Magoun went up to Lily's little sleeping-chamber, and watched her a second as she lay asleep, with her yellow locks spread over the pillow. Then she spoke. "Lily," said she—"Lily, wake up. I am going to Greenham across the new bridge, and you can go with me."

Lily immediately sat up in bed and smiled at her grandmother. Her eyes were still misty, but the light of awakening was in them.

"Get right up," said the old woman. "You can wear your new dress if you want to."

Lily gurgled with pleasure like a baby. "And my new hat?" asked she.

"I don't care."

Old Woman Magoun and Lily started for Greenham before Barry Ford, which kept late hours, was fairly awake. It was three miles to Greenham. The old woman said that, since the horse was a little lame, they would walk. It was a beautiful morning, with a diamond radiance of dew over everything. Her grandmother had curled Lily's hair more punctiliously than usual. The little face peeped like a rose out of two rows of golden spirals. Lily wore her new muslin dress with a pink sash, and her best hat of a fine white straw trimmed with a wreath of rosebuds; also the neatest black open-work stockings and pretty shoes. She even had white cotton gloves. When they set out, the old, heavily stepping woman, in her black gown and cape and bonnet, looked down at the little pink fluttering figure. Her face was full of the tenderest love and admiration, and yet there was something terrible about it. They crossed the new bridge—a primitive structure built of logs in a slovenly fashion. Old Woman Magoun pointed to a gap.

"Jest see that," said she. "That's the way men work."

"Men ain't very nice, be they?" said Lily, in her sweet little voice.

"No, they ain't, take them all together," replied her grandmother.

"That man that walked to the store with me was nicer than some, I guess," Lily said, in a wishful fashion. Her grandmother reached down and took the child's hand in its small cotton glove. "You hurt me, holding my hand so tight," Lily said presently, in a deprecatory little voice.

The old woman loosened her grasp. "Grandma didn't know how tight she was holding your hand," said she. "She wouldn't hurt you for nothin', except it was to save your life, or somethin' like that." She spoke with an undertone of tremendous meaning which the girl was too childish to grasp. They walked along the country road. Just before they reached Greenham they passed a stone wall overgrown with blackberry-vines, and, an unusual thing in that vicinity, a lusty spread of deadly nightshade full of berries.

"Those berries look good to eat, grandma," Lily said.

At that instant the old woman's face became something terrible to see. "You can't have any now," she said, and hurried Lily along.

"They look real nice," said Lily.

When they reached Greenham, Old Woman Magoun took her way straight to the most pretentious house there, the residence of the lawyer, whose name was Mason. Old Woman Magoun bade Lily wait in the yard for a few moments, and Lily ventured to seat herself on a bench beneath an oak-tree; then she watched with some wonder her grandmother enter the lawyer's office door at the right of the house. Presently the lawyer's wife came out and spoke to Lily under the tree. She had in her hand a little tray containing a plate of cake, a glass of milk, and an early apple. She spoke very kindly to Lily; she even kissed her, and offered her the tray of refreshments, which Lily accepted gratefully. She sat eating, with Mrs. Mason watching her, when Old Woman Magoun came out of the lawyer's office with a ghastly face.

"What are you eatin'?" she asked Lily, sharply. "Is that a sour apple?"

"I thought she might be hungry," said the lawyer's wife, with loving, melancholy eyes upon the girl.

Lily had almost finished the apple. "It's real sour, but I like it; it's real nice, grandma," she said.

"You ain't been drinkin' milk with a sour apple?"

"It was real nice milk, grandma."

"You ought never to have drunk milk and eat a sour apple," said her grandmother. "Your stomach was all out of order this mornin', an' sour apples and milk is always apt to hurt anybody."

"I don't know but they are," Mrs. Mason said, apologetically, as she stood on the green lawn with her lavender muslin sweeping around her. "I am real sorry, Mrs. Magoun. I ought to have thought. Let me get some soda for her."

"Soda never agrees with her," replied the old woman, in a harsh voice. "Come," she said to Lily, "it's time we were goin' home."

After Lily and her grandmother had disappeared down the road, Lawyer Mason came out of his office and joined his wife, who had seated herself on the bench beneath the tree. She was idle, and her face wore the expression of those who review joys forever past. She had lost a little girl, her only child, years ago, and her husband always knew when she was thinking about her. Lawyer Mason looked older than his wife; he had a dry, shrewd, slightly one-sided face.

"What do you think, Maria?" he said. "That old woman came to me with the most pressing entreaty to adopt that little girl."

"She is a beautiful little girl," said Mrs. Mason, in a slightly husky voice.

"Yes, she is a pretty child," assented the lawyer, looking pityingly at his wife; "but it is out of the question, my dear. Adopting a child is a serious measure, and in this case a child who comes from Barry's Ford."

"But the grandmother seems a very good woman," said Mrs. Mason.

"I rather think she is. I never heard a word against her. But the father! No, Maria, we cannot take a child with Barry blood in her veins. The stock has run out; it is vitiated physically and morally. It won't do, my dear."

"Her grandmother had her dressed up as pretty as a little girl could be," said Mrs. Mason, and this time the tears welled into her faithful, wistful eyes.

"Well, we can't help that," said the lawyer, as he went back to his office.

Old Woman Magoun and Lily returned, going slowly along the road to Barry's Ford. When they came to the stone wall where the blackberry-vines and the deadly nightshade grew, Lily said she was tired, and asked if she could not sit down for a few minutes. The strange look on her grandmother's face had deepened. Now and then Lily glanced at her and had a feeling as if she were looking at a stranger.

"Yes, you can set down if you want to," said Old Woman Magoun, deeply and harshly.

Lily started and looked at her, as if to make sure that it was her grandmother who spoke. Then she sat down on a stone which was comparatively free of the vines.

"Ain't you goin' to set down, grandma?" Lily asked, timidly.

"No; I don't want to get into that mess," replied her grandmother. "I ain't tired. I'll stand here."

Lily sat still; her delicate little face was flushed with heat. She extended her tiny feet in her best shoes and gazed at them. My shoes are all over dust," said she.

"It will brush off," said her grandmother, still in that strange voice.

Lily looked around. An elm-tree in the field behind her cast a spray of branches over her head; a little cool puff of wind came on her face. She gazed at the low mountains on the horizon, in the midst of which she lived, and she sighed, for no reason that she knew. She began idly picking at the blackberry-vines; there were no berries on them; then she put her little fingers on the berries of the deadly nightshade. "These look like nice berries," she said.

Old Woman Magoun, standing stiff and straight in the road, said nothing.

"They look good to eat," said Lily.

Old Woman Magoun still said nothing, but she looked up into the ineffable blue of the sky, over which spread at intervals great white clouds shaped like wings.

Lily picked some of the deadly nightshade berries and ate them. "Why, they are real sweet," said she. "They are nice." She picked some more and ate them.

Presently her grandmother spoke. "Come," she said, "it is time we were going. I guess you have set long enough."

Lily was still eating the berries when she slipped down from the wall and followed her grandmother obediently up the road.

Before they reached home, Lily complained of being very thirsty. She stopped and made a little cup of a leaf and drank long at a mountain brook. "I am dreadful dry, but it hurts me to swallow," she said to her grandmother when she stopped drinking and joined the old woman waiting for her in the road. Her grandmother's face seemed strangely dim to her. She took hold of Lily's hand as they went on. "My stomach burns," said Lily, presently. "I want some more water."

"There is another brook a little farther on," said Old Woman Magoun, in a dull voice.

When they reached that brook, Lily stopped and drank again, but she whimpered a little over her difficulty in swallowing. "My stomach burns, too," she said, walking on, "and my throat is so dry, grandma." Old Woman Magoun held Lily's hand more tightly. "You hurt me holding my hand so tight, grandma," said Lily, looking up at her grandmother, whose face she seemed to see through a mist, and the old woman loosened her grasp.

When at last they reached home, Lily was very ill. Old Woman Magoun put her on her own bed in the little bedroom out of the kitchen. Lily lay there and moaned, and Sally Jinks came in.

"Why, what ails her?" she asked. "She looks feverish."

Lily unexpectedly answered for herself. "I ate some sour apples and drank some milk," she moaned.

"Sour apples and milk are dreadful apt to hurt anybody," said Sally Jinks. She told several people on her way home that Old Woman Magoun was dreadful careless to let Lily eat such things.

Meanwhile Lily grew worse. She suffered cruelly from the burning in her stomach, the vertigo, and the deadly nausea. "I am so sick, I am so sick, grandma," she kept moaning. She could no longer see her grandmother as she bent over her, but she could hear her talk.

Old Woman Magoun talked as Lily had never heard her talk before, as nobody had ever heard her talk before. She spoke from the depths of her soul; her voice was as tender as the coo of a dove, and it was grand and exalted. "You'll feel better very soon, little Lily," said she.

"I am so sick, grandma."

"You will feel better very soon, and then——"

"I am sick."

"You shall go to a beautiful place."

Lily moaned.

"You shall go to a beautiful place," the old woman went on.

"Where?" asked Lily, groping feebly with her cold little hands. Then she moaned again.

"A beautiful place, where the flowers grow tall."

"What color? Oh, grandma, I am so sick."

"A blue color," replied the old woman. Blue was Lily's favorite color. "A beautiful blue color, and as tall as your knees, and the flowers always stay there, and they never fade."

"Not if you pick them, grandma? Oh!"

"No, not if you pick them; they never fade, and they are so sweet you can smell them a mile off; and there are birds that sing, and all the roads have gold stones in them, and the stone walls are made of gold."

"Like the ring grandpa gave you? I am so sick, grandma."

"Yes, gold like that. And all the houses are built of silver and gold, and the people all have wings, so when they get tired walking they can fly, and——"

"I am so sick, grandma."

"And all the dolls are alive," said Old Woman Magoun. "Dolls like yours can run, and talk, and love you back again."

Lily had her poor old rag doll in bed with her, clasped close to her agonized little heart. She tried very hard with her eyes, whose pupils were so dilated that they looked black, to see her grandmother's face when she said that, but she could not. "It is dark," she moaned, feebly.

"There where you are going it is always light," said the grandmother, "and the commonest things shine like that breastpin Mrs. Lawyer Mason had on to-day."

Lily moaned pitifully, and said something incoherent. Delirium was commencing. Presently she sat straight up in bed and raved; but even then her grandmother's wonderful compelling voice had an influence over her.

"You will come to a gate with all the colors of the rainbow," said her grandmother; "and it will open, and you will go right in and walk up the gold street, and cross the field where the blue flowers come up to your knees, until you find your mother, and she will take you home where you are going to live. She has a little white room all ready for you, white curtains at the windows, and a little white looking-glass, and when you look in it you will see—"

"What will I see? I am so sick, grandma."

"You will see a face like yours, only it's an angel's; and there will be a little white bed, and you can lay down an' rest."

"Won't I be sick, grandma?" asked Lily. Then she moaned and babbled wildly, although she seemed to understand through it all what her grandmother said.

"No, you will never be sick anymore. Talkin' about sickness won't mean anything to you."

It continued. Lily talked on wildly, and her grandmother's great voice of soothing never ceased, until the child fell into a deep sleep, or what resembled sleep; but she lay stiffly in that sleep, and a candle flashed before her eyes made no impression on them.

Then it was that Nelson Barry came. Jim Willis waited outside the door. When Nelson entered he found Old Woman Magoun on her knees beside the bed, weeping with dry eyes and a might of agony which fairly shook Nelson Barry, the degenerate of a fine old race.

"Is she sick?" he asked, in a hushed voice.

Old Woman Magoun gave another terrible sob, which sounded like the gasp of one dying.

"Sally Jinks said that Lily was sick from eating milk and sour apples," said Barry, in a tremulous voice. "I remember that her mother was very sick once from eating them."

Lily lay still, and her grandmother on her knees shook with her terrible sobs.

Suddenly Nelson Barry started. "I guess I had better go to Greenham for a doctor if she's as bad as that," he said. He went close to the bed and looked at the sick child. He gave a great start. Then he felt of her hands and reached down under the bedclothes for her little feet. "Her hands and feet are like ice," he cried out. "Good God! why didn't you send for some one—for me—before? Why, she's dying; she's almost gone!"

Barry rushed out and spoke to Jim Willis, who turned pale and came in and stood by the bedside.

"She's almost gone," he said, in a hushed whisper.

"There's no use going for the doctor, she'd be dead before he got here," said Nelson, and he stood regarding the passing child with a strange, sad face—unutterably sad, because of his incapability of the truest sadness.

"Poor little thing, she's past suffering, anyhow," said the other man, and his own face also was sad with a puzzled, mystified sadness.

Lily died that night. There was quite a commotion in Barry's Ford until after the funeral, it was all so sudden, and then everything went on as usual. Old Woman Magoun continued to live as she had done before. She supported herself by the produce of her tiny farm; she was very industrious, but people said that she was a trifle touched, since every time she went over the log bridge with her eggs or her garden vegetables to sell in Greenham, she carried with her, as one might have carried an infant, Lily's old rag doll.